S0-BOA-120

THE NYLON HAND OF GOD

THE NYLON HAND
OF GOD

STEVEN HARTOV

Copyright © 1996 by Steven Hartov

All rights reserved. No part of this book may be reproduced or utilized in any form or by any means, electronic or mechanical, including photocopying, recording, or by any information storage or retrieval system. For information, address Writers House LLC at 21 West 26th Street, New York, NY 10010.

eISBN: 978-0-7867-5401-4

Print ISBN: 978-0-7867-5400-7

Cover design by Michael Scowden

Also by Steven Hartov

FOR AL ZUCKERMAN
My agent behind the lines

Acknowledgments

My thanks to Lieutenant Colonel (ret.) Shaul Dori; Ory Slonim, Special Consultant to the Prime Minister; Brigadier General Yigal Presler, Advisor to the Prime Minister on Anti-Terror Warfare; Colonel (res.) Ranan Gissin; Sergeant Major Didi Lehman; Yaakov "K"; Fred Pierce; Dr. Donald Drouin; Detective Tim Connelly, NYPD; "Arthur"; Erster Polizeihauptkommissar Bernd Pokojewski; Eric Sabbe, EKHK G. Haiber–Bundeskriminalamt; Dr. David Th. Schiller; Sergeant First Class Jerry Ginder; Major Robert Oles; "Mustaffa"; Claire Wachtel; and of course, the *real* Ruth.

This work was reviewed by the IDF Military Censor.

The Hartov espionage trilogy is comprised of *The Heat of Ramadan*, *The Nylon Hand of God*, and *The Devil's Shepherd*. This new release reflects the original hardcover manuscript, unedited and unabridged. For the many loyal fans who've inquired about the fates of Eytan Eckstein and Benni Baum, their adventures will continue in an upcoming book. For more information, please visit the author's site: www.stevenhartov.com.

Have pity upon me,
Have pity upon me, O ye my friends;
For the Hand of God hath touched me.
Job 19:21

Prologue
New York, Late November 1992

Moshiko Ben-Czecho knew that his death was imminent, but he refused to surrender to his shameful sensation of fear.

There was no visible threat in evidence, he had no reason to be afraid, and he was determined to lock the rising paranoia in that corner of his mind reserved for fantasy, premonition, and weakness. He would slam the door of his subconscious on that paralyzing viper, so that no one might see it, smell it, hear its insistent hiss. He would simply ignore it, as if it did not exist at all.

Yet it was there. Like the faint scent of electric air, when there is thunder in the wind. Like the sound of bird wings in the dark, when the careful steps of something large and powerful break no twig in the undergrowth.

Moshiko understood—for his training was thorough—that this essence of fear was a physiological response to some sort of environmental stimulus. His brain was bypassing its own logic, alerting his body to its possible destruction.

Already his adrenal glands were injecting his muscles with a significant boost in power. Heart rate was up, increasing oxygen flow to his extremities. His pupils were dilating to take in more light, auditory canals expanding to absorb faint sounds, and olfactories stretching to snare the smallest particles of a predator's breath from the atmosphere. And even as his blood raced through his limbs, the arteries were also constricting, so that the slash of a blade or the plowing of a bullet would not result in a fatal gush from his wounds.

His body had required only a few milliseconds to prepare, and now the secondary phase was engaged. The decisive phase.

Fight or flee.

But Moshiko Ben-Czecho, because he was a security officer at the Israeli Consulate General, did not have the luxury of choice. He could not flee. And inasmuch as the dread sweeping over him like a malarial chill did not stem from any discernible danger, he was determined to outwit his instincts.

Today, Moshiko decided, he had absolutely no reason to be fearful. It was a day like any other, the late-autumn morning a mirror of a hundred others that had gone before. No consular routines had been broken, no alarms had sounded in the hallways, no diplomatic crises had encroached upon the denouement of a long workweek sliding toward the Sabbath. Yes, his vocation made him the potential target of gunfire or sabotage, but much like a professional test pilot, he, together with his fellow members of the General Security Services, lived with that danger, while for the most part ignoring it.

The Consulate General and Permanent Mission to the United Nations occupied five floors of an unexceptional skyscraper on Second Avenue in Manhattan. It resembled a typical Israeli government office, transported to the West intact. The interior walls were of thickened concrete slabbed over with plaster, the floors of cracked linoleum tiles that looked like leftovers from a warehouse fire sale. The heavy wooden desks were scuffed and scabbed by thousands of dripping tea mugs and careless cigarettes, and hardly any chair in the place had its twin.

The finger-soiled walls, which displayed few attempts at decor except some aging black-and-whites of elder statesmen and laboring kibbutzniks, were freely utilized like the Wanted boards of U.S. post offices. Stuck up every which way were notices from one department to another. Personnel advised secretaries that their overtime was getting out of hand. Security reminded diplomats that their movements should be properly logged. Information warned everybody that all contacts with journalists had to be cleared by *them*.

As dictated by realpolitik, the consulate was also a secure facility, the hard-shelled outpost of a country at war, deep within the architecture of a stalwart ally. It was a maze of secret passageways and escape routes, with video cameras poking their snouts from every corner and X-ray machines scanning incoming mail for explosives. There were more pistols in desk drawers than in the mansion of a Colombian drug lord.

It was a schizophrenic entity, an island of love and paranoia that warmly welcomed its friends, while patting them down in search of armed enemies. Moshiko's job involved the latter, somewhat distasteful, necessity.

He was enduring the last ten minutes of his shift on the fourteenth floor of the building. This was the first level of the consulate, the entrance through which Israelis trudged to renew their passports, foreigners appeared to submit visa applications, and the parents of young Israeli-American men came to beg that their sons be excused from military service (the embarrassed boys usually hung back, looking at their shoes). The general public was restricted to this area, for above were nestled the diplomatic enclaves, the secure communications centers, and the quiet caves of Mossad officers, with their smiles as thin as their economic covers.

Moshiko's post was the first line of defense, for no visitors, whether bicycle messengers or White House presidential advisers, simply wafted into the consulate. The double doors of a passenger lift opened onto a large antechamber *cum* security screening room, an oblong space bordered by plastic chairs, overflowing ashtrays, cheaply framed propaganda posters from the Ministry of Tourism, and an Israeli flag drooping from a pole. Across the rectangle of worn blue carpet, the facing wall was dominated by a double-thick steel door held fast by an electromagnetic lock, and a large picture window of bulletproof plexiglass.

The window was a new addition to the facility, the outcome of a nasty little skirmish between the Foreign Office and the GSS, known by its Hebrew acronym, Shabak. Up until recently, all visitors had suffered the equivalent of bowing before Oz, as they were viewed by cameras and queried by intercom, an indignity that the GSS insisted was an effective psychological deterrent. But the diplomats successfully argued that although the country was still technically at war with twenty Arab states and terrorist factions, her face abroad should not be one of a panicky prison warden. The peace process was taking center stage in the world's media, and consulates, though they might indeed be small fortresses, should not *appear* to be so.

To a man, the New York GSS officers hated the "aquarium." And as one of the members of the team, Moshiko had to endure his share of shifts, when he would sit behind the glass feeling like a lonely bank teller guarding Fort Knox. He did not have much faith in the impregnable qualities of the window. In Lebanon, he had seen what a simple rocket-propelled grenade could do to an armored personnel carrier.

On the Israeli side of the Perspex, he perched behind a counter in a small, dimly lit room. A row of video monitors showed him images from other parts of the facility. A microphone poked up from the countertop, so he could speak to visitors in the waiting chamber, and a red telephone sat beside a "panic button." To the best of his knowledge, no Shabaknik had ever pressed it, for it would be like ringing the scramble klaxon at an air force fighter base.

Below the frame of the wide window, a shallow steel drawer was set into the concrete and could be pushed to the outside for deposits of passports or identity papers. Beneath that, a row of photographs was propped in the shadows. The grainy shots were of active anti-Israeli terrorists. Not the political masters such as George Habash or Ahmed Jabril, but the men who had proved their mettle in actual hijackings, bombings, or shootings. Moshiko glanced at them often, seeing them not so much as the enemy as the antimatter to his own existence.

In a waistband holster clipped to his belt he wore a Beretta .22 caliber automatic. The weapon's stopping power was questionable, but within the confines of the consulate you did not want your rounds passing right through a terrorist and killing some unfortunate New Yorker who had come to volunteer for banana-picking duty on a kibbutz. Besides, in keeping with Israel Defense Forces tradition, you were not expected to hunker down and outmarksman an attacker to death. You were expected to *charge*.

There was a running joke among the Shabakniks about designing a bullet that would kill terrorists, wound diplomats, and bounce off anyone else. Not that these young men viewed their endeavors as a game, but as with any dangerous activity, some self-deceptive levity was necessary, even as they remained alert as hunted gazelles during every second of their shifts. The routine was exhausting, yet if you faltered, that could well be the moment that you, and those you had sworn to protect, would die.

In the year that Moshiko had worked at the consulate, hardly anything of substance had occurred. One explosive device had been mailed to the consul general and immediately detected and defused. One overwrought fan of Louis Farrakhan had stepped from the elevator waving a plastic pistol, which he had wisely dropped before being nearly executed by Moshiko and two of his comrades. It was hardly a chain of mishaps that boded ill for the immediate future, so Moshiko did not understand why he was breathing as if he had just run the obstacle course at Wingate.

Perhaps it was the very *lack* of action that had him spooked. He had had that feeling before, lying in ambush near Marj Ayoun, just before his tour was over and he was about to go home. Yes, that was it, a foolish superstition, like that of a businessman who had flown too many times without a mishap, an unsubstantiated sense that the odds were shifting.

He sat in the armless swivel chair, looking down at his hands where they rested on the countertop. The building heat was adequate, yet his fingertips fluttered and his left knee bounced above his tapping heel. There was a small annoying tic in the corner of his right eye, and his pulse throbbed some kind of message in his ear.

"*Zeh lo ritsini.*" He assured himself that the affliction was not serious. "*Atah stahm mishtagaya.* You're just losing your mind."

Determined to outwit his forebodings, he embraced a false calm, harking back to the teaching of his hand-to-hand instructors. The body was not a temple; it was a slave to be mastered. He began to breathe diaphragmatically, hissing the long breaths in and out, slowing his heart rate. He drew his fingertips together and commanded them to a stillness, as he did each week on the pistol range in Nassau County.

"Hey, Maharaja Yogi. Try to stay awake for your last ten minutes."

Moshiko nearly bucked from his chair, but he managed to quickly feign composure. He looked up to see the image of his boss reflected in the window. Hanan Bar-El, a short, muscular forty-year-old given to dark shirts and flowery ties, stood framed behind him in the open doorway of the booth.

"I was practicing *Krav-Maga*," said Moshiko as he set his hands into the first position of Contact-Combat.

"Well, don't punch anything expensive," Bar-El warned playfully. As GSS chief of security for New York, he was not prone to smiles. But Moshiko was one of his favorites. "And let those poor misguided Russians in. See you Monday."

Moshiko waved over his shoulder as Bar-El closed the door.

He looked out through the window at the five visitors in the waiting chamber. Four of them were a family of Russians, the young parents fussing over a pair of toddlers whose winter clothing made them look like small stuffed bears. These days most Russian Jews sought the golden promise of America, yet here was a family who had made it to Manhattan but longed for Jerusalem. A former refugee himself, Moshiko was still touched by such naive idealism.

"Mr. Penkovsky?" He keyed the microphone and spoke in English. "Please come in." He touched a button beneath the counter, the magnetic lock buzzed, and the Russians rushed through the door with a bounce that made him feel momentarily like a gatekeeper at Disney World.

The remaining visitor in the chamber was a girl, who looked to be less than twenty. She was wearing bright-yellow boots and a blue wool ski cap. As Moshiko watched, she pulled off the hat, shook out a stunning stream of red hair, and smiled up at him. He waved back briefly.

So where was this mortal danger?

It did not exist.

He looked at his watch.

Six minutes to go.

As his apprehension slowly faded, Moshiko allowed his mind to engage in a forbidden pastime. It began to wander, as he reflected with a blend of melancholy and hope on the not too distant future. Soon his life as a Shabaknik would end, yet something with more promise would begin. . . .

Moshiko had long ago come to the realization that he was not going to have an illustrious career in the Israeli intelligence community. He had been born in Czechoslovakia as Moshe Kubis, the son of a Christian father and a Jewish mother, which according to biblical tenets made him a member of the Tribe. At the age of seventeen he had emigrated to Israel and Hebraicized his family name to complement his new life.

When Moshiko (a nickname for the Old Testament name Moses) had completed his compulsory three years of army service in the Golani infantry brigade, he applied for duties with the Special Operations wing of AMAN—Israel's Military Intelligence branch. Almost immediately it appeared that his East Bloc background would thwart him, yet by a stroke of luck, one of his vetters was a Major Benjamin Baum, who as a child of the Holocaust was partial to renegade refugees.

"Kubis?" Baum's brows had arched as he perused Moshiko's dossier. "As in *Jan* Kubis?"

"My great-uncle," Moshiko had muttered, bracing himself to be thrown out on his ear.

"My *boy*." Baum was stunned, for in addition to being a brilliant AMAN officer, he was also an amateur historian of the war years. Jan Kubis was a Czechoslovak hero. It was Sergeant Jan Kubis who had been parachuted by the British OSS into the Czech forests on a winter night in 1941, the point man of a secret mission called Anthropoid. And it was also Kubis who had managed to mortally wound SS Obergruppenführer Reinhard Heydrich, the Nazi Butcher of Prague, before being killed himself in a shootout with the Gestapo.

Baum quickly found a position for Moshiko with the physical-security detachment of Special Operations, as well as a place at the Sabbath table in Baum's Jerusalem home. However, the regulations of an intelligence service at war could not be completely circumvented, and when it became clear that Moshiko's security clearance would restrict him from the adventures to which he had aspired, the major helped him transfer to Shabak.

Much like Britain's MI5 or the American FBI, Shabak handled counterintelligence. However, it was also responsible for supplying armed guards to El Al passenger flights, air terminals, consulates abroad, and close protection for heads of state. Young men fresh out of IDF combat units often became "GRs" (as the pistoleros were slanged), for widely accepted if less than patriotic motives. You could travel the world, taste foreign women, and save up some shekels. A few managed to rise through the ranks to become regional security chiefs, and some even returned to Tel Aviv and careers in the more sophisticated venues of spy hunting and mole trapping. But Moshiko no longer entertained such illusions.

He was, however, harboring a secret from his coworkers, for which at times he felt pangs of guilt. He was going to resign altogether from the service. Worse than that, and perhaps smacking of treachery, he planned to stay on in New York and go to university.

The reason being Kathleen.

They had found each other at a Halloween party, to which Moshiko had been invited by an American friend studying at NYU. He arrived straight from work on a rainy night, so unlike the other revelers, he wore no costume, not even a cheap plastic mask.

He was the enigmatic stranger, tall and well built, with wet black hair and blue eyes. Kathleen had long chestnut hair and Irish-cream skin, a freckled nose that poked from a pink bandit's mask. She wore a purple dress and carried a magic wand, and she came right up to him and tapped him on the head.

"And who are you supposed to be?"

Moshiko held a glass of vodka, crackling over fresh ice, while R.E.M. blared "Losing My Religion" through the miasma of undulating bodies. And feeling somewhat protected by the anonymity of the others' costumes, he answered spontaneously, if a bit foolishly.

"A secret agent."

"Oh, really?" Her mask tipped from his head down to his feet, then back again. "So where's your costume?"

His response was extremely unprofessional, but perhaps it was at that moment that he realized he wasn't making a career of this anyway. He pushed back the flap of his unconstructed blazer, showed her the pistol on his right hip, then closed it again and smiled.

"Wow." Kathleen stood still for a long moment, then lifted the mask from her face. "Where did *you* come from?"

But Moshiko did not hear her query, for he was entranced by those eyes.

Later, his recollections of the late evening played over in his mind a thousand times, his very favorite film. Her small apartment, the memory of his fingers, the wet wool of her coat as it opened, her breath in his ear, the cool smooth skin that grew warm to his own touch.

In Israel, he was nothing out of the ordinary. Every other young man was like him. Almost every girl he knew carried her own pistol next to her lipstick.

But here, to Kathleen, he was James Bond. She could not get enough of him. . . .

Moshiko realized with a start that he had been lost in fantasy for some moments, his daydream so hypnotically real that now he crossed his legs and leaned forward, hoping to deflate the evidence of his erotic enthusiasm. It would not do for him to go striding back through the consulate, on his way to sign out, with a bulge in his trousers and a flush to his face. He would save that for later. He and Kathleen had long planned for this slippery weekend at an inn on the southern shores of Connecticut.

The double doors of the elevator slid open, and for a moment, when no one appeared, he again had that unwelcome sensation. His fingers tightened at the edge of the counter. He stared through the glass, then stole a glance at his watch. One minute. It was nearly 12:30 P.M. of a Sabbath eve. No more "customers" after 12:30. No more.

He snorted at his own stupidity when the figure stepped out into the waiting chamber. For the man was a Hasid, a devoutly religious Jew, replete with a wide black hat, long curling *payis* twirling down in front of his ears, and a bushy beard dripping rivulets of rain onto the carpet. From neck to ankle, the Hasid was enveloped in a long black woolen frock coat.

Just another throwback to the nineteenth century, thought Moshiko with some relief. *About as dangerous as a starving poodle.* For indeed the man looked as if he had just stepped from the cobblestoned streets of an ancient Polish shtetl.

Except for the shoes. *Is it a religious holiday?* Moshiko wondered. The man's feet were cradled in sopping sneakers, the plain canvas-and-rubber basketball type. On certain days of observance, the religious took care to wear no skins of animals.

As the Hasid strode slowly across the floor, Moshiko quick-scanned the face. Hundreds of such men passed this way each week, preparing their pilgrimages to the Holy of Holies in Jerusalem. They did not even appear on the GSS threat scale. If they waited too long inside the consulate's passport section, you could often find them wrapped in a *tallis*, praying over by the windows.

Moshiko stared at the man's features, an attempt to match them to his expectations.

The nose was wide and flat, the skin not quite as pale as the usual sallow hue of men who bent their eyes to prayer books in gloomy rooms.

Something else. The dark eyes glistened, their pupils cavernous, the white orbs veined with fine yellow lines hinting at a touch of jaundice. It was almost a dreamy look. A blank, unseeing stare.

A man lost to God, Moshiko decided, even as he watched the Hasid's closed mouth, something playing at the corners of the lips. A twitch.

The Hasid stopped a foot from the window. The redheaded girl looked up from a paperback book. Moshiko touched the microphone button.

"*Shalom.* How can I help you?" he asked in English.

The Hasid did not move or speak. His nostrils flared slightly with breath still steaming from the chilled air in his lungs.

Moshiko cleared his throat. "*Efshar lazohr l'cha?*" He offered aid once more, this time in Hebrew. For perhaps the Hasid was Israeli born, just a visitor to Brooklyn. Here for a passport renewal. Going home.

No response.

Moshiko was debating whether to summon Bar-El, when the Hasid slowly reached into a pocket of the frock coat and came up with a folded piece of paper.

For God's sake, he's a deaf-mute. Moshiko chastised himself with a mental shake of his head. He slid the teller's drawer out to the poor fellow, who dropped the paper inside. Then he pulled back on the steel tray, extracted the note, and looked down at it.

The scrawl was wavy, as if the hand that had scribed it was palsied. The letters were in large Hebrew script, just two words, but he could not discern their meaning. Was it a name? Maybe it was Yiddish?

And even as he pronounced the phrase aloud phonetically, his heart thundered up through his body.

"*Allahu Akbar.*"

God is Great.

The war cry of Islam.

Moshiko snapped his head up, but the yell was choked in his own throat. For now, pressed against the glass, were the wet smeared features of the Hasid's face, a smile spread from cheek to trembling cheek, and two rows of silver-rimmed teeth that flashed against the fluttering tongue, warbling something he could not hear.

He saw the Hasid's fist reach up to the top button of his coat, where fast as the claw strike of a jaguar it gripped the small plastic disk and pulled. And Moshiko was already launching himself backward, his hands pushing against the counter with every adrenaline-poisoned muscle in his arms.

But he knew that it was too late.

The Hasid's coat must have been quite a burden to him, for it weighed twenty pounds more than on the day it was purchased. It was lined with forty strips of Semtex-B, a moldable plastic explosive of Czechoslovak manufacture that burned at a rate of twenty-four thousand feet per second.

The detonator, a necessary booster to ignite the primary charge, was a fulminate-of-mercury blasting cap, cocooned with three more like it inside a pack of Marlboros stuffed into the Hasid's vest pocket. The coat button was tied to a wire lanyard that closed a simple, battery-powered circuit.

The Hasid disappeared into a sun of thundering heat that dissolved his own blood and bone, as well as that of the redheaded girl. A hundred blades of lightning flame leapt out at the walls of the waiting chamber. And true to the claims of its manufacturer, the security window did not shatter. It completely left its frame and flew intact, like a giant piston, into Moshiko's booth.

And in that final microsecond, before his world went black, before his body impacted with and passed right through the wooden door behind him, Moshiko realized . . .

He should have listened to his instincts.

Part One: HOGs

Chapter 1: Jerusalem

Lieutenant Colonel Benjamin Baum watched a final breath of pewter winter light as it sank below the stony turrets of the Cathedral of Saint Trinity. The silhouetted spires were capped in brilliant green ceramic domes, and from each crown another finger poked a golden crucifix into the falling night. Yet it was not the massive architecture that held Baum's gaze, for he had squinted pensively this way a thousand times before. Rather, it was the rare vision of the structure's eaves being dusted with snow, and the certainty that this unusual day, much like his career in the army, would soon fade forever.

With a heavy palm, Baum smeared a circle of fog from his office window, discovering once again that the church resembled an upturned hand of Christian Orthodoxy sinking into a Judaic sea. It sat atop this promontory of Jerusalem called the Russian Compound, so named in deference to the Eastern pilgrims who had once sought refuge here. The cathedral was a stubborn anachronism, for the Compound now held a ring of other buildings, their inhabitants less deferential to their deity than the monks who swung their incense maces inside the church's battlements.

A low, flat structure at the Compound's western side housed the interrogation rooms, communications centers, and dark and desperate holding cells of the National Police. To the east, a central court of high stone chambers echoed with the thunder of gavels, as judges sentenced restless queues of terrorists and thieves.

And to the south, amid another block of bureaucratic buildings whose worn brass shingles lied to wayward visitors, the Special Operations wing of Israeli Military Intelligence still held its temporary residence. After five years, AMAN's Special Operations personnel, its officers and analysts, its wizards, watchers, secretaries, and janitors, no longer dreamed of the promised new facilities. It might well be that somewhere down in Tel Aviv, a modern lair of steel-and-Plexiglas, plush-carpeted suites would soon spring up. But given the realities of Israel's construction trade, the strikes and slowdowns, and the fact that the country's best laborers were Palestinians, forbidden to work so sensitive a project, most of AMAN's SpecOps people had long resigned themselves to call Jerusalem their home.

Of course, to Benni Baum the promise of a new seaside facility would not have moved him, for he had always called Jerusalem his home. He had come here as a child of the camps, thankful now that his first recollectible images were of a sun-burned city of wondrous hills and alleys, shorts and sandals, the air a heady draft of desert dust and pine.

There were cities on this earth whose faces never felt the sting of certain seasons, and he recalled how, long ago, before that first November chill, he too had thought Jerusalem blessed with endless sun. The images were for the most part true, of stony shadows thrown by a cloudless azure sky, of palm fronds waving above bronzed Israeli beauties, of pink-veined granite magically translucent in the white, bright days of six-month summers. And even as the winter came, it did so in bursts of effort between sunny days that would be spring in any other place.

Yet once each year, on a day that Baum always relished with a child's glee, it was as if God could not restrain his brush stroke, and it snowed. And on that day Jerusalem became like a sultan's sandstone palace, sitting on a cloud of cream.

"Are you converting to Christianity, Baum? Tell me now, so I can downgrade your security clearance."

Lieutenant General Itzik Ben-Zion's rumbling tones echoed off the walls of Baum's office. Benni sighed, yet he did not immediately turn.

"Actually, I was praying for a stay of execution. No particular denomination."

He looked down at his hands, where he clutched a sheaf of papers, memories in triplicate. No one would ever need them, for everything was being swallowed by computers now. Still, he was quite sure that on one glorious day the hard disks, RAMs, and LANs would all come crashing down and there would be a mad scramble for fountain pens until someone straightened out the mess.

"No one is forcing you out, Baum."

Benni turned from the window, eyeing his commander. Yes, his decision to retire was voluntary, but there were those who would revel in his departure.

The general stepped into the office, bending his head to clear the frame. He was the tallest officer of any that Baum knew, which alone gave him some unwarranted recognition. His full head of wiry black hair was going salt and pepper now, but his hawkish nose still preceded every entrance like a tank's cannon, his dark eyes and slanting brows completing the image of a giant bird of prey. The circles thereunder had grown darker with the years, yet the lines above his cheekbones remained shallow, as if he preserved his youth by the dictates of fashion modeling. Don't smile unless you have to.

Rank and power were the treasures Itzik coveted, yet as those coffers grew, his spiritual well had diminished. Yes, he was at last a general, but his wife had finally divorced him and his children kept their distance. Whatever unappreciated happiness had once been his now resided in someone else's home.

"I was referring to Operation Moonlight." Benni suppressed a cynical leer. It was common for AMAN officers to wear civilian clothes, but ever since making general, Itzik almost always wore his uniform.

"Well, it's too late now." Ben-Zion placed his fists on his hips. "That mission is running."

"We should look at it again."

"We have *looked* at it a thousand times. Let's not beat a gift horse."

"I think you are mixing metaphors." Benni regretted the comment as soon as it escaped his mouth. Challenging Itzik was a fatuous little habit he could not shake, which was why he would be leaving AMAN as a lieutenant colonel, while men twenty years his junior already wore three "felafels" on their epaulets.

"You're doing it again, Baum." The general jabbed with a finger, while Baum dipped his head, attempting a mimed apology. "But this time you and your partner are not going to screw this up for me. We are going through with it."

Benni shrugged. Itzik was clearly still rankling over the recent power struggle that had resulted in the cancellation of one of his operational brainstorms. He had wanted to put a long-range reconnaissance team into the western Iraqi desert, to ascertain the revamping of Saddam Hussein's Scud capability. Baum and his partner of many years, Eytan Eckstein, had killed the project by proving that the human risk was too great, instead striking a deal with the Americans to provide satellite coverage of the area.

It was not the first time they had caused one of Itzik's "babies" to be stillborn. Yet Baum's and Eckstein's field successes had also enhanced Itzik's reputation, so no doubt the general harbored mixed emotions regarding Baum's leaving.

"We *should* go through with Moonlight," said Benni, the sheaf of papers fluttering as he gesticulated with his beefy arms. "But I just can't fathom why the *other* side is also so anxious."

"Yours is not to reason why." Itzik's finger was still trained on Benni's nose. He holstered it in the pocket of his trousers and said, "*Hofshi l'chol ha'avodot*"—"Dismissed to all tasks"—an IDF expression forbidding further discussion. He turned to leave, then remembered why he had come. "And I reviewed your request to bring Eckstein out of Africa. Denied."

"May I ask why?"

"You know why. You two are dangerous together."

"To whom?" Benni wanted to keep his mouth shut, but in Itzik's presence the message from his brain to his lips was always waylaid.

"I am not going to discuss this, Baum."

"You think you should keep us apart? Like cheating schoolboys?"

"No!" Itzik shouted. "Putting you at different desks isn't enough. You two have to be separated by continents!"

"I thought he might be able to help us with this." Benni kept his own voice even. "Maybe see something we've missed."

"Moonlight is *yours*." Itzik was still yelling, a technique no longer effective once you got used to it. "You've handled it alone until now, and you will finish it that way."

And before Baum could outgun him with tactical brainpower, the general strode from the office and slammed the door.

"*Ken ha'mefaked*. Yes, Commander," Benni grunted, without a hint of deference.

He sighed, once more looking at the papers in his hands. He was having trouble forcing the stuff into the burn bag, which hung more than half empty from an aluminum frame.

Procrastination was a new habit for Baum, one he did not like. He barreled through his missions in the same way he still played weekend soccer, leaving breathless teammates and opponents in his wake. With his wide bald head and Dumbo ears pitched forward, his massive shoulders hunched above a belly full of Maya's schnitzel, his trunky fifty-two-year-old legs bruising those of boys half his age, he thundered through his play, as through his work, with the mischievous eyes and quick grin that made him look more like the bratwurst seller he might have been, had he stayed in the country of his birth.

Benni never let wait until the morrow an effort that could be handled *now*, no matter the discomfort. A few disgruntled AMAN officers disliked him for his bluntness, while envying his successes. There was no one in the unit who did not respect him. His superiors never wondered what he was *really* thinking.

So being hampered by hesitation was a strange sensation. In nearly thirty years of intelligence work, he had never entertained a vision of these final weeks. Like other men of action, he had assumed, even hoped, that his career's end would come upon him mercifully. Something loud and quick.

But this? A few desultory days of file pruning?

Well, at least he would not have to endure the torturous ritual of clearing out a closet full of boots and ranks and dress uniforms. As a *katam*, a special duty officer in AMAN, he had not worn a uniform in years. The last time had been in 1986, at a quiet ceremony in the office of the Prime Minister. Eckstein had stood next to him, his arms encased in plaster casts, muttering something about a medal from the Likud Party being equivalent to an Iron Cross. A dubious distinction.

Benni raised the sheaf of papers high above the burn bag, barked "*Kfotz!*" like the jumpmasters at Tel Nof, and dropped the pile into the receptacle. Pleased with this small victory, he put his thick fingers to his wide hips and looked around.

He had never liked the office anyway. It was too big, and it was up on the third floor, too far from the troops. But Ben-Zion had insisted that if Baum was going to run Operations, he would have to sit up here with the rest of Olympus.

Of course, Benni always took a bad situation and twisted it by the throat. His cavernous "private" office became a sort of free-for-all conference center for all the *katamim* under his command. He had quickly cured the boardroom atmosphere, having his subordinates haul in filing cabinets, bookshelves, extra desks, wall maps, and two green steel combination safes, for he insisted that intelligence officers worked better in smoke-filled, claustrophobic spaces. A comfy operations room invited you to kick back and ponder a problem, while a stinking cell made you drive for a solution so you could escape to fresh air.

The IDF had an egalitarian, no-saluting, wrinkled-uniform reputation that smacked of insubordination, and Benni encouraged the tradition, for it often catalyzed into stunning field coups. In most Western nations, a soldier could expect to face his commander across a polished floor that served as a canyon between the ranks. Benni had replaced the CO's desk with a T-shaped structure of tables, the head serving as his work space, while his team perched on plastic kitchen chairs surrounding the leg, a design that proclaimed, "Okay, I'm the boss. But go ahead, argue with me."

Baum hated the idea that his team members might say "Yes" to him when they meant "No," or "Good idea" when they really wanted to scream, "*Hishtagata?* Are you nuts?" For many of his planning sessions, he placed someone *else* at the head of the T, while the rest of his crew paced, swigged Cokes, and blew a choking fog of cigarette smoke.

Department legend had it that General Ben-Zion had once thundered into Baum's office with an order, only to find the colonel's driver ensconced happily in his chair, boots up on the blotter and wearing the uniform of an air force major. Baum, Eckstein, and the rest of their team were dressing in the singlets and shorts of a soccer club, an armorer was filling their gym bags with mini-Uzis and magazines, and the general had backed out without saying a word, apparently deciding that ignorance was the better part of valor.

Yet Baum's socialistic style did not prevent him from driving his crew like a chain gang overseer, and indeed the clearest clues to his work ethic were the road construction signs he had affixed to his doors. No engraver had ever carved a nameplate for him and at present the only evidence that herein lay the bustling lair of the Chief of Operations was a small red metal triangle nailed to the door side facing the corridor. It had been lifted from the concertina wire girdling a minefield on the Golan Heights, its meaning clear to any foolhardy interloper: Unless you are a professional and know exactly what you're up to . . . Stay Out.

The door suddenly creaked open, and Benni stiffened, for another visit by Itzik would surely unleash his worst insubordinate demons. But the head that poked inside belonged to Raphael Chernikovsky.

The small, balding, bespectacled officer, known to all by his departmental sobriquet, Horse, was Benni's top analyst and troubleshooter. He suffered the unenviable task of sitting in on all of Baum's planning sessions, then tearing the proposals apart with astute critiques. It was an unpopular though indispensable position.

"*Shabbat Shalom*," Horse offered as he slipped in like a shy wraith. He was carrying a laptop computer, and one white shirttail was half out of his trousers.

"To you too, *Soos*," said Benni. He glanced at his watch, annoyed that even on the cusp of a weekend he could not indulge his melancholy in peace. "What's up?"

"Well," Horse fumbled, smearing a wisp of red hair over his shiny scalp. "It's about your retirement party."

Benni rolled his eyes. He did not want to even think about such a funereal soiree. "Aren't those things supposed to be a surprise?"

"I . . . Sure, I guess so. But no one thinks it is possible."

Benni folded his arms, pondering the backhanded compliment. After all, he *was* the grand master of conspiracies. "Yes. Well, do whatever you want. I'll play along."

"Here in the office? Or would you prefer a restaurant?"

"Let's talk about it next week." Baum waved a hand in the air.

"We only have two weeks."

"Go home, Horse. It's Shabbat."

"Okay. But the girls will want to prepare. They have been asking—"

"Go home!" Benni boomed, and Horse stiffened as if he had touched a damp electrical plug. He backed up to the door and struggled for the flip handle.

"Sure, Benni. Have a nice day off. I will see you Sunday."

"Yes."

Horse was now halfway out, shielding himself behind the doorframe. "Uh, how did it go with Itzik?"

"Smooth as a rhino's ass."

"Oh. So Eckstein will not be joining us?"

"No. He stays in Africa."

"Oh. Too bad."

"Your dinner is getting *cold*." Benni's voice began to rise again. The door decapitated Horse's shadow, and his rapid footfalls echoed away.

Benni frowned, aware that he should follow his own advice and depart. It was a Friday eve, the Sabbath had begun, and his office held that terrible stillness of a sports stadium long after the main event. There were other sounds, from far away, for the three main floors and basement labs were always haunted by the lonely men and women who had to keep the thing alive. Here and there a telex chattered, a telephone rang, a printer spat decrypted text from a computer. But all in all, the building barely breathed, settling into its welcome weekend coma.

He looked around and decided that the task, though simple, was too daunting for today. Maya and his two sons, Yosh and Amos, were holding *Shabbat* dinner for him. Some other time, a few small boxes, and all his personal effects could easily be packed into his car.

His walls did not hold a single plaque, no trophies, medals, or citations, though there were plenty of those gathering dust in the attic of his home in Abu Tor. Instead, his priorities were displayed by a few pictures on a shelf behind his desk. First came early black-and-whites, himself not slim but muscular, in groups of uniformed comrades. Then the smiles of his family shone brightly from Agfacolor hues. And finally a few darker candids of Benni and Eckstein against the backdrop of several foreign cities.

There was, however, a single item propped against one corner of the room, of which even Benni was much too proud to relegate to a rusty footlocker.

The long black iron tube was reminiscent of an oboe, its bottom half cocooned in polished wood and splayed into a bell-shaped horn, with two thick pistol grips, a trigger, and a pull-down hammer jutting from the heavy body. Its mouth held a green metal phallus head, the nose cap a deactivated detonator. It was a Rocket Propelled Grenade 7-D, a Russian antitank device that had become the favorite of terrorists from Belfast to Baghdad. This particular *Reaktiviny Protivotankovyi Granatomet* had never actually been fired at Israeli troops or tanks, its fate reserved for glories greater than a single battlefield catastrophe.

The weapon's master had arrived in Israel back in 1986, but to Benni, those days of Ramadan still came to him in waking dreams. Each time he touched the puckered bullet scar that creased his belly, he remembered Operation Flute and breathed sighs of relief.

Benni stared at the RPG. He wondered if the fingerprints of Amar Kamil might still be found there, next to those of himself and Eytan, who together had in private moments hefted the device, shaking their heads in silence at each other.

A gap of nearly fifteen years divided Baum and Eckstein, yet even with their very first handclasp of so long ago, they had known that they were destined to be partnered. Both men were German born, and both had shed the dusty uniforms of combat officers for the anonymous glories of AMAN, knowing that they would spend their lives assumed by friends and relatives to be the boring bureaucrats of some redundant government institution.

They experienced, if such a thing existed, a melding of the minds, a quasitelepathic language that had them functioning as one, the resultant power doubled. It was a phenomenon Benni had previously found only with Maya, and that was after an adult lifetime of wedded joy and discourse. His relationship with Eckstein was born of blood, toil, danger, and that foolish, unimpeachable trust a man must have for his own parachute, if he intends to jump at all.

It had nearly come apart one winter day in Munich, when, too eager to scratch the name of Amar Kamil from Israel's elimination list, they had caused the death of a decoy placed before their path. Ben-Zion's punishment had been to banish them to menial duties. Yet, in a very real sense, Amar Kamil himself had saved them, returning to the land of his birth and raising Operation Flute from the grave.

Their renegade reputations remained intact. Down in the small cafeteria on floor two, the bogus cover of a comic book, drawn by one of Benni's artistic analysts, was still taped to the wall. It showed Baum's and Eckstein's heads poking from a single body, whose muscled arms waved pistols, James Bond attaché cases, and streams of computer paper, HATEOMIM HANORAIM—The Terrible Twins—exclaimed the cartoon title.

For General Ben-Zion, it was painful to watch the glories that he coveted heaped upon two men who obeyed barely one third of his orders, argued with another third, and ignored the rest. He could not disband a union that brought kudos from the Knesset, but he *could* promote them. They rose in ranks and the increase in responsibilities caused the separations in assignments.

So Benni was a lieutenant colonel now, running Operations. Eckstein was a major in command of his own AMAN team, and had been sent to Ethiopia on a long-range mission, the importance of which Baum could not contest. Yet the colonel missed his right hand, his right brain, and he assumed that Eytan also suffered the phantom pains of amputation.

Perhaps it was a sign—the separation, the falling winter night—that it was time to go. No other partnership would ever be the same, and Maya well deserved an end to many nights alone. Not that she had endured her trials in silence, mind you, but she had done most of her yelling at his photograph, while he was away.

In just a few short weeks, Baum would be gone. No man was irreplaceable, and his ego, always held in careful check, did not permit the luxury of assuming that he would be missed for long.

Yet who would run Operations? Who would lead the teams of Queens Commando into the wastes of foreign deserts, the alleyways of enemy capitals? If Eytan Eckstein stayed with AMAN, he might well sit behind this desk someday. But Benni had his doubts.

Baum was nothing of a diplomat, but Eckstein was even less so. You had to be able to pilot a desk in AMAN with the skill of an F-16 jockey. As far as office politics were concerned, Eckstein was a kamikaze.

"Well," Baum whispered, half aloud, "he'll have to fly alone." But he wished that he could have his old partner as his copilot, just once more.

There was a single file sitting on Baum's tabletop, a thick packet inside a brown clasp cover, stamped with the title OR YAREACH—Moonlight—and a slash of SODI BEYOTER—Most Secret. He had intended to sign it out and take it home, but now he thought better of it and walked the file over to his safe. All the details had been hammered out, and with a bit of luck this mission would soon be put to bed.

The Israel Defense Forces still had six prisoners of war being held by enemy factions across the Middle East. In a country of less than five million souls, every life was precious, and the IDF's reputation was built on its commitment never to leave a dead, wounded, or captured soldier in the field. This obsession gave the man or woman at arms a sense of security, but it also gave the enemy a terrible advantage. An Israeli prisoner's barter value in the political souks was greater than a wing of fighter planes.

All of the prisoners were being held by terrorist factions, in turn controlled by Arab confrontation states. Three of the men had been blown from their tanks in 1982, at the battle for Sultan Yakoub, a mountain town in Lebanon that turned out to be a Syrian armored porcupine. The Syrians made a gift of the three Jews to Ahmed Jabril, chief of the Popular Front for the Liberation of Palestine—General Command. President Hafiz al-Assad insisted that he had no influence over the notorious terror chieftain, even as Jabril took Turkish baths in Damascus with the commander of the Syrian Mukhabarat.

The fates of two more servicemen were less clear, the identities of their captors the subject of some argument between AMAN and Mossad. This made the probabilities of rescue slim, so it was hoped that a policy of filling Israeli detention camps with captured terrorists would prod the opposition into an uneven swap. Yet no one on the other side seemed all that interested in recovering their Arab brothers, and they held on to their Israeli prisoners like amateur thieves with a priceless van Gogh.

The frustrated Israelis even threw all their efforts into a bid to broker the release of American and German hostages held in Lebanon, which finally succeeded. Yet the hopes that Israeli prisoners would emerge with all the rest were shattered, and the crestfallen diplomats and intelligence officers went home with thank-you notes from Washington and Bonn.

At last, one of the Israeli POWs was returned to the bosom of his family. He was a Druze soldier from a proud mountain village in the Carmel, and he came home in a box. Samir had been beaten to death by his captors, but the government still agreed to free two hundred dangerous men, in exchange for a memory.

The sixth man was perhaps the most famous prisoner of war since Israeli agent Eli Cohen had been hanged in Damascus. Captain Dan Sarel was a member of the Israeli navy's elite naval commandos, a small unit whose menu of services offered high-altitude night parachuting, long-range scuba navigation, and close-quarter combat skills that would frighten a rottweiler.

On a moonless night in 1986, Sarel's Flotilla 13 team had breached the Lebanese waters off Junieh, attacked a terrorist command post of Amal militiamen, and destroyed it under a storm of enemy flares and tracers.

In the tradition of Israeli commanders, Sarel had then pushed his reluctant men into their Zodiacs, while he headed back into the madness to retrieve the body of a fallen comrade. Within seconds he was cut down by a burst of Kalashnikov rounds and snatched away by eager Amal fighters. The IDF command brought up everything they had, turning a secret mission into a blatant rescue effort that raged throughout the night. But at dawn, the exhausted gunship pilots turned for home and the missile boats withdrew from the smoking shoreline. It was clear that Dan Sarel, if he still lived, was on his way to the Bekka Valley.

Sarel's trail, unlike that of the other soldiers in captivity, did not go immediately cold upon his taking. The commander of Amal, Mustaffa Dirani, was in dire need of equipment for his warriors, and he correctly assessed the cash equivalent of an Israeli commando with the highest IDF security clearances. When Sarel survived his multiple wounds, an auction ensued, yet no other lip-smacking terror chief could match the government of Iran for buying power. Tehran quickly paid the top bid of $350,000, then had Dirani turn the Israeli captain over to Hizbollah, the orphan terror wing of Iranian Islamic fundamentalism.

The Israelis knew that Tehran still pulled the strings, but they adhered to the rules of the game and turned to the puppet Hizbollah. Yet it was an iron doll that could not be moved, even when Israeli commandos from the elite Sayeret Matkal—General Staff Reconnaissance Unit—kidnapped Sheik Sa'id, the movement's spiritual leader, from his bed in southern Lebanon.

For years Benni Baum had watched in frustration as other officers dedicated life, limb, and careers to the recovery of Dan Sarel. The captain's wife, holding a five-year-old daughter never touched by her father's hands, made international appeals on television. Jews worldwide carried poster pictures of the captain during Israel Independence Day parades. Non-Israeli diplomats made appeals to the Iranians, only to be rebuffed across carafes of coffee and gulfs of mistrust. The name Dan Sarel became a symbol of the lost Israeli warrior, whispered in cafés in Tel Aviv, broached by Mossad agents risking their necks in unfriendly places, scoured for by AMAN researchers among the tons of intercepts pouring in from telephone, fax, and satellite traffic.

Nothing.

And then, one cool September morning, the message made its way from a grit-lined Arab hand into a soiled Jewish palm. It happened at the abandoned Lebanese village of Abu Zibleh, a cluster of bullet-pocked cement huts where Israeli paratroopers came to hone the arts of breaching rooms with assault rifles and grenades.

An IDF lieutenant stopped his men with a raised hand and a shout of "Cease firing!"

A Lebanese farmer stood quietly nearby. From his shoulder hung an ancient shotgun, from his right hand a lifeless pigeon, from his left, an envelope. The lieutenant read the letter, shook the farmer's hand, gave him a fifty-shekel note as proof that they had met, and without further comment ordered his men to saddle up.

The deal was simple, clear, too good to be real: Dan Sarel, in exchange for Sheik Sa'id, plus one thousand aircraft tires for F-4 Phantom fighter jets, one hundred Sidewinder missiles, and fifty TOW antitank systems. The note was signed by Abu Yasir, the nom de guerre of Sa'id Abbas Mussawi, general secretary and operational commander of Hizbollah. Mussawi had no aircraft larger than hang gliders, so it was clear that the tires and Sidewinders would only be counted by his men en route to Tehran. As for the TOWs, no one really expected Israeli tank commanders to provide the terrorists in southern Lebanon with a high-tech executioner's ax.

But being children of the Levant, everyone understood this to be merely the opening gambit in the dance of the bazaar.

As the nature of the demands were purely military, the mission fell—after a squabble with Mossad—to AMAN and Special Operations. Benni Baum selected one of his men, a former Matkal commando, to carry the return note—a request for a formal meeting. Dressed in the clothes of a Lebanese farmer and armed only with a pistol, an air extraction beacon, and the legs of a sprinter, he slept alone at Abu Zibleh for three nights, until the pigeon hunter returned. . . .

At the first secret encounter between unofficial representatives, held in a seaside café on Cyprus, only two Israelis were in attendance. One was an attorney, Advocate Ori Neviim, who was trusted by Hizbollah because he was not an employee of any official Israeli body, but had labored for the release of POWs on a purely voluntary basis. The other was Lieutenant Colonel Benni Baum, who had been chosen as Chief of Security for Moonlight. The Minister of Defense had mentioned that Hizbollah's point man, Sheik Tafilli, had been educated in Frankfurt. Itzik Ben-Zion proposed his German-born Chief of Operations as Tafilli's opposite number.

While ten Israeli AMAN officers and Matkal commandos hovered anxiously out of sight, Baum and Tafilli quickly established a rapport in *Hochdeutsch*. They each absolutely refused the other's conditions, and the four Shiites and two Israelis left the café, pleased that progress had been made—at least in Middle Eastern terms.

After three more meetings, in Monte Carlo, Athens, and Palermo, Ori Neviim had reduced the Hizbollah demands to acceptance of the imprisoned Sheik Sa'id, three hundred pairs of tires, and four tons of nonlethal battle gear, such as combat webbing and field first-aid kits.

The Israeli politicians and general staff were terribly suspicious, and Ori Neviim warned that Hizbollah's move was, essentially, a separate peace. Other groups, such as Islamic Jihad and Hamas, might certainly attempt to foil such a deal.

Baum insisted, to the initial shock of his employers, that the exchange take place at *sea*. He reasoned that while the ability to attack an exchange site on any continent was common to all terror teams, the sea power of such factions was negligible. When Baum presented his argument at another emergency Council session, complete with maps, little ship models, and his bellicose yet irrefutable logic, the commander of Israel's navy said, "And here I thought us White Hats had all the brains. *Kol ha'kavod, Baum*. All the respect to you."

And so it was that in less than two weeks' time, an Israeli missile boat carrying Sheik Sa'id would drop anchor off the northern coast of Morocco. A Hizbollah freighter flying a Liberian flag and hosting Dan Sarel would coast to a halt, and it would be reminiscent of the old cold war exchanges at Berlin's Checkpoint Charlie. Baum would cross by flexible connecting bridge or Zodiac to take Sard in hand, and Tafilli would do the same for Sheik Sa'id.

Baum would be back in his office, packing up his photographs, and home in time to read the splashed headlines of a story in which his name would never appear. . . .

Benni spun the old-fashioned dial on the big steel safe and placed the Moonlight file inside. He closed it, lit a cigarette, took one last look at the snow-covered cathedral, and was heading for the door when it swung open.

"Good thing I caught you." Itzik Ben-Zion filled the frame again. He closed the door and backed up against it.

"Don't worry, Itzik," said Benni, assuming that the general wanted to reiterate his ban on Eckstein's participation. "I won't make a break for it."

"It's a bad piece of news." Itzik never softened a blow. "Just came in encoded, but all the papers will have it in an hour." He paused.

"*Nu?*" Baum placed his fists to his hips, while the cigarette hung from a corner of his mouth. Bad news was how he earned his keep.

"A bomb attack at our consulate in New York," Ben-Zion continued. "Two dead, five wounded, one seriously. It looks like a suicide attack. . . . As a matter of fact, a human bomb."

Now Baum understood, but he was not diving into this with Itzik just yet. "It's *not* Hizbollah," he stated.

"Who says?"

"I say." Baum tried to control his exasperation. "At this point, if they want out of the exchange, they know they can just pick up the phone or send another fucking farmer to Abu Zibleh. They don't have to go blowing up people in Manhattan, *koos shel ha'imayot shelahem*." He added the Arabic curse on their mothers because he was not quite convincing himself.

"*And* he was dressed as a Hasid," said Ben-Zion.

"A Hasid?" Baum's eyes widened, and he almost laughed. "Nonsense."

"It's on the GSS videotapes." While Benni's brow furrowed, Itzik spilled the worst of it. "The seriously wounded man is a Shabaknik. It's Moshiko Ben-Czecho. He's just hanging on. Lost a hand and an eye."

Baum opened his fists and dropped his arms to his sides. He inhaled a long breath and took the cigarette from his mouth. He had fostered Ben-Czecho, encouraged him, coached him. The faces of other men and women who had been crippled by his nurturing flickered briefly through his memory. When would he ever learn that a recommendation to the services was not the same as helping a young man into college?

Itzik finally moved from the door. He sat down on the conference table, while Baum continued staring into space. "Give me one," said Itzik quietly, and Baum reached into his breast pocket and fished out the pack of Time in slow motion. Itzik lit up with his own lighter.

"He keeps asking for you, Baum," said the general, in an empathic tone that few ever heard from his lips.

Benni turned to his boss, their narrowed eyes meeting through the smoke. What was Itzik saying? Was he telling Baum that Moshiko needed his adopted father figure at his side but that it was out of the question with Moonlight on the horizon? That would be typical of Ben-Zion, so Benni just waited, and watched.

"Shabak and Mossad will already be all over this like flies on camel shit," Itzik said.

"That's right. No reason for AMAN to stick its prick in too."

"However, given the priority of Moonlight, if my Chief of Operations suspects that this act *could* be the work of Hizbollah, or a rejectionist faction, and that it *might* have some bearing on the exchange . . . well, that's another story."

Okay, Baum, Benni cautioned himself. *Don't cut off your own nose.* "Well, it *might* be Hizbollah," he said. "It would be insane, but so would any man who takes them off the suspect list without seeing the evidence up close."

Itzik nodded slowly. They were making a deal, and Baum would owe him, which was a rare and precious IOU to have.

"Moshiko keeps asking for you," Itzik said again.

"I heard you."

"He may not live very long."

"So why am I standing here?"

"Three days, Baum." Itzik raised a warning finger. "No more." Then Benni hesitated, feeling as if he were about to buy a used Mercedes from a taxi driver. Was this some sort of setup? Was Itzik trying to get him out of the way while he turned Moonlight over to another officer or ran the mission himself? But so what? So Benni would not get that one last shoulder clap from the Prime

Minister. It wasn't as if he would have to scratch the chapter from his memoirs, because he couldn't write them anyway.

New York. Yes, the most important thing right now was to get over there and hold Moshiko's remaining hand. And just as important, a piece of information most probably forgotten by the boss, was Ruth.

Benni's only daughter was working on a Ph.D. at Columbia University. She had been there four years now, and they had not seen each other for two. But it was not the physical distance that separated father and child.

They were not on speaking terms. It was a pain that caused Benni, at least twice a day, to rub a spot on his chest like a man who has eaten too much *hareef*. Some mad bomber far away was offering him a chance to save a soul, and he knew whose soul that was.

"Agreed," said Baum. "Three days."

"And you'll report to me from the consulate," Itzik ordered.

"As soon as I get there."

"And if Tafilli gets cold feet from this and wants to push up the timetable"—Itzik wagged the same finger—"you're on a plane."

"First flight out," Baum promised. He looked at his commander. Perhaps Itzik had learned something from his own personal misfortunes. *Sorrow changes all of us*, he thought.

The general stood, went to the door, opened it, and yelled "Yudit!" at the top of his lungs. He never used an intercom. It was a power thing. Then he turned to Baum. "There's a military flight out of Ben-Gurion in one hour. I can hold it for fifteen minutes, but no more."

Baum walked behind his desk, bent to a lateral file drawer and pulled a worn, prepacked valise from inside. When you came to Queens Commando from some other combat unit, your "war kit bag" was exchanged for a suitcase. Instead of clean fatigues, boots, grenades, and ammunition, it held clothing with foreign labels, "backstopping" papers that upheld your cover, toiletries from foreign countries, and a trio of passports, none of which was Israeli. If you had to put a pistol in there too, the chances were fifty-fifty that you were not coming back.

Benni picked up the phone and called Maya. He told her he was leaving for three days and he held the phone away from his ear and grimaced while she yelled at him. Then he shouted back, "I'm going to see Ruth."

There was silence for a while, then Maya said something in German, then Benni said, "*Ich liebe dich auch*," and he hung up.

Yudit appeared in the doorway. She had black curls and bright eyes and a disposition that had made it possible for her to hang on as Itzik's secretary for two years—longer than any other young soldier had ever suffered it. She treated the general like a senile father, and he enjoyed it even as he growled at her. It was as if he still had one child who tolerated him.

"What is it, Itzik?" she demanded. "I have a date."

"You'll have to cancel," he ordered. "Baum here has to get to the airport. Now. You'll drive his car."

"Benni," she implored, "why can't you drive it there yourself? Really."

"I can—" Baum began.

"No you can't," said Itzik. "We're short on vehicles, and I don't want one sitting in long-term parking for no reason. Now move." And with that, Ben-Zion strode out into the hallway, having recovered his wits after suffering the temporary discomforts of his own sentimentality. "And *call* me, Baum," his departing voice echoed.

Benni shrugged apologetically, wrestled into a leather car coat, and hefted his valise.

"I am sorry, my dear," he said as he touched Yudit's shoulder and headed out the door. "If we hurry, you might make it back to your date in time for the good parts."

"Why, Colonel Baum!" She addressed him with facetious formality. Yudit was twenty-four now and an officer, but she had been working with Benni since her first months in the army. He was like a favorite uncle. "It so happens that I am still quite virginal."

"Of course," said Baum. "So is my wife."

She laughed, closed the office door, and slipped her free hand through his heavy arm. As they headed toward the darkened stairwell, Benni tried to maintain the levity.

"Well, at any rate," he said, "think of the overtime you'll be making."

"A fool's fortune," she scoffed, for if the Israel Defense Forces actually paid such bonuses, she would have been as wealthy as a princess.

She looked up at Baum, expecting to continue their banter. But she saw that he was not smiling, his eyes unfocused, on something far away. Something lying in the shadows.

She had seen that look before, when he was flying off to bring back a body rather than a trophy.

Chapter 2: New York

Martina Ursula Klump dined alone, in the farthest corner of the room.

She had a predilection for the last compartment on any Continental train, the dark and cramped repose of final seats inside the tails of airplanes. She preferred the apexes of triangles, where all approaches funneled toward her scrutiny, bringing friends and foes alike into sharp focus.

She had her back to the wall, and usually she was most comfortable that way. Yet tonight her position seemed doubly precarious.

She brought a glass of red Traviche Oak slowly to her mouth, the chiseled tips of her blond hair drifting from her collarbone toward the goblet's stem as she tipped her head. Yet her metallic-gray eyes failed to focus on the smooth white stucco walls, the polished oak tables and chairs, the waiting water glasses tucked with precisely folded napkins.

Instead, she dropped her gaze to the stack of newspapers piled at the table's edge. The cover of the *New York Post* showed a middle-aged man supporting his grief-stricken wife at their daughter's graveside. The headline postulated in three-inch scarlet letters: JEW VS JEW??

Fools. Martina silently chastised the paper's editors for their careless speculations, even as she wished against all logic that they might be correct. A tidy conclusion to the mystery of this bombing would certainly ease her discomfort, but she harbored no such delusion, for the investigators in place would quickly look beyond the Hasid's frock coat for the wolf who no doubt wore it. The saboteur's technique too much resembled her own signature, and because she was innocent of any involvement, the rage of being plagiarized was multiplied.

Until this moment, all the pieces of her plan had been clicking nicely into place. Now everything was in jeopardy, an unwelcome sensation, as if she sat in a rocker at the prow of a schooner.

She set the wineglass down, raising her eyes to the wall chandeliers throwing flickers over etchings of riding gauchos, framed prints of Buenos Aires, and the pelt of a mountain cat hung beside the lanyards and stones of a *bola*. Perhaps the Argentine Pavillion was a nostalgic venture into memory, but Martina indulged the digression without shame. It was one of the only restaurants of its kind in New York, lost among a hedgerow of Brazilian haunts on West Forty-sixth Street. She did not go there often, but when she needed to ponder in an ambience that soothed, she would wait until the business crowds had gone and the only other customers were a few lonely Argentine expatriates.

The music was always the same—pianos, accordions, and Carlos Gardel's warm tenor vibrato, trembling with the soft tango rhythms of years long gone. And the waiters were all immigrants, sad quiet men in black trousers and vests, billowy white shirts, and crisp bow ties. The one who served Martina bowed and called her *Señorita*, and then he kept his distance.

She felt the waiter's sidelong gaze upon her, from far away behind the thick oak bar, and she knew that any fantasy of his was chilled by her demeanor, for nothing in her face or form suggested need or friendship. Draped neatly across the finials of her chair, a black leather Andrew Marc jacket framed her upper body, whose athletic curvature was softened by the folds of a white turtleneck. Her legs, long yet sinewed like those of a tennis player, were crossed at the knee and concealed to the ankles beneath a slim black woolen skirt. Her boots were high and laced through many eyelets, with a sole like a runner's shoe.

Martina never wore a heel unless she absolutely had to.

Like lacquered nails, lace underclothes, and finger rings, makeup also held a lowly place in her fashion lexicon. Her high North European cheekbones, long eyebrows darker than her hair, and slightly cleft chin made artificial emphasis redundant. Although the Middle Eastern sun had added some fine etches at the corners of her eyes, her skin was smooth and thirtyish, six years younger than her passports would have shown, had they been genuine. Her nose was balanced to her features, although its tip was somewhat sharp, and her mouth was very wide, turning slightly downward at the corners.

Empathy was not a trait she projected, yet she did have a smile in her repertoire, a bright and flashing thing that she could summon on demand. But she kept that smile hidden, wearing it behind her lips the way New York women wore expensive necklaces, tucking them away to discourage sprinting snatchers.

Martina wore no jewelry besides a silver Rolex watch, although that choice was not in deference to Manhattan street thieves, for she could summon bursts of speed that would leave a mugger gaping. Her body was a tool of her profession, kept taut and lubricated by the running that she favored for its lack of ties to gyms and gear. Still, fleeing was the last response with which Martina faced aggression, for in addition to the Walther P-38 that made her handbag heavy, she had been schooled in hand-to-hand techniques devised for maiming, rather than dissuasion.

She was a woman for whom liberation meant continuing to live as she always had, with the exception of some months in Germany's Bruchsal

Penitentiary, an anomaly she intended never to repeat. Her independent outlook had not altered much since teenage years, nor, hardly, had her appearance, although she had learned that men were quickly fooled by fashionable costumes and sexual misperceptions. A man who saw her crop-haired Wanted poster in the antiterror halls of the *Bundeskriminalamt* in Wiesbaden would fail to match it to the face that dipped once more toward the newspapers, though no surgical wizard had ever touched her features.

She had also bought the *Times* and the *Daily News*, but the *Post*'s postulations would most likely list her name among the suspects, if that was in the cards at all. Despite the eyewitnesses, Uri Dan, the paper's Israeli correspondent, was scoffing at the idea that the bomber had indeed been a Hasid. He listed motivated men of Hizbollah, Hamas, and Ahmed Jabril's PFLP-GC, while on the editorial page Evans and Novak spun a web of reasoning for Zionist conspiracies, a ridiculous theory that the Israelis might have bombed their own consulate. A double spread of inside photos showed the lifted fists of gleeful Amal fighters in Sidon and the bug-eyed visage of Arafat as he sidestepped a full denunciation of the carnage. But nowhere in these pages, or in those of any other paper, did Martina's name appear.

Yet the absence of a public accusation did not comfort her. She eliminated all the journalistic clutter, distilled the facts, and assumed unpublished details. She knew the minds of Israeli professionals, who had once splashed her photograph across worldwide newspapers after a similar bombing in Buenos Aires. And since she *had* prepared that device, she had not minded the strange sensation of having her scent sniffed publicly by bloodhounds. Here the very absence of her name was more ominous, and she could picture the fingers flipping through her file in Jerusalem.

A lone suicidal bomber, a clever and concealed device of molded C-4 or Semtex, a mule in a guise that would grant him close proximity to a wary target. When the modus operandi was examined, she knew that she would be there on the top-five list of suspects.

She certainly could have done it.

But she had not.

The waiter crossed the floor, carrying a silver tray of appetizers and an *Empanada Argentina*, a steaming meat pie shaped like a clam. He placed the tray before Martina and stood back, smiling as he asked, a little too familiarly, "*¿Qué tal, señorita?*"

"*Bien, gracias,*" she said, and although her mouth made something like a smile, her eyes stayed fixed on his so long that he blushed, bowed, and fled back to the bar.

Her gaze was useful as a tool of measurement, for persons of weak character were quickly unnerved by it, and the low voice that emanated from her wide throat could also be unsettling. To Argentines her Spanish pegged her as a stunning *compadrita*, while Germans equally assumed her to be one of their own. Her English had been eroticized by years in Paris, and Americans often thought that she was French, Belgian, or even Scandinavian. The camouflage was useful.

Martina watched the waiter scurry to a family of new customers, and she almost wished he had been someone more magnetic. Her work surrounded her with men she could not touch.

As she moved her chair closer to the table and smoothed a napkin over her lap, she felt the small pucker scar beneath her skirt, just below her navel. The hole was the result of a small-caliber wound she had acquired during her escape from Bruchsal, and since then she had allowed few men to see it. Those with whom she had slept since that frantic flight from Germany had all been fascinated by the hard nipple of pink flesh.

Her late husband had always glossed over the wound, because he had scars of his own.

She flushed the thoughts of failed erotic ventures from her mind and broke the back of the *empanada*, forking bits of smoking meat into her mouth. Something else pricked the inside of her nostrils, and she looked up to see a woman at a nearby table lighting up a filterless with a match. The scent of sulfur sent her briefly on a flickering excursion, the smells and sounds rushing by like scenery past a roller coaster car. . . .

She felt her fingers trembling over deadly clay, and faraway concussions smacked her ears. The oily stench of motorcycle rubber breached her woolen mask as sweat stung the skin beneath her leathers and her pistol bucked in the speeding wind. Nausea rose with the sickening wrench of tearing muscle, the snarl of dogs, the clang of gates and locks, and then the dawn air thrilled her over the pounding of her sprint and she tumbled with a punch of soaring power in her groin. The agony gripped her again, the cold steel of a truck bed, the torture of pocked roads, the blessed stab of a needle into flights of soaring darkness. And finally the whiteness of the Levantine sun, the throb of sinews on the mend, the gentle popping of distant rifles. And the smell of sulfur from the guns . . .

In the halving of a second her eyes refocused on the newspaper. But for a moment she saw the glossy pages of another publication. It had been more than a decade since that copy of *Stern* had screamed its story, yet she remembered every word and photograph. Hers, and those of Friederike Krabbe,

Barbara Meyer, and Inge Viett, all splashed beneath a banner, DIE FRÄULEIN AUS P-38—The Girls from P-38—as if their favorite pistol were an alien planet. And for her talents with sophisticated destructive devices, she had been anointed with her nom de terror: "Frau Seafore." Mrs. C-4. The Bride of the Plastic Explosives.

Yes. She *could* have done it.

But she had not.

And for once she could not identify the motive, and certainly not the capability, of any other competitor. She knew the secret of the Hizbollah prisoner exchange with the Israelis and was sure the fundamentalists would hold their radicals in check. The Arafat camp was already waving a white flag, and they would hardly sully it with Jewish blood. Most of the anti-PLO rejectionists were well intentioned yet ill equipped to handle such audacity. They could not even properly hijack a boatload of senile tourists.

Martina had herself been contracted to scuttle the upcoming exchange, and she assumed her employers to have tactical wits, so it made no sense that *they* would muddy up the playing field and make her mission doubly hard to execute. Yet her own technique had been mimicked in this bombing, and the imitation infuriated rather than flattered her. Someone not only had stolen her thunder but might cause the enemy's wagons to be drawn into an impregnable cordon.

The appetizers had lost their attraction. Martina's stomach fluttered, and she dropped the fork on the plate, sat back expelling air between her lips, and finished off the red Traviche in one long swallow.

"*Unwichtig.* Unimportant," she whispered with forced conviction. "*Der Fisch muß flußaufwärts schwimmen.* The fish will swim upstream."

From the telephone and toilet alcove of the restaurant, a man emerged into the dining area. He looked around, was brought up sharply by his own image in the mirrored wall behind Martina's head, then came forward to her table.

Mussa Hawatmeh was clearly ill at ease in his new pin-striped navy suit, white shirt, and gray silk tie, but Martina had insisted that he learn to eschew jeans and leather jackets for such businesslike occasions. He unbuttoned his suit coat and took the seat at her right elbow, while she examined his freshly cut and gelled hair, the closely shaven olive skin, his dark eyes and youthful features. She was pleased, for he looked like the wealthy cousin to a prince of the House of Saud, or perhaps an ethnic businessman from Rio de Janeiro, or even Tel Aviv.

He settled stiffly in his chair, folded his fingers together, and placed them on the table edge. Then he glanced over at Martina and frowned, like a boy whose mother was forcing him to wear short pants to school.

Martina laughed and raised a finger that brought her waiter at a trot.

"*¿Por favor, señor?*" The waiter this time stood a meter from the table, as if staying outside the range of her gaze. He looked only at Mussa.

"He'll have an Escudo," said Martina, and when Mussa began to raise a hand in protest, she caught his wrist in a swift, firm grasp. "Yes," she emphasized. "And bring him also a *bife de chorizo*. Medium rare."

"*Muy bien.*" The waiter walked away.

Mussa raised his eyes to the ceiling. He appeared to be praying for clemency.

"Escudo is a good beer," Martina said in the measured German that Mussa had learned under her tutelage. "And you must learn to drink it, along with anything else that is offered you in company." She paused when he seemed to be ignoring her instruction. "*Sieh mich bitte an.*"

He obeyed and focused on her, and her tone returned to one of sympathetic coaching.

"In America," she continued, "a man who refuses a drink can only be one of two things; an ex-alcoholic or a Moslem. There is a time to put aside the rules of the *Sharia* in favor of the mission." She touched Mussa's hand again, this time more gently. "This is something that your enemies have always understood. How else could the Jews do battle on the Sabbath?" Her solid stare bored into Mussa's softer gaze as the waiter placed a tall glass of amber liquid on the table. "You must, at the very least"—she whispered now—"match them faith for faith, and will for will."

Mussa took the glass and with nauseous anticipation swallowed a gulp of the blasphemous brew. Martina smiled and swept the foam from his upper lip with her finger.

So much work, she thought. *So many barriers to penetrate.* She wondered if her men could ever rise to the occasion, put aside the superstitious tenets of their culture and religion to serve the greater purpose of Koranic laws that she, too, respected, yet saw as latticework on which to climb to greater glories.

In Lebanon, she had adopted these fledglings and transformed them, taught them languages and foreign cultures, electronics and improvisational ordnance. She had instructed them not only in the offensive driving of cars and trucks and motorcycles, but also in the mechanics of enhancement and repair, the crucial tactics of mobility. She had slapped them for the rust upon their gun barrels, and had she not been a woman in a Moslem world, she would have kissed them when their AK-47s were oiled and on target.

It was Martina who had seen the lack of foresight of their masters, the weakness in the hierarchy of Hizbollah that bound the anxious fingers of her warriors. It was she who had taken them away, formed an impenetrable cell of guerrillas whose ideals could never be subverted. They looked upon their mentor as something of a queen, while she viewed herself as more the mother of this group that called itself Yadd Allah. The Hand of God.

It was a name that she knew was probably at this very moment being whispered in the operations rooms of worldwide Western intelligence agencies. But if her men would live up to the promise of their title, they had to learn that Allah's will was sometimes best served when his laws were subverted.

They had learned to lie for Him. They had learned to kill for Him. And now that they were here upon the ramparts of his enemies, could she teach them to ignore Him?

There was so little time.

"Is he coming?" she asked as Mussa took another, smaller sip of the beer.

"Yes, he's on his way," he answered sullenly, as if he had suffered a reprimand.

She wondered for a moment if she had not erred, selecting for her pack of wolves all males. Their dedication and courage were unmatched, yet they lacked the finer instincts and determination of their female counterparts. She had worked for many years with the women of the Rote Armee Fraktion and knew that in a pinch, when all seemed lost, no man could match a woman for the ferocity of a cornered lioness. But on the other hand, those dens where females ruled were volatile, and no one woman kept control for long. Here, the boys bent quickly to her will.

With the exception of the legendary terror mistress Leila Khaled, there were few women on this earth who had successfully commanded groups of Moslem warriors. And although the boosting of her own ego was not the object of Martina's efforts, with some modest satisfaction she had allowed her men to anoint her with the code name "Leila."

She looked up at the entrance to the Pavillion. A small man stood next to the bar. His hair was white like seagull feathers, swept back from a brow made leathery by wind and sun. His vested gray wool suit, white collar, just a bit too large, and plain black tie were caped by a long blue winter coat. His gold-framed spectacles gave him the air of a Zurich clockmaker. When he saw Martina, he picked up the soft attaché at his feet and started forward.

Martina noted that the man she knew as Omar had replaced his plain brown cane with a less modest walking stick. This one was straight and tapered, with a polished metal tip. She had often wondered why such a sprightly fellow would need an aid at all. Now she decided that it was just a decorous weapon.

She reappraised the man who had been functioning as cutout, hiring her services for a third party, negotiating and consulting with her for many months. She had come to regard him as merely a pleasant messenger, but given the recent explosive events, she wondered now if his harmless demeanor camouflaged a threat, like a carnivorous flower.

As the dapper Arab bowed and took the seat facing her, she saw that the stick's ivory pommel was a bust of Ludwig van Beethoven.

"*And* you have good taste in music," she opened in English without greeting or preamble.

"I am of that generation." Omar shrugged as if apologizing, while he set the briefcase between his feet.

"A drink, *señor*?" The waiter was at his shoulder.

"Too strong for this heart." The old man waved a hand politely, and as the waiter left he added, "And bad for the soul."

Mussa grunted and removed his hand from the glass of Escudo.

"And a good evening to you, my young friend." Omar bowed to Mussa, who just dipped his head in reply.

"He is not feeling very well," Martina explained.

"Oh, I am so sorry."

"Actually, neither am I," she added.

"Is it the weather?" Omar turned his head, offering a sympathetic ear, but the disarming smile beneath his slim white mustache did not fade. "At times, this city can make Hamburg seem like a summer playground." He pronounced it "bley-ground," the substitute of *b* for *p* the clue that gives away all speakers for whom Arabic is the mother tongue.

"It is the *political* winds," Martina said, and she glanced down pointedly at the *New York Post*. The waiter returned with sirloins for her and Mussa. She forked her strip of meat and cut across its backbone, the blood welling up around her blade.

Omar watched her hands, and she studied his face, but she found only inquisitive interest, with no hint of guilt or discomfort.

Martina did not absolutely know who Omar represented, which was standard field procedure. He was of Palestinian descent, so she assumed his master to be of the ilk of Abu Nidal, or perhaps Abu Ibrahim, whose chief bomb maker, Mohammed Rashid, had once been tutored by her very own RAF cell in Germany. One of these men, who would loathe an Israeli-Arab rapprochement of any kind, might well have suggested her for the job, and she was wise enough to understand the use of this elderly buffer. But she would have been a fool to allow propriety to prevent her from some accusative probing.

"I wonder who might be so foolish as to commit so terrible an atrocity," she wondered in encoded politesse.

"It is a shame," said Omar, taking up her tone.

"Especially when peace seems in the offing."

"Perhaps close at hand."

Martina chewed a piece of meat, while Mussa watched his elders like a silent ball boy. He had quickly lost interest in his own meal.

"Such secret deals are precarious enough," Martina continued, a thin reference to the prisoner exchange.

"A house of cards," Omar agreed.

"Then who would do this strange thing now? This thing that so resembles my cachet. What would your guess be?"

The old man stirred in his seat, repositioning a troublesome limb. He touched his mustache, pursed his lips, and looked up at the ceiling.

"Our troubled King of Babylon?" he posited, thinking of Saddam Hussein.

"Too busy licking his wounds to risk a final retaliation for his recent Scud festival."

Omar nodded and refocused on Martina's face, where he was met with an accusatory glare.

"I assure you, my daughter," he said—and Martina stiffened at the parental endearment—"that I am no wiser than you on this matter. But since *we* know about the secret arrangements that will soon take place, it is good sense to think that others might know too. Not so?"

She did not answer. Except for the rippling of her jaw muscles, she moved no more than a hunting cat.

"This act," Omar continued as he tapped the *Post* with a finger, "seems quite desperate. It is surely an attempt by someone who objects to the coming arrangement to throw the train and all its passengers from the track."

"And are you saying that it might succeed?" Martina whispered, sensing Mussa's body go stiff as he, too, understood the implication. "Are you saying that I may soon find myself on line at the New York Unemployment Office?"

Omar laughed. He could not help himself, for the image of Martina, in her fashionable clothing, filling out a form where under "Skills" she might write, "Terrorist—References available upon request," filled his eyes with tears that he dabbed away with his handkerchief.

His amusement did not improve Martina's mood, for the idea that the prisoner exchange might be canceled due to the consular attack would mean that her own contract would be voided. Yadd Allah would be left begging at the back door of some mosque in Jersey City. However Omar answered now, if it was a lie, she would have to read it on his face, in his body.

He leaned toward the table, placing his fingertips together as if in prayer, and he spoke into Martina's eyes like a kindly old professor imparting wisdom to a doubtful student.

"Politics has many levels, my dear, and the animals of politics have their public voices. Below those voices, they have spirits, where their truths live. The voices, so I hear, are even now hurling accusations at the United Nations. But the *spirits* carry on unchanged. *You*, too, are expected to carry on, despite some fears that you may have now."

Mussa recoiled into the back of his chair. He suddenly had to pee, in part reaction to the beer, but mosdy because he had witnessed Martina's rage before, and this old man's deprecation of her courage could ignite unpredictable reactions. But her hand reached out and held him still.

"I assure you, Omar, that I am not a nervous bride," she said. "However, it is a common fact that *men* do often panic just before the wedding. Their own fears that they cannot possibly be faithful cause them to cheat, to commit dangerous dalliances, sometimes on the brink of the ceremony."

"Well, *this* groom is true to you," Omar insisted, finally showing some impatience.

"Then who is insulting me with imitation? I do not mind the chase, Omar, but I wish to be told when the dogs are running."

"I do not *know*," he snapped. "But I suggest you just *ignore* it."

Omar's vehemence seemed genuine, and Martina finally nodded, the matter closed. She waved at the waiter, then mimed the bringing of a handled cup to her lips, formed a *C* with her hand, and held up three fingers.

No one spoke until the man had removed the plates and deposited three cappuccinos.

"*Prost.*" Martina raised her cup and sipped as her companions echoed the toast. Her smile smoothed the troubled waters, and she carried on with the wedding analogy. "So, as we have discussed, this affair is a lavish one. I will need to place deposits. Flowers alone are a fortune these days."

A half-million dollars will buy a lot of flowers, Omar thought with some cynicism as he toed the briefcase. "The funds are here," he said. "However, as we also agreed, the bank would like to have some short details of the expenses and festivities."

Martina reached down for her purse, and Mussa watched her hands. He had known her for ten years, but he still could not anticipate her actions. She might have made some silent calculation, could well surprise and shock him, as she often did.

She came up with a folded piece of paper, very small and flimsy, and handed the slip to Omar. He carefully unfolded it, peered down for a moment, then removed his glasses and held one lens like a magnifying glass.

The little page was filled with typed English words, the list long, detailed, and precise, as he would expect of a German "consultant." He did not react to the equipment: M-16 rifles of such and such capacities, uniforms of particular grades, components for electronic devices he would never fathom. There were four vehicles that were fairly common and the listing of an aircraft lease, multiplied by hours. He took note of the flat rentals in Helsinki and the prices of French passports on the black market.

But all of that was overshadowed by the lone descriptive sentence at the bottom of the page. He squinted hard and moved the paper closer to his face, and when he raised his head, his eyes were wide and emphasized his silence.

"Is it all very clear?" Martina asked as he stared at her.

Omar nodded once.

"Will you remember it?"

"I am not likely to forget," he whispered.

Martina reached once more for her handbag.

Y'allah, mâ baka fiyi, Mussa thought as he squirmed. *I can no longer stand it. I'll piss in my pants.*

Martina plucked a filtered Kent from her purse and lit it with a gold electronic lighter.

"So unhealthy, my dear," Omar warned, though he was pondering dangers far greater than smoking.

"I'm trying to quit." She lifted the glass ashtray from the table's center and drew it near, sheltering it with a cupped hand. Then she recovered the paper from Omar, dropped it into the receptacle, and touched the cigarette to its skin. The flash paper flared for a millisecond, leaving only a tiny pile of ash. The ignition must have burned her fingers, but she did not flinch.

"Perhaps I should not have been so confident." Omar looked at the ashtray as if it were a wrecked luxury car he had driven too fast. "I may not recall all the pricing details."

"No matter," said Martina as she stubbed out her prop. "They fluctuate like the stock market. And besides, as we agreed, whatever balance remains is reserved for my estate. As I told you, I have personal matters that will require attention in the event this bride meets a sad fate. Which is a possibility, wouldn't you say?"

"Regretfully, I would." He seemed to have lost interest in the charm of Martina's company, and as he gathered his coat over his shoulders, he gestured at the briefcase that would remain. "That should suffice you quite nicely. And please, do contact me when this phase of the project is complete."

"There will be no need. You will read about it in the newspapers."

Omar regarded her for another moment. "Go with God," he wished.

"If She wills it." Martina smiled.

The old man made a sound in his throat, raised himself upon his stick, and walked quickly from the restaurant.

Mussa reached for the briefcase and passed it to Martina's side. She was reminded briefly of Von Stauffenberg's attempt to kill Adolf Hitler, and she glanced quickly inside to make sure that it contained only envelopes of cash.

"*Los*" she said to him, having witnessed his discomfort, and he shot from the table and headed for the rest rooms.

She settled back and sipped the cappuccino, listening to the soft, accordionlike notes of the *bandoneon*, exhuming melancholy thoughts of her own losses. . . .

And once again she saw her parents whirling through a crowd of dancers in fine black suits and scarlet gowns, arching against each other, with proud, exaggerated postures, in the clinches of the tangos born in brothels of the Orilla. She saw again their happy smiles and felt the ruffles of her own party dresses, the sense that in this magic land called Buenos Aires nothing could encroach upon the triangle of love that was her family. There had been no hint of danger then, even though she was aware that her parents and their friends lived in Argentina as members of a society removed, like royal dukes and duchesses cast adrift from their own fatherland.

Her father offered her no more than adoration, a love and sense of confident security equal to that lavished on her mother. He was a man respected for his scientific brilliance, often whispered to in German consultation by men who sought his wisdom, expressed their fears as times changed after someone named Perón had gone, and were comforted by Doktor Otto Klump's reassurances that their world would be unaltered.

He was a calm and ordered man; not arrogant, but stubborn, yes. And even when Martina began to miss the dwindling parties, and the "discussions" started up between him and Katharina, he refused to move from their home in Vicente López or seek anonymity in some slum like San Fernando, where houses were no more than stucco huts on lawns of rocky mud.

Martina carried on, singing German nursery rhymes at home and chattering her perfect Spanish in the school she skipped to every morning.

And then her world turned inside out. A day in May 1960. A day to be remembered, when suddenly her father's courage cracked. The telephone calls began, the whispers in the dark of late-night visitors, men who had seemed so erect and powerful, their faces now pale and creased with worry. A tragedy had befallen one of their circle, and he was gone somewhere, taken by some vengeful force, and Martina hid behind her door, confused. And very soon their friends fled, parents with whom her parents had danced, children who had ridden ponies on her birthday. She heard her mother's hissed insistence, her pleading of names such as Paraguay and Brazil. Yet her father would not run again, he said.

And then his work at the laboratory was gone, and with it all her mother's smiles. And finally her father's confidence ended with a pistol shot. The very weapon that lay nestled in her handbag . . .

She no longer felt the fury, and her sadness very, very rarely brought on tears. Yet she wondered once again at what might have been, who she would have become instead, had he lived.

She realized that Mussa had resumed his seat, his face now turned to her expectantly.

"*Sprich du. Bitte.*" She offered him the opportunity to speak his piece.

"It is far too dangerous, Leila," he said.

"Really?"

"Please, don't mock me."

Martina dropped her facetious expression, crossed one knee, and folded her hands over it. All ears.

"Yes, it is," Mussa continued. "And you know it too. Once again, I object to the entire plan. We will all simply be killed, without hope of success." There was a thin film of sweat on his upper lip, and he wiped it quickly with a napkin.

"Without risk, there is no reward," said Martina.

"That is a meaningless slogan." He pressed on, angry now at being patronized. "And another thing. Bringing your mother into this, in *any* way, defies all rational security procedures."

"Your German is really improving."

"As my brother's brother"—Mussa gripped the table and raised his voice—"I must state my *complete* opposition to this."

Martina was unmoved by Mussa's plea. They had had this argument before, but she knew exactly how to defuse him.

"And as your brother's brother," she said quietly, "you are obliged to support me in my life's endeavors. At least, that is, according to the Koran. So if you are truly a servant of Allah . . ."

She left the conclusion hanging as Mussa sat back in his chair, looked at the ceiling, and muttered something under his breath.

"*Ach. Trottel!*" Martina spat, but she was already past this victory of wills and looking at the entrance to the dining room, where a young man was striding toward their table. He was short and wore a leather motorcycle jacket, his body girded with a messenger's pouch, and he carried a helmet under one arm. He was smiling stupidly.

"*Masalkhair,*" the young man said brightly in Arabic as he plopped clumsily into a chair.

"*Guten Abend,*" Martina replied slowly in German. "Why don't we just put up a shingle here that says, 'Yadd Allah—Open Nine to Five'?"

The young man blushed for his indiscretion.

"I told you, Iyad, to meet us *later*. At the flat."

"But I thought you might want to see these now." He rubbed his helmet-matted hair. "I've been out there all day, and they just came out of the one-hour."

"You'll get a medal," Martina sneered, but she put out an open palm.

Iyad fished into his canvas bag and came up with two packets of color prints. Soon after Martina had heard the news of the bombing at the Israeli Consulate, she had sent her men into midtown to observe discreetly the unfolding of events on Second Avenue. She had ordered photographs of all the arrivals and departures at the site, for she sensed that the incident might somehow impede her own activities. She did not have great faith in Iyad's streetcraft, but he was a good photographer, and the swarming of press outside the consulate would provide ample cover.

She sat back from the table and placed the photographs on her lap, then slowly shuffled the images that showed the passage of the day as morning winter light faded on wet faces into shadows of the evening. The pictures were close and very clear; policemen with their bored expressions, the placards of some Jewish protest group, the Israeli consul general flanked by young men looking tense and sleepless, the New York City police commissioner speaking into a microphone that had a large NEWS 4 banded to its collar.

And then she stopped. Her back slowly came erect, as if something with many legs were crawling up her spine.

She stared at the print for a very long time, so long, in fact, that Mussa and Iyad stirred in their chairs, yet they did not dare to speak. She looked at the picture, then at the one before it and the one after it, but she returned to it and held it fast while her heart rate slowly, very slowly, returned to something like a normal rhythm.

There was no mistaking him. He should have worn a hat. She had not seen him for a very long time, but the face of Major Benjamin Baum—perhaps a Colonel now—was not one that she would soon forget. It would make perfect sense for him to participate in such an investigation, yet the coincidence set up a shrill vibration in her body, the antithesis of reuniting love. This was certainly a reconvening she had always hoped for, but on her own terms. He might be here to view events unrelated to her in any way, but Martina knew that where she was concerned, Benni Baum, or Hans-Dieter Schmidt, or whatever he was calling himself now, was a very dangerous man.

"*Markierstift.*" She held out a hand to Iyad, while her eyes remained fixed to the photo, and he handed her a red china marker of the type used on contact prints. She slowly circled the bald head, thoughtful frown, and bulky shoulders. Then she leaned toward Mussa and placed the picture in his hand.

"Track him," she whispered, and she held his gaze until he felt the burn.

"And don't lose him."

Chapter 3: New York

"Tell me something, Bar-El. Is this a goddamn *language* problem?"

The sounds of screaming sirens had long since receded from the barricaded portico of 800 Second Avenue. Yet inside the blackened antechamber of the Israeli Consulate, it seemed that a quick call for an ambulance might soon be in order, as Jack Buchanan's tirade threatened to turn physical.

Buchanan was the Special Agent in Charge of the New York FBI field office, and his mispronunciation of the Israeli chief of security's name was blatantly intentional. He said "Barrel," when even the most jingoistic Texan would have easily grasped that it was like a cattle brand: BAR-L.

"Is that what this is, Bar-El? A *language* problem?"

Hanan Bar-El stared back, affecting a dumb look that invited Buchanan to make a fool of himself. The two men were separated by no great distance, as there was barely enough breathing space for all the investigators there to stake a claim of jurisdiction. The atmosphere was thick with burned synthetics and the anticipation that ripens the air before a cell block riot, and Buchanan's voice was threatening to bring down a ceiling already precarious with structural damage.

The floor, walls, and dropped acoustic tiles of the antechamber were charred to the color of barbecue coal. The carpet looked as if it had been mowed with a laser blade, and wherever the inferno of detonating Semtex had encountered synthetic resins, the substances had drooped into puddles of their former selves, so the remaining chair parts and poster frames had taken on the qualities of Daliesque dreamscapes. The combined effect was like the inside of an oven where a large birthday cake had been left on High while its amnesiac baker set out for vacation.

On the far side, the consulate's steel entrance door was discolored yet intact, a counterpoint to the gaping hole immediately to its left, where Moshiko's bulletproof window had thundered through his security booth like a flying house in a tornado. The steel window frame was twisted, the shorn ends of telecom wires gleaming in the glare of Crime Scene spotlights like the orthodontic braces of a screaming teenager.

Buchanan and his minions outnumbered their Israeli counterparts. He stood in the center of the chamber, six foot one, his short brown hair going gray, his hazel eyes set close together in a slabby Celtic face. The veins in his neck bulged above a starched white shirt, regimental tie, banker-gray suit, and cream raincoat. The SAC's anger was a tool he utilized each workday, but in recent months he had discovered the emotion greeting him at dawn. His fiftieth birthday was approaching, and there was nothing he could do to outwit the calendar. Add to that this dispute over territory he considered his turf, a splash of racial hatred, and he was ready to blow.

"Do I have to get a *translator* up here?"

The American men and women constituting his task force winced with the FBI chief's outburst. You could certainly take the Israelis to task for many things: arrogance, lack of manners, their dismissal of all opinions not their own. But suggesting that they lacked intelligence or linguistic talent was bound to put you on the losing side of an argument.

"Only if you wish to add insult to injury," Bar-El replied evenly.

He stood defiantly before the shattered booth. It was cold in the room, yet he remained jacketless, his gray shirtsleeves rolled to the elbows, his fingers smeared with soot. Knuckles on hips, he had the air of a combat officer who had lost a man, blamed himself, and knew that the battle was far from over.

He was flanked on both sides by his security team, large GSS men emulating their boss's attitude. They, too, had shed the blazers that concealed their sidearms, their pistols and spare magazines now in plain sight. Given the circumstances—and being Israelis—no man's raised voice was likely to impress them. So as Jack Buchanan ranted, they looked decidedly bored.

"All right. I'll say it *real* slow. This is New York City, in the State of New York, in the United States of America. This is *not* fucking Tel Aviv." Buchanan shrugged off his raincoat, while Bar-El's men instinctively watched his hands. "There has been a *crime* committed here. A crime of local and national importance, which makes this both a local *and* a federal issue." At this point he waved his badge. "And as I am the senior agent of the *Federal* Bureau of Investigation for this district, I have complete jurisdiction over this crime scene. Is that clear?"

The GSS man to Bar-El's right raised his palms to applaud. Hanan's own hand flicked out and preempted the gaffe.

"What is clear to me, sir," said Bar-El in a measured tone, "is that you are standing on property which falls under the category of diplomatic integrity." His smooth English seemed to enrage Buchanan further.

"*That* is your territory." Buchanan shot a long arm toward the blackened steel door. "*This*"—he pointed at the floor—"is New York State." He took a moment to turn slowly, looking into the faces of four men and women wearing blue parkas stamped with *ATF*, three uniformed NYPD cops, three more NYPD detectives, two Crime Scene men carrying armloads of gear, and four more FBI field agents. None of them dared defy his authority in what was clearly escalating into a dangerous confrontation, but their faces showed uncomfortable queries of "What next?"

"Now," Buchanan pronounced as he again faced Bar-El. "I will give you all one minute to clear this area, return inside your facility, and allow my people to continue their work. One minute. And then I will place all of you under arrest."

"*Sh'enasseh*," one of Bar-El's men uttered clearly in Hebrew. He locked his thumbs into his belt, his right hand favoring the Browning High-Power he used for close protection details. This time Bar-El made no move to quiet his man.

"What the *hell* did he say?" Buchanan demanded.

"He said"—Bar-El translated—"'Go for it.' "

Buchanan's jaw dropped; he was a man unused to having his gauntlet picked up. Thirty years of political infighting had given him a well-oiled tactical brain, and he realized that his own self-assurance had just resulted in the calling of his own bluff, leaving no option but to carry out the threat. What would the Director say? Friend to the President, jet-setting sophisticate, a former judge, who wore out his tuxedos at cocktail parties hosted by friendly embassies in Washington. It would not please the boss, heaping scandal on disaster.

Fuck it . . .

And then Buchanan was rescued from his own momentum.

"You better cool it, Jack."

It came from the corner of the room near the steel magnetic door, where a large, curly-headed man in his forties was rocking back and forth on the balls of his feet, squinting up at something on the ceiling, his hands jammed into the pockets of a green trench coat. In looks, he might have been one of the Israelis, except that his voice emerged in plain northeastern American.

"Who said that?" Buchanan's hand halted in midsignal to his troops. He was sure that the Israelis would not draw their weapons, but he hoped they would resist, and he was looking forward to the nostalgic blood and tumble of a close-quarter bar fight. Yet the voice confused him.

"Simmer down, Jack. Way down."

Buchanan placed his palm over the chest of his deputy, a tall black man named Gold, and shunted him aside. And then he recognized the figure in the corner.

"What the hell are *you* doing here?" the SAC thundered, then swung on his troops. "Who the hell let the Agency in here? What's the matter with you people? You've probably got a goddamn news reporter in here too, for Christ's sake!"

Buchanan's task force furtively glanced at each other as if someone had just passed gas at a funeral.

"It's a federal matter," said the man from the corner. "As you so tactfully stated."

"This is *not* an Agency issue." Buchanan waved his arms, his bunched raincoat whipping the ceiling. "You stay the hell out of this!"

Yet the man ignored Buchanan, stepping slowly forward as he watched his own feet. The reflector lights revealed some gray now in his brown curls, some deep lines at his eyes suggesting a past of squinting through binoculars.

"Mr. Bar-El," the man said quietly as he turned toward the Israeli. "I apologize on behalf of my colleagues. It might be a good idea to bring your Consul General down here."

"You what?" Buchanan sputtered.

"I wanted very much to do that, sir," Bar-El responded. "But she is at the mayor's office for a news conference."

"You apologize?" Buchanan crossed to the CIA officer in one long lunge. "You apologize on *my* behalf? Let me tell you something about these fucking people, *Mister* Langley—"

"*Jack.*" The CIA man snapped it like a warning shot and lowered his voice. "You are on the edge now, Jack. The very edge. Go ahead, look down," he suggested, though of course Buchanan did not oblige, his cheeks only reddening further. "You see what's down there, Jack? *Rocks.* Big, jagged boulders, just waiting for you to fling your whole fucking career onto them."

Buchanan's fists balled, the knuckles white as skinned onions. Yet he was reprieved once again as the charred elevator doors slid open. His people parted down the center of the room, anxious to give their boss an alternate target.

Benni Baum stood alone inside the elevator. He was wearing his off-white turtleneck and well-worn car coat, carrying his soft valise in one hand. In the other he held the visitor's pass issued by a police sergeant in the lobby. He had donned his reading glasses and was examining the document, a forger's habit acquired while serving a stint in AMAN's "art" department.

"What the hell is *this* now?" Buchanan said in a low grumble. "*Death of a Salesman?*"

The Americans burst into exaggerated laughter, for although the beefy Baum hardly resembled a Willy Loman, they snatched the opportunity to break the fevered tension.

Benni snapped his head up, and the laughter subsided. The assembly did not know who he was and assumed he had taken offense, but the expression on his face was not a reaction to them.

It was the stench. The heavy, nostril-wrinkling smell of explosive gases dissolved in heat, of human elements never meant to be grilled, blood and bone and flesh burned past well done. He had smelled it all before, in Zion Square and at the Coast Road Massacre. In Beirut, Belfast, Jerusalem, the explosion sites that he had come upon as investigator, visitor, or grieving countryman. And still, each time he smelled it, and more and more as the years passed, his expression reflected rage, but was as much a concentrated effort to stem the urge to vomit.

The elevator doors began to close, and Benni slammed them back into their recesses. A Crime Scene man stepped forward and offered him a pair of light blue drooping objects that looked like hotel shower caps. Everyone was wearing the hospital booties, and Benni handed the man his valise, slipped them on, and stepped out.

With a quick glance at the postures, Baum assessed the confrontation. He placed a smile on his face, walked right past Buchanan, and held out his hand to Hanan Bar-El.

"*Shalom*, Hanan," Benni said warmly. Peripherally he saw the large man who had been facing Buchanan fade into a darkened corner.

"*Yoffi lirot ot'cha*. Great to see you," Bar-El responded with double sincerity, continuing in Hebrew. "And how should I call you?"

"By my name," said Benni. He would not be using a cover in the United States. There were too many American intelligence officers who knew him, and such behavior on Allied territory would be considered bad form. "You were expecting me."

"Badash notified me after you called him."

"Good," said Baum. Uri Badash was Chief of Operations for Shabak and a good friend, but Benni would never tolerate an officer from another branch barging in on AMAN operations, so he always extended the same courtesy. "Now," he said as he took Bar-El by the elbow. "Why don't you step out of that line of gorillas. It's looking like the Civil War in here."

Bar-El's men grinned, and even Hanan could not suppress a smile as he followed Baum over to Buchanan. Benni stepped up close to the tall FBI man and thrust out a large hand.

"Benjamin Baum."

"Jack Buchanan." The SAC's face was still set in a sneer, yet his arm was being pumped by a powerful piston. He showed Baum his badge. "Head of FBI for this region."

"A pleasure." Baum stuck his hand into a pocket and came up with two business cards, handing one to Buchanan and the other to Bar-El.

In the upper left corner was the menorah-and-leaf-cluster symbol of the Government of Israel, while the raised blue letters in the center said simply: BENJAMIN BAUM—SPECIAL SECURITY ADVISER TO THE PRIME MINISTER. No address, just fax and telephone numbers. While Buchanan examined the card, Bar-El raised an eyebrow.

"*Kartees yaffeh, Baum.* Nice card," he murmured.

"Yes. Is the ink dry?"

Bar-El rubbed a thumb across the lettering. "Seems to be okay."

"So, Mr. Baum." Buchanan straightened up to ramrod posture. "How can I help you?" It was not an offer to serve. It was a suggestion to state your business and get out.

"I sink, perhaps, zat *I* can help *you.*" Benni's spoken English was heavily accented in German.

Buchanan frowned down at Baum. The Israeli's big bald head, bull neck, and wide shoulders no longer reminded him of a street salesman. "I'm not too sure you can help, Mr. Baum. We were just having a nonmeeting of the minds."

"*Ja.*" Benni's eyes crinkled. "My age is not yet affecting my nose." He touched the soccer-flattened appendage with a finger. "If you would excuse my lack of manners for just one minute?" And he turned toward Bar-El.

Buchanan looked out over his troops and briefly rolled his eyes.

"*Nu,* Hanan?" Benni prodded Bar-El in Hebrew. "Give it to me quick."

"This son of a whore—"

"Hanan." Baum raised a warning finger. "There are a number of NYPD detectives who speak fluent Hebrew."

Bar-El flicked his eyes over Buchanan's troops.

"This *gentleman* is the only problem here. Yesterday it was all fine. The EMS people were great, took good care of Ben-Czecho. Then the first NYPD people came in, and we were all working together."

"No conflicts?"

"The New York cops are pros. They liaise with consulates every day, and they know where the borders are."

"But they don't have the labs for this, right? They can't extend their authority."

"Right. So the task force shows up. And this guy barges in like Napoleon and decides that *we* don't have the authority to investigate an attack on our own territory!"

"Keep it calm, Hanan," Benni soothed.

"He was about to arrest us."

Benni blinked, and then he laughed in one long burst that turned the heads in the room. "*Arrest* you?"

"You heard me right."

Baum put a hand on Bar-El's shoulder. "You should have let him, Hanan. Then you'd never hear of him again."

"Well, you ruined it for me, Baum." Bar-El smiled. "Now you owe me."

"Okay. I'll try to fix it up here, if you don't mind."

"The business card says you're the boss."

"Nonsense," Benni scoffed. "This is your facility."

"Well, Uri Badash insists you're a magician, so let's see some magic."

Benni took his hand from Bar-El's shoulder and rubbed his jaw. "Just one more question. Who removed the body of the terrorist?" He had learned from hard experience that the corpse of an attacker often yielded greater clues than recovered weapons or explosive residues.

"*Bodies*, Benni. And they weren't exactly that, either."

"Bodies?"

"Yes, the girl too. The city medical examiner took them out."

"What girl?" Benni whispered. Casualties were not just numbers to him. Everybody in Israel seemed to know everyone else, or at least a close relative or friend.

"A young woman. Nineteen. Here in the waiting area."

"One of ours?"

"American girl. She came for a work visa. You haven't seen the papers, have you?"

"I haven't stopped moving."

"There was more left of her than of the bomber," said Bar-El. "Enough to bury."

Benni put his hands into the pockets of his coat and looked at the silly shower caps encasing his shoes. *Children*, he thought. *We are eating each other's young.* He turned to the FBI agent and switched back to English.

"Okay, Mr. Buchanan. I believe I understand the complexities."

"From whose point of view?" Buchanan crossed his arms.

"Sir," Benni said in a conciliatory tone. "Given that I hold the rank of colonel in my country's military, I would never be so ungracious as to ask a man of *your* rank and responsibilities to justify his position."

The flattery had its effect, and Buchanan dropped his arms. "Appreciated."

"And so, my recommendation." Baum lifted his hands, indicating the gloomy antechamber. "This area is technically United States territory, a portion of real estate of the City of New York. Correct?"

"That's correct."

"The area including and beyond that wall," said Baum as he gestured at the smashed security booth, "which also contains valuable physical and forensic evidence, is the property of the State of Israel. Also correct?"

"I said so myself before you got here."

"We will relinquish *this* area here to your investigators."

Bar-El's men looked at their boss, pleading for his intervention. But Hanan shut them up with a hard stare.

Benni continued. "And our people will have full jurisdiction over anything that is found on the other side."

"That's exactly right," said Buchanan too quickly, thinking he had been empowered by a political simpleton.

"However," said Baum, raising a finger, "there are conditions."

"What conditions?"

"Your people will be assigned an Israeli liaison, to whom all evidence will become available without question."

Buchanan hesitated. "Well, I don't know . . ."

"And our people will be assigned an American liaison, who will operate under identical conditions."

With the offer so reasonable, Buchanan was hard pressed to object.

"And," Baum added, "the choice of an Israeli liaison is yours, if you please."

Buchanan thought for a moment. He could have it all his own way, with one small hitch, and of course he would feed the Israeli liaison exactly what he felt like and no more. The Director would be pleased. It did not take him long.

"I choose you," he said as he jabbed a finger at Baum.

"Me?" Benni managed to look incredulous.

"You said it yourself, Colonel Baum. Rank and responsibility. And *you* seem to be a reasonable man."

Benni looked over at Bar-El and shrugged. He turned back to Buchanan. "All right, sir. *Ja*, as you say."

"Good enough." Buchanan began to don his raincoat.

"Accordingly, if you don't mind," Baum continued, "I will select an American as your liaison to us."

"Be my guest."

Baum effected one of his short Germanic nods, then turned slowly, perusing the strange faces in the room. He finally faced Buchanan again, but he was pointing over his shoulder.

"I will accept that man, over there."

Buchanan turned. Baum was gesturing at the CIA officer.

"No way." The SAC shook his head. "Not him."

"Why not, if I may ask?"

"He's not from my group."

"Then what group is he from?"

"He's not from my task force," Buchanan snapped.

"I'm from Langley," said the voice from the corner.

"Ah," said Baum. "I see. Well, that is good enough, it seems to me."

"No way," Buchanan repeated, his ire on the rise again.

"Mr. Buchanan," said Benni, yet now his tone was also changing. 'I will not be handling evidence *here*, and *he* will not be handling evidence over *there*. We will simply be informational conduits, a task for which I am sure we are both competent. I choose him."

"Forget it," Buchanan spat. "And you know what?"

"Yes, yes. I see." Baum cut him off, holding up a hand. "We will just take a short break, then, while I telephone our ambassador in Washington and have him call the White House with your complaints. Shall we?"

Buchanan opened his mouth, but nothing emerged. His jaw worked for a moment as he thought, *I'm gonna be fifty. In three weeks. Fifty. I don't need this shit. I don't even care. Fuck it.*

"You three!" He pointed at the uniformed cops and started issuing orders. "Two of you can go back downstairs. ATF, I only need three of you here. Lab stays too." He thrust his jaw at an NYPD detective. "O'Donovan, choose your own team." His eyes flicked toward the Israeli contingent. "And watch them like hawks. Gold," he murmured now, "let's get the hell out of here."

He brushed past Baum as someone stabbed the elevator button. The doors opened and Buchanan stepped inside, tore off his booties, and flung them back out onto the burned carpet, where a Crime Scene man picked them up gingerly and placed them in a plastic bag. The men and women who followed their boss removed their foot condoms more politely and, jammed to overflowing, the elevator closed.

A cloud of dust swirled past the reflector lights in the wake of the departed investigators. And then, as if released from a frozen dimension, Buchanan's remaining subordinates began moving to their tasks.

The uniformed cop took up a post near the elevator. The two Crime Scene men opened their heavy toolboxes. First they distributed surgical gloves to the Alcohol, Tobacco, and Firearms personnel and the NYPD detectives. Then they both donned the old active infrared night vision goggles, took up filtered flashlights in their hands, and began examining the burned carpet, looking like alien insects in search of a meal. An Explosives Ordnance Disposal expert from the Redstone Arsenal came up with miniature colored pennants and began to mark the blast area. The outer fringes would be blue, closer to the source of the detonation would be red, and ground zero, in front of Moshiko's booth, would be yellow. The three NYPD detectives huddled to one side and produced notepads.

Bar-El walked over to Baum, wearing a satisfied smile. "Just like David Copperfield."

"I haven't read it since I was a boy," said Benni. "What's the allusion?"

"I meant the magician." Bar-El laughed as Baum waved off the compliment.

"Well, a deal is a deal." Benni cocked his head toward the steel entrance door. "Let's go inside."

"Aren't you supposed to *liaise* here?"

"All in good time."

The passport and visa section of the facility was closed and devoid of personnel. Still, the urgent sound of ringing telephones echoed everywhere. Whenever Israel endured a crisis, from the rescue of Ethiopian refugees to a war in the Gulf, it seemed that half of the three hundred thousand Israeli expatriates in the Greater New York area called in to volunteer. Pilots wanted to fly, nurses wanted to nurse, and paratroopers were ready to do anything requiring muscle. But today the phones warbled away unanswered, for there was nothing anyone could do.

The reception area was fairly intact, with the exception of a line of blast trajectory leading from Moshiko's booth to a bank of windows at the opposite wall. Jagged sections of the booth's door were scattered about like plywood puzzle pieces, and where Moshiko's mangled body had come to rest against the far wall, the remnants left by Emergency Medical Service lay untouched. Empty infusion bags sat in amoebic stains, and a pile of blood-soaked bandages still oozed serum. A flat, army-style olive mattress was soaked to a dark umber, and on it lay the tatters of his jeans, blazer, and shirt.

For a moment, Benni stared at the pair of black sneakers that lay on their sides. Then, as the GSS men stepped across the carnage and went back to their posts, he felt the cold wind slicing through the shattered windows, turned toward the passport section, spotted an empty office, and crooked a finger at the man from Langley.

Baum walked into the cubicle, set his valise on the wooden desk, and turned as the CIA officer closed the door and folded his arms. The two men looked at each other for a moment, and then both their faces were crossed by wide mischievous grins, like those of twin schoolboys who had once again duped an unsuspecting teacher.

"Making friends all over the place, huh, Benni?" Arthur Roselli laughed as Baum walked up to him, and they clasped each other's shoulders with grips like sumo wrestlers.

Baum stepped back and shook his head. "When I saw you, Arthur, I was sure I was going to blow the whole thing."

"You handled it like Solomon, you old renegade," said Roselli. "That asshole didn't know what hit him."

"If I am a renegade," Baum warned as he wagged a finger, "then *you* are sounding like a traitor."

"*He's not from my group!*" Roselli mimicked Jack Buchanan's growl, and the two old friends laughed again.

Arthur Roselli had, for three years, been the Central Intelligence Agency's chief of station at the American consulate in Jerusalem. He and Baum had first been introduced at one of those diplomatic cocktail parties that resemble Halloween, where all the intelligence officers are pretending to be something else. Sometime later, Roselli had approached Baum one to one, seeking his aid in an extremely delicate issue. The CIA suspected that an American immigrant serving in the Israel Defense Forces was passing information on U.S. weapons systems to a Romanian intelligence agent. The soldier was caught by Baum and turned, and thereafter Roselli became Baum's "playback feed," distorting the intelligence that continued to be purchased by Bucharest.

It was not long afterward that Baum found himself in Roselli's shoes, asking the CIA man for help with Operation Flute and the quest for Amar Kamil. Without Roselli's aid, Benni and Eytan Eckstein might well have wound up as corporals in the reserves, checking women's pocketbooks for explosives outside Cinematheque.

Eventually, Roselli had been recalled to Virginia and promoted to head the Agency's counterterror program. The two had remained in touch, primarily through secure communications links. But during the Gulf War, when the Scuds began to fall in Israel, Roselli's first phone call upon detection of an Iraqi launch by CIA satellites was always to wake the Baum household so they could don their gas masks.

"How did you know I was coming?" Benni asked with pleasure.

"I didn't at first," said Roselli. "I was going to send one of my men up here, but then Uri Badash called me."

"Hunh. I will have to give that Shabaknik a lecture about security," Baum said facetiously. "He thinks he is my social secretary."

"And thanks for making me that fucking Buchanan's employee," said Roselli. "But I won't be able to hang around."

"You're welcome." Baum grinned. "I also have only three days. But your FBI compatriot will be happy to replace you with one of his own. We will feed him what we want and send you the real Mac . . . MacDon . . . How is it?"

"McCoy. And that's exactly what Buchanan intends to do to you, big shot."

"We will see." Baum's eyes crinkled.

Roselli suddenly grew solemn. "Hey, I'm sorry about your casualties, Benni."

"*Our* casualties, Arthur. The girl was an American."

"Yeah."

"Moshiko was a soldier. He was aware of the risks."

"Badash tells me you knew the kid."

"*Know*," Benni corrected. "I just came from the hospital. Went there straight from Kennedy." He lit two cigarettes and handed one to Roselli.

"Ahh, a taste of the old country." Roselli dragged on the Israeli brand. "Is he going to make it?"

Benni was silent. He was seeing Ben-Czecho's broken and bandaged form lying in the NYU intensive care unit. Drugs dripped into his arms, and monitors blipped like faint signals from a lost spacecraft. The boy's eyes were wrapped in gauze. He had been trached in the throat on the floor of the consulate, the hole sutured now, and he was breathing on his own, but he could only utter the occasional hoarse whisper from dry lips.

Benni had taken a piece of ice from an aluminum pan and gently moved it over Moshiko's mouth. Then he spoke to him, and the tremendous effort to smile that screwed up Moshiko's burned face had brought a glisten to Benni's eyes.

"*Ani kahn.* I am here," Benni repeated a few times. When Moshiko reached up and tried to clutch him with his right hand, Benni avoided the bandaged stump and gripped his forearm. Except for professional secrets, the two men had never held much back from each other, and Benni was not going to allow some strange doctor to perform his fatherly duties.

"Moshiko, listen to me," he said gently as he bent toward the ravaged face. "You are not going to use this hand again, my son. Not ever. It is gone. But I think you knew that, didn't you?"

Moshiko's arm went limp, and Benni laid it at his side. Certainly the shock of amputation had been surging through Moshiko's medicinal barriers for hours, telling him by way of pain what no bold mouth had yet dared utter. He nodded twice to Benni, a quiver dimpling his chin.

"And no crying." Benni squeezed the young man's shoulder gently. "The salt will make it harder on your eyes. And you *are* going to see again." Moshiko's face turned toward Benni's voice. "Yes, you will. The doctor swore to me." He did not think it necessary to say now that it would be through one eye only. "Oh, and Uri Badash sent a message. He says you'll just have to learn to shoot lefty and gives you thirty days to get back to work."

For the first time since the explosion, Moshiko's brain offered him an image to replace the ghoulish grimace of his attacker, and he smiled a real smile. It must have pained him awfully, for the skin over his cheeks was still oozing through scales of fresh scab, but he managed it. He lifted his left hand and raised a thumb.

"Good." Benni touched the top of Moshiko's head, the black hair still caked with dried blood. "I have to get over to the consulate, but I'll be back. Is there anything you want to tell me? Anything you saw that I should know?"

Moshiko lay still for a moment. Then he moved his lips, and a sibilant whisper emerged.

Benni bent over and placed one of his large ears above Moshiko's mouth. "Again."

Moshiko repeated himself, and Benni straightened up, a frown creasing his forehead. Now he was whispering.

"Did you say *Allahu Akbar?*"

Moshiko managed another nod.

"He said it to you?"

Moshiko lifted his left hand and mimed a writing implement.

"He wrote it down?"

Moshiko wagged a finger.

"It was already written?"

Moshiko formed the "okay" sign with his fingers.

"He gave it to you." Benni imagined the transaction at the security drawer. "It was a note."

Moshiko raised his thumb.

"*Mitzooyan.* Excellent," said Benni. "Where is it?"

The young man waved his hand. The note was gone, burned, dissipated by the blast.

"Of course." Benni patted him on a bare shoulder. "Rest now. You are brilliant. I'd kiss you, but I think I'll leave that up to this gorgeous young thing."

He looked up and smiled at Kathleen, who was sitting in a vinyl armchair on the other side of the bed. Only immediate family members were allowed in the ICU, but she had claimed that she was Moshiko's sole relation. She did not understand the Hebrew exchange between her lover and this burly man who looked like a villain from a James Bond movie, but she had watched the way he touched Moshiko. Like a father. And when he smiled at her, she smiled back....

"Yes, he's going to make it," Benni said now to Roselli. "There was a girl there with him. Very beautiful. He will be all right. I could tell by looking at her."

"Good," Roselli said, but he was wondering if he himself would want to survive such a maiming.

Benni stubbed out his cigarette in a soot-caked ashtray. "We should go." He made an effort to smile. "Before people start to talk."

"Wait a minute, Baum. You haven't solved this thing yet."

"What do you mean?"

"A *theory*," Roselli pressed. "Baum without a theory is like flapjacks without syrup. What's your assessment?"

Benni shrugged. "You know me, Arthur. Slow-witted."

"Yeah," Roselli scoffed. "Right."

Baum had known that Arthur would want to engage in speculations about the bombing, and he wanted to avoid such a discussion. He could not share details of the upcoming prisoner exchange, and therefore denying that Hizbollah had a hand would seem unreasonable. Given Moshiko's story about the note, it seemed unreasonable to *him*.

"Well," Benni said, "it could have been any number of groups."

"Oh, come on. You feed 'Suicide Bomber' into our system, and the only thing you get is 'Moslem Fundamentalist' flashing at you like a runway beacon."

"Perhaps." Benni demurred.

"You had the same thing in Argentina last year," Roselli prodded, as if he had to remind Baum of recent history. "Although if I remember right, you guys tried to flush some German girl from the bushes."

"That was just a decoy." Benni waved an arm and started again for the door.

"Wait a minute." Roselli reached out and pulled at Baum's coat. "I've got a present for you."

Benni turned to look at his old friend as the conviction that indeed it might be time to retire washed over him. It was a sensation of weariness, as if he was losing the ability to dissemble, as if Arthur was pulling on the cloak of deception that he had always worn so comfortably.

"It's not a Zippo with your name on it." Arthur smiled. "It's a tooth."

"Excuse me?"

"A *tooth*, Baum." Roselli opened his mouth and tapped one of his large white incisors with a fingernail. "Buchanan's people are out there trying to bag everything, but it's stuck in the ceiling right outside the entrance door."

Benni's eyes narrowed as he understood the significance of such a find, and he knew that Roselli was of the same mind.

AMAN's research department was the best in the Middle East, retaining Israeli experts in every professional field that might prove useful in intelligence operations. Some years back, an American officer had been taken hostage in Lebanon, and as a crude demonstration of sincerity, the kidnappers had mailed a severed finger to the American embassy in Tel Aviv. Even before taking a print off the digit, Roselli had brought it to Baum.

AMAN had summoned the "Hand Man," an elderly doctor who had survived his years at Auschwitz by developing an unusual expertise that amused the SS. He could be shown a man's palm and tell you if it belonged to a coal miner, a crematorium cleaner, or a camp guard. Since the war years, he had extended his repertoire.

"This is not the finger of an American officer," the old survivor had pronounced. "It is the second digit, right hand, of a Lebanese farmer. You see? It even has a ridged callus from a scythe handle. Cedar wood, of course . . ."

"Don't tell me you haven't got a Tooth Man too," Roselli demanded.

"We do, at that," Benni confessed, "although I think he uses an autoanalyzer and a microscope."

"Right. And that tooth can buy you a lot of leverage."

"Perhaps." In fact, Benni knew that with a list of the compounds used to fill the tooth, he could have the general location of the dentist who did the work, and therefore the origin of the bomber, determined within one hour.

"Your perhapses are getting too coy for me, Benni." Roselli slapped his friend on the back. "Let's move."

They walked back out into the waiting area, where the wind from the shattered windows was pushing some torn propaganda booklets around the reading tables and overturned chairs. Hanan Bar-El was helping two of his men seal up the holes with black plastic garbage bags and masking tape. He spotted Baum and Roselli and walked over.

"You two know each other?" he asked bluntly.

"Eyes of a cop," Roselli commented to Benni as he jerked a thumb at Bar-El. He stuck out a hand and introduced himself.

"You nearly saved my ass," said Bar-El.

"Bullshit," Roselli sniffed. "I just don't like gunfire in close quarters." He cocked his jaw toward the blown-out booth. "So what's your first instinct on this thing?"

Benni tried to deflect the speculations. "It is probably a bit early to round up the usual suspects." He kept the conversation in English, even though Roselli's Hebrew was quite functional. "Right, Hanan?"

Bar-El ignored Baum's reticence. "Hizbollah. I still think they did us in Argentina, we didn't fuck them enough for it, and now they're getting cocky."

"What about this Jew-against-Jew thing that's in all the papers?" Roselli wondered.

"Oh, come on, Arthur," Baum scoffed. "Three years in Jerusalem, you ought to know us better."

"You lived in Jerusalem?" Bar-El raised his eyebrows.

"He was studying at yeshiva," Benni said with a straight face.

"I know it sounds insane," Roselli admitted. "But keep it on the list for now."

"At the very bottom," said Bar-El. "What do *you* think, Benni?"

Baum was forcing himself to ponder the possibility that Hizbollah, or some offshoot thereof, was trying to scuttle their own prisoner exchange. But for the sake of Captain Dan Sard, he wanted to reason their participation out of it. "I think that I had better look before I leap."

A woman crossed through the passport section and approached the three men. She was small, in her mid-thirties, with jet-black hair pulled into a tight ponytail, dark eyes, and no makeup. She spoke to Bar-El in Hebrew.

"Hanan, I just took a call from Tel Aviv. National Police are sending two bomb people over on the next El Al."

"*Yoffi*," said Hanan.

Roselli looked down at the attractive woman and extended his hand. "Art Roselli, from Washington."

The woman regarded his proffered hand with an amused expression, then shook it once in a strong grip. "Natalie Shapira, from Ramat Gan."

Roselli laughed.

"Arthur is a friend," said Benni to the woman. Shapira was the head of the consulate's public relations unit that dealt with a voracious New York press. She was also one of the resident Mossad agents, a double duty that often turned her working days into twenty-hour marathons. She and Baum had encountered each other at various Israeli intelligence seminars.

"A rare and beautiful thing, a friend," said Natalie as she looked squarely up at the big American.

"Natalie is chief of our Information Department," said Bar-El.

"And I must go *inform*." She smiled and walked away without further pleasantries.

"Pretty spook," Art murmured to Benni.

Baum looked at him quizzically. "What makes you say 'spook'?"

"You just got here, and you two know each other. But you didn't *greet* each other."

"I am definitely losing my touch." Baum shook his large head.

Bar-El headed back to his office, hopeful now that the National Police *chablanim* would soon arrive and collect all their evidence. Then he could clean up and have the consulate back on its feet by Monday.

Baum and Roselli walked back out through the steel entrance door. "You're going to need an ally out here," Roselli said, sotto voce. "I'll point you in the right direction."

The ATF people had marked off the blast area, a tricolored flower of pennants. The Crime Scene men no longer wore their goggles, having placed minute explosive residue into small plastic boxes. They were now filling three large garbage bags with bits of clothing and other recognizable debris. The bags were taped and marked: *Female. Male. Other.*

The EOD man from Redstone had his own bag. Benni eyed it longingly, for it would contain any wires, microchips, or detonator parts that could give the bomb designer a "signature."

Roselli walked Baum over to one wall, where the three NYPD detectives were squatting over an object partially covered with white plastic.

"What you got?" Roselli asked in as harmless a tone as he could muster.

"Girl's sneaker," said a detective without looking up. He was prodding the object with a pencil eraser. "Part of her's still in it. Wanna look?"

"I'll pass," said Roselli.

One of the men stood up, brushing off the knees of his suit trousers. He was tall and slim, yet he appeared taut beneath his white button-down and conservative paisley tie. *Like a boxer*, Benni decided. The man looked to be about thirty-five, with short blond hair that would have branded him a fascist in the America of the seventies but, with its finger-combed gel, was now classified as chic. He had green eyes, some red in the thick eyebrows, and a smooth Irish complexion, still pink with the cold. Benni feared that he was looking at a younger clone of Buchanan, until a wry grin appeared on the young man's lips.

"Quite a performance, Roselli," the detective said. "I like the Darth Vader routine."

"The better to scare you with, my dear," said Arthur as he offered his hand.

The detective just waved back, showing his surgical glove.

"Detective Michael O'Donovan," Roselli announced with a flourish, "meet Benjamin Baum."

The young man said only, "Colonel," as he glanced at Baum.

"You two seem well acquainted," Benni said in an effort to warm the atmosphere.

O'Donovan looked at the CIA officer, then breathed something that might have been a sigh. "From days gone by," he said quietly. Then he squatted and rejoined his fellow detectives.

Roselli caught Baum's attention, looked down at O'Donovan's back, and thrust out his chin. *That's your man*, he signaled. Benni mouthed sarcastically, "Thanks a lot."

The two walked back over to the darkened corner where the CIA agent had been standing before Baum's arrival. For a long moment, they stood in silence.

"Can I smoke in here?" Roselli suddenly called out to no one in particular.

"They're your lungs," one of the detectives answered.

Roselli produced a pack of Camel Lights and fished a cigarette out with his lips. As he raised his lighter, he paused and flicked his eyes at the ceiling. Benni looked up as the flame flared briefly.

Embedded in the blackened acoustic tile was a small white object the size of a large kernel of corn. Something metallic was apparently part of its composition, for it gleamed as it reflected the flame.

Benni looked back at Arthur with widened eyes. He had already judged the distance and knew he could not reach it. He hunted in his coat pocket, took out his house keys, and slipped a small penknife from the ring. Arthur palmed it with the dexterity of a pickpocket, but he still had to wait.

The diversion came within a minute. Suddenly the elevator doors opened and a blinding flash made the investigators throw their arms up defensively.

"Jesus Christ—what the fuck!" someone shouted.

"*Daily News*," said a singsong female voice from inside the elevator. "Smile, everybody!"

"Block the camera, for Christ's sake," O'Donovan said. He was not yelling. He had seen it happen too many times. And the uniformed cop had already thrown his girth across the open elevator doors.

Roselli reached up and popped the ragged tooth from the foam core. Baum was already holding out a handkerchief, and he moved it quickly, caught the object, and slipped it into his coat.

"Your men let me up here!" the woman was squealing.

"And my men will let you out," O'Donovan replied as he returned to his work.

"We have freedom of the press in this country," she shouted as the big cop hammered on the elevator buttons and the doors closed.

"You are free to leave," O'Donovan mumbled.

"Fucking vultures," someone growled.

Roselli nodded at Baum. Then he put his fingers on Benni's arm and pushed him a little in O'Donovan's direction, like a father coaxing a shy toddler at a birthday party. He winked at Baum and walked back into the consulate.

O'Donovan was rising from the sneaker, taking off his gloves.

"Let's call the M.E. back over for this, Jerry," he said to one of his detectives. "Might tell us more about the concussion."

"Where's the phone?" the detective called Jerry asked.

"Go on inside," Benni offered. "To the right, on any desk in the passport section."

"Thanks." The detective was buzzed in.

"Mr. O'Donovan," Benni said as he approached the young man.

"Mike," the detective corrected.

"Mike, then." Benni gave the cop his best fatherly smile. "Tell me, were there any other victims? Wounds, and so forth?"

"There was a Russian family." He was still eyeing Baum with cautious detachment. "Sustained some ear damage."

"That is all?"

"They were inside the consulate," said O'Donovan. He picked up his suit coat from a plastic ground sheet, rolled down his shirtsleeves, and buttoned them. "I think some of your people suffered shock trauma, but nothing serious." The small emphasis on the word "your" made Benni realize that this would not be an easy friendship to cement.

Baum backed up a bit, looking at the floor and speaking as he moved, so O'Donovan was forced to follow him as he maneuvered into his jacket.

"I wonder," said Benni, when they were removed from the rest of the group, "if you could spare half an hour for me?"

O'Donovan looked at Baum's face as he pulled his tie out from inside his shirt. The Israeli's tone was not obsequious; it was more like a suggestion to share information. He had seen how quickly the man outmaneuvered Buchanan, and the SAC was mean-spirited, but he was no idiot.

"What's on your mind, Colonel?"

"Benni, if you please. Do you have a car?"

"Outside."

"Good," said Baum. "Give me a lift, and I will offer you a small present."

O'Donovan examined Baum for another moment. No good detective rejected an informant, no matter how duplicitous the source might seem to be.

"And it's not even Christmas," he murmured as he turned to his colleagues. "Frank, when the medical examiner gets here, try to wrap this up. Two uniforms should be here round the clock. I'll be back anyway in half an hour."

The task force members watched O'Donovan as he swept a hand toward the elevator. "After you, Colonel."

"It's Benni," Baum insisted as he hit the button.

"Yeah," said the detective, as if an alchemist were offering him bullion at a discount. He took off his booties, recovered Baum's from him, and dropped them into the Crime Scene bag.

O'Donovan did not care much for this whole scenario. He had been to the Middle East. Not enough time had passed, and there was no one and nothing from that part of the world that he had liked or cared to remember.

As the elevator doors began to close, O'Donovan looked across the gloomy tunnel of the antechamber, through the mangled window frame of the security booth, and into the brighter daylight of the consulate.

He saw Arthur Roselli's silhouette facing him from the other side of the blown-out cubicle. The shadowy figure offered a weary salute.

O'Donovan shot him the finger.

Chapter 4: Columbia University

The face that filled the eyepiece of Mussa Hawatmeh's powerful Steiner monocular caused him to draw an inadvertent breath, for he had not expected to find a thing of such beauty connected to the lumbering target of his assignment. He focused on the features of the young woman, assessing from her expression that the exchange taking place at two hundred meters' range was not the chance encounter of two strangers, yet he was unsure if the rush of his pulse came from the discovery of a tactical advantage or the simple response to a stunning female. And of course there was no way for Mussa to know that the face delivering his momentary pleasure caused its owner such regular discomfort.

In fact, Ruth Baum was the sort of young woman who sometimes wished that all of humanity were blind.

There were so many women on this earth who tried every morning to live up to a magazine-cover ideal, spending hours before mirrors, applying subtle hues of makeup to emphasize hollows that should exist and did not, to raise the planes of faces too flat. To strengthen lips too thin, eyes too small, throats born sagging, chins left wanting.

But Ruth had fallen into that other category, the one she should have thanked the heavens for instead of cursing them regularly. She decried the envy of her friends, responding to their compliments with such dismissals that they soon learned to still remarks about her looks, and she so distrusted male attention that only those brave souls who could weather ego batterings were left alive on her social battlefield.

If beauty was truly in the eyes of the beholder, then Ruth labored counter to the efforts that might please those who beheld her. And still she was unsuccessful.

She was of medium height and weight, yet her proportions added illusionary inches to her proud posture. Her feet were small, her legs slim and rising to a youthful waist and stomach. Her hands were strong and unmanicured, her breasts just a bit too full for her own sense of economy, and her skin a pale amber, permanently tanned where years of desert exposure would remain a lifetime tattoo.

Ruth tried to calculate a narrow range of fashion, loose-fitting jeans and jackets to camouflage all lines that curved away from straight and narrow planes. Her bulky sweaters in the winter and T-shirts nearly to her knees in summer did much to keep her secret safe, but there was nothing she could do about her face.

Her auburn hair fell well past her shoulders, a curtain that often drifted in her way. She would tuck the strands behind an ear, and then the high plane of her forehead and her emphatic eyebrows offered up her intelligence. Her large azure eyes above high cheekbones were nearly always clear, despite the late nights spent hovering over texts, and her slim nose sloped up immeasurably just before the tip, a remnant, she supposed, of some distant Christian German ancestry. Her lips were just too full, a wide bow that annoyed her, their only grace being that they were perfect for the flute she used as therapy when life became too burdensome for her to concentrate on studies.

The expression she cultivated appeared to be a grim assessment of everyone's intelligence. Yet Ruth Baum's greatest problem when it came to suppressing her own beauty was that she loved to laugh, and her wide bright smile foiled her entirely.

Ruth's years in America had not much altered her view of the world or stilled the tensions that were birthrights of Israeli citizens. To most Israelis, America was a place where one could shed the choking memories of battle, the probabilities of death from any hostile border. Since the ill-conceived war in Lebanon of 1982, the desire to make *yeridah*—literally "going down" from the State of Israel—no longer bore the stigma that once caused emigrants to make the move in secret. Israelis had been leaving the country in record numbers, their motivation clear: escape.

Ruth's reasons for resettling in New York were similar, yet after struggling through the better part of the Graduate School of Arts and Sciences' master's-doctorate training program in research psychology, she had been brought to the realization that her own "escape" was a very private one. It was also clear that no degree of professional success or creature comforts would ever free her from the bonds of her past.

She had come here to study, hoping in the process to leave her darker self behind. But by now she had accepted one of her professors' simplistic description of the human mental condition: The airlines may lose all your luggage, but your emotional baggage is always carry-on.

Still, although the daily drudgery of study had become oppressive, she enjoyed the life at Morningside Campus. The lawns and hedges of the spacious courtyards were English in their manicured geometry, the stone and brick and marble architecture Washingtonian in its elegance, and somehow an invisible academic moat discouraged the violent forms of human life that lived outside.

It was like a retreat, and while Ruth was anxious to receive her degrees, she was not looking forward to being thrown from the nest.

There were many international students at Columbia, yet few of them had ever served as officers in wartime armies, none of them as military intelligence analysts attached directly to the offices of a chief of staff. No other woman had ever worn the rank of captain while monitoring the progress of a commando raiding party as she huddled with a team of sweating colonels in a subterranean operations room. Ruth rarely expounded on her experiences, but word got around, and the beauty she denied was cloaked in an additional air of mystery.

She knew that her tendency to seek anonymity was the inheritance of her father's professional habits and would not necessarily benefit her academic progress. She was not effusive, but she also was not shy, and coming from a society where everything was open to debate and everyone's expertise a target for challenge, she bridled at the "professor as God" mentality of the American system. She had to teach herself a degree of tact that she certainly had *not* learned from her parents.

For the most part, however, she could not remain inconspicuous, for many of her instructors were heterosexual men. At first it was her eyes, and then the soft and throaty Israeli-accented English that drew their curious necks from the collars of their cardigans.

She tried not to take advantage of her congenital trousseau, but after her first year of struggle she decided that any benefit accrued from her professors' unrequited feelings was beyond her control. She had committed only one sexual error, having slept with an associate professor, and though she quickly lost interest in his nervous performance, she had to stretch it out until semester break. She sometimes remembered now, with a smile, how during that autumn term she had claimed menstrual afflictions of impossible duration. She got her A and ended the liaison, and now she kept her distance from them all.

Not that every member of the faculty found her fetching. On American campuses, Israel was no longer viewed as the David of the Middle East, and she was occasionally taken to task for simply hailing from a "fascist Sparta." One Russian-born instructor had made the mistake of equating her opinions on a matter of schematic psychology with her origins in an oppressive, siege-mentality society.

"If I'd wanted to argue politics, Professor," Ruth had responded, "I would have gone to the School of International and Public Affairs."

The tactic earned her back slaps after class. Having revealed his prejudice, the pompous man could not possibly give her a lesser grade just because she was Israeli.

Socially, Ruth was well ensconced. After a few false starts born of petty jealousies, she had won the respect of those fellow students who had also survived the program. She retained just a few friends who served as confidants, while making herself available to the numerous classmates who, for some reason, sought her counsel on issues personal and professional. Perhaps it was the depth of her eyes, the suggestion that her experience far exceeded her time on earth. But what endeared her most was her availability as the target of a gibe. She enjoyed a sarcastic tease, and she could take it just as well as give it.

Just after the first lecture of a new professor, her friends would gather round and imbue her with manipulative traits she did not have.

"So how're you going to play this one, Ruth?" This was usually Paul Desmond, a Cornell graduate who spent a lot of time wishing he were at Harvard. "Cold bitch? Warm and shy?"

"Dominatrix," Ruth would answer simply, as the small group walked from Schermerhorn over to Uris Hall for coffee.

"Whips and leather?" Lisa Borowitz was Ruth's roommate in the two-bedroom they rented together on West 112th Street.

"He'd have cardiac arrest," a woman named Kit commented on the elderly professor. Kit was a transfer from Georgetown, tall, blond, leggy, and cynical.

"Mental torture, then," Ruth decided.

"Yeah, you're good at that." Paul waved and split off, heading for the gym to squeeze in a workout.

"He loves you," Lisa said to Ruth as they watched Paul depart.

"*Sheh hazion omed, hasechel yored*," Ruth muttered in Hebrew.

"Which means?"

"As the cock rises, so the intellect declines," Ruth offered with a demure smile.

Kit laughed. "You're such a delicate flower."

Ruth had no interest in Paul Desmond, nor in most of her other male classmates. She found it difficult to relate to the average American male, for she came from a place where by the age of twenty-one most young men had shouldered terrible responsibilities, made life-and-death decisions for themselves and others under their command. American college men still retained the high school immaturities that Israeli boys shed within their first weeks in the army.

Still, she did not reject all advances out of hand, and when occasionally she found herself attracted to *both* the mind and the body of an American, she expressed her desires unabashedly. Ruth enjoyed sex, and coupled with the lack of frequency with which she partook of it, her desire could reach a fever pitch.

Unfortunately for Ruth, most of the relationships did not endure for more than a few weeks, as her partners became demanding of time she did not have. Postgraduate work at Columbia was extremely expensive, and she had to work.

Foreign students in the United States were granted limited work visas, but Israelis abroad could find employment in their own government facilities without restrictions. And so she shuttled back and forth from the *Mishlachat Habitachon*, the Israeli Defense Mission in midtown, which was primarily responsible for purchasing American-made supplies with the millions provided in grants and loans from the U.S. government. Ruth served as assistant to a retired IDF general, who was kind enough to allow her to steal whole blocks of time to keep up with her studies. He was also sharp enough to realize, after his first and only gaffe, that Ruth did not want to be reminded that being the daughter of Benjamin Baum offered her any advantage.

In addition to this, she discovered that her talents in English brought further financial benefits. Other foreign students employed her to "edit" their papers (penning the original works could result in her expulsion); some of them were quite wealthy, and no one squabbled over her prices. She was often amused when a cousin to the Crown Prince of Oman would hand her five hundred dollars as a tip for editing a paper that took her barely an hour to bring to top form.

And still there were times when the financial burden nearly broke her will, and she came very close to calling her parents in Jerusalem and asking for a loan. But the idea that her father might answer and she would have to ask him for help stilled her hand. Instead, she reluctantly fished a credit card from her wallet, took a cash advance, and paid for the next round of academic credits at exorbitant interest rates.

Ruth no longer felt that resorting to such measures was the knee-jerk, regressive behavior of an angry child. If her years studying human psychology had taught her anything, it was that resentment for parental misbehavior had to be explored, understood, and vented. She and her father had hardly communicated at all since her coming to America, yet she understood her own feelings now and she hoped someday to have the opportunity to face him as an adult and "dirty the air."

She realized now that her years of resentment had not begun to foment until she herself was an intelligence officer. It was then, sometimes standing watches that saw days pass into nights in The Hole, far below General Headquarters, that she saw the depths of her own childhood deprivations. She watched as field rank officers embraced their work with near erotic fervor, ignoring phone calls from their wives, missing children's birthdays, and to

Ruth it was like suddenly being introduced to her father's mistress, a hag called "duty," who had stolen her childhood.

And for what? Had Israel found a minute's peace for all his absences? Had his explanations that he was "fighting" for her security dulled the pains of his inattentions? Had his professional successes, so secret that he would not share them, been worth her scorching feelings of unworthiness? It was during those long hours of fluorescent days that never ended, before computer screens of blinking coded traffic, listening to the urgent radio contacts of agents in the field, that it suddenly struck Ruth in the heart like a Jerusalem December wind. She looked around at the intense expressions of these men and finally saw her father for what he was.

He could never remember the names of her girlfriends. He barely grunted when she received an *Aleph* in a class. Her flute was nothing more than background music, and when at last the boys started to come around, he had not even looked up long enough to suffer a twinge of fatherly jealousy.

But enemy orders of battle? He knew them by heart. The résumés of terror stars? He could recite a thousand details. She was sure beyond a painful shadow of a doubt that the brain of Benjamin Baum, master counterterrorist, contained reams of telephone numbers and addresses, agents' real names and their covers, mission plans and backups, safe houses and dead drops, weapon types, muzzle velocities, one-time pads, matrix codes, and the mind-numbing duplicitous plots for creating double agents, inserting them, extracting them, and, yes, eliminating them when "duty" deemed it necessary.

Oh, yes, she was sure he had never shirked a rendezvous. But her high school graduation? He had missed it.

Her father was not an unaffectionate man; he kissed and hugged his children freely. But when Ruth recalled the bearlike embraces and the wet smack of his lips on her cheek, these symbolic efforts made in passing from one appointment to another further enraged her. They required no more emotional effort than the repacking of his suitcase, and God knew for how many strangers he had also feigned affection, while simultaneously planning their demise.

On only one occasion had he actually expressed some pride, and that was when she had been selected for the Intelligence School at Training Base 13. Yet even then he clearly viewed his daughter's military career path with the arrogance of a contractor whose son has finally agreed to take over the business. It was expected.

Ah, but when she announced her intention to muster out of the army, study abroad, and settle in America: *that* he noticed. Suddenly Benjamin Baum was on his feet! He was a child of the Holocaust, Israel had given the Baums everything they had, there was only one place on this earth for a Jew to feel secure and proud, and what right had Ruth to join that throng of selfish cowards who would abandon their homeland! The fights were thunderous, yet mercifully short, for Ruth's greatest inheritance was her stubborn resolve.

And then she was gone.

For a while she experienced a terrible sadness, most of it focused on her mother. Maya Baum had labored hard to fill two roles, and it was surely through her compensatory efforts that Ruth and her brothers had escaped emotional crippling. However, as Ruth studied in her chosen field, even her pity for her mother was tempered, for she felt somewhat like the child of one parent who had abused her while the other stood by and witnessed it. . . .

Yet on this early-winter day in the fourth year of her studies, Ruth Baum was not thinking about her past. She was focused on the immediate future.

She sat at one of the small round tables in the psychology library on the ground floor of Schermerhorn. The room, with only a few reading tables, yellow vinyl armchairs, and steel stacks of periodicals, was not a full-fledged research facility. In general, Ruth rarely frequented libraries, for she had never been able to concentrate in such an atmosphere. To her, a large space crowded with concentrating minds was anything but silent, a bombardment of neural beams and heightened sexual energy where young and horny students hunched together, trying to ignore their groins.

But if she found the psychology library empty, she would settle there, searching for substantiation of her upcoming master's research project. The paper was a high-risk venture, and she was looking for a way in which to make it palatable.

Presenting a master's thesis on terrorist psychology would simply not do, for it would fall outside the bounds of "political correctness" and might endanger her progression to the doctorate. However, she thought now that she had a title that would dupe her academic overseers: "A Pattern of Early Growth Stimuli in Politically Violent Action Group Members."

It was still risky, yet she could not help it. She was fascinated by the subject of terrorism. Her personal library was filled to overflowing with titles in Hebrew, English, and German: Uri Dan's *Etzba Elohim*, Robin Wright's *Sacred Rage*, Stefan Aust's *Der Baader-Meinhof-Komplex*. The hard disk of her personal computer was jammed with a database of international terrorists and psychological profiles, and too much of her overburdened finances went to telephone bills that were slave to her modem. Having failed to force the obsession back into the realm of "hobby," she had decided to put it to academic use. Without consciously realizing it, she was well on her way to becoming a competitive authority on the subject.

"Oh, if *Abba* only knew." She would sometimes picture her father's stunned reaction had she been able to tell him about her secret love. But she'd be damned if she would volunteer the information. Someday, she would just mail him her first published book on the subject.

She sat back now and rotated her neck as she stretched her arms. She dropped her hands onto her worn black denims and looked at them.

"Well, I guess it's in the jeans," she whispered, then smiled at her own pun as she began leafing through a pile of periodicals. She always got a kick out of *Schizophrenia Bulletin*, especially since she herself felt like a patient at times. She liked *Motivation and Emotion*, a small publication written without ego. But today the article titles seemed to sway before her tired eyes: "The Effects of Hormones, Type A Behavior Pattern, and Provocation on Aggression in Men."

"*Ya Allah,*" she whispered. "*Ma assiti l'atzmi?* What have I done to myself?"

A group of chattering students pushed their way through the library turnstiles. Ruth gathered her materials and snaked her arms into a camel-hair coat.

She hunched against the wind and headed for the main administration building, a huge white edifice on the same plateau as Schermerhorn, with Athenian cupola and columns at the peak of two wide flights of marble steps. Her favorite spot for solitude was on a stair just inside the spacious foyer, where all sounds were softened by the vast cavern and she would be able to concentrate. She walked quickly around the building's flank, watching her Doc Martens crunching patterns in the dust of early snow.

She missed Jerusalem, even as she fought it harder with each passing day. The letters from her mother were not enough, the photographs of her brothers in uniform only made it worse. She wanted to pull on a T-shirt, shorts, and sandals, to walk down Ben-Yehuda in the blinding white of spring, to find a man she understood and loved and trusted. To hold his hand and stroll the exotic alleyways as she had once done with her father, when her longings for his return were answered and he would spend a smiling morning of exploration with her. She wished that she could transport herself to Abu Tor, even for an hour, just to see her house, her mother, her brothers, to be sure it all still existed and was there for her.

At the top of the wide stone steps, just outside the entranceway of the building, she suddenly stopped. She blinked, pushed the hair back behind her ear, and blinked again. A flood of heat rose from inside her coat to her chilled cheeks, and her heart began to hammer so that her knees nearly buckled.

Her father was standing in the center of the marble hill, looking up at her. He was cradling a bouquet of red roses.

They sat together in the smoking section of the Cosmopolitan, a self-service coffee shop on Broadway near the corner of 114th Street. The floor was red industrial tile, the chairs were of bent metal tubing, and cheap Tiffany-style chandeliers hung from the ceiling like spacecraft from the planet Woolworth. Ruth liked the two brothers who owned the place and took pickup orders from behind the greasy glass counter. They always smiled and called her "our beautiful smart girl," without being wolfish.

She was extremely proud of herself, so much so that she felt as if she had actually grown taller. She had not run to her father, thrown her arms around him, or cried, yet neither had she allowed her resentments to cause her to turn her back on him. Instead, she had calmed her racing heart and slowly descended the marble stairs. Her father's face revealed his insecurity, hopeful yet afraid, like a field marshal surrendering his sword.

Ruth stopped a step above him, looked into his eyes, then glanced at the flowers.

"*Ha-indianim matziim mikteret shalom.* The Indians usually offer a peace pipe," she said.

"The florist didn't have one," said Benni, unsure if his daughter might not simply throw him backward into a somersault.

"Well, at the very least you should surrender your pistol."

"I am unarmed, Ruti."

His nervous smile faded, and as Ruth watched his face, she saw a look in his eyes that, certainly, few had ever witnessed. It was a plea. In the last two years, his age had finally come to those eyes. He had not lost a kilogram, nor had his bulky muscle dwindled, but somehow he looked smaller. She knew then that her own self-image had grown.

She did not kiss him or touch the roses, but she took his elbow and led him toward the Broadway gate of the university. During the long silence of the stroll, and until they actually entered the coffee shop, Benni still expected her to hail a cab, push him into it, and slam the door.

They ate hamburgers and sipped cherry Cokes. Benni suffered through the enervating small talk, while Ruth was on the "high ground," enjoying his discomfort. Baum was the sole survivor of his German family, and Maya of hers, so there was little fodder for gossip. And Ruth refused to smooth their conflict over with a skein of idle chatter, saying only that her academic program and her life in New York were both successful.

She did probe him about her mother, Yosh, and Amos, a respite for which he was grateful. And he relayed some anecdotes about her brothers' failed romances, which amused her.

"And how is the great General Ben-Zion?" she asked, for she often viewed her father's commander as something of a Machiavellian influence.

"Sour, as usual," said Benni. "But still healthily ambitious."

"And Eytan?" Eytan Eckstein was the only coconspirator in her father's world whom she truly liked. For a large part of her adolescence, she had even loved the handsome, quiet agent, with his blondish hair and sad eyes, a secret crush that set her young heart pounding whenever he appeared at the door to the Baum household.

"He was sent abroad on assignment," said Benni.

"Without you?"

"Without me."

"He is the good side of your soul, you know, *Abba*."

Benni looked at her. He had not heard a term of endearment from his daughter's lips in a long, long time.

"I know," he said. "I miss him. But not as much as I miss you."

Ruth did not smile, her expression suggesting: *You should continue on this path.*

"You've become so beautiful," her father said. "It's hard for me to look at you."

"It's not my beauty that's making it hard for you, *Abba*. It's twenty-six years of mistakes. Most of them yours." She waited until he nodded. "And we will have to discuss that. Another time, but soon. We'll probably need a few days. Do you have the courage?"

After a moment, in which Benni imagined the flood of anger and issues that would tumble out of Ruth's mouth, he said, "I have it."

"Good." She finally smiled at him. "Temporary stay of execution."

Benni relaxed a bit. They finished their lunch, and Ruth got up to fetch coffee. "So how did you find me?" she asked as they caressed the steaming white cups.

"The postgraduate office sent me to the psychology center. Some kids there suggested the main building. They were very helpful."

"*Meragel.* Spy," Ruth said. She reached out, took one of Benni's Times, and lit up.

"I've heard the antismoking campaign here actually gets violent at times," he commented.

"My father says smoking enhances concentration." She repeated his favorite excuse for continuing the habit.

"True, but no American man will want to kiss you."

"I do it to keep the kissers at bay."

"Me too," Benni said, and Ruth laughed. His image was anything but Casanova.

"Well, a few good men *have* braved the battle smoke," she offered.

"May God go with them." And then he quickly stuttered, "I–in a positive way, I mean."

Ruth reached out and touched his meaty hand. "Of course. *Und so, Herr Oberst.*" She changed the subject in German, which along with Hebrew and English was one of the tongues of the Baum household. "What secret mission brings you to this land? Though naturally I expect a good cover story."

I'll tell you two truths," said Benni.

"That would be novel."

Benni ignored the gibe and went on. "I'm here for the consular bombing. But I just used that as an excuse to see you."

Ruth watched his eyes, a technique learned from him. "And had there been no bombing?"

"I would have come anyway." It was not a lie. The rift had pained him, and before the end of the year he would have been on a plane. "*Eema* has really suffered from this." Ruth's mother was clearly pushing Benni to make amends, but Ruth accepted that a stubborn nature needed prodding.

"I know," said Ruth. "She writes to me." Then she let him off the hook. "So tell me about your theories. I've been working at the Defense Mission, and everyone has an opinion."

"At the Defense Mission?"

"Secretarial."

"I see." He would not offer her any money just yet. She might take offense. "Well, let's see. What *do* I think?"

Benni instinctively looked around the coffee shop. The closest person to their table was an elderly woman, squinting at the obituary column of *The New York Times*. A young, dark-featured man was squeezed into a corner table, well out of earshot. Even so, he lowered his voice and detailed the attack in Hebrew. He told her about Moshiko, the bomber's Hasidic guise, and the American girl who was killed in the explosion. He left out the part about Moshiko's note and was about to change the subject, when Ruth suddenly began to interrogate him in a way that furrowed his brow.

"Tell me about the device, *Abba.*"

"The device?"

"Semtex? C-4?"

"We don't know yet. Probably Semtex."

"Fingerprints?"

"You mean, did he touch anything?"

"No, I mean a signature," Ruth said. "Odd wiring. A detonator. Anything left?"

"Well, the Americans are going to try to put it all together."

"They put TWA 206 back together and still came to the wrong conclusions." She meant the jumbo jet that had been blown out of the sky over Hornesby, Scotland. Benni did not say anything, so she continued. "And what about this 'Hasid's' face? Did Bar-El get it on video?"

"You know Hanan?"

"His Shabakniks work with ours at the mission. Well?"

"Yes, uh, it's on his tapes. But the man was wearing a shtreimel, and the camera was up high."

"How about a description from Moshiko?"

"He's temporarily blind. He could make a description, but he wouldn't be able to confirm a drawing yet."

"Have him do it anyway, while it's still fresh. A subject's visual recollections are more accurate when his eyes are closed, at any rate."

Benni did not respond. He was beginning to see his daughter in a strange light that made him squirm in his chair.

"Did the bomber say anything?" Ruth continued.

"Not that we know of." It was a partial lie.

"Very unusual. He got up to the window, didn't speak, and blew himself up without so much as a 'Fuck all of you Zionist dogs'?"

"Apparently."

"So you're telling me," Ruth said as she sat back and exhaled a long plume of smoke, "that a suicide bomber attacks an Israeli diplomatic facility, makes no statement, and then no one claims responsibility?"

"Those are the facts."

"As you have them."

"As I know so far."

"Atypical," said Ruth.

"Yes, you could say . . ."

"Sounds like Argentina," she added.

"Yes, as a matter of fact . . ." Benni stopped in midthought, "How much do you know about Argentina?"

"Probably as much as you do," said Ruth. That bombing was still a perturbingly unsolved riddle. She stubbed out her cigarette, folded her arms, and squinted up at the ceiling.

A frightening instinct flashed through Benni's mind. His daughter was behaving like a professional, so much so that it superseded the explanation of her own military experience. Was it possible that she was still employed by the government? Could she have been recruited by Shabak or Mossad without his knowing? Nonsense. Impossible.

"Tell me, Ruti," he said now, very softly. "I would never insult your powers of logical deduction, but how is it that you are so 'up' on this subject matter?"

Ruth had been determined not to tell her father about her "hobby." But he had come to her in an effort to reconcile, and she suddenly found the withholding childish.

"My master's thesis is going to be an analysis of terrorist psyches. But I warn you, *Abba*," she quickly added, as she pointed a loaded finger at him, "don't you *dare* express an iota of pride."

Benni stared at her, his jaw slack. He could certainly understand why she would think him proud, and a twinge of that emotion did register. Yet most of what he felt was a quivering chill, like a fighter pilot whose son had just declared his intention also to fly the supersonic coffins.

"Close your mouth," Ruth said. "There are flies in here."

"I will be very anxious to read it," was all he could manage.

"So," she continued, "you have a suicide bomber, Semtex, no political capital. Take a guess."

"I don't *know yet*," Benni answered like a squeezed informant. "Maybe Hizbollah."

"Too easy."

"Ahmed Jabril, then. Abu Ibrahim."

"Possible. Using a decoy signature, perhaps. But I don't think so."

"So, Ruth." He was becoming just a bit annoyed now, keeping it in check. "Why don't you tell me what *you* think?"

"Sounds like Martina Klump to me," she said.

"Excuse me?"

"Martina Ursula Klump, the German woman. Born in Argentina, emigrated to Europe. Frau Seafore, the bomb mistress of the RAF."

But Benni did not need a bio on Martina Klump. He had heard Ruth quite clearly, and her words sent a wild current from the base of his spine to the thick skull bones at the back of his bald head.

"What makes you say Klump?" he whispered.

"Modus operandi. In particular, a penchant for designing sophisticated explosive devices, which are then used in attacks for which no credible suspect claims responsibility. Let's see . . ." She rubbed her forehead with her thumb and fingers, trying to picture her database file on Klump. "Fatherless, I believe. Seems to me he was a German scientist. Committed suicide, a definite impact on her psyche. She started out with Action Directe in the mid-seventies, then went with the Rote Armee Fraktion, perfected her skills there. I think she was captured, did some prison time in Germany, then escaped and went to ground in the early eighties. She was spotted in Lebanon, training Hizbollah suicide bombers."

Ruth looked up to see her father staring at her dumbly. The roses lay on a corner of the table, and he was unconsciously deflowering one with his left hand, rolling the petals like bloody flesh between his fingers.

"Human suicide attack is still a rare terrorist technique," Ruth continued. "In all our years of warfare, only a few Palestinians have ever done it. The only other such recent act was the killing of Prince Gandhi by a female Sikh separatist, and it was widely speculated that Klump was hired to prepare the attack. Don't you read the papers, *Abba*? Or at least your own files?"

"Mmm." Benni had one elbow on the table and was holding his jaw. "I'll have to think about that." But he was already thinking about it, and his physical pose was an effort to suppress the shiver that would certainly show if he did not hold on to himself.

He was thinking of Martina Ursula Klump, and why he had not immediately placed her on his list of potentials. Because he had denied the possibility, that was why. She might have crossed his mind, and he had sent her packing right out the other side.

He was thinking of Germany in the autumn of 1981, when he and Eytan Eckstein had gone to Wiesbaden to inform the *Bundeskriminalamt* of an upcoming RAF rendezvous, during which Klump could be ambushed and taken alive.

He was remembering a small town in southern Bavaria, the railroad tracks near Bad Reichenhall, himself and Eckstein watching through binoculars as a squad from Grenschutzgruppe-9 chased Martina Klump along the rain-soaked trestle, and she turned and stopped and dropped her pistol, her motorcycle jacket opening as she threw her hands into the air and the snarling Alsatians brought her to the ground.

He was seeing her again, inside the isolation cell below the massive castle that was Bruchsal Penitentiary. Alone with her, an arrangement made by his good German friend Bernard Lokojewski. Just Baum and Klump together, sealed in a cocoon of concrete that held nothing but an iron bed, walls so thick that no one but God could eavesdrop. Martina wearing nothing but a canvas frock that could not possibly be torn to fashion a noose.

He was seeing her face, the burning eyes made hollow by years of fugitive existence, the blond hair cropped close and boyish to her skull, the lips that would have proved, despite the canvas bag, that she was a woman, had they not been drawn so tightly into a thin line of distrust.

He was living it again, that awful night in Munich after Klump's escape. It is the last night of Oktoberfest. He and Eytan hurry to the Hauptbahnhof, hoping to be lucky against all sense of reason.

There are twenty-seven platforms in a train station the size of five jumbo-jet hangars, the giant walls fitted with flickering neon ads for Panasonic, Überlinger, *Süddeutsche Zeitung*. The train to Berlin has come in late from Ansbach and is being held so wobbling revelers can make the already crowded yellow cars. The passengers are jammed into billets of red-upholstered seats and steel overhead racks, the windows curtained with soiled brocade. Pools of vomit smear the cobbled slate platform, and those too drunk to make the train are sprawled on wooden slat benches.

Benni stands at the mouth of the platform and watches as Eytan searches every car, staring into the windows as the beer-soaked passengers watch him watch. Eckstein is wearing jeans and a cream-colored sweatshirt, but his green trench coat dissolves his intention to look like a concerned boyfriend.

Eckstein surely knows that if Martina is aboard, she may be that man in the jeans suit with the curly brown hair, slumped behind *Die Welt* in a darkened compartment. Or she might be that old woman with the soiled beige pocketbook, who keeps her back to him and sips from a bottle of Pilse. Or if Lokojewski's information is correct, she might be dead.

Eytan's distant figure jumps down onto the tracks and comes up on the other side. Finally, as his weary form approaches, Benni overhears two swaying teenagers wearing those enormous Oktoberfest felt hats. One juts his chin at Eckstein.

"*Er ist BKA*. He's a BKA agent."

Benni would smile, if not for the chasm of hopelessness in his gut. *Good guess*, he thinks bitterly. *Right profession, wrong country*.

Revelers begin to yell their pleasure as the black-rimmed doors slam one by one, a final whoop as the party ends. The blue-uniformed conductor climbs aboard, and the train rolls out, all electric, no sound but the squealing bogie wheels. Two women on the platform wave white handkerchiefs as the caboose recedes.

Eytan looks at Benni and says something in German.

"Fort."

Gone . . .

"*Abba*. I said think, not brood."

Benni snapped himself out of it. "Yes." He forced a smile and touched a finger to his temple. "Well, it is a very intriguing idea."

"Would you like to see my files on the subject?" Ruth asked, trying to keep any hope out of her voice.

"Certainly."

"I'll show you my apartment." She quickly pulled her book bag up onto her lap. "It's two minutes from here."

Benni gathered up the surviving flowers. "Ruti," he began hesitantly. "You know, I'm only here for three days. It's not much time."

"Of course." She was prepared, had expected it. The excuse, like the signature song of Groucho Marx: Hello, I must be going.

"How about joining me?" Benni suddenly proposed. "I'll be working, but at least we can be together."

Ruth looked at her father. *This* she did not expect. She would have to miss work. There was a paper to edit. But she could spend some time with him, as an adult, maybe even as a peer, living some reality. She would have to skip a couple of boring lectures.

Her mouth spread into the wide grin that always made Paul Desmond's heart hurt.

"Okay," she said warily. "But no secrets."

"It's a deal. No secrets."

"Liar."

Benni laughed. He got up, bent across the table, and kissed her on the forehead. They left the Cosmopolitan arm in arm.

Mussa Hawatmeh exited the coffee shop a minute later. It was cold, and it took a couple of nervous kicks to get the big Suzuki bike to turn over. But then he rode very slowly down Broadway, and he watched the man Martina hated, and the girl, as they crossed the avenue, went halfway down West 112th Street, and entered a small apartment building.

He was shivering as he pulled the motorcycle onto its kickstand near a public telephone, dropped a quarter in, and waited a long time until his rings were finally answered.

He smiled as he spoke.

"I think I have just found a pearl in your ugly oyster."

Chapter 5: The East River

Omar Bin Al-Wafa wanted out.

To be transferred to another assignment, to be relieved of his duties, even to be sent home in disgrace. It did not matter anymore. He was old, he had served his masters well, and enough was enough. He well understood that the role he played was a living lie, but even his duplicity had its limits. His last encounter with Martina Klump had shaken him to his core, for he sensed that he was being used to set her up for a fall, and he would not be able to face a mirror if they turned him into a murderer of courageous children.

The tip of his cane clicked on the icy sidewalk as he descended with care along the last appendage of Forty-second Street between First Avenue and the FDR drive. His spectacles were coated by the fog of his own breath, and the tufts of white hair beneath his black beret completed the impression of an eccentric French tourist whose senility had led him to an area not meant for strolling septuagenarians.

He appeared to be an inviting target, yet his dark mood had raised his blood pressure and sharpened his reflexes.

He turned the corner down by the Robert Moses Playground, its high wire fences and empty courts black beneath a moonless night. The homeless under the causeway had not even made a fire, too cold to come out from their shelters of cardboard boxes and plastic sheets. He was alone, with the exception of the pair of ridged rubber soles he heard tiptoeing carefully behind him. Cars were darting intermittently along the drive, but Omar knew that in this satanic city they would not stop to help even if a killer was strangling a naked toddler.

Omar suddenly halted. Then he turned and faced his attacker squarely. The junkie also stopped, just five feet away, smiling through a short beard. He was very large and wore a woolen watch cap, some sort of worn field jacket, torn blue jeans, and combat boots. Omar lifted the walking stick and shifted it to his left hand, gripping it at the middle of the shaft.

The junkie was amused by the old man's defensive posture, but did not much feel like getting rapped on the skull by the cane's ivory pommel. He pulled out a six-inch switchblade, held it near his leg, and pushed the button. The blade clanged as it flipped down and gleamed.

"I'm twice your size and half your age, grandpa," he whispered. "So just give me the cash and we'll skip the fucking dance."

Omar reached over with his right hand, gripped the cane head, twisted, and pulled. And then he was holding a very long, tempered steel sword as he dropped his little body into a fencer's stance.

"*En garde*," he said, in an alarmingly controlled tone.

The junkie instinctively leaped backward, landing in an awkward crouch that sent a flush of rage to his face. He raised the knife to eye level.

"Okay," he snarled. "I can dig it."

Yet before he could make his first probing lunge, Omar extended the sword, and a web of bright-blue lightning, accompanied by a wicked crackle, arced across the concealed prongs near the point of the blade.

The junkie froze. *Oh, shit*, he thought. *Not this again.* Just a week ago a young woman had stunned him with one of those fifty-thousand volt pocket zappers. One second he was reaching for her necklace, and the next thing he knew, he was sprawled on the sidewalk in a puddle of his own urine.

Omar suddenly yelled like an enraged baboon and lunged forward, driving the flashing épée toward the junkie's throat. But the young man was already sprinting away, and he disappeared through a white cloud of his own breath.

Omar stood still for a full minute, watching the streams from his lungs curl through the air, the fading footfalls of his assailant echoing in his brittle ears. He nodded to himself, and had he not been overburdened by his broodings, a smile of satisfaction might have spread his frozen mustache. He had not had a physical confrontation like this in perhaps twenty years, and he was pleased to discover that his hands were still steady. He inserted the blade into the wooden scabbard and slammed it home with a flourish.

He looked up at the sky, the low ceiling of midnight clouds hued amber by the lights of a city that never rested. For a moment, he closed his eyes and replaced the bitter wind from the black river with the warm breezes of a *khamsin* skipping off the Sea of Galilee. He did not care for the cold, but he could endure it, as he had done in many winter capitals of the world. For always in his mind was the promise of the Middle Eastern climate, waiting to embrace his bones at the end of every journey.

"And I will again return there soon," he whispered. "But not as a Judas."

At that moment, warmth arrived in a form more immediate and practical. A dark-blue Lincoln Continental slid down the street alongside the United Nations compound. It turned the corner, its brights flashed once, and Omar stepped forward. The rear door opened, and he slipped inside.

"*Lailtak sa'idi.*" A voice bade him good evening from the darkened corner of the compartment. "*Kif halak?*" It asked after his welfare in a Farsi-accented Syrian dialect.

"*Ilham' dilla mashruh.* Thank Allah, well," Omar answered as he settled back into the leather cushion.

"*Shai?*" A hand extended a glass of dark tea, and Omar understood why the interior of the limousine seemed bathed in a low fog. Yet he declined the refreshment.

Omar's host leaned forward, his face appearing in the dim light from a door panel. Ali-Hamza Asawi had soft and unlined features, short black hair, and a narrow jaw covered by a manicured beard. Although his vision was perfect, he often wore plain metal spectacles to further enhance the academic appearance he cultivated. His black wool three-piece suit was typical of Iranian diplomats, a white, collarless shirt was buttoned at his throat, and the only bow to Western decadence was a taupe cashmere scarf draped around his neck.

Asawi's diplomatic cover was as a press attaché and assistant to Mohammed Ayatollahi, Iran's ambassador to the International Atomic Energy Agency. He held full credentials as a professor of journalism from the Sharif University in Tehran, and he actually lectured there on occasion, but his tenure had little to do with higher learning.

Ali-Hamza Asawi was chief of psychological and counterintelligence operations for the Western Hemisphere division of SAVAMA, the Iranian Revolutionary Secret Police. After the fall of the Shah, SAVAMA had been quickly organized to replace the SAVAK, whose American- and Israeli-trained agents had all been executed or exiled. The new intelligence organization could now hardly be distinguished from the old, even surpassing it in fanaticism and cruelty, although its political bent was the polar opposite of its predecessor's.

Although just forty-two years old, Asawi had risen rapidly to one of the most powerful posts in SAVAMA. AS an infantry captain in 1979, he had virtually no intelligence background when he volunteered for the Ayatollah Khomeini's fledgling secret police, which was sorely lacking in trainers and advisers. Asawi proposed a simple plan, rapidly approved. He imprisoned the former head of SAVAK's PsyOps and Counter-Intel program for a full year, promising a pardon and redemption before God if the agent would reveal the secrets of his trade.

He spent nearly every day of twelve months with his former enemy, culling the arcane arts of false flag operations, populace subversion, disinformation, communication interceptions, and technical acquisitions forbidden by international law. When the interrogation was finally completed to his satisfaction, he thanked his "mentor" and had him executed in a public hanging.

For the past few years, Asawi had appeared to be engaged in an effort to support Mohammed Ayatollahi's contention that Iran had the same right as any other nation to improve its lot through technological advancement. The small research reactor at Sharif was, he insisted, nothing more than that. And even though Iran's enormous oil supply could keep its lights aglow for a thousand years, who but Allah could say that she did not deserve the benefits of peaceful nuclear power?

However, Asawi's talents lay in deception rather than scientific enlightenment. He flooded the U.S. Department of Commerce with requests for purchase approvals: an ES/9000 computer from IBM, circuit boards from Textronix, timing devices from Rockwell. And while he kept FBI, Treasury, and Customs agents busy battling with industrial lobbyists on Capitol Hill, he sent his agents out to acquire vacuum pumps and balancing machines from Leybold and Schenck in Germany, supermagnets from Thyssen, beryllium from Semipolotinsk, and M-9 missiles from North Korea.

A few American components did make it through to Sharif. And thanks to the lack of oversights, many crucial European items were shipped to Ispahan, the sealed Iranian city of mosques and minarets, where the efforts to create a nuclear weapons capability were in full swing. But at this rate, Asawi and his masters knew that they would enter the next century without seeing a mushroom cloud blossom over the sands of Dasht-e-Lut.

Asawi finished his tea and replaced the glass in a holder of the limousine's liquor bar, which held only mineral water, a few bottles of Snapple, and a brass *finjon* sitting in an electric warmer.

"Be on your vey," he instructed the driver, in an accent that often caused Americans to mistake him for an Indian. There was no partition between the compartments, but he felt secure that the black chauffeur would not comprehend a Syrian dialect. The car belonged to the Iranian mission and was electronically swept each day. The drivers were switched every week, hired through an American cutout.

The limousine made a right turn onto Forty-first Street and headed west into midtown. Omar did not bother to inquire about its destination, for he had accompanied Ali-Hamza Asawi on a hundred seemingly aimless meanderings. He had strolled with Asawi through the streets of Paris and nearly frozen with him on a chairlift in the Alps. Once, they even hired horses in the south of Spain and trotted off onto the beaches near Málaga to be assured of distance from prying ears. In fact, Omar realized that in all the years he had been working for SAVAMA, he had never once met Asawi in any building that remotely suggested the People's Revolutionary Government of Iran, or in any office that was more than a transitory cubicle rented by his control for the occasion.

Omar had arrived in Tehran in 1968, when thousands of disenfranchised Palestinian Arabs had sought refuge throughout the Middle East, hoping that their exile would be temporary. Being of partial Iranian descent, he had felt comfortable with the people and their culture, although his birthright was not forgotten as he became a street policeman, rose to the rank of detective sergeant, and gained a professional reputation regarded as apolitical by Iran's new mullahs. His fervor for the Palestinian cause put him in good favor with the revolutionary government, and although he was about to retire, a recruiter for Asawi swept him up. At the time, one did not refuse an offer to aid in the resurgence of fundamentalist Islam.

On the whole, Omar was grateful to be active at an age when most men resigned themselves to *sheshbesh* games on street corners. Ali-Hamza Asawi had always treated him with respect, and he had never asked Omar to undertake a mission that might conflict with his Palestinian nationalism. Yet now Omar's conscience was overpowering his need to feel useful.

Still, it would not be easy to resign. Although he had become a full-fledged Iranian, he and his sons and their children were considered of foreign descent, and his employment in SAVAMA assured them all a great security.

"And so, my friend." Ali-Hamza Asawi began the debriefing in Arabic. "How is our Mrs. Seafore?" Even though the driver was linguistically "deaf," Asawi would use no proper monikers.

"She appeared quite shaken by the bombing," said Omar. He removed his beret and opened his coat. The limousine was comfortably warm, and the lights of passing traffic drifted by the smoked windows like hazy torches in a midnight demonstration.

"Shaken?" Asawi sounded surprised.

"Well, perhaps 'offended' would be a more appropriate word."

"How so?"

"She thinks the incident may somehow interfere with her own mission."

Asawi smiled. "And so it shall," he said softly.

Omar turned in his seat so he could see Ali-Hamza's face. Even though his suspicions were threatening to burst from his mouth, he could not afford to face his control with false accusations. He rested his walking stick on the upholstery and patted it with his hand.

"By the way, Ali-Hamza," he said. "This article came in very handy tonight. I was nearly mugged."

"Really?"

"Just before you arrived."

"Good!" Asawi was truly pleased. "Now perhaps my men will understand why I do not give them aftershave as going-away presents for missions to New York. I have your permission to relay the story?" the Iranian asked.

"*Khadamtak sharaf*. To serve you is an honor." Omar smiled, and then he quickly switched subjects. "But tell me, Ali-Hamza. Don't you think that the Israelis might actually suspect Mrs. Seafore of involvement?"

The pleasure remained in Asawi's eyes. "Perhaps."

"But she was not involved." It emerged from Omar as an unconvinced statement.

"No."

"Yet the attack *does* have the earmarks of one of her efforts."

"If I have done my job properly," said Asawi without further elaboration.

That was it, then. Martina's instincts had been on the mark, her anger justifiable. She suspected that her employers were funneling her into a trap, while Omar had denied it in his naïveté, an unwitting buffoon. He gathered his courage.

"Ali-Hamza," Omar said as he stared straight ahead. "I wish to be relieved of this assignment."

Asawi hardly raised an eyebrow. He was not surprised, for Omar Bin Al-Wafa was essentially a kindly man with a sense of justice. For this reason, he was rarely privy to the purpose, or the impact, of an assignment. "Is your conscience troubling you, Omar?"

"I do not wish to be the instrument of this young woman's destruction," Omar declared.

"She is not a woman," Asawi said. "She is a weapon, and she is well paid to be utilized as we see fit."

"I do not wish to participate in this," Omar insisted.

"Then we will discuss your termination *after* I have properly debriefed you."

The implication was not lost on Omar, and he settled back with a sigh. Ali-Hamza was correct; one did not withdraw from a running mission, no matter one's distaste. But if Omar were to be forced to continue, at the very least he wished to understand. He was used to Asawi's elaborate manipulations, but this one genuinely confused him. Martina had not perpetrated the bombing, but Asawi had placed her signature upon it. To what end?

"So, Omar," Asawi continued, "did you sense in your meeting that our lovely lady might guess the true nature of your representation?"

"Not at all."

"She believes that your motives are pure? That your background is genuine?"

"It *is* genuine. As is my accent—not that she could really discern such subtleties."

"Why not?"

"A few years in Lebanon do not turn a German into an Arabic scholar." Omar shifted in his seat. Ali-Hamza's debriefing had taken on the annoying grate of interrogation.

"And she did not make further inquiries as to the identities of your 'employers'?"

"She is believing what she wants to believe." Omar's voice rose a bit. "That I am a Palestinian, and a representative of one of the Rejection Front leaders."

"But you *are* a Palestinian," Asawi said with a certain disdainful authority.

"And you are a Persian," Omar shot back, and the driver looked up into his rearview mirror. "But *first* we are Moslems, faithful only to Allah—"

Omar stopped himself. Ali-Hamza was regarding him with a thin smile. The Iranian raised a finger and wagged it at him. "Got you again, Omar Bin Al-Wafa."

Omar slumped back into the seat, embarrassed. "My age is making me brittle," he sighed.

"We are never too old to learn. Your emotions linger too close to the surface," Asawi gloated. "But I am sure that as a detective you also addled the brains of a few prisoners."

"Do you think of me as a prisoner?"

"Don't be foolish," Asawi snorted, though in fact he viewed the old man as exactly that, a hostage to SAVAMA's wishes and commands. They were both fully aware that the status of Omar's family depended on the merits of his service. "Now, give me the details of the good lady's plans."

The limousine turned right on Sixth Avenue and moved slowly north as Omar recited verbatim the list that Martina had shown him. When he got to the sentence that summarized her action plan, Asawi leaned forward as if he had not heard.

"Repeat that," he said.

"She intends to acquire a prototype man-carried antiship weapon for use against the prisoner exchange."

"A 'prototype' weapon?" Asawi was squinting now at the floor.

"A sort of minitorpedo."

"A *minitorpedo*," the Iranian enunciated carefully. "And how does she intend to 'acquire' this device?"

"She is going to hijack it."

"From where?"

"From a U.S. naval facility. Somewhere in Europe, I believe."

Now Asawi began to laugh. He placed his hands on his knees, sat back into the corner of the seat, and actually shook with laughter.

"This is no joke, Ali-Hamza," said Omar.

"It is absolutely ridiculous," Asawi managed.

"I assure you that she is a driven woman. She has planned every detail and is fiercely determined to make it work. And from what I could see, Yadd Allah will do her bidding. Like panting dogs they will."

"Yadd Allah," Asawi sniffed.

"And there was one other thing," Omar continued, wanting to be relieved of the pressure of accountability because he could never write anything down. "Her budget. It appeared that there would be funds to spare, but Mrs. Seafore hinted that she had needs of a personal nature. In the event of her death, she said."

Asawi nodded. He was silent for a while, and he twisted open a bottle of Snapple, poured himself a glass of the berry-colored liquid, and sipped as he pondered.

"Are you aware, Omar," he said at last, "that our lady friend has a mother?"

"All of Allah's servants have mothers," Omar replied, knowing that he would soon be lost again in the labyrinth of Ali-Hamza's mind.

"Yes, my friend. But *her* mother is alive and well. And living here in New York."

The revelation stunned Omar. Intelligence operatives who worked at the "sharp end" of the business—contract agents, wet-work specialists, terrorists for hire—were extremely wary of exposing their loved ones to their professional associates. The irony of employment in intelligence—and this phenomenon was common worldwide—was that as soon as an agent demonstrated blind commitment by perpetrating extreme acts, he or she instantly became a liability. Family or friends could be used as leverage tactics. In Martina Klump's case, Omar had come to think of her as an unnatural phenomenon, a being without origins who had somehow emerged from the political miasma of the extreme left. To him, she was like Macbeth's executioner: not of woman born.

"How do you know this?" he asked, although the question sounded childishly naive even as it left his lips.

"My friend," said Asawi, "we would hardly have you employ such a dangerous asset without first having a considerable file on her. She may not have become an 'Arabic scholar,' as you put it, in Lebanon. However, during those years she certainly exposed a great deal of herself to our associates."

Ali-Hamza always referred to the members of the Party of God as his "associates." There was a tone of disdain there, as if Hizbollah's peculiar brand of religious zealotry was an anomaly to the cosmopolitan SAVAMA officer. Omar had the impression that Ali-Hamza used Hizbollah for his own ends, while remaining aloof from their political aspirations.

Hizbollah was, after all, the creation of a team of Iranian Revolutionary Guards who had been sent to Lebanon under the direction of SAVAMA in 1982. The present Hizbollah negotiator for the upcoming prisoner exchange, Sheik Tafilli, reported directly to Sa'id Abbas Mussawi, operational commander of the organization. Mussawi in turn reported to Mohammed Hussein Fadlallah, the spiritual father of the movement. And while Fadlallah claimed complete independence, he accepted "suggestions" from Mohammed Javad Larijani, the Iranian presidential adviser on intelligence affairs.

If SAVAMA required that Hizbollah should undertake a particular task—even something so distasteful as surrendering Israeli captain Dan Sarel in an exchange—Ali-Hamza Asawi's position gave him the power to actually issue directives to Fadlallah through Larijani.

"Yes, of course," said Omar. Still, the knowledge of Martina's mother's whereabouts was not a piece of information he cherished. He wondered how the German woman would react if she thought her mother's name was being invoked in an operational discussion. The speculation did not comfort him.

"And a mother's love is a powerful thing," Asawi added.

"Yes," said Omar. *But not powerful enough to keep her sons from slaughter.* He was thinking of the one million Iranian men who had been sacrificed in the bloody confrontation with Iraq. He was seeing the endless graves that stretched to the horizons of Tehran, the sad portraits of the fallen staring out from metal-and-glass frames above the flat stones. He was thinking of his own niece, a broken woman left with icons instead of sons.

Asawi reached into the pocket of his suit jacket and extracted a small leather-bound notepad. As he printed something carefully with a Mont Blanc, he asked, "Her list suggested that her operation would take place in Europe?"

"So it seemed."

"Then it will occur on American soil," he concluded confidently. And he issued his next directive to Omar. "This is what I would like you to do. Make contact with our infamous debutante and inform her that your Palestinian masters believe her plan to be foolish."

Omar waited for the rest of it, while he thought: *Why not ask me to simply smear myself in goat's blood and go for a swim in a shark pool?*

"Tell her," Asawi continued, "that a great deal of money has been invested, her plan will never work, and she should stick to more mundane ideas—such as frogmen and limpet mines."

"Frogmen and limpet mines," Omar repeated weakly, like a psychiatric patient under hypnotic suggestion.

"Yes. And when you have done that"—Asawi tore off the small rectangle of blue paper and handed it to Omar—"call the New York Police Department's hot line. Do *not* call 911, for you will merely speak to a dispatcher there. Make it one of the publicized numbers—Crime Stoppers, or Cop Shot." He pointed to the slip of paper now in Omar's hand. "Give them that name, and that address, and say no more."

Omar looked down at the note, suddenly feeling his age, just as he had so strongly felt his youth not twenty minutes earlier. He was being instructed to first insult an unpredictable contract agent and then expose her vulnerabilities to the enemy. Now was the time to reiterate his refusal of this mission. Yet even though he was not so concerned for himself at this stage of his life, he also held the lives of his family in his hands.

"With all due respect, Ali-Hamza," Omar said quietly, "such pressure is likely to make her crazy."

"Precisely," Asawi quickly replied. "And if the Israelis believe that she was instrumental in the bombing—and with this small but generous clue you shall provide, that is a conclusion they *must* draw—they will pursue her with typically vengeful enthusiasm."

Omar removed his spectacles, closed his eyes, and rested his head on the seat back. He had worked for Ali-Hamza Asawi for a long time, and he had never been bold enough to ask for the whole picture. However, this time he wanted to comprehend, for the sake of his own motivation. He had to understand why the Iranians had first arranged for the prisoner exchange, then set in motion a plot to destroy it, and were now applying pressure to their own proxy!

"I apologize," Omar sighed. "I am a bit tired." He paused. "I know, Ali-Hamza, that it is not my place . . ."

"But you wish to understand."

"Yes. I confess that for once I do."

"You are correct. It is not your place."

Omar opened his eyes, turned his head, and smiled weakly at Asawi.

Asawi returned the smile. "I sympathize. Blind obedience is for the very young, but you cannot know everything, my friend."

"Of course not." Omar replaced his spectacles, and Asawi, seeing that the old man had once again embraced compartmentalization, decided to risk some generosity.

"This much I can tell you. We care very little for the return of Hizbollah's Sheik Sa'id, and certainly less for an Israeli commando."

"Yes." Omar listened carefully.

"That prisoner exchange is nothing more than cover. A way to distract the efforts of Israeli intelligence. Do you follow?"

"Thus far."

"Good. Now furthermore, if there is someone who is trying to *thwart* the exchange, the Jews will redouble their efforts to *protect* it. They will be forced temporarily to refocus their intelligence resources, redesignate manpower. Hopefully, for a time, they will neglect *other* areas."

"Yes, that makes sense." And suddenly Omar did comprehend. For a moment, he had forgotten that Ali-Hamza's talents lay in deception. No part of Omar's assignments was ever directly related to the primary mission, whatever that might be.

"And finally," Asawi explained in a light crescendo of self-satisfaction, "one selects a delegate—in this case our honorable Mrs. Seafore—who is difficult to dissuade once set upon her course. If we then place obstacles in her path, her determination will increase, making our true mission that much easier to execute."

"*Mashallah.*" Omar held up one of his small hands. The word meant "Bravo," but it was not said facetiously. "I understand. It was stupid of me . . ."

"Don't apologize." Asawi waved a hand. "And have no fear. I would not have told you more."

"I have no need to know."

"And you will carry out these next small tasks?"

"With skill, I assure you."

"Allah reward you for me."

The briefing was over, and the two men settled into a comfortable silence.

The limousine had passed Times Square and was weaving through the theater district. Awasi told the driver to enter a parking garage on West Forty-seventh Street and drive through it to the next block. He was accustomed to being followed by American counterintelligence watchers, and any car that mimicked this act would be easy to spot.

The Lincoln drove north once again, and Omar could not help wondering as to the nature of a mission so significant that it required a red herring of global proportions to mask it. The car had grown very warm inside, and he opened his window for a few breaths of air. They passed a construction site protected by a long fence of plywood slabs, the boards covered with posters by the ghostly paste-wielders that one never actually saw. The Angelika 57 theater was hosting a retrospective of American features from the early cold war era, and a bold title against a background of red cloud flashed over and over again.

Atomic Café . . . Atomic Café . . . Atomic Café . . .

Omar closed the window.

For most of the last decade, SAVAMA's efforts had been concentrated on two primary missions: fomenting a Moslem fundamentalist revolution throughout the Levant and acquiring the Bomb. Omar had surmised that many of Ali-Hamza's missions involved the acquisition of nuclear components. However, Iran had not yet succeeded in its quest to join the international nuclear clique, and SAVAMA was most certainly engaged in tapping an alternate nuclear vein.

Perhaps one of the splintered Soviet republics was finally desperate enough to sell the Iranians a warhead or two? This would certainly fall within Ali-Hamza's area of operations, as would the concept that such a transaction would have to be masked by another event. Otherwise, the Israelis would pull out all stops to halt the delivery.

Omar was suddenly gripped by a sensation of constriction. He thought of his grandchildren, living under the specter of an Iranian government that was always less than stable and certainly did not need to have nuclear toys at its disposal. But then, he was just an old man doing the will of Allah.

He decided that if his mission was successful, he would have to move his family. Again. Another exile. There were rumors that the Israelis and the PLO were holding secret talks. More than ever now, he found himself hoping for their success.

The car coasted to a stop. Omar looked over at Asawi, who shrugged in slight embarrassment.

"I am sorry, Omar," he said. "Procedures, you know. We are only a few meters from the main road." He touched a button, and the electronic door locks popped up. He smiled. "I trust that you will not need your cane again for anything but walking."

Omar opened his door and stepped out, pulling his beret onto his head as he looked around. Through the black fingers of the trees he could see the white lights of Tavern on the Green. He was in Central Park.

"And Omar," said Asawi from the black rectangle of the compartment. "I am pleased that I was able to dissuade you from leaving our employ. *Auda' nak.* Farewell."

"*Allah yihfazak.* God keep you," Omar replied as he gently closed the door. He straightened up, took his bearings, and began to walk.

Asawi watched the little figure recede toward Central Park West. Then he waved at the driver, and they proceeded in the opposite direction.

He reached for the telephone, dialed a number, and spoke in Farsi.

"Book me on the next flight to Tehran."

He snapped the cellular into its cradle, opened the cabinet under the bar, and came up with a small flask of Dewar's. He poured himself half a tumbler, neat, then tuned the radio to a country-and-western station, sat back, crossed his ankles, and sipped.

He did not care to be in New York when Martina Ursula Klump began to vent her rage.

Chapter 6: The USS Intrepid

The hurtling roar of the flaming Japanese Zero had long since faded into the Pacific winds, the jagged wound where the pilot had plunged his spinning machine through the flight deck of the carrier now cauterized and healed. Where a burst of smoke had choked surviving sailors, the only cloud that hung there now was of multicolored balloons. Where the flash of a two-thousand-pound bomb had murdered half the crew of the hangar deck, Christmas bulbs festooned the steel cavern. And where frightened fire crews had battled floods of raging aviation fuel, struggling barmen fought to quench the thirsts of partygoers.

The thundering impacts of war were merely memories now, and the great centerpiece of the Pacific Fleet had been made over into a sea-air-space museum, her keel embedded in the sludge of the Hudson River, her flanks fettered to the dock at Pier 86. Filled with artifacts of American aeronautical history, the flight deck crowded with silent aircraft, she was an incongruous fixture of the west side of Manhattan.

The museum usually closed at dusk, yet various organizations had discovered an exotic atmosphere in which to hold rousing social bashes. By night, especially during the holiday season, revelers dressed to the nines arrived at the *Intrepid's* gangways.

This evening it was the Soldiers', Sailors', and Airmen's Club of New York City, whose party organizers gleefully wondered if the ship might actually pitch and roll at her moorings. Even though the major television networks had finally stopped showing that video clip of a smart bomb diving into Saddam Hussein's Air Force Intelligence headquarters, the pride of Desert Storm was still fresh enough to attract a thousand veterans to one last postwar bash.

The night was still and clear, though had there been precipitation, it would certainly have fallen in burry flakes. Inside the pier's entrance gate, the flight deck of the carrier loomed high overhead, its aircraft's wings and tails jutting into the sky like a netful of shark carcasses. The sloping sides of the hull were bathed in the green glow of ground lights, and the four entranceways to the ship were bright-yellow rectangles at the tops of zigzag gangways.

Many of New York's municipal VIPs were attending the event, for the chance to revel among uniformed American warriors was an opportunity too rare since 1945. Limousines drifted through the gate, a contingent of NYPD cops checked the credentials of guests on foot, and officers and other ranks in full regalia enjoyed the white-gloved flash of a Marine MP salute.

A figure hugging a large metallic Coca-Cola cylinder skirted the long parade of revelers, begging pardon as he waddled toward one of the policemen. The hood of his black sweatshirt was drawn tightly around his face, covered further by a USS *Intrepid* crew cap, and the back of his red museum parka was emblazoned with the ship's silhouette. The wet cough of a winter cold racked the man's hunched shoulders, and as he stopped for clearance, a policeman winced under the spray of spittle. "Come on, man. Effin' thing weighs a ton," the crewman whispered hoarsely. The cop waved him through with a gesture of disgust.

The crewman moved more quickly now, past the limos in the parking lot, until he slowed near the stern. The caterer's truck was parked nearby, and he waited until a trio of shivering cocktail waiters appeared at the tailgate to be handed armfuls of replenishment. Then he fell in just behind them as they weaved their way up through a crowded gangway, parting the partygoers with "Comin' through! Heads up!"

He passed through the double entrance door and was met by a blast from the horn section of a big band. The party inside the hangar deck was already in full swing. Marines in blue dress tunics, army officers in buttoned-up olive, and naval aviators in winter black twirled women wearing sequined gowns beneath the flashes of a disco ball. Huge military displays, including a Gemini space capsule and an array of antiship missiles, were suspended from the flight deck like Christmas ornaments in the salon of a giant. A full dance floor of interlocking wooden planks had been laid, so that as the band segued into "Stompin' at the Savoy," the iron cave erupted in the thunder of a stampede. The orchestra was jammed atop the roof of a ten-foot observation deck, and a solo trumpeter fired high C's down into the crowd.

Around the perimeter, cash bars had been set up like field messes. The crewman worked his way toward the nearest table, where a perspiring bartender spotted him and shouted, "Thanks. Anywhere." He set the canister down and stepped away to watch the crowd. A steady trickle of servicemen hurried toward the rest room at the stern. Visor down and hands jammed into the pockets of the parka, he followed.

As with most naval vessels, the latrine had been designed for volume rather than aesthetics. Banks of urinals and stalls wound back and forth, and he had to squeeze past soldiers washing at the sinks. He found an empty stall in a far corner, went inside, locked it, tore off the baseball cap, and quickly freed the choking drawstring of the hooded sweatshirt.

Martina Klump shook her head violently, her blond hair cascading in a yellow halo until she stopped and it settled over her face. She blew out a long breath, swept the strands from her eyes, and continued with her task.

She removed the parka and hung it on a steel hook. Her high-heeled pumps, which had been slung beneath her armpits from a black string running across her neck, joined the parka. From the belly pouch of her sweatshirt she pulled a folded Bloomingdale's shopping bag, a lipstick, mascara tube, perfume vial, a folding hairbrush, and a black box purse on a long silver chain. She set the collection down on the cover of the commode.

Very carefully, she pulled the sweatshirt over her head. The hem of her black tube gown had been raised and pinned to itself beneath her arms. She slipped her sweatpants down to her ankles. Her stockings were unmarred, the clips and garter belt in place, the emerald silk undies that matched her bra still as wanton as she'd planned. Of course, the sweat socks and sneakers did nothing for the image, but that would soon be rectified.

She unpinned the dress and smoothed it down. It was long-sleeved to the wrists, but its elasticity would leave no doubt regarding her figure. She reached up and touched her throat, finding the strand of pearls intact.

She removed her sneakers and socks, pulled her feet from the sweatpants, freed her pumps, and slipped them on. The folded remnants of her *Intrepid* crewman went into the bottom of her shopping bag, and from the small vial of Estée Lauder she daubed her throat, wrists, and underarms, then applied the mascara without a mirror. When she finally took a deep breath, unlocked the stall, and stepped out, she was carrying only the bag, the purse, and a posture of arrogant bravado.

She strode past two large Marines who were gripping the flush handles of their urinals as if the ship were swaying in a storm. Then she stepped up to the nearest sink, dropped the shopping bag, and leaned into the mirror to apply her lipstick. She was pleased with her emergence, a doubtful butterfly now reassured, and as she quickly brushed out her hair, she realized that the gaping faces of three army officers were staring back at her from the glass.

Martina smiled as she turned to them, recovered the bag, and said, "As usual, gentlemen, the line in the ladies' room is *unbearable*."

She strode from the latrine, giving her gait enough hip to elicit a drunken wolf's bray. At this rearmost section of the ship, caterers hustled like a frenetic mortar team at the crux of an infantry battle, stripping packings from cocktail canapés, chips, and dips. Martina pressed her shopping bag into a pail of torn Ritz boxes.

She plunged into the crowd, walking along the shore of the dance floor. Couples staggered laughing from the fray and others hurried into it, and within a minute she had spotted twenty other blondes in sleek black dresses, but she was not discouraged by comparisons.

Martina knew that she could probably have dispensed with her deception as the museum employee and just purchased a ticket for the event. It was unlikely that she had been tracked as she emerged from the building where she rented a flat under a cover name, rode two different subway lines to the Lower East Side, hailed a taxi, and stopped at a deserted corner in the restaurant supply section of the Bowery, where Iyad handed her the canister. Nothing in her surroundings had alerted her. At times, her own tradecraft annoyed her for its paranoiac caution, yet it was ingrained and she performed it by rote, like the warm-up of a musician before a concert.

More and more, she sensed a discomfiting linkage between herself and the consular bombing, for the concept of coincidence was not in her lexicon. There was a troubling thread there, set to humming at high pitch by the photographic image of Benjamin Baum. She recognized the tune. The lyric would come later.

And Omar's message, whispered during a brush contact on a crowded bus, certainly had the opposite of its intended effect. How dare he and his masters tell her how to run a mission? *Frogmen and limpet mines?* The idiots. As a professional, she would have accepted a simple order to abort, but she reacted with disgust to the insistence on a change of tactics. *I am a surgeon. If you've hired me, then shut up, go to sleep, and let me cut.* She had wanted to kill him right then and there, but he was only the messenger, and she chose not to respond at all.

She reached the first drink table and circled to the bartender's flank. Despite the cluster of male hands stretched out to him like beggars, he ignored them and said, "Ma'am?"

"Stoli, please." Martina smiled. "Rocks."

She took the drink, lifted it in a silent toast to a Marine lieutenant who was glancing at her chest, and steadied the glass when she realized the ice was trembling. It would be her only alcohol of the evening, yet she wanted it now and drank it quickly. Her quake of nerves surprised her, no different than a schoolgirl's at a Sadie Hawkins dance. She knew how she looked; the mirrors did not lie. But Mussa's words had set her to wondering if she could do it, the memory of their morning argument adding anger to her doubts.

"You do not have to do this, Leila." His voice had grown louder as he watched her lay out her "gear."

"I do."

"Not this way."

"What way, then, Mussa?"

"A mugging will work just as well."

"Ah, I see." She had scoffed. "Four men struggling in the street. That will not attract attention."

"We can follow him. To a deserted place."

"And suppose his plans do not include such a place? If he enters a taxi and disembarks at the Plaza Hotel?"

Her logic infuriated him, her will to use her body even more so.

"Then we can lure him." Mussa grasped hopelessly, falling neatly into Martina's strategy.

"Precisely what I have in mind, Mussa."

"But not *this* way!"

"Why not? He will be a military man, and *your* way will bring on a fight and we will have ourselves a torn and bloody uniform."

"*Sharmootah.*" He hissed it as he stomped away from her in disgust.

"What did you say?" But she had certainly heard the Arabic for "whore."

"It is the way of a harlot!" His face was bunched like a frustrated child's as he screamed at her.

Martina watched him, scorching him with her eyes until he turned away and collapsed into a chair. In Lebanon, she had had men flogged for such insubordination, until they learned that she was not from the same mold as their subservient sisters and mothers of the Shia villages. No one of Yadd Allah ever challenged her this way now, but Mussa was not just another soldier, or a simple underling. He was family, a tie in Moslem heritage not so easily broken by widowhood.

Martina had been wedded to Hussein Hawatmeh, Mussa's oldest brother. Granted, the union had been brief. There had been no nuptials to speak of, no cottony chiffons, blushing bridesmaids, morning coats, or pipe organs. No limousine to whisk the couple off to sunny isles for languid lovemaking and fantasies about their future. It was a ritual of respect, a public promise before God, for Martina and Hussein wanted each other, yet could not breach the moral codes they preached. So the bride wore the veil and *jallabiya* of the Beka, and the groom wore camouflage. A muezzin warbled from a minaret as a mullah blessed them in the sun, which glinted sharply back from lathed steel, for the wedding party carried Kalashnikovs instead of flowers.

Perhaps no black widow's mate had ever been more doomed, for when Hussein met Martina, his headstone was already being chiseled. His indoctrination as one of the Isargaran—Lovers of Martyrdom—had been completed at the Marvdasht facility near Tehran, his offensive-driver training honed in Assayda Zaynab, near Damascus. It was left up to Martina to complete the process, send her men to reconnoiter the Israeli positions north of Marj Ayoun, select a vehicle that would mirror one the soldiers usually waved through, carefully design and mold the composition of RDX Hexogene and Pentaerythritol TetraNitrate, as well as build in the double-insurance detonator that would be activated by Hussein's own hand but could also be exploded by remote radio control should the martyr's courage fail him.

She realized somewhat later that the mission had been a test: not of Hussein's loyalty and courage, but of her own. And not long after the concussion had wiped him and twelve Israelis from the earth, she decided bitterly that he in turn had been subjected to a trial of his indoctrination, ordered to wed and bed this foreign woman, thereby testing both their mettles. Not that it mattered, for his ardor for Martina's body could not have been injected by any North Korean psychologist. And she, too, was surprised at her desire for him, and at the grief that followed. She had rebirthed herself in Lebanon, and with that transformation came an adolescent passion, the unencumbered desire that besots teenage heads and is rarely matched for later lovers. And between the day that Hussein first descended from a dusty jeep into the camp, and the dusk just four months later when he left in much the same way, Martina fought against the hope that he might flee, leave her a note begging forgiveness for his cowardice, a pledge of love greater than for Allah, a promise to rendezvous at some faraway place, in a near year.

But instead he killed himself as planned. It was quite a test to put to a young bride.

The event also shocked Mussa Hawatmeh, waking him from a slumber of submission to Hizbollah, and while in public he celebrated at Martina's side, together they secretly mourned. They decided never again to be manipulated by unseen hands and took their loyal men away, first to enclaves in the south, where they engaged in battles of their choosing, and later out of Lebanon altogether. But Mussa could not escape the tenets of his culture. According to Islam, he was now responsible for Martina, the widow of Hussein.

Martina knew that had they continued living in the Middle East, she would have been obliged to marry Mussa. Yet inasmuch as she was having none of that, he was surely doubly frustrated. Did he love her? Perhaps not, but he surely loved the memory of Hussein, and the idea that Martina would bed another man, even for the sake of the cause, was abhorrent. . . .

She looked into the bottom of her glass, watching the last of the Stolichnaya drain into her mouth. The flutter in her stomach told her that she was risking much more here than her own ego, for having insisted on this course of action, she now had to prove it operationally correct. With the crucial stage of the mission about to be launched, it might be dangerous to face her men empty-handed.

It had been some years since she had seduced a stranger. Her figure was in fine form, her face belied her age, and the scent that rose from her throat had a sultry tang. But like a retired sniper, she wondered if she could still hit the mark.

Relax, she ordered herself. *This field is full of stags. Take your time.*

The band slid gracefully into a Viennese waltz, and she found herself looking up into the face of a tall, elegant man offering her an elbow.

"May I be so bold, ma'am?"

He was physically wrong for her purposes, much larger than Mussa. His sandy hair was flecked with gray and his uniform was the dress black of the U.S. Army Corps of Engineers, but he would be good enough for a warm-up.

"You may." She set her glass on the drink table and took his arm.

The field-rank officers siezed the floor, for apparently those of lower echelons were untrained for the strains of Strauss. Martina's partner scooped her back, joined his free hand to hers, and began to spin her. He was proud, graceful, and quick, his gaze fixed upon some distant point as they rose and fell over swells of three-quarter time. He moved in silence, like a soldier of another generation. The room's perimeter became a kaleidoscopic haze, and clasped against a Prussian posture, the ebony cloth and shiny brass, Martina danced again with her father. . . .

His features never dimmed for her, unlike those of so many others of her past—forgotten lovers, fallen comrades, and even Hussein. Although she had been only five years old at the time of his suicide, his image had been scorched into her memory. She recalled her slippered toes upon his polished brown shoes, her chin planted in his belly, looking up into the false severity as Papa played her prince, his jaw thrust out and away, his spectacles gleaming in the light of a chandelier, the smile at the corners of his eyes, and the brush of hair so great and thick it was like the coat of an aging raccoon. But they had never danced like this, and she still longed to feel the flow of his pride, had he lived to see her grown.

She knew so much more about him now, for as she reached her teenage years she had sought out every detail. Of course, her mother had survived, but by that time Katharina Klump's descent into an alcoholic oblivion had blurred her memories, frustrating Martina with contradictions. Apparently, the wife of a German officer lived in blessed ignorance, asking few questions about her husband's career.

The truth, as it emerged, was a simple story of a man of science, whose brilliance would have brought him glory had the flag outside his ministry waved stars and stripes instead of a swastika. Dr. Otto Klump was holding a prestigious physics chair in Berlin when the NSDAP swept through German politics, offering talented scholars a choice: the boundless research coffers of a burgeoning war machine, or academic oblivion. Though unimpressed by uniforms or ranks, the doctor was a slave to his own scientific curiosity. And who could dismiss such an offer, to exchange an old bench of stained beakers and Bunsen burners for a staff of fifty researchers? And so he went to work as one of Albert Speer's *Wunderkinder*, reporting directly to Karl Saur, chief of the Technical Department in the Ministry of Armaments.

The ministry was a physicist's paradise, where, encouraged by Adolf Hitler's rapture for secret weapons systems, fertile imaginations conceived of television-guided missiles and smart torpedoes. Klump and his colleagues drafted designs, constructed models, cursed failures, and leapt with joy whenever some wild fantasy actually *flew*, while they remained carefully ignorant of Nordhausen, where their successes were replicated by thousands of dying slave laborers. It was a cauldron of brilliance, hampered only by the lack of as yet unborn computers and microchips, and the advance of the Allied armies.

And suddenly, one day, Dr. Otto Klump went from Führer's pet to fugitive. The American Army's Counter Intelligence Corps was sweeping across the scorched German earth like an avenging angel, and one by one the architects of the Nazi war machine were plucked up and subjected to *Selektion*: interrogation, trial, prison, execution. But Otto Klump was not a runner, and he sent Katharina south to her sister in Bavaria, while he waited for the young Americans in their peaked caps and trench coats.

He spent nearly a year at Chesnay, a palace on the grounds of Versailles converted into a detainment center by the U.S. Army. Many of the German scientists were processed through this central clearinghouse, where Allied interrogators extracted knowledge that might aid them in the inevitable conflict with the Soviet Union. Complete cooperation could gain one a slot in Project Overcast, a secret program devised to bring worthy Germans and their families to America for anonymous employment in the U.S. defense industries. The alternative was that you could find yourself wearing headphones in the defendants' box at Nuremberg. When his turn came, the doctor made his play, redrawing each of his designs down to the last rivet.

Yet the payoff never materialized. President Truman, having already allowed a thousand former Nazis to grace America's shores, decided to close the door. Klump was shown to the gate, informed that he had two weeks to clear out of Europe (for what the Americans declined to have, they also wished to deny the Russians), and given the name of a contact in a "ratline," an escape organization that would get him to Argentina. It was strongly suggested that he venture no closer than that to the United States.

Another man might have been embittered, but Klump considered himself lucky. He was alive, liberated, and he fetched Katharina. Soon they found themselves as pillars of a growing German exile community in Buenos Aires. Juan Peron's government was sympathetic and his arms industry thirsty for talent. The Klumps had their first and only child in 1955, and they flourished.

The Allies had treated Otto and his relocated compatriots with such objectivity that they were lulled into forgetfulness about their other, less sympathetic judges. The Jews. But the Israelis, after stitching up the gaping wounds of Holocaust and fighting off their neighbors, had *not* forgotten. Otto Klump had been a scientist, first, last, and always, and he had viewed the Nazis' anti-Semitism as a distasteful lever with which to place and keep themselves in power. But when the Israelis began to hunt, and Adolf Eichmann disappeared, only to reemerge behind a glass booth in a Jerusalem courtroom, Klump knew that the earth would offer no more ratlines. His comrades fled, his employment disappeared, his optimism collapsed, and he found his final solace in a bullet.

The smiling toddler whom he had called *meine kleine Prinzessin* was—except for a helpless mother with a shattered heart—alone. . . .

"You're leading."

Martina looked up, realizing that her partner had coasted to a standstill and was smiling down at her. "Not that I mind, ma'am. But we ought to come to an agreement."

"Oh, I am so sorry." She put a hand to her mouth and forced a girlish giggle. "I am lost in the music, and my feet betray me." She offered her arms submissively. "Please."

"Are you French?" the officer asked as he began to spin her again, slowly.

"Yes," she said. "And at times, so are my manners."

He laughed and opened his stride as Martina concentrated on remaining supple. She was not quite finished with her memory, so she ended the recollections of her father as she often did, with a silent prayer for forgiveness.

For many years, while underground with the ultra-extreme German left, she had rejected and divorced him. Her female comrades had convinced her that Nazi Germany was a male-dominated, racist abomination, the antithesis of their righteous view of global liberation. But with maturity, she had come to the conclusion that all effective political movements contained the same cast of characters. Few leaders were idealists, most soldiers pure in that they announced their killing natures by their garb. And her *Papa* had been neither, just a professor, a good man who loved her and had been frightened to death....

Across the crowded dance floor, she suddenly saw the object of her quest. A naval officer in formal dress, black double-breasted blazer with shiny brass buttons, rows of chest ribbons, gold braiding near the cuffs. His skin was smooth and dark, his hair short and gleaming. He was not too tall, and he held his triangular back erect as he gripped a homely, chattering brunette and moved as if praying for a switch to disco. He was not exactly Mussa's twin but could easily serve as a photo stand-in.

As Martina's partner turned her again, she moved into the navy officer's field of vision and focused on him hard until he looked her way. She smiled at him, a knowing grin of sympathy, and in turn he flushed a bit, smiled back, and rolled his eyes.

The couples passed, while Martina glanced back over her shoulder to find the navy man still looking at her. She longed now for the waltz to end, for her new-found love could not be allowed to escape. Then she calmed, knowing he was not going anywhere, not after she used *that* smile.

A sea of uniforms, and yes, she felt some kind of strange elation, perhaps a remnant of the Argentine soirees of her childhood. A part of her adored them for their foolish simplicity, their childish games of glory. All soldiers were strutters, their egos pinned to their chests.

Except for Benjamin Baum.

A *Schwein* who passed himself off as a faithful bloodhound, a vulture cloaked in the joviality of a dodo bird. A coward who belonged to that netherworld of soldier spies who coveted their rank and power as did tank commanders but were loath to risk their sacred skins in battle. A liar who left his uniform somewhere in a Jerusalem closet while he donned the costume of a father, friend, or lover, deluding himself that God had granted him a license to betray for the sake of the mission.

A rattlesnake who did not have the decency to rattle.

Ten years had passed since the dogs brought her down at Bad Reichenhall. But it had taken far less time for Martina to assemble the pieces, to realize that the episode that nearly ended in her death had been, from the start, the impious plot of Hans-Dieter Schmidt, or Hugo Klein, or Benjamin Baum, all one and the same, of Israeli Military Intelligence.

Not by random order of the German Ministry of Justice had she first been remanded to Preungesheim Three, the women's section of the Justizvollzugsanstalt prison complex in Frankfurt. It was an unusual choice for a terrorist with a DM 50,000 price on her head; not a remote and isolated facility but a walled-off suburban block in the northern section of the city. And there in the female quarters, lulled by the false aesthetic decor, the purple paint, and the cotton curtains, it had been no accident when she first heard her name carried on the wind through the bars. She climbed onto her cot and pressed her nose to the chill air, to hear it clear as gunfire. The male degenerates locked in the massive blockhouse of Preungesheim Two, pounding on the walls as they sang it over and over: Martina Ursula Klump, Martina Ursula Klump, *Marteena Ursoolah Klaahmp*. Had they read of her incarceration in a newspaper? Could they have known of her whereabouts through the radio or television?

No. Not bloody likely. It was part and parcel of Baum's plot. The prosecutors became alarmed that the RAF would attempt to free her, and she had to be moved, ever closer to his gallows.

And whose idea, then, was it to ship her off to Bruchsal, that sprawling brick fortress with its massive ramparts and medieval turrets for the machine-gun-toting guards? For her own security, they said, as she peered from the transport wagon, its only passenger, and entered the hideaway that nearly became her tomb. Was she truly so naive? Or was she then, as before, in the power of the absence of her father, even in her violent courage susceptible to the false kindness of men of his generation? Baum had hatched this final humiliation, to secrete her in a facility for *male* murderers and rapists, to strip her of her dignity, to have her locked away inside her cell, forbidden even from communal meals or exercise with the cream of Germany's scum.

And then, the prize. The deal. The ultimate insult. Major Benjamin Baum, arriving to the rescue, her savior. You will not be harmed, he had said. It has all been arranged, he assured her. Your escort on the soccer pitch will be felled by your groin kick, the helicopter will sail over the northern wall and never touch the ground, and you will be on it and gone within twenty seconds. And the delicious secret of this place is that even if the guards are tempted by reflex to bring it down, they will never open fire, because a children's hospital sits fifty meters outside that wall, and God help them if they cause a crash.

She had only half believed him then, and should have heeded her own cynicism. But she was deep inside the isolation cells, with Baum's warm German tones, his talk of children, his Münchner jokes, his oath that if she would trust once more and talk to him of matters of the recent past, she would be free to begin her life anew.

If she would just trust . . .

And then she was sprinting across the exercise field, the cold wind of rushing rotors on her face, her faith renewed as the silhouette leaned forward from the guard turret and she saw the spitting submachine gun and felt the full metal jacket lift her by her guts. Screaming his name, cursing his race, she somehow crawled to the skid and hung on as her blood streamed down her legs, and they flew.

There is a children's hospital, he had said. Baum cared for children? He cared for nothing but his own agenda. Baum knew pain? She wanted him to feel the wounds of his own betrayals. Baum said "trust"? She longed to etch the word in his chest. *Vertrauen.*

If she was blessed with the opportunity, she would teach him about love. And loss . . .

Martina's partner was bowing to her. The waltz had finally ended, and she answered his gesture with a smile and a dip of her knees.

"A drink?" he offered.

"The ladies' room," she said with an apologetic shrug, and she waved and walked away.

She moved toward the stern but almost immediately swung back and began to cruise along the hangar deck's perimeter. She found him standing off to one side of a bar table, sipping a scarlet drink, his patent-leather shoes set firmly apart and his dark eyes scanning the dance floor. She could easily envision him at the bridge of a vessel. She smoothed her dress again and straightened her shoulders, striking all thoughts from her mind but the desire for this nautical stranger. She made as if to pass him by, stopped just off his port beam, smiled, and gestured at the officer's cap tucked under his arm.

"Are we leaving already?"

The navy man looked down at his cap, then back at her. "*We*, ma'am?"

Martina laughed, a rich sound from her throat. "It's European English. I mean *you.*"

He grinned back at her. Very white teeth. "Well, *we* were thinking that we're a lousy dancer and we've crushed enough toes for one night."

"Really?" Martina's frown showed her disappointment. "And I thought you held your own very well with the lady." She made an obvious effort to see the fingers of his left hand. "Your . . . ?"

"A stranger," the navy man said, and realizing that she meant business, he began to search her eyes.

She held his gaze for a moment, then recovered her smile and said brightly, "That looks good."

He glanced down at his drink, reached the bar table in one stride, and ordered, "Bloody Mary," in a tone with which Martina imagined he also said "Hard to starboard."

The barman served him quickly to make him go away, and he offered the cold glass to Martina. She took it in her left hand as she extended her right.

"Sandra Russel," she said as she felt his grip, sea-weathered and strong.

"Rick Delgado."

"Happy holidays." She touched her glass to his, and they both sipped. "It *is* good." She licked a bit of tomato pulp from her upper lip. "Ensign?"

"Lieutenant."

"I apologize. The ranks confuse me."

"I guess that makes you a civilian." He touched her elbow, and they stepped away from the bar crowd.

"I confess."

"And not from the States."

"So what am I doing here?" She sighed as if weary of this recitation. "Well, my father is English, my mother French. I work for the attaché at the French Consulate, and he insisted that I take a ticket and charm some of his American comrades."

"And how are you doing?"

"My feet hurt!" They did not, but Martina dipped like a skier, took off her heels, held them up like felled rodents, and said, "Ahh."

The bandleader's chipper voice suddenly echoed over speakers.

"Okay, folks. We've got over a thousand of you here, so odds say we have at least three birthdays." A waiter zoomed onto the dance floor on a pair of Roller-blades, holding a white cake with spitting sparklers high over his head. "Birthday boys and girls on deck!" the bandleader shouted, as the crowd oohed and applauded. The musicians launched into a blasting version of the Beatles' celebratory tune, some bashful guests were coaxed out by their partners, and the rest joined them in a raucous flail.

Martina took Delgado's elbow. "Can we skip this one?" she asked, as if he had been keeping her on the boards all evening.

"Sure."

They strolled toward the bow as they sipped their drinks, through a section of the hangar deck that held a maze of displays. Large-scale ship models shone from long glass cases, and grainy photographs of sea battles papered the walls. A poster from the early forties showed a muscled ironworker, fist upraised. *Avenge December 7!*

"There are still some good wars," Martina offered as she looked at the colored print.

"Hmmm." Delgado smiled ironically.

"My grandfather was in the OSS," she responded defensively. "He died near Paris in 1944."

"Yes." The lieutenant stopped to assuage her. "That one was a 'good' war."

"And the Gulf?"

"In some ways."

"Were you there?"

"On a destroyer."

She moved him forward again, looking down and bobbing on the carpet as if to relieve her aching feet. "I have learned not to ask too much of military men. Their secrets make them . . . how should I say? Nervous."

"I don't have a lot of secrets."

"We shall see." She briefly squeezed his arm and sipped her drink without looking at him, careful not to promise too much, too soon.

They arrived at the forward section of the hangar deck. Most of the space was occupied by two perfectly preserved airplanes, a Curtiss torpedo bomber and a Grumman Hellcat. Beneath the Hellcat's high wing a rack of rockets were slung, and in the shadow below, a Marine corporal was gripping the red, sequin-covered rump of a girl while she explored every tooth in his head with her tongue.

Delgado tried to turn away, but Martina trapped him with the intense grip of a rewarded voyeur. They watched for a long moment, and then she came to her tiptoes and put her mouth to his ear.

"Is that what they mean by kissing under the *missile* toe?" she whispered, and Delgado started to laugh so hard that he had to pull her away. They were still laughing as they returned to the dance area, where the band had now settled into "Moonlight Serenade."

"Now, this is more my speed," he said as they watched the languid swaying of the couples.

"One dance," said Martina. "And then I will let you go."

"I'm in no hurry."

"*I* may be, I warn you." She hinted at inebriation she did not feel, for with all the touching of her glass to her lips, she had imbibed nearly nothing.

They set the drinks down on a chair, and she took his hand and walked him onto the floor. She turned to face him, and still holding her shoes on the pegs of two fingers, draped her arms over his shoulders and looked up into his eyes. Neither was smiling now, and Delgado joined his hands behind her waist, letting his cap fall against her buttocks, and they danced.

The spotlights on the disco ball dimmed, and Benny Goodman's nostalgic ballad was accompanied by a gentle throb of hues, the swish of dresses, and the murmurs of the swaying crowd. Placing her cheek against the cloth below Delgado's collar, Martina let her warm breath flow over his throat. She pressed the cushion of her breasts against his chest and smiled to herself as she made it happen, feeling his erection as it began to push against her belly. His body stiffened and embarrassed, he tried to retreat with his hips, so she slowly dropped a hand, slipped it around his waist, and tightened him against her until she heard him swallow hard.

"Where do you have to be?" she whispered.

"Nowhere." His voice was hoarse. "I'm on leave until Monday."

"Then no one will miss you, Lieutenant Delgado."

"No." And knowing that they were quickly working out the logistics, he added, "But I'm at the Brooklyn Navy Yard. The BOQ."

"Be what?"

"Bachelor Officers' Quarters."

"You have a roommate?"

"Yes."

"I have none."

"Where do you live, Sandra?"

"Close enough."

They danced in silence for a moment, and Martina pressed her other arm across his wide back and held him that way. His enthusiasm had not diminished. Her voiced dropped to a serious tone.

"But you must tell me two things, Lieutenant."

"Fire away."

"Do you know how to handle a garter belt?"

"God." He nearly choked on the image. "I think I can manage."

"And one more question." She lifted her face and placed a finger on his cheek. "Do you practice safe sex?"

"Yes," he said, his eyes glistening with the blaze of a tortured animal.

"Good," said Martina. "Me too." And as she brought his head down, and just before she pressed her lips against his mouth, she whispered, "No fucking while skydiving."

The cab ride had been a blur of tangled hair, fingers, and tongues. Martina hardly released his mouth, drinking in his lips with a persistence that made Delgado wonder which of them was the sailor. He held her breast through the cloth of her gown, and when she pushed up harder against him he dropped his hand to her knee, gathering the dress there, and then moved toward her thigh, over the exotic clips she had promised and into the satin that was damp with her genuine excitement at near victory. The cabbie, who had chauffeured hundreds of randy couples in his time, kept his bored attention to the streets and said only, "Nearly there, folks," as he turned onto East Sixty-second Street, hoping to avoid the ugly task of cleaning semen from his back seat. At that point, with a final long groan, Martina slipped her hand into Delgado's trousers and gripped him, knowing that a man so hard sees little of his surroundings.

And now they were on the bed in Sandra Russel's modest studio, the bunched uniform sprawled across an armchair like a deflated scarecrow, Martina's garter belt and bra straddling the pile of his shoes and cap on the carpet.

When she first saw his muscled body, she had quickly decided to proceed at her leisure. The timing was hers, and she sat down on the corner of the coverlet and pulled him in to bury his face in her while she slipped her dress over her head, then she lay back and asked for him to do the rest, and he had stripped her in a frenzy and then entered her. She was amazed when she came before he did, loving him for a moment, the way a hunter loves the bird he follows in his sights.

And after he came, with a painful cry freed by drink and her urgent encouragement, she pushed him onto his back and quickly brought him back to full staff.

Now he gripped her waist, stunned with pleasure as she rode him. She rose and fell, her fingers digging at the muscles of his chest, faster, although she was not really coming now. Yet Delgado could not discern a mimicry as he thought of his incredible good fortune, and he watched her mouth as it uttered small screams, louder and longer, until she finally shouted, "*Jetzt! Jetzt! Jetzt!*"

The door to the apartment burst open, just six feet from the bed, and three hooded men were inside. Heaven knows what Delgado thought as the point man swept Martina through the air and onto the floor with a single backhand swipe. And then they had replaced her, silently pummeling his head with blackjacks that sent him quickly into unconsciousness.

They trussed him with duct tape, mouth, arms, hands, legs, and feet. Then two injections of Sodium Pentothal, bordering on lethal, and they placed his heavy form in a body bag, left a foot of zipper open for oxygen, and locked him in a clothes closet that was surprisingly empty for the flat of a fashionable woman.

There was not much housekeeping to do, for Sandra Russel's drawers held only dust, and everything else was a disposable prop. They folded Delgado's uniform, took his shoes, and held their breath as they checked his wallet. It was a treasure trove of U.S. Navy credentials.

Finally, the three men removed their balaclavas. Mussa stood in the center of the room, using the woolen mask to wipe the sweat from his face. He was still breathing heavily, and he smoothed his wringing-wet hair with his fingers and looked over at Martina with a squint of satisfaction, a superior grin of arrogance. Yes, her way had worked, but she had also proved to him that when he branded her *sharmootah*, he was not wrong.

She was wearing a blue silk robe, her arms folded across her chest. Her cheek still hurt where Mussa's watch had smacked into the skin, yet that did not anger her.

It was his expression, and those of her other two men, who watched her now with sheepish grins, having witnessed their commander in a position no soldier should ever see.

There was only a second to regain control, and then it would be lost, perhaps forever. Martina stepped up to Mussa, cocked her right arm back; and slapped him with a force that sent him sprawling on the bed.

He pulled himself slowly to his elbows, then touched his face, staring up at her in stunned disbelief.

"I would not want you to enjoy your work too much," she said.

Chapter 7: New York Police Department

The midtown north detective squad occupied most of the second floor of a lackluster precinct house on West Fifty-fourth Street, and those of its members who had envisioned their investigative careers amid the historical architecture of old New York were slow to overcome their initial disappointment. No feature film studios ever sent location scouts here, no police show crews dragged klieg lights through the quarters too cramped for camera dollies, and not a single Manhattan photographer in search of grainy reality had ever shot a cop at MTN. The squad room had all the character of an urban high school converted to a reformatory.

There was not a stick of structural wood in the entire space, no heavy balustrades or creaking plank floors, no cathedral ceilings or arching windows through which the sunlight from the rivers could shaft through swirls of cigarette smoke. The squad room was a long rectangle of linoleum and painted cinder block, narrow windows with metal cross-frames, and rows of steel desks and chairs ordered with all the imagination of a fly-by-night real estate office. Every desk lamp had the same corrugated neck and fluorescent head, exuding the same warmth as a dentist's X-ray.

The pervasive decor was paper, reams of it, white and buff rectangles stuck up on the walls, piles sliding across glass blotter covers, manila files overflowing wire baskets, and the pink and blue copies of Supplementary Complaint Reports rolling in and out of humming Selectrics. No photograph, colored poster, or even the classic Rockwell print of New England cop and child, graced any spot to ease the eye. There was nothing irrelevant to NYPD business, by order of the lieutenant, who was determined to demonstrate that all the softer aspects of her gender had been retired.

All in all, the Midtown North squad room was bland to the point of demotivation, an opinion offered by an IAD psychologist who toured the precincts. There was hardly evidence to differentiate the place from any other municipal bureaucracy, except for the occasional pistol butt poking from a waistband or the ten-foot temporary lockup cell. However, the final word on layout belonged to the squad's lieutenant, king of the realm. Or in this case, queen.

A uniformed cop, bundled up for the winter, her nightstick, cuffs, and holster clanking like a horseless knight, hauled herself up the stairway and passed two prim black women typing reports at the squad room's entrance. She turned right and knocked shyly on a door with an engraved plate that said, simply, *Sergeant*.

"Come on." A voice vibrated through the glass.

Aside from the lieutenant's office at the northeast corner of the squad, Detective Michael O'Donovan's cubicle was the only private room on the floor. It was hardly an executive suite, being just large enough for his desk, a standing coatrack, a low bookshelf, a metal filing cabinet, and a "guest" chair. There was a mesh window that looked out over the squad, the view occluded by Wanted posters and police-artist sketches taped to the glass from the outside. Below the window, two computer terminals sat on a slim counter, and unless O'Donovan had hung his Sheraton Hotel DO NOT DISTURB card on the doorknob, the admin women often squeezed between his desk and a Compaq to run down a license plate or a fingerprint record. Behind O'Donovan's head were corkboards covered with notices and rosters. A pair of dot-matrix printouts served as nameplates, displaying *Sgt. O'Donovan* on one and *Sgt. Ramos*, with whom he shared his tasks, on the other. The fuzzy print was a reminder that nothing was engraved here, and job security depended on performance.

"It's a phone message from the desk, Sergeant," said the uniform.

O'Donovan was reading a powder-blue DD5, an update on an unsolved homicide. He retrieved the slip without looking up. "Thanks," he murmured.

The uniform turned for the door.

"Officer," said O'Donovan.

"Yeah?"

"Leave it open." He smiled at her. "And stay warm." She blushed and lowered her head as she left.

O'Donovan pursed his lips, wondering why all the female uniforms in mid-town looked like trolls, while the women down at One Police Plaza looked like Charlie's Angels. Then he stopped wondering. He knew why.

He read the desk sergeant's neat print, frowned, mumbled "Terrific," then balled the paper and threw it into his wastebasket. "How did I catch *this* cluster fuck?" He dropped the "Five" sheet on the desk and laced his fingers behind his blond head, arching back until his cartilage cracked. He looked up at the low ceiling and took a couple of long, slow breaths.

Michael O'Donovan's plate was already so full that just the thought of it was causing painful intestinal sensations. He was the sergeant in charge of the MTN squad, which meant that he ran the show, even though a lieutenant was the titular boss. Just like in the military, the noncoms did all the work. It was O'Donovan's responsibility to assign detectives to cases, supervise the progress of investigations, dispatch the radios, equipment, conversion cars, make sure the paperwork was up-to-date, and liaise with all the other department units that might be called in on a case. Of the more than 2,500 cases that MTN caught each year, it seemed to O'Donovan that fewer and fewer were "grounders," easy solves that wrapped up fast and went to court. With the upsurge of violent crime and the flood of cheap firearms in the hands of younger and wilder sociopaths, the bulk of robberies and homicides was falling into the "mystery" category—the unsolved open files for which a man like O'Donovan felt responsibility and shame. He wanted to do well, which did not mean the attainment of rank or glory. To O'Donovan, doing well meant accomplishing his mission.

He had mustered out of the army in 1980, an embittered twenty-three-year-old who had fully intended a lifelong military career. Yet he had returned to his native New York, plowed through his B.A. at John Jay, gone straight to the Academy, and finished up his six months near the top of his class. Then it was two years in uniform, another year in plainclothes with Auto Theft, and he was given his gold shield while still at patrolman's rank. O'Donovan was going to the apex, one of the SID special outfits, a task force like Joint Terrorism, Robbery, or Narcotics. He was not going to be one of those "hair bags" who kicked back, served out their twenty, and retired to some houseboat in Florida.

Yet here he was, halfway through his own twenty, and it seemed that every time he got a foot in the door, his damned conscience would yank him back. Just recently he had sunk his teeth into a big ten-thirty at a local Chemical Bank branch, six armed men who shot the old guard and took off with nearly a million. O'Donovan would not let go, working round the clock as he pushed the squad's nine men and one woman until they nailed the perps in Brooklyn. Some hotshot from the Major Case Squad had taken notice, inviting O'Donovan to make his move. But with his squad floundering in backlogged cases, he was left struggling to cover the chart—the schedule of detective shifts and assignments—instead of kissing the right asses in the proper downtown watering holes. Someone else had gotten the Major Case slot.

And now it was flu season. O'Donovan's chart had holes in it you could drive a truck through. He often found himself on the street, covering the types of crime scenes he had not attended to in years. Fit and healthy, as one might expect of an ex-Special Forces sergeant, he was cursing his own fortitude. The sergeant over at the Seventeenth Precinct was down with pneumonia, and O'Donovan had been ordered to cover that chart as well, which was doubly difficult since a third of the Seventeenth's squad were out on a steal to Organized Crime.

And that was how he had wound up catching this bomb thing at the Israeli Consulate, which was in the Seventeenth's jurisdiction. It was big, an opportunity to go Joint Terrorism Task Force. And O'Donovan wanted nothing to do with it.

"Hey, O.D." Jerry Binder stuck his head around the edge of O'Donovan's door. Binder was a muscle-swollen forty-five-year-old who never missed his daily routine bench-pressing 230 pounds. "You do lunch yet?"

O'Donovan jerked a thumb at a wire basket overflowing with Fives. "Can't get out from under."

"Come on," Binder coaxed. "We'll hit the deli. Two pounds of nice lean corned beef on rye." He flopped his black eyebrows, which almost made O'Donovan laugh. Binder's huge jaw, evil grin, and thistle-thick black hair always reminded the younger man of Sergeant Rock of comic book fame. Binder was also a Special Forces veteran, a fact that had instantly bonded the two men. It was Binder who had graced the sergeant with the nickname "O.D.," for Olive Drab.

"Can't make it, Binder," said O'Donovan without apology. "I'll order up."

Binder stepped into the doorway, straightening his tie and looking hurt. "You ain't S.F.," he accused. There were only two kinds of people in Binder's world, Special Forces and All Others, and his greatest insult was to place you in the latter category. "Can't be." He shook his head as if O'Donovan's rejection of corned beef was the final clue. "I wanna see your DD-214." He meant the sergeant's military record.

"You're gonna get it with a side order of .38s, if you don't get out of my office."

"Ha!" Binder pounded his pectorals like Tarzan. "Bounce right off!" He dropped his hands. "Which reminds me. When the fuck are we gonna get nine-millimeters?"

"You don't need a nine," said O'Donovan with a grin. "As a matter of fact, we should take your issue away from you. It's redundant."

It was only a partial joke. When perpetrators saw Binder's fullback form bearing down on them, they usually surrendered without his having to draw his service revolver.

"*Itchy Bahn*," said Binder, a holdover phrase from his two tours in Vietnam, which he used as an all-purpose "Right on."

"Hey, Jerry," someone called from the squad room. "Ten-one your wife." PD code for "Phone home."

Binder turned. "I always give her ten, Mancuso," he said. "And she wishes it was just one less."

"All right, all right," O'Donovan scolded. "We have ladies here."

Frank Mancuso joined Binder in the doorway. He was a slim thirty-year-old of northern Italian descent, with sandy hair, a manicured mustache, and an easy smile that always made him the "good cop" in any interrogation.

"Don't sweat it, O.D.," said Mancuso. "Lou's in Martinique, or wherever the hell she went."

The lieutenant was on vacation, which was usually a license for the rise of profanity.

"And don't call her *Lou*," O'Donovan warned with a pointed finger. "You remember the last time."

"Yeah." Mancuso actually looked frightened as he recalled the gaffe.

"You'll *never* make sergeant," said Binder as he went off to make his call.

"Hey, Sarge." Tim Griffin loomed in O'Donovan's doorway. A large Irishman who had emigrated long ago from Boston, with his white hair and pink features he could probably have retired to an easy life of playing cops for the local soap operas. Griffin had already put in twenty-five years, but he liked the work. "What's up with the beard case?" In NYPD parlance, beards were Jews.

"*Which* beard case?" O'Donovan asked impatiently. Midtown North covered the diamond district, and the squad had fifty cases that could fall into that category.

"*The* beard case," said Griff. "Boom."

"Stuff's just starting to come in."

"What'd the M.E. say?" Mancuso asked.

"Two DOAs had fragmentation wounds, fatal compression, usual bullshit," said O'Donovan. "Bomber wasn't even whole, but the M.E. took some shrapnel out of him and the girl. You saw the girl."

Mancuso scrunched up his nose. He did not want to remember much of what he had seen. "How about lab?"

"FBI's got most of that. Arson/Explosion wants in, but the feds have their own EOD, that guy from Redstone. Our forensics can't compete with that D.C. lab." O'Donovan shrugged. "We'll probably just get old news."

"Yeah," Griffin agreed, with the cynicism of a veteran. "I don't even know why Joint Terror's letting us touch it."

"Our DOAs, our case," said O'Donovan.

"Not even," Mancuso corrected. "It's the Seventeenth's."

"And I'm running their squad for now, so we'll keep it."

"Lucky us," said Griff. "Hey, did you voucher that scummy tooth?"

"What tooth?" O'Donovan asked innocently.

"Come on, Detective. Did you?"

"I was logging at the scene." Mancuso joined O'Donovan's conspiracy. "Don't remember a tooth. Do you, O.D.?"

Griffin looked at both men, then shook his head slowly. "If you kids are doing an end run, you better be ready to take some kind of heat if it doesn't pay off."

Tim Griffin reminded O'Donovan so much of his own father that when the big Irishman spoke in tones of admonition, it made him feel like a five-year-old on the verge of a spanking.

"Hey, Griff," O'Donovan said now, just to offset his insecurity.

"Yeah?"

"Voucher this." He raised a middle finger from his fist. Mancuso laughed, but Griffin did not. He just shook his head again.

"Okay, troops!" Binder clapped his hands together as he reappeared. "Did my homework. Let's *deedee*."

"You coming to lunch?" Mancuso asked O'Donovan.

"Yeah, take a break," Griffin prodded.

"No, I am *not* coming to goddamn lunch," said O'Donovan. "What is this, a surprise party?"

"Is it your birthday, Sergeant?" Binder asked.

"No."

"Then suck a burger at your post." He grinned, saluted, and added, "*Sir.*"

The three detectives moved away to gather their coats and gloves. O'Donovan returned to his Fives, shaking his head as the men's chatter receded down the stairwell.

"Speaking of parties," Griffin was asking. "What's on for Christmas?"

"Probably a four-to-four at P. J. Moran's," said Mancuso bitterly.

Binder began to sing. "Jingle bells, mortar shells, Charlie's in the grass . . . You can take your Christmas and shove it up your ass . . ."

The laughter and voices echoed away as a door slammed.

On most days the profane banter of the squad could raise O'Donovan's mood and swing it out into a higher, lighter orbit, where he could view his ugly world with objectivity. But he was feeling more and more like the Dutch boy with his finger in the dike. He stared down at the blue paper before him, rereading the details without digesting: *Jenkins, Timothy M/W/24 Homicide by Handgun. Sept. 1, 1990.* There was a color photograph of the crime scene stapled to the file folder, a shot of the Columbus Circle subway stop, four chalk circles around spent shells on the platform, a pool of blood, yellow barrier tape, and the helpless postures of detectives and uniforms, hands in pockets, staring at their shoes for answers. The body was not in the Polaroid, for the young tourist's friends had quickly carried him up the stairwell and rushed him to St. Luke's-Roosevelt in a cab. He was already dead, but the people who love you are always slow to surrender.

The squad was going to wrap this case and had already picked up four of the six black perps, who had killed Jenkins for his cash so they could go dancing at Roseland. None of them was over fifteen years old.

Such successes were supposed to bless O'Donovan with the Job's only true reward, except that they were grossly overshadowed by the hundreds of open mysteries. Department regulations stated that you could not close an unsolved case, so the files multiplied like an alien, incurable disease: precarious piles on desks, bound stacks with no hope of a home, rainbow pages protruding from cabinets like wagging, accusatory tongues.

O'Donovan wanted to burn them all. He wanted to lock his door and never have to face the citizens at a scene again, with their childish trust forever shattered when their stereos and TVs were taken from their apartments and no one even bothered to dust for prints.

The bombing at the Israeli Consulate might just be the springboard to a better professional life, if he could muster the political savvy to leverage a transfer. He knew that while a task force job was viewed as sexy, it would also harbor frustrations, yet the idea of focusing on a single area of investigation appealed to his assaulted soul. You could become an expert, instead of a dilettante. A sleuth of a single AO, instead of a jack-of-all-crimes.

O'Donovan's father, a devout Irish Catholic who had spent thirty years on patrol and had come to be called the King of Bed-Stuy, had always told his son that to advance into the upper echelons you had to be much more than a good cop. You also had to know whose hand to shake, which beers to buy, when to show your "moxie," and how to hold your tongue.

His father had never gotten out of uniform. The O'Donovans were not known for holding their tongues.

Yet perhaps O'Donovan's first stumble toward the Joint Terrorism Task Force had been fortuitous. . . .

He had been over at the Seventeenth, checking the previous shift's "60" sheet, when the call came in. A uniform patrolling in an RMP on Second Avenue had heard the explosion, hustled to the scene, and breathlessly radioed the desk. O'Donovan quickly advised the Detective Bureau and his own precinct that he was responding and took off. He jockeyed his car the wrong way up Second, and Binder and Mancuso nearly front-ended him as the two cars skidded to a stop in front of 800. Civilians in shirtsleeves were holding tissues over their mouths as they streamed from the skyscraper.

"Frank," O'Donovan yelled to Mancuso as he grabbed Binder. "Call Fire."

"Did it." Mancuso was halfway out of the driver's seat, still holding the mike.

"Then put ESU on standby."

"Ten-four."

"And EMS."

"Watch it!" Mancuso yelled, and O'Donovan turned and jumped back. An Emergency Medical Service crew nearly dumped him as they raced into a side door with a trauma board like a pair of mad surfers.

"Frank, get some uniforms out here," was O'Donovan's last order as he and Binder pushed their way into the building. The sergeant did not expect to nab a bomber. For all he knew, the explosion had been caused by a gas leak. But if the damage was the result of a crime, he had to maintain the integrity of the scene, control the flow of civilians *and* cops. Careless intruders could destroy crucial evidence. "Remember," his father had often repeated, "when you go in, you bring something with you. When you leave a scene, something is lost."

Binder flashed his gold at a building security guard, who danced out of the way, but the elevator was down and the detectives had lost the EMS people.

"You police?" A wiry young man addressed them in heavily accented English, then he saw the badge. "Follow me." He ran around a corner, pulled open a door, dashed into a stairwell, and Binder and O'Donovan ran after him. O'Donovan noticed that the youth was wearing a pistol, and he realized that this was not going to be just another case.

The two detectives were in good shape, but the Israeli kid took the stairs three at a time without faltering. When they passed the eighth floor, Binder managed to grunt, "I—hate—youth."

The first moments inside the consulate's labyrinth were suffused with a flat silence, interspersed with muffled shouts, the curdling sound of children crying, and the rasp of their own breathing. They followed the security man down a long hallway and into the passport and visa section. The two EMS men and three civilians were down on the floor, working over a crumpled, bloody form. A gray cloud carrying flimsy curls of burnt epoxies hung below the ceiling like an inverted lake mist, moving quickly out a bank of shattered windows to the left. From the right, two figures emerged from what appeared to be the blast area. They were wearing black rubber gas masks and carrying red fire extinguishers.

One of the men dropped his cylinder, tore off his mask, and said, "*Koos shel ha'ima shel ha ben-zonah,*"which O'Donovan and Binder did not understand. But they had both been to war, and they watched the Israeli with empathy as he charged for a men's room door.

The second man removed his mask, walked to one of the punctured windows, and stood with half his face outside, taking in air. O'Donovan realized that the man was speaking to him and Binder.

"Muzzerfokker killt a girl," he said.

O'Donovan moved to him. "Where?"

"In zeh waiting area." The Israeli looked back over his shoulder.

"Okay," said one of the EMS technicians. "Let's strap him to the board and get a gurney."

"Forget zeh gurney," a civilian Israeli said quickly. "Down zeh stairs. Zehr are five of us."

"Right," an American voice replied.

"*Which* motherfucker?" O'Donovan asked.

Hanan Bar-El turned from the window. "Zeh one out zehr in little pieces." He watched the black-and-crimson face of the wounded man as it passed by on the stretcher. He murmured something to the unconscious figure, then said to O'Donovan, "Maybe zeh bastard finished my man here too."

Then the quiet ended. Sirens flooded up from below, and the clatter of equipment crescendoed as panting firemen charged in wearing inverted air tanks and using their picks as hiking sticks. A wide-eyed uniform showed, then a sergeant from the Emergency Service Unit, then Bomb Squad, and Arson and Explosion, wearing their stenciled jackets like movie stuntmen.

It was O'Donovan's scene, and he immediately took over, calling Mancuso up to log while Binder acted as muscle. After the area had been declared secure, Crime Scene was already working when Jack Buchanan strode in with his troops.

O'Donovan half expected the SAC to try to relieve him, but he was pleasantly surprised.

"You in charge?" Buchanan asked.

"O'Donovan. Midtown North."

"Buchanan. Joint Terror. You have homicides, right?"

"Two, so far. One might be the perp."

"You know our drill?"

O'Donovan knew. The JTTF worked in pairs of NYPD detectives and FBI agents. The task force had major "juice" and would easily supersede other authorities on such a politically loaded case.

"Yes," said O'Donovan.

"Okay." Buchanan nodded sharply. "So we'll work everything but the DOAs. You'll work that angle. We'll be linked up on progress. You want to clear it?"

"After the fact."

"Good man. What's your name again?"

So Buchanan had watched O'Donovan run the scene. He had apparently been impressed, because by Saturday morning, and before the confrontation with the Israeli security people, he had bent to the detective and whispered:

"This works out, Sergeant, and I might offer you a chance to blow off chain snatches for good. We're short." Then he winked and walked away. . . .

The telephone rang, and O'Donovan twitched. He looked at it for a moment before picking it up.

"Midtown North."

"O'Donovan?"

"You got him."

"Jack Buchanan."

O'Donovan straightened up, thinking of another of his father's expressions. *If you dream too much of the devil, he will appear.*

"What's up, sir?"

"What you got so far?" Buchanan asked.

"Lots of canvasses. License plates around the scene, half checked out clean so far. Four outside witnesses, all said the guy was solo. I know the Israelis say no way this guy was really a Hasid, but I think we should run his description, maybe in Brooklyn."

"Police artist? A composite?"

"The Israelis have a videotape, Mr. Buchanan."

"Jack." The FBI man paused, knowing that *he* would not be successful on that end. "Think you could get a copy through that Colonel What's-his-name?"

"Baum?"

"Yeah. Baum."

"He's coming over here today." O'Donovan tried not to let his distaste show. "Just got a message."

"Work him, Mike. It's Mike, right?"

"Yes, sir. It's Mike."

"Work him, Mike. Run it out like the whole case is yours. Then just feed me, okay?"

"Ten-four."

"Good man."

Buchanan hung up.

O'Donovan replaced his handset, a sensation of itchy discomfort creeping under his collar. There was something about Buchanan, something that his father would have pegged instantly and not liked at all. There was no way to tell if the FBI agent regarded him as a promising additional resource or as a convenient slave to be forgotten once the crop was in.

He decided that it did not matter. The Chief of Detectives had approved the linkage, and Buchanan had just issued a liberating order: Run it out.

But what about Arthur Roselli, the CIA man who had let his disdain for the SAC pour out in mixed company? Had Buchanan forgotten about the "deal," whereby Roselli was supposed to serve as liaison to the Jews? No, men like Buchanan did not forget having their arms twisted. The FBI agent was simply bypassing Roselli and replacing him with O'Donovan.

But Mike O'Donovan could not easily bypass, or forget, Arthur Roselli. They had history together that no internecine squabbles could erase. . . .

Sand in the midnight wind. Billows of sand, twisters of desert chalk loosened by the turbine storms of giant steel propellers. Jet streams of rock particles pummeling his face, filling every crevice between neck and collar, flowing up beneath his buttoned sleeves. No oxygen to breathe, just a suffocating sea of dust, mocking his squeezed eyelids and nose as it collected in muddy clumps between his teeth, filled his ears, and turned his face into a cracked grimace.

Thunder. The unholy power from twelve jet engines of six giant RH-53D Marine Corps helicopters, the violent whopping of their blades joining the higher scream of sixteen more fan turbines on the black wings of four C-130 transport planes. A chorus of iron Valkyries setting up a vibration in the Iranian wasteland that jellied knees and turned your guts to water. A sound so thick you could nearly touch it, so all-consuming that it was like wearing stereo headphones, through which some demonic torturer pumped the howl of a typhoon.

And still he smiled.

"We are here," he said, though no one heard him and he could not hear himself. "We are going to do it."

It was not yet 0200 on the morning of April 24, 1980. For nearly six intolerable months, fifty American citizens had been held hostage in Tehran, all blindfolded, shackled, prodded, and kicked for the amusement of a madman called Khomeini. The incomparable might of the Great Satan made impotent by the rusty gun muzzles of a ragtag throng of Pasdarans. Yet in less than forty-eight hours, the community of nations was going to be served with a reminder that America was not the whipping boy of the third world. The United States Armed Forces' Joint Special Operations Detachment "D" for Delta had landed by night on the desert salt flats at Posht-e Badam. Operation Eagle Claw was under way, and when it was over, the Israeli raid on Entebbe would look like an assault on a kindergarten.

First Sergeant Michael P. O'Donovan was not actually a Delta "operator." He was a light and heavy weapons specialist with a twelve-man A-Team of the Tenth Special Forces Group Airborne, part of the First Battalion stationed at Bad Tölz, West Germany. Mike had certainly wanted to go Delta, along with every other young Special Forces adrenaline junkie when he first heard that Colonel Charles A. "Chargin' Charlie" Beckwith was putting something very special together over at the Fort Bragg stockade, which had been emptied of prisoners to accommodate the fledgling counterterror force. The Tenth's CO, Othar Shalikashvilli, had encouraged his SFers to try out for Beckwith's outfit, but there was an age minimum of twenty-two, and O'Donovan's birthday was painfully far off. So he had waited and watched, feeling like a frustrated junior high school student as the big kids went out for varsity ball. And then he was stunned when SF professionals, master sergeants and captains, Vietnam three-tour combat veterans, returned from Beckwith's selection course with bruised egos, shaking their heads. Only one man from the Tenth made the first cut, and Mike buried the dreams of Delta in his footlocker.

Almost two years passed, and Operation Eagle Claw was already well into the planning phase, when a piece of disturbing intelligence reached the Stockade. Not all of the fifty hostages were being held at the U.S. embassy compound on Talleghani Street. Three men—the U.S. chargé d'affaires, L. Bruce Laingen, Political Officer Victor Tomseth, and Security Officer Michael Howland—were secluded separately in the Iranian Ministry of Foreign Affairs, a few blocks south of the embassy. Beckwith did not have enough trained Delta operators to effectively split his operation, so he called on the Tenth SFGA to provide Eagle Claw with a Special Assault Team. "Shali" selected O'Donovan's A-Team for the job.

Training began in late November of 1979. O'Donovan's captain treated the exercise as just another "problem," saying nothing revelatory. But the team's instincts were tuned to changes in their normally secretive routines. There were plenty of facilities at Bad Tölz for constructing mock targets, but for this problem they went elsewhere. They traveled by night, in separate cars with civilian German plates, wearing climbing clothes and carrying their weapons and gear in colorful rucks. They rode south along the Lenggries road and turned west toward Jachenau on a winding mountain track, where they practiced their assault on a four-story abandoned factory building whose broken windows howled in the Bavarian wind. They always returned to Bad Tölz before dawn, slept a few hours, and then worked the problem on paper. Their captain would update the team with fresh "intelligence," but unlike other exercises, he did not seem to be concocting it with their "Excess Officer," the XO.

"There are three prisoners, twelve guards, all on the second floor," he would announce, and depart. Then he would return. "Correction. Fourteen guards, six on floor two, eight on floor three." The team would rework the plan, travel and rehearse all night, and the next day would dawn with fresh surprises. "Disregard all previous. There are three prisoners, all on floor three, two in the room on your plan designated 'Shade,' one in the room designated 'Sunset,' two guards in 'Shade,' two in 'Sunset,' five in 'Stroke,' five in 'Dawn.' Opposition weapons are G-3s, possibly some .45s."

The building in the mountains changed too. One night the team found its third-floor windows girded by iron balconies, so they used rubber-coated grappling hooks to set climbing ropes for scaling. On another night, the iron rails were declared unstable, so they switched to quick-assembly, single-pole aluminum ladders with bipod feet and protruding "L" rungs.

There was none of the heavy sighing or bitter jokes that always accompanied tactical changes, for the captain issued the news without his usual acerbic humor. In addition, and early on, he made it clear that any man caught discussing the "problem" with an outsider, including the Tenth's CO himself, would be on his way back to Fort Devens faster than you could say "Regular Infantry." Someone sent out snoopers to test the team's discretion, other men from Bad Tölz, whose proddings were rebuffed with polite "Fuck off's."

And then, one miserable icy night in February, all whispered speculation ceased. The CO himself appeared at the mock target, along with a civilian "guest" whom the A-Team's captain introduced.

"This is Arthur from Langley, no last name. He has worked extensively in the area of operations, knows our three prisoners personally, and will go in with point." The captain coughed and paused for effect. "Gentlemen, as of tonight we are officially attached to Delta. We are going to free the hostages in Iran."

When the war cries died down, Art Roselli became the thirteenth man in O'Donovan's A-Team. He had piles of photographs—of the prisoners and their prison, of Tehran, Desert One, Desert Two—as well as a wealth of knowledge retained from two years at the Tehran embassy. His cool and humorful demeanor, and the overpowering sense of mission now felt by the team, made him instantly part of a family that usually disdained intermarriage.

The very next day, a U.S. Army cook serving the chow line at Bad Tölz made the mistake of inquiring about the "heavy vibes" coming off of the A-Team. Roselli and O'Donovan reached across the aluminum soup counter, picked him up by his field jacket lapels, pulled him over the split-pea, and dumped him on the floor.

There were no more questions after that.

The helicopters were very late, and when they finally arrived at Desert One, only six of the eight had survived the horrendous flight from the USS *Nimitz* through the blinding sandstorm of a *haboob*. But they were nearly all refueled now from the fat rubber blivets in the bellies of the C-130s, and O'Donovan and his team squinted at the hellish first stage of Eagle Claw with a hope undiminished by bad omens. An Iranian fuel truck had been stopped on the Yazd-to-Tabas road with a Light Anti-Tank Weapon, and its plume of burning gasoline made the huddled groups of Delta operators flicker like dancers under the strobes of a giant disco. A civilian bus had also been stopped, and somewhere its forty-odd elderly Iranians and children huddled under the guns of American commandos.

The assault teams were all dressed alike, wearing navy watch caps, black field jackets, blue jeans, and scuffed boots. They had shoulder-patch American flags, which would remain covered by duct tape until the raid commenced, but without insignia and half blinded by the turbine technostorm, they had to press nose-to-nose and shout in order to identify each other or issue orders. It was like a controlled riot in someone's airport nightmare.

O'Donovan was hunched over, trying to protect his "child"—a Colt Commando cut-down version of the M-16 assault rifle—from the driving desert grit. He wished that he could have cocooned the entire weapon in Saran Wrap. Most of his team were sitting on the ground, waiting for the order to board the choppers, yet Mike could alight for only a few minutes, and then he would be up again, pacing, watching, going over it once more in his mind. He longed to be airborne, inside the relative peace and quiet of a roaring RH-53D, on the way to Desert Two in a valley near Gamsar, where they would hole up until next nightfall. And then the Special Assault Team would separate from Delta, ride into Tehran in a Volkswagen minibus, pull up outside the foreign ministry, and . . . He tried not to think further. They had done it all a thousand times.

A man was cruising along the huddled figures of O'Donovan's team, bending low as he searched for the right face. By the curls poking out from beneath his wool cap, O'Donovan recognized Art from Langley, who peered at him twice until he remembered that the Irish kid had dyed his blond hair black.

The large intelligence officer put a hand on Mike's shoulder and they placed their heads mouth-to-ear, like fishermen in a nor'easter.

"I don't like it," Roselli shouted.

"What? Say again?"

"I said it looks *negative*. Red and Blue are starting to load, but Eagle is on the satcom to Hammer, and he's not happy."

Roselli meant that two of the Delta elements had begun to board the choppers but Colonel Beckwith was talking by satellite communications link to Major General James Vaught, the Joint Task Force commander, and something was not right.

"What's the rumor?" O'Donovan yelled.

"Hydraulic problem. Only five flyable choppers."

O'Donovan pulled his head back and squinted at Roselli. The CIA man nodded. Eagle Claw had a minimum equipment manifest, below which it would be no go. Six choppers, not *five*.

It happened very quickly after that. O'Donovan's captain appeared and, without a word, bent to each man, making a double slashing motion across his own throat. Except for the curses of frustration that they swallowed with grit, no one spoke as they rose, gathered their gear, and followed their detachment commander across the salt flats and into the black belly of a C-130.

A Marine chopper that had been refueling off the Hercules began to rise away as O'Donovan set foot on the steel cargo ramp of the plane, and he closed his eyes against the cloud of desert that billowed from the prop wash. And then the chopper's turbines drew unnaturally near and he snapped his eyes open as a sound like a chain saw cutting through an oil drum thundered back from the C-130's cockpit, a giant white fireball rolled back across the laps of the Blue Element men already seated, and the air force pilots and crew disappeared in a torrent of exploding fuel and ammunition. Then it was madness heaped upon devastation.

O'Donovan backed out of the plane, slipped, and fell under a crush of screaming men, lost his gear bag and came back up. Then he saw the huddle of waving arms, some of them already aflame as commandos tried to crawl from the burning wreck, and he ran back in. He found himself alongside Art from Langley, struggling with a man who fought them like a drowning swimmer as he screamed, "My weapon! My weapon!" and tried to return to the blistering flames as Redeye missiles cooked off and went sailing out into the night like giant Roman candles.

Somehow, all of Delta's Blue Element escaped, along with O'Donovan's team. Many of them rolled in the dirt to smother hungry patches of sparks and tore smoldering watch caps from their singed hair. They regrouped and attacked again, ignoring the flames that crawled toward aerogas, pulling burned and screaming Marines from the torn chopper, leaving three in the unapproachable inferno and five more air force crewmen, who they prayed had died instantly with the first explosion.

O'Donovan did not recall much of the rest with clarity. What returned to him for years of dreams was the tunnel of the C-130 fuselage, now dark and thrumming with a siren call of "Failure. Come aboard," then bursting upon him like a tidal wave of white horror. The nightmares usually ended there, for the rest had been a slow, shocked crawl as he burrowed, like all the men, deep within himself. The endless flight back to Masirah Island off Oman, Charlie Beckwith's tirades of frustration, which most understood and ignored, another flight, to Wadi Kena in Egypt, and finally the long haul back to Langley Air Force Base in Virginia. It was all a blur of slumped postures, lifeless steps, shaking heads, and worthless consolations. It was exactly like a funeral. A meaningless ritual, for the loved one was gone.

O'Donovan returned to Germany, but he knew that his career in SF was over. If he stayed, he would forever try to overcome the shame of Desert One, and there was no way to do that, so he mustered out. Ten years later, when the troops set off for Desert Storm, he felt no pangs of regret. He pitied them their adventure, for he despised the Middle East, and he knew that many of them would soon be his comrades in loathing. . . .

O'Donovan was staring without focus when Binder, Mancuso, and Griffin sauntered back into the squad room. Binder popped halfway into his office and tossed a paper bag on the desk.

"Didn't eat, did you?" he said, like a hapless mother.

"Thanks."

"Sure. Corned beef. And Sergeant?"

"Yeah."

"Get a life." Binder grinned and pulled away, peeling off a midlength leather coat as he whistled.

O'Donovan smiled as he opened the bag, then it faded as the dig hit home. A life. He had one, but what did it mean? For whom did he really struggle on? Most of these men had families. Their wives and kids came first, and *then* the Job. O'Donovan had been married once, to a girl he met at John Jay. She was a sweet Irish kid, the answer to his mother's prayers. But Terry had never heard of posttraumatic stress syndrome, and her handsome, somber ex-soldier had frightened her out of the house in less than a year. Now he lived alone in a studio on the Upper West Side, avoiding relationships by hiding in overtime.

A life.

Komack, the desk sergeant, appeared in O'Donovan's door. The huge cop filled the frame as he placed his hands on it like Samson at the Philistine pillars.

"Your *guests* are here, Sarge."

O'Donovan managed a desultory thumbs-up as Komack pulled a strange face, eyes wide and brows raised, and withdrew.

The Israeli colonel called Baum stood outside in the squad room. He was wearing the same leather car coat as before, his hands jammed into the stretched pockets as he perused the room with a small smile on his lips, as if some nostalgic flash had crossed his mind. There was a brown fedora on his large bald head, yet the hat did not quite fit the image. It looked like a gift someone had forced him to wear. It should have been Tyrolean gray, with a green feather.

O'Donovan rose from his chair, walked to his open door, and then stopped, instantly confused.

Next to Baum stood a young woman. She had been facing away, yet as she turned now, the detective's gaze became fixed upon her. She was wearing small brown hiking boots, blue jeans, and a camel coat, over which flowed long auburn hair. Her eyes were Caribbean blue, her sculpted cheeks were flushed with cold, and she wore no makeup to emphasize the bow of her mouth. Her long, dark eyebrows might have offered a hundred different comments, yet as she looked up at him, unblinking, nothing in her expression changed.

O'Donovan's first thought was that she must be someone's case, a complainant wisely concealed by one sly detective from the rest of the squad. She had probably been summoned by some playboy like Mancuso for an unnecessary follow-up. A stunning lipstick model who'd had her toy poodle stolen.

"Detective O'Donovan." Baum sounded jovial as he stepped forward and extended a meaty hand.

"Mike," the sergeant corrected as he snapped his attention back to Baum and shook.

"*Ja*, Mike," said Baum. "And how are you?"

"Busy, Colonel." O'Donovan was about to select some lucky bastard to tend to the young woman when Baum put a hand on her shoulder.

"Detective, I would like you to meet my daughter, Ruth. Ruth, this is Detective O'Donovan." He said the last part as if swallowing the admonition *Now shake his hand like a good girl*.

O'Donovan looked at her again and blinked. "I'm sorry?" He bent to her, thinking, *How the hell does* she *come from* him?

"Ruth." She offered her hand, and the grip was firm and cool. "Like in the Bible."

He felt her low voice in his knees, and something of his thoughts must have shown, for her cheeks darkened a bit more.

" 'They asked me how I knew . . . ' " Binder was rolling a Five into his type-writer and singing the opening of "Smoke Gets in Your Eyes." O'Donovan shot him a look, and he stopped.

Benni Baum ignored the spark that flashed between his daughter and the American. "I hope you don't mind . . ." He placed an arm around Ruth's shoulders.

"No, not at all," said O'Donovan.

"Good. Shall we talk?" Benni asked.

As he grabbed an extra chair and ushered his guests into his office, O'Donovan looked over, to see Binder holding his mouth and Mancuso covering his eyes. Griffin shrugged at him hopelessly, like the father of juvenile delinquents.

O'Donovan closed the door and maneuvered behind his desk. Baum took off his hat and coat and hung them on the standing rack. The Israeli colonel sat, wiping his large pate with a handkerchief. With his ice-blue eyes, slabby face, and roll-neck sweater, he reminded the detective of one of those Russians from the Rego Park squad, who could flip instantly from Santa Claus to Rasputin, depending on necessity.

"Ms. Baum?" O'Donovan offered to take Ruth's coat.

"I am still cold," she said. She sat down next to her father, crossed her legs, and folded her arms.

"Ruth is a student here at Columbia," said Benni proudly.

"Oh, really?" O'Donovan tried to guess her age. "Which program?"

"Psychology," said Ruth. "Master's slash Ph.D." Her accent was distinctly foreign, yet she pronounced her English vowels and consonants properly in a rich alto tone.

"We don't normally bring guests along," said Benni. "But Ruth and I do not see each other much." His daughter looked at him and smiled slightly. "And as she is also a former army intelligence officer, she is always an asset." He reached out and patted her knee, while O'Donovan tried to picture her in uniform, then swallowed once as he tried *not* to picture her shedding it.

"Very interesting," said O'Donovan, trying to wade quickly through the small talk. "Then we're all veterans. So . . ."

"Tell me, Mr. O'Donovan." Ruth was scanning the bulletin board behind his head. "Must detectives have university degrees?"

"Not necessarily. I have one from John Jay."

"So, then," she continued as she spotted his and Ramos's printed "name-plates," "may I ask why you are only a sergeant?"

O'Donovan squirmed. "Well . . ." He was about to launch into an explanation of civil service ranks versus NYPD command responsibilities, then sensed that she was throwing him a curve. "There was a lot of intermarriage in my family," he said in a flat, serious tone. "Mental retardation, low IQs."

Ruth examined his grave expression for a moment, then burst into laughter, tilting her head back and covering her chest with one hand. Baum was also smiling.

"I apologize, Mike," said Benni. "Do you know Israelis?"

"Not intimately."

"We are blunt, as you can see. But we are also sincere. People often think of us as pigheaded and arrogant." He lifted his palms. "They are correct. Still, on the good side, we have no false manners, no *politesse*. When we say 'drop by,' we expect you to show up. Our friendships are usually ended only by death."

O'Donovan was taken aback. Maybe he would reconsider his categorization of all peoples who lived east of Greece.

"I have been warned," he said, smiling.

"Yes," said Ruth. "You have." She turned to her father and commented, "*Ben-adahm nichmahd*," which vaguely meant, "Nice guy." Benni segued to business.

"So, Mike. What is the progress?"

"Well, Colonel . . ."

"Please. Benni," said Baum. "Let us consider this an intelligence operation. No ranks. Agreed?"

O'Donovan shrugged. "I'll try." He had never addressed an American colonel as anything but *Sir* or *Boss*. "So far there are no hard leads. The Joint Terrorism Task Force is leaning hard on their snitches, trying to get something from one of the Arab groups."

"He means informers," Benni said to Ruth.

"I know, *Abba*," she replied patiently.

"Joint Terror," said Benni. "Mr. Jack Buchanan?"

"Yes."

"Mmm." Benni pulled an earlobe. "And your participation?" O'Donovan had been very close-mouthed when he gave Baum a lift up to Columbia.

"I work the homicide angle. Simple detective work. Profile of the bomber, or maybe someone else who wired him up."

"You see?" Ruth elbowed her father, who ignored her.

"And the explosive device?" Benni asked.

"The FBI labs and the Redstone Arsenal people do most of that, but since our M.E. has the bodies, Forensics here in New York looks at the shrapnel too."

"What do they have?"

"Well . . ." O'Donovan hesitated for a moment, the years with Special Forces having ingrained a reticence to share such information. But Baum would smell a holdback from ten miles out, and if O'Donovan did not give, then he was not going to get. "We have Semtex as the primary, with traces of RDX, so they think the detonator was a mercury fulminate cap with an RDX base charge. No microchips or receiver parts were found, but there was some battery acid in the bomber's corpse. Looks like a simple self-detonation to me. No radio control."

"Yes, I would agree," said Benni. He had spoken to Hanan Bar-El that morning. The EOD men from Tel Aviv had already come to the same conclusions. "You seem to know your explosives, Mike."

"Army," said the detective.

"And what exactly did you do in the army?" Ruth asked.

O'Donovan looked at her, paused, and said, "Not very much, I'm afraid."

The statement was so swollen with regret that Ruth decided then and there that she wanted very much to hear more about O'Donovan's life. She watched his light eyes as they lost focus for a moment, his reddish brows forming a small crease above the bridge of his nose. His dirty-blond hair was thick like the coat of a husky, and the way his razor had left a line of fuzz across one cheekbone made her want to reach out and touch his face.

"And our dental work?" Benni pressed on.

"Should be ready by now. Could you pull the door open?"

Benni complied, and O'Donovan called out to the squad room. "Binder, send Davis in here."

"Yes, *sir*," Binder replied facetiously, but he walked quickly to the rear annex of the room, and soon Aaron Davis appeared in the doorway. A very tall black man in his early forties, Davis wore gold-rimmed glasses, and had a penchant for Armani suits. He was an elegant, intelligent detective, and considerably more mature than the rest of the crew. O'Donovan did not trust Binder or Mancuso to maintain respectful demeanors in Ruth's presence. Davis, on the other hand, had absolutely no interest in white women. He referred to them all as "tuna in water."

"My liege?" The detective offered his services in an operatic bass.

"Where you been?" O'Donovan asked.

"Back of the bus." Davis often retreated to the annex to concentrate on his reports. O'Donovan smiled.

"Aaron Davis, meet Benjamin and Ruth Baum. They're from Israel."

"A pleasure." Davis bowed to their nods, thinking, *Crazy white folks marrying teenagers.*

"Davis, check the Teletype. Should be a printout for me from Epstein in Forensics. It'll just be a list of chemical compounds."

"On it."

O'Donovan sat with the Baums for an awkward moment. Then his stomach growled, and he slapped it with his hand and ordered, "Quiet."

"You should eat." Ruth gestured at the bag from the Stage Deli.

"That's all right. I can wait."

"I'll join you if you are shy. My father picked me up before I had time for lunch."

"In that case . . ." O'Donovan began to open the bag.

"Another black mark against my parenthood," Benni sighed.

"And my book is already full," said Ruth. She stood up, opened her coat, and shook it off onto the chair. She was wearing a forest-green turtleneck, and when O'Donovan saw the upper half of her body he quickly turned to the task of unfolding wax paper from the sandwich. "But I'll bet *you* ate. Didn't you, *Abba?*" she added.

"You know me, Ruti." Baum pinched his own girth. "Pockets full of cookies."

Ruth grinned as she stepped to O'Donovan's desk. Her teeth were very white, and small dimples appeared on her cheeks. He divided the sandwich and gave her half.

"*Beteyavon.*" She sat back down and took a bite.

"Sorry?" O'Donovan popped open a Coke can.

"It means *Bon appétit.* Do you always eat Jewish deli?"

"Binder out there has converted us. He's a *landsman.*" The Baums' surprised stare made O'Donovan laugh. "We work the diamond district. You pick up the slang."

Ruth chewed and nodded slowly at him, as if she were building a file.

Aaron Davis reappeared, bearing a single Teletype page. "This must be it, O.D."

"Thanks. And stick around." O'Donovan wanted to shift the balance of discomfort. Davis leaned against the doorjamb.

The Teletype said only:

LABORATORY TO MTN SQUAD. ANALYSIS OF COMPOUNDS AND STRUCTURE. (It did not mention a tooth outright, for O'Donovan had asked Epstein for the results outside of channels.) MATURE BIO PRODUCT: ENAMEL 8%, DENTIN 47%, PULP 23%, NON-PRECIOUS ALLOY PULPOTOMY FILLING 21%, INC. NICKEL, BERYLLIUM, SILVER, COBALT. MINUTE TRACES CARBON AND HUMAN BLOOD TYPE B NEGATIVE.

The list ended with two words in the lower right corner: NO CONCLUSIONS.

O'Donovan sat back and blew out a sigh of frustration. "Terrific," he mumbled. He passed the printout to Baum, who looked briefly at the page and pointed at O'Donovan's phone.

"Do you mind?"

"Be my guest."

"Overseas?"

"It's on the arm," said O'Donovan. Ruth raised an eyebrow. Every profession had its own patois.

Benni stood up and bent over the desk, punching numbers into the soiled beige instrument. "My people may be able to decipher this quickly."

"And who exactly are your people, Colonel?" O'Donovan decided to match his guests' bluntness.

"Where did you serve in the army, Mike?" Baum countered with a question as he waited for Jerusalem to pick up.

"Special Forces."

"*Those* kind of people," said Benni. Then he began to chatter quickly in Hebrew. He picked up a pencil from O'Donovan's desk, jotted a number on the back of one of the detective's calling cards, and hung up. He waved the Teletype sheet. "I would like to fax this, with your permission."

"Couldn't read it to them, Mr. Baum?" Davis asked proprietarily.

Baum turned to the dapper detective and smiled. "Open satellite calls can be easily pulled from the atmosphere, Mr. Davis. But fax intercept devices are very expensive, as well as fussy. It decreases the odds."

Davis showed his palms in surrender. "Out of my league," he said. He looked down at Ruth, and then at O'Donovan. "Maybe yours too, O.D."

"Show the colonel the fax machine, Aaron." So much for Davis's discretion.

The tall detective led Baum from the office. Ruth took a sip from the Coke can and handed it to O'Donovan, waiting to see if he would wipe the top or just add his lips to her imprint.

"So, Michael," she said as she balled her napkin and arced it into his wastebasket. "What is *your* theory?"

O'Donovan swigged from the can. "Honestly?"

"And professionally."

"The bomber was dressed like a Hasid. Maybe he was one. Occam's razor."

"The most obvious conclusion is often, et cetera, et cetera." Ruth nodded. "And motive? Or affiliation?"

"Not personal. Maybe religious, or a connection to one of your right-wing groups."

"Like the JDL?"

"It's possible."

"Yeshiva boys with complexes." Ruth scoffed like a dismissive psychologist.

"Even the incompetent can be dangerous."

She looked at him, then shifted her chair to face him head-on as she tucked a rope of hair behind her ear.

"Let me tell you something about Jews," she instructed with a smile. "We may self-flagellate, but we don't self-detonate."

O'Donovan laughed.

"It is an absolute," Ruth insisted. "I will stand by it."

"I hope I don't prove you wrong."

"Wager."

"Pardon me?"

"I will bet you."

"I'll take that bet. How much?"

"Dinner."

The smile fled from O'Donovan's face. He felt the deep blush rise from his chest and up over his cheeks.

Ruth looked down at her hands and shook her head. "I am sorry," she said, admonishing herself. It was just that he reminded her so much of the young Israeli men she missed. Men of purpose, with a reserved yet ready humor. He was very handsome and had a concealed strength, like some of her father's comrades. He reminded her of Eytan Eckstein. She looked up. "I shouldn't have. But you don't wear a ring, and policemen usually have pictures on their desks, wives or children . . ."

"It's all right."

"You know, I come from a country at war. Life can be very short. We jump sometimes."

"Ruth." He stopped her. "It's a bet."

She watched him for a moment. "You are being polite."

"No." He swallowed. "I'm trying to match your courage."

"Fine." She slapped the tops of her thighs. "If I win, you cook. I'm a *rotten* cook. If *you* win, we go out. Fair?"

O'Donovan laughed again. "Fair as a skeet shoot for the blind." Ruth's mischievous smile had made him feel somehow lighter.

Baum returned with Detective Davis, rubbing his thick hands together.

"It went through," he said. "We have some very talented dental forensics people. They could have a point of origin within fifteen minutes."

O'Donovan looked doubtful, and he noticed a similar expression on Davis's face as the tall man cleaned his glasses with a purple handkerchief.

"What are *your* theories, Colonel?" O'Donovan asked as he retrieved the original Teletype.

"Well . . ." Benni pursed his heavy lips. "May I smoke?"

O'Donovan opened a drawer and placed a glass ashtray on his desk. Baum produced an unfamiliar cigarette box and lit up as Davis wrinkled his nose.

"I am tempted to say Hizbollah." Benni began to pace in the very small space. Of course, he preferred to completely strike the Party of God from the suspect list, given his high hopes for Moonlight. "But that is the most obvious choice." He stopped pacing and squinted at the two detectives through a ribbon of smoke. "Do you know them?"

"Not personally," said Davis. "But we read the papers."

"Iranian proxies," O'Donovan grunted.

"Yes," said Benni. "But I am leaning toward the more obscure. Perhaps Hamas, very active in our country, in the West Bank. Very violent. The Red Eagles would be good candidates, or Islamic Jihad." He was fishing for another truth. One that might lead him comfortably away from his own instincts. "Abu Nidal is still quite dangerous. He recently had Yasir Arafat's chief of security, Abu Iyad, murdered in Tunis. He would do anything to stall a rapprochement between us and the PLO, including running an operation like this one and false-flagging it."

"I lost you," said Davis.

"Disguising it. Making it look like someone else." Benni mimed a rectangle with his hands. "A *sill* job?"

"A frame-up," O'Donovan corrected.

"*Ach, ja.*"

"You are reaching, *Abba*," Ruth scoffed.

The three men looked at her. Benni smiled patronizingly.

"Ruth has ideas of her own," he said. "In addition to studying psychology, she is also an amateur antiterrorism."

"Amateur simply means unpaid, *Abba*," she retorted. "Given your salary, that almost puts you in my league."

Davis laughed.

"I should have spanked her more," Benni said wryly.

Ruth ignored them. "Detective O'Donovan here thinks the bomber was actually a Jew."

Baum looked at the American. "Really?" he asked, as if O'Donovan had just claimed an abduction by alien beings. "How absurd."

"You see?" Ruth pointed at O'Donovan. "I like Italian, by the way."

The detective cut her off quickly. "You haven't mentioned *your* suspects, Ms. Baum."

She hesitated for a moment, then turned to her father. "*Mootar li?*" She asked his permission to put in her "two shekels," but it was more of a professional courtesy than the subservience of a child.

Benni raised a palm and shrugged. He was almost instantly regretful.

"My own theory is rather more simplistic than my father's." Ruth crossed her arms over her chest as O'Donovan fought to keep his focus on her face. "And I believe it is more in line with your investigation." She looked up at Davis. "After all, as homicide detectives, you are probably more interested in catching a killer than in implicating a political group. Correct?"

"You got it," said Davis.

Ruth's appeal to the policemen's motivation was not lost on Benni. He resumed his seat, knowing where she was going with this and wishing it were otherwise.

"I think the bomber was just a male mule," said Ruth. "While the *bomb maker* is a woman."

O'Donovan leaned forward. "A woman?"

"Martina Ursula Klump." Ruth pinched the bridge of her nose, closed her eyes, and recalled the details she had just reviewed from her database. "Born in Buenos Aires in 1955, only child of a former Nazi physicist and his wife. Father commits suicide in 1960, mother reacts with extreme depressive anxiety and alcoholism. The fatherless daughter feels orphaned." She opened her eyes for a moment and lifted one finger in the air. "This, by the way, is a common thread among radical female terrorists." Then she resumed her Rodinian pose. "Ms. Klump attends the Sorbonne around 1973, is recruited by Action Directe, a budding French terrorist group. She does not fully matriculate, transfers to the University of Frankfurt, becomes involved with ASTA, the General Committee of Students. She writes some radical articles for *Konkret*—it's a leftist German magazine-and is picked up by Baader-Meinhoff."

She looked up to be sure the Americans were following her. Davis made a reeling-in motion with a finger, and she continued.

"Klump has inherited, or learned, her father's abilities with explosive devices. She designs, builds, and detonates a number of bombs for the Red Army Faction. She has an affinity for plastics, usually stolen from U.S. Army facilities in Europe, and becomes known as *Frau Seafore*—Mrs. C-4." Ruth formed a small brick shape with the fingers of her joined hands. "Sometime in the early eighties, she is captured by GSG-9."

"Ulrich Wegener's commandos," said O'Donovan.

"Right." Ruth smiled at him and continued. "But somehow she escapes before trial."

Benni shot from his chair, startling everyone as he lunged for the ashtray and stubbed out his cigarette. One simple sentence from his daughter's mouth, and ten years of nightmares for him. *But don't stop her*, he warned himself. *Not now.* He sat back down, waved an apology, and lit up another Time.

Ruth watched him for a moment, his cool blue stare a mirror of her own. She went on.

"She disappears, but is later spotted training terror cadre in Lebanon. Some experts ascribe suicide bombings there to her handiwork. She leaves Lebanon, and her trail goes cold."

"Like Carlos," O'Donovan offered.

"Yes, except that Ilyich Ramírez Sánchez is believed to have retired."

"But this Klump hasn't?" Davis asked.

"No."

"So why do you connect her to this?" O'Donovan asked. He was very impressed by Ruth's knowledge, but it was purely academic. She had no case, as far as he could see.

"Well, let's look at it as *you* would." She held up a finger. "Motive: money, as she is known for providing work for hire, and politics, a long history of acting on behalf of extreme leftist and anti-Zionist groups." Another finger came up. "Means: her proven expertise. Just three years ago, an Indian head of state was killed by a suicide bomber, and it was believed that Martina was the technician. Only last year, the Israeli Embassy in Buenos Aires—please note the location—was destroyed by a car bomb identical to one designed by Klump for an offshoot of Hizbollah in 1984. Her photograph even appeared in Israeli newspapers, which are often used as tools by our intelligence agencies. They were probably trying to . . . how would you say it? Squeeze her."

Benni said nothing. He was regarding his cigarette as if the tobacco had been cut with camel dung.

"And finally"—Ruth now held up three digits, like a Girl Scout salute—"opportunity. She is a linguist and holds probably at least three legitimate passports—Argentinian, French, German—and who knows how many forged papers. No offense, but your customs officials at Kennedy might as well be blind."

Davis looked at O'Donovan and pulled a face. "From the mouths of babes."

"She is likely not alone," Ruth added. "It is suspected that Ms. Klump heads her own cell of freelancers, her former students from Lebanon."

"It's not *that* easy to just come walking in here," O'Donovan said defensively.

"With all due respect, Michael," Ruth corrected him, "you board a foreign airliner in, let's say, Nairobi, bound for New York. Halfway over, you tear up your Tunisian passport, which costs about five hundred dollars on the black market, and flush it into the wind. At JFK you claim refugee status, sign a promise to return for an immigration hearing, and then simply disappear. I could bring an *army* in here."

"I don't think you *need* one," Davis said, looking impressed.

"Jesus," O'Donovan whispered. He had listened to Ruth's performance with growing alarm, yet it was not the information that shocked him. It was the source of its delivery. *Out of your league*, Davis had said.

"Well!" Benni clapped his hands once. "As you can see, my Ruth weaves a good story. However, I could paint you three other scenarios equally as convincing. You know . . ."

"Put your money where your mouth is, *Abba*," Ruth said.

Baum tried to cut her off with his glare, yet his heart sank as he realized that his parental powers had been all but castrated. She was absolutely unmoved by his displeasure.

"You could get us the latest updates on Klump." She began to work him into a corner.

"Could you do that?" O'Donovan jumped on the idea.

"Well, I suppose . . ."

"Of course he could," said Ruth. "He can get anything he wants."

"Would it have her recent movements?" Davis asked.

"There is really no way to tell." Benni desperately searched for an escape route.

"Unless you ask," Ruth pressed.

"Ruti," Benni turned on her in Hebrew. "*Tafsiki im zeh*. Stop with this."

"*Lama? Mi mah atah mefached?*" She knew her father too well. Accuse him of being afraid, and he would jump from a skyscraper just to prove you wrong. "Just call again, *Abba*, and ask for the last page of the file," she pleaded in a phony, manipulative purr that really annoyed him.

Benni sighed and pushed himself out of his chair. He was seeing a fat file inside his safe. There was a single word on its cover, TANGO, and across that, a red slash of Most Secret. But what did it matter, really? Only a chosen few could access his safe, so at best a sanitized print from the AMAN computers would be relayed. Why not? It would prove nothing.

He reached for O'Donovan's telephone again. He was well past the journeyman's rank when it came to disguising his emotions, yet he had to concentrate to camouflage his disquiet.

In his own office in Jerusalem, a thin male voice answered. It was Raphael Chernikovsky, aka Horse. Benni pictured his steel glasses and thin, unsmiling mouth.

"*Soos! Manishmah?* Horse! How goes it?"

"Hans," Horse said without a reciprocal greeting. He automatically resorted to the use of one of Baum's covers, for the benefit of potential interceptors. "The boss has been asking about you. Wants to know when you're coming back."

"Tell him a month, just to annoy him."

Horse did not laugh. One of Baum's favorite hobbies was stirring the wrath of Itzik Ben-Zion, a diversion for which Benni's troops often paid the bill.

"How is the conference going?" Horse asked. Special Operations officers quickly learned a coded lingo reserved for open phone lines. When encryption devices were unavailable, there were categorical vocabularies in plain language. Benni fell right into step.

"Pretty boring so far," he said, meaning that the investigation had not yet borne fruit. "I slept right through a lecture about hard drives." No concrete leads or conclusions from the American end.

"So how can I help you?"

"I need a marketing pitch."

"Which one?"

Benni cleared his throat. "Tango."

There was silence on the line. At this point, standard procedure dictated that Horse must resist. He could not know if his commander might be a captive, under duress, so he would need three prearranged cues in order to proceed.

"Where is it?" Horse asked.

"My right-hand drawer, under the photo of Mrs. Schmidt."

"One moment," Horse answered, although he did not move from his chair at Baum's conference table. The framed photo of Benni's wife confirmed that it was indeed him on the line, yet no operational file of any kind would be left in a desk drawer, and they both knew it.

Baum's mention of Tango was, however, very unusual. Horse was one of two AMAN personnel, including Eytan Eckstein, who knew that Tango was a restricted file kept in Benni's safe. *That* file was the genuine and complete article, while the SpecOps computer held an "edited" version.

"I don't have the key," said Horse, trying to discern if Baum meant the full Tango file in the safe.

"You won't need it," said Baum. "It's unlocked."

Okay. So Benni meant the computer version, to which all SpecOps officers had access.

"Is there a phone number where I can reach you?" Horse asked.

"One, oh, three, oh, seven, two, four."

Horse jotted the numbers down, backed up one digit from each numeral, and came up with 0929613, Benni Baum's military identification number. Second confirmation.

"Got it," said Horse. The final confirmation would be more esoteric. Baum would have to recall an experience shared by him and Horse alone, to which no one else in the department was privy.

"You know, *Soos*," Benni now said, brightly, "there's a girl here at the conference."

"Yes?"

"She reminds me of that little brain from Athens. Leena was her name?"

Baum could almost hear Horse blush. The analyst was not known for his sexual exploits, yet he and Baum had once been holed up overnight in the Greek capital, waiting for Eckstein and his team to come in from Crete. As they sipped away their time in the hotel bar, a bubbly young waitress working her way through a computer science degree had struck up a conversation with Horse. At the close of her shift, she had invited him up to her quarters to play with her laptop. Benni and *Soos* were sharing a room, but Baum slept alone that night.

"Yes." Horse coughed. "Leena. So what part of the brochure would you like?"

"Just the most recent sales figures." Benni meant the last pages of the computer file, which would have the latest updates on the subject's whereabouts and movements. "I'll give you a fax." He relayed the number.

"Take me a few minutes," Horse said. "*Beseder?*"

"*Meya chooz.* Hundred percent. Send everyone my regards."

"Don't forget to call the boss," Horse pleaded.

"How could I?" Benni sneered, and hung up.

Baum turned to the detectives, who had listened politely to a Hebrew conversation that meant nothing to them. Ruth, however, was eyeing him with critical disdain for his childish machinations.

"Thank you, *Abba*," she said, knowing full well that he could easily manipulate the transmission to his own advantage. "Can I have a cigarette?"

Benni handed her the pack of Time and a plastic lighter. O'Donovan felt a wash of relief when he saw her light up. How many women had literally backed away from him when he revealed his own habit?

The door burst open. Jerry Binder started to speak, then he waved a big hand through the cloud of smoke. "Jesus Christ, somebody call the friggin' fire department."

"What is it, Binder?" O'Donovan asked.

"You better get out here, O.D. You got a flash from the Wheel."

O'Donovan rose from his desk, and his guests moved out into the squad room so he could extricate himself.

A man with his hands cuffed behind his back was being escorted up the stairs by two detectives gripping his dungaree jacket. He had stringy red hair and a wild glaze in his eyes. As they passed, he looked at Ruth and mumbled, "I'd like to fuck *that* in the ass." Without missing a beat, one of his escorts stuck out a foot, and he smacked down onto his face with a scream. "Gee, sorry," said the other detective as they dragged him toward the lockup.

Frank Mancuso strode in from the annex, holding up a Teletype printout and a fax in Hebrew characters. Binder took the fax and handed it to Benni Baum.

"This's gotta be for you," he said. "Rest of us are godless."

Ruth stepped up to read over Benni's arm. Baum broke into a wide grin, waving the fax like a racing pennant.

"Well," he said triumphantly. "I have yet to meet a Hasid who has his cavities filled in Tehran."

"No shit?" Aaron Davis dropped his reserved demeanor and snatched the sheet from Baum, as if expecting some linguistic miracle to reveal its secrets.

"Okay, *Abba*," Ruth said, unable to fully disguise her disappointment. "But that still does not preclude Klump's involvement." Then she looked over at O'Donovan, realizing she had just won their bet.

The detective was not joining in Baum's celebration. Binder, Mancuso, and Griffin had all crowded around him and the urgent Teletype from the Manhattan Bureau of Detectives. O'Donovan dropped the paper to his side and looked first at Baum and then at his daughter.

"Someone just called Crime Stoppers. That's our 577-TIPS number. They log it downtown and relay it to the squad on the case." He lifted the paper again and read the transcript.

" 'Received 1:45 P.M. Detective Frankel at One Police. Caller: male. Accented English, estimate Middle East or Eastern Bloc. Relay to Detective Michael O'Donovan MTN. Detail follows.' " O'Donovan cleared his throat. " 'Caller: I have information about the bombing at the Israeli Consulate. Frankel: Would you care to identify yourself, sir? Caller: It is an address. Mrs. Katharina Klump. One sixty-seven East Eighty-ninth Street. Frankel: Sir? Would you? Sir? [Caller disconnected].' "

There was a long moment of frozen silence. Neither Binder, Mancuso, nor Griffin understood the significance of the tip, but Ruth's hypothesis was fresh in the minds of O'Donovan and Davis. Both men slowly raised their heads to look at her, like gazelles smelling a lioness in the rushes.

She put a hand to her mouth and whispered, "*Elohim*," stunned by her own prophetic accuracy.

O'Donovan's eyes narrowed at Baum, and Davis voiced his thoughts. "It's too damned good to be true."

"Uh huh," O'Donovan murmured.

"Of course." There was a flash of anger in Ruth's voice. "My father came here, blew up his own consulate, and now we're solving a phony case for you, just to make a good impression."

"Whoa, lady," Binder said. She shot him a fiery glance.

O'Donovan backed down quickly. "That's not what we mean, Ruth."

She cocked her head, about to demand an elaboration, when her father spoke up.

"Detectives, it may be a gift horse." The last thing he wanted was to run with Ruth's hypothesis, but his mission was to solve the bombing and if possible bring in the bomb maker. All personal considerations had to take a back seat. "You can look it in the mouth, or you can ride it."

"Fucking goddamn police brutality!" The fresh prisoner shouted from the lockup. No one seemed to hear him.

"So who's this Katharina Klump?" Binder asked.

"The mother of your bombing suspect," Ruth answered in a barely audible voice.

"What suspect, boss?" Mancuso asked O'Donovan.

"Brief you later." The sergeant turned to Ruth. "She lives here in the city?"

"Apparently. If your caller is genuine."

"Frank." O'Donovan handed Mancuso the Teletype. "Run the name and address."

"Got it." Mancuso moved away.

"I want a fucking lawyer!" the prisoner whined. "And I'm hungry!"

"How'd ya like some Mace for dinner?" someone growled at him.

Griffin slipped away, responding to another detective's wave from across the room. The small group stood in silence, waiting for Mancuso's confirmation. Davis acquired an ashtray, which he carried from Ruth to Benni, like a priest passing the alms basket. They stubbed out their cigarettes as Griffin returned holding two fresh sheets of fax paper.

"More good news from the Holy Land," he said.

Ruth took the pages and glanced at her father, who nodded and said, "*Totsee et ha'mekorot.* Omit the sources." She read the first page of Hebrew print and began to censor and translate simultaneously.

"There are no confirmed sightings of the subject since 1987. In 1985, she was spotted three times in Algeria, where it is speculated that she has some sort of headquarters or command post." This was fresh fodder for Ruth's files. She came to a reference to information supplied by the German BKA and omitted the origin, according to her father's warning. "In 1986, her mother disappeared from Buenos Aires." She glanced up to be sure that her audience had taken note. "Between that date and November of '87, Martina was seen once in London, once in Lisbon, and twice in Hong Kong." She handed the first page to her father.

"If you're a 'businesswoman' running the Europe-to-Asia route," O'Donovan postulated, "what's your most likely travel hub?"

"The Rotten Apple," said Binder.

"Pardon?" Benni looked at the big man.

"New York," Ruth said absently. But she was staring at the images on the second page. With the growing popularity of the fax machine, scanned photos in AMAN computers could be digitized and printed like Veloxes, in tiny dots of black and white, for transmission purposes. The prints on the fax were amazingly clear.

The first photograph was of Martina Ursula Klump, age 26, dated 1981. It was a frontal shot taken upon her capture by GSG-9, showing blond, close-cropped hair, hard light-colored eyes, and a defiant mouth. The other three photos were numbered surveillance shots.

Number one showed a young woman drinking from a mug at an outdoor café. She had long black hair, sunglasses, and a mole next to her left nostril.

Number two was a profile of an elderly woman wearing a kerchief and peering into a shopping bag.

Number three was a grab shot of two figures on a motorcycle. The "pilot" wore full leathers, his goggles and half helmet resting on a completely bald head. A stunning, summer-clad blonde gripped the motorcyclist from behind, but a thick black arrow pointed down at the *driver*.

Ruth said nothing as she slowly handed the sheet to O'Donovan. For the first time in her life, she felt as if she was crossing that dark tunnel from headquarters intelligence to the realities of the field, from the safety of the data bank to the exposure of enemy territory. For the first time, she stood at the edge of her father's world.

She looked over at him, and her heart began to pound when she saw his expression. His eyes said, *I should have left you at home, my love.*

"Holy Christ," said Binder as he looked over O'Donovan's shoulder.

"You could put out an APB," said Griffin. "But what the hell would you say?"

"I think I got it!" Mancuso said brightly as he returned. "It's a nursing home. Klump wasn't a match, but I called and did my Social Security routine. They've one old German woman answers to the name of Katharina, registered as Frau Oberst."

"Frau Oberst," Ruth said. " 'The Colonel's Wife.' " She turned to her father. "*Otto Klump war ein Oberst?*" she asked in German.

Benni shrugged. "*Du weißt es besser als ich.* You know better than I," he lied, as he began tearing the first fax page into thin strips.

"Hey!" O'Donovan protested.

"He has memorized it," Ruth said quietly.

O'Donovan waved a "never mind" and turned to his troops.

"We're not gonna put out any APB. We're going to sit on the address." They would begin a surveillance on the nursing home.

The detectives split off to gather their coats, and the energy in the squad room immediately began to shift. Voices rose, drawers opened and closed, as car keys and speed loaders found pockets and holsters.

"You want me to advise the Bureau?" Mancuso called out, referring to the Bureau of Detectives.

"Affirmative." O'Donovan went into his office and emerged wearing a dark-blue topcoat and carrying Benni's and Ruth's outerwear.

"How about TTF?" Binder asked.

"Negative for now," said O'Donovan. "Our homicides . . ."

"Our perp," Binder finished.

"You want backup from the Nineteenth?" Griffin asked. "Some Anti-Crime people?"

"Later," said O'Donovan. "If we roll over past midnight."

The group reassembled outside O'Donovan's office, buttoning their winter clothes.

"Jerry, get the pump," said O'Donovan. "If she shows, she might bring her friends."

Benni watched the large detective trot away to a back room. As he returned carrying a shotgun, Baum muttered in Hebrew, "*Afiloo bli chavreyah, zeh lo yazor l'cha.*"

The detectives looked to Ruth.

"Even without her friends," she translated quietly, "that won't help you."

The men squinted at Baum, who seemed to wake from a dream as he turned to them, tried to smile, and shrugged.

"Let's move," said O'Donovan. But as Baum and Ruth began to fall in behind the detectives, he suddenly stopped.

"Hold on a second." He put out a hand and touched Benni's arm. "Colonel, I don't think you can . . ."

"I am your liaison. Remember, Detective?" Benni said, though he showed no overt enthusiasm. "And do you think you can spot her without me? If you do, well then . . ."

"Okay," said the detective. "But Ruth is out of it."

She grabbed O'Donovan's coat sleeve. "Why?" she demanded, but he would not turn to her. He knew he wasn't strong enough, and he focused on her father, who was already descending the stairs after the other men.

"Colonel." O'Donovan pleaded.

Baum stopped and turned. "Let her come," he said. Then he looked at his daughter, weighing the value of the bond they would seal versus the potential danger. "Let her," he almost whispered, then he trotted down the stairs.

O'Donovan clucked his tongue. Ruth still held his sleeve, and she yanked once to force his acquiescence. He ran his fingers through his hair and sighed.

"If we move in," he said in as stern a tone as he could muster, "you can't come. You'll have to wait in the car."

"Fine."

"It could go all night."

"Fine."

"It'll be very *cold*." One last, hopeless attempt.

Ruth slipped her hand inside his elbow and flashed the smile that O'Donovan was beginning to wish he had never seen.

"Keep your motor running," she said.

Chapter 8: Yorkville

The ragged blade of a midnight wind stabbed at the corners of Martina Klump's eyes as she rode against the face of an approaching storm, the air so cold it seemed almost liquefied as it battered her black jeans and stiffened the denim to a crackling shell. It dove around her gloves and sawed at the skin beneath her leather cuffs, charged under her visor and slapped her cheeks, and it freed the strap at her collar and played a wild paradiddle on her helmet with the cross-buckle.

And still her thighs were warm beneath a layer of polypropylene leggings, the friction heat that rose into her groin as comforting as a midnight Jacuzzi on the porch of a Bavarian *Skihaus*. The splendid tremble came from the horsepower of a big black Suzuki, a king among the species of machine she favored above all other modes of transportation.

A motorcycle offered bursts of speed untethered by the weights of luxury appointments. It invited insolent dismissals of traffic lane conventions, ghostlike slips through narrow alleyways, and even the ability to outrun sprinting men on stairways. And although the season was at its peak of cruelty for riding, she was reluctant to dismount, for she would feel again like a grounded hawk, left only with its talons.

She eased back on the throttle, turned right on East Eighty-fourth Street, and coasted to a stop just short of Second Avenue. She left the engine running, for Iyad sat behind her and would take over as pilot. She looked down at his gloved hands clamped over her stomach, watching the frozen arms draw slowly apart. When they had mounted the motorcycle, he had been reluctant to embrace her as a proper passenger should. Now he was having trouble releasing himself.

She hopped onto the sidewalk, bouncing a few times on her black Reeboks. Iyad lurched forward and grabbed the handlebars, while Martina recovered her black Cordura rucksack from his back with all the ceremony of stripping a battlefield corpse. She thrust the sleeves of her motorcycle jacket through the straps, then gripped the back of his neck as she flipped his helmet visor up.

His face was a bug-eyed mask of numbed flesh, frozen and frightened half to death by her lust for speed. She lifted her own visor and blew on him with her mouth a wide O, as if cleaning a pair of glasses. Iyad worked his cheek muscles and tried to smile.

"*Ist es besser?*" Martina asked.

He nodded, and their helmet visors clacked together.

"*Gut*. Now listen." She kept her lips very close to his, yet no one would mistake her posture for affection. "If I return, fine. If not, or you see someone or something not right, take half a spill and lose the bag." She patted the brown leather saddlebag draped across the gas tank. "And then, Iyad. If you are followed . . . lose *them. Clear?*"

He nodded again. Martina handed him her helmet, and walked away.

She forded the sparse traffic on Second Avenue, pulling a teal ski hat onto her head. She clipped along to bring the blood back into her legs, and when she reached First Avenue she turned right, continued a few meters, then stopped. She turned slowly, as if momentarily disoriented, yet she was far from lost.

A freezing night and a late hour were Martina's favored choices for a risky rendezvous. Few pedestrians strolled the streets, and watchers would be easily spotted stepping quickly back between parked cars or into the shadows of buildings. Except for taxis, drivers would have no motive for a leisurely cruise, for even the irrepressible Manhattan prostitutes would be too chilled to ply their trade.

She looked at the corner of Eighty-fourth Street, but no man or woman stumbled out into her view, no vehicle slowed. She walked north now, turned left on Eighty-fifth Street, bending once to tie a lace that was not errant as she glanced back between her knees.

As she turned right again on Second, a pang of mourning struck her as she looked up at the gray facade of the Yorkville Savings Bank. Half of the steel letters above the clock were gone, the remaining characters spelling just KV LLE now. Manhattan's proud old German colony was dead. It remained but for some kindly soul to please inform the patient.

Yorkville had once been the pride of the city's German-born, its ten-block enclave on the Upper East Side a constant festival of *Gemütlichkeit*, where the food, music, and language of the Fatherland were abundant for homesick Berliners or budding Germanophiles. In Yorkville, you could always find a meal of *Kartoffelsuppe* and *Schweinshaxen*, wash it down with a *Dunkel* beer, and go on to hear a string quartet play Mozart at Our Lady of Good Counsel. On Steuben Day, the city's bands marched proudly down Lexington Avenue, and during Oktoberfest, groups of men in lederhosen staggered from the Heidelberg to dance a drunken jig.

Martina had chosen New York City as her mother's final residence because it lay at the hub of her travels. All of Katharina's Buenos Aires friends had passed on, she had slipped into semi-dementia, and New York seemed the most practical and secure selection. The discovery of Yorkville was an added bonus, although Martina realized now that even in the early eighties she should have sensed its mortal decline.

She usually rode in a precautionary chain of taxis directly from the airport to the Edelweiss Rest Home on East Eighty-ninth. On foot now, she could see the effects of the gentrification virus. The Heidelberg Gasthaus was still there, but it was overpowered by an aluminum-and-glass copy center. Turning left onto Eighty-sixth, she was shocked. The Ideal Restaurant, where she had once smiled over a sizzling schnitzel as an old accordionist sang folk tunes, had been blown out by a boiler explosion. The Bremer House, where you could buy a Strudel, a case of Pils, or even an Iron Cross with oak leaf clusters, if you knew how to ask, was now a sprawling pizza parlor.

She stopped at the corner of Third Avenue as a roller of wind thundered down Eighty-sixth from Central Park, lifting swirls of crackling litter. Bending her head into it, she squeezed her eyes shut, trying to strike distracting melancholy from her brain. A yellow cab cruised by, the driver slowing as he inspected her optimistically, then sped away. She took her hands from her pockets, turned north on Third, and walked.

She was carrying $150,000 in a manila envelope, tucked inside her ruck along with a complete change of attire, full sweats in pink that she could don quickly in an alleyway. Ferrying such funds on the dark streets of Manhattan did not unnerve her, for inside her jacket and beneath her purple ski sweater, her P-38 rested in a waistband holster clipped to the band of her jeans.

She hoped that the money would last. If she was forced to stay away for as long as five years, it would be enough to cover her mother's room and board. If she was killed, the retainers she paid to a wealthy Lebanese lawyer in London would be put to use. Mr. Farad had a sublime lock on a British police medical examiner, and the corpse of an appropriate homeless woman would be identified as that of Martina Oberst, while her mother would receive £200,000 sterling as a death benefit from a British insurance firm. But if she was captured, tried, and imprisoned . . .

That had happened only once. It would not happen again.

Yet the image of her mother sitting in her rocker, watching the window, waiting for a daughter who would never come, suddenly closed her throat. It surprised her, and she choked back the sob. *Mutti, I will not abandon you*, she promised silently, for the frail little form with her white curls, mottled cheeks, and large blue eyes of deceptive clarity could no longer comprehend the verbal assurances. She had been lost so very long ago, her mind frozen to the days when Otto, her beloved, lived and little Marti adored her, as she still did.

Martina had long ago forgiven her mother's helplessness after Papa's suicide. For even though she had felt equally widowed, her youthful gall made her survival a given, while her mother had no future without him. At first she had raged against the drink that allowed her mother to retreat into her dreams, and fearing that she, too, might be dragged into despair, she fled. Yet later on, as she grew and learned and reflected, and loved her father even more, she had refocused what she felt for him and given it to *Mutti*. Otto had adored Katharina so, and Martina had to keep his only legacy alive.

She smacked the corners of her eyes with the heels of her gloves, smudging the sentiment away. This would not be the last time she would ever see her mother. It would *not*.

She crossed the corner of Eighty-seventh, sidestepping the boots of a homeless man who was lying on a subway grating, trapping the rising heat inside a gray army blanket. Only the eyes in his black face and the top of a leather flying helmet poked out from the cuff of greasy wool.

Aaron Davis watched Martina pass, then he reached down to the Motorola tucked between his knees, clicked the mike button twice, waited a beat, then two more clicks. It was only a "heads up" signal, which he had already performed twelve times in the past four hours, whenever young women of a certain weight and height, with faces that might be dangerous, had passed his way. He had changed out of his suit in the surveillance van, taken his position, and declined offers to be relieved, except once to urinate and grab a slice of pizza. The rest of the squad thought he was loony, but the hot grate was the best spot on the "sit."

Martina glanced once at the avenue as another cab cruised by. Nothing about the vehicle triggered any recognition that it was the same taxi that had passed by before.

She marched on, wanting to arrive already, to see *Mutti* and make her smile, to give her the small box of liqueur-filled chocolate bottles wrapped in colored foil, to hug her for as long as she dared and be gone. With her own mission running now, there was risk in every predictable encounter. Once this was finished, she could fret over a hundred other questions that remained unanswered.

Omar had not flagged her for another contact, but then she had made it clear that there was no need. She wondered if her anonymous employers had swallowed her decoy intention to snatch the missile from a European base. As a function of her operation, this was not key, although a deception was better for security.

Then there was the all-important issue of the real device, its movements and location. The portable antiship missile was still in prototype, although its tests had all been flawless. It was a concept based on the American TOW, the Tube-launched, Optically-sighted, Wire-guided antitank missile used with devastating effect by the United States and her allied infantry troops. In this case, the Hughes Corporation had adopted the design for use by elite naval commandos, such as the SEALs. Minnow One, as the prototype was coded, was relatively small, came attached to an inflatable skirt with an optional, propeller-driven sea sled, and could turn a single courageous frogman into a lethal submarine.

Martina paid a considerable annual stipend for information about such weapons systems. Her source was a man named Sam Tamil, the owner of a security and consulting firm called DDS. Tamil had an international reputation as the most spurious security con artist in the Western world, a charlatan who sold nonfunctional tracking devices to the families of kidnap victims and could reputedly market night-vision goggles to the blind. DDS did, however, possess a data bank of technical information whose purloined tidbits could be purchased at exorbitant prices. And Tamil himself had an Achilles' heel—his own sacred skin. He never refused a cash down payment, even for top-secret, proprietary information, but once the money was in his account, you merely had to threaten his life and he would deliver.

In London, Tamil had shown Martina the forbidden specs for Minnow One. She had swallowed a gasp when she saw the drawings, for her father's diary had mentioned his designs for a similar device he had called *Der Fliegende Fisch*—The Flying Fish. The Nazi weapon had never passed the blueprint stage, but when Tamil touted the Minnow, she knew that it would be her weapon of choice. She did not expect him to actually acquire one for her, so she offered him $50,000 for a year's schedule, updated monthly, of the weapon's depot sites and testing scenarios. Soon after the funds were transferred from her Swiss account, she warned Tamil that any informational error, or a leak to any authority, would be discussed with his son Abraham at the elder Tamil's funeral. The schedules arrived in timely fashion at her private postal box in Manhattan.

Every aspect of her plan that could be ensured by guile, threat, money, or deception had been checked and double-checked. Yet she was only one woman, and for such a complex project she was forced into reliance on others. And all of them men.

In less than forty-eight hours, the first stage of her three-part plan would have to proceed flawlessly: the assembly of materials, rapid movement over long distances, precise timing, and a healthy dose of something whose existence she disdained—luck. Factors that were uncontrollable troubled her most. Was Lieutenant Delgado dead or alive? She realized now that she should have opted for his death, although her reasoning at the time seemed logical: a corpse begins quickly to emanate an alarming stench, while a heavily drugged man is less likely to succeed in summoning help. Yet it was possible that he had been found, and his life was a loose end.

Benjamin Baum provided the most insistent upset to her calm, for being again in the same city with him made her feel like a mouse locked in a boa constrictor's cage. What was he really doing in New York? Had he come only as a result of the bombing? And if she was the object of his quest, how could he have known of her whereabouts? It was possible that Yadd Allah had been penetrated. Oh, yes, certainly she could bear witness to the Israeli's ability to manipulate a doubt, to corrupt a conviction until the victim was turned, trapped. Yet who among her flock would risk treachery, when they knew full well how she would deal with them? And she was so cautious, so compartmentalized. None of her men save Mussa was aware of more than his own private assignments, not one would know the impact of the mission until they were all armed and on the road. Only Mussa realized that Martina's mother still lived. And could he ever betray her? It was not possible. He was a religious man, and his deity bade him obey.

Near the corner of Eighty-ninth Street, she passed a white panel truck with *Manhattan Cable TV* stenciled on its flank. She glanced into the passenger window and saw the driver slumped against his headrest, a yellow hard hat tipping toward his snoring mouth. It was Detective Jerry Binder, stuffed into an MCTV coverall.

Across the corner, the Yorkville Deli was the only neighborhood concern still open at the late hour. Beyond its foggy glass, the backs of two men were hunched over paper cups that sent swirls of steam past their wool caps. The shorter figure triggered bitterness once more, but then she heard the thrum of Iyad's motorcycle echoing closer as it ascended Third Avenue, and she quickly turned down Eighty-ninth, taking her emotion with her.

Benjamin Baum. If only she had never met him, who knew what might have been? If only she had seen him early on for what he was, not been weakened by his persuasive powers, had parried his psychological thrusts, his subtle, unrelenting hints at her guilt by association, which whittled her defenses, made her supple to his seductions and his promises. If only she had known then what she had learned through pain: that they were all the same, both sides, *all* sides, vicious dogs who served their masters while wearing shiny tags stamped patriotism, or loyalty, or love, when in fact they only lusted after the power that licensed them to bite and rend. What might have happened to her then? Would she have grown out of her radical youth, wearied of the fugitive life, retired on one blessed sunny day when she saw a toddler in his mother's arms and realized her own true and simple desire? She would never know now. And Benjamin Baum had sealed it so.

She walked along the sidewalk of the cross-street, a dark and icy slope of muted cars parked among molehills of trampled snow. Passing a dull gray Fairlane, whose engine hummed and coughed, she peeked at the young woman huddled beneath a draped coat on the back seat, then hurried onward and downward. The row of five-story houses were packed together on the north side like old book spines on a shelf of black sky: tan, red, and gray rectangles. Each one wore a mask of rusting fire escapes, and the buildings butting up against the Edelweiss offered handholds and short leaps, for Martina had not chosen the rest home solely for its comforts.

She stopped at the foot of the cement steps rising up to the glass door of number 167, a building with a red-brick facade, a crisscross of iron fire balustrades, and a small brass shingle with *Das Edelweiss* engraved in script. She heard Iyad's Suzuki pass behind her, as the boy, of questionable intelligence, hopefully heeded her instructions. He was to stop halfway down the block, park the bike, and enter the foyer of a building across the way, from which he could observe. It was not too much to ask, even of a simpleton. Yet had her manpower not been strapped, she would have utilized Jaweed or Fouad.

She unzipped her jacket, tugged once at the front of her sweater to be sure it was not snagged, took a long cold breath, and walked up the stairs.

The entrance cubicle of Das Edelweiss was like that of any moderate Manhattan residence. The second door was also glass, electronically locked, and to one side of the foyer was a long lime reception counter before an administrative office. An elderly night manager in a worn blue blazer completed the impression of a European pension gone to seed. He looked up from his newspaper, squinted at Martina, and buzzed her in.

From the moment she saw his face, she knew. He did not start, or leap for a telephone, but he smiled as he straightened up in his chair, and the expression was a touch too enthusiastic, the corners of his lips trembling over his dentures. An elderly Germanic watchman, upon seeing a young woman in leather regalia cross his threshold near to midnight of a Sunday, should have frowned with suspicion.

She felt the downy hairs along her spine arching and a hollow pop as her auditory canals yawned open in alarm. She pulled off her ski hat as the blast of overheated air hit her from the foyer, and as she crossed the strip of maroon carpet, her eyes quickly sought out every shadow in the ancient lobby, behind its green armchairs and its drooping potted trees.

"*Guten Abend*," she said as she placed her left hand on the lip of the reception counter. Her right thumb hooked under her sweater to the butt of her pistol as she bellied up close to the bar. *Just push off with the left, draw as you roll, come up shooting.*

"*Willkommen, Fräulein*," said the night manager.

She waited a beat. Nothing happened. The old man continued to regard her through his heavy black spectacles, his gray hair wild as if he had been nervously finger-combing it. Yet his smile was in place, and she thought for a moment that she might have erred, until she saw the corners of the newspaper he held fluttering like butterfly wings in a breeze.

She looked along the darkened corridor toward the elevator, then back at the entrance doors. Nothing. She quickly slipped out of her rucksack.

"I am here to see my mother."

The night man apparently felt an admonition appropriate. "It is very late."

"She doesn't sleep much."

"Yes. None of them do."

Martina waited for the next logical question, but he just looked at her.

"Katharina Oberst," she said.

"*Ach, ja.*" He dropped the paper and pushed his chair back. "Five C?"

"Five A," she corrected.

"*Ja, das stimmt*," he said, as if she had unfortunately passed a trick quiz.

"But first I would like to put something in her box."

The night manager sighed and Martina's alarm increased. He clearly wished to be rid of her. She quickly opened her rucksack and placed the envelope on the counter.

The old man picked it up and extracted himself from his chair. He pulled open the office door and started inside.

"*Der Schlüssel*," Martina said.

He stopped and turned. "*Bitte?*"

She was holding a small brass key in her gloved hand. He came back to retrieve it, and this time her cold gaze erased the chalky smile completely from his face. He muttered something as he hobbled into the office and found the numbered brass box, using his key in one hole and hers in the other. When the envelope was secured, he was startled to find her standing at his heel.

She pocketed the key and returned to the counter, yet now she did not look at him at all. The money was behind steel and safe by law. She could kill the old man, and still that trust belonged forever to Katharina. Of course, she had no intention to do so, but the stench of betrayal was on him, and it made her blood run hot and quick.

"Aren't you forgetting something?" she said as she watched the elevator.

"*Entschuldigung?*"

"The book."

"Oh, yes." He hefted a large visitors' ledger, opened it to the proper place, and tried to smile again as he offered a pen.

She turned and stared at him until he retreated a full step. Then she took the pen, drew only a long black line across the page, dropped it, and walked away.

The night manager sat down, pulled open a metal drawer, and found his flask of schnapps. He took a long swig, then kept his fingers on the entry buzzer. He watched the main door with longing. The policemen had told him to do nothing, but he had a terrible urge to grab the telephone, dial 911, and flee.

Martina walked past the single elevator, the shiny brass mailboxes, as she reset the ruck upon her back and stuffed her gloves into her jacket. She reached up under her sweater, gripped the cold butt of her P-38, yanked open the service stairway door, and lunged inside.

Nothing. She looked up at the ascending brown metal banisters, breathing softly as she waited for a shadow, some hint of sudden retreat.

Silence.

She began to sprint up the heavy steel stairs, always looking upward, her mouth closed and her respiration steady, the only sound the creaking of her leather jacket, past the fire extinguishers, the landings.

She stopped at five and listened. A muffled television set filtered through the door, but aside from that no hasty footsteps, no scrapes of tensioned spines pressed up against walls. She stepped into the corridor.

Clear.

She felt her heart now, pressing hard against the elastic of her running bra. She longed for the chill of her motorcycle ride, as the overheated building caused her sweat to run in itchy rivulets from her armpits.

Perhaps she was wrong, and the superstitions of encroaching age were finally upon her. Perhaps caution itself had become a danger, so draining when one heeded its voice. *Be ready*, she coached herself. *But be calm.*

She was at the rear of the building, facing the corridor of flowered wallpaper, the cream ceiling with its shameless fluorescent fixtures. She dropped her hands to her sides, straightened from a partial crouch, and walked.

Her mother's small one-bedroom was at the front, where Martina had insisted it be, paying a small premium for the privilege. It had a picture window from which *Mutti* could enjoy the changing seasons and Martina could observe the street below. She walked up to the door. It was not locked, a house rule in places where the tenants often fell, fracturing bones.

She turned the glass knob and gently pushed it open.

The first thing that hit her was the odor, a waft of mothballs and wool curdled by the overheated atmosphere. Then she smiled as another scent mingled with the first, the tang of thick black coffee, the grounds boiled freely with a floating egg-shell, just the way *Mutti* always liked it.

She closed the door behind her. The only light in the room was thrown by a shaded lamp on a tall brass pole, next to the arm of a scallop-backed love seat that she herself had purchased some years before. The seat faced away from her, and over its arch she could see the low glass coffee table, its surface polished to a diamond sheen. The mahogany china closet was still in place against the right wall, and a drum table with maritime hardware counterbalanced it on the left. The rest of the decor consisted of framed pictures covering every horizontal surface, including the radiator cover below the window. Silver frames, brass frames, teak frames, photos so familiar that she needn't glance at them to know their contents.

The larger ones were all of *Papa*, here in woolly suits and fedoras, there in shorts and flannel shirts, a coil of climbing rope across his shoulders. In some he hugged a young and radiant Katharina, in others he glowed from the adoring gazes of his wife and a pigtailed toddler. He posed with other men in shirtsleeves, hovering proudly over drafting tables, and in all of them, with the exception of a stark black-and-white in which he wore the uniform of a Wehrmacht *Oberst*, he smiled broadly.

There were other pictures, some art prints clipped from books, of scenes Bavarian; none was Argentinian, as if that period had been stricken from history. And there were a few portraits of a young woman who might have been Martina but was actually a photographic twin selected from the files of a Paris advertising agency. Martina had substituted the stranger for all mementos of herself, placing her faith properly in her mother's failing eyesight.

She watched the tall back of a birch rocker as it gently nodded at the picture window, where a few flecks of flurrying snow were beginning to touch the darkened panes. The muted strains of Beethoven's Fifth drifted from an old radio, yet she knew the selection was coincidental. The tuning dial had probably not been touched this year.

She stepped softly to the left and through the darkened archway of the tiny bedroom, her muscles tightening as she quickly scanned the space, pulled open the bathroom door, then reemerged somewhat relaxed. She walked over to the rocker, gently stopped its movement, and smiled as she looked down.

"*Grüß Gott, Mutti,*" she whispered brightly as she bent and kissed the silky tangle of white curls.

Katharina looked up from her knitting, and without stopping her reedy hum in accompaniment to Ludwig van, or registering anything more than warm pleasure in her shiny eyes, she smiled.

"*Grüß Dich, Schatzi,*" said Katharina, as if her daughter had merely been gone shopping for the afternoon. "*Ein schöner Abend, stimmts?*"

"Yes, *Mutti,*" Martina agreed. "It is a beautiful evening." And not wanting to expose herself too long before the window, she quickly knelt on the floor and turned the rocker to her. Her mother mouthed surprise at the pleasant little ride, and Martina could see that she was knitting a quilt that had no pattern and was filled with holes and wayward loops of blue yarn.

"So how do you feel?" Martina placed her hands on the bony knees beneath a pink flannel housecoat.

"How?" Katharina asked, as if the question was part of an oft-repeated game. "O-o-old," she sang as she bent forward and placed her forehead to Martina's.

They laughed together, and Martina squinted hard in an exaggerated smile. She watched her mother's eyes, still china blue as they must have been so long ago in mountain German air, searching for a sadness, a knowledge that her daughter might be troubled, alone, in danger, at risk. It was not there.

"But not *s-o-o-o* old," her mother added. Martina leaned forward and kissed her jowly cheek. Then she quickly shrugged off her backpack, fumbled with the buckle, and came up with the long box of chocolate brandy bottles.

"I brought you something." She placed the box on her mother's lap, but Katharina did not even look at it. Instead, she reached forward with a gnarled hand and touched her daughter's face.

"*Meine Liebste,*" she said.

Martina covered the hand with her own fingertips and closed her eyes for a moment, imprinting the touch upon her memory. Then she twisted where she knelt on the worn carpet, donning the ruck as the barrel of her pistol pressed into her pubis, reminding her that she should not dawdle. She took both her mother's hands into her own.

"*Mutti,*" she said, trying to penetrate with one final thrust of clarity. "I will have to go away."

"*Ja, natürlich.* Try to bring a cake, Marti. For the coffee."

"No, *Mutti.*" Martina squeezed a bit harder. "I mean, maybe for a long time."

"Oh, yes. I know, darling. But you always come back, don't you?"

"Yes, *Mutti.* I do."

"And you will bring some sweet surprise?"

"I will try to bring something very special."

"And visit with me, for just a little while?"

"I always do, *Mutti.* Don't I?"

"Yes. You are a good girl. Just as your friend said."

"Yes."

Martina felt the rush of something in her chest. Her friend. What friend? She had no acquaintance who also knew her mother, yet she fought with every muscle in her face to maintain her expression, her voice even and undemanding. "My friend."

"*Ja,* such a nice man." Her mother wagged a playful finger. "*Ein* gentleman," she said, as if warning Marti not to break his heart.

"He is." Martina's voice was a hoarse rasp as she wrestled with her smile. "Isn't he?"

"*Ach, ja.*" Katharina giggled.

"Herr Franz," Martina said, one last hope that this friend was born of fantasy.

"Yes," her mother said, then she shook her head. "*No. Herr Klein.*"

Martina leapt to her feet. Klein. Hugo Klein.

Benjamin Baum had been there.

And then she heard it, even as she worked to silence her own blood and bring the building sounds to the fore. She had already felt it, ignored it, like a veteran Californian dismissing the tremors. The quick tread of footsteps from the distant stairwell.

She spun and walked toward the door, her smile turned to a savage lip curl as she unholstered the P-38. She was about to cock the slide when she heard the creak of the rocker behind her. Her mother had risen from the chair and was following her.

"Marti?" Katharina's voice was still bright, untuned to the radical atmospheric shift.

Martina turned, laying the pistol along her right thigh as she reached out and cradled her mother's chin.

"Go sit, *Mutti,*" she whispered, every microsecond an eon of delay. "Go." She kissed her mother hard on her forehead. "I will be right back."

She waited until Katharina turned back toward the window. Then she pulled open the door.

The apartment door immediately to her right also opened, and the figure of a young man froze halfway out the frame. He was tall and blond, wearing a tie and a long coat, and for a moment she thought that the German BKA had pursued her here. In his right hand he held a chrome revolver pointed at the floor, in his left a small walkie-talkie, and a gold badge gleamed from his belt. His eyes gripped Martina's face, then flicked over her shoulder, and she knew that he was frozen by the presence of her mother beyond her back. She raised the P–38 to his gaping mouth and cocked it, the echo of the slide ringing in the corridor.

O'Donovan launched himself backward into the vacant flat, crashing to the wooden floor as the Motorola went skidding away. He snapped out his foot and caught the edge of the open door, slamming it as he crabbed backward and gripped his pistol two-handed between his knees, his breath pouring from his mouth.

Martina kept her weapon trained on the door as she reached back with her left hand, found the knob, and closed her mother's flat.

At the far end of the corridor, the stairwell door flew open and two large figures spilled into the corridor. Martina's pistol swung to them like a battleship turret, and they stopped, iced silhouettes in the harsh fluorescent light.

Benni Baum was wearing a ragged army field jacket and a dark wool cap. Jerry Binder's huge bulk protruded from behind, the yellow hard hat a blazing target he had forgotten to discard.

Benni was unarmed. He slowly straightened up, opening his hands to the sides, his palms upturned. He saw the barrel of Martina's pistol, a tiny orifice as large as a train tunnel, but he blurred it from his vision and focused on her eyes, the fiery blue glass unblinking above nostrils stretched like a wild mare's, a mouth drawn tight.

"Drop, Benni," Binder whispered between clenched teeth. He had not brought the shotgun into the rest home, but his pistol was in his hand, concealed from Martina's view. "I'll take her."

"No," Benni instantly replied. "Not here."

Benni took one step forward, a movement so slow and measured it was like the ballet of a mime. He stretched his fingers further, no tricks up his sleeves. He spoke in German.

"Martina," he said as gently as he could, while his heart already felt the impact of the coming bullet. "*Hör mich an.* Listen to me."

For a second he had hope, for she did not move. But then her face went darker, her chin rose, and she shouted.

"*Nein!* Not again! Not to *you!*"

Binder grabbed Benni's collar and slammed down onto his back, pulling Baum with him as Martina's shot exploded in the corridor, a blinding flash and a concussive ring as the round cracked above their noses and split the wall behind them. They rolled away from each other and Binder was up, his pistol fumbling for a shadow as Martina dove into the apartment to her left. O'Donovan charged out from the flat across the way, saw Binder's gun, and flattened himself against the corridor wall.

In the street below, Martina's gunshot was only a muffled report, no more than a firecracker in a clothes closet. Yet everyone who had anticipated it knew what it was.

Ruth had emerged from O'Donovan's Fairlane, and she jolted backward with the dull crack and froze, staring up at the Edelweiss. Panic claimed her instantly as she imagined her father's crumpled body, and she leapt for the entrance of the building. Her feet flew out over a patch of ice as Aaron Davis gripped her upper arm to hold her back.

"Let me *go*," she snapped, but the tall man squeezed until she stopped her squirm. He was also staring upward, the walkie-talkie in his free hand suddenly crackling with O'Donovan's strained whisper.

"Aaron, call ESU. We might have a hostage thing up here."

"Ten-four," Davis whispered back.

He and Ruth snapped their heads around to the roar of a big motorcycle. True to Martina's instructions, Iyad had broken cover to mount the bike, yet he panicked now as his overthrottling drew the focus of Frank Mancuso, whose assignment was to watch for Klump's backup. Wearing a black ski parka and a baseball cap, Mancuso sprang up from a maintenance stairwell across the street and began to run down the sloping macadam between the parked cars. He drew his revolver and shouted something as the big Suzuki roared away, its rear wheel fishtailing wildly.

Iyad suddenly remembered that he was supposed to lose the saddlebag. He wanted to just toss it away, but Martina had strictly forbidden so obvious a decoy. He decided to tilt the bike and help the bag slip off, then made the mistake of turning to look behind, where a mad figure was gaining quickly on foot. The rear wheel skidded over a patch of snow, and then the whole machine was listing hard to the right as the engine guards sparked on the pavement, and the Suzuki tunneled under the running board of a parked Jeep Cherokee.

Iyad yelled as something sharp tore through the jeans of his left leg. He thrashed for a moment like a downed steed, then freed himself. He pulled once on the handlebars with everything he had, but the motorcycle was locked beneath the car. He got up and sprinted for Second Avenue, his arms flying as he tore off his helmet and hurled it away.

Inside the darkened flat next to her mother's, Martina saw the glint of a plastic dinner plate on a tray, snatched it up, inverted it, dropped it to the floor, and with a toe kick jammed it under the door.

From the flat's bedroom she heard a weak and frightened cry, "*Wer ist das? Wer ist das?*" but she sprang to the salon window and threw one palm to the wooden slats. Freshly painted, it would not budge, and she spun back on the room, spotting a large wooden knitting chest. Sensing the intentions from the corridor, she aimed her pistol at the door, closed her eyes to mitigate the flash, and fired another shot. Then she holstered the P-38, picked up the chest, and, twisting once around like a discus thrower, hurled it at the window, where its impact sent pounds of glass and spools of colored yarn out into the night.

O'Donovan and Binder had squeezed their backs to opposite sides of the doorframe in the corridor. Binder was holding Benni at bay to his left, and they all stared down at the carpet, showered with wooden splinters from Martina's hollow-point. The door to her mother's flat began to open, and O'Donovan reached out and slammed it. The detectives gripped their revolvers two-handed now, and when they heard the window explode, O'Donovan nodded.

Binder lifted his right knee and bucked his foot back like a mule. The door flew on its hinges, a warbling geriatric cry came from somewhere inside, and O'Donovan charged in behind his outstretched weapon.

Wind whipped in through the jagged maw of the window, white streams of snow crisscrossing outside in the black air.

"Jerry, take the stairs," O'Donovan ordered.

"Roger that," said Binder as he turned, expecting to have to manhandle Baum away. But the Israeli's feet were already pounding down the corridor, and he followed at a hard run.

In the street, Ruth and Davis heard the sailing glass and ran to the western corner of the Edelweiss, where the building was separated from its neighbor by a twelve-foot gap. Mancuso joined them, carrying the saddlebag and panting in the frigid air, and the trio gawked up at the distant image of Martina's legs as they disappeared over the last rung of an iron ladder curling over the roof.

Davis's radio was at his lips. "She's going up and over, Sarge."

"No shit," came the hoarse reply, and then O'Donovan appeared on the fire escape, more glass raining down as his coat snagged on the window shards.

He flattened himself against the brick face, edging quickly toward the ladder. He looked up, then down at the faces far below, his hair wild and the open coat whipping like a cape as he stuffed his radio in a pocket. He made an encircling motion with his left arm, and then he began to climb.

The entrance to the Edelweiss sprang open, and Ruth turned to see her father, his face set in something like that ferocity he showed on weekend soccer pitches, yet frightening for its lack of intramural fun. He charged right past her, thundering up the hill toward Third Avenue, with Binder close on his heels.

"Davis!" Binder shouted breathlessly, stunned by the heavy Israeli's speed. "You and Mancuso, the other flank!" Davis and Mancuso instantly sprang away in the opposite direction, as Griffin's cab turned into the street and raced after them. Ruth was alone. She looked around for a moment, hearing the approaching sirens, seeing the rectangles of light popping up in the neighboring buildings. She took off after Benni.

Martina did not hesitate. She had walked the route before, and now she merely had to run it. The gap between the rear of the Edelweiss and the mirroring brownstone on Ninetieth Street was too wide to leap, but just one building to the east, the void closed to less than ten feet. She ran along the hard-packed snow and hurdled the dividing wall onto the next roof.

Halfway across that expanse, she slowed, hearing the pounding of the policeman's feet behind her, his shout stolen by the wind as she curved to the left, picked up speed, and launched herself from the eave, arching up like a long-jumper as the black alley flashed below. Her feet cleared the lip of the far roof and she executed a perfect parachute-landing fall in the snow, onto a calf, thigh, hip, rolling as her clamped ankles followed over. She stayed down, drew her pistol again, waited until she heard the quickening pace of the policeman's feet as he prepared to mimic her leap, then stood full up and pointed the P-38 across the gap. His mouth opened wide and his arms flailed and he slid down onto his back in a spray of white cloud. She did not need to fire. She had killed his momentum.

Zigzagging now in the event that he would try for a shot across the gorge, she sprinted over the roof of 210 East Ninetieth and skidded to a stop at the ledge. She stuck her head out over the five-story drop, looking west, then east. Nothing yet. But they would come.

She holstered the pistol, clutched the ice-glazed iron ladder, and swung over, locking the vertical spars between her insteps and sliding down to the first fire escape platform. Then she ran to its iron staircase, gripped those banisters, lifted her feet, and schussed down it, sailor style. In ten seconds she was hanging from the lip of the final platform, ignoring the pain in her torn palms as she dropped ten feet to the sidewalk.

Baum rounded the corner from the avenue with Binder at his heels and Ruth a close third. But Martina had far less of an expanse to cross.

The slim skyscraper of Ruppert Towers stood just across the street, set back thirty meters from the sidewalk. A driveway curved toward the bright glass lobby, the asphalt bordered on the right by a chest-high brick wall. An expansive private park led away from the top of the wall, with twisting brick paths and the bare trees of a small urban forest.

Yet she waited on the south side of the street, her left hand stinging on the snowy trunk of a car, crouching enough to obstruct their aim, but not so much that they might lose her. The trio thundering down the street from her left curved in her direction. From the right, a pair of men came steadily up the hill, their arms pumping with exertion, followed by a yellow taxi.

Her breath was coming hard now, less from the strain of flight and more from her fury. *In my mother's house,* she nearly cried aloud. *My mother's house!* She fought the urge to just step into the street and open fire. *Wait,* she commanded herself. *Wait.* They had to close the range.

Baum was four car lengths away and the men to the right not much farther when Martina moved, driving everything into her legs as she raced across the street, grimacing with pleasure as she heard a cry of frustration from behind and above, the cop who had chased her pounding on a fire escape as he watched. Her slamming sneakers and the grinding of her leather drowned out the shouts of her pursuers, and with one hand on the driveway wall she was up and over, head down and flying through the park.

Benni still led the pack, as Jerry Binder tried to match the colonel step for step. Ruth was not far behind, unsure of why she also ran, an actor in her own nightmare, which had suddenly spun to life before her eyes. Davis and Mancuso passed her now, closing on Binder and Baum with their revolvers held high like Olympic torches.

Benni reached the wall, slammed his palms down, launched himself up, and rolled onto his side, the momentum carrying him back up on his feet. Binder finally passed him, having taken the height in one tremendous leap, and the two men hurtled after the receding silhouette in the park, their breaths coming like locomotive plumes, their middle-aged hearts warning them that it would have to end soon.

Through the black tree trunks they could see a high metallic fence at the border of the park. It curved to the left, where in the distance it was bolted to the side of Ruppert Towers. To the right, it led back to Ninetieth Street.

Beyond the fence there was nothing but black air, as the built-up park dropped off into a canyon of open lot. Binder had a flash of hope, that Martina Klump had erred. She would be trapped. But Benni was no fool for optimism.

Martina's sprinting figure reached the fence, yet she did not hesitate. She leapt up on the chain link like a spider, pulled herself onto its horizontal spar, stood up to full height with her arms spread like a swan diver, and jumped. There was a resounding clang as her body impacted with a towering light pole six feet from the fence, and she corkscrewed down and away.

Binder slammed against the chain links, knowing he had nothing left with which to emulate the woman's feat, and he rattled the metal with his big hands and roared, "Motherfuckingsonuvabitch!"

Benni joined the big American, looked down, then slumped onto his back in the fresh coverlet of snow, trying to breathe. . . .

Twenty feet below, Martina's black soles touched the deep lane that forked to a parking lot beneath the towers and also out the other side onto Ninety-first Street. She was already running again, keeping close to the building as she stretched out into a rapid lope.

The escape route had worked, but her satisfaction was spoiled by those other emotions that twisted her face into a mask of rage.

"You want to play *family* games, Benni?" she whispered as she ran off into the night. "*Two* can play."

Chapter 9: The Lexington Avenue Grill

Lieutenant Colonel Benjamin Baum looked down at his hands. They rested at the edge of the small dining table, turned upward for his inspection, the hair-matted backs lying listlessly against the white tablecloth. They were slabby things, the digits wide and stubby like cheap cigars, the palms lined like a dry riverbed. A flat gold wedding band was locked behind a bulky knuckle of the fourth finger on the left, and only surgery of flesh or metal could free it now.

Baum wondered how his long-dead parents could have ever dreamed such hands might fly across the delicate teeth of a piano, or how the women he had known had allowed these hooves to fumble over their breasts. These hands that were so comfortable gripping pistols, tweaking radio dials, jabbing at trembling subordinates, snatching at the collars of the accused. A hundred different currencies had been dealt from them like blackjack cards, some lives clasped protectively by them forever, while others were allowed to slip between the fingers with no more ceremony than a quick dust-off on trouser seams.

Like the hands of a renowned character actor, they belonged to one man while gesticulating for so many others. They were the hands of a pudgy toddler called *Bibi*, and those of a boisterous bull called *Benni*. They were the hands of Hans-Dieter Schmidt, Hugo Klein, George Harrington, and those of Antoine Arbre, Maxwell Pine, and Nigel Trunk. Some of these personas were deceased now, some temporarily retired, yet all of their identities survived in ledger-sized safe boxes, and every act they had committed—murders, flashes of heroics, deceptions, and seductions—was etched into history just as if all six had been full flesh and blood, wandering a course from birth to death.

But they all shared this same pair of ugly hands, and as Benni stared past the fleshy blades that would have been the envy of a tae kwon do master, he was truly stunned. On the table lay a large white plate, with a lovely slice of steak streaming juices around a hill of mashed potatoes. A crisscross of baby asparagus completed the gourmet-magazine layout, and all of it untouched.

For the first time since he could remember, Benni had lost something that not one of his personas had ever neglected, despite pressures, dangers, or even incapacitating illness.

He had lost his appetite.

A dinner knife and fork lay bracketing the meal, and Benni slowly gripped the handles, raising them erect. Yet his culinary weapons refused to do battle, and he sat there looking like a prisoner protesting in the mess hall of a penitentiary.

He raised his eyes and looked across the narrow dining room, the water glasses shimmering from a rushing subway, the businessmen aglow with a day's worth of takeovers, puts, and calls. A long oval bar of blood-red teak lay as sentry to the Grill, a hundred wine and beer glasses racked above it like stalactites. There was no dividing wall between the restaurant and the lobby of the Loews Summit Hotel, and he watched as a pair of tired El Al pilots, peaked caps pushed back on their gray heads, hauled their crew cases toward the reception desk. The Loews had replaced the Lexington as the Israeli government's unofficial New York hostelry. It was newly renovated, metallic and spotless. Benni missed the Lexington.

A flash of desert umber caught his eye, and he looked up at the silent screen of a giant TV, another CNN report on the stranded UN nuclear inspection teams in Iraq. No other diners appeared interested in this now passé drama. When the stock ticker loped across the screen, then they would look up.

Benni surrendered, laying the utensils back down. He raised a finger, and in a moment a sprightly blond waitress in a buttoned vest and tight white collar appeared.

"Can I help you, sir?"

He tried to smile. "May I get a drink, please?"

"Perrier?"

"Beck's."

"Certainly."

He reached down absentmindedly into the pocket of his car coat, coming up with a pack of cigarettes. He frowned at the red-and-white box of Marlboros, remembering that his Israeli stash was exhausted. He lit up, murmured, "Out of Time," and sneered at his own pun.

The call from Itzik Ben-Zion had woken him long before dawn. It was not the timing that disturbed him, for his profession precluded any notion of undisturbed sleep. Rather, it was Itzik's tone, and his message.

"That's enough, Baum," the general growled without greeting. "Back here tomorrow."

"This is just getting hot, Itzik," Benni attempted without real hope. "Some very interesting developments."

"Have you seen your daughter?"

"Yes."

"And Ben-Czecho?"

"Once. I'll see him again today."

"Good. A team is coming in to replace you."

"You know, Itzik—"

"And of course I don't have to remind you of the priority mission. Back here tomorrow. That's an order." *Click.*

It did not really matter. There was no way for Benni to explain to his commander why the bombing had taken on such significance. In order to do so, he would have to unravel a decade's worth of knotted lies, and even then the general would have correctly emphasized the "priority."

The waitress set a fluted glass on the cloth and quickly filled it from a tall green Beck's. Benni watched her hands, thinking how the Germans stretched out beer pouring like extended foreplay, the Americans got it quickly over with, and Israelis always slugged it from the bottle.

"Is your dish all right?" she asked with some concern.

"The dish is fine," said Benni. "And I am sure the food will be also." He winked at her, and she waved a hand and left. He returned to a comfortable frown.

His final visit with Moshiko had not uplifted him. The boy was fully aware of his injuries now, the drug intake only a skein of comfort over the throb of violent amputation and the horror of a lost eye. The jokes about Moshe Dayan's unhampered sexual and political achievements fell flat.

Ben-Czecho had been moved into a private room and was up on his feet. Yet now that his survival was assured, the impact of his maiming was not a future for which he gave thanks.

Within a week, he would be shipped back to Israel for rehabilitation at Tel Hashomer. Benni promised to put in a call to his old friend Naftali Rossman, the war-crippled head of that hospital unit, who had worked wonders with thousands of Israel's young casualties. He also assured the boy, without mentioning Martina Klump, that the investigation was progressing nicely. And he tried to assuage Moshiko's vengeful comments with the reminder that his attacker had already served his sentence, having blown himself to bits.

Moshiko merely grunted in response to these attempts. The ever-present Kathleen, her youth and beauty looking drawn and fatigued, sat thumbing through the Israeli tourist brochures that some well-meaning soul had brought her from the consulate. The images of a foreign land and culture assured her only that she would never see her wounded warrior again, and she watched him pace before the window, his hand fidgeting behind his hospital robe, his eye staring out at the snow, their love stretching thinner across a cavern of unshared experiences. . . .

Benni took a long drag from the Marlboro, parted his teeth, and a thick ribbon of smoke leapt into his nose like a genie returning to his lamp. A woman across the room glared at him, yet he was sitting in the proper section, and he held her righteous gaze and sipped from his beer until she turned away in disgust.

Perhaps the alcohol would return his stomach to its natural ravenous state. This hollow lack of desire was an odd sensation, yet he was well aware of its cause. He was abandoning an operation, an act equivalent to an obstetrician taking a dinner break in the midst of a breech birth. It was an anomaly, a crime against his own nature.

There was little comfort in the reasoning that the bombing was a sidebar. Yes, he had come here to comfort Moshiko and for a rapprochement with Ruth, but as was frequently the case in his fluid world, the rules had changed midgame. That challenging unpredictability was the factor that had drawn him to this profession, yet here he was, retreating from the field, walking off the playing pitch.

Another churning pain smoldered somewhere below his esophagus, but it was not the pricking of a ballooned ego, for Benni had never regarded himself as a one-man show. At this stage he would have hunkered down, set up a field command post, and called in his specialists. These pangs of guilt issued from the duality he felt toward Martina Klump.

Her involvement in the bombing made no operational sense. *And it does not have to,* he told himself as he swirled the liquid at the bottom of his glass. The act could certainly stand alone, a work of violent sculpture in the vast gallery of Middle Eastern politics. Yet as Ruth had said, without a claim of credit it was meaningless. Without the artist's name inscribed, the piece would have no value.

The timing of the attack, on the verge of the watershed prisoner exchange, might just be *tziroof mikrim*—combined occurrences, the Hebrew nod to acts of fate. Yet like all good rabbis and intelligence professionals, Benni denied the existence of coincidence.

"*Ach*, Martina." His lips moved slightly as he set the empty glass on the table, realized the Marlboro had burned down to his fingers, and lit up a fresh one with the stub. "If only I could talk to you."

He understood her thirst to wreak vengeance upon him, for in her place the same wretched fire would burn in his heart. But what would make her think that a bombing in New York would sting him in Jerusalem? There was no way she could have had a schedule of the consular routines and dispatched a human grenade to maim Moshiko, even if Benni's connection to the boy was known to her. And if by some frightening penetration of Israeli networks that information was in fact available, such a flimsy strike at Benni was foreign to her courage.

If only he could have explained to her, apologized. Just a few short minutes, and he knew he could convince her that Bruchsal had been a horrible mistake. His word, despite what she might think, was not given lightly. There had been no reason to deceive her into believing that her escape route was secure, while arranging for a marksman to take her down. An appeal from his government, and she could have been simply locked away for life. A quiet conference with Bernard Lokojewski, and she could have tragically "committed suicide" in her cell.

Her bitterness was comprehensible, even her embrace of the Lebanese terrorists and acts of murder against Israeli troops. He had the power to suppress her crimes and grant absolution, but first she had to *listen* to him. He felt like the parent of a child who had joined a radical cult, and short of snatching her away to a rehabilitation camp, there was no way to deprogram her.

The Tango file. He cursed it now, the thick sheaf of reports, transmissions, commentaries, double encoded and as indecipherable as the Dead Sea Scrolls to anyone but himself. It lay there in his Jerusalem safe like a mummy wrapped in rotting swathes of lies. How he wished now that he had shared it, even with Itzik Ben-Zion, for he carried the shame of its responsibility alone. And also in that airless tomb lay that other file, Moonlight, the details of the prisoner exchange rushing onward to fruition, threatened by dangers that he sensed yet could not pinpoint.

The image came to him, and he slumped back in his chair and dropped the cigarette onto a butter dish. A tango in the moonlight. They were intertwined somehow, Martina and the exchange, and they flashed by, twirling in embrace, just like the essence of that torrid dance, breast-to-breast, clutching and then stamping apart, caressing while their hands concealed stilettos.

But what connection? How? If only Eytan Eckstein were with him now, together they could reason it out. How often had they managed it, in so many foreign capitals and slums, inhaling clouds of cigarette smoke and carafes of coffee as they tunneled through the night until a mental labyrinth surrendered? He tried to conjure his partner's voice from half a world away.

"*Nu*, so Martina ran the bomber," said Eckstein inside Benni's head.

"Who says?" Baum countered silently.

"We'll take it as a given."

"Why?"

"Stop resisting, Benni."

"Okay. What's her motivation?"

"Not personal. She can't guarantee your involvement."

"Political, then."

"Fine. It's a unilateral act."

"Then why doesn't someone take credit, Eytan?"

"Okay. Strike that. It's operational."

"Target?"

"The prisoner exchange."

"She can't know about it."

"But she does, Benni. You're in denial."

"Okay. Then who's running her?"

He could imagine Eckstein thinking, rubbing a hand up the back of his blond head.

"No one runs her anymore," said Eckstein's voice. "She runs herself."

"Okay, so who's *financing* her?"

"Uh, Hizbollah."

"Runs counter to logic."

"Fine. Jabril, then. Nidal, Abbas, the Palestinian rejectionists."

"Doesn't really fit with the exchange. You're back to unilateral, Eytan. But don't forget the bomber was Iranian."

"Fine. So you answered your own question."

"The Iranians?" Benni was squeezing the bridge of his nose, eyes shut, conducting his silent symphony. "Why them? They control Hizbollah, they obviously sanctioned the exchange, they want the military cargo even if they don't give a shit about Sheik Sa'id."

Eckstein's spirit voice did not immediately reply. "They have some *other* motivation," his ghostly whisper finally declared.

But Benni could not fathom that, and the dialogue faded. He just could not separate himself, play both parts successfully.

He tried to stagger on alone. If the bombing *was* an attempt to scuttle the exchange, then that effort had failed. Accordingly, would there not be other attempts? Itzik was right. He had to get on home and tend to this from "inside the perimeter."

Still, Martina's role in synchronous events continued to grow. There was the matter of the motorcyclist who had lost his machine and fled. The recovered saddlebag had contained meaningless personal items and one incriminating lead that could not be ignored. It was a well-thumbed map of Boston, with a penciled circle within which fell that city's Israeli Consulate. Despite Baum's protests that such a blatant breach of Martina's security must surely be a decoy, Hanan Bar-El had no choice but to treat it as a new threat.

The fresh team from Tel Aviv had already arrived, and Benni had briefed them at the hotel. They were Mossad people for the most part, as Ben-Zion had agreed with the "civilians" that this was jurisdictionally an intelligence issue on foreign soil, and AMAN had other fish to fry. Most of the young agents were British-born Israelis, and Benni was impressed by their tailored suits and English aplomb, remembering his own recruitment in the sixties, when the "office" had to put you through a course in how to knot a tie and drink an aperitif.

They had thanked him for his input, then huddled with their GSS and NYPD counterparts, preparing to head north for Boston. Benni had to suppress the egotism that had him wishing for their failure, so that he would be recalled to wrap up the case.

"*Shvitzer.*" He chastised himself with the Yiddish slang for a narcissist. He was already thinking like a retiree, jealous of the vigor and enthusiasm of the young.

Deciding to take another stab at his meal, he plowed up a healthy pile of the potatoes. They tasted like cold, wet plaster, and he caught the waitress's eye and pointed at his empty beer glass.

If he had to leave, he wished that he could do it now, head straight for Kennedy and catch the late flight to Ben-Gurion. Yet another event prolonged his suffering.

Just after Itzik's wake-up call, the phone in his hotel room had rung again. This time it was Lieutenant General Avraham Yaron, the IDF's military attaché at the Israeli Embassy in Washington. Yaron greeted Baum like an old army buddy, which was appropriate since he had been Baum's squad leader during basic training three decades before. Their career paths had often crossed, spilling over into reciprocal invitations to weddings, brises, and bar mitzvahs.

"*Akshev!* Ten-hut!" Yaron boomed into the phone.

"Avraham!" Benni smiled despite his foul morning mood.

"You weren't going to visit me, were you, Baum." The general's tone was playfully wounded.

"You were next on my list, I swear. But Itzik's dragging me home."

"*Jobnik.*" Yaron insulted Baum's commander with an army term meaning "noncombatant," then his voice grew serious. "Well, now you'll *have* to visit me."

"How come?" Benni sat up on his bed, fully awake.

"First of all, Hanan Bar-El flashed our chief of security down here. Something about Boston, which on *my* map is in Massachusetts, but he still has our Shabakniks running around like they're expecting a Syrian invasion. You know about it?"

"Yes."

"Thought so. I'd like to hear the story from a cool head. But that's not why you're coming here."

"*Nu?*"

"A package arrived by overnight courier," said Yaron. "Addressed to you."

"So?" Benni said with some confusion. "Have someone send it on to Jerusalem in the pouch."

The general laughed once, a snort without mirth. "No can do, Baum. The thing has no return address, a hefty weight to it, and it's covered with stamps. *Lebanese* stamps."

Benni understood that such a parcel would be automatically tagged "suspicious" and not forwarded anywhere until it was examined. "Oh," he said. "No return address?"

"That's right," said Yaron. "Why? You got relatives in Beirut? Just *your* name and *my* address, thank you very much. The sappers have it in the basement, but they want you here for the opening ceremonies."

"Yes, I understand."

"Something relevant to that fucking fiasco up there, Baum?"

"Might be."

"Good. Then swing on down. You might want to have a look inside, if it doesn't explode first." The general said this with the flippancy that comes of over-exposure to incoming artillery.

"All right," Benni sighed. "I can catch a shuttle tonight. Is there a flight out tomorrow?"

"Of course!" Yaron shouted. "This is Washington, not Petach Tikva." He paused. "And Baum?"

"What?"

"You weren't going to visit me. *Were* you?"

"Go to hell, Avraham."

"Down for thirty!" The general laughed, harking back to the good old days when he could torture Baum with push-ups. . . .

So now this too, Benni thought while the waitress refilled his beer glass. He did not even want to speculate on the meaning of the package, but he had the uneasy feeling that he was wearing a nose ring and Martina was tugging at it, turning his head, drawing blood.

All of this was just very poor timing, a series of occurrences jerking him from his trajectory. He had planned on devoting this last evening to Ruth, a quiet dinner over which they could arrive at some personal conclusions. That was the worst of it, that he and his daughter had just begun to dissolve the obstacles that had kept them apart for years, and now he was severing the tie again before they could seal a fresh pact.

This short time together had been far from ideal, hardly a quiet camping trip in Galilee where they could stare at the stars while he confessed his parental mistakes. Yet they had been immersed together in operations, witnessed each other's talents and foibles. Perhaps she understood him a bit better now, perhaps he had gleaned the depths of her disappointments. He had always loved her, always been proud, and now he knew that a parent, stingy as he might be with praise in his professional life, had to verbalize those feelings to his children. A child could not be expected to discern love or encouragement. She had to be told.

That was what Ruth was trying to tell him, that it was not too late, that she would forgive two decades of ignorance. She was giving him another chance, yet now the opportunity to speak his heart was being snatched away, and he was not sure that she would grant him a rain check.

And what of Yosh and Amos, his two sons, already in uniform? Had he raised them in that same atmosphere of friendly neglect? He was sure that he had. Were his excuses of the call to duty enough to assuage their loneliness in his absence? He doubted it profoundly. Would his poor example of manhood and fatherhood turn them into parents who also patted their toddlers' heads in passing, while they laced up their combat boots and went back to their units? One a paratroop recruit now, one a pilot candidate. He had taught them to replace intimacy with sacrifice.

Benni had never shared with anyone, not even Maya—*especially* Maya—that his most terrible fear was losing one of the children to untimely death. As a young father, he had been awakened by horrific nightmares of auto accidents, suffocations, terrorist attacks on their nurseries. And like every soldier determined to survive, he had suppressed those fears, camouflaged the ugly secret.

Yes, I am afraid for her, he admitted now. Ruth lived in a city rife with horrors that made Jerusalem seem like a Vermont village by comparison. Add to that equation a woman like Martina, and although Ruth was only on the periphery, his fears began once more to rise in his chest.

If only O'Donovan had reacted properly when he had the chance, this nightmare could have been swept away.

And that was another factor that churned his stomach juices. O'Donovan. There was no ignoring the fact that the American and Ruth had begun to form a bond. It was hard enough for a father to accept a daughter's sexuality, yet this potential union, with all its verbal jousts and hungry gazes of an onrushing tryst, deeply worried him. All Benni needed now was for Ruth to marry an Irish Catholic and wind up living in America for the rest of her life.

Ruth O'Donovan. The sound of it made him miserable.

"I haven't seen that pose since Maccabi Tel Aviv lost the basketball cup in 'seventy-nine."

Benni looked up to see Ruth standing directly across the table, somewhat pleased at having caught her father in so vulnerable a posture. His elbows were on the table and his head was in his hands, and he quickly placed them in his lap and smiled up at her.

"*Erev tov, yefefiah sheli.* Good evening, my beauty." The compliment was genuine, for as she pulled out a chair and slipped into it, he could see that her inherent physical traits had been further enhanced by grooming. Her hair was freshly washed, she wore a blue silk blouse beneath her camel coat, and the hemline of some sort of skirt revealed too much thigh.

"*Abba.*" She leaned across the table and kissed him on the cheek.

Perfume. And her blouse was not buttoned to the throat. Benni dipped his head around the table and glanced at her legs. "You're wearing a dress."

"It's a jeans skirt, *Abba.*"

"You look very nice." *Stockings?* Could not be. Not *Ruth.*

"Thank you." She placed a small leather bag on the table and pointed at his plate. "That must be your second serving." She had never seen a steak survive in his presence for very long.

"Yes." He smiled weakly. "I already had the shrimp pasta."

Ruth raised a doubtful eyebrow. Like most Israelis, her father was none too keen on crustaceans.

"Would you care for a drink?" The waitress appeared at her shoulder.

"A gin and tonic, please," Ruth said, switching momentarily to English. She turned back to her father. "So here we are again, *Abba.*"

"I am so sorry, Ruti." Benni squirmed, sure that she was going to reprimand him for his untimely departure. "I wish that I could . . ."

She placed her hand over his fist and stopped him with her smile. "It's all right, *Abba.* Really." She spotted his Marlboros and plucked one from the pack. "You know, in the past three days we've spent more time together than in the past five years."

Benni nodded, holding his breath like a defendant as the jury foreman rises from the box.

"It was very good." Ruth's eyes sparkled at him. "Much more than I could have expected."

He had a profound urge to pull his daughter to her feet and crush her to him. Yet he just sat there, stunned by her magnanimity.

She lit the cigarette, sat back, and blew out a stream of smoke. "Ahh." She sighed with pleasure. "*Hoo-kanah*. The best brand."

Benni smiled. *Hoo-kanah* literally meant "Someone else bought them."

"So did you get a lot done today?" he asked, determined to maintain the friendly atmosphere.

"Caught up on all my homework, like a good girl." She reached down to the floor and moved a small white shopping bag to his side. "There's perfume in there for *Eema*. And I got Yosh and Amos both Maglites for the army. Don't leave it in an airport lounge somewhere."

"I won't."

"I also gave you a copy of my thesis proposal." Then she added somewhat self-deprecatingly, "Might help you sleep on the plane."

"Nonsense. I'll be fascinated. Thank you."

She shrugged and looked out at the other patrons.

"Would you like something to eat?" Benni offered.

She turned back to him, a hesitation in her eyes. "I thought you had to go."

"Well, yes."

"That's all right," she said quickly. "I'll get something later."

He sensed some sort of embarrassment in her tone, a censorship. Yet he did not press her. "I was going to catch the late-night flight back home, but I have to go to Washington now."

"Really? And how is it going? Any further word of her?"

"No." He very much did *not* want to discuss Martina. "And really, I am sorry we can't have dinner."

"Oh, stop it, *Abba*. You've apologized twice in two minutes. It scares me."

Benni obeyed and forced a smile. He watched his daughter as she looked up at the silent television screen. Why was she being so complaisant? Where was her anger, her childlike admonitions? He was more comfortable with those emotions, in light of this strange acceptance of his departure. It was almost as if she could not wait for him to go.

"Ruti?" he suddenly said brightly as he pushed his plate of cold food aside, folded his hands together, and leaned forward.

"Yes?"

"How about coming with me?"

A small furrow appeared above her nose. "To Washington?"

"No." He grinned foolishly. "Home."

"I can't take time off now, *Abba*. I'm in the middle of—"

"Not a vacation," said Benni, still afloat on his deluded optimism. "I mean permanently."

Ruth slowly withdrew toward the back of her chair, regarding him as if she had spotted fangs in his mouth.

"No, really," said Benni, not heeding the warning signs. "You could go to Jerusalem U. We'll get you your own apartment."

"*Abba.*" She began to shake her head.

"There's an excellent program on the Mount Scopus campus. My department uses the chief psychologist up there."

"*Abba,*" Ruth said more strongly, her words expelled from between clenched teeth. "You are *ruining* it."

"Why?" He pressed on, propelled by his own emotions now, his fear. "Why not?"

"*Because,*" she snapped as she violently stubbed out her cigarette. "I am not some child who needs to be monitored by Mommy and Daddy."

"That's not what I mean."

"That's *exactly* what you mean."

"You don't understand the dangers."

"*What* dangers?"

"Have you been blind the last three days?"

"No, I haven't been blind, *Abba.*" She leaned toward him now, the fire in her eyes. "I have not been blind at *all.* You've tried to treat me like a child every step of the way. You were angry every time I tried to contribute."

"That's not true." Benni wagged his head. "You don't understand." There was no way for him to explain his predicament. He could not give over enough facts to mount a reasonable defense.

"Oh, I *do* understand," Ruth snapped. "I think you're jealous. You can't stand having me compete on the same level."

"Nonsense." Benni dropped a hand on the table, making the cutlery sing.

The waitress had sneaked inside their confrontation and slipped the drink to Ruth's side. Ruth snatched up the gin and tonic, took a long slug, and stuck out her chin. "I'm afraid it is not nonsense," she said with a psychologist's superiority.

"Ruti," Benni tried again, ignoring her huff when she heard her childhood nickname. "I am only concerned for your welfare. You can call it drama, if you like, but there is a very dangerous woman on the loose. She knows me well, and she might threaten you too."

"Oh, please!" Ruth expelled a sarcastic laugh. "I've been riding the New York subways for years, and you never worried about that!" Her raised voice turned the heads of some other patrons. The language was foreign to them, but a fight was a fight in any tongue.

Benni sat back, lowering his head. "Yes I did," he muttered, and the rest followed in unverbalized confessions. *I was scared breathless. Always. Forever. Every day, from the minute you were born.*

And all at once he was stung by his own ineptitude, how quickly and clumsily he had torn the scab from a healing wound. We must be eternity's fools, he thought, to dream that there might ever be peace, when I can't even maintain a three-day cease-fire with my own daughter. What gave him the right to be so bloody arrogant? What psychotic insecurity made him strive for command, for control, for positions where his word was always the last one? What kind of pathetic cowardice had he unleashed upon Ruth, trying to shackle her like some helpless autistic? He should have simply said, "I am worried about you. I love you and I am frightened of dangers beyond my control. But you are a grown, intelligent, resourceful woman, and I trust your judgment."

His shame brought a deep flush to his face. He would apologize once more, say it all, even if it fell flat. He raised his eyes to look at her and was momentarily heartened to find a smile at her lips. Yet she was not looking at him.

Detective Michael O'Donovan was crossing the floor. The tall American was clearly off duty, sporting a black turtleneck, blue jeans, and a woolen baseball jacket with green leather sleeves. The significance of this casual attire was not lost on Benni, whose optimism faded quickly to a dark resentment of the intrusion.

O'Donovan walked up to the table, avoiding Ruth's eyes while she followed his face.

"Colonel," he said, offering his hand across the dinnerware.

Benni reluctantly reached out to take it, and his knuckles brushed his beer glass, which began to topple. O'Donovan saved the spill with a quick left-handed lunge.

"Close call," the detective said modestly as he pulled out a chair.

"Good reflexes," Ruth complimented with a smile.

"*Aval lo maspeek tovot.* But not good enough," Benni murmured. Ruth shot him a look that would have singed his hair had he had any left.

"Hello there," O'Donovan said brightly to Ruth. He was fully aware of the chilly atmosphere and trying to stay above it.

"Hello to you."

Benni watched their eyes connect. He had the ability to read three layers of subtext in a greeting, but this one was an open book.

"Like a drink, sir?" The waitress was at the detective's shoulder.

O'Donovan pointed at Ruth's glass. "What's that?"

"Gin and tonic," she said.

"Same for me."

Benni felt his stomach flip.

"Well, Colonel." O'Donovan leaned forward. "I'm sorry to hear you had to cut it short."

I'll bet you are, thought Benni with disgust, yet he just shrugged. "The fortunes of war."

"Yeah," said O'Donovan. A long silence ensued until his drink arrived and he raised it. "Here's to that. Something we all know too well."

Ruth clicked her glass against O'Donovan's. Benni declined to toast, and he suddenly demanded in a flat and scornful tone:

"Why the hell didn't you shoot her, Michael?"

Ruth and O'Donovan froze, the glasses at their lips.

The American lowered his drink, his expression no longer so friendly.

"I told you, Colonel."

"*Abba*," Ruth warned her father.

"Why, Detective?" Benni asked again, not daring to glance at his daughter. "Yes, as you said, the line of fire. But if you had just overcome your sentimentality . . ."

O'Donovan opened his mouth and looked away in astonishment. Then he pressed his anger down, summoned a patient smile, and turned back to meet Baum's glare.

"I'll tell you this much, Benni."

"*No*." Ruth reached out and placed her hand over O'Donovan's forearm, her choice of sides clear as she leaned toward her father and growled, "I certainly wouldn't put it past *you*, *Abba*, to shoot a daughter in front of her own mother!"

Benni blinked, pursed his lips, and nodded. He rose from his chair. His valise was next to his leg and he picked it up, adding the small shopping bag to the same hand. He stood there for a moment, looking at the bag, while Ruth stared at her clenched fists. O'Donovan watched him.

"Please excuse old soldiers," Benni said softly, raising his head. "We don't fade gracefully." He walked behind Ruth's chair, looked down at her, then bent and kissed her hair. She did not move. "I have to get to Washington," he said flatly as O'Donovan got up. This time Benni offered the hand, a silent apology.

O'Donovan understood that Benni's outburst clearly had little to do with him, or Martina Klump, or anything else but Ruth. He felt sorry for Baum, as well as relieved that he would take his dark cloud with him.

"Good luck, Colonel," he said, pumping Benni's hand. "It was a privilege."

"The same," said Benni.

"We'll try to do you proud."

Benni gripped the detective's hand very hard and looked into his eyes.

"I cannot protect her anymore," he said, without gesturing at Ruth. "But *you* can."

He waited until O'Donovan nodded once. Then he released him and walked from the restaurant.

Out on Lexington Avenue, Benni did not need to look for a cab. The yellow sedans were parked in a line at the curb before the hotel entrance. The night was bitter, yet he stood for a moment on the sidewalk, trying to flush the pain in his heart with long drafts of the icy air. The avenue was busy, the cusp of a workday evening, with streams of holiday shoppers taking advantage of the pre-Christmas store schedules. No one glanced at him, no figure waited in the distance, feigning disinterest. And still the few gray hairs at the back of his neck tickled their warning. He could hear Eckstein's whisper inside his mind: "*This* bear has a tail."

But he could not spot the watcher. He was losing his touch, yet somehow the loss did not trouble him as it should have. He suffered that bitter resignation of all old warriors, who awaken one day, in the offensive quiet of retirement, wishing they had fallen in battle.

The first cabbie approached him. In keeping with professional precaution, Benni declined the ride.

He got into the second taxi, bound for La Guardia Airport, Washington, D.C., and perhaps parts, as well as parcels, unknown.

Chapter 10: The Grill

Ruth's father was gone, yet the pall of his parental obstinacy remained behind, hanging above the table like the cordite clouds she had once witnessed in the war-torn hills of Lebanon. She stared into a blurred distance, wondering if there would ever be a time when they would meet on an equal plane. Could a man who had diapered her as an infant ever view her as a human being apart and self-sustaining? And would she ever find a way to truly snip her own umbilical and defuse his disapprovals with powerful calm?

How long would it take? He was no longer young, well into that phase of life where work-obsessed men often burst their overlabored hearts. Would she soon stand beside his bedridden form, making one final attempt to penetrate those large unhearing ears?

She closed her eyes and swallowed, remembering that she was not alone, forcing the vision and emotion back down. *There will be another chance*, she told herself. *We started something good here.* . . .

Yet only yesterday a gunshot had nearly slashed the future at its roots, and in *Abba's* business, tomorrow could bring the same. His lifestyle parried with premature death. It angered her, then brought on fear, then dissolved into despair.

She felt a set of fingers pressing gently on her forearm. Michael O'Donovan was still there, his reddish brows knit together in empathic concern. Ruth looked at his Gaelic face and wanted to run. What the hell was she doing here? What childish attraction to this "greener grass" had made her fantasize any true connection between them? She had spent her day staving off images of sexual play with this man, then wasted a full half hour primping like a debutante. To what end? It could only fizzle in an emotional cul-de-sac.

She slowly drew her arm from his fingers and put her hands in her lap.

"I'm sorry, Michael." She tried to smile kindly. "I think the mood has passed."

He registered no disappointment, no evidence of a punctured male ego. He nodded slowly as he spoke.

" 'O you kind gods. Cure this great breach in his abused nature.' " He recited without drama, as if every NYPD detective held Shakespearean soliloquies in reserve.

"*Excuse* me?" Ruth watched his mouth return to its smile, a sensation of disembodiment under her skin. As if she had witnessed a man momentarily possessed.

"It's from *King Lear*," he said.

"*King Lear*."

"Yeah. Shakespeare."

"I know the author, Michael. It's the *actor* who surprised me." Despite her mood, she decided to delay her urge to bolt. She reached out for her drink. "Something they teach you at the Academy?"

"My father was a fan." O'Donovan also took up his glass. "Big Irish street cop. Hated television, made us spend an hour reading every night after dinner. His favorite gag was pulling doctors over for traffic violations. He'd let them talk down to him for a while, then he'd recite *Henry* V while he wrote out their tickets."

Ruth smiled. "He sounds like fun."

"He was."

"Oh. I'm sorry."

"Rest his weary soul," the detective intoned in an Irish brogue, as he raised his glass toward the ceiling. "And Mother's with him."

The atmosphere dipped once more as Ruth was reminded of Benni's mortality. She frowned. "So is that how you see *my* father? The poor old Lear, tormented by his daughters, railing against the storm?"

"No," O'Donovan replied with surprise. "It's how I view *you*. The wronged Cordelia, trying to reach him."

Ruth regarded him for a silent spell, somewhat stunned. Still wrapped in her comfortable cloak of self-recrimination, she was unprepared to be understood. And the source of support was so incongruous, a man she hardly knew, a police detective whose exposure to daily cruelties should have deadened his emotional availability. Yet she had seen American men do this before. They studied women's magazines. They often knew what to say.

"Don't tell me you're one of those sensitive, liberated men, Michael," she said doubtfully.

O'Donovan raised an eyebrow. "Well, I guess you could ask my detectives. They might answer you when they're done laughing."

"That's what I thought."

"It doesn't mean my sympathy's some kind of ploy."

"So what is it?" Her residual bitterness had left her spoiling for a fight.

"Maybe it's just identification," he said. "We probably grew up in similar homes."

"Hmmm." She doubted that anyone could appreciate a childhood under Benjamin Baum's parentage-in-absentia.

"But it's interesting that you find it threatening." His tone was pensive, not challenging at all.

"And why do you think that is?"

"I don't know, Ruth." He shrugged. "You're the psychologist. Examine it."

She sipped her drink and stared at the glass. *I don't need this*, she thought. *A cross-examination by some amateur analyst.* She felt the anger swell, then suddenly recalled her father's reaction to her own barb not ten minutes ago. *Just like your old man, huh, Ruth?* she challenged herself. *Truth hurts too much?*

She pushed a strand of hair behind her right ear as she looked over at him sheepishly. Her wry smile was greeted by his, and she knew why she wanted to run. She was prepared for a primitive attraction here, but had not bargained for a man with a brain and a heart as well.

"You know, O'Donovan?" she said. "You might be too much for me. I could be out of my league."

"Funny. One of my guys suggested the same thing. In reverse."

"Fair warning, for both of us."

"Let's wing it," he suggested.

"Fine." She waved her hand as if sweeping away all recent unpleasantness. "*So*, I believe you owe me dinner."

"The case isn't closed yet."

"Oh, come on!"

"Maybe the bomber was an *Iranian* Jew." He tried to sound serious.

She pointed at him. "Welsher."

"Okay, okay." He held up his palms. "Let's order."

"I'm not really hungry."

"Jesus!" He rolled his eyes in mock disgust.

Ruth laughed. "Tell you what. Another drink, then we'll pick a place. A different place."

"Fair." O'Donovan signaled the waitress and pointed at the empty glasses.

The Grill was filling to capacity as hungry shoppers came in off the street. A line of chattering New Yorkers hauling bags of wrapped gifts had formed at the maitre d's station, some begrudgingly being siphoned off to the lower dining level. A medley of old Perry Como carols drifted over from the bar, and the waitress deposited two more drinks along with a check, a suggestion to either order dinner or make way.

O'Donovan raised his fresh drink. "Merry Christmas."

"Happy Chanukah," Ruth countered as they touched glasses. "We're a little early, though, I think."

"It gets worse every year," said O'Donovan. "Someday we'll be singing 'We Three Kings' in July."

"In my country, we haven't commercialized Chanukah yet."

"As it should be."

"No admiration, please. Plenty of us picnic at the beach on Yom Kippur."

"Well, us Catholics appreciate creative sacrilege."

"I was just a kid in 1973," Ruth remembered. "On that Yom Kippur, half the country was in synagogue. The Arabs were smart, launched an attack, and by evening the whole army had gone from prayer to slaughter." She shrugged. "Gives you kind of a 'fuck you' attitude toward God."

"Careful, lady," O'Donovan warned.

"Why?" she scoffed. "What can he do? Send me to Lebanon?"

O'Donovan chuckled. Jerry Binder often used the same expression, with Vietnam as the tag.

"So, Michael." Ruth looked at him with an impish expression.

"Yes?" He shifted in his chair, ready to parry a coming barb.

"Got a cigarette?"

With some relief, he fished into the pocket of his baseball jacket. "Just a Camel."

"A camel will do when a Mercedes will not."

"Come again?"

"Expression from home." She accepted a light, and O'Donovan took one for himself. "Did you think I was going to ask something personal?"

"Doesn't scare me."

"How's your sex life?"

The detective coughed. He prolonged it a bit while he stalled for time, and Ruth grinned.

"Sorry, but I did warn you yesterday," she said.

"Yeah, I know. Blunt as a ball-peen hammer."

"A what?"

"It's a tool." He was about to describe the shape, then dropped his hands. "Not important."

"I will withdraw the question."

"No, it's okay." If she wanted to bring up the subject, he was not going to run from it. "My sex life." He pondered for a moment. "I'd describe it as . . . festive."

"Festive?" She widened her eyes, imagining costumed orgies.

"Yeah. I usually get lucky on major holidays."

Ruth laughed, impressed by his modesty. She was certain he could do much better than the rare tryst.

"And yours?" O'Donovan asked, fully expecting her to unfairly claim, *None of your damned business.*

"Mine?" She leaned on an elbow and placed her chin in her palm. "I would describe it as *selective.*"

O'Donovan nodded, avoiding her eyes while they smoked. Selective. What did that mean? Was she saying that he might be one of the few, or that he should not get his hopes up?

"Let's change the subject," said Ruth.

"Okay," he quickly agreed.

"Let's talk about your army career."

The optimism faded from his face. "Maybe we should go back to sex."

"Later. First we'll exchange some army lies."

O'Donovan looked at his hands. "Do we have to?"

"I think so."

He knew what she meant. The military was so obviously a large part of his history, his character, and hers as well, that they were not going to get very far by skirting the issue. He glanced at the nearby tables, then pulled his chair closer, while Ruth, who had been swaddled in such behaviors, leaned in as well.

"I was nineteen when I volunteered for the Eighty-second Airborne Division," he began, "twenty when I got into Special Forces. . . ."

He glided quickly over the mundane aspects of army life, for Ruth had surely undergone a similar experience. Yet when he returned once again, as he had on so many tortured nights in his bed, to that hellish twilight on the salt flats of Desert One, the Story emerged as it never had before. His confession bolted unbridled, in streams of repressed smells and images, unrelated bits he sensed would be understood as no priest or army comrade had ever done. Before, he had always censored his pain. Yet here, confronted by a woman who hailed from a warrior tribe, he surrendered to a fantasy that God had finally sent a battle-scarred angel who could understand and perhaps absolve him. He would tell it all at last.

Some time later, he finished his story, his hands still, the cigarette a gray snake of brittle ash. Now Ruth's fingers rested on *his* forearm.

"It was cruel, Michael," she said gently.

"Yeah," he whispered.

"I have heard this story before."

"Well, it's no secret."

"No. I mean that I have *heard* it. AMAN intercepted all of the transmissions from the Iranian desert that night. I wasn't in the army yet, but I've heard the tapes. It was terrible."

He looked at her, his eyes narrowing as he thought to close the window to his soul.

"Are you ashamed, Michael?" she asked. Her face was very close.

"No," he began to lie. Then, "Yes. Or at least I was. For a long time. Now I don't know. Bitter, I guess."

"Sad," she ventured.

He nodded. She moved her hand along his arm until she covered his fingers.

"Can I tell you something?" she asked, not really seeking permission. "You are part of an outlaw class in your society. Maybe the Gulf War will change that, I don't know. But your experience is still a lonely one here, so this thing has become a shameful secret to you." Her other hand joined the first, to hold him as she continued. "I was an intelligence officer. I worked in The Hole at Tel Aviv headquarters, monitoring mission progress. We rarely tell the world about our failures, but for every Entebbe I listened to, there were three small disasters. For every supercommando raid splashed across the world headlines, I heard half a dozen fiascoes."

O'Donovan watched her eyes as they glistened, felt the warmth of her hands as she went on.

"That sickening calm of the commanders while they start off, and then the noise, the gunfire, the confusion. I've wanted to cover my ears, to scream, to run from the damn room. Right out of the army. Right out of the country. I've heard the helicopters, the kid lieutenants crying, sergeants yelling for medevacs while their soldiers bled to death. And sometimes, when I couldn't take it anymore, when I felt like some voyeuristic whore down there in my antiseptic hole, I'd grab some other pathetic officer and we'd rush to the hospital, to meet the wounded, carry them from the choppers just so we wouldn't go stark raving insane."

A tear left her right eye, and she made no move to stop it as the bead dropped from her cheek and stained the blue silk above her breast. He continued to stare at her, immobilized.

"You're not alone in this world, Michael." She slowly wagged her head from side to side. "You simply haven't met all of your soul mates." Then she blinked, released his hands, wiped her face with her fingers, and took a long pull from her drink.

They sat inside a private silence for a while, watching the scurry of the waiters, listening to the ring of silverware, the release of laughter held in check throughout an urban workday. O'Donovan experienced a wave of relief. He did not have to keep his secrets locked away, unshared for fear of judgment. There were others out there, women who would *not* be frightened by his dreams, for they had night-mares of their own. A life with someone like her would begin on a different plateau. How wonderful, he thought, to be free to fall into a somber mood of memory. "What's up?" she would ask. "Just Iran," he would answer. She would nod in understanding, maybe kiss him with her beautiful mouth. "I know," she would say. "I know."

Then all at once that fantasy was replaced by melancholy, as he realized that here no paths could lead to that Utopia. Her interest in him was surely fleeting, and probably her presence in New York as well. Her permanent satisfaction here was about as likely as his finding happiness in a Bedouin encampment. A love affair with her would be like a cruise ship romance: all-encompassing, while the band played and the moonlight sparkled on the sea. Then, speared by reality in the harsh light of dry land. *Ruth O'Donovan.* He shook his head. He might as well be falling for a Martian girl.

"Would you like to talk about your father?" he offered, searching for a subject to kill the mood of intimacy.

Ruth looked at him and raised an eyebrow. "Or how about bleeding ulcers?"

"No, really," said Mike.

"No." She shook her head. "Really."

"Okay."

"I'll just work myself up."

"Sure."

She sighed. "But maybe I need to get past that." She crossed her arms. "He wasn't home a lot. But like lots of Israeli kids, we weren't special. I have two brothers. They're in the service now." She picked up her handbag, found a tissue, swiped at her nose, and then crumpled it into a ball. "When he *was* home, he acted like any other father with a crazy work schedule. He never talked about it, as if he was just a dentist or something. *Aw, just another wisdom tooth, kids.*" She turned toward O'Donovan, closing her fists. "But he wasn't a dentist, or a lawyer, or a bus driver. We *knew* what he did, and he wouldn't share it. He couldn't, but it still hurt. Me, at least." She waved a hand and frowned. "Silly childhood psychosis."

"Your trouble isn't trivial," said O'Donovan, "just because you know what it's called."

Ruth made to answer, then stopped herself, thinking that no *shagitz* had the right to be this stunning, this smart, with a heart so large, shoulders like those, eyes so blue. How dare he have the audacity to become more in these few minutes than the promise of a night or two of amusement? Where the hell could they ever hope to go with this thing?

She reached out with her thumb and finger and gently gripped his chin, feeling the soft sand of his shave. "Remember this, Michael," she whispered, with the intensity of a demanded oath. "Wherever you are, whenever it happens, with whatever woman you have them. Be first for your children."

"If it happens," he agreed, his lips barely moving.

"It will. Make a pledge."

"I promise." He reached up and touched the wrist that hovered near his throat. "If you'll make one too."

"What?"

"That your daughters, if they're like you . . . won't touch men like me and then walk away."

It took her a second, but then she understood. She raised herself from her chair and bent forward. She hesitated when her mouth was very close to his, their gazes wide as their pulses began to tremble, and then he met her. Their eyes closed and they touched their lips together, sighing gently into each other, a sweet taste of smoke and ice, sealed by incredibly soft heat.

Ruth slowly pulled away, her hair trailing from his cheek as she sat. His eyes were still closed, and she watched expectantly as they fluttered open. He took a long breath, placed his right hand over his heart, and mouthed something.

She leaned forward. "Pardon me?"

"Call nine-one-one," he repeated as he held his chest. Then he grinned through his blush.

She smiled back. "I'll race you to the ambulance."

"Ahem."

They turned to the sound of apologetic throat-clearing. The maître d', a young man wearing an olive double-breasted suit and a short brown ponytail, was standing at a tactful distance. He smiled down at them.

"Evening, folks."

They nodded.

"If you'd care to order dinner, could I impose upon you and offer a table for two?" He gestured across the room. Mike and Ruth looked at one another, each trying to read the other's eyes. "Or maybe if you'd just like another drink,

I could suggest the bar? Next round on the house." He was still smiling, even though they were becoming a financial liability.

O'Donovan could have flashed his badge, and the man would have gone away. But his father had taught him that such behavior was what made the public eternally suspicious of policemen.

He handed the maître d' enough cash to cover the tip as well.

"Thanks so much," the young man oozed as he withdrew.

"Happy holidays," said O'Donovan.

"Do you have another place in mind?" Ruth asked.

"Not really. How's your appetite?"

She looked up at the ceiling. "Maybe a little aroused."

"Little Italy?"

"Kind of far." Her face took on an attempt at innocence. "Tell you what. Even though you lost, I won't make you cook."

"Wise choice."

"There's a good Chinese place on the Upper West Side."

"Great."

They both stood, buttoning their coats, pulling on their gloves. Ruth took his elbow and looked up at him.

"I live nearby," she said. "We could take it out."

"To your place?" He wanted to be sure, make no clumsy assumptions.

"I could show you my database files."

He grinned at her. "The modern equivalent of 'etchings'?"

"I don't know what you mean."

"I'll explain it later."

"Fine," she said. "Lay on, Macduff."

"Hey! You're quoting the Bard!"

"I'm a college girl."

They walked from the Grill, arms locked and bodies close together.

At the far end of the Grill's oval bar, a small man perched on a stool, the fingers of one hand playing over his upper lip, as if reading Braille across the freshly shaved skin. It was a strange sensation for Fouad, as he had always worn a full black beard since adolescence. Yet the mission demanded an unpious naked face, and he only hoped that he would be forgiven.

As he watched the tall American and the striking Jewess embracing immodestly and making for the door, one might have thought that the discomfort of a fever caused his next action. He glanced down into the well of the lower-level dining area, raised an icy green bottle of O'Doul's nonalcoholic beer, and rolled it across his forehead.

Ten feet below and thirty feet away, a trio of diners sat at a corner banquette. The wide backs of two well-dressed men were exposed to the crowd, while across from them a woman appeared to be enjoying the attentions of her "double date." Her hair was long and straight, black as Siberian mink fur, with a crop of bangs cut low across coal eyebrows. She wore tinted, blue-framed glasses above a carefully painted maroon mouth. Her dress was a thick gray knit, with a hem to her crossed ankles.

The woman held a long white cigarette, whose glowing tip made little arcs as she chatted animatedly, smiled at her escorts, and sipped from a wineglass. Nothing in her posture indicated that she had seen Fouad's gesture from the bar, although just afterward, she toyed briefly with a gold electronic lighter, and ignited its flame twice.

Fouad dropped a ten onto the bar, slid quickly from his stool, and hurried after the couple. He could see them through the hotel's glass facade, getting into one of the cabs at the sidewalk. That was fine. He would be inside Muhammed's follow car before the man panicked and took off without him.

The woman at the banquette reached for her purse. She extracted a digital beeper, switched off the volume, and propped it up so she would be able to clearly see the liquid crystal readout.

She looked at the two large young men and almost laughed, for they still maintained those fixed silly smiles with which they had been responding to her meaningless chatter for nearly an hour. One of them had just received a large platter of chicken salad, the other a dish of pesto pasta. Yet both meals remained untouched.

"Now we wait," said Martina. The two men looked at her, immobile. "Eat your food."

They rolled their muscular shoulders and bent gratefully to the task, as if she had been starving them.

"Take your time," Martina chided, and they slowed the rapid shoveling of their food. She thought of how the Central Intelligence Agency had acronymed her operators as HOGs, and for a moment she wondered if the Americans had somehow been privy to their eating habits. Then she smiled again as she envisioned the policeman who had chased her, and the daughter of Benjamin Baum.

No need to hurry, she mused silently. *Those two will dance before they fuck.*

Ruth and Mike had not, in fact, danced. Yet they had not hurried, either.

In the long taxi ride northward, their conversation diminished as they approached Ruth's neighborhood, the anticipation drawing each of them privately inward. They stopped at the Chinese restaurant on Broadway, a Cantonese place, called Ping Tung, and as they waited for their order they stood before a large aquarium, staring at a menagerie of bulbous-eyed goldfish, neither of them really thinking about ocean life.

They walked to Ruth's apartment, hunched against the crosstown wind, arms unlinked now, with Mike carrying the brown shopping bag. Number 550 was a large old building without a doorman, and Ruth, hugging a pair of soda bottles, found her keys and shouldered open the heavy door. They rode the old broom-closet elevator to the third floor.

Her apartment, at the end of a long hallway, brought shudders of relief. Its spitting and creaking radiators had filled the modest space with warmth, and as Mike stripped off his jacket he was struck by the resemblance to his own place, twenty blocks south. The paint was the same, layers upon layers of that beige cream, as if all Manhattan landlords filled their buckets from a communal vat. A large Persian carpet supported modern yet unmatching furniture in the living room. Above a small tan couch, a large aerial photograph of Jerusalem was framed under glass. A blond coffee table was nearly obscured by psychology texts and loose papers. Six earthenware urns held bouquets of dried flowers and thistles, as if no one had the time or inclination to water here.

Mike looked across the narrow salon to its far end, where a pair of open doors revealed small separate bedrooms.

"Got a roommate?"

"In name only," said Ruth as she hung their jackets and recovered the bag from Mike's hands.

"Where is she? Or *he*?"

"*She* is temporarily absent."

She pulled the chain of a standing lamp and walked toward an archway leading to a kitchen alcove. "She's in love."

"Do you like her?"

"Like her?" She stopped before entering the kitchen, frowned, and turned, searching for something. "She's funny, accommodating, Jewish, and absent. If I was gay, I'd marry her."

He smiled as he watched her focus on the coffee table. She walked to it, lifted a foot, and in one deft motion swept all her books and papers onto the floor. She placed the bag on the table, brushed her hands together, and grinned at him.

"Dinner is served," she said grandly.

"Too fussy for me." He moved to the couch. "I like it informal."

"Speaking of which," said Ruth as she looked down at her skirt, "I'm changing. Be right back."

As Mike pulled the contents from the oil-stained bag, Ruth reemerged from her bedroom sporting blue jeans and a gray Columbia sweatshirt. She was barefoot. To him, she could not have looked sexier had she been wearing a silk bikini set from Victoria's Secret.

She turned on a small television and they sat together on the couch, watching a local news report as they demonstrated their lack of chopstick dexterity. Though barely four days old, the bombing at the Israeli Consulate had been relegated to third tier, after the latest White House link to Iran-contra, and a more regional flap over the mayor's tennis vacations. There was no mention of last evening's shootout on the Upper East Side. No wounds, no news. Gabe Pressman, whom Ruth liked very much, finally raised the bombing issue. But he was inclined to interview another journalist, Robert I. Friedman of *The Village Voice*, whom Ruth despised for his career built on self-hating exposés. Friedman declared that the bombing was the work of Kahane-following fanatical Jews, and Ruth booed him roundly.

She tasted Mike's beef and snow peas and said, "*Fooyah!*" He countered by trying her triple-starred lobster, and promptly gulped half a glass of soda.

She turned off the television and warmed up the compact disc player, inserting a medley of nostalgic Israeli folk songs rendered by Arik Einshtein. When a languid wartime longing for a girl and home played in the background, Ruth translated for Mike.

> *I have a girl named Ruti,*
> *Who waits for me on those shores . . .*

There were no further confessions of painful army histories. They shared some simple childhood experiences, searching for similarities that really were not there, smiling at the images of each other in those awkward, helpless years of prepubescent frustrations, schoolings, summer camps, discoveries. And when they reached the teenage years, where both had certainly been preoccupied with the wonders of the opposite gender, they fell to silence.

"How about some mud?" Ruth said when they had finished the meal.

"Is that an offer for a facial or a wrestling match?"

"Coffee. Turkish style."

"You cook?"

"Let's not exaggerate."

She moved to the kitchen, and Mike was content to sit on the couch, listening to the guitars and the soft melodies sung in her language. The singer's voice was warm, the tones like Italian or Greek. Mike had fully expected the disconsolate whines of Arabic ouds, and he was somehow ashamed. He knew that his ignorance could not be remedied in an evening.

He watched Ruth's back through the archway as she stood before the stove, her hair thrown back over her shoulder, repeatedly lifting the conical brass pot as she brought the brew to the boil and then snatched it away before it overflowed. When she inserted a spoon into the *finjon* and began to stir, and her bottom swayed like an orchestra conductor's, he had to look away.

They were seated together again, sipping the sweet dark "mud," when she pointed across the room.

"There's my monster."

Mike had not really noticed the computer before. Such devices had become as mundane as bathroom commodes. It sat on a small desk tucked beneath an H-shaped bookcase, which looked as if it might buckle under its burden of volumes.

Ruth walked to it, pulled out a caster chair, and turned on the cpu. Then she stretched her fingers like a pianist and began to play.

"I'll call up the juicy stuff," she said as she waited for the computer to awaken. *How long is it going to take him?* She tapped on the rim of the keyboard. *I already kissed him once, and I'm not going to do it again.* "I use D-Base Three, but I'd like to upgrade." *If he was Israeli, we never would have made it to the food,* she complained to herself. "I really need a faster machine." *On the other hand, if he were Israeli, it would have been over in ten minutes and he'd be complaining about the cold food now.* "Here we go. Let's look for Mistress Klump." She began to type instructions: Search for Terror; Change Directory to German; Change Directory to RAF. *Maybe it's the garlic.* She ran her tongue across her teeth, mistyped a word, slapped the keyboard, and began again. *Come on, Michael. Say something. Do something, or I'll pack you off!*

"It's in Hebrew, for God's sake."

Ruth stiffened. He was standing behind her. She could feel his body brushing her back, his voice vibrating down through the top of her head.

"Not for God's sake," she said. "For security."

"Well, I can't read it." His fingers came to rest on her shoulder.

"I can translate." Her voice emerged in a thick whisper. *Careful what you wish for,* she warned herself now, a small alarm spreading heat to her face even as she wished more fervently. "This stuff is sensitive, you know."

She felt the hair being swept gently back from her right shoulder, and then his fingers touched her throat, moving to her chin. She tilted her head back and looked up.

"So are you," Mike whispered as he bent his head. "Despite the facade."

And then he kissed her.

At first their mouths were tentative, a light touch without hunger, without movement. Then Ruth pressed her bare feet to the floor, and as the chair turned, their faces swept around, their lips parted, they stole a glance into each other's eyes, and joined again. She reached up to his face and held it to her own as he knelt between her knees.

Their mouths could not be stopped now, their fingers at each other's faces, eyes, hair. Ruth opened her lips and sank into a dream of tastes, a flood of warm swirls, the food, the coffee, the sweet liquids of his mouth. She held the back of his head and strove to envelop him, and then she slid away and kissed his eyes, his brows, his hair, as his lips found her throat and they slipped to the floor.

He rolled onto his back and she came with him, her hair cascading over his face as she gripped his waist with her thighs and bent to him again. He was conscious of the blood rising in his groin, but it was her face, that face that he longed for, had wanted to touch from the second he first saw it. And now he was free, released at last from a prison of propriety, and as they kissed again he touched her cheeks, swept the backs of his fingers across her neck. And then he gripped her shoulders and gently pushed her away, because he had to see her eyes again.

She opened them. They were even bluer than before, wide with her breathing. She sat up and swept her hair up and back with a forearm, and they both shuddered for a moment.

"You're warm," Ruth decided hoarsely. She reached down to his waist, and he arched as she pulled the turtleneck over his head in one determined sweep. Then she looked down at the red-blond hair of his chest.

"So are you," he said, and they both reached for the hem of her sweatshirt.

She sat up straight again. She was wearing a modest white brassiere, yet such was her figure that no undergarment had a hope of stemming desire.

"Oh, Lord," Mike whispered as he looked at her, wild strands of hair across her flushed face, her wide navel fluttering with the sprint of her heart above his belt buckle.

He wanted to wait, to please her, to take his time. As long as it would take her to be ready, to signal him, to draw him into her. It would be her decision. He wanted to give her patience, gentleness, the conviction that he was there for her first, and for himself only after that.

It was as if she read his mind.

"I know who you are, Michael O'Donovan," she said. "What kind of man you are." She kissed him softly. "Don't show me your patience. I want you *now*."

Crushing his mouth with her own, she reached up behind her back with one hand, and the white cotton fell away. The rest of their clothes came off without their lips ever separating. Their electrified skin suddenly encountered the bristle of the carpet, and all at once Ruth rose, took his hand, and walked quickly to her bedroom. She flicked off the light as she turned to catch him.

They stood beside the bed for a moment, lips more gently together again. Then they fell onto Ruth's white sheets like trapeze lovers drifting onto a net, and after a moment they both arched and gasped as they were joined in a stunning relief of plunging heat.

When it was over, so quickly that it had seemed like a lightning strike, they lay there bathed in a sheen, their limbs entwined as they listened to the echoes of their ragged lungs inside the small bedchamber. Her damp hair was draped across his neck and shoulders, and as they peered through the dark at each other's faces, each doubted that the other could possibly have climaxed in so short a time. It had been like a traffic accident, a volatile burst of energy leaving only fleeting images of the event, the reverberations of the physical impact, and a flood of adrenaline.

As with all first-time lovers, the tension had been slain, the doubts dispersed. Now they could take their time and drive anticipation back to its peak.

They began once more, with light touches, kisses that drifted from their joined mouths to find and taste the unlearned planes of their bodies. After a long while, their mouths met again. Ruth slithered above Mike, her breasts brushing his chest as she began slowly to rock, then she groaned as she swept him up and posted like a determined equestrian. He held her face, kissed her chest, watched her, knowing that he could give her what she wanted. Her eyes squeezed shut, her long eyebrows nearly met as a deep crevasse formed above her nose, and she began to whisper in Hebrew as her hair whipped.

"*An ba'a. Ani ba'a.*"

She threw her head back and her arms went stiff as stone, and as she trembled there, Mike suddenly heard an echo to her ecstasy.

It was another cry. Similar, yet without pleasure. The long pleas of a woman's voice. But it came from outside, from the hallway beyond the apartment door. He pulled Ruth down to him and hugged her hard, and as she began to speak, he said, "Shhh."

She lifted her head to listen. "I hear it too," she whispered.

They lay still as hunters in the undergrowth. It came again, a thin female cry, a long stream of "Ohs," each one punctuated by a small bang, as whoever was out there pounded weakly on Ruth's door.

She pushed herself up onto her hands. "*Yo*," she whispered, an Israeli exclamation of discovery. "Maybe it's Lisa."

She sprang off him and bolted to her bedroom door, yanking a white terry-cloth robe from its peg. Quickly she slipped into it and tied the belt at her waist as Mike lifted up on his elbows.

"Doesn't she have a key?" he asked, assuming correctly that Lisa was Ruth's "perfect" roommate. It struck him as more than odd that the woman would reappear near midnight, bleating outside her own apartment.

Yet Ruth was already striding for the door, perhaps bolstered by the presence of "her" detective. Mike was not so reassured, and as he watched her peer briefly through the peephole and quickly turn her dead bolt, he leapt from the bed and struggled into his underwear, thinking of the backup .38 in his jacket pocket.

The hallway light spilled into the living room, and for a moment, before Ruth sprang forward and knelt, he could see the small soles of a woman's sneakers. The scuffed cleats were punctuations to a curled-up fetal ball, a body writhing in pain.

He was shamed by his momentary suspicion. Striding across the carpet, he could see the entire length of the corridor. Not a single door had opened. *New Yorkers*, he thought with disgust.

As he reached the doorway, seeing Ruth kneeling over the sufferer, he felt a swell of pride rise in his chest. A surprising wave of elation brought a smile to his face, a conviction that this night was the beginning of something wonderful.

He stepped through the doorframe, and a ten-inch iron bar blurred from the left and cracked against the bridge of his nose. He actually heard the ring of metal against his bone, the massive explosion inside his head as a flash of yellow lightning burst behind his eyelids. His hands flew out as he reeled backward, and as his wrists smacked the doorframe he reflexively gripped for a hold. Yet another blow came from the right: a fist, a foot, the butt of a brute head—he would never know, for the impact to his solar plexus sent him hurtling. Now another blow as his spine met the floor, yet another as his head bounced. He opened his mouth to yell Ruth's name, but no breath remained in his lungs, and his naked arms were gripped, his shoulders pulled to the nauseating tear of muscle, and he was dragged.

Ruth barely had the time to turn her head.

She had been trying gently to uncurl the groaning woman, to examine her face huddled behind an arm. Reaching out, she had stroked the tangle of black hair, for she could see the smear of blood below her nose. The pathetic figure was wearing a stained gray coverall and a purple ski cap.

Ruth was whispering, "It's all right. We'll get an ambulance," when she heard the rush of clothing behind her and a smacking blow that snapped her head around. Seeing the two huge men pummeling Mike, she froze for just a split second, then opened her mouth to scream.

All that emerged was a choking gasp as a hand locked around her throat. She twisted back toward the prone woman, while her eyes bulged and the tears welled, and she felt herself being lifted, her hands scratching and pummeling at the viselike wrist.

Martina's thumb was embedded so deeply in the soft flesh that no sound at all escaped Ruth's gaping mouth. She flailed with her arms, tried to kick out with her feet, but Martina, her teeth set in a death's-head grimace, lifted her and propelled her backward toward the open door.

Ruth's fright flooded into panic, yet she managed to lock her fingers on a clump of the woman's hair, and for a split second she had hope as she yanked with every vestige of her strength. But the hair and the hat came away, and a gurgling, silent cry leapt from her, for at the root of that powerful arm, the face from the German prison photo grinned wickedly.

Martina pushed Ruth's failing form easily into the apartment now. She kicked the door closed with her foot, raised her free hand, and struck down with a glass syringe, plunging the needle through Ruth's robe and into the flesh below her collarbone.

It was not the drug that had an instantaneous effect.

Ruth fainted from the horror.

Chapter 11: Brooklyn

The polished wooden beads of a *masbaha* clicked together inside Mussa Hawatmeh's hand, the muted chatter of the rosary like a string of worries being counted on the abacus of a doubtful Oriental accountant. He was no more cognizant of his fingers fiddling with the spheres than he was of his own bare footfalls across the floor, the bristle of the carpet between his toes, or the Persian pattern as it blurred in his vision and he strove with all his will to forgo another glance at his wristwatch.

He reckoned that in all the violent seasons of his life, no lethal device had ever so unnerved him as this small clock at the end of his arm, in the midst of this endless night. The tires of an automobile whispered from the street, and for a moment he paused, gripped the beads, raised his head, and listened. Yet the watery light rippled quickly across the curtained windows, and hope faded.

Mussa sighed and resumed pacing his cage, the long sitting room of a dilapidated house at the corner of Carlton and De Kalb in the Fort Greene section of Brooklyn. It was one of many such neglected homes, abandoned by owners who had watched the crime encroach upon their lives and fled to sunny parcels of orange groves and armadillos. The elderly couple who had gratefully accepted six months' rental in advance no longer viewed their property the way Martina Klump did—as a safe house.

The four stories of chipped red brick and gabled roofs sat upon a raised copse of frozen and neglected gardens, the image of a haunted lair enhanced by a black ironwork fence. The isolation had attracted Martina, for she was unconcerned by the plague of roaming hooligans, confident that potential vandals would test her men only once. Instead, it was the curiosity of neighbors that could thwart her, and to that end the massive, bolted driveway gate had sealed her choice. The macadam curved from the side street into a large two-car garage, from which a walled-in portico led to the kitchen. If one was careful, the troupe of a small circus could reside here, with no comings or goings observed except for the occasional movement of vehicles.

Although their time in residence was to be very short, Martina had instructed that no member of Yadd Allah was to use the front door of the house. That privilege was reserved for herself, as resident of lease, and Fouad and Iyad, who always entered and exited in painters' coveralls. A sign announcing *Renovations by McFee and Sons* had been posted on the frosted weed crop, and a thick sandwich of plywood was propped against the front porch next to a pile of two-by-fours. All of this would serve to cover the occasional buzz of saws from inside and the ring of hammer heads on steel.

For the sake of cover and camouflage, it might have seemed a wiser choice to set up camp in the Moslem enclave of Jersey City or among the pita and *halâwi* merchants of Atlantic Avenue, where a few more Levantine faces would blend like pebbles in a rock garden. Yet those neighborhoods were rife with FBI watchers and Mossad informants, while here in this forgotten strip of Brooklyn, Martina and her HOGs would remain unnoticed. She had also chosen the secluded outpost for psychological reasons, wanting her men to remain alert in their discomfort, their senses undulled by familiar sounds, smells, or tastes. She wanted them sharp as commandos behind enemy lines, reflexes wound to a high pitch in isolation.

Thus far, she had been correct. No breach of privacy had sent them scurrying, no friendly neighbor or beat policeman with a curious nose. Now just a single hour remained, and the undisturbed preparations for *Unternehmen Skorpion*—Operation Skorpion—boded well for its success. However, Mussa was not heartened by the progress, for the Scorpion herself was late.

He succumbed to his nerves and raised his wrist, staring at the steel face of his watch. Five minutes past two. In the same hand he held a short-range Motorola, and he pressed the transmit button and whispered.

"*Ashma kân?*"

He looked up at the high ceiling, trying to discern on which floor Muhammed paced, peering from the darkened windows. After a moment, the walkie-talkie crackled.

"*Mâshi.* Nothing."

Mussa frowned and looked around his jail, thinking that at worst, Martina's failure to appear would mean a closure of this verse, the freedom to abandon and "disinfect," each man to make his own way home. If that was God's will, they would someday reconvene on a hill in Lebanon to ponder the "what if"s. And if she had been taken, then it was not for lack of warnings on his part, her vengeful digressions having led her into ambushes he could not describe vividly enough to frighten her. And no failure could be placed at the pious feet of Yadd Allah, for despite her driving them like exhausted cattle, they had accomplished each and every task in perfect detail.

He watched them proudly now as they moved quickly, shadows laboring in silence. In the center of the sitting room sat a long dining table, upon which the black dress blazer of a naval officer gleamed beneath an aluminum reflector. Nabil, the group's technician, who held degrees from Cairo University, was wearing jeweler's spectacles and inspecting a complex set of wiring and antennae sewn into the jacket lining. His small body darted from the uniform to an open black attaché case, its exposed false bottom lined with a slab of dull yellowish clay. Next to the attaché lay a modified electronic address book, from which two short wires led to a small bulb. Nabil flitted back to the uniform, squeezed something with his fingers, and watched as the bulb glowed brightly and burned out with a pop.

The engineer nodded, switched off the palm computer, secured its button with electrical tape, and carefully replaced the bulb with a pair of small brass tubes. Then he gently buried the tubes in the clay, replaced the false bottom of the case, and folded the wires, laying the computer inside. A sheaf of papers and a text on U.S. naval operations joined the lot, and he closed the case and snapped the catches.

He peered up at Mussa over the tops of his spectacles, and as he pointed with one finger at the case, with another he wagged the warning *Be very careful, my friend*. Although the device was now disarmed, once Mussa threw the computer's switch, he would be carrying his own death at the end of his arm.

Mussa turned to where Salim, Ali, Jaweed, and Yaccub knelt on the floor of the sitting room beside a gleaming mahogany coffin. The men wore olive-drab T-shirts and camouflaged fatigue trousers, but they had not donned their boots, for they had yet to pray. Their hair was cropped, their beards gone. The fair-complexioned Ali had dyed his crew cut to wheat blond. Jaweed was born of a half-Circassian father, and his red hair and freckled face would have made an O'Malley proud. The other men looked like muscular American boys of Italian or Puerto Rican descent.

Their breaths clouded the chill air as they bound and tagged folded bundles of black mourning suits, each identified by number to avoid a mixup. Along the wall of aging flowered paper, six M-16A1 rifles were racked, butts to the floor, each flash suppressor capped by a mottled Marine fatigue hat, each butt stock taped with two magazines of 5.56 mm ammunition. Nearby, six Motorolas identical to Mussa's sat in recharging cuffs.

In America, you can buy an army, Mussa thought with a blend of cynicism and gratitude. *But you can't buy this.* He turned to a pair of carpenter's horses supporting a long slab of plywood, which was covered in thin mattress foam and tailored with billows of white nylon. In the middle of the slab lay a headless body, in fact a medical mannequin whose posterior half had been shaved off with a surgical bone cutter. This left the chest, abdomen, frontal thighs, shins, and the full feet and arms intact.

The body had been slipped into a white neoprene diving suit to give the "corpse" the feel of rigored flesh. It was now clothed in an ebony burial suit, the white-gloved hands lacing fingers across the chest, the polished shoes poking up from depressions. With the soft nylon caressing its sides and legs, the half-man offered a convincing illusion. Except for the final detail. Just above the empty collar, a cantaloupe-sized hole in the wood remained unfilled. It would be up to Iyad to provide that distasteful punctuation, and God help him if he failed.

The four "Marines" had laid their bundles in the bottom of the coffin, and now they walked to the slab, lifted it, and returned to the sarcophagus. They carefully lowered the "deceased," and his nylon quilt married perfectly to the coffin's lining.

The whine of a laser printer drew Mussa's focus, and he walked out through the archway of the sitting room, past a curved stairway, toward a rectangle of light. Inside a former sewing room, a tall and spindly boy named Fahmi sat before an IBM PS2 and a color Textronix printer, at each elbow a tilted drafting table. The worktops held reams of colored papers and purloined letterheads, but the bottles, brushes, and styluses of a classic forger were not in evidence, for Fahmi was a technical artist of the modern world.

Most of his works were now complete, creations that would prove their artistry by being glossed over as genuine. The license plates were nothing short of spectacular, alphanumeric portraits designed on graphical software. The letters and numbers appeared to be raised, for each character was shadowed. He had printed them on heavy plotter stock, trimmed and glued them to aluminum rectangles, applied three layers of clear lacquer, and finally smeared the finished products with dapplings of mud.

Mussa's naval credentials required no alterations, for they belonged to the genuine Lieutenant Rick Delgado. However, Fahmi had made good use of the officer's civilian documents as samples. There was now a driver's license and registration for the hearse, limousine, Ryder rental truck, and a late-model Chevrolet repainted as a navy staff car.

Re-creating the wallet documents carried by U.S. residents was not very difficult, for Americans laminated by habit and therefore the paper stocks did not have to match the originals precisely. Nearly every municipal seal was available to the American public through over-the-counter clip art, and the laser was sufficient even for the forgery of a coroner's death certificate.

The passports, however, were another matter altogether, for one could never underestimate the enthusiasm of a U.S. Customs inspector. To duplicate the various stocks, fibers, water seals, and infrared cues, most intelligence agencies employed a full "art department." Fahmi had neither the time nor the equipment for such a venture, so he had devised an alternate, albeit expensive plan for Yadd Allah's extraction from U.S. soil.

Over the course of the last month, they had arrived through New York and Miami in the prescribed manner of asylum seekers, using black market Afghan and Tunisian passports, which they promptly shredded into aircraft toilets. Each "refugee" had then walked happily past U.S. Immigration officials, clutching his signed promise to return for a hearing.

Fahmi, on the other hand, came through as a well-dressed French tourist, using the legitimate papers of his Parisian residence. Sewn into the lining of his down coat were twelve genuine blank Maltese passports, each gold seal of twin dolphins having enriched a corrupt minister from Valletta by five hundred pounds sterling. Every member of the group now carried one, complete with a U.S. entry stamp of Fahmi's design, in the jacket of the mourner's suit that was to be his escape garb.

Fahmi was grateful that he had overextended his budget and purchased an extra passport. For sure enough, Martina had found a need for it.

He was perspiring now, despite the chilled house, as time was very short. He wiped his fingers on his fatigue trousers and checked the freshly affixed photo of the young woman. Mussa had done well, using a telephoto until he obtained a full frontal image with the eyes focused directly on the lens. Now for the final detail. Fahmi printed a duplicate of the U.S. Customs and Immigration stamp for entry into Kennedy Airport, after having first reversed all of the courier letters and matched the red hue of the month. He quickly rolled a film of alcohol across the warm typeface, placed it facedown over a blank page in the passport, and rubbed briskly with a marble stone. When he peeled the plotting paper away, the positive image was indistinguishable from the worn metal stampers used by officials. He filled in the space above "date" with a black pen, then waved the little booklet in the air to dry it as he turned and grinned at Mussa.

Mussa bowed to his artisan, managed a deceptively calm smile, then walked back toward the foyer. He glanced again at his watch and winced. Two-twenty.

The atmosphere in the large house was strangely dormant. All of the windows were heavily draped and further sealed with black darkroom cloth, which prevented their work lights from stirring curiosity but also hushed the house's sounds to flat murmurs. The aluminum reflectors threw cones of yellow haze through which cigarette smoke twisted, and with the muted exhortations of Arabic as background, it all reminded Mussa of a Syrian field hospital, the kind of place for which he had no nostalgic longings.

He started when a finger touched his forearm, and he whirled to find Nabil holding the naval jacket like a manservant. Mussa grunted, then offered his arms, moving slowly with concern for Nabil's wiring. The engineer quickly enveloped him and closed the brass buttons.

"We are almost ready," Nabil murmured as he came up with a whisk broom and began to brush the blazer. "But again I must say, respectfully, that I believe we are more likely to martyr ourselves than to overcome a contingent of American Marines."

He lifted Mussa's left arm and bent it at the elbow, turning the wrist and folding the cuff back. A small metal ring, like the arming pin of a hand grenade, protruded from the lining and was held in place by stitches of thread. "Once you throw the calculator switch, Mussa," Nabil briefed in a cautionary tone, "the briefcase is armed. Then you must simply slip a finger inside the ring and pull very hard." He reached up and patted the left breast pocket of the tunic, where Mussa felt a slim metal box press against his chest. "A steel cable will release a spring switch on the transmitter. It is soldered there and cannot slip out, but should you somehow dislodge the ring *before* you arm the case, when you *do* switch on the calculator . . ." He stopped, shrugged, and looked up at the ceiling.

Mussa was not particularly alarmed, for he had full confidence in Nabil's failsafe abilities. He was more concerned with the engineer's preamble of doubts.

"You must have faith," he said, placing a hand on Nabil's shoulder. "With a bit of luck, the Americans are now focusing their protective efforts on Boston."

"If they found Iyad's decoy," said Nabil doubtfully as he plucked a wayward thread from the tunic.

"They did. And they must follow it up."

"But the young fool lost the motorcycle."

"Yes, but it will take time to trace it. And we will be gone."

"One way or another." Nabil smiled at his own gallows humor. Then his eyebrows drew together. "So where is she, Mussa? Why this digression of hers? I do not understand, and neither do the others."

Mussa looked over at the other men, who were systematically destroying remaining articles: mannequin parts, extra uniforms, and maps whose courses had been memorized.

"Leila has her reasons for following this path," he said, though he himself disagreed with many of her methods. "Besides, we cannot lose." He smiled down at the engineer. "If we martyr ourselves, we will be called to Paradise. If we succeed, the results are the same."

"*In sh'Allah*," said Nabil.

Mussa patted the engineer's cheek, a signal that the time for introspection was past. Nabil nodded, sighed, and returned to his work. There was a powder-blue baby carriage standing near his worktable, and he threaded a needle and bent into the pram.

Mussa looked down at his body, the sharp creases of the uniform and his incongruously bare feet below the trousers. In truth, he did not have much faith in his own words of reassurance. Martina's cold professionalism had been supplanted by something else, an obsession that seemed purely personal. She had some sort of need to avenge a past wrong, and her aplomb had been contaminated by the presence of this Israeli AMAN officer. Until the bombing at the consulate, she had never mentioned him to Mussa, and since he was privy to most of her history, this skeleton emerging from her closet unsettled him. He shook his head as he raised his watch once more. *Well*, he thought, *at least the cause is pure.* His eyes widened with alarm when he saw the time, and he snatched up the Motorola and was about to key the button when it crackled with Muhammed's voice.

"She is here!"

With a ragged exhalation of relief, Mussa strode to the dining table, picked up a Beretta 92-F, and held it behind his back—the arrival of a comrade could always be followed by that of the foe. The far kitchen door leading to the garage portico swung open, and she strode through the galley and into the salon, followed by the burly Youssef and Riyad.

For a moment the men froze as they stared at their lioness. She was every bit the American male: blond hair cropped and gelled against her skull, aviator glasses, and even a small mustache. She was wearing a New York Yankees baseball cap, a dark woolen jacket with leather arms, and a mechanic's coverall. Had she found herself aboard an aircraft carrier, Mussa was sure that no deck crew would have stopped her from taking off in a fighter plane.

She stood in the archway, then swept off her glasses and snapped, "*Zurück an die Arbeit!* Back to work!"

The men recovered from their brief lapse, their limbs moving in jerky haste as Martina growled again. "We have to be on the road. In thirty minutes!"

She removed the cap and came at Mussa, tearing off the mustache in a swift motion that made him wince. She stopped very close to his face, then retreated a full step and looked him over.

"Very nice." She spun him around like a head tailor examining the work of an apprentice. "Where are the shoes?"

"We were going to pray," said Mussa, facing her again.

"Pray in your heads. There isn't time."

She moved away, taking off the baseball jacket and dropping it to the floor as she found the marked bag that held her Marine uniform. No one but Mussa dared glance at her as she unzipped the coverall, stepped out of it wearing only a running bra and briefs, and began to don the fatigues.

She buttoned the fly of the trousers, frowning at the gap between her stomach and the waistband. The agitation of the past four days had stripped her of kilograms she could not afford to lose. When she tried to insert the tongue of her web belt through the brass buckle, her fingers foiled her. "*Scheißer*." She cursed herself until she finally succeeded, then yanked the belt so hard the cinching pained her.

She quickly pulled an olive T-shirt over her head, glanced at her watch, and tried to push the panic down. But they had so much to do yet, so far to go. She wanted desperately to be on the road, for she had no one stationed at the target area who could contact her with calming assurances. There would be one chance only. The timing had to be divine.

"Nabil, is Mussa's coat ready?" She sat down on the floor and pulled on a pair of green military socks.

"He is wearing it," Nabil replied, his voice muffled, as his head was still inside the baby pram.

"Just answer!" Martina snapped, betraying her agitation.

He looked up and blinked. "Yes, Leila."

"And the power sources?"

"Fresh batteries in everything."

"And it all works?"

"Perfectly," he declared without hesitation.

"*Gott helfe dir*," Martina warned, although she knew the threat was hollow. If Nabil's equipment failed, the reactions would be instantaneous and deadly, with far more impact than her wrath. God help *me*, she thought. She was used to working carefully, methodically, anticipating moves and countermoves. Yet now she felt trapped into discarding essential cautions.

"Where is Fahmi?" she asked as she laced a pair of Vietnam-style jungle boots.

"I am here," replied a voice from behind her.

"The documents?"

"Everything is done."

"Where?"

"The licenses and registrations are in the glove boxes. Passports are in the pockets of travel clothes."

"Mine?"

"In your coat. It hangs with the skirt and blouse on a peg in the truck."

"And the plates?"

"On all the vehicles, plus switch sets in the boots."

She turned her head and looked up at the spindly boy. His face exuded faith in his own professionalism, and she wanted to rise and hug him. Instead, she nodded her approval, even though she longed for a strong caress. Her insecurity could not be quelled by any checklist.

She was absolutely certain now that she had been set up as the patsy for the consular bombing and that Benjamin Baum played a pivotal role in that ambush party. Her mother's safety and future were in question, while with the Americans and Israelis snapping at her heels, there was little she could do to parry them. She had only one card up her sleeve, yet this ploy seemed so weak to her now, so desperate, that as she roughly pulled on a mottled fatigue jacket, she found herself struggling against a threat of tears. *No!* She stopped herself. *Never! I will not let them see that.*

"Mussa?" She controlled her tone. "The aircraft."

"Booked and waiting."

"And you are sure the package arrived?"

"I sent it by special courier. And since your 'friend' has headed for Washington, you can be sure he is not going to visit the monuments."

Martina stopped fiddling with her clothes and looked at him: so young, so brave, ready to follow his brother's fate. Wearing the stolen uniform of an American officer who had no doubt expired by now, an act that would certainly mean the electric chair if he was taken prisoner. She had to rise to that, to match that courage. If her mother's welfare was to be assured, she had to survive this episode *outside* prison walls. She had been paid, the funds committed. Her only choice was to execute Skorpion successfully and leave its victims cursing as Yadd Allah flew.

"And did you take the pearl?" Mussa asked, although he hoped Martina had abandoned this wild insurance policy.

"The jewel is on ice." For the first time since her arrival, something like a smile crossed her lips. At least that improvisation had worked sublimely.

Mussa frowned. "What do you mean, 'on ice'?"

"In the limousine."

"Alone?"

"Fouad is baby-sitting." She turned now to the men who had gathered near the rifles at the far end of the salon. As Youssef and Riyad had just arrived with her, Ali, Jaweed, Yaccub, and Salim were roughly dressing the two large men in their uniforms.

"Salim!" Martina shouted, and the tall Lebanese whirled his head around. "Why do you answer to that name?" she challenged, as he stared at her. "Are there American Marines named Salim?"

"No, ma'am," Salim drawled in a southern accent he had practiced while watching *Heartbreak Ridge*. "Thought you said *Gyrene*."

"And you?" She pointed at Yaccub, a wide, muscular twenty-six-year-old of Syrian birth.

"Fazio, Anthony. Three-two-five, seven-six, one-seven-oh-one." Yaccub spat the words in a hoarse growl. "Second platoon, Bravo Company, First of the Third. Security."

The rest of the men had drawn themselves to attention.

"You." She pointed at Jaweed. "Get a uniform and gear to our man in the limo."

"Yes, ma'am," said Jaweed as he scrambled for the bag with the name Foster marked on it.

"And I did not see the staff car." She wondered if there was something they had actually missed, one correction she might make to remind them of whose mind was superior.

"I parked it two blocks away," said Nabil.

Martina spun on him. "Two blocks away? Are you mad?"

"It was my decision alone," he declared bravely as he threw his shoulders back. "It is the one car that should not be seen pulling into or away from this house."

"And if it is *stolen?*" She advanced on him.

"There is a Club on the wheel."

"And if the tires are *slashed?*" She was nearly nose-to-nose with him now.

"Four spares in the garage." He did not dare move, a man with a tarantula crawling on his neck.

Martina looked at him, then reached up with her right hand and touched the side of his face. Mussa winced, expecting Nabil to receive a blow for his independent efforts, but Martina suddenly placed her lips to his cheek and kissed him. Then she pulled back and smiled, an expression matched by all those around her.

"There are no better," she whispered. She stopped herself from expressing further sentiments and turned away. "My first coat and the galoshes, please?"

"In a valise," said Nabil, still holding a flush of pride in his cheeks. "I will place it on the back seat of the staff car. I did not want it to be stolen."

"Of course," said Martina. She looked around the sitting room once more, and as her gaze fell on the gleaming coffin, and she slowly walked to it, the spines of her men stiffened. She raised the heavy lid, held it open for a moment, then gently closed it. She stood staring at the polished wood as she asked, almost inaudibly, "Where is the head?"

No one answered her, the house itself as silent as a grave. She raised a hand and slammed it onto the coffin.

"Where is the head?!" she shouted. "Where is it? And where is that idiot Iyad?"

"He will come." Mussa tried to assuage her. "He is late."

"Late?" She turned on Mussa. "*Late?*" She lifted her arms and then slapped the sides of her trousers. *That accursed simpleton,* she yelled inside her mind as she began to pace. *He meets us in the open, prattles in Arabic, nearly fucks up the decoy, then loses the bloody motorcycle.* She cursed herself for keeping him on after his first acts of buffoonery. Not only had he delivered a stolen bike to authorities who could run it down; now he had *failed* to deliver the key to Yadd Allah's escape. She put her fingers in her cropped hair and tried to think.

Just then, Muhammed's Motorola signaled Mussa's, the crackling whisper followed by an urgent rap on the front door. Mussa ran to it, turned the knob, and Iyad nearly fell into the foyer.

His hair was slick with rivulets of rain and sweat. He was breathing very hard, and though he surely felt the stab of Martina's glare, he avoided her eyes and pleaded to his comrades instead.

"I am sorry." Iyad shook his head and looked jerkily around. "I am sorry." He placed a black physician's satchel on the floor and stripped off his raincoat, revealing the green scrubs of a hospital orderly. "I could not do it." His hands trembled at the ends of his arms, the palms turned up in supplication. "The autopsy room was overflowing with doctors," he whined. "The morgue was like a train station." He fumbled in a breast pocket for a cigarette, then lit it with a wavering match, trying to delay the flurry of curses that he knew would shortly follow. "These New York drivers are worse than Lebanese. So many accidents tonight."

Martina walked to him, her eyes skipping over his worthless form as she focused on the black satchel and snatched it up. She opened it. It was gaping. Empty. Nothing.

She dropped the bag and turned away, her fists clutching at the air as if pumping the black balloons of blood pressure gauges. Her eyes flicked from the coffin to Nabil's worktable and his power saws, and on into the distant kitchen. There, on the Formica cutting surface embracing two large sinks, she could see the empty metal colander Nabil had welded to a small steel tripod. The mortician's kit was there, the makeup, the alcohol and embalming fluids. The macabre tools gleamed back at her in the harsh light of the galley.

If the coffin charade was not complete, the ruse imperfect in any way, they would never get off the ground. They would never leave the shores of America.

She looked at her watch, the surge of her heart seeming to race the second hand. *Just one miscalculation?* She begged the question silently as her chest constricted. *Just this one, and I am finished?*

"I am sorry, Leila."

Iyad's whisper seemed to drift above her head, yet she appeared utterly calm, unmoved. Her hands had fallen to her sides. She raised some fingers and dropped them again. *Could this be forgiveness?* the men wondered as they watched her. She glanced up at Muhammed, who had descended the stairs halfway and stood watching from behind the banister, like a child cowering while his parents fight.

She walked slowly to Nabil's worktable, where a large bottle of Gatorade sat open and nearly empty. She lifted it and looked through the plastic, then raised it to her mouth and finished off the green liquid.

She turned and walked back toward Iyad, the empty bottle swinging from her fingertips, the eyes of her men following her like swimmers wary of a shark. Yet a smile had returned to her mouth, something like a sympathetic squint to her eyes.

"I am sorry," Iyad said again, somehow more relaxed now that Martina had not in fact exploded. "But a human head?" He actually snickered. "It is just not so easy."

"It's all right," said Martina as she raised her right hand. "It's all right."

She stopped a meter from him, smiling still while he shrugged and looked down at his feet. Then she reached into her waistband, pulled out her P-38, inserted the barrel deep into the mouth of the Gatorade bottle, placed the plastic rump against his chest, and fired.

The report was not as loud as the stamping of her men's feet as they jumped back in shock. Iyad's body arched and planed through the air, his cigarette spun away like a pinwheel, and his arms windmilled for a second before he impacted with the wooden floor of the foyer. A surge of air rushed from his lungs, his legs twitched a few times, and then he was still.

"It's all right," Martina whispered once more as she tucked the pistol back into her trousers. She waved the small cloud of smoke aside with her hand.

"Yours will do nicely."

A deceptive winter sun dusted the Potomac with muted white light, bringing to Prince Georges County a false spring warmth that nearly fooled a few Maryland warblers into prematurely opening their throats. The early-morning sky framed the black river trees in blue, offering the illusion that somehow three more months of cold had been skipped, like scuffed tracks on an old gramophone record. Yet the southern oaks showed no buds, the breaths of grazing horses rose into the air like locomotive plumes, and no Marine on duty at the Naval Surface Weapons Center at Indian Head was beguiled into discarding woolen underwear in favor of summer issue.

Like most military dawns on the Maryland peninsula, this one was cold enough, and it kept the balance of NSWC personnel caressing coffee mugs inside their white wooden barracks. The center was not a typical naval base, being inhabited for the most part by scientists, engineers, and officers with armada combat ribbons. They lived a civilized existence, passing a modest workday in their laboratories, and at this hour the garden lanes and parking lots were silent. The sole breach of peace was committed by that branch of the populace whose job it was to keep the secrets secure. As always, the Marines were the first ones up.

Two vehicles, their engines coughing softly, rumbled slowly out through the triangular park that formed the gateway to the center. The transfer of a secret prototype from Indian Head to the proving launch near Dahlgren was supposed to be executed without fanfare, and the appearance of the lead vehicle certainly denuded the mission of its glamour. The Hum-Vee, a light armored all-purpose utility truck, still retained the sandy colors of its brief stint in Desert Storm. The Hummer had a penchant for barrel-rolling, and this one had done so off a high dune in Kuwait, its bumps and bruises giving it the air of a competitor in a military stock car race.

The squat Hum-Vee was followed by a more conventional deuce-and-a-half, a six-wheel, canvas-covered truck in woodland camouflage. The vehicles were occupied by six men of a rifle security company, plus one laboratory technician from the center. The lab man dozed in the Hum-Vee's cab, while the Marine escorts remained erect on their seats, drifting like dormant guard dogs, lids half closed, fingers twitching over their M-16s.

Lance Corporal Mark Milliken kept the boxy vehicle in second as he passed the large NSWC welcome sign, a bronze silhouette of a feathered tribal chief. He rolled to a stop next to the brick guardhouse, where a barrel-chested black sergeant of the Charles County Sheriff's Department slid the booth's door open. Milliken tilted back his fatigue cap, showing bristles of corn-blond hair. He handed the sergeant a travel order.

"Nice morning, huh?" the cop offered as he reached for a steaming mug and brought it to his lips.

"Better'n driving in snow," Milliken commented. Some of the Marines resented the decision to have the center's gate guarded by civilians in Smoky hats. But not Milliken. The cops were sharply creased and polite in the extreme, but he had once seen a pair of them handle an intruder with the swift violence of an urban drug bust.

"What's your destination?" the sergeant asked.

"The center at Dahlgren."

"ETA?"

"Hour at the outside. I'm gonna take Route 210, then 225, then 425, then 6, then 301. Piece of cake if we beat the bridge traffic."

"Uh huh." The sergeant checked the orders now to verify the route. "Whatch-yuh carrying?"

Milliken grinned. Although this transport was routine, the nature of his mission was not up for discussion, and the cop knew it. He looked over at the lab man snoring in the passenger seat, then back at the sergeant.

"One geek, six leathernecks, and a large dildo."

The sergeant laughed. "Roger that." He tapped a small transceiver console. "Have your people give me a shout when you make port." Everyone who worked around the center picked up navalese.

"Will do," said Milliken as he put the Hum-Vee in gear. Standard procedure was to maintain radio contact with the Marine net, but he always kept the cops in the loop. If there was trouble on the road, the Charles County cherry tops could be there long before the MPs got their shit together.

Milliken signaled a "wagons ho" with his left arm, and the deuce followed him as they picked up speed, heading northeast on Route 210. The morning wind began to whip into the Hum-Vee, and he closed his window and settled back to enjoy a sunny ride through the Maryland countryside.

Detail at the NSWC was basically a bore, and after the first few security hops hauling supersecret weapons around, the missions quickly lost their glamour. The lieutenant tried to keep the men on their toes with NIS reports about terror threats and attempts made against U.S. military cargoes. Yet all of those events took place in Europe, Central America, or the Philippines. In these parts you were more likely to impact with a stray cow than be assaulted with harmful intent.

Milliken had had his war. True, most of it had been spent sweating in a tin can off the beaches of Kuwait, but in the end the Marines had finally gone ashore. There were a couple of noisy firefights, although Milliken's company spent a lot of time getting sunburned while guarding enemy PWs. Still, there would be plenty to tell his kids about, when he had them.

By comparison, Maryland was R&R, without much recreation to speak of. It did not take long to see the sameness of each mile—the litter-free roads lined with red-brick strip malls, Pizza Huts, Mickey D's, liquor stores, and video arcades. The only solace here was that the high school girls were abundant, bored, and precocious enough to appreciate the body of a man who could do sixty push-ups in as many seconds. Marines never tired, and neither did Susie Upham. Milliken now smiled through his workdays, anticipating the Saturday nights with his leggy senior. He was a short-timer with thirty-two days to go, and he and Susie had some plans that included a motorcycle.

He slowed for the right turn onto 225, making sure the deuce was close, passing the Lone Star Café, where he and Susie spent many nights swaying near the jukebox and mingling scents and sweat.

In the rear section of the deuce, there was not much protection from the wind. Although the heavy canvas roof was tied down firmly to the steel bed, the chill knifed up through the hems and whipped around the cargo compartment. The rear flap was secured with loops of 220 parachute cord, the corners untied so the escorts could periodically check the road.

A very tall black Marine sat on the corner of the starboard slat bench, bending his head through the small triangle of light. As the small convoy turned off 210 onto 225, he watched a black limousine and a hearse, coming from the opposite direction, follow them into the turn. He closed the flap, turned up the collar of his field jacket, then sat back and gripped the butt of his M-16, which was jammed between his legs, barrel down to the steel floor.

"Nice day for a funeral," he muttered.

"Come again?" A second Marine, short, wide, and muscular, sat on the opposite bench.

"Limo and a meat wagon with running lights." The black Marine raised his voice above the rumble of the undercarriage.

"You always cheer me up, Humason," the shorter man sneered.

"My job, Del Ray, my man."

The Marine called Del Ray smiled. "Security threat? Should we take 'em out?"

"They already dead."

Del Ray nodded. Then he pointed to the peculiar manner in which Humason held his weapon. "And you can flip that thing around, Hum. This ain't no chopper. You ain't gonna shoot no rotors off."

Humason looked at his rifle. "I know it. I was thinkin' 'bout shooting myself in the foot." He lifted a large boot, placing it on the canister that was secured between them on the truck bed: a wide olive fiberglass tube about a yard and a half long. The "business" end had a closed clamshell nose, while the rear portion had a circular vented blast skirt. Jutting off from the middle of the launch cocoon was some sort of optical tracker sealed in flexible black plastic, and below the device a compressed rubber skirt hugged the tube like a hot dog roll. The entire unit was clamped to a wooden cradle with steel straps.

"Come on, this life ain't that bad," Del Ray admonished. Then he pointed at Humason's boot. "And get your damned foot off the government property. Skipper finds cleat marks on 'at thing, he'll have your ass *and* mine."

Humason reluctantly slipped his boot from the tube, then reached out to smooth away the scuffs. He raised his bass voice, simulating their lieutenant's nasal Yalie tones.

"Deliver the fish, *gentlemen*," Humason whined. "Do not *sell* it. Do not lose it."

Del Ray laughed and clapped his gloves together. "Pretty good," he said. "Pretty good."

"Little fucker's an asshole," said Humason.

"He's an officer. Watchyah want?"

"An' what the fuck's this thing anyway?" Humason wondered, waving a hand at the yellow stencil on the tube: UNITED STATES NAVY—RESTRICTED PROTO.

"Don't know." Del Ray shrugged. "Looks like a Dragon," he said, referring to the widely issued infantry antitank weapon.

"Look like my daddy's dick."

"You wish," Del Ray sneered.

"Yeah?" Humason challenged, pointing at his own crotch. "You wanna see *this* prototype?"

Del Ray ignored him, leaning toward the canvas back flap and peering out. They flashed past a sign on the far side of the road: *North Maryland 425—Snow Route*. The two-lane blacktop wound between stacks of sleek pines. About a hundred yards back, the dull headlights of the limousine and the hearse danced over a crest and then disappeared as they cruised into a curve. Del Ray closed the flap.

"We're on four-two-five," he said. "Halfway home."

"Six more months," said Humason, "and I *am* home."

"Three more, I'm in Norfolk," said Del Ray. He also wanted out of the Corps, but he wanted *in* to a more elite outfit.

"Yeah." Humason snorted bitterly. "You'll make SEALs, and I'll be a college professor."

"Hey. Corps's been good to you, Hum. Might even get you a job."

"Like what? A fireman?"

"Wear the colors, my man," Del Ray advised. "Don't diss the Corps. You See Gee See," he sang the Code. UCGC—Unit, Corps, God, Country.

"See *this*." Humason made a masturbatory motion, closed his eyes, and rested his head against a rattling support. . . .

Up ahead in the Hum-Vee, Milliken held his speed down along 425, though he was tempted to run flat out along the curving dry blacktop. The road surfed gracefully over rolling crests, but the following deuce had a high center of gravity, and causing it to hustle and maybe spill its lethal cargo would mean brig time, no Susie, and maybe no post-Corps erotic rides on a throaty bike. He glanced in the rearview and saw that Chuck Norman, the deuce driver, was trying to match him tread for tread, so he slowed some more and reached for the handset of a PRC-104 mounted between him and his passenger.

"Bravo Two, don't kiss me." Milliken smiled into the transceiver. "One round'll get us both."

"Roger, One." Norman's voice crackled back over the PRC's speaker, and the deuce dropped back.

They passed six more miles of wide-open fields, winter grass flattened into rows of black mud, stubborn patches of snow clinging to split-rail fences beneath the clement sun. Stained and warped clapboard houses sported tire swings in their front yards and fleets of old cars up on cinder blocks.

They descended a long shallow stretch, approaching an intersection and a two-way stop. The NSWC lab man, perhaps sensing a crossroads through his slumber, stirred and lifted his head. He was a fully bearded man wearing a ridiculous white coat that pegged him for his profession. He turned his knuckles in his eye sockets.

"Where are we?" he muttered.

"Ironsides," said Milliken as he stopped and idled the Hum-Vee. Before him, Route 6 passed from west to east. At the southwest corner of the intersection, a short post was affixed with a painted portrait of a country steeple, an arrow pointing toward Nanjemoy Baptist Church. On the southeast corner, a ramshackle white house looked as if it should have been condemned, yet fireplace smoke leaked from its crumbling chimney and heavy sheets whipped from a line in the yard.

"This dump has a name?" the lab man asked.

"All God's chillun," Milliken commented.

He hesitated, for a yellow Ryder rental truck was approaching the intersection from the west; although the truck had the right-of-way, the driver chose to let the military vehicles make their turn. Milliken waved in thanks, noting the camouflaged sleeve that returned the courtesy.

"Guy's a jarhead," he said as he put the Hum-Vee in gear.

"Probably moving his family," said the lab man.

"To better parts, if he's lucky," the corporal sneered.

He looked at his watch as he took the left turn and decided to make up some time. The deuce was close enough, and he gunned the powerful Hum-Vee as the road through Ironsides began to slope. There was not much here: a silent white volunteer firehouse set back off the road to the left, one low flat garage with rusty gas pumps that was clearly out of business. Not a soul in sight, probably no more life than when the place was a sharecroppers' haunt over a hundred years before.

"How much farther?" the lab man asked as they entered the tiny village.

"Hilltop, Welcome, then we'll be on 301," Milliken answered as he struggled with the gearshift.

"Coffee?"

"We'll hit a joint in Port Tobacco on the way back."

He was just getting up some speed and passing a small gray roadside barn on the right, when he yelled.

"Holy shit!"

A woman suddenly appeared from behind the barn. She was cloaked from neck to ankles in a long black coat, her head wrapped in a purple kerchief, a pair of black sunglasses and her white nose the only facial features exposed. This incongruous apparition marching out in front of Milliken's Hum-Vee would have been enough to shock him into fibrillation, but she was also pushing a large blue baby carriage, coming right on as if she was blind, deaf, and deranged.

Milliken stamped the clutch and jumped on the brake at the same time, leaning hard to the left as he swung the wheel. The nose of the Hum-Vee dipped hard, and the rear wheels sprayed a patch of wet sand as the steel body skidded to the right. The lab man's hands shot up to the roof, and the lone Marine in the cargo compartment tumbled to the floor.

"Mother *fucker*," Milliken yelled as his tires friction-burned on the blacktop. The woman's image flashed just ten feet forward of the right fender, and even though the vehicle came to a rocking halt, she went down. He saw her topple to her right, as if the wind of his near impact had tackled her, and the baby carriage went with her.

More tires screeched, and Milliken twisted his head around, expecting the deuce to rear-end him. But the six-by had stopped a few lengths back, with the high yellow body of the Ryder behind it, and he realized that the sound had come from in front.

A green military staff car had come barreling over the hill at him from the east and careened to a halt. As Milliken gripped his steering wheel and tried to catch his breath, the driver's door of the car opened and a navy lieutenant in full dress stepped into the road. He was carrying an attaché case, and he looked extremely outraged as he marched straight for the corporal's cab.

"Oh, am *I* fucked," Milliken whispered as he stared at the approaching officer. "Susie, you can visit me in the can."

He suddenly realized that he had to make an effort to help the fallen woman, or they would add dereliction of duty to the court-martial charges. He unsnapped his seat belt, reached for the door handle, and popped it open.

"Stay where you are, Marine." The naval officer had a hand out like a traffic cop as he reached Milliken's cab. He yanked on the door, nearly pulling the corporal with it, and he roughly swung the briefcase up and pushed it into Milliken's chest. "Hold this and don't *move*."

Milliken said nothing as the lieutenant strode away. He closed the door and gently placed the briefcase atop the metal box of the PRC. He looked over at the lab man, who was blowing out air and shaking his head.

"Oh, man, am I fucked," Milliken mouthed again as he began to pray that the woman was all right.

Mussa strode around the bumper of the Hum-Vee. Martina lay curled up in a fetal ball next to the baby carriage, much too close to the vehicle, but there was nothing to be done about that now. He knelt in the road with his thighs pressed up to her rump and bent over her. Her sunglasses reflected his white peaked cap, her mouth an expressionless line, one hand on the trigger grip of an Ithaca twelve-gauge pump swathed in a blanket inside the carriage. He let his full weight crush her as he placed a finger inside his left sleeve, found Nabil's pin, and pulled.

There was a second's delay, then a sharp, hollow bang shook the roadway, followed immediately by a high-pitched squeal that came from the rending of metal and the expulsion of gases from inside the Hum-Vee. The vehicle's fuselage buckled outward like the waxed skin of a milk carton, a gas cap twirled off into the sky, and both cab doors flew open and banged against the body. A small fountain of orange flames and black smoke enveloped the cab and licked out through the shattered windshield, but there was no geyser of cloud, no chunks of shrapnel to speak of. Nabil had done his homework. Just enough plastique. Not too much.

The concussion did not cause Martina to hug the blacktop in a cringe of self protection. It signaled her, and before the echoes of the explosion rang back from the sparse buildings, she was scrabbling out from under Mussa's weight, yanking the shotgun from the carriage, and sprinting away in a crouch to avoid having her clothes set afire. She stopped ten meters up the road and spun around, clutching the Ithaca two-handed. Then she straightened up and strode back toward the burning Hum-Vee, looking like a housewife in some urban cop's nightmare.

Mussa rose to his feet and steadied himself, staring for a moment at the burning vehicle. No cries emerged from the inferno, but the pop of a rifle round cooking off snapped him back to action. He looked for Martina, saw her coming on, and quickly crossed her path, circling around the Hum-Vee's left fender as he unholstered his Beretta.

In the cab of the deuce, Chuck Norman's mouth was agape. His windshield was spider-cracked, and he reached up to find that his glasses were gone. The concussion had split them in half at the bridge, and he could feel the tickle of blood snaking down the side of his nose. His comprehension was lagging behind the realities. He did not get it.

"My fucking God," was all he could utter. One second, Milliken had stopped to avoid smearing a pedestrian, and the next second, hell. A navy lieutenant was walking toward Norman's cab now. On the right side, the woman, looking perfectly healthy and gripping a dark-gray pipe, strode through a cloud of smoke. In the sideview mirror, the blurred forms of armed Marines were sprinting up from behind the yellow rental truck.

Then he got it.

He spun to his passenger, a nineteen-year-old kid just transferred from Quantico.

"Perris!" Norman yelled. "Get the fuck out!"

The confused youth, desperate for elaborating orders, turned to speak. But Norman was already unholstering his sidearm and jumping down from the cab. Perris sobbed something and followed suit, clutching his rifle as he heaved on his door, stomped down on the running board, and launched himself into the road.

Martina stepped in close to the truck to avoid peppering its precious cargo and caught Perris in midair with a blast from the Ithaca. His body crabbed sideways and fell flat to the road, where his face bounced and his M-16 went spinning away like a rotor. She pumped the Ithaca at her hip, stepped over the body as the ejecting shell ricocheted off the deuce, and she went on, moving out to her left as Ali led Salim and Yaccub at a run from that side of the Ryder. On the far side, Jaweed led Youssef and Riyad up that flank. They were all moving too fast, the sheen of adrenaline in their eyes.

"Careful!" Martina shouted at them. "The cargo!"

A single pistol shot echoed close from the other side of the truck, and she spun toward it, until she heard Mussa shout, "Clear!"

In the rear of the deuce, Del Ray and Humason were lost. They were good Marines and would have fought like banshees had they realized the truth of the event. But no one was issuing orders, and they were faced by six Marines sticking rifle barrels in their faces.

"One helluva fuckin' exercise," Humason grunted as he freed the canvas flap, placed his hands on his head, and kicked out the tailgate pin, letting the steel door fall and bang on the bumper.

"Exercise, shit," said Del Ray as he also assumed the position and hopped to the ground next to Humason, who glanced over at him, bewildered.

Del Ray had barely straightened up when Jaweed butt-stroked him in the jaw with an M-16. But the American weapon was not designed for close-quarter abuse and marine skulls, and the stock split with a crack as it sent Del Ray sprawling and unconscious.

"Hey! You fuckin—" Humason began to shout, yet it turned to a wheeze as Ali plunged his rifle barrel into the big man's solar plexus. Humason sat down hard in the road, fell on his back, and rolled onto his side.

"Disable him," Martina ordered as she turned away and began to jog back up the hill.

Ali thumbed the safety to semi, stepped back, and fired a round into Humason's thigh. The Marine jerked hard, but he did not scream.

"Move!" Martina shouted over her shoulder as she ran for the staff car. Her kerchief sailed out into the road and the glasses also spun away, leaving her cropped blond head bobbing over her black cloak.

Mussa bested her speed, and he was quickly inside the staff car and turning it around in the roadway, slowing for her as she reached the passenger side, yanked on the door, and dove in.

The deuce-and-a-half, fully occupied now by its new owners, jumped jerkily forward, then cruised slowly around the burning Hum-Vee. Rounds were still cooking off inside the smoking wreck, their echoes like a distant, hesitant firefight, and the gasoline was beginning to burn, leaking streams of fire into the road. Riyad was driving the deuce, and he gave the Hum-Vee a wide berth, then came back off the shoulder, picked up speed, and chased after Mussa's car.

The black limousine emerged from where it had halted back at the junction. It cruised to the left of the Ryder, picked its way around a corpse and shards of glittering glass, then joined the procession, followed closely by the hearse.

Humason rolled slowly onto his stomach and came to his elbows. Tears ran off his big cheeks and onto the cold tar. He looked over at the abandoned rental truck, its cab doors open on their hinges. Then he turned his head to where the deuce had been. Del Ray lay on his back in the road, peaceful, like he was catching some rays. Chuck Norman's boots poked up from a shallow ditch in the far shoulder. That new kid, What's-his-name, was laid out flat across the double yellow line, three shiny rivulets of liquid crawling away from his body.

Through the curling smoke of the blown-out Hum-Vee, which was really starting to go now, he could see the staff car, leading its convoy of murderers, just disappearing over a distant hill. From the passenger window of the car, the black shape of the woman's coat fluttered out into the air, billowed like a pirate's flag, then drifted to the road in a heap.

He reached down with his left hand and found his Motorola in its pouch, struggling to free it, trying to ignore the rippling agony lancing upward from his thigh and the hot puddle soaking his lap against the macadam. He dragged the black box to his mouth and pressed the transmit button.

"Bravo Base," he whispered. "This is Bravo Two. We got a bonfire here." He took a long, slow breath, trying to keep his head up. "I say again. We got a *bonfire.*"

Then he passed out.

It did not really matter. The walkie-talkie was dead, and he didn't have the range anyway.

Chapter 12: Washington, D.C.

An undulating quilt of mist crawled slowly over the barricaded property of the embassy of Israel, the white evaporation drawn by an unseasonable sun from the snow between the forecourt cobblestones. A light morning breeze drove it through the iron perimeter fence and across the gardens scanned by all-weather cameras, until it finally curled and dissipated against the sand-colored granite walls.

Benni Baum sat in the rear of a taxi at the corner of International Drive and Van Ness, squinting at the building through unrested eyes. The engine idled, the driver tapped his fingers on the wheel, the meter was running, and still Baum did not move.

The regal residence of his nation's representatives reminded him too much of an Ottoman fortress. Despite its modern half-moon windows and the Israeli colors fluttering in the breeze, it was no less than a prison, isolating them from the rest of the diplomatic community. It was his final way station before returning gratefully to the normalcy of routine, yet he sensed that within these walls waited secrets best left unexplored. He felt like a rookie teenage player of Dungeons and Dragons, vortexed by false leads that offered only further riddles.

Benni hesitated, looking down at his wrinkled trousers. His unpressed blue shirt and creased paisley tie suggested a man who had slept in his clothes, in a chair, which was precisely the case.

On the previous night, he had checked into the Ritz-Carlton in a snit of vengeful mischief. For most of his career, Benni had heeded the naggings of stingy AMAN comptrollers, staying in flophouses and cheap pensions, yet as he headed into Washington from National Airport, he suddenly decided to stick it to Itzik Ben-Zion. The general would froth when he saw the bill, and Benni might just tell him to go to hell.

He had settled into his room, then remembered that in Washington a suit would be the uniform of the day. His blue serge was a mess, but rather than summon the laundry valet, he pulled it from his valise along with a wrinkled oxford shirt, dressed in them, then stood in the bathroom for ten minutes while the hot shower roared into an empty tub. Yet the steam treatment did little for the patchwork of creases, and he came out breathless, fell into an armchair, then dragged his valise over and plucked Ruth's thesis proposal from the pile of his own maps and notebooks.

And there he had sat, marveling at every page, stunned by her felicity with the English language and her profound analyses of terrorist psychology. When he succumbed to the urge to call her, he saw that it was past 1:00 A.M., thought better of it, and read on. At some point, he slept. He dreamed of her, as a happy child, a stunning teenager, an angry woman. And then she turned into someone else, and he awoke to the sun, a full ashtray, the taste of stale Scotch, and a pain in his temples. . . .

Now he stared at the embassy, manacled by his own reluctance. The entrance drive for diplomatic vehicles was closed off by a massive black gate on trolley wheels. Outside, a District of Columbia cop appeared in Benni's view, taking up a position between the taxi and the gate. He realized that if he prolonged his loitering, he might soon be dragged to a station house for questioning.

"*Kadima.*" He ordered himself into the fray, paid off the driver, and got out. The sunny breeze stung his bloodshot eyes as he carried his battered valise across the road, forcing a smile at the policeman. The cop nodded glumly, eyeing the suitcase, yet he did not intercede. That was up to the Israelis inside the compound.

The gate held an access door for visitors on foot. Benni was about to press the intercom button when the lock buzzed, and he looked up at the smoked windows, assuming that General Avraham Yaron had given the order.

He crossed the wide forecourt, entered the building, and dropped his passport in the drawer at the security booth. Still harboring the superstition that he carried bad luck to youthful warriors, he declined to engage the GSS officer behind the Plexiglas in pleasantries.

"Would you like us to hold your suitcase, sir?" the young man offered.

"Yes," was all Baum said, and another Shabaknik appeared, to politely retrieve the bag.

He stepped through the next magnetic door, into the cavernous vault of the embassy's foyer. It had been designed for press conferences, cocktail parties, and even appearances by the Israel Philharmonic, yet today it was just an empty hangar. Symmetrical staircases led up to a girdling balcony.

"Baum!"

Benni looked up to see Avraham Yaron leaning over the balustrade. "*Bo,*" the general ordered as he waved a hand, and Baum made his way up the stairs, unable to force his legs into a pace of appropriate enthusiasm.

The office of the military attaché was a wide affair designed for the reception of Pentagon counterparts. It had a large, plush couch faced by a long coffee table, wooden armchairs, and a rolling trolley of coffee carafes and soft drinks. Yaron's desk was stately, a counterpoint to the general's tastes at home, where he was more comfortable surrounded by ammunition-crate stools and steel filing cabinets encrusted with sand. The papers on the green blotter were ordered behind a line of four telephones, while brass plaques from a dozen IDF combat units and framed photographs of Israeli weapons systems covered the wall.

The general was wearing that peculiar woolen IDF dress uniform issued only to officers who host foreign dignitaries. He was apparently scheduled for such an event today, and he looked down at his own bladed creases when he saw the smug smile on Baum's face.

"Like a clown, eh?" Yaron said, with the expression of a shorn poodle.

"Not really your style, Avraham," Benni agreed.

"Oh? I didn't know I *had* style."

"You don't," said Baum. They grinned at each other and shook hands. Yaron was aging, yet he retained his full crop of soft brown hair, graying only slightly at the temples. His facial wrinkles, hardened by the years of squinting in the sun, were overshadowed by two long scar scimitars across the left cheek. Yaron's smile was quick, yet if you did not know him, the lips, torn by grenade shrapnel, could make you unsure as to the intent.

The general pointed at the couch, and Benni backed into it and slumped down. The mess of his attire caused Yaron to comment as he poured two cups of coffee, settled into a chair, and crossed his heels on the table glass, making it shimmer.

"You look like shit, Baum."

"*L'chaim*," said Benni as he sipped the dark brew.

"Seriously." Yaron came up with a pack of Time, lit one, then tossed the box to Benni, who sighed gratefully as if he had been thrown a life preserver. "I've seen you more relaxed in the Golan after a six-hour bombardment."

Benni blew out a stream of smoke and looked up at the ceiling. "Life was simpler then, wasn't it?"

"And shorter, for a few of us, if you remember."

They smoked in silence for a few moments. "Well, Avraham," Benni said, "I'm retiring soon anyway."

"Sure, Baum," Yaron commented wryly. "When Itzik marches you out at gunpoint."

"No. Really."

"Whatever you say, *Bibi*." Yaron did not buy the scenario of Baum contentedly sunning himself on a beach somewhere. "*I'm* the one who's retiring. This is my last stop."

Benni nodded. "I know it."

A general officer who had held major IDF commands, such as Chief of Paratroops and Infantry, was often given a foreign posting as his last career stop. Military attaché to the United States was the pinnacle of such assignments. There was nowhere to go after that.

"So maybe we'll open a business together," said Yaron.

"Small arms? Communications gear?" Benni suggested with a disdainful tone, as every other hackneyed IDF colonel seemed to gravitate toward such ventures.

"I was thinking more along the lines of string bikinis," said Yaron, and both men enjoyed a raucous laugh. "Anyway, to business." He placed his feet on the floor and stubbed out his cigarette. "That pain in the ass of yours, Ben-Zion, called again this morning. Made me promise to deliver you to Dulles for the next plane out."

"Ahh. Home," said Benni with all the enthusiasm of an extraditable.

"You two working on something big?"

"A minor conspiracy."

"Don't tell me about it," said Yaron. "I'll just get jealous and wind up bucking for a field command again."

"I won't," said Benni, although he knew that Avraham would not really expect him to share compartmentalized issues.

"So, they're almost done with your package." The general turned toward the open door and shouted, "Sheila!"

After a moment, a chubby brunette wearing a peach-colored pantsuit appeared in the doorway. Her features reminded Benni that the general's wife insisted that his secretaries be less than comely. The tactic was questionable, as it failed to blind him to the attributes of other women, but it did put a respectable face on his office environment.

"Yes, Avraham?" Sheila inquired.

"Get Nadav in here, please."

"He's coming up the stairs now."

Yaron waved a hand like a dismissive crown prince. Sheila withdrew without taking offense.

A tall, slim man entered the general's office. He was wearing the "uniform" of all GSS chiefs of security abroad: an inexpensive dark suit, soft shoes with rubber soles, and a Sears tie. He had short red-blond hair and a mass of freckles permanently darkened by years in the fields of his kibbutz.

Nadav halted in the doorframe, planting his palms at the sides as if launching himself from the door of a C-130.

"*Boker tov.* Good morning," he said brightly.

"Nadav, this is Benni Baum," said Yaron.

"Ah, our 'recipient,' " said the GSS man, meaning the addressee of the suspicious package. He marched toward Baum, who half rose from the couch, shook hands, and fell back into position. Nadav spotted the coffee trolley and made straight for a carafe. "You're a friend of Uri Badash." He poured himself a cup and sat down next to Baum. "He mentioned you in a telex."

"Yes." Baum sighed. "But it seems more like he's keeping an eye on me. Maybe he thinks I'm a mole."

"Maybe," said Nadav. Uri Badash, as chief of Shabak counterintelligence, was tasked to suspect everyone, everywhere, all the time. "Are you?" he asked playfully.

"Well, my kids certainly treat me like an enemy agent," Baum complained.

Yaron laughed. "That's their job."

"And they're good at it," both he and Benni punch-lined simultaneously. Nadav smiled, realizing that the two men had a history together.

"Well, Benni," said the security chief. "Your gift has been scanned in the basement." The package had been examined by X-ray and an electronic explosives detector. "Nothing showing, but my sapper's still taking his time."

"It's all clear?" Yaron asked.

"In theory." Nadav reached for Yaron's pack of Time and removed a cigarette. He had quit smoking, because he had to lead his men in daily physical training and they were of a growing generation of nonsmokers. He toyed with the white stick. "But you never know. They're making pistols out of plastic now and detonating Semtex with electronic greeting cards."

Benni grunted. "So it could still go off."

"Why do you think I'm up here drinking coffee?" Nadav quipped. Yaron and Baum smiled at the Shabaknik, knowing that he had hovered over his sapper until the likelihood of a detonation dropped to near zero.

Yaron turned toward Baum. "So what's the flurry up north?"

"Well . . ." Benni relayed the recent events superficially, revealing nothing of the secret prisoner exchange or of his dualities with regard to Martina Klump, and not invoking Ruth's name at all. When he wrapped up with the details about the map of Boston, Nadav shifted uncomfortably in his seat.

"If that map points to Boston," said the GSS man, "then I'd say Washington is the more likely target."

Baum stared at him, suddenly aware that he should have made a similar assessment.

"I'm going to put those extra men on, Avraham," Nadav added. Due to the bombing, he had already placed the Washington GSS on higher alert, yet Baum's information reawakened his professional paranoia. He rose from the couch.

"We're having Capitol Hill people here today," Yaron warned. "Let's not make the place look like Spandau."

But Nadav ignored the general and headed for the door. The army had its concerns, the diplomats theirs, and Shabak had a job to do. "Don't care if it looks like Ansar," he said, referring to an Israeli prison that detained Palestinian terrorists. "I'll be frisking senators by lunchtime."

"Relax, Nadav." Yaron's attempt to soothe him was stopped by the appearance in his door of a young man who rarely ventured onto the diplomatic floors. He was a communications technician serving in a remote cubbyhole on the top floor of the embassy, part of a team whose function was to transmit and receive encrypted messages from Tel Aviv. As a sidebar, they intercepted transmissions to and from the embassies of confrontation states, as well as any other local traffic of interest.

The young man was short of breath. He took off his glasses and wiped them on the end of a stained brown tie as he pulled the office door closed. He hesitated, apparently frozen by the expectant stares of three superiors.

"*Nu?*" Yaron demanded as he came to his feet.

"Uh, Avraham," the young man stuttered, the acceptable lack of formality failing to assuage his discomfort before the general. "We've just picked up something you might . . . I thought maybe you'd want to hear."

"Yes?" Yaron put his fists on his hips.

"There's an alert on, to all American military forces in the area. It was hard *not* to pick it up. It was all over the traffic." He seemed somewhat embarrassed, like an entrapped voyeur.

"What is it?" Yaron's annoyance was on the rise. "Are they deploying to the Gulf again? *What?*"

The young man sputtered more quickly now, wishing he had done this by in-house telephone.

"Apparently a terror group has attacked a U.S. Navy weapons convoy. If I'm getting the codes right, the slang, you know, a number of Marine escort guards are dead. And there seems to be a total media blackout on the event, as maybe some sort of weapon or missile might have been stolen."

The technician had no more to relay, and his arms fell limp, as if he had finally confessed to damaging his father's car. Yet he did not move, apparently expecting some advice, instructions, a blessed order.

"*Ya w'Illi.*" Nadav whispered an Arabic expression imploring God as he turned to look at Yaron. His suspicions of the Boston "decoy" had just come home to roost.

"It's probably not connected," said Yaron.

"And my prick's not connected to my balls," Nadav retorted.

Benni said nothing at all, though he had risen to his feet and the cigarette between his finger and thumb was squashed to a thin strip, the smoke curling up over his arm. He wanted to rally to Yaron's side, to join in the assumption of coincidence, yet he could not. Images of strands of plotting string coursed across a map of the northeastern United States; clock faces and distance calculations formed flipping equations in his head. A woman flew into a night sky full of snow and corkscrewed down a lamp pole, while the charred bodies of Marines were pulled from dusty rubble, then turned to those of young Israeli men with the yellow stencils of IDF on their bloodied fatigues. A couple tangoed in the moonlight, and a pistol barrel flashed into his eyes as he squeezed them shut.

A hollow bang forced his eyes open again. Someone was rapping on Yaron's door.

"*Kaness!*" the general shouted, and the communications technician jumped aside as another man entered the room. He was wearing jeans and a heavy flak jacket, his hair pasted to his scalp by sweat, but he had left his visored helmet elsewhere. The sapper carried a large padded envelope, upon which sat a shallow white box, its interior swathed in tissue paper as if it contained a dress shirt. Unaware of the dramatic news just relayed, he beamed with the pleasure of having bested the grim reaper once again.

"Who's the birthday boy?" the sapper asked.

Yaron cocked his head at Baum, and the sapper approached Benni like a sommelier, offering the package. Baum tried to keep his fingers from trembling as he reached up and slowly unfolded the tissue paper.

In the bottom of the box was a book. It was hardbound, with a glossy black jacket. The top half of the cover showed the forehead, arching dark eyebrows, and wide, angry eyes of a female face. She stared out at him, her nose and mouth obscured by a raven veil. The bottom half of the cover was splashed with the neon letters of the title.

Shoot the Women First.

Benni stared at the gift, a published treatise on the histories of female terrorists. He was dimly aware that his compatriots had crowded in for a look.

"Book-of-the-Month Club?" the sapper joked, but Baum heard only his own blood roaring in his ears. He withdrew his hands from the paper and slowly stuffed them into his trouser pockets as he continued to stare at those eyes, and his vision blurred.

"Avraham!" Someone was yelling for Yaron. "Avraham!" Yaron spun to Sheila's imprecations echoing from the hallway.

"What is it?" he yelled back.

"The phone, for God's sake!"

It was only then the men realized that one of the general's instruments was jangling in its cradle. He sprang to it as Sheila called again: "It's patched in from the operator."

"Yes?" Yaron pressed the handset against his head and stuck a finger in the other ear as he squinted. "What? Who?"

Then he turned to Baum and extended the phone.

"It's for you."

Baum walked across the floor, his shoes suddenly heavy as a pair of ski boots. He pulled a hand free from his trousers, wiping the sweat on his shirt as the black instrument beckoned him from the end of Yaron's arm. He slowly placed it to his ear and closed his eyes.

The first sound was the warble of a satellite transmission, the pips and squeals of very long distance and miles of air. Then the voice brought him erect as if an electrical bolt had lanced him from the floor.

"Baum?"

It was a female voice, almost friendly in its tone. For a moment, he had hope that the caller would deliver him from this frightful spiral, lift him from a vessel that thundered onward into a storm, that the voice belonged to anyone but *her*.

"Yes?" he whispered.

She spoke in German, and hope turned to ash.

"This time," said Martina Klump, her voice echoing as if from the bottom of a mine shaft, "you are *my* prisoner. And if you do anything, anything at all—leave Washington, cancel the exchange, call in your troops—I *swear*, your wife will never forgive you."

The line went dead, the sound gone hollow and devoid of electrical life. Baum looked at the receiver, replaced it on the cradle, and then his short struggle to comprehend was suddenly over as he expelled an animal sound and began to scramble inside his suit jacket for something.

"What is it, Baum?" Yaron strode back to him, seeing the flush of panic on his friend's face. "What's going on?" He reached out to put a hand on Benni's arm, which flew up to ward him off.

"Outside line," Benni croaked. "Outside!" He was flipping through his small telephone notebook like a stockbroker about to lose a fortune.

"The red phone." Yaron pointed. "It's direct."

As Benni scrambled for it, Avraham turned to Nadav and mouthed, "The *doctor*." The GSS man hesitated, but Avraham Yaron had known Benni Baum for all their adult lives, and he had never witnessed a reaction like this before. "*Zooz!*" he snapped, and Nadav sprang for the office door.

Benni dialed Ruth's apartment in Manhattan. When her phone began to ring, he backed up to the desk and leaned on the edge, scrabbling at his tie, trying to take in oxygen. On the seventh unanswered ring, he dropped the receiver to the desktop and once more flipped through his booklet.

"Benni?" Yaron attempted again, more softly now. But Baum just shook his head violently.

He dialed again.

"Midtown North," the desk sergeant answered.

"Detective O'Donovan," Benni snapped.

"Who's calling?"

"Benjamin Baum," said Benni, then pronounced it again. "Ben-ja-min Bowem."

"One minute."

It was less than that, only a few seconds, until Aaron Davis's tired and remorseful voice came on the line.

"Colonel Baum?" He waited for Benni's response. "Aaron Davis here. Colonel?"

"Yes," Baum whispered.

"Mike O'Donovan is in the hospital, sir. We've been trying to reach you."

Benni could not speak, and there was a long exchange of breaths while Davis gathered his nerve.

"But it's worse than that, Colonel." The detective sighed, and his voice fell to a faint apology.

"Your daughter has been kidnapped."

Part Two: Nylon

Chapter 13: Ethiopia

Major Eytan Eckstein's eyes were as blue as the ripples of Lake Tana, a resemblance even more precise now that the African sun had arched into the late-morning sky and the waters sliding slowly toward the great falls of Tessissat were burnished by the windless heat. Across the vast expanse of what in other lands might have been called a sea, the yellow haze obscuring distant ridges was of the same dust that encrusted Eckstein's brows, and the papyrus boats hovering in the shallows mirrored the pink flecks of fatigue half hidden by his squint.

He had driven south through half the night from Asmara, the only city in the land of the Lion of Judah that retained the tastes of its many failed European conquerors. He had filled the gas tank of his forest-green Renault jeep, then fueled his own belly with a bowl of pasta, yet the mountains of the Gondar Province each night abandoned their warmth, and neither the food, the jeep's worn canvas roof, nor his woolly sweater was enough to keep his teeth still. But the cold was ally to a tired driver, and its constant jab had kept him from toppling into the gorges of Wolkefit Pass.

Now the devil of another day was well engaged, the December heat swinging toward its apogee, and the Renault's roof was rolled onto a cross-spar, the heavy navy sweater flung into the back seat. Despite the rays that nearly beat him blind and air so thick it sluiced around the windscreen like the backdraft from a jet afterburner, Eckstein no longer felt the urge to doze, for an oppressive day was more his element than a shriveling night. He had been born in Germany, but in Israel his body had learned to blossom in sweat.

Though a field-rank officer of the Israel Defense Forces, Eckstein bore scant resemblance to his peers in other branches: no polished brown boots, epauletted olive tunic, or smartly angled red beret to hint of those nostalgic airborne days before he joined the Special Operations branch of AMAN. His hair could be properly described as "dirty" blond now, thickly dusted by the mountain track and long enough to gather into a tail held by a black rubber band at his neck's peeling nape. The sleeves of his gray sweatshirt had been cut off at the shoulders, the fading purple letters on the chest bisected with a blade for further ventilation. Thus, NYU had been reduced to *NU*, coincidentally a Yiddish exhortation of impatience. A pair of cargo-pocketed khaki shorts ended at the middle of his sunburned thighs, and his tan canvas boots had been carefully purchased for their French labels. A New York Yankees baseball cap, a pair of black-framed Ray*Bans, and the blue Domke camera bag that bounced on the Renault's passenger seat all enhanced the cosmetic image cultivated here, the accoutrements of "cover."

Yet despite the lack of a uniform, Eckstein, like all his coworkers, continued to regard himself as a soldier. The term "agent" was rarely used by AMAN professionals, except in reference to their civilian counterparts. The word embodied questionable elements, like marketeers of theatrical talent, real estate, or life insurance.

Eckstein picked his way slowly along the only thoroughfare of Gondar, the provincial capital just north of Tana. The cluster of single-story plaster buildings with their roofs of bleached wooden slabs formed a "city" not much larger than the *Shuk Hapishpishim* flea market in Tel Aviv. Human and animal pedestrians ruled the road, and Eckstein held his speed to a crawl as he gently weaved between a family's wooden cart, pulled by a mule, and a strolling pair of patriarchs poking the dust with the tips of their gnarled *dulas*.

When he reached the southern outskirts of the town and picked up speed, he checked the rearview and decided that no other vehicle had followed him into Gondar, or waited on the single road that was the only path through the *wayna dega*—the high plateaus of brown tabletops and green scrub that looked so much like the northern Negev. A small bald boy waved at him and beamed the ready smile so common to these alleged descendants of King Solomon and Sheba, queen of ancient Ethiopia. To Eckstein, the inhabitants of this cruelly climated land were unusually beautiful, their soulful eyes reflecting a difficult fate. Yet the thought that troubled him now as he returned the boy's wave was that *his* Caucasian face, and his vehicle, were becoming too familiar features of the area. He wondered if the local shepherds had already anointed him with some colloquial nickname, for if so, then his operational days here were numbered.

In Addis Ababa, Bahir Dar, and Asmara, those who did address Eckstein knew him only as Anthony Hearthstone, a British-born and Munich-schooled photographer, which accounted for his perfect English tinted with hues of *Hochdeutsch*. Tony was a Christian moniker he had used before, having coupled it with the surname Eckhardt for work on the European continent. Yet Internal Security had decided that Mr. Eckhardt needed retiring, so another easily recallable approximation of Eckstein had to be concocted. "Cornerstone" was too blatant a translation, so Hearthstone was born in the Cover room at headquarters.

He was, to all who encountered him now in Africa, a fit and friendly photojournalist freelancing for *Stern* out of Hamburg. He appeared to be in his early thirties, though he was actually past thirty-eight, and his assignment for that magazine was to continue covering the hardships of the Horn. This made him an odd remnant of the flood of television, radio, and print people who had hovered here like desert flies when the drought was at its murderous peak, then quickly migrated to the war in the Gulf, and never returned. The journalists had left Ethiopia, but the famine had not.

That starvation, with its impact on the remaining pockets of Ethiopian Jews who had not been spirited to Israel during the airlifts of Operation Solomon, was the true focus of Eckstein's purpose here. The Israeli government continued to view the ingathering of exiles as a mission equal in importance to any other venture, and intelligence operatives often found themselves decompressing from anti-terror operations, only to be reassigned to the extraction of a besieged Jewish enclave from some distant, hostile environment. Such missions were regarded as the purest expressions of the nation's soul, and Israeli soldiers and agents undertook them with the same fervor they applied to thwarting a conventional enemy military assault.

Eckstein had already been in country for nearly two months, as commander of a SpecOps team tasked with the rescue of one such group of *Beta Israel*, the Ethiopian Jews more commonly known as *Falashas*. His operation had nearly foundered upon a number of treacherous obstacles, yet today he had set those troubles aside and drove with an urgency demanded by the message he had received in Asmara.

Each night at the stroke of twelve, no matter his fatigue or the inconvenience of location, Eckstein sought the high ground of his environment. On the top floor of a ramshackle hostel or a hilltop overlooking the Rift, he would set up his small Panasonic Single Side Band 18, drape the wire antenna over a tree limb or metal water pipe, affix his earpiece, and tune in the BBC World Service. For five minutes he would actually listen to the "main points," for he might have to justify his eccentric habit with a recitation of the headlines. But at precisely four minutes and fifty seconds past the hour, he would punch a preset frequency and listen for another full five minutes, for that was his only link to his true self.

On most nights he simply stared into the darkness, hearing blank static as he chewed a flap of the sourdough pancake called *injera* or sipped a barely alcoholic bottle of *talla* beer. Then he would pack up the little civilian receiver and go about his business.

But on the previous midnight plus five, as he squatted on the dark balcony of a pension, he had suddenly straightened up and nearly dislodged the plug from his ear. The voice was very faint, a sandy whisper in the night, but its slow and careful American tones were directed unmistakably at him.

"Bavaria, this is Modigliani Art. Call the ball, man, at two-niner-zero, two-seven-six, two-four-one-four. I repeat . . ."

Eckstein scrambled in his cargo pocket for a notepad and a pencil, jotting down the proper name and numbers, which at first glance confused him. The message was repeated twice more, while he closed his eyes and tried to make out every nuance of the words oscillating with the mountain winds and weather. Then the hollow static returned, and he waited out the remainder of the five minutes, though he expected no repeat performance.

Bavaria.

It was certainly directed at him, for he had used that code name for one long, turbulent period of his career. Yet only a select group of his comrades was privy to that knowledge, and this bass American voice bouncing from the stratosphere could not be matched with any other in his mind's roster.

Modigliani Art.

The contact had identified himself as if expecting Eckstein's recognition. Yet to the best of his knowledge, he had never encountered such an odd moniker—except perhaps as the title to a museum exhibition, where the words would have been ordered more gracefully.

And *Call the ball, man?* He repeated the phrase in a half-whisper, yet the only identification he could make was with the common radio instruction given to American naval aviators as they approach an aircraft carrier, an order to the pilot to declare that he was on course to set his plane down. So what was the intention here? That Eckstein should "come in for a landing"? The lack of clarity was maddening.

And finally, the numbers: 290-276-2414. They resembled no familiar telephone listing of any continent, but in keeping with departmental wireless practice, Eckstein added a digit to each numeral and came up with: 301-387-3525.

He sat down on the cool plaster balcony, produced a Mini Maglite, and cupped the bulb, staring at the numbers. Three-zero-one. An American area code, followed by seven more digits.

And then it came to him.

Modigliani Art. *Italian Art.* How many men did he know who fit that description and whose voice rang so familiar now? Just one. Art Roselli, former CIA Jerusalem chief of station.

And it was not "Call the ball, man," Eckstein realized as he slapped his forehead and silently chastised himself in Hebrew, a language he had not used in sixty days. Rather it was "Call the *bald* man."

An urgent message, so categorized because it broke over a frequency reserved for his ears only, authenticity confirmed by the use of his very private code name. A plea reaching out through a million other bits of floating impulses, a message from *Art Roselli* to call *Benni Baum* at a telephone number in the United States.

Eytan was somewhat stunned by his decryption, and as he removed the earplug, wound the wire, and packed the Panasonic back into its case, his train of thought wound through a pass of questions. What sort of event would have brought Benni Baum to contact him here in Africa? Baum had no part in Eckstein's *Mivtzah Yermiyahu*—Operation Jeremiah—so the need was probably unrelated. Had Baum in fact discovered something relevant to his mission, he would have relayed a standard encryption through the major's commo link from Jerusalem.

Ever since being separated by Itzik Ben-Zion, Benni and Eytan had secretly supplied each other with the points and modes of contact for whatever missions to which they were assigned. Yet each knew that the other would only break into that compartmentalization under emergency circumstances. Could this have something to do with Eytan's family? He shuddered, yet the years in intelligence work had taught him not to indulge in speculative panic. And why a relay from the United States? What was Baum doing there? He should have been up to his ass in Moonlight—the recovery of Captain Dan Sarel—of which Eckstein was supposed to know nothing at all. And finally, why was their old ally Arthur Roselli making the contact on Baum's behalf? Eytan might have assumed that Baum was somehow incapacitated, except that "the bald man" now waited impatiently by a telephone. Perhaps Roselli had made the contact because only he had access to the proper transmission gear?

Eckstein stopped excavating his mind and squinted at the dial of his Breitling. He had a full twelve hours in which to select a secure contact station. It was standard procedure to allow a man in the field half a day to answer a contact, for his *mahfil*—his control—could never know the full situation on the ground. If the English message had included the code word "pomegranate"—a translation from the Hebrew slang for hand grenade—then Eytan would have signaled his team members, destroyed his gear, and headed for a predetermined extraction route from Africa. But no such alarm had been sounded.

He had planned to sleep until dawn and then begin the long drive to Addis Ababa, but after a quick calculation, he decided to drum up a meal and depart at once. By noon he could be in Bahir Dar, at the southern tip of Lake Tana. Even if every telephone line in the province was down, the digital link at Dar's airport would be functioning.

He packed up his camera gear, filled his ruck with three days' worth of underwear and socks, made certain to include some very relevant reading material, and left the pension. . . .

He drove briskly now along the lower ridges near Addis Zemen, his boots kicking up small swirls of dust from the clutch and gas pedals, the gearshift chafing his palm under a sticky glue of grit and sweat. He focused on the winding highway, glancing at the vast geographic phenomena that fated the Ethiopians to a life of challenge. To the east, the wide forestlands that briefly flourished after September rains were slimmed and browner now from a constant diet of sun, the fields of yellow flowers gone. To the west, the surface of Lake Tana was flat and bright as polished steel. A flock of pink flamingos touched their black beaks to the water's edge, the reflections of their spindly legs giving them the odd double forms of alien mosquitoes.

On the long slope rising toward the road, a shepherd boy led two burros laden with dry bundles of firewood branches. Waiting for him on the shoulder was an adult couple, the man wearing the bleached shawl of a *shamma*, the white skirts of the woman's *k'ami* shaded by a straw umbrella.

As Eytan passed, he knew that the parents smiled down at their son, for the boy's bright face reflected their pride as he struggled upward with his prizes. A pang of longing struck his heart, for while he tried to focus once more on the road, he saw the black curls of Simona's hair framing her blue eyes, and the wide dimples of his son's cheeks beneath a tousled mop of blond hair so much like Eytan's own. Oren was well into his fourth year now, and Eytan was grateful that most of his recent assignments had not taken him far from Jerusalem, nor for extended periods of time. His feelings for his wife had always been remarkably intense, even during times of conflict. But until the arrival of Oren, Eytan had never imagined a devotion so powerful, a love that could not be tempered in the least by his own dark moods, his son's occasional bouts of inherited recalcitrance, or thousands of kilometers' distance and weeks without contact.

Too often he pictured Simona, alone in their bed in Talpiot Mizrach, the Jerusalem moonlight striping her body. An image replayed itself daily, of Oren scampering happily off to *gan* with his Mickey Mouse backpack bouncing on his bony shoulders. And Eytan knew that while Simona provided the fatherless apartment with comfort and joy, inevitably she would find their little boy staring at the black-and-white photograph of Eytan on the coffee table in the salon, asking in his sweet, reedy voice: "*Matai abba yavoh habayta?* When is Daddy coming home?"

Yet all soldiers, if they intended to survive the profession, had to be able to strike such emotional encroachments from their minds. If you could no longer accomplish that, then it was time to retire. The frequency with which Eckstein found thoughts of his family nearly filling his eyes had begun to cause recalculations of his future. In two more years he would have put in a full twenty in the Israel Defense Forces, when many officers took their pensions and with the relative youth of four decades set off upon second lives and careers. In addition, dangerous fieldwork was voluntary, and you could simply request extraction from such challenges and "fly a desk," as Benni Baum sneeringly described office combat. But Eckstein was excruciatingly self-aware, and he knew that the same blood that had once driven him to volunteer for the paratroops, and then again for Queens Commando in Special Operations, would always run in his veins. He would have to leave the army altogether, or he would constantly be sticking his ever aging neck out.

Another factor that weighed on him was that Benni Baum was himself about to retire. And in truth, their segregation from each other had changed the game so much that Eytan's enthusiasm had waned. He had not lost belief in his missions, but his ability to execute a task without his "better half" was being sorely tested. It seemed to him that he and Baum had been fated to function as a single entity, and although neither man had yet found the courage to voice that conviction to the other, Eytan would bet all his accumulated field bonuses that Baum felt the same.

Benni Baum would never admit that he needed the input of another specific comrade, yet his rantings to Personnel as he repeatedly assembled identical rosters of teams, with Eytan always as his second, were evidence enough. Eckstein and Baum were two halves of a single brain that simply functioned in low gear during their separations. The relationship was more than the father-and-son meld of successful family businesses. It was really too close to be sensible, and now the distance was too damned far, and that was why Eytan raced along the highway toward Bahir Dar.

After another half hour of speed that was drawing off his last reserves of concentration, he sighed with relief and slowed to a more reasonable cruise. He was approaching the outskirts of Ethiopia's most rapidly expanding city, and he could see the spiderwebs of utility lines that crisscrossed over the low buildings, the textile factory that was attracting country laborers tired of their battles with the land. He glanced at his watch, satisfied that he still had plenty of time. Yet one could not yet rely on the fortitude of the telephone system, and he would seek out the very first instrument. If that failed, he would continue on to the airport in hopes of more regularly maintained technology.

A small gasoline station appeared on the lake side of the road, and Eckstein decided to give it a try. He spotted a telephone line running from the roof of the station's single-story pink pastel building to a nearby pole. In addition, a white plastic sign hung over the open doorway, the bright-red Amharic letters advertising a roadside café. He could water his "horse," feed his grumbling stomach, and hopefully put his disquiet to rest.

Parking the jeep well away from the pair of old pumps, he turned off the engine and swung his legs out over the oil-stained earth. He sat for a minute, expressionless, rubbing the long pink scars that curled around his right knee. It had been over five years since a burst of Skorpion-68 rounds had nearly crippled him on the highway between Munich and the München-Riem airport, and he was fully recovered now, even holding his own in a couple of spontaneous soccer matches with the locals. Still, any prolonged position brought the cramping back to the joint. He stood up and suppressed a grunt, removed his Yankees cap, wiped his slick forehead with the front of his sweatshirt, and reset the hat. Then he reached into the jeep for his camera bag and rucksack and walked into the building.

Emerging from the harsh light of noon into the gentle gloom of the café, Eckstein was momentarily blinded. He could hear the low hum of an electric fan, and above that the bubbling notes of a *washint*, the long wooden flute played by shepherds to calm their flocks of oxen. The relative cool of the space brought instant relief. He pulled off his Ray•Bans, leaving them to dangle at the ends of a black cord.

There were only four wooden tables, a pair to the right and left, attended by folding metal chairs of rusty tubing. A peeling color poster of the great Blue Nile falls was glued to one wall next to an ironwork window, through which sharp shafts of light threw prison-cell stripes over the concrete floor. Against the rear wall, a small wooden counter rose to bar height, and a young boy's head and shoulders poked above the scuffed top. He had a crop of nubby hair covering his dark scalp, wore a bright-blue cotton shirt thick with dried sweat, and was concentrating on the gnarled flute. Glancing up at Eckstein and smiling through his eyes, he finished his lick with the discipline of a prodigy practicing for a recital.

Eckstein approached the counter. There was no cash register, only a wooden drawer divided for denominations. A small caged fan turned slowly at one end of the bar, and there was no telephone in plain sight, though that did not immediately alarm him.

"Hullo, mate," said Eckstein brightly. He already had a fair grasp of Amharic, as that was the predominant dialect of the Ethiopian Jews. However, other citizens shared a score of tribal tongues, so in most urban areas the lingua franca was a pidgin version of English.

"Helloo, meester." The boy grinned. "You need petrol?"

"Something to eat first, I think."

"You like *wat*?" The indigenous stew was a spicy mix of lentils, peas, and beans, with an occasional egg thrown in and a few chunks of mystery meat if you were lucky. Actually, Eckstein longed for a plate of hummus and a cold bottle of Maccabee, yet that was only a fantasy here.

"Sounds lovely," he said, and the boy placed the long *washint* on the counter and skipped through an archway into the "kitchen," which looked to be no more than a burlap tent at the rear of the building.

Eckstein walked to the nearest table and set his rucksack and camera bag on the floor. He returned to the counter and called into the back room.

"My friend."

The boy emerged, wiping his hands on a cotton rag. "Yes, meester?"

"Got a telephone, by any chance?"

The boy reached beneath the counter and set an ancient European model before Eckstein with as much pride as if he had produced the golden crown of Solomon himself.

"Fabulous," said Eckstein, although the existence of the old phone proved nothing yet. Ethiopians often displayed appliances, whether or not they actually worked. He fished into his shorts pocket and came up with a wad of mixed Ethiopian and American dollars. The boy waved a hand at him.

"You pay after," he said.

"I'm calling collect," said Eckstein, which was standard procedure, as the number and charges would appear only on the recipient party's bill. "But I still want to pay for the use."

The boy frowned at him and shook his head.

"The *other side* is paying," Eckstein tried to explain as he pointed off toward some distant shore. "But I want to pay *you* too." Actually, he just did not want to be interrupted during the conversation. He fanned the wad of bills like a blackjack dealer and said, "Go ahead, pick a card."

The boy's eyes widened at the peacock tail of currencies. He looked up at Eckstein, who grinned at him and nodded. The boy snatched an American twenty from the deck, and when the foreigner did not move to take it back, he laughed a happy warble and scampered into the kitchen.

Eckstein removed his small notebook and a mechanical pencil from his pocket and placed them on the counter. He picked up the handset and swept the zero around the rotary dial. When the operator in Bahir Dar came on, he stated his wishes and read off the number, then waited for nearly a full minute as he pictured her searching for a free line on an old plug switchboard. He heard her Amharic-accented English in the foreground, the inquiries of an American operator in the background, and then a discomfiting silence as an agreement to accept the call was negotiated.

"Hello?" Benni Baum's voice was unmistakable, even with the crackles of multiple relays.

"I thought I told you never to call me here," Eytan quipped in English as relief swept over him.

There was silence from the other end.

"Boss?" Eytan's brow furrowed as, not knowing whether Benni might be using cover, he fell back on this general verbal address.

"Hello, Tony." Benni's tired voice sighed. "Thanks for getting back."

"What's up?" Eytan asked.

"Well, things are very interesting."

Eytan did not reply for a moment. After so many years together, the two men had developed a private working code in addition to the encryptions supplied by the office. A situation described as *interesting* was dangerous, dreadful, and horribly screwed up. An event delineated as *boring* would have indicated the standard difficulties of their profession. This was clearly an emergency, and the muscles of Eckstein's shoulders tightened.

"Well, that's good," Eytan said in a flat, unenthusiastic tone. "Life should always be interesting," he added, meaning quite the opposite.

"Hunh," Benni grunted. His timbre was so depressive that Eytan's alarm multiplied.

"Where are you, by the by?" Eytan asked.

"In a hospital."

"Oh? Who's the patient."

"I am."

Eytan said nothing, hearing his own breath, trying to suppress his forebodings.

"It's all right," said Benni. "I'll be getting out tomorrow."

"What was the problem?"

"Never mind that, Tony," Benni said impatiently. "I have some changes in the price lists for the medical supplies. Do you have the catalogue?"

Eytan stared at the telephone cradle, dimly aware that the Ethiopian boy now carried a steaming bowl of *wat* from the kitchen to his table. Benni was reverting to code. Whatever was going on, it was serious enough that Baum wanted to relay it encrypted, and he did not feel that the transmission was secure. There were, of course, no "medical supplies" involved. The reference to changes on a price list simply meant that Eckstein was to take down a series of numbers. The "catalogue" was the code key in his rucksack.

"Yes, I have it," said Eytan as he prepared to write.

"Ready to copy?" Benni asked.

"Ready."

"Good. Beginning on catalogue page sixty-four, then . . ."

In the upper left corner of a blank page in his spiral-bound notebook, Eytan jotted the numeral 64. Then he moved the pencil to the right-hand edge of the sheet and began to list numbers vertically, in very small print, as Benni read them off.

"Thirty-six, two, twenty-four, eight, six, eleven, zero . . ." Baum read off twelve more numerals, sighed, and said, "Next. Bandages."

Eckstein flipped to a fresh sheet, moved to the right margin, and listed fourteen more numbers.

"Syringes," Baum intoned flatly, and Eckstein repeated the process, then twice more for "surgical supplies" and "antibiotics." As Eckstein quickly recorded the codes, he briefly wished that Benni had selected a market subject more in keeping with his cover as a photographer. Then he realized that Baum had already considered that, deciding that the bulk of foreign conversations coming from the Horn involved medical relief, while a list of Tri-X, Agfacolor, and lenses would stand out among the transmissions.

At last there was silence from Benni's end.

"Is that it?" Eytan asked.

"That's enough, I think." .

"Give me fifteen minutes or so," said Eckstein. "Then I'll let you know if we can afford the increases."

"Fine."

"Will you be there?" Eckstein asked flippantly, as yet unaware of the state of Baum's dilemma.

Benni snorted and hung up.

Not one quip, thought Eckstein. Not a single sarcastic retort to show that Baum was still in control, which he always managed despite the gravity of a situation. Eckstein could not remember ever hearing The Bear sound so desolate.

He looked up, to find the boy regarding his notepad with curiosity. He smiled at him. "Got any water, lad?"

"A bottle?"

"Yes."

"No." The boy shrugged. Then he smiled hopefully. "I have Pepsi."

"Super." Eckstein slapped the counter and moved to the table. He sat down with his back to the rear wall of the café and pulled the earthenware bowl of *wat* over to his place. His appetite had been supplanted by his anxiety to decode Baum's message, yet he picked up the large metal spoon, shoveled a pile of lentils and gravy into his mouth, and said, "Hmmm, fab," as the boy grinned and placed a warm can of soda on the table. A heavy shadow crossed the front windows of the café as a large yellow pickup truck rumbled up to the gas pumps. The boy hurried out the door.

Eckstein picked up his rucksack, opened a side pocket, and came up with a slim paperback novel. It was the orange-spined 1975 Penguin edition of Ernest Hemingway's *A Farewell to Arms*. The copy was well worn, actually on the brink of molting from its bindings, but Eckstein had repaired the cover with black electrical tape and reset the binding with carpenter's glue. He could certainly have acquired a newer version of the classic, except that it was identical to Benni Baum's copy and could not be substituted for the sake of aesthetics.

A book code was one of the oldest and most primitive tools of the intelligence trade, yet it remained among the most secure methods for message transmissions. Two operatives holding identical copies of any publication, whether it be *Newsweek, Vol de Nuit,* or the Bible, could encrypt and decrypt in relative safety.

The sender began by first writing out his message vertically, the words and phrases taking on the forms of "down" columns in a crossword puzzle. Then he selected any page of the printed manuscript and began to encrypt, carefully matching each letter of his message to the first identical one that appeared in a line of text, and noting the number of the location in that line, including periods but not spaces between words. If a letter failed to appear in a given line, the sender noted a zero as a "null" and carried on. The resultant matrix of numbers could be further encrypted by math, but that was rarely necessary. Interceptors found these codes to be maddeningly unbreakable, for the letters never appeared in the same numerical positions, and there was no hope of decryption based on repetition. Without the book to match the code, you were lost.

Eckstein took the first number that Baum had selected as his "catalogue" page, 64, subtracted one from each digit, and turned to page 53 of

Hemingway's semiautobiographical tale of an American ambulance driver serving with the Italians during the First World War.

CHAPTER 10
IN the ward at the field hospital they told me a visitor was
coming to see me in the afternoon. It was a hot day and there

He noted Benni's double confirmation, the word "hospital" in the first line. Then he set the first page of his notebook against the margin of the print and began to decrypt. He had used this method rarely, yet retained the ability to quickly count words as summed groups, slowing only as he approached the required number. In the first line, the thirty-sixth letter was *m*. In the second, the second letter was *o*. In the third, the twenty-fourth letter was also *o*.

His five columns of numbers corresponded to five consecutive pages, the breaks having been cued by Benni's changes of medical requirements. The process took less than five minutes, during which Eckstein did not try to read the phrases forming in his notebook but kept one eye half cocked on the doorway, through which he could see the Ethiopian boy chatting with the driver of the pickup.

Eckstein closed the novel, the cover of which showed a large red cross and part of a photograph below the title. The picture was of Hemingway himself during the Great War, fully uniformed and recovering in a wheelchair from his leg wounds. The cracked image reminded Eckstein of his own long recuperation, wheeling himself impatiently around the sunny grounds of an IDF military hospital.

He replaced the book in the rucksack and closed the pad as the young proprietor trotted back into the café.

"Is it good?" the boy inquired as he passed by, clutching a sheaf of bills.

Eckstein shot him a thumbs-up as he popped the top of the Pepsi and downed half the can, quenching the spicy fire of the *wat*. The boy grinned, rooted behind the counter for change, and skipped back out the door.

Eckstein took a breath, opened the notebook again, and quickly read the five rows of decryption.

M	B	H	E	I
O	L	A	N	A
O	U	S	R	M
N	E	T	O	L
L	Q	A	U	O
I	U	K	T	S
G	E	E	E	T
H	E	N	Y	
T	N	R	O	
A	B	U	U	
C	A	T	R	
T	C	H	A	
I	K	H	.	
V		O	O	
E		S	.	
		T		
		A		
		G		
		E		

He sat for a long while, blinking at the rows of words, reading them over again, wondering if he might have made an error. Yet even one or two decryption mistakes would not have altered the profundity of the message. He could feel the thump of his left breast against the damp cloth of the sweatshirt, the strange crawl over his forearms, and the heat that was suddenly so oppressive, undimmed by the shade of the café or the fan that whizzed behind him like a carnivorous fly.

Moonlight active. The prisoner exchange was "go," counting down to a date as yet undisclosed to him.

Blue Queen back. Martina Klump had emerged from a self-imposed operational exile, and use of her old code name meant she was functioning again as opposition.

Has taken Ruth hostage. Eckstein failed to absorb this, could not believe it. Had to, or the only counterconclusion was that Benni had lost his mind. Ruth, that stunning and magnetic Baum for whom Eytan had always had feelings that were borderline fraternal. As she had grown into womanhood, he was grateful for their gaps in age, and the relationship between himself and Benni that hexed all indulgence in fantasies. She had once, as a late teenager, blatantly informed him that she intended to marry him, an objective that seemed finally to wane upon his wedding to Simona. Ruth had gone off to study in New York. Benni was now in America as well. But how the hell in God's name . . . ?

En route your A.O. Martina Klump had kidnapped Ruth and was traveling with her to Eytan's area of operations? To Ethiopia? No, Benni was generalizing. Somewhere in Africa. But to what end?

I am lost. There was no subtext in that. Baum was clearly at wit's end, a confession that Eckstein never thought to hear, read, or have revealed, even if his old comrade was drawing his very last breaths.

"*Elohim ba'shamayim ayzeh fashlah,*" he exclaimed silently in Hebrew—"God in heaven, what a screw-up"—as he tried desperately to assemble the frantic phrases into a logical progression. The prisoner exchange, years of collective effort by all of Israel's military, diplomatic, and intelligence arms, and with Baum as its point man, was about to bear fruit. Somehow, Martina Ursula Klump, all but forgotten along with the tattered Tango file in Baum's safe, had come forth once more, and for some reason was connected to Moonlight, a danger to its execution. Her fate and Benni's were intertwined again; perhaps Baum had tried to thwart her and the Blue Queen had countermoved by taking a precious pawn. *Of course* Benni was "lost." His hands were expertly manacled. Any reaction on his part might result in the death of his daughter.

Eckstein looked at his watch. Nearly fifteen minutes had passed, though he had no doubt that Baum would sit by that telephone for hours until he called again. He found himself patting the pockets of his shorts in search of cigarettes, then remembered that he had quit. He knew too well that by sharing this deadly ambush, Benni had placed him at the heart of a conundrum. If Eytan decided to consult with Itzik Ben-Zion in an effort to enlist departmental aid, the general might justifiably postpone or cancel the exchange. Without knowing Martina's intentions there, Eytan could not predict her reaction. Would such an effort buy Ruth time? Would it result in her death? Was there a window of days in which to mount a rescue? Or did merely hours remain, or ineffectual minutes? And if Eckstein did *not* relay this quandary to Itzik, could that withholding result in tragedy for Israeli prisoner Dan Sarel?

Then, of course, there was the issue of Eckstein's own mission, Operation Jeremiah. True, he and his team were waiting out a lull pending the arrival of two crucial individuals from Europe, but he could not take leave and go gallivanting off now while Jeremiah was running. Such an act would be unforgivably remiss, a danger to his comrades in the field, an invitation to a court-martial.

The image of Ruth Baum's face suddenly superseded his reason. He saw her again as a young soldier, appearing proudly at the door of Benni's home on her first leave. He saw the features that could return a man to belief in the wonder of Genesis, the smile so powerful it seemed capable of illuminating a moonless night.

He saw her cringing under the barrel of a pistol.

He got up and sprang for the counter, where the Ethiopian boy was just lifting the telephone to return it to its hiding place. Eckstein grabbed the instrument and, in reply to the boy's shocked look, quickly produced his wad of cash, peeled off an American twenty, and said, "Just one more, okay?"

The boy took the bill, laughed, and again disappeared into the kitchen.

It seemed forever until Benni once more came on the line.

"How do those prices strike you?" was how Benni answered.

"Shockingly high, if I have them right."

"You have them right."

Eckstein took a long breath. "They are a problem."

"Yes. They are."

"I have a question."

"Ask."

"Is the astronomy project directly linked to these other changes in the weather?" He was asking if Moonlight was tied to Martina, and therefore to Ruth's abduction.

"It is," said Benni.

"Then if there is an eclipse of the moon, we may not see Venus?"

So many years of working together made communication possible by the improvisational use of hints. "The moon" was obvious. Venus could only be Ruth.

"We may not see that planet again." Benni's voice wavered.

Eytan paused, trying to imagine the depth of his friend's pain.

"I see," he said. "That's what I feared."

"Fear." Benni expelled the word with disdain. "There's a better term for it."

Terror, Eytan thought instantly. "Well," he said at last, "I'm due a vacation."

"Wait a minute—" Benni began, but Eckstein rode right over him.

"I'll be leaving the capital tonight." Eytan's tone made it quite clear that his move was irreversible.

"You have work," Benni protested, though his tone was unconvincing, his hopes too tenuous to mount a proper protest.

"It can wait. In twenty-four hours, I'll be where Rick met Ilsa for the last time."

If Baum did not immediately realize that Eytan meant Casablanca, Art Roselli was an old Bogart fan, and he would figure it out soon enough.

Benni said nothing for a moment, and Eytan wondered if his old friend had lost his nerve, that his fear was crippling him, that he would decline to face the bull just once more. When Baum finally spoke again, this time in German, Eytan heard the choked tones of emotion.

"Our boss will bust you to corporal," Benni warned in a whisper.

"Well," Eytan answered in the same tongue, "rank has its privileges."

He replaced the telephone on its cradle, picked up his ruck and camera bag, and headed for his jeep.

Chapter 14: Bethesda, Maryland

"Just give it to me, Baum."

Jack Buchanan's voice was like the slow scrape of a woman's fingernails across a long dry blackboard. The words were carefully disjoined above a background hiss swollen with intent, as if someone had maliciously proffered a violin and bow to a malcontent.

"Give it all to me *NOW*, everything you've got, and we can skip the ugly formalities."

Buchanan could not yell, a restriction that certainly cramped his style. Yet this "interview" was being held in a private room of the Step Down Cardio-Thoracic Unit of the National Naval Medical Center, and although his powers as an FBI SAC sliced through state and federal barriers, he was fully aware of the protocols. Bethesda was fully staffed by U.S. Navy and Marine Corps personnel, the sprawling facility regarded as just another vessel by the uniformed doctors, nurses, and orderlies who served "aboard her." The NNMC was even "commanded" by a rear admiral. Being a former Marine himself, Buchanan was attuned to naval law and trying to behave like a civilian reluctantly piped across the gangway.

"You have what I have," Benni Baum lied. Having once been interrogated for a full week by Stasi agents in Leipzig, he was tempted to make a mockery of Buchanan's threats. Yet the sarcastic humor with which he usually faced such menace had taken leave of him.

He lay on the large pneumatic bed, fighting the urge to jump into his clothes and run from the facility—to the airport, to somewhere, anywhere east, toward Ruth. He stared up at the red and yellow stripes that joined the cream walls and spotless ceiling, one slabby arm across his bare chest. A tube dripped sucrose from a hanging bag into his wrist, and the EKG electrodes were still taped to shaved patches of his skin, though he was no longer hooked up.

Beneath the blanket, Benni's left hand still clutched the balled-up sheet of legal pad upon which he had encoded his message to Eckstein. He wished now that he had destroyed it, but after Eckstein's call at 3:00 A.M. and so many hours without sleep, he had quickly succumbed to a flat, immobile slumber.

The sudden breakfast arrival of Buchanan and his angry circus had taken Benni completely by surprise. His copy of the Hemingway classic lay on his night table in plain view, but the sweat of his palm would soon turn his encryption to a mealy, unintelligible wad.

"Bullshit," Buchanan snorted. He rose from the red polymer chair at the foot of Baum's bed, thrust his big hands into his trouser pockets, and stepped to the wide window. He suddenly parted the Venetian slats with a loud crackle, staring out as if expecting enlightenment. The gloom of the room was unaffected, as the rainy morning was having difficulty pushing through the night.

"Why don't you let *me* try, Jack?"

Benni turned his head. The voice came from the sharp face of a wiry bearded man leaning against the closed bathroom door. He wore scabbed blue jeans, black combat boots, and an army field jacket, yet the thumbs hooked into his belt exposed the butt of an automatic pistol, spoiling his "construction worker" getup. His name, as he had offered it, was Denny Baylor, and he was an agent of the Naval Investigative Service. Altogether, there were six men in the room in addition to Buchanan. They stood or sat about, with pencils poised above evidence pads, like reporters at a breaking news conference. Yet they all had that restless, hungry air of attack dogs awaiting their master's signal.

Benni sympathized with their frustration. In fact, he could not quite understand their polite reticence. Had the situation been reversed, an Israeli naval weapon hijacked and Israeli soldiers murdered in ambush, he would have had his hands around someone's throat, patient or no patient.

His emotions here were split straight down the middle, a schizophrenic fissure above which his loyalties swayed like a mouse clinging to a pendulum. The problem was clear, yet unsolvable in any good conscience. To the left, his allies had been raped, and aiding them in their counterstroke might possibly save Dan Sarel from steaming to his own death.

To the right, Ruth's life.

The choice was obvious, though every word and action now forced another precarious step out onto a high wire. He knew that his deceptions would soon disgust him. He looked at Baylor and shrugged.

"You could use drugs," Baum suggested. "But you will most likely just get confessions about my love life. Very boring, and in Hebrew. How is your Hebrew, Mr. Baylor?"

The NIS agent stared at Benni and chewed an unseen glob of something tucked into his cheek. He raised a middle finger from one fist, but rather than aiming it directly, he stroked the bridge of his nose with it.

The response from the other men was less casual. Their spines stiffened, and Benni regretted his cavalier tone, which now caused an atmospheric shift.

"You're right, Jack. This is bullshit." Special Agent Charles Gold, Buchanan's tall black deputy, had been leaning against the wall behind his boss's chair. He unfolded his tweed-jacketed arms and threw them up. "Let's skip this and take it to the NSC." He pointed at Baum. "Drag his attaché over to the White House and get some action. We don't have time."

Spurred by his deputy, Buchanan spun from the window. "Do you understand what is happening here, Baum?"

"I do."

"A secret prototype has been *stolen*, Colonel. Men have been killed." Buchanan was bending at the waist, an effort to prevent himself from approaching the bed. "The hijackers were led by a woman. You *know* that woman."

"I understand the event," Benni tried to assuage. "And the consequences."

"No you don't, mister," said another NIS agent, who was pacing out a small track near the closed door of the room. Unlike Baylor, he was dressed in a blue suit, white shirt, and regimental tie. Peter Cole was Baylor's commander, and with his short black hair, quarterback features, and Oklahoma drawl, he could have stood in for a country-and-western star. "No you don't. Or you just don't give a damn because they weren't *your* people."

Benni reached for the bed controls and raised the upper portion of his body. "I apologize if I gave you the impression that I don't care," he said. "That is not the case."

"Well, it damn well *seems* like the case," Gold pouted.

"Gentlemen, do not read my mind," Benni warned. "You will get it wrong. I want this woman as much as you do."

"Then spell it out!" Buchanan nearly yelled.

"You know as much as I do," Benni dissembled again, feeling an encroaching sense of guilt. "As much as the Germans do, or Interpol. It's all in your own files, I am sure."

"But what's her objective?" The third FBI official in the room was Hal Novak, who served as the Bureau's counterintelligence liaison to the Pentagon. He sat on the other bed of the room's pair, his back to the Israeli, his voice controlled and level despite his anger. "What's she planning to do with it?"

"How the hell should *I* know?" Benni snapped, finally beginning to resent the implications. He was being treated like a multiple bank robber who had stashed his take in a secret hideaway, yet he suddenly realized an opportunity to elicit some information for his own needs. "Are you telling me, gentlemen," he asked quietly and with genuine concern, "that this prototype is functional? That it can be armed and fired by just any ambitious thief?"

There was no immediate response from anyone in the room, though Benni quickly scanned their faces for a hint of confirmation. In the far corner, to the

246   The Nylon Hand of God

left of the wide wooden door, was a stainless-steel sink, above which a mounted shelf held tongue depressors and a box of surgical gloves. A man who had not been introduced by name leaned against the trough, apparently taking little interest in the "debriefing" as he toyed with one of the hand condoms, snapping its elastic fingers like party balloons. Very large, he wore a dark-blue turtleneck beneath a brown Australian outback raincoat, and his slightly graying thick black hair was pulled back from his wide face into a ponytail. Benni assumed this man to be a representative of a special operations team that might be tasked with recovering the navy's missile, perhaps an officer from SEAL Team Seven. By the looks of him, the life of one Israeli girl would not even appear on his score card of obstacles.

One other man sat closer to Baum, on the edge of the empty bed to his left. He was small and bald, and even though he was nattily dressed, he reminded Benni of Horse, who was no doubt fretting terribly now in Jerusalem. Dr. Werner Carswell was director of the Minnow Project at the Naval Surface Weapons Center at Indian Head. He carried a large soft briefcase swollen with papers, as if somewhere therein might lie the recipe for the rescue of *his* kidnapped child. As he held his thick glasses and nervously flipped the frames open and shut, he looked up at Peter Cole for a signal. He received a cautionary nod.

"Well, Colonel"—Carswell sighed reluctantly—"let's just say that the Minnow was designed for simplicity. Of operation, that is. It's actually an extremely sophisticated concept, combining some of the TOW features, such as goniometer tracking of a modulated IR lamp on the projectile, which signals changes to the fin surfaces as the operator locks on optically. But then, you also have some features from the Hellfire RB-17, the whole dual mode thing, you know, antiradiation slash infrared seeker, which is auto backup if the operator can't remain stable. *And* there's the unitary antiship warhead, naturally."

Benni blinked at the little man, a gesture that brought a small smile to Denny Baylor's lips and a flush to Dr. Carswell's face as he realized that his enthusiasm had carried him too far.

"Nice work, Doc," said Peter Cole as he rolled his eyes. "But I think the colonel was looking for a plain old yes or no."

"Of course." Carswell cleared his throat. "Well, all of that is packaged to be very user friendly. I wouldn't call it a cinch for the simple infantryman, but it *would* be for the simple SEAL."

The big ponytailed man in the corner emitted a pained grunt, which confirmed Benni's assessment of his Military Occupational Specialty.

"So you are saying, Doctor," Benni coached, "that our terrorists could easily figure out how the Minnow works, and use it?"

"Well," said Carswell, "your Israeli troops use our own Dragon. If you issued one to an untrained man, could he use it?"

"The firing instructions are printed on the launcher," said Baum.

"Same concept." Carswell shrugged.

"The instructions are *printed* on the damn thing?" Buchanan asked incredulously.

"A prototype is designed to test all aspects of the concept, sir," said Carswell in defense.

"Jesus H. Christ," Charles Gold whispered.

For a moment, Benni thought that the men were turning inward, focusing on their own lax security. But Hal Novak, whose job it was to seek out security breaches in the defense establishment, addressed the room.

"People, odds are she *already* knows how to use it," he said darkly. "Already knows everything about it. No smart woman buys a diamond without first looking at it through a jeweler's loupe." Novak rose from the bed and turned to face Baum. He was wearing a brown corduroy three-piece suit, complete with a vest-pocket watch. His thick gray hair and mustache filled out the image of a "hanging judge" from a rough East Coast city. His counterintelligence post demanded patience, suspicion, and brainpower. "I think, Colonel, that Martina Ursula Klump had inside information. She knew what she wanted, and when and where to shop for it."

"I agree," said Baum. "So you should probably begin looking immediately at your Weapons Center personnel."

"I'm looking at you," said Novak, not bothering to conceal his intent.

"Then your vision is *blurred*." Benni raised his voice as he rolled onto his left side and returned Novak's attempt to stare him down.

Outside in the hospital hallway, a soft double bell rang out a code call for a Stat team. To Benni, it sounded like the signal for a boxing round as the Americans commenced a verbal assault.

"Why *did* you come over here, Baum?" Buchanan demanded.

"You know why, Mr. Buchanan. To investigate the consular bombing."

"Did you know Klump was involved?" Charles Gold jumped in.

"I am still not convinced that she was," said Benni. "The bombing and the hijacking may be purely coincidental." He no longer believed that, yet he could not reason out a logical connection between the two events. Why would Martina tip her hand so clumsily?

"Yeah, right," Denny Baylor snorted. The lump in his cheek was revealed to be tobacco, as he spit a short brown stream into a paper cup.

"I think you knew she was here, Colonel," Hal Novak accused. "And you knew what she was up to."

"I'll second that," said Peter Cole.

"*Gott im Himmel*," Baum grunted as he pulled his left hand from beneath the blanket and folded his arms across his chest. By now the paper ball was a clammy wad of pulp, and he felt free to knead it in anger. "So you all *really* think that an Israeli officer, an *allied* officer, would come here with full knowledge of an impending attempt to steal a secret American weapon and not *share* that with the Defense Department? Does that make sense?"

"Hey, you guys got your own agenda," said Baylor simply, as if Baum were the head of a Mafia family, a different moral culture.

"And when you had Beirut in eighty-three," Hal Novak added, "two hundred and fifty Marines bought it, while your people probably had a heads-up call on every major terror action going down."

"And we warned you *twenty fucking times!*" Benni finally bellowed, feeling like he was now defending the honor of his nation rather than his own familial interests. "If you place your men in a war zone, forbid them to chamber ammunition, and they are blown up by an unopposed maniac driving a truck bomb . . . search your own damned souls!"

"Hear, hear," the large SEAL grunted from his corner, obviously harboring similar opinions regarding ridiculous rules of engagement.

"But for the sake of argument, Baum," Jack Buchanan broke in, "let's say you *did* know that this Klump was after the Minnow."

Benni blew out a long breath, dredging up his last reserves of patience as he laced his fingers over his stomach. "Mr. Buchanan," he said slowly, "you *have* no argument. For the simple fact is, I had no idea that your Minnow even *existed* until you so generously revealed it to me right here in this room."

Buchanan held Baum's gaze, while the other men glanced at each other, wondering who was going to catch hell for *that* little security breach.

Baum had spoken the truth. He'd had no foreknowledge of the Minnow, nor of Martina's intention to steal it, though now he certainly suspected her intentions for its use. He did not, of course, reveal his depth of knowledge of her background, details of the Tango file that might soon mean all the difference. At any rate, the fact that Otto Klump had been a scientist who conceived of such weapons long before technology allowed their fruition was irrelevant. And the idea that Martina would covet such an irony, as the icing on her cake, was beyond fantasy.

"But I agree with Mr. Novak," Benni pressed on. "*She* did have knowledge of the weapon. And all of us, as intelligence officers, can draw the conclusions. Either you have an enemy agent inside your military, perhaps even a paid informant who revealed this information to Klump, *or* you yourselves have already presold the Minnow to some other customers. Perhaps a third world nation? Perhaps an Arab nation?"

As it happened, both of those suppositions were accurate, although only Dr. Carswell and Peter Cole could confirm the last part of Baum's theory. Cole chose to bluster.

"That is pure bull, mister," he growled as he placed his fists on his hips.

"Really?" Benni wondered. "For an investigator who should be thinking exactly along those lines, I think you protest too much."

"And *I* think you're just trying to draw off the heat," Cole spat.

"With finesse, Baum." Buchanan shook his head. "With finesse."

Once more Benni found his calm. Yet as he looked squarely at the men, he suffered profound disappointment, the hurt of a mistrusted yet essentially loyal friend.

"Gentlemen," he said quietly, "heat means nothing to me. I am trying to work with you, but the atmosphere here has brought me to the sad conclusion that a call to my embassy's attorney might be in order."

The men watched him, some of them thinking now that this had not been managed well. They had followed Jack Buchanan's lead, echoing his allegations like a wolf pack. No one had thought to play the cliché role of "good cop," and they now were faced with a defiant prey who would not be brought to ground. The nameless SEAL team officer had already decided that under other circumstances, he would enlist this Baum's aid in setting up joint exercises with the Israeli naval commandos. Peter Cole, on the other hand, did not know a hard case when he saw one, nor when to change tactics.

"You want to talk lawyers, Colonel?" he challenged. "We've got a great one over at Justice. Digenova barely whetted his appetite on Pollard."

Cole's allusion to the American intelligence analyst who had been convicted of spying for Israel brought the sting of bile to Benni's throat. Benni turned to him with a battery of daggers in his eyes.

"I will consider your remark as a formal breach of diplomatic protocol, sir," he said. "And given the presence of American deep-cover agents on *our* soil, whom we have politely allowed to play with *their* toys, I will advise the Prime Minister that they are now fair game."

Benni was bluffing, for low-priority counterintelligence was the purview of Uri Badash and the GSS. But he caught Hal Novak's momentary blanch and could only wonder what it meant. In fact, Novak was screaming *Stop!* inside his head, for he had recently discovered that the Defense Department's supersecret espionage wing, the Intelligence Support Activity, had two deep-cover agents actually serving in elite units of the Israel Defense Forces.

There was a knock on the door, and Peter Cole stepped away as it was pushed open. Benni could see the arm of a uniformed Marine guard, but his heart sank as a nurse stepped shyly into the room. She looked at no one as she walked through a silence thick as sour pudding, placed an electronic thermometer in his mouth, and waited for the readout.

His dismay deflated him as he lay back on the pillow. *Where the hell is Arthur?* He pleaded silently, wondering why Roselli had not arrived to help him counter Buchanan's attack. The CIA agent had left the hospital the previous evening, indicating only that he had some ideas about Benni's next course of action. Yet now Baum found himself trapped in a room with these men who obviously viewed him as a convenient scapegoat, and he wondered if his spontaneous tactics of the previous morning had been poorly chosen. . . .

His reaction to Martina's phone call had been genuine, and Aaron Davis's sickening news of Ruth's kidnapping had buckled his knees, causing him to slump to the floor of Avraham Yaron's office as a wave of nausea spun from his bowels and up into his head. Yet even as Yaron yelled once again for the embassy physician, Benni was able to calculate. He could not reveal the truth to any of his own comrades, not even to a blood brother such as Avraham. And nothing short of hospitalization would assuage Itzik Ben-Zion's impatience for his return.

He managed to give Yaron the contact number for Roselli at Langley, and within minutes a navy ambulance was speeding north on Connecticut Avenue, transporting him to the Bethesda facility.

Baum's state of shock was not feigned. The ambulance paramedics confirmed it by his blood pressure, and as he breathed heavily through a plastic oxygen mask, his wild thoughts were dulled by the inclusion of a sedative via an IV. He vaguely recalled the turn into the rolling grounds of the hospital, a glimpse of the sand-colored Bethesda tower as they swept by, the muttered curses of the driver when he saw that the emergency entrance was blocked by deliveries of the more gravely injured.

The ambulance swung to the NNMC's main entrance, halting before a massive glass facade that reflected that day's unusual winter sun, and Baum squinted painfully as they rolled his gurney from the wagon. The images and sounds blew by: the thump of rotor blades, Art Roselli's face bending over his own, Avraham Yaron's worried expression joining the American's, the hiss of hydraulic doors, and the barking of orders. A huge American flag hung from a balcony above the wide lobby, curious civilians stood from their armchairs to watch the drama, a square blue pennant showed the hospital's motto: "Caring Is What We Do Best."

He passed the better part of the day on the third "deck," in the Coronary Critical Care Unit, strapped to a high bed inside a glass-fronted cubicle. Testing revealed no threatening fibrillation or telltale muscle damage, and Benni sent Avraham packing off to send a message to Itzik Ben-Zion and then to host his congressmen, while Roselli stayed on.

At last, when the navy doctors had raised his status to stable, Benni was allowed to confer quietly with Arthur, who showed little surprise as his old friend relayed a string-of facts that might have seemed hallucinatory had they come from anyone else. Roselli had spent a life exposed to contorted plots, and he had developed quite a tolerance, yet finally his emotions caused a squint of empathic rage to hood his dark eyes.

It was Arthur's idea to contact Eytan Eckstein, his suggestion to utilize Langley's transmission capabilities. Benni gave over the frequency and contact time, and Arthur hurried away to meet the 4:00 P.M. deadline, for Addis Ababa was eight hours ahead. Before he left, he promised to return at the first opportunity, pending some arrangements he thought it wise to prepare.

"In the meantime," he warned, "be ready for the jackals. They will come."

As he left the CCU, he spoke to a doctor and arranged for Benni to be moved to a room on the other side of Three West. He noted the room number and that of its private telephone, then showed his identification to a chief petty officer. He sternly emphasized that the Israeli patient should be moved only to that designated room and that the posting of a Marine guard might be wise.

In the late afternoon, Benni was transferred to his new quarters. He was mildly sedated, unaware that Jack Buchanan and Charles Gold had already shuttled down from New York, their fervent requests to question him denied till morning by a strict "No Visitors" order from the navy doctors. Following a dinner that remained untouched by Baum, Roselli called once to check the line, assure Benni that the "telegram" had been sent, and state cryptically that he was "shaking the trees."

Later, as the night rolled in with a blanket of winter clouds, Benni found the strength to hobble from his bed. Holding his IV bag aloft with one hand, he rummaged through his valise, which had been delivered by one of Nadav's GSS men, and extracted a legal pad and his copy of *A Farewell to Arms*.

It took him a long time to devise his message to Eckstein and to properly encrypt. His concentration flagged repeatedly, and when at last he reversed the process, and it came out right, he was drained of strength and hollow of spiritual sustenance.

Still, he did not sleep. He waited, with the room lights full and glaring, afraid he might fail to be awakened by the telephone. The hours were a tortuous voyage through his life, images of his family with which his other self, the professional, tried to battle as he strove for logic, sought a plan, devised a counterstrike, and strained to discover the traps. Alone.

Yet he was a helpless pauper of information, and not having enough to even begin devising a proper strategy, he was faced with submission to a monster he had held at bay forever: defeat.

By 2:00 A.M., the ideas were dead, the image of Ruth having replaced all others, hovering above him as he prayed that she still breathed. He lay there barely moving, his palms pressed into his eyes. Once or twice his chest heaved in a sob, and he felt the sting of liquid between his cheeks and the course skin of his hands. He stayed that way until Eckstein called, then called back again, and finally an injection of hope allowed him to find peace. By the mercy of God, he did not dream. . . .

"It's normal," said the nurse as she withdrew the thermometer and quickly exited through the cordon of grave men.

There was a moment of silence after her departure, then Denny Baylor muttered, " 'Bout as normal as a beer party in Mecca," referring not to Baum's temperature but to the events of the past twenty-four hours.

Jack Buchanan grunted. He was once more staring out the window.

"Colonel Baum," he began, for the first time making an effort at cordiality, "our conflict here is giving succor to the enemy."

Benni, who had expected a renewed assault, raised his narrowed eyes. "I agree," he said. "Every minute rewards her with distance."

"At Mach speed," Charles Gold added.

Benni looked at Buchanan's deputy. "Then she is airborne, I assume?"

"A hired executive jet," said Buchanan. "But we don't think the pilots were in on it. She probably commandeered it over the Atlantic." He turned from the window and fixed his impatient gaze on the ranking NIS officer. "Jump in anytime, Cole."

Peter Cole's face hardened in objection to this cooperation, but he flipped a page on his pad and summarized in staccato.

"They took our transport vehicle in Ironsides, about fifteen klicks from the weapons center. Headed north and ditched it, plus a bogus staff car, before they hit Route 225." He looked up at Baum, remembering that the man was foreign, and added, "This is in Maryland."

Baum nodded, and Cole continued.

"They showed up clean and dry at a civilian airstrip near Pomonkey. Had a limousine and a hearse, passports, cleared customs, loaded a coffin aboard, and took off."

"A coffin," Baum whispered, as the flesh of his neck began to crawl.

"The Minnow would easily fit," said Dr. Carswell, and Benni resumed his breathing.

"Cleared customs?" Charles Gold's head tipped forward. Charter flights were rarely inspected prior to departure, and then only if on-site customs personnel had a reason to search. "That field's international?"

"No," said Cole. "But they were flight-planned for Málaga, and she probably didn't want to risk any outbound hitches, so she advised a mobile inspector."

"*She* called in customs?" Hal Novak's eyes widened.

"Yup," Cole replied.

"Balls," Denny Baylor whispered in appreciation.

"What about the truck and the staff car?" Novak asked. "Can we get prints off them?"

Cole shook his head. "Wiped, or they wore gloves. A Marine survivor says the car was driven by a naval officer, but we're sure the getup was lifted. There's a young guy in a coma up at NYU Medical, fits the description of an AWOL lieutenant. A nosy super found him in a body bag."

"*Christ,*" Buchanan said, as if hearing this for the first time.

"What happened to the hearse and the limo?" Novak probed.

"Drove away," said Cole. "Haven't picked them up yet."

So she has left men behind, Benni thought as he instinctively looked at the window. Martina's threat had not been hollow. She could have him watched and know if he left United States territory.

"May I ask?" Benni said quietly as he kept his face averted from his visitors. "Was there a description of the travelers?"

"Two women, nine men," Cole answered.

"No more details than that?" Benni worked to keep his voice steady.

"We showed a photo of Klump to the airfield personnel and got a positive ID. No match on the other female. Most of the men were Middle Eastern. *Ayrabs,* according to the gas jockeys at the strip."

"Hogs," said a deeper voice, from the vestibule near the doorway. The men turned to the source of this odd invective.

Arthur Roselli stood just inside the door, his hands in the side pockets of a blue anorak, the shoulders black with rain. A pair of sunglasses hung from a pink elastic tube around his neck, incongruous considering the weather, suggesting the carefree fashion sense of a ski coach.

Benni heard the sharp intake of air through Jack Buchanan's nose, yet the SAC held his protest in check. Baum's own breath expelled in a slow leak of relief.

Roselli looked around. He recognized the FBI officials but not the NIS men, Carswell, or the silent SEAL. He produced an ID wallet from his pocket, flipped it open, and murmured, "Roselli from Langley," as if that was the silly high sign for entry into a college frat house.

"HOGs, gentlemen," he said. "Klump's men. She was attached to Hizbollah in Lebanon early to mid-eighties. Pulled out with her own splinter group. Freelancers. Call themselves Yadd Allah, Hand of God. Get it? HOGs." He looked directly at Buchanan and added, in as nonthreatening a tone as he could manage, "But I assume you know all that, Jack."

Buchanan had a choice to make. He could rekindle his hatred, or just let the embers glow until a more convenient day. His conflict with Roselli went back nearly twenty years, to a time when the Bureau had wanted to ensconce its own mole-hunters at Langley, and the CIA had reacted like a housewife threatened by her husband's hiring of a nubile au pair. But in fact the mistrust was "cultural," animosities sown long before by J. Edgar Hoover, whose agents had ruled the roost of domestic *and* foreign intelligence until World War II, then resented the encroachment of the new Central Intelligence Agency and its Yalie playboy spies.

"That's right," said Buchanan. "We have pretty much the same thing." He rubbed his square chin. " 'HOGs' is new to me."

"Agency nomenclature," said Roselli, and warming to the truce, he smiled. "You know us. Crazy for acronyms."

Buchanan grunted, yet his attempt at a smile looked more like intestinal discomfort.

"So what's the feeling across the river?" Charles Gold asked.

"The feeling," said Roselli, "and that's all we have, is that this isn't a heist for resale. She didn't take the Minnow for another end user."

"How do you draw that conclusion?" Dr. Carswell asked hopefully.

Roselli looked at the scientist. He had never seen the man before but correctly pegged him as a "computer nerd," and a sworn-in member of this sad clique.

"The weapon's a prototype," said Roselli. "One of a kind. It's not like the Redeyes we've got floating all around now because we handed them out to the Afghans like candy."

Peter Cole raised an eyebrow, impressed that Roselli would publicly take issue with an Agency policy.

"Any third party who takes delivery knows that all of our intel assets will be out there looking," Roselli continued. "And every one of our pissed-off SOCOM operators will be itching to kill to get it back."

The gates of mercy shall be all shut up, thought the nameless SEAL in the corner. He was an Annapolis graduate.

"And if anyone uses it against a vessel," Carswell interjected, "there will be residue to identify the Minnow, even if it has to be dredged up."

"Right." Roselli looked over at Buchanan. "And then you'll probably be able to run the user down." The compliment was not backhanded, for no one could compete with the FBI's forensic capabilities.

"We sure as hell will," said Gold.

"So it's not for resale," Roselli concluded. "She's going to use it herself, because she doesn't give a shit who knows."

"Balls," Denny Baylor whispered again as he chewed the tobacco lump.

"You've got another theory?" Roselli turned on the bearded agent, assuming the remark to be a dismissal of his assessment.

"I was commenting on her nerve," said Baylor.

"Ahh." Roselli nodded. "That she's got." Then he addressed Baum directly for the first time. "Right, Colonel?"

"*Knollen.*" Benni used a descriptive German obscenity and raised a fist to show the testicular size.

The door opened once again, and Baum wondered if the entire Pentagon was going to try to squeeze into his room. When he saw that the new visitor was Detective Michael O'Donovan, a flush of anger rose to his face. He had sworn O'Donovan to look after his daughter, and the man had failed the test of a simple bodyguard. Lusting after her he could manage, but keeping her out of harm's way was too much to ask. Then he suddenly realized that his anger was misguided, a projection of his own guilt. But that self-awareness was then replaced by a shiver of insecurity, for O'Donovan might reveal that Ruth had been taken, a fact that had to be kept from Jack Buchanan.

His fears were immediately allayed, for although O'Donovan looked at him with a pained expression of apology, he also casually drew one finger across his lips, indicating that they were sealed.

"O'Donovan!" Jack Buchanan peered across the room. "Is that you?"

Roselli sidestepped, praying that the detective would hold his own.

"In the bruised flesh," said O'Donovan. The bridge of his nose was covered with a white cross of surgical tape, and patches of purple skin below his eyes looked like the deflective smears on a football player's cheeks.

"Who's this?" Charles Gold asked.

"It's O'Donovan," Buchanan said incredulously. "Midtown North." He turned back to the detective. "What the hell happened to *you?*"

"Car accident," O'Donovan answered plainly.

"You're a cop?" Peter Cole asked, trying to make some sense of the relationships.

"NYPD," Buchanan answered in O'Donovan's stead. "He was working on the consulate bombing."

"Is he cleared for this?" Cole demanded with childish propriety.

"He's with me," said Roselli.

"But is he *cleared?*" Denny Baylor emphasized, backing up his boss.

Roselli spun on the young NIS agent. "He's ex-SF, Tenth Group, clearances up the ass." Everyone in the business knew that Special Forces operators had to survive the same vetting as the Agency's most clandestine agents. "We were together at Desert One," he added for effect. "Where were *you?*"

Baylor just blinked at Roselli. In 1980, he was a junior in high school.

"You been briefed on the latest, O'Donovan?" Buchanan asked.

"Affirmative," said the detective.

"Thoroughly," Roselli interjected.

"Then you know what we've got here." Buchanan focused grimly on O'Donovan, not terribly pleased to see a man whom he had recently treated like a gofer. "Wish you'd nailed this bitch last week. Then we'd be preparing for indictments, instead of burials at Arlington."

O'Donovan's eyes narrowed, an expression that caused him physical pain. His voice dropped to a heavier caliber.

"*I* was just working the homicide angle. Remember? *You* run the terrorism task force, *Jack.*"

Buchanan's lips worked soundlessly. Then he shut them.

"There isn't time for this," said Hal Novak. "Roselli, what's your target assessment? People are waiting to deploy."

Art Roselli rubbed his jaw, raising his eyes across the room to Benni. They had planned this next part carefully, but it was unrehearsed. "Well, we should assume that every American vessel between here and the Red Sea is at risk. Any ship exposed to open water of, let's say . . . what's the effective range?"

"The Minnow requires one hundred meters to arm itself," said Dr. Carswell.

"One hundred meters of open-water exposure," Roselli concluded.

"Shit," said Peter Cole. "That's hundreds of targets."

"Pssss." The nameless SEAL released a sound like a submarine blowing ballast. His men could never cover such a list of maybes.

"But I think," said Roselli, "that our guest here might be able to narrow that." He folded his arms as he continued gazing at Benni.

"I believe I told you, Mr. Roselli," Benni said through a tight mouth, "that this particular risk is *ours* alone. An Israeli affair."

"The target risk might be yours," said Roselli, "but the device is ours."

"What's the deal here?" Jack Buchanan asked in frustration. "You two know each other? What the hell you talking about?"

"We've had contact before." Roselli colored his tone with displeasure. "And we have our differences on this."

"No fucking surprise," said Buchanan.

"Come on, Baum," said Roselli with more urgency. "Give it up. Tell them, or we're all off on a wild-goose chase."

That was exactly what the two men had planned, although it had been Baum who was more reluctant to squander the resources of American Intelligence and Defense. He was fairly certain of Martina's intended landfall, the site from which she would jump off to assault Moonlight in the Mediterranean. Carrying her stolen American prize, she would certainly not set down in any European or African nation where there was a significant American presence, or in any area where Israelis could comfortably operate.

Algeria was openly hostile now to both countries, given its Moslem fundamentalist propensity, so the section of the Tango file suggesting Martina's mobile command post in the Algerian Sahara appeared likely. Benni could, in fairly good conscience, withhold this guess from his interviewers, while Roselli had the authority to focus certain CIA reconnaissance assets on Algeria without specifying the motive. Yet Baum still did not feel comfortable with a more elaborate deception.

However, Arthur had reasoned that without concocting a full decoy, they could not deflect American attention from the secret prisoner exchange or the deadly predicament of Ruth. These people had to be given an alternative target.

"All right," said Baum with exasperation. "All right." He looked up at the ceiling as if begging forgiveness for the coming transgression. "Martina Klump has a bone to pick with us—with Israel, that is, and with the German government as well. As you all know, she was once a wanted member of the Red Army Faction. A joint Israeli-German operation resulted in her capture and imprisonment. She has sworn vengeance."

It sounded awfully melodramatic as he said it, but that part was not far from the truth. He inhaled deeply, as if the next revelation would require all his moral strength.

"There is a clandestine deal about to be consummated between Bonn and Jerusalem," he lied. "The Israeli Navy has purchased a pair of customized attack submarines from Germany. We are scheduled to take delivery next week, in Bremerhaven." He raised his bare arms to show that nothing was left up his sleeves. "Those submarines, gentlemen, or one of them, are most probably Martina Klump's target."

As if disgusted by his own indiscretion, Benni dropped his hands onto the bed with a thud.

There was a short silence, then the men reacted like a basketball team that had nearly forfeited a game due to the fouls of one player. They groaned, someone smacked his forehead, and a string of low curses echoed in the stuffy room.

"Jesus fucking Christ, Baum!" Buchanan resumed his comfortable rancor. "You've been holding that back?!"

"Could've saved us this whole damned square dance," Peter Cole muttered.

"*We are* capable of discretion, Colonel," said Hal Novak.

"I *told* you, Baum," Roselli chastised.

Benni chose to address Novak's comment. "I'm sure that you are," he said. "And I am sorry. However, you must understand the sensitivity here. We have sworn to Bonn not to reveal this sale. Left-wing elements in Germany's government are very powerful, and a vote of no confidence could result." He paused. "I admit that I might have told you sooner. But I was not at liberty to do so."

"Well, thank you for *sharing*." Buchanan's voice oozed. His mood was lifting, for at least the target was not American.

"And there are further complexities," Baum continued as he completed his ruse. "We cannot warn the Germans of this danger, for they might withdraw from the deal. We need those boats. And," he added, looking chagrined, "due to some past indiscretions, we have sworn not to operate on German soil."

Roselli picked up his cue. "So you're saying that Israeli security teams can't be at the site, at the sub pens? Not even for defensive purposes?"

"Skeleton sub crews," said Benni. "And nothing more."

"All right," said Buchanan, pulling his lip thoughtfully. "All right. At least we've got something to chew on." He looked at Roselli. "Langley, did your sky eyes get anything on the aircraft."

"Negative so far. We also ran it by the FAA, but they had no distress signal from any airplane in Atlantic sectors. Plus, yesterday's weather was a break after heavy storm systems, so lots of backed-up traffic took to the air. It was a mess."

"What about humint?" Peter Cole asked Roselli about information coming in from field agents.

"We've already got assets checking out every potential European strip, within reason, of course. I suggest you do the same."

"We will," said Cole as he puffed up a bit. He turned toward the nameless SEAL in the corner and began to make a suggestion. The man was gone. "Where'd he go?" he muttered.

"Knives to sharpen?" Denny Baylor speculated scornfully. He had once wanted to be a SEAL himself but he had been cut during "Hell Week" in Coronado.

"Gold," Buchanan said to his deputy. "We'd better get in touch with our people in Germany. What's the nearest major city to that port?"

"Hamburg," Benni offered, but watching the Americans take his and Arthur's bait, he desperately wanted them to be on their way, for his urge to come clean was powerful. He moved his hand to the nurse's call button and surreptitiously pressed it.

"I'll contact the consulate there," said Gold.

"And let's put the Pomonkey descriptions together and fax 'em," Buchanan added. "No, better, let's get the airfield people to D.C. and work the Identi-Kit."

"Right," said Gold as he jotted on his pad.

Benni suffered a chill as he pictured an image of Ruth's face being distributed along with those of the other "suspects."

"Think I'll head over to the Pent," said Hal Novak, pulling on a tan trench coat. "See if they'll take some suggestions."

"You do that," said Buchanan with inappropriate authority. Novak looked up with a reproachful glare.

The door was suddenly thrust open, yet this time no timid nurse appeared. The woman who entered wore olive slacks and a lime-colored, epauletted uniform blouse. She was tall and officious, with short brown hair cut close to a handsome face. She wore captain's bars and a stethoscope, and she marched over to Baum's bed carrying a clipboard.

"What's the problem, Colonel?" she asked as she glanced at his chart.

"No problem, Doctor," Benni said, as if he had punched the call button inadvertently. "I am feeling a bit tired, though."

She walked to his side, flipped his wrist over, pressed two fingers to the pulse, and looked at her watch. After ten seconds she issued an order without glancing up. "Everybody out."

Dr. Carswell snapped up from the other bed and began gathering his papers as if he had been scolded by a nun. The other men stole looks at each other, yet they also began to file toward the door. Roselli and O'Donovan hung back.

"We have work to do," said Buchanan, turning back to Baum from the door. "But don't go anywhere." He was eyeing Roselli suspiciously.

"I would not dream of it," Benni promised, and as the FBI man squinted at him and finally left, he blew out a sigh.

"Seems fine." The doctor removed her hand. "Any difficulty breathing?"

"No," said Benni.

"Pain?"

"Negative."

"That's U.S. military parlance." She almost smiled at him. "Very good. How do you say it in Hebrew?"

"*Shlili.*"

"*Nachon,*" she replied in the same language—"Correct"—and in response to Benni's stunned expression, she explained, "Three months in Haifa with the Sixth Fleet."

"Wow," Roselli exclaimed. "See, Baum? You can never be too careful."

The doctor frowned at the two remaining interlopers. "You too," she said as she flipped a thumb toward the door and gathered her clipboard. "He should rest."

"I just want to chat with them," Benni begged. "A few minutes."

"Just a few," said the captain, backing toward the door. "While you're in here, Colonel, your heart is *mine.*"

Baum smiled and saluted as she departed.

"Your *heart* is *mine*?" Roselli whispered to Baum through a grin.

Benni shrugged, while the CIA officer's smile faded as he recalled the details of the Klump case that Baum had painfully revealed only yesterday. The issues of the hijacked Minnow, Ruth's kidnapping, and the secret prisoner exchange were bad enough, but they were layered over a background that made Baum's position impossible. He felt great sorrow for Baum. He had met Benni's daughter on more than one occasion in Jerusalem, and he could imagine the excruciating crush of conscience gripping the old warrior's heart.

Michael O'Donovan was standing back from the foot of the bed, examining his shoes. Benni looked at the young detective's battered face, the bruises set off by the pallor of his winter skin. He recognized the genuine pain of a remorseful lover, and he was about to speak, when O'Donovan looked up.

"Colonel, I don't know how to say this . . ."

"Then don't say it, Michael." Benni absolved him. "What's done is done. You can share the details of it later, if it will help us. We have to move forward now, and quickly."

O'Donovan looked at him for a long moment. "Right," he said.

Benni motioned for Roselli to come closer, for he was genuinely tired and had to lie back on the pillow.

"What now, Arthur?" he asked in a near whisper. "Eckstein is on the way to Casablanca, though God only knows what he expects of me there." He pinched the end of his bulbous nose as if to ward off emotion. "I am afraid to move from here."

O'Donovan slipped up to the bed and also lowered his tone. "You really think she's got watchers here, Colonel?"

"The agents confirmed it, Michael." Benni sighed. "She left men behind."

"Yeah," Arthur agreed. "We have to assume that." He reached for Benni's telephone and dialed a number.

"So why don't you have your people just pick them up?" O'Donovan asked Roselli impatiently. "They must be right around here somewhere, staying close to the colonel."

"It's *Benni*, for God's sake," Baum admonished yet again. "And he cannot just pick them up. That could cause Martina to act. . . ." He trailed off and frowned at his clenched fists.

"My *people* have other *ways*," said Roselli. Then he spoke into the telephone. "Okay, Tripod," he said, and hung up. "Can you smoke in here?"

"Only if you want to die by that woman's hands," Baum muttered, meaning his hard-nosed physician.

"Could think of worse ways to die." Roselli laughed, but he put the Marlboro box away in his pocket.

None of the men spoke for a moment, each of them lost in his own inner conflicts. Benni turned to O'Donovan.

"Don't you have to get back to New York, Michael?"

"Sick leave," said O'Donovan.

"Uh huh," Benni grunted. Then he sputtered with exasperation. "*Ani moochrach livroach me po.* I've got to get out of here."

"*Savlanoot*. Patience," said Roselli, which surprised O'Donovan, as he had no knowledge of the agent's stint in Jerusalem.

The door opened to the sound of the Marine guard's uniform snapping as he came to attention, and three men strode crisply into the room. They wore the spotless green tunics of Marine Corps officers, and Benni cursed under his breath as he suspected another delegation arriving to plunder his mind. He reached for the call button, but Arthur quickly stayed his hand.

"Welcome aboard, gentlemen," said Roselli with a bright smile.

The men grinned back as one of them saluted and clicked his heels in Chaplinesque style. Baum and O'Donovan peered at the men more closely.

The first officer was a lieutenant colonel, the second a major, and the third sported gleaming captain's bars. Each wore a peaked cap, and their physical similarities to one another were obvious. None of them over five feet eight inches tall, they had broad shoulders and heavy, muscular girths. They were clean-shaven, and their wide faces shone with rain and mischievous expressions.

"Remember Flute?" Roselli asked Baum as he looked his men over with pleasure. "Gave me an idea."

Baum squinted at his friend, confused by his reference to the operation in 1986 when the two had cemented their bond. Then he realized the nature of Roselli's gambit, and he snapped his head back to the three "Marines."

"Shell game." Roselli crossed his arms. "Gentlemen," he said to the officers. "This is Mike O'Donovan, and the prone fellow is Lieutenant Colonel Benjamin Baum."

The three men nodded politely. They were Agency employees, men who had worked for years with Roselli in various clandestine capacities. The "captain" smiled.

"I'm Moe," he said.

Next to him, the "major" picked up his cue. "I'm Larry."

"So I guess I'm Curly," said the third man, as he reached up to remove his colonel's cap. His head was almost completely bald, except for a few fringes of gray straying back behind his large ears. Both O'Donovan and Baum gaped at the evident similarity between the CIA man and Benni.

"Just did it this morning," said the "colonel" as he ran one beefy hand over his freshly shaved pate. "My wife *hated* it."

The other two officers began to laugh. Roselli followed suit, and both O'Donovan and Baum were unable to suppress their own wide grins.

"It looks very attractive to *me*," said Benni. "Very."

The laughter settled into throat clearing, a lighter mood of cautious optimism as the burly agent stepped forward. A strange air of witchery hovered as his and Baum's faces, like those of brothers reunited after a spell of decades, neared each other.

"Well, Colonel," said the agent as he began to unbutton his tunic and pointed at the hospital mattress, "hope that bed's comfortable."

Chapter 15: The North African Coast

The Dassault Falcon 900 executive jet soared on a surface of frigid black air, its mirror-sharp chestnut underbelly nudging the buffets at 33,000 feet, its steel wings swaying from port to starboard as it dodged the peaks of Atlantic winds. The sleek nose and polished windshields of the mechanical hawk reflected a hard high moon as it dove through waves of stratosphere, and the thundering heat of its tri-jets left a long, curving wake of vapor behind the blade of its tail.

The falcon flew effortlessly tonight, yet no higher than the spirits of Martina Ursula Klump. She watched the reflection of her own smile in the porthole, an expression that finally showed release from months of tension. Yet as her eyes flicked down through the quilt of clouds to the surface of a darkened sea, her body refused to be still.

She reclined in a butter-cream leather seat that would have seduced most travelers to sleep, but the toe of her boot tapped the air, her shoulders and thighs swayed beneath the dark wool of her long dress, and as the crescendos of the Allegro assai of Beethoven's Ninth filled her headphones, she began to conduct. Her eyes closed, her head bobbed, the black bangs of her wig thrashed across her forehead, she lifted her fists, and the London Festival Orchestra and Chorus were hers. She commanded them, drove them on until they obeyed, melded with their maestro, and finally roared together in a stunning Germanic climax.

She slumped back, breathless, and as she tore the headphones off she opened her eyes to find Salim across the cabin isle, frozen to his own seat as he regarded his commander with shock. She began to laugh, and then she threw her head back and let it come, roaring until the tears streamed into her ears.

At last she recovered, laced her fingers together, and stretched. Just above her a video monitor displayed the progress of the Falcon, a white line crawling over an electric-blue map toward the green contours of the Strait of Gibraltar. Past the monitor, the crystal cabinets of the jet's galley reflected the blinking diodes of a CD player, and through the forward door she could see Mussa's wing tips resting on the cockpit floor, his body hidden behind a bulkhead in the crewman's jump seat. Just past his legs, the starched white shirts of the pilots framed a carnival of cockpit displays.

Martina pivoted and continued to survey her vessel. She had chartered the French-built aircraft solely for its size and range, yet the airborne estate was fit for a duchess.

I have done it. She slapped her thigh as once more Salim came into view, his body cocked, prepared to spring to her command. She smiled at the contrasting posture of Muhammed, asleep in the bucket facing Salim, arms dangling, fingers brushing the rich red carpet. *I fooled them all, escaped the chase of a hundred American hounds, took their precious toy, and left them ranting to themselves.*

She stopped turning and faced fully aft, adoring the men who occupied this luxury so well deserved. The cabin walls tunneled away, brocaded in a cream material of irregular texture like the skin of a rare animal. The curved ceiling held panels of reading lamps and air nozzles plated in gold, while the lower walls were lined with polished cabinets of red gum wood. Four more leather seats surrounded a thickly grained dining table extending from the port fuselage. Yaccub, Jaweed, and Ali played a game of cards on half its surface, while Nabil sat next to them, ticking quietly on the keyboard of a Compaq laptop. The cabin was cool, and the men still wore the dark jackets of their "mourning" suits, their activity suggesting wealthy young princes aboard a flying casino.

Beyond them, half a bulkhead obscured most of the Falcon's small bedroom, yet she could see the thick black pipes of Riyad's and Youssef's trousered legs, and across from them, on a couch whose lush upholstery matched the carpet, the soles of the girl's shoes.

Once I trusted Baum, she remembered, the bitterness diluted by sweet vengeance. *Now I've trussed him.* She slid back a gold ashtray cover, lit up a slim Du Maurier, and depressed the button to recline her seat, indulging the nostalgia of Skorpion's first-stage success.

We are all here. And alive, she marveled, like an outrageously lucky combat commander. Then she frowned at the thought of Iyad. *Well, not all so lively.* His head had made the trip, but his body was folded into a refrigerator in the basement of the Brooklyn safe house. Yet in death, Iyad had proved himself to be ten times more useful than when he still drew breath. Martina's smile returned again as she recalled the American customs inspector, briefly raising the coffin lid, then dropping it again as if he had glimpsed the corpse of Count Dracula himself.

Without that final touch of verisimilitude, who could say where they would be now? She could not be judged by the moral tenets of Judeo-Christian ethics, that phrase itself being laughably oxymoronic. Any Imam who witnessed the blind faith and selfless courage of Yadd Allah would have blessed her act as a necessity of Jihad.

Of course, it was also not wholly true that all of her men had made the roll call. Fouad and Fahmi had to remain behind to drive the limousine and hearse from the scene, because abandoning the vehicles would have alerted inquisitive minds at the airport, and Baum also had to be convinced that an observation post remained on American soil. There was the risk that they might be captured, but absolutely none that they might talk. And they would be reunited, all of them, she assured herself. They would sip mint tea on the balcony of the Imperial in Beirut, their faces aglow with the sun sliding into the Mediterranean as they laughed together and remembered.

How smoothly it had all run, more like a Hollywood film than an actual mission, which were usually fraught with mishaps. She saw herself again, walking through the black smoke of the burning Hum-Vee, unstoppable as a battle tank. She saw her men flooding toward her, drawn by her power as they swept human encumbrances aside and executed their moves. The wind buzzed through her sweat-soaked hair again, whipping into the staff car as they sped from the ambush site.

And then they were off the road, in a secluded copse behind a barn, having all switched costumes inside the vehicles, submerging the uniforms and weapons in weighted duffels to the bottom of a pre-reconnoitered pond, bolt-cutting the Minnow from its cradle, snuggling the fish into the coffin, the coffin back into its idling caisson, then each man checking his own and his partner's attire and documents, looking for potential giveaways. And they were off again, for the airport.

They had stopped once more at the roadside, for she had to be certain, and she marched around the vehicles, peering in the windows. "Straighten your tie," she instructed Jaweed. "Your shoes are muddy," she informed Riyad. "Don't carry the girl," she coached the men again. Ruth was conscious, but her glassy eyes and limp head warned of a potential swoon, too much melodrama for even the most bereft young widow. "Just grip her elbow, and make sure she knows I will shoot her if she makes trouble." She handed Ali an ammonia capsule to break under the girl's nose, and he took it as he said, almost apologetically, "Your wig is crooked." Martina thanked him and spent the last minutes before the arrival at the airstrip preening, while the men cleaned their hands and faces with alcohol wipes.

She barely remembered the boarding of the jet, just snatches of images, like those of her own wedding. It all proceeded in slow motion, because that was the pace she had demanded. After all, it was a funeral procession, not a bank heist. The airstrip personnel were not accustomed to hosting wealthy clients or aircraft of the Falcon's size, yet because of the solemn nature of the business, the crop-duster pilots and weekend Cessna jockeys kept a respectful distance. Only Martina and Mussa spoke, and though the Falcon pilots doubted that the coffin would fit into the rear cargo hold, Nabil had researched it to the last centimeter.

He had bought a folding metal stand for an electric piano and now set it against the forward bulkhead of the hold, propping one end of the coffin on it, the angle allowing the outer door to close with a pneumatic hiss.

"Well, I'll be damned," the chief pilot exclaimed, scratching his head.

"*Blessed*, I should think," said Martina as she thanked the customs inspector, who just shrugged, still confused as to why he had been summoned by this aristocratic woman, when he usually found himself engaged in nasty exchanges with irate travelers.

She remembered, with a sense of pride, the faces of Fouad and Fahmi, resolute, chins uplifted, as they stood by the hearse and limousine and watched her walk toward the jet's stairway. She could not bid them farewell, hug them as she wished, but at the last second she found the excuse. She walked to them, proffering a "tip" as would befit a customer of her stature, and as the hundred-dollar bills were exchanged, she shook their hands with such power that the squeezes would remain in their memories.

And then the door closed, the Falcon turned onto the single long runway, and she held her breath until it finally rose into the early eastern sun, barely clearing the Maryland pines. . . .

She squinted through her cigarette smoke, focusing again on the small female feet in the aft chamber. The image raised the discomfiting specter of another loose end, her mother, who remained helplessly alone in Yorkville. Yet *Mutti* was most likely safely adrift in her senile reveries. She may have been questioned briefly by the Americans, but they would have quickly realized the limits of her contributions. The pathetic, lawyer-laden American justice system would deem her mother useless as a witness, forbidden as a pawn. They might watch her in fruitless hope, but ultimately they would have to leave her be.

The Falcon bounded gently as it passed through a pocket of low pressure, and the girl's feet twitched once, like the limbs of a dreaming dog. The injection she had been given just after boarding would be wearing thin now, yet with Youssef and Riyad as baby-sitters, Ruth Baum was hardly a threat. Martina looked at her watch. Less than an hour remained . . .

Ruth also sailed aloft among the clouds, yet they were the high, wispy cirrus of chemical dreams. The sun was white and sharp and far away, a brilliant dot against a shimmering azure sky. Her hands stretched out before her as she floated, her fingers brown from the beach holiday that had begun some time ago, yet had no limit, no sad anticipation of its end. A slim silver ring flashed on one finger, cotton sleeves billowed over her forearms, and the cool vapors tickled her cheeks as she flew under the power of her own ecstasy.

She looked down at the seductive layer of cloud, bent her head, and settled onto a creamy bedsheet, the scent of fresh laundry and the sweet pungency of a man's aftershave rising from the pillow. The bed, an endless mattress without corners or borders, rose up gently and fell again. She felt a weight on her back, a soft nudge, and she rolled over, reaching up to touch the smooth muscles of his shoulders, the downy hairs at the nape of his neck. The rocking came again, yet now it was their rhythm, together, entwined, as she drew her head back, stretched her throat, and sighed.

The bed bucked hard, but suddenly she knew it was not love. The sun went out, day to night, quick and horrible, like a coffin lid slammed down over a coroner's miscalculation. Her hands scrabbled at the air as she tried to surface, and then she heard Mike's voice calling to someone, but it was *not* his voice, the accent strange.

"She's up. She's up."

Her eyelids were glued. She brought her palms to her brows and smeared them up. The darkness was replaced by blinding pins of light, then a hovering black mushroom. She saw the woman's face inches from her own, the wide mouth, the black hair, and she screamed.

Martina's fingers dug into Ruth's shoulders as she pulled her up into a sitting position on the couch. Ruth's head sank forward; a hand pushed her forehead back. Just beyond Martina's breast, a huge man leaned forward, reaching out for her. A wave of nausea clenched her as she retched and slid to her knees. Someone cursed, a door was kicked open, fingernails pinched her armpits, and she crawled into a small room. A gold sink was to her right, a hand turned her head to the left, but there was only a heavily upholstered seat there. She could not hold it any longer, yet suddenly the seat flipped up to reveal a steel commode, and she regurgitated nothing but saliva and coughed until her tears met at the bridge of her nose.

At last, the rebellion of her body subsided. A damp cloth poked through the tumble of her hair and swiped over her mouth. She slid slowly back and sat on her heels, her arms trembling as she gripped the commode for support. She heard the suffocated whine of jet aircraft engines and it all came back to her full force, like the hollow dread of a mourner waking to a dawn that would not bring relief, could not roll back time.

Elohim. Oh, God. She shook her head once, and a liquid whirlpool swirled in her brain. *I'm still here.* She remembered her last wakeful state, as she walked toward the airplane, wanting to cry out but for the hand that gripped her elbow, the woman's face that watched as it escorted, the brows knitted in concern above eyes that threatened death.

That had been real, the wedding bed a dream.

She opened her eyes. She was wearing a long black dress, spotted with liquid. Where is *Abba* now? Her silent plea brought a flash of anger, some strength to her arms as they steadied. Yet she quickly wondered the same of Michael, which evoked her last image of him, being thrashed by those men, his half-naked body arching back into her apartment. What had they done to him, the *bastards*? Had they killed him? Left him on her floor to be found by those other policemen, who should somehow have been there to stop this? How had they all allowed it, let her be taken by these maniacs?

There was only one answer. They were dead. Both of them. Her father and Michael. She felt the beginning of a sob, then swallowed it, hard. No. *Abba* had gone to Washington, to the embassy. No one could harm him there, and by now he would know she had been abducted. She was alone, yes, but only here, not in the entire world. For now she was helpless, yet she still had power over her own mind. She could weep over Michael, or hope that he, too, had survived. She chose life, to give her strength.

Large, callused hands encircled her forearms, and this time she steeled herself as the man helped her to her feet. She did not know Youssef's name, but she recognized the huge head of short black curls, the flat nose and heavy lips. It was the same man she had seen in profile as he swung something into Michael's face. She searched the eyes and found them to be not cruel, just large and dull, the expression of an obedient guard. She would ask him about Michael, but later. He would tell her with his eyes.

The woman gripped her waist from behind, and she stepped forward as a chill snaked over her flesh. The big man backed up, ducked through a passageway, and she saw the length of the plane. Male heads poked into the aisle from both sides of the tunnel, turning back to stare at her like movie patrons disturbed by a drunken heckler.

"*Setzen Sie sich,*" a voice commanded as her body was steered to the left, and she hazily wondered why the woman assumed she knew German. Seeing the wine-red couch, she felt her knees go liquid again, and she sank into it as the aircraft bucked. *Pregnancy*, she thought, and she dropped her head back on a cushion and closed her eyes. *This must be what it's like.* The incongruity of the image surprised her, and she remembered an old teenage fantasy, of a love affair with Eytan Eckstein, daydreams of having his baby. Eckstein. If he were here, he would walk through this flying can of terrorists and shoot each one between the eyes.

She heard the pop of a metal tab, the hiss of carbonation. Someone gripped her jaw, and she looked up to find the German woman hovering over her, holding a can of Coke like a TV actress on Channel Hell.

"Drink," said Martina. "If you are good, no more drugs."

Ruth took the can, and the sweet cold liquid buzzed down her raw throat. Martina placed her hands on her hips.

"*In Ordnung?*" she asked, like a jaded night nurse.

"Things go better," Ruth whispered.

Martina nodded. She turned and said to someone, "She will be no trouble," and she marched briskly away.

I am going to kill you, Ruth swore silently as she watched Martina's receding back. . . .

The Falcon pilots were not particularly alarmed by the eccentric behavior and odd composition of their passengers, or by the uncommon instructions issued by the woman who ran the show. When you worked for Jetstar Aviation, Inc., you knew that you were no more than a glorified chauffeur. Jetstar was a charter service, and anyone who had the cash could hire you out. Each job brought new passengers, another boss, king or queen for a day. There were weird dietary demands, cinema tastes for the VCR from Disney to porno, antismoking fanatics who wanted the ashtrays sterilized, fat men who ordered up boxes of Macanudo cigars.

Joe Dawson, the man in the left seat, had flown A-4 Skyhawks for the navy in Vietnam. His copilot, Chip Bergh, had jockeyed air force F-4 Phantoms, though he had been too young for the "Southeast Asia Games." Neither man had wanted to put in the commercial airline years needed to make chief pilot, so they had opted for the type of flying that reminded them of their military years: you never knew where you were headed next.

This job was a little stranger than most. First of all, they always flew with a steward or stewardess, who tended to the passengers. Canceled by the customer. Then, they had been told to file a flight plan from Salisbury Airport in Maryland to Málaga, Spain, so they had topped off the tanks and run a full preflight in Baltimore, while Dawson punched the "From" and "To" codes into the AFIS system, coming up with fourteen legs over an easy 3,250 nautical miles, just under seven hours with a 33-knot tail wind at 37,000 feet. But just prior to takeoff, the point of departure had been changed to a strip in Maryland that did not even show up on the vector charts. Bergh quickly flipped through the Jeppesen Airway manuals, finally locating a diagram of Pomonkey, which did have a 5,000-foot macadam strip. But as he showed it to Dawson, he pointed out a printed warning. Caution: Strolling dogs on the maneuvering area.

Dawson looked at him.

"*Strolling* dogs?"

"Woof, woof," Bergh replied.

They were ex-fighter jockeys. They shrugged and took off for Pomonkey.

The coffin was a surprise, even more so because it fit into a cargo hold that had been designed only for a cartload of luggage. Dawson had a rule, that he would haul anything but guns or drugs, yet the customs inspector saved him from having to ask embarrassing questions. Anyway, this group did look pretty funereal, and he and Bergh slipped their "serious masks" over their usual jocularity and headed for Spain.

The woman was polite, very businesslike, and beautiful in that hard way that reminded Dawson of female navy officers who had run the gauntlet of male fraternities. Just after takeoff, she'd entered the cockpit and issued some odd orders. He and Bergh were to forgo wearing their lightweight headsets and instead listen to incoming radio traffic over the cockpit speaker and respond using hand mikes. All communications were to be pumped through to the headphones at the jet's dining station, and since one of her guests was ill, they would kindly ask before using the bathroom. Other than that, happy flying.

When the woman had gone, Bergh shot Dawson a look. The pilot responded with an eye roll: just another crazy client. For an instant, the thought of a hijacking crossed his mind, but that was a wacky notion here, as this wasn't a commercial flight. There was no need for the woman to commandeer them, as she was shelling out big bucks for the ride and they would go wherever she wanted, fuel and landing facilities permitting. That same devil-take-it attitude that had kept Dawson's gray eyes unmarred by crows' feet, his black hair thick, and his age difficult to pin down returned to him quickly. He was about to make an off-color remark to Bergh about "Bat Girl," when the woman returned with a dark, serious-looking fellow who sat down in the crew seat, folded his arms, and watched them fly. The guy never moved, for six hours, not even to take a leak.

At one point, about two hours over the Atlantic, Dawson had tried to engage the young man in conversation. The pilot loved the Falcon 900 and he reveled in showing her off, but this particular model had one flaw that never failed to make a client laugh. The cockpit digital warning chip had been programmed by an engineer with a lisp. You could punch a button and test the warnings, the flight deck filling with the processed voice of the programmer. Instead of "Stall! Stall!" this one said, "Thtall! Thtall!" Rather than "Don't sink!" it cried, "Don't think!" No matter how many times they repeated the act, it always broke up the clients. The guy in the jump seat didn't even crack a smile.

Martina appeared in the doorway of the flight deck. She leaned one shoulder against the frame and looked forward through the wide windows.

"How is it going, gentlemen?"

Dawson turned his head. The woman's voice was low and full, sort of a French accent with sharp edges. Her straight black hair obscured most of her face. "Just fine, ma'am," he said. He was curious about the other woman's scream and had glimpsed her being helped into the head. "How's the young lady?"

"She will be all right." Martina's eyes stayed focused forward. "Some bad dreams. Airsick."

"Sorry about that," said Dawson. "We'll be dropping altitude soon, hitting some more bumps. She the widow?"

"Yes."

"Tough break." He clucked his tongue. "Young guy?"

"Brain hemorrhage," said Martina. Mussa shifted in his jump seat.

"Jeez," Chip Bergh empathized.

Martina brought a hand to her lips, and Dawson realized she was holding a cigarette.

"Ma'am," he said uncomfortably, "I'm required to ask you not to smoke on the flight deck."

Martina turned her face to him, and the blank blue eyes drove an icicle into his groin.

"Then ask," she said quietly.

"Ma'am," he began again, knowing it could cost Jetstar a fat account, "please don't smoke on deck."

She smiled at him, but only with her lips. No teeth, no eyes. Then she twisted toward the galley, tossed the burning butt into the spotless sink, and resumed her position, staring forward as she recited like an FAA inspector.

"An inadvertently dropped cigarette might cause the pilots to have to attend to a fire during crucial flight operations."

"Right, ma'am," said Dawson. "Glad you understand."

"Although you are on autopilot anyway. Correct?"

Indeed, the Falcon's yokes moved gracefully, untouched by either pilot's hands. The aircraft's control surfaces had been run by the Honeywell FMS computers since Maryland, following the AFIS plan. The pilots simply monitored the EFIS video and clock-style displays showing altitude, pressures, fuel, weather, progress, and vectors. They would take control only for evasive traffic maneuvers, or thirty minutes out from landing.

"Yeah," said Dawson, feeling an inexplicable embarrassment. "We're hightech."

"Where are we?" Martina asked.

" 'Bout a hundred miles from Gibraltar," Chip Bergh said. He did not look at the woman. He wondered if she gave Dawson the creeps too.

"We will be changing course," said Martina.

"Pardon?" Dawson bent his head to the right, as if his hearing were impaired.

"We will be changing course. We are not going into Málaga."

"We're not," the pilot said flatly.

"We will refile for Oran," she said.

Bergh looked at Dawson, his eyebrows creasing above his nose.

"It is a city in Algeria," said Martina. "On the northern coast."

"Do you want me to notify Málaga?" Dawson asked, although such a procedure was unnecessary. This was not a commercial flight, with a crowd of passengers' kin anxious for its arrival.

"No," said Martina. "Unless your wives are waiting for you."

The pilots said nothing. They also did not act quickly enough.

Martina squatted as Mussa pulled his feet back to give her room. She pointed to the horizontal console between the pilots' seats and addressed them in a patronizing tone.

"Would you like me to do it *for* you, gentlemen?" She gestured at the keyboard below one of the Honeywells. "You simply look up the new destination code through AFIS, refile from your last way point, push AP here for Autopilot, then NAV here for Navigation, and this lovely machine will do the rest."

Joe Dawson's face colored to a crimson that usually only his teenagers managed to elicit. He had to work at keeping his voice even.

"You've done some flying, ma'am."

"A hobby," said Martina. She stood up again. "Oran is nearly due west of Gibraltar, perhaps one vector change and an additional two hundred and forty-two nautical miles."

"We'll need clearance," said Dawson.

"No we won't. We will not actually land there. Approximately forty miles out, you will turn right onto a new heading and proceed to a smaller strip."

Dawson sighed. "And where's that, ma'am?" He glimpsed Bergh's hand balling up on his knee. Jetstar had thirteen pilots, and *they* had the luck to get stuck with Amelia Earhart.

"Farther south. You will have ample fuel."

Suddenly she touched Dawson's shoulder, squeezing it as she bent her head down and smiled at him. It took all his willpower not to shake her off, as he decided she must be the kind of lover who likes to make men yell.

"And you don't have to bother with the FMS, Mr. Dawson." Her breath was laced with cigarettes and coffee. "My man in the back is printing out your new flight plan." She turned to the dour youth in the jump seat and said, "*Rûh,*" which was a word from no language in Dawson's lexicon.

Mussa got up and walked quickly aft as Martina settled herself into his seat. She crossed her legs, leaned one elbow on her knee, and fingered the strand of pearls near her throat as she focused on the pilots, whose shoulders now showed the tension she had anticipated. The cockpit speaker volume was set to minimum, yet as the Falcon nudged into the evening Mediterranean air traffic, the transmission chatter began to pick up, like a restless Broadway audience during an overlong intermission.

Dawson and Bergh silently awaited instructions, while each of them secretly wanted to cut out of autopilot, take the controls, land at Málaga, and look for other employment. Maybe a Federal Express gig, where the letters and parcels couldn't jerk you around. It was not the first time that Joe Dawson wished he and his copilot shared some obscure foreign language that could not be understood by a client. But he realized that even if he and Bergh shared Swahili, mumbling it to each other would probably just tick the woman off.

Mussa reappeared in the doorway of the flight deck. He handed Martina two copies of a printout from Nabil's laptop, whose hard disk contained flight plan software similar to AFIS. The new plan was laid out in a matrix of three short legs, showing the proper vector for each, distance, flight time, fuel required, airspeed, ground speed, and the "comfort factor" of avgas remaining upon arrival. The legs began over Gibraltar, turned south before Oran, passed over Tlemcen, turned south-southwest over Figuig, and ended at the edge of the Algerian Sahara at a place designated as *Skorpion.*

Martina thought for a few moments, unconsciously waving the papers under her throat as if cooling her skin.

"All right," she said to Mussa in German. "Cut the cabin lights and tell the men to stay alert."

Mussa retreated to his tasks, while Martina resumed her forward vigil. She was not interested in nature's canvas of night sky. She knew that if her flight had been pinpointed by American military forces, U.S. Navy fighters would try to intercept her here, where their carriers plied the Mediterranean and there were many Allied bases into which to force her down. Behind her, the brightly lit passenger compartment turned to a purple cavern as her men swiveled to the windows, watching for the flames of afterburners. She handed Dawson one of the printouts.

"Drop ten thousand feet," she ordered like a submarine captain. "Shallow glide path on the first heading."

Dawson and Bergh were actually relieved to take control from the Honeywells. They felt better easing up on the white throttle spools, handling the yokes rather than watching their disembodied jinking.

"Give me the Oran tower frequency," said Martina. "It is one one seven point one."

Bergh made the radio adjustment.

"A microphone," said Martina.

Dawson was tempted to say "Aye, aye, sir," but he just unclipped the hand mike and passed it over his shoulder.

"Oran, Oran," Martina said into the mike. "*Ici Vol Nanci Neuf Zero Zero France Jardin.*"

She continued to transmit in a clipped Parisian French, which Dawson understood only vaguely despite his four high school years of the language. From the pleasant, almost jocular responses she received from the Oran tower, it was clear that she had full clearance for Algerian airspace.

"*Nanci Neuf. Fin,*" she said, and she handed the microphone back to Dawson by briefly resting her wrist on his shoulder. "You can drop down to twenty thousand."

The pilots continued their descent, paying closer attention now to engine performance, checking heat and pressure. The Falcon power plants rarely failed, but aeronautical superstition held that the gremlins showed up at the most inconvenient times.

"Would you like us to make the next turn on your mark?" Dawson asked. He had not intended the question to sound facetious, but Martina was a hunter of the fragile male ego.

"Sarcasm could cost you your gratuity, Mr. Dawson," she said. "Just follow the plan. It gets rather tricky near the end."

Chip Bergh was wearing a Jetstar flight cap of the classic captain's style. He reached up and pushed it back, scratching the crown of his head, then took it off and laid it on his right thigh. He waited a while, searching the fuel gauges until he found Martina's face reflected in one of the glass lenses. When she turned her head and called out something to one of her funeral cortege, he quickly hung the cap over a small red metal housing on the far right corner of the cockpit's dash.

Dawson glanced over at his copilot, who continued staring innocently ahead. A smile snatched up the corners of Bergh's mouth for only an instant.

The housing above Bergh's knee protected a large toggle switch, with the options ARM, ON, and RESET now obscured by the cap. In the event of a crash, the emergency beacon would be activated automatically. But the switch could also be thrown at the copilot's will, sending out a constant nonvoice signal over the international emergency frequency of 121.50.

Bergh had spent most of his air force time flying out of U.S. bases in southern Europe. The charts of that continent, as well as of the African one below it, were still fresh in his memory. He knew that once you crossed the Algerian coast and headed south, the desert came up real quick. There were not even semicommercial strips past Béchar. They would be low on fuel, and the Falcon's tri-jets were fussy about sand.

Dawson held his course for another ten minutes. The Falcon was not exactly in a screaming dive, but the airspeed was up over five hundred knots and he let it ride, because they were not going to make an approach into Oran. No need to tiptoe. He bolstered himself with the thought that the sooner they delivered this bizarre entourage, the sooner he and Bergh could rotate back to Oran, refuel, find some place to "crash," and head home to Baltimore at dawn. And if the woman's eccentricities sucked their tanks dry, she would just have to whip out her AmEx card and spring for a fuel truck.

Forward and below, the North African coast was shrouded in a puffy bustle of winter Mediterranean cloud, the obscured cities a lighter glow trying to penetrate the cotton. The Falcon was really starting to buck now. Dawson heard a soda can clang and roll off a surface back in the passenger compartment. The woman sat in the jump seat, unfazed by the turbulence. She wasn't buckled in, and he was not going to suggest it. Anyway, he was convinced that even if he barrel-rolled the airplane, she would just hang on and grin like some Tilt-A-Whirl junkie.

At exactly forty point four one nautical miles out from Oran, he made a hard ninety-six-degree right turn and came onto the new heading. The woman got back into the act.

"Good," said Martina. "Now, as you can see by the plan, you have two forty-two point four nauticals to your next way point." She slipped off the jump seat and came to her haunches again. "At your present speed, this leg should take just under thirty minutes."

"You ought to strap in, ma'am," said Chip Bergh. "It'll get rough when we break through the cover."

"I *have* a mother, thank you," said Martina. "Just fly."

You should fly through the fucking windshield, Bergh thought, as he just nodded like a dashboard doll.

"At the end of this leg," Martina instructed, "you must be down to thirty-five hundred feet."

"Thirty-five," Dawson confirmed. *Just go with the flow, Chip,* he tried telepathically to coach his younger partner. *Just go with the flow.*

Martina watched the instruments vigilantly, cross-checking the progress against her plan. Other than Vietnam vets who had spent a lot of time in the bush, Dawson had seen few men who could squat like that for so long. With the cloud cover tapering off in the distance and the endless black desert reaching out to them, he had a fleeting vision of the woman crouching on a dune, wearing one of those Lawrence of Arabia robes and a white headdress. Halfway through the descent, she rose for a moment and called aft in the language he now assumed to be Arabic. Someone handed her a black purse, and she resumed her unladylike pose, while Dawson wondered if she was going to powder her nose, then found himself speculating as to what kind of underwear she wore, if any at all.

It took all four of the pilots' hands to hold them on the second half of the leg, while a crosswind tried to push them southeast and a ragged layer of cumulus swatted the undercarriage. On other occasions when they had ferried executives through such nauseating vibrations, the high-paying passengers often raised their voices in alarm. Not a whisper came forward from the darkened fuselage. For condensation over an arid land, the vapor was as thick as clam chowder, and the pilots flew IFR, hoping there were no rocky peaks unaccounted for by the woman's computer flunky. When the cockpit windows began to patter, Dawson reached for the wiper switch and found his wrist stopped by Bergh's hand.

"It's sand, Joe."

"Jesus Christ."

"It twists up from the desert floor."

"Terrific. I'll just get out and put the filters on the intakes."

"Just keep cool, Mr. Dawson," said Martina. "We will clear out of it in another thousand feet."

Dawson white-knuckled his yoke, yet it was from anger, not fear. He wanted to stand the Falcon on its tail and send the bitch somersaulting all the way back to the head.

But she was right again. They suddenly broke from the clouds, and while the grit still tickled the windows and the wind did not release them, the flat contours of the land came into sharp focus. To the right, a low range of craggy mountains curved out and then returned in the distance like a burnt banana. To the left, an endless pattern of gentle brown waves was highlighted by long, oval troughs. The wastes looked harmless at this altitude, but the shadows meant that the dunes were huge.

A very slim black line followed the lee of the mountain range and faded into the distant landscape. Across the entire panorama, maybe five pinpoints of light indicated civilized outposts. They could have been towns, or hotels, or, more likely, Bedouin bonfires.

"Make your turn," Martina ordered.

The Falcon banked gently to the right, turning forty-five degrees onto the next heading. They straightened out, receiving a jarring pocket blow for their troubles.

"You have sixty-one nauticals until landing," she said. "Come back on the power."

"I *have* a mother," Dawson snapped, unable to contain himself any longer.

To his astonishment, the woman barked a single laugh.

"Touché," she said. "Give me a frequency of one-one-one point two."

Dawson handed her the mike. She began speaking, in Arabic this time, while he craned his neck, searching for the landing lights. Nothing. Just that black ribbon between the mountains and the dunes.

"Where's the strip, lady?" He no longer gave two shits for Jetstar's public relations.

"You will see it in a minute," said Martina. "No downwind or base legs. It is a straight approach. But you will need the Fowlers."

Dawson turned his head and looked at her. The Falcon's wings were equipped with additional flaps, called Fowlers, on the leading edges. They were used only for extremely short field landings. Martina was holding the mike, looking back at him with her head cocked like an innocent lapdog's.

"How long is this strip?" he demanded.

"Long enough."

"It's not an airport?"

"Not in your sense of the word."

"No tower?"

"It is a two-lane blacktop. Perfectly wide, straight, and acceptable," she said.

He stared at her for a moment, then turned back to his controls. His face was set at the edge of a decision. When he glanced over at Bergh, the slight shake of his copilot's head confirmed it.

"I won't do it, ma'am," said Dawson.

"You won't?" She sounded curiously surprised.

"No," he stated with clipped finality. "You didn't advise Jetstar about any of this." Then he added, in homeboy tones, "Just *ain't in* our contract."

"I see," said Martina thoughtfully. "Well, then. Would you be so kind as to give me some volume?"

Bergh turned up the cockpit speaker. He smiled. They had won. Dawson was already starting a gentle left turn. They were heading back around to the north.

Martina spoke into the mike.

"Skorpion, this is Stinger. If you read me, kindly reply in English. Over."

"Stinger, this is Skorpion," replied a heavily accented voice bathed in static. "Read you loud and clear. Over."

"Tell me, Skorpion," she said offhandedly. "This aircraft is a Falcon 900. Are you familiar with the model?"

"Oh, yes, madam," the voice replied with enthusiasm.

Oh, yes, madam, Dawson mouthed silently. He was thoroughly disgusted now with the whole goose chase.

"Well, then," Martina queried. "If I kill the pilots, do you think I can bring it in?"

"Oh, certainly, madam. That aircraft practically lands itself."

Dawson and Bergh both spun their heads around, their jaws dropping for a second, then clenching back to tooth grinding. Martina had removed her wig. What they saw now was the same steely face, yet crowned with a thick crop of blond bristles. She held a very large pistol in one hand.

"Fuck," said Bergh as he snapped back around to the controls.

Dawson continued to stare at her.

"You are out of your mind, lady," he said through his teeth.

"Absolutely," Martina agreed, although only ice remained in her voice. "And I have a fat life insurance policy that covers air disasters. No children, and no 'loved ones.' I will shoot you as soon as kiss you, and I would much rather shoot you."

Dawson believed her. He turned back to his airplane, muttering, "They don't pay us for *this* bullshit."

"Now continue your foolish maneuver," said Martina. "And make it a full three-sixty. You are low on fuel."

They were back on course in less than a minute. As they approached the black ribbon at two thousand feet, Martina instructed, "Come left and follow the road."

Dawson complied. There was a good moon now and sharp contours, but it wasn't enough to set down by. He was no longer thinking about a drink in a hotel bar and a soft mattress. He was trying not to "buy the farm."

"What about cars?" he muttered.

"There will be no traffic."

"We need some illumination here."

"Don't whine, Mr. Dawson. Just throttle back and drop the gear."

The wheels slid down and locked, while the tri-jets struggled to keep the Falcon flying at its approach pitch.

"No spotlights," Martina ordered, and Bergh shrugged, removing his hand from the wing projector switches.

She spoke Arabic again into the mike. After a moment, a long stretch of straight road just a thousand meters ahead was washed by the yellow glare of twenty landing beacons, set out in perfect order along both shoulders.

"Now *that's* more fucking like it," Dawson whispered as he and Bergh worked furiously to bring the Falcon on line. While their fingers stabbed at toggles, Bergh quickly added the transponder beacon to the frenzy, but Dawson was too busy to notice. He had certainly made his share of successful carrier landings; it was just that he had sworn off ever doing it again.

They were well below the right-hand ridgeline now, the slopes rushing by as the updraft tried to lift the starboard wing. They wrestled with it and came in flat and high, a hundred feet above the first beacon, as snakes of sand whipped across the road and they ignored them, pushing the Falcon down. It was going to be a hot and hard landing, but they could not tell how much room they had, and they needed four thousand feet of friction starting *right now*.

The road was not flat. It bowed up in the center, and Dawson corrected to keep the screeching outboard wheels astride the hump, holding the nose off until he absolutely had to set it on the winter-cracked macadam. The engines howled in reverse, and the fuselage sounded like it might buckle over the pebble washes, but as sand twisters beat at the cockpit, the pilots nudged the brakes until the last beacon came up, and they stamped down hard. The Falcon stopped, but not before slipping to the left in a tire scream that left it tilted toward one shoulder while a cloud of dust settled over its wings.

Silence. No one in the back applauded.

Dawson and Bergh sat very still, finally expelling two long exhalations between tight lips.

"Very *good*," said Martina as if a pair of clumsy flight students had surprised her.

"What now?" Dawson murmured.

She did not reply, but her finger pointed forward of the Falcon's nose.

From behind a high dune, a pickup truck rumbled out into the road, turning to show its fender to the airplane. In the open back sat a man in a dark field jacket. A black kaffiyeh covered his head, one corner of it drawn up over his face. He held an AK-47 assault rifle in his lap.

On the rear of the truck's tailgate, a large piece of plywood had been mounted. It was painted white, and its high black letters read, in English:

FOLLOW ME

Ruth had to be helped down the Falcon's stairway. The drug residue in her veins, the lack of food, and the final adrenaline surge of the rough landing had short-circuited her leg muscles. Impatient with her hobble, Youssef turned at the bottom of the gangway, put his hands under her arms, and lifted her to the ground like a toddler.

Although the cabin of the jet had been dark, the undulating plains of the Sahara were darker. The moon had gone behind a coastal bank of clouds, and no man-made light shone from any quadrant. She squinted into veils of shadows that reminded her of a midnight swim at the bottom of an unlit pool.

But she knew desert when she smelled it. The jet's engines had shut down, and a cold, lifeless wind swept the burnt gases away, bringing the flat scent of dry rock and parched thorn to her nostrils. The stillness of a desert night was unmatched in nature, for no leaves rustled, no insect wings buzzed, no small feet pattered through undergrowth. If you heard a slither, it would be when the snake was at your toes.

Of a thousand earthly deserts, she had no idea upon which one she stood. But it was surely *not* the Negev.

She started when the stairway was cranked back up into the jet. The pilots had not emerged, but Ruth assumed that they were part of Martina's "crew." After the landing, the aircraft had taxied for a long time over hard-packed sand, a gently twisting wadi whose floor had been worked over by spade and shovel. Yet here at the wadi's mouth the earth was loose and softer. She heard the clang of a grappling hook, then the whine of a distant winch, and the plane began to move again, its tires crunching loose stone as its big body receded, dark and lifeless like a beached whale.

"Clean the intakes and get the nets over it."

Ruth turned to the sound of the German voice. She could see more clearly now. She was standing at the edge of a wide bowl of house-high dunes, its flat floor the size of a soccer field. Along the far side, before the foot of ridges, a low row of mounds jutted up from the floor like fresh graves. Each mound had a small metallic cap, like a conical Chinese straw hat, protruding from its spine. Her attention was drawn to Martina, whose figure appeared as a black silhouette striding across the flat sand.

Ruth shivered. No desert, despite its midday heat, retains its temperatures long past sundown. In winter, the contrasting dangers can be brutal, from death by heat stroke to crippling hypothermia. Youssef released her arm for a moment, took off his suit jacket, and draped it over her shoulders. Then he gripped her again, harder, so she would not mistake preservation of a hostage for kindness.

She could see other figures now, shadows moving purposefully across the sand bowl. From behind her, some men grunted as if hefting a weight, then passed by in front carrying a long box on their shoulders. Martina stopped them.

"Take it to the hole, put it in the aircraft, and remove Iyad for burial. Then seal the doors. I want to keep the dust off it and check the circuitry tonight."

The men hurried with their burden. They did not follow the path of the jet, but shuffled in a different direction altogether. There was *another* aircraft? Then Ruth realized that Martina had not used that word. She had said *Hubschrauber*.

"*Willkommen.*"

Ruth winced, snapping her head back to the voice. Martina stood before her at a detached distance. It was too dark to read her expression, but her short blond cut seemed to glow around her skull. She still wore her funeral dress, yet despite the bitter wind she did not hunch or embrace herself. Her arms hung down, loose and relaxed. In her right hand she held a pistol as casually as a hair dryer.

"Your quarters are being readied," Martina said.

Quarters? Ruth glanced around. She saw nothing that resembled a building, a barracks, or even a tent.

"You were an unexpected guest," Martina added by way of explanation.

For some reason, Ruth snatched a crumb of comfort from the remark. The woman's operation was clearly not improvisational, but at least her abduction had not been part of the planning. Then the hope quickly diminished. What difference did that make here and now?

She found her voice.

"Can I ask where we are?"

"You may ask," said Martina, though she clearly felt no obligation to answer. She turned and looked off in the direction of the towed Falcon, and Ruth followed her gaze.

Five shadows were approaching across Martina's "parade ground." The two figures in the middle appeared to be stumbling along, their hands clasped strangely before them, while three other men seemed to be supporting them. The wind carried the muffled sounds of American voices raised in anger, and as the men neared, Ruth could see the white shirts of the pilots beneath their open flight jackets. Their hands were bound at the wrists. They were clearly *not* part of Martina's crew.

"You and your humps have crossed the fucking line, lady!" Joe Dawson spat as he lunged forward and was checked by an octopus of arms.

"I see that you are much braver on the ground than in the air, Mr. Dawson," Martina said. There was a smile in her voice, and Ruth looked at her.

"Fuck *you*," Chip Bergh spat.

Martina laughed. "As you say in your vernacular, you should be so lucky." She switched to German. "Riyad, take them for a long walk east. At least five kilometers."

Ruth's head twitched back toward the men. Martina's goons were holding the black bodies of machine pistols. For a moment, she had thought she would be sharing her predicament with the pilots, finding comfort in numbers. Yet her eyes widened as the Americans were spun around. They were being led off to execution, and Ruth's character burst through her own survival instincts.

"No!" she shouted, then yelped as Youssef's hand dug straight down to her bone.

Dawson spun his head around, but he was pushed and fell to his knees. Riyad pulled him up, and the death squad progressed away toward the dunes as the wind stole the sounds of tramping feet and violent curses.

Ruth had partially slumped with the pain in her arm, but now she drove up and to the right, yanking free for an instant. Martina's hand shot out and grabbed a fistful of the front of her dress, pulling their faces close with amazing strength.

"Don't kill them," Ruth pleaded. "You don't *have* to. Why do you have to? Don't!"

She lost her voice as Martina turned and hauled her, walking briskly across the sand. Ruth tripped over her own feet but was kept aloft by the momentum.

"They won't be killed," Martina said.

"Don't!" Ruth begged again, Martina's claim not having registered. "*Please* don't. They might have families, children. You can't—"

"I *said* they won't be killed!" Martina stopped short and jutted her face toward Ruth's, causing Youssef to nearly topple them all over from behind. "They are going to be set free."

She held her posture until Ruth's body relaxed. The girl was sniffling, and as she hung her head, Martina found herself impressed by her foolish courage. In the face of the pilots' deaths, she had forgotten the proximity of her own.

Martina reached down and took Ruth's hand. Then she led her at a brisk march toward the northwest corner of the sand bowl.

Ruth's strength was gone. Her emotion had drained her reserves to a parched, numbed well. She walked, feeling Martina's grip and the big hands on her back. She saw the ground suddenly fall away into a shallow ramp, then they were going down into a dark trench, the meager light all but gone now as they passed beneath a net stretched over the passageway.

Maybe the pilots were not going to be executed. Maybe they would be set free. But here in this winter desert, it would mean practically the same thing.

"They'll freeze to death," Ruth murmured in a final, feeble protest.

The sounds of rusty hinges reached her ears, and just ahead, a gray square of subdued light appeared in the subterranean pitch. Martina pulled her toward the chamber, the smile in her voice once more.

"I only need one bargaining chip, my dear," she said.

Chapter 16: Casablanca

In the course of his middle-aged life, Hans-Dieter Schmidt had successfully negotiated a thousand passport controls.

As the director of marketing of a Munich-based pharmaceutical concern, Schmidt's pursuit of foreign customers had kept him abroad for much of the past twenty-five years, and now the crossing of a border should have evoked no more excitement than a stroll to the local post office. In countless lines of weary, foot-shuffling passengers, he had acquired a posture and an expression of passive disinterest. Whether in Larnaca or London, Sofia or Saigon, a democratic enclave or a hotbed of tyranny, he had learned to ignore the petty arrogance of customs apparatchiks and the steely glares of jackbooted border guards. He projected the impression of a rumpled, nonsubversive visitor and had rarely been detained for even a cursory inquiry.

So this morning's arrival at Casablanca's Mohammed V airport should have educed no more adrenaline than the train ride from Salzburg to Vienna, yet Schmidt knew that it was the most important crossing of his life, and he wondered if his hammering heart might give him away.

From the arrival ramp of Royal Air Maroc's Flight 205 to the escalators descending to the customs hall, the endless corridor was populated by pairs of khaki clad border police, smoothing their mustaches as they scrutinized each face. At the foot of the escalators, where ragged queues extended back from the control desks, the gargantuan gold obelisk jutting down from the vaulted ceiling looked very much like a guillotine. And although Schmidt carried no contraband of any kind, beyond the visa clerks a final X-ray scan of incoming hand luggage was being conducted, causing beadlets of sweat to break out on his brow.

Perhaps it was vague recollections of a childhood at Dachau that rekindled the sensation of fate at the mercy of oppressors, as he searched for the correct answers to questions that might be posed. He reread the front page of *France-Soir*, growing ever angrier at the bureaucrat who languidly compared photos to faces, checking information on a nationally linked computer. And then he found his bubbling indignation had been totally unwarranted, as he was passed through with the whack of a visa stamper and a cursory "*Bienvenu.*"

Breathing like a liberated convict, Schmidt recovered his valise from a carousel, went out into the main concourse and straight to the currency exchange window. He armed himself with five hundred dirhams, strolled to the information desk at the hub of the mall, and thumbed through brochures of the Maghreb until the American finally emerged from customs, shouldering his way through a throng of locals. The tall blond man was easy to spot, as North Africa was still suffering a paucity of tourism as a result of the Gulf War, and most everyone else was wearing a *jallabiya*.

Schmidt followed him out the glass entrance doors into a welcome North African sun. The American waved off the teenagers who offered to carry his Tourister, and the German did the same, until they found themselves side by side before a line of Mercedes taxis.

The American spoke. "Want to share?"

"Why not?" said Schmidt.

They got into a battered cream sedan, the driver assumed their objective to be the heart of Casablanca, and he was off. The chunky German turned to the lanky American.

"Ahh, the Middle East warms my bones," said Benni Baum.

"Compared to New York, it leaves me cold," said Mike O'Donovan.

Benni nodded. "*L'hôtel Sheraton, s'il vous plaît,*" he said to the driver, and the rest of the ride was as devoid of conversation as the bedroom of a couple on the verge of divorce.

Benni's appearance on Moroccan soil was not in itself a high-risk venture. Of all the Arab states, Morocco was regarded by the Israelis as the least confrontational, its monarchy paying lip service to Arab unity, its newspapers supporting the Palestine National Congress with desultory editorials. In the *mivtzaim* (operations) room of AMAN's SpecOps headquarters, a large map of the earth covered one wall, with countries considered high risk for Israeli operatives shaded in varying hues of red. Morocco was a very pale pink.

Israel and Morocco had maintained a covert link for many years. GSS teams had trained King Hassan's close protection details, Israeli advisers from the World Bank had been seconded to Rabat's Ministry of Economics, and even Yitzhak Rabin had made a secret pilgrimage to Hassan's palace, disguised in a "Beatle" wig and black-rimmed glasses that were still the butt of jokes in the Mossad's "costume" department.

When AMAN Special Operations teams began their indoctrinations in street-craft, they cut their teeth in Israeli cities, then moved on to European capitals. Those men and women who showed promise in tracking, shaking watchers, and proper handling of dead drops then graduated to low-risk "unfriendly" cities, such as Casablanca and Tunis. If you could not handle yourself in Tangier, then you were certainly not going to Damascus. These relatively harmless practice sessions did not mean, of course, that the Moroccan

Sûreté Nationale would look kindly on Israeli operators launching an unauthorized mission from their sovereign territory. For the sake of the world stage, if such an endeavor was discovered, it would have to be punished by incarceration. The unlucky participants would surely be repatriated, but only after an acceptable term in a malodorous Moroccan prison.

When Eytan Eckstein had served a two-year stint as head of SpecOps Training, he enlisted Benni's aid to run three teams through their paces in Casablanca. The two men had headquartered at the Sheraton, and although today they had made no arrangement to meet there, the colonel knew his major's mind. . . .

As for Michael O'Donovan, the U.S. Special Forces was essentially a combat recon and indigenous liaison outfit, and he had not been extensively trained in intelligence tradecraft. However, in his ten years on the streets of New York City he had accumulated more "hunting" experience than most field agents acquire in a like period of intermittent assignments. He had some German and French, and although he did not know exactly what Baum and Roselli had in mind for North Africa, he was determined to participate.

His sense of duty to the NYPD had been replaced by a horrible crush of responsibility, a hunger to save the woman who had seen so quickly into his soul. Their lightning union of minds and bodies had given him hope that there might be someone meant for him, and although fully aware that the relationship might fail even a brief test of time, he mourned as if Ruth had been struck down by a hit-and-run driver, then snatched away, still breathing. He had let her be taken, she was out there somewhere, and he would not rest until he saw her again.

At first Baum resisted his inclusion in the mission, but O'Donovan made it very clear that he would not be left behind. The detective threatened to dog him across the entire globe, and if that did not work, he would go over to Jack Buchanan, blow Benni's scenario, and join the cumbersome government effort that would surely result.

"Well . . ." Baum relented at last. "I suppose an angry New York cop might be useful."

Art Roselli quickly supplied O'Donovan with a new passport and backstop material in the name of Michael Connolly, a corporate attorney from New York specializing in mergers of pharmaceutical ventures. He also provided a letter from a New York surgeon prohibiting O'Donovan's participation in all police activities for thirty days, which was delivered to his lieutenant. She promptly called his apartment, but spoke only to his answering machine. He had not gone home again from Washington. . . .

The face of Casablanca had not changed very much since Baum's last visit, its skin the same alabaster of grand Moresque civic structures and white Franco-Mediterranean facades. A few more unsightly moles of modern business towers had sprouted from its folds, the arms of its French-style boulevards reached farther out toward Azemmour and Rabat, and the date palms of the medians had flourished untrimmed. But the city was still like an immortal, matronly ship captain's widow, slowly spreading its girth in its perch by the sea, smelling of sun-broiled fishnets, chugged diesel, and the salt of a damp breeze.

Although most of the Maghreb still bowed to conservative Moslem mores, Morocco, as the gateway to the Iberian Peninsula, seemed to have been granted dispensation by the Imams for the sake of commerce. Casablanca flourished in a schizophrenic flaunting of its license. The towering mosque of Hassan II was evidence of a billion-dollar devotion to monarch and Allah, while the kosher restaurants of the city's remaining Jews overflowed with patrons who no longer feared repression. Yes, there were still Moslem women here who wore the veil, but many sported the more fashionable, rainbow-colored *jallabiyas*, with no head coverings at all, and just as many strolled along in business suits and immodest skirts. In stark contrast to Tehran, there were no Religious Police here who might shoot a woman for wearing lipstick and eye shadow.

Lisbon, Geneva, and Vienna had all seen service as neutral playing grounds for the secret struggles between fascist and democratic, communist and imperialist ideologues. Beirut had also taken a turn hosting the shadow warriors, but she had died in twenty years of civil war and foreign invasion, and even the most foolhardy mercenaries were still loath to do business there. But Casablanca's gleaming 1930s architecture, the winding alleys of a mysterious Casbah, and her palm fronds waving to the spill of French and Arabic tunes remained as a backdrop to the cliché. The city was safe haven to diplomats and arms dealers, thieves and entrepreneurs, smugglers and spies.

At the corner of Avenue des Forces Armées Royales and Rue Colbert, Baum and O'Donovan walked into the cavernous lobby of the Sheraton Hotel. It was already late in the morning, and businessmen were gathering in the open coffee-and-sandwich salon. The wide reservoir of a fountain splashed and bubbled, and the chatter of parrots in hanging cages mingled with the tunes of a recorded jazz ensemble, so that the high walls hummed like a combined dance café and Caribbean zoo.

They strode to the reception desk at the far end of the lobby, a chest-high rectangle of polished stone, manned and womaned by blue-blazered Moroccans. Registration forms were filled out, Baum guaranteeing payment with a "Schmidt" gold Visa card, which was registered to a Frankfurt account.

While O'Donovan watched the lobby traffic with a distracted frown, Benni tried not to look across to the gift shop on the far side. There was a postal box mounted on the wall, and a European man wearing an American A-2 flight jacket and black jeans was inserting postcards into the slot. His dark-blond hair was pulled back into a ponytail.

The desk clerk handed Benni a pair of plastic room-access cards.

"Seven-eighteen, Herr Schmidt," said the clerk.

"We are smokers," Benni warned.

"So are most of our guests." The clerk smiled broadly. "Morocco is still civilized."

"*Merci beaucoup.*"

"*Avec plaisir.*"

A young porter hefted their bags, but as the trio neared the elevators, Benni handed him twenty dirhams and said in French, "Thanks. We need the exercise." The boy backed away, a palm placed over his chest.

Eytan Eckstein followed into the elevator, but he moved straight to the back of the mirrored cubicle, and he and Benni did not make eye contact. O'Donovan glanced at the third man's reflection, the sunburned expressionless face, eyes hidden behind pilot-style sunglasses. He knew that Baum was anxious to meet a fellow AMAN officer here, but this man could not be the major of record. He looked more like a German terrorist or, at best, a Swedish rock-and-roll drummer.

Benni and O'Donovan exited onto the seventh floor, and when they reached 718, Benni stopped to insert the plastic key as O'Donovan turned his head and stiffened.

The third man was coming on quickly. O'Donovan twisted back to Benni and flicked his eyes in warning. But Baum just casually said, "I hope this one is better than that dump in Tangier," opened the door, took the American's elbow, and roughly pushed him into the room. The ponytailed man came in on his heels, Benni slammed the door with his foot, and he and the intruder embraced in a bear hug that expelled their air.

Baum and Eckstein parted without a word. Benni walked straight to a television on a polished bureau and, without glancing at the accommodations, said, "Ahh, place looks very decent." He turned on the TV, found the European music channel, and Peter Gabriel's "Sledge Hammer" rang off the walls.

"Beds look comfortable too. Don't you think, Michael?" Benni coached, and when O'Donovan just stared at him dumbly, he made a flapping gesture with his hand, as if he were working a sock puppet.

"Yeah," said the detective, at last picking up his cue. "Real nice."

Eckstein had no idea who this bewildered American fellow might be, but he was in Benni's charge and it was not the first time Baum had shown up to a rendezvous towing a *tomech*—SpecOps slang for a foreign but loyal assistant. Eckstein removed his sunglasses, approached O'Donovan, and smiled behind a finger forbidding dialogue, then he gestured at one of the double beds. O'Donovan shrugged and sat down, feeling, for all his NYPD rank and experience, like a child on the first day of grade school.

A strange ballet followed, with Baum and Eckstein moving quickly, as if repeating a mime routine they had often taken on a road tour. It reminded O'Donovan of the initial search of a crime scene, without the banter.

Neither of the Israelis really suspected that the Moroccan Mukhabarat would take enough interest in them to monitor their activities. But hostile agencies also had a foothold in Casablanca, and Martina Klump was certainly not funding her efforts with the profits from a McDonald's franchise. Someone was supporting her, and whether that banker might be the Syrian, Iraqi, or Libyan government, technical aid might also be lent. So the two men proceeded out of professional habit, like pilots running a preflight check.

Benni began by closing the wide window draperies, then he unplugged every lamp in the room, which submerged the space in a brown gloom lit only by the spill from recessed bulbs in the foyer.

Despite the popular notion that high-tech wizardry allows for miniature, battery-powered room bugs of unlimited endurance, most such devices are still secreted in harmless appliances and run off standard electrical current. Removing the plugs reduces that risk by a certain percentage. Another popular option is to conceal line-powered microphones inside electrical boxes behind the plug plates. Benni was not about to unscrew all the plates in the room, so he went to his valise and fished out a thick cellophane packet. It was certainly reasonable for a middle-aged salesman to carry a supply of Dr. Scholl's sole inserts, and he peeled the backings off a handful of foam pads and gently covered each receptacle.

Eckstein came out of the bathroom, where he had run the shower while he finger-searched the light fixtures, plumbing lines, and cavities beneath the sink, bidet, and toilet tank. Careless operatives often thought a closed bathroom to be a safe haven for discussions, so these areas were frequently targeted by acoustical interceptors. His search could only be cursory, so he eliminated the risk by leaving the water on, exiting, and shutting the door.

O'Donovan watched as Baum and Eckstein now regarded each other across the large room. Both men were wishing they could have smuggled in a portable sweeper, which would have greatly simplified their efforts. AMAN's wizards now produced a very fine model, essentially a multiband receiver with an incremental scanner and a directional antenna. The operator donned headphones, flooded the room with prerecorded music from a portable tape player, and proceeded to "sweep" every wall, carpet, and stick of furniture. If a transmitter was functioning, eventually the scanner would intercept the frequency, and the operator would hear his own taped music being played back into his ears. But these devices were very expensive, and though usually disguised as Walkmans or CDs, they were not issued to field operatives without a commanders' assent. The department comptroller refused to risk having some third world customs inspector confiscate a sweeper for his teenage daughter.

Like tired boxers, Baum and Eckstein retreated to opposite ends of the suite, turned, and began again.

Eckstein used his Maglite to inspect the standing closets in the foyer, then was pleased to find that a full-length mirror was merely hung from a hook and could be lifted away from the wall. Baum opened the radiator below the windows, pulled the cushions from a love seat, ran a pencil point through the upholstery cracks, then lay down beneath a coffee table like a car mechanic. Eckstein got up on a chair and swept his beam over the air conditioner grate, while Baum removed the drawers from the writing table, inspected it, replaced them, then set the telephone down on the bed and gently smothered it with two pillows. Both men now went to their knees, and like blind men searching for a lost cuff link, they touched every centimeter of carpet, poked under the beds, and caressed the furniture, windowsills, and picture frames with more delicacy then either of them had shown a woman in a very long time.

The whole security dance took less than twenty minutes, but by the time it was over, both men had worked up a sweat. They were not foolish enough to feel carelessly comfortable, yet with their wits and experience as the only available tools, they had done what they could. Benni opened the minibar, handed Eytan an orange juice, and popped the tab on a can of soda water. He gestured at O'Donovan, inviting the American to help himself. A British veejay was now babbling nonsense and nearly poking his nose out from the TV screen. Benni turned up the volume, and Eckstein joined him in a corner near the draped windows.

Benni leaned back against the sill and looked up at his younger comrade, realizing that if only their operational union had never been broken, he would probably not be in this predicament. Fate would likely have taken a different course. Ruth might still be in her New York apartment, trotting off blithely to classes, ignorant of O'Donovan's existence, comfortable in her antipaternal hostility. Safe. Yet if this was a crueler reality, it was best faced with Eckstein, and it was hard for Benni to keep the emotion out of his voice. They conversed in low Hebrew tones full of subtext.

"*Asoor l'cha l'hiot kahn.* You shouldn't be here," said Benni with a pained smile.

"Neither should you, my friend." Eytan meant: in such a terrible position. "Who's the bruised bodyguard?"

"A New York detective," said Benni. Eytan glanced at O'Donovan, who was now smoking a cigarette and staring blankly at the television. "He was working on the consulate bombing. Itzik sent me over there to liaise."

Baum relayed the rest of the details in a clipped shorthand. He was reluctant to expound on the relationship between Ruth and Mike, but it was key to the sequence of her kidnapping. Eckstein tried not to react overtly, but sexual images lie close to the surface of a man's mind, and he could not help reappraising the American. It was not lost on Eckstein that, despite the haircuts, he and O'Donovan were physically similar. The detective still wore a strip of white plaster over his nose bridge, and there were purple patches under his eyes. The bandage was as blatant as a Sikh's turban. He would have to lose it, and a woman's compact would camouflage the rest.

O'Donovan looked over at Eckstein, who touched the fingers of his left hand together and made a motion of plucking a grape from a low vine, the Israeli gesture that means: *We'll get to you in a minute.*

"I don't suppose you've had any ideas," Benni said hopefully.

"Even without the facts, I've got some infrastructure going."

"Always the renegade," Benni complimented. "I *do* have the facts, though I've made no contacts yet, except for you. The 'Mafia' will do what he can."

Baum was referring to Art Roselli, but Eytan also realized that Benni assumed his partner's preliminary efforts were purely out of channels. He looked at Baum, unsure that the colonel would be able to function with calm clarity, given the circumstances. He was about to confess his doubts, and reveal the actions he had already taken, when there was a rapid knock at the door.

Baum was moving to shoo away a probable chambermaid, when Eckstein touched the burly man's chest and held him in place. His eyes apologized. "I'm not always the loose cannon you think I am," said Eytan. He walked to the door.

When he opened it, General Itzik Ben-Zion strode into the room.

The commander of Special Operations dipped his head as he passed through the foyer. There was no obstruction there, but previous encounters with door-frames had ingrained the defensive habit. He was wearing a pearl-gray double-breasted worsted suit, a white shirt with European collar, and a blue silk tie. The temple frames of stylish sunglasses disappeared through his stiff salt-and-pepper curls, yet he was also carrying a lightweight London Fog, as even Casablanca could readily change its tune in the winter months.

Benni had not seen Itzik out in the field or, for that matter, out of uniform in many years. He looked like a Sicilian don en route to a conference of the Families. But it was not the general's attire that drew Baum's focus. Rather, it was the fact that Eckstein had clearly blown the whole scenario to their boss, including Ruth's abduction, placing her life in further jeopardy by casting her fate to the winds of Itzik's ambitions. Stunned and feeling betrayed, Baum folded his arms and sliced into Eckstein's soul with a withering glare.

"I had to, Benni," said Eytan. "It was too complex, too many factors, Moon-light not the least of them." Baum said nothing. "There are other risks, other lives at stake," Eytan continued. "You *knew* you'd have to share, but there wasn't time to talk you into it."

Baum's expression gave no quarter, though beneath his squint of anger he realized that Eckstein was right. He could not have brought himself to consider anyone or anything but Ruth. He would have sacrificed Dan Sarel. Someone had to act on behalf of the logical part of his mind, which was temporarily crippled.

Ben-Zion approached the two men, stopped, and cocked his head back toward O'Donovan, who saluted him wearily and returned to the television.

"What's this?" Itzik demanded, as if the American were a rubber doll.

"*Tomech*," said Eckstein.

"*Niflah*. Wonderful," Itzik grumbled sarcastically as he threw the raincoat over the back of the small divan. "I love unvetted witnesses."

"He's in one hundred percent. And he doesn't have the language," Eckstein reassured.

Ben-Zion ignored him and turned to Baum. The general assumed that his men had swept the room, but the television blared, and they drew their heads close, like defense attorneys discussing a tactic in open court. He should have used their cover names, but he wanted to cut quickly into Benni's defenses. He removed his sunglasses.

"Eckstein here says you might want to tell me something about the Tango file, Baum. And you had better tell it straight."

Benni looked up at his towering boss, the dark eyes set in that unblinking, don't-bullshit-me glare he often used to jelly the knees of headquarters staff. Then he glanced briefly at Eckstein, whose pained expression and slight nod were those of an accomplice encouraging confession. This was it. It was over. He felt the years and the lies and the burden of his secret unwinding like the sliced strands of a rubber-band ball. The man who had resisted hostile interrogations without giving up a single secret now found himself confessing like a philanderer.

"Martina Ursula Klump was ours," Benni said to Itzik. Then he walked to a writing table, picked up an ashtray, came back around the love seat, and settled his rump on the edge of its headrest. Itzik shifted, to once more tower over his colonel, while Eckstein stared at the window draperies as if he could see through them to Casablanca's seaport.

"Come again?" Ben-Zion said, squinting as he bent his head.

"Klump was ours." Benni lit up a cigarette and blew the smoke from the corner of his mouth.

"What do you mean, *ours?*" Itzik demanded with growing alarm.

Benni looked at him squarely. "She was my agent. I turned her."

Ben-Zion blinked. Although the magnitude of this revelation was already beginning to dawn, he resisted the onrushing implications. The general lived on secrets, coveted them, used them for professional and political leverage. He prided himself on knowing the hidden treasures of all the compartmentalized units that funneled their whole truths only to him. It was not possible that any of his men, even the Terrible Twins, could have kept such a thing from him.

He straightened up and turned to his younger subordinate.

"What's he talking about, Eckstein?" he asked, as if Baum had been speaking Cantonese.

"Listen to him," Eytan replied curtly.

"It was nearly twenty years ago, Itzik," said Benni, as he held his cigarette and watched the tip burn. "Before I came over from the civilians." Benni had begun his intelligence career as a Mossad officer, then was co-opted by AMAN chief Shlomo Gazit to help form a Special Operations branch for military intelligence, initially called Unit 509. "We were working out of Paris, trying to penetrate Action Directe. She was fresh in from Buenos Aires, a student at the Sorbonne. Her father had been a Nazi engineer. We got to her while she was still a leftist recruit."

Ben-Zion was fully familiar with the scenario. During the student revolutionary years of the late sixties and early seventies, the children of former Axis fascists were coming of age. They were often confused, riding the radical political fence, sympathetic toward third world, anti-imperialist efforts, yet secretly appalled when Arab terrorists murdered Israeli schoolchildren, echoing their parents' crimes. At times, that guilt could be played upon.

Itzik shook his head, lit up his own cigarette, and exhaled with a rumbling sigh. He knew that there was more, much more. "And I suppose you bought her ice cream at Yad Vashem," he said sarcastically. The Holocaust museum in Jerusalem was a must stop for Israeli tour guides shepherding nonbelievers.

"Twice," said Benni. It was still common practice to bring foreign assets secretly into Israel for indoctrination. They were often photographed there in the company of uniformed officers, an insurance policy to guard against the opposition's trying to "triple" them back.

"*Ya' Allah*," Ben-Zion whispered, realizing now that Baum was not talking about a brief period of youthful turmoil during which the girl had turned over a few names and addresses. She was not a simple *shtinker*, Israeli slang for a stool pigeon. She had been recruited, trained, and run by Baum. "*Kfoolah amitit?* A real double?" Itzik squinted at Benni, not quite believing it.

"Full-blown," said Eckstein. He moved from the window and closed in. Itzik's ego was about to be bruised.

The general tried to reassemble history. Martina Ursula Klump, notorious German terrorist, suspect in scores of European attacks, RAF bombings, actions in Lebanon. Could this be true, that one of his own sections had been running her under his ignorant nose? He tried to distill his wounded pride from the potential vat of kudos. Could it really be that while Mossad teams kept Klump near the top of their elimination lists, she was being handled by his own pigheaded Baum? It was *fantastic. A* German fanatic with a price on her head, in reality an **AMAN** asset! He might actually get a smile out of the Prime Minister.

"How did you do it?" he asked Benni with undisguised awe.

"Do what?"

"*Turn her.*"

Baum hesitated. Then he blushed and looked at Eckstein for help.

Itzik's eyes flicked between the two officers. "What is it?" Images of blackmail and torture leaped to his mind. "What did you use?"

Benni sighed. "The natural tool of the trade," he said, as he looked at the floor.

Itzik's mouth dropped open. "You *seduced* her?"

"He had hair then," Eytan interjected, by way of explanation.

Ben-Zion slapped a palm to his forehead and slowly turned a full rotation. "Oh, that's *precious.*" Sex was certainly at the top of the list of recruitment techniques, but it was usually left to the experts, the lover boys, department *femmes fatales*. The image of his bulldog colonel successfully bedding *anyone* was too much to bear. "Oh, this is *rich.*"

But Benni was unable to view the events with lighthearted nostalgia. Until this moment, only Eckstein had shared the secret of Martina's turning, and he realized that no rationalization of patriotic duty had ever allowed him to forgive himself. No, he had not always been a beefy, bald, thundering field commander. He remembered the years, into his thirties, when the flesh of his wide body was trim over muscle, his face smooth, and his eyes unwrinkled, when he could tap into a gentle charm that blinded women to his aggressive appearance. He remembered that self, and a young, inexperienced German girl, alone in a Paris flat. The doorbell said Schmidt, the rent was paid by the Israeli government, and she cried when she orgasmed. Ruth was already beginning school by then, Maya cared for three children in Jerusalem, and he wondered if lust was the price of duty, or the reward.

Ben-Zion jammed a hand into a trouser pocket and began to pace between the love seat's back and the window. He tapped his cigarette, dumping ashes on the floor, and he appeared to be speaking to his shoes.

"Okay," he said. "I'll bite. You turned Klump. But from what Eckstein tells me, she's not so crazy about you anymore. Give me the rest, quickly."

Eckstein picked up the cue, knowing that it would be just too painful for Baum.

"Benni ran her till 1982," said Eytan. "She moved from Paris to Frankfurt, got into Baader-Meinhoff, and stuck with it right through the RAF. She was out in the front lines, but she maintained contact. She was damned cool, and her merchandise was always hot."

Tip-offs about pending terror actions were categorized by temperature. If an agent's *mafil*, her control, declared that her information was "hot," it had to be treated as accurate by his commanders, without identifying the source. There followed the difficult decisions, whether to act on that tip and risk blowing the anonymous agent, or hold off and pray for low casualties.

"Yes, yes." Ben-Zion continued to pace. "When did *you* come into it?"

"Later," said Eckstein. "Near the end."

"Uh huh," the general grunted. They had done it again, these two *manyakim*, running a renegade operation in his kitchen while he snored in the bedroom. They were *determined* to give him heart failure. "It went sour, I assume," Itzik said with a certain satisfaction.

"She was in very deep," Eckstein continued. "We think it just got too scary for her. She started to miss contacts, blow off meets. They were printing pictures of her in *Stern*, and she just went dead."

"I decided to bring her in," Benni whispered. Then he cleared his throat and found a fuller voice. "I just sensed that she would go for it."

Itzik stopped pacing and looked at Baum. He almost commented, *Or you just wanted her back in your bed.* But seeing Baum's haggard expression, he stifled the remark.

"I managed to get a coded contact to her," Baum continued. "It was early in '82. We were in Germany. Remember?"

Itzik rubbed his brow above closed eyes.

"Joint venture with the BKA," Eytan prodded. "Rolling up a Jabril network?" The general nodded, and Benni went on.

"It was very difficult. We had to track her and do it on the street. It took a long time, but Zvi Pearlman pulled it off." Benni paused. Pearlman was dead, and they all missed him. "It was one long fucking week, but she answered with a flag."

"I don't know if you remember," Eckstein said to Ben-Zion, "but she was captured by GSG-9 in Bad Reichenhall. That was our setup, with the BKA. The rest of it—the trial, the sentence, the transfer to Bruchsal—was all cover."

"Really? So who was so damned cooperative in Wiesbaden?" Itzik asked, trying to keep abreast of the German counterintelligence connection.

"Lokojewski."

"Huh," Itzik grunted. "*Another* renegade. His father was an SS colonel, you know."

"The son has more than made up for it," said Benni.

"And her escape?" Itzik pressed. "That I remember."

Benni sighed, his shoulders sagging as he lit up another Marlboro.

"I fucked it up. They had her in the subbasement at Bruchsal, the psychiatric holding cells. No one even knew she was there." He saw her again, the hollow eyes, shoulders shivering in her burlap bag. "I hadn't made contact throughout the trial phase, so she didn't trust me at first. But she came around. I promised her the standard package. Told her she would have to arrange for the escape herself, through the RAF, so they would buy her right up to the end. But then we would pick her up, she would get new papers, all the back pay, and it was a lot. If she wanted, she could spend her life sunning on the beach in Netanya and picnicking with Wolfgang Lodz." Benni's voice fell to a whisper again. "I swore to her, Itzik. And I meant it. . . ."

Ben-Zion stared at Baum, and he actually felt sorry for him. To some men, losing an operative was like losing a child.

"A German guard was switched at the last moment," Eckstein concluded. "He wasn't briefed, and he opened fire. Brought her down, but she got up and made it to the helicopter."

No one spoke for a few moments. Eckstein, wishing he had a cigarette, chewed his lip instead. He looked over at O'Donovan, who had fallen asleep on the bed, his sneakers still placed on the floor. *Ex-soldier*, Eytan assessed. *Probably airborne.*

Ben-Zion backed up to the windowsill, leaned against it, unbuttoned his suit coat, and folded his arms. He looked up at the ceiling and began to nod slowly, as if he were praying, while he rapidly extrapolated the rest of the sad scenario.

"I get it, Baum," he said. "You run this girl, this woman now, for years. Maybe she's in love with you, maybe not, but she's in very deep, out there on point, and you're her lifeline. But you never bring her in, right? You leave her out there."

"She was irreplaceable," Eckstein said, although he did not need to defend the tactics. Itzik himself would have left his own mother in Baghdad if she could transmit hot merchandise. "Her stuff probably saved a hundred lives. Maybe more."

"Then she breaks," Ben-Zion went on. "Goes under. But you reel her in one more time, get her to trust you again. Then she gets shot, and from her point of view you're a duplicitous Jew bastard who set her up for a hit. Good so far?"

Benni said nothing, although Itzik did not pause long enough to hear a rejoinder.

"Now she's *really* pissed off, gone forever. Winds up in Lebanon, with Hizbollah, then Yadd Allah."

Benni knew what was coming, but he just took the blows in silent penitence. They had not shared the truth with their commander, and he was justifiably absolving himself of the responsibility.

"And there isn't enough blood on earth to quench her rage," said Itzik. "Unless it's *your* blood, Baum. So you've finally turned her, all right. Turned her into something that for ten years she only pretended to be. A sworn enemy of the State of Israel."

"I think that's a bit dramatic," said Eytan.

"Really, Eckstein?" Ben-Zion spun on the major. "Hell hath no fury, my young friend. You can check with my wife."

The judge and jury had spoken. Itzik suddenly straightened up, walked to the minibar, and rummaged through the bottles. He came back popping the tab on a can of Imperial beer.

"So you'd better tell me now what all this has to do with the Tango file," he said as he sipped.

"Tango was Martina," Benni murmured.

Itzik stopped in mid-swig. He looked over the top of the can and licked foam from his upper lip. "Excuse me?"

"Yes," Eckstein confirmed.

The color rose dangerously to Ben-Zion's face. Sure, it was standard procedure to camouflage the identity of an asset, especially a double. The real names and bases of operations were changed, and sometimes there was even a "shadow file," kept in the control's safe. But when briefing him on Tango's status, Baum and Eckstein had always appeared to be confiding in him, bemoaning the loss of a *male* asset, a *Belgian* who was working the European terror networks and had supposedly been caught and killed. The memos all referred to the male gender, and one even included a physical description. His ire broiled as he recalled once bragging about Tango to his Mossad counterpart.

"Then who the *fuck* was Paul Krimmant?" Itzik growled.

"It's an anagram," said Eckstein. "From the letters of her name."

Ben-Zion stared at Eckstein, then turned the heat of his gaze on Baum. Though they were downtrodden now, he pictured them snickering behind his back after God knew how many file briefings.

"I hate you two, you know," he said simply. "I really do." He pointed a long finger at Benni. "If Ruth wasn't involved in this, I'd pack you both off home and sing an aria at your courts-martial."

Benni and Eytan watched the general as he tipped his head back, finished the beer in one long guzzle, and crushed the can in his large hand. He tossed the aluminum carcass into an empty wastebasket, but the ring was muffled by the MTV veejay, who still chattered on. Ben-Zion placed his fists on his hips as he came to a decision.

"You fucked this up, Baum," he said. "So now you fix it. Moonlight is going to run, as is."

The significance of that statement did not escape Itzik's officers. Their commander cultivated the image of an emotionless warrior, but he had kids of his own. For Ruth's sake, he would not change the time or place of the prisoner exchange.

"Your ex-girlfriend has a dangerous toy now, Baum. And she had better not get to use it."

Benni's eyes widened. How did Itzik know about the Minnow? Benni had not even briefed Eckstein yet on those details.

"Avraham Yaron works for the army," Itzik responded to Baum's expression. "Not for you. He flashed us from Washington."

Benni nodded. There was no betrayal there. Had Avraham known about Ruth, he would have kept his mouth shut.

"Now, this is how it will run, people," Itzik continued. "The exchange is going to come off, as scheduled, and come hell or high water, you had better tend to this little problem." He took one fist from his hip, looked at his watch, and began to wag a finger. "I don't even want to *hear* about this, except maybe next month at Ben-Levi's wedding." He was referring to the nuptials of one of the cipher clerks. "You have less than seventy-two hours. Anything or anyone you use is up to you, but *no one* who's on the payroll. *Baroor l'chem?*"

"It's clear," said Eckstein. Ben-Zion was giving them a dim green light. On the other hand, he was cutting them off, forbidding all use of departmental support. "But we are going to need a few things, Itzik. Expensive things."

"Use your fucking gold card," the general snapped.

"Come on, Itzik . . ." Benni growled.

"Okay then, Baum. How much is in your pension fund?"

"You know how much."

"That's right, I do." The general nodded as he thought. "Tell me, did Horse know about any of this?" The reference was to Benni's troubleshooter.

"Maybe some of it," Eckstein reluctantly volunteered.

"Good," said Itzik. "As of right now, he is suspended without pay. If he happens to show up here carrying a hundred thousand, it will be out of *your* own pocket, Baum. And if later on, by some miracle, Mr. *Paul Krimmant's* back pay reimburses your account, don't ask me about it."

"Thank you, Itzik," Benni whispered.

"Don't thank me! I could murder you both and get a medal!"

Itzik stretched up to his full height, buttoned his suit jacket, and recovered his raincoat. Benni rose to face his commander, and Eytan joined him at his side. Both men wanted to shake the general's hand, but they were afraid to break his spell of self-deception. Itzik took his sunglasses from his pocket and put them on. He shook his head once, and headed for the door. He stopped and turned halfway across the room.

"You have created quite a monster, gentlemen."

"*Es ist unser Ebenbild,*" Benni muttered in German.

"What did he say?" Itzik demanded of Eckstein.

"In our own image," Eckstein said.

The general grunted, and then he was gone.

Chapter 17: Casablanca

By midnight, the owner of the Café de France would normally have been closing his establishment. His four waiters, in their livery of black trousers, olive wool blazers and vests, white shirts, and black ties, would have damp-clothed the Formica tops of forty tables, carried piles of chipped demitasses on shoulder trays to the tired barmen, and dumped a hundred ashtrays clotted with butts. They would have lowered the metal shutters that walled off the café from the sidewalk, and outside, between the high concrete pillars at the edge of the street, rolled the huge red visors stamped with Coca-Cola logos up into the overhanging roof.

They would have been relieved to be finally off their burning soles, but even though the clock tower in the Place Mohammed V struck the witching hour, it was not to be. Far away and half a day behind, the Royal Moroccan soccer team was joining battle in Brazil. The Café de France had a large-screen TV, and the place was teeming as if for a lunchtime sitting.

Benni Baum did not mind the crowd. On the contrary, he was comforted by the clatter of dishware, the glottal shocks as Moroccan tongues struck soft palates, the muffled roar of the Renaults, motor scooters, and *petit taxis* that funneled through the vast square that was Casablanca's hub. The wind that dodged around the red weather banners and into the café carried a port perfume of sea air and scorched petrol, mixing with *café noir* and tobacco as it snatched up the hopeful shouts of *"Coup du Monde!"* when Morocco finally scored.

It was widely held in the Israeli intelligence community that more successful operations had been planned in open cafés than in soundproof briefing rooms, a tradition born of the concept that it was harder for the opposition to acoustically target an improvised meet than a fixed base of operations. Indeed, the overburdened AMAN comptroller had once seriously proposed acquiring a restaurant franchise rather than continue to face the mountains of luncheon receipts that smothered his desk each Friday.

The main floor of the café was packed shoulder-to-shoulder, which was also fine with Baum, as the waiters had to set him up on a balcony at the top of a curved stairway. Aside from the trickle of patrons quickly using the men's room between game quarters, no one else was up there, because the television below was partially obscured by a buttress. However, the entrance of the café was in plain sight, and as Baum's visitors wandered in, each of them repeated a similar mime. They scanned the main floor, saw no one they knew, finally looked up, and were beckoned by Eckstein's finger.

The small group of High Atlas mountain trekkers—for certainly by their bright alpine sweaters, neon belly pouches, and dark anoraks they could be nothing else—had gathered around three tables pushed together by the accommodating maître d'. The man's presence temporarily stifled their "touring" plans, as he had returned to the balcony, unfurled a camel rug, and was bowing toward Mecca as he recited the *rakatin*. Benni Baum, who sat at the head of the joined tables, leaned the back of his metal chair against the rear wall and drummed his fingers on his knees. When the pious Moroccan finally rose and recovered his rug, Baum smiled at him and bowed his head in a gesture of respect.

Baum's party was not yet complete, so he waited, not wanting to have to rebrief anyone. He was anxious to start, yet a modicum of calm had returned to his troubled heart, for in truth he had not expected to have a team assembled so quickly. He looked to the far end of the joined tables, where Eckstein straddled a chair and rested his chin on his arms, pretending to watch the match while he kept an eye cocked on the front entrance below.

Benni regretted his earlier accusatory outburst, in which he had challenged Eckstein's decision to stop over in Tel Aviv en route from Addis Ababa. And he had quickly apologized when the major recounted his activities while briefly on Israeli soil. Eytan's visit was so short that he had not even seen his own wife and son.

Eckstein had begun his military career as a paratroop officer, and those years at the sharp end of the IDF had ingrained the habits of mission preparation. More often than not, operations were canceled at the last minute, but you learned to prepare your men and equipment with the very first rumors of impending action. If you were ordered to stand down, then the only price your troops had paid was a few liters of sweat.

Eckstein had scant information with which to plan properly, but he knew that Ruth Baum was being held by Martina Klump, somewhere in North Africa. That was more than enough to assemble a team, men who had close-quarter combat experience and dual nationalities, as Israeli passports would have prohibited travel to the Maghreb. He had also accurately guessed that upon being briefed, Itzik Ben-Zion would be reluctant to inform his own superiors, for such a revelation would put irreversible gears in motion. The prisoner exchange—Itzik's next plateau toward the peak of chief of staff—might be put off. And while Baum's many friends in high military places might decide to mount an official operation to recover his daughter, that plan would be subject to cabinet approval. Ruth did not exactly constitute a planeload of hijacked Jews, and who knew what political squelching could occur in the corridors of the Knesset? So if Itzik was going to support a rescue attempt, it had to be one he could deny, and therefore Eytan's telephone calls were made, even *before* he saw the boss, to men not presently "on the payroll."

The bulk of Israel's army is composed of reservists, men and women accustomed to finding in their mailboxes small brown envelopes summoning them to a thirty-day stint. They are also given a coded call sign that may be broadcast by radio or television during an emergency. The members of small elite units are often summoned informally by a phone call from their operations officer, saying only, "*Anu zazim*. We're on the move."

Eckstein was able to make contact with most of his prospective candidates, even those who had relocated to Europe for employment purposes. Yet the bulk of the men were still in Israel, and all of the conversations were short and more or less the same.

"Didi, it's Eytan."

"*Ma-enyanim, ben-adam?!* How are you, man?!"

"Fine. Listen, are you busy?"

"As hell, as always. What's up?"

"Something big. It'll take three days, minimum."

"Shit. I have law boards tomorrow."

"Benni needs you."

"I was gonna flunk them anyway. Give it to me."

"Okay. Go to Ben-Gurion, pick up a ticket for TWA flight 883 to Paris, leaving at 0620."

"Want me to charge it?"

"I already paid. Ticket's under David Lerner."

"*Chutzpahnn.*"

"Then catch the first connector to Casablanca. That you'll have to pay for. Maybe we'll reimburse you."

"*Ooh-ah.* A self-paid vacation."

"Check into the Hotel de Paris on Rue Branly. Show up at the Café de France in Place Mohammed tomorrow at 2400. The rest is gear. Want to copy?"

"Hey, don't insult me. I just memorized fifty torts."

The unquestioning replies to Eckstein's obscure summonses should not have surprised him, although he was always pleased to find those fluids of loyalty and self-sacrifice still running through Israeli veins. Decades of warfare had not yet slimmed the lines of young inductees volunteering for dangerous duty, and even with these mature veterans, their reflexive response to the call of "Follow me!" had not slowed. Eckstein was well aware of the secret peace negotiations slowly bearing fruit on previously entrenched fronts, but he wondered if peace, when it finally came, would alter the character of the Israeli nation for better or for worse. . . .

Benni lit up a Casa Sport, a local filterless cigarette that had the bite of a Sobranie and the aroma of dried sheep droppings. He looked at his watch and decided to give the last man five more minutes, then they would start without him.

To his right, Horse was finally returning to his usual state of somber reflection. Over the past twelve hours, the little operations analyst had been batted about an emotional racquetball court.

First, while still in Jerusalem, he had been summoned to take a telephone call from the commander himself, whose tinny voice hailing from some long-distance relay was all too clear in its intention. Ben-Zion informed Horse that he was, as of that very moment, suspended indefinitely without pay, and he should leave the premises. With Benni Baum out of the country and no one else to bat for him, Horse meekly complied, praying for elucidation in the near future. As he was wandering bent-backed and spiritually deflated toward the main entrance of the SpecOps building, he was stopped by one of the *ksamim*, a wizard from the subterranean workshops where tools of the trade, such as minicameras, transceivers, and detonators, were disguised as wristwatches, Walkmans, and fountain pens.

The man handed him a soft briefcase with a shoulder strap, which appeared to be empty. "Be careful," the wizard said. "There's a hundred thousand dollars in the lining. Go home." Now thoroughly confused, Horse boarded his regular bus to Gilo, but before entering his apartment house, he was beckoned over to a car, in which sat two of the gorillas from "Peaches," the SpecOps internal security detail.

"Go upstairs and pack," said the beefy driver. "Three days' worth, climate like Jerusalem. Take your time. Ten minutes."

Even though Horse himself was by now a captain, he tended to snap to orders like a recruit. The two men sped him to Ben-Gurion Airport, a nauseating careen during which they handed him a travel packet containing his cover passport, which was Hungarian, appropriate support papers, a ticket for the short El Al hop to Cairo, and another on Egyptair to Casablanca. They made him repeat his contact instructions three times, but no one ever mentioned Baum, and by the time Horse was entering Moroccan airspace, he was paranoiacally convinced that Itzik had made him a sacrificial cash courier. He was going to deliver a payoff and might never come back.

When he walked into the Café de France, high on adrenaline and shivering from the wind, he nearly fainted when he saw Eckstein's face smiling over the balcony rail. Now he sat at the table, reunited with his "family," safe and secure, though certainly in harm's way. He studied the *Lonely Planet* guide to Morocco, Algeria, and Tunisia.

At Benni Baum's left elbow, a small, dark-haired man screwed a cigarette into a black holder, bit the onyx between his teeth, and lit up with an electronic lighter. Lieutenant Colonel Shaul Nimrodi, former OC of the IDF parachute school at Tel Nof, was one of those rare diminutive men who never felt the need to over-compensate for his size. The youngest of twelve children born to an Iraqi rabbi and rebbitzen who had *walked* to Jerusalem from Baghdad, Nimrodi had discovered early on that his flashing smile could quickly disarm opponents while his quick brain moved in for the kill. He had served as an airborne officer for twenty-five years, and given the thousands of recruits who had followed him out the jump doors of every transport aircraft in the IDF inventory, he was something of a national celebrity. In Israeli airports, restaurants, and movie theaters, he was still warmly accosted by paunchy reservists who clapped him on his small, muscular back and thanked him for quelling the most fearful moments of their lives.

Nimrodi's humor under pressure was legendary, yet the respect he commanded was also due to his insistence on rigid discipline and the stunning rage he could summon whenever unprofessional laxity appeared. He had been known to keep an entire company at attention for three hours under an August sun for neglecting the instructions of a rigger.

In the course of his career, there was not a single major Israeli airborne operation in which he had not played a crucial role. From the Golan in '67 to Suez in '73, from Entebbe in '76 to Beirut in '82, Nimrodi was summoned when history could not wait for loadmasters to consult their technical manuals. The chief of staff would task the chief paratroop and infantry officer, who in turn would task Nimrodi, no matter who else stood in the chain of command.

"We have to put the 202nd regular battalion on the ground at Sidon tomorrow at 0700," the CPIO would say.

Nimrodi would jut his cigarette Roosevelt style, squinting up through the halo of smoke, tap one set of fingers with his thumb, and come up with a calculation.

"We'll need six C-130s, each with one support APC, six G-111 cargo chutes per vehicle, drop the M-113s from the ramps at six hundred meters altitude, then bring the troops into a landing on the strip, line astern. We'll put in Pathfinders and Para Recon first from two C-47s for LZ marking and security, but no parachute drop for the main force. It'll give us more room for ammo and heavy MGs and mortars, maybe an additional two thousand kilos per bird. Estimate thirty minutes tops for the main-force delivery."

"Can you *do* that by tomorrow?" the CPIO would ask doubtfully.

Nimrodi would simply grin, and the long crevasses that spidered down from his eyes to his jaw were always the signal that caused his superiors to reply with a beaming "*Kadimah!* Forward!"

Nimrodi had finally retired with his pension, and at the relatively young age of forty-six he had no plans for a second career. He had fully intended to spend the next ten years with his wife and three daughters, touring the world, playing backgammon at the beach, dabbling in the stock market, and then he would see about a modest business venture. But his telephone never seemed to stop ringing, and officers in uniform and civilian clothes kept appearing at his door in Nes Ziona. Men like Benni Baum, with whom he had worked on a number of tricky insertions and extractions, would not allow him to lapse into comfortable sloth. At the present time he was working as a consultant for Akorda, a transport corporation owned in proxy by AMAN, which was contracted to the government of Mauritania. He was a free agent now, taking orders only from his own conscience, and Eckstein's telephone call had resulted in a quick hop over to Casablanca to see if he could help out an old comrade in arms.

Nimrodi looked over at Benni and raised his right wrist, showing Baum his watch.

"Just another five minutes, *Baba*," said Benni in English. Nimrodi was traveling under a false Iraqi passport supplied to him by AMAN in 1991, when the entire parachute brigade was preparing for a drop into the western Iraqi desert, a mission that never materialized. The document stated his identity as Ahmed Tabri, but the Arabic nickname for "Papa" had stuck with him since an operation in the Jordan Valley in 1968, during which he had worn a kaffiyeh and led a recon team of Arabic-speaking commandos.

Nimrodi smiled at Baum, shrugged, and sipped from a steaming glass of black coffee. "I am in no hurry, my friend," he said in a surprisingly deep voice. When he spoke English, his accent sounded curiously French, and since it emanated from a face that was angular and large-featured, he was often compared to the actor Jean-Paul Belmondo. "But you will want to begin this soon."

"Yes," Benni agreed. He looked down the row of tables, where the men were bending their heads together, quietly recalling other missions and adventures. "We can manage as is, but the last man is bringing the real time product."

"Knowledge is power," Nimrodi agreed. "We will wait."

Michael O'Donovan was not seated with the rest of the contingent. Although more intimately linked to this venture than any of them, he felt the outsider and was in no mood to exchange pleasantries with seven strangers. He stood off to one side of the balcony, between tables on which empty chairs had been upturned like the corpses of poisoned roaches. He sipped a beer, smoked, and stared blankly down at the crowd of soccer fans.

"It wasn't a malfunction. It was a panic cutaway." The man to Nimrodi's left, David "Didi" Lerner, was expounding on a parachuting incident with one of his former army comrades. Lerner was a wide, muscular Israeli of Australian birth. He was prematurely bald, but his youthful face suggested that maybe he shaved his head for "style." Lerner was still a reserve sergeant major with Sayeret Matkal, the ultrasecret General Staff Reconnaissance Unit, which was technically in the AMAN order of battle but reported directly to the chief of staff. One of Israel's top experts in high-altitude parachuting, he now ran a marginally successful free-fall club called ParaGo. The business teetered on the edge of bankruptcy, because Lerner was much more interested in jumping than in marketing his services for Independence Day demonstrations. With a wife and child to support, Didi had decided to go for a law degree, though he had little faith in his ability to pilot a desk for long without getting *kotzim ba'tachat*—thorns in the ass.

"That's what I thought too," said Amir Lapkin. "He was hardly out of the plane when he cut it away. He didn't even let the main fully deploy, so everyone thought it was collapsed."

Lapkin was also half "Anglo-Saxon," as the Israelis refer to those citizens whose native language is English. Born in Toronto, he had been brought to Israel as a child. Lapkin's dark features and a long mustache that drooped to his jowls gave him the look of a Mexican bandit. He had served as an officer in Lerner's Matkal team, but as with all such units, rank meant nothing to their relationship. He was a gardener in civilian life, but he spent a lot of time packing chutes for ParaGo and maintaining his national marksman status at the Olympic pistol range in Herzaliya. He had a rumbling voice and a dry wit made sharper by his unsmiling, deadpan delivery.

Two more men sat across the table from Lerner and Lapkin. Although they were also Israelis, their Nordic features and clipped conversation in

Hochdeutsch suggested descendants of Gestapo officers rather than Holocaust survivors. Ari Schneller was tall, nearly white-blond, and German born. He had served in the IDF parachute recon force of the Thirty-fifth Brigade, and on three previous occasions he had been attached to Benni Baum to work briefly as a "hard man" for operations in Germany. After mustering out of the service, he had relocated to Vienna and started a security firm, supplying technical services and armed escorts, trained by himself, to the heads of Viennese banks. Disarmed by his classically Aryan looks, Schneller's older clients sometimes took him into their confidence and reflected on the "good old days." He relished these incidents, giving the old Fascists plenty of rope, then pointedly announcing to their stunned gapes that he happened to be not only a Jew but an Israeli commando as well. Eckstein's call had offered a welcome respite from the Austrian social and climatic chill.

Schneller argued with Rick Nabbe over the merits of the Glock 9, a plastic pistol whose grip Nabbe insisted was designed only for Texans. Nabbe's military background was similar to Schneller's, for he had also served in Sayeret Tzanchanim. He was Belgian born, medium height and wide, wore his brown hair in a Julius Caesar cut, and sported steel-rimmed spectacles with wraparound earpieces. He was equally quick of humor and reflexes, and was known to defuse operational dangers by impersonating Peter Sellers's Inspector Clouseau.

He had not worked directly for Baum but had occasionally been summoned by AMAN when SpecOps was planning operations on French soil. When French engineering industries were irresponsibly supplying Saddam Hussein with nuclear processing components, Baum had recommended Nabbe to the Mossad. He was most proud of having blown up a factory warehouse containing Baghdad-bound centrifuge components in Lyons.

Nabbe had taken a two-year contract as a close-protection expert in Frankfurt. He was sometimes called upon by Germany's GSG-9 to instruct the antiterror commandos in combat quick-draw, but mostly he was sick and tired of being treated like a butler by touring rock-and-roll stars. Eckstein's cryptic telephone suggestion that this project would overshadow Nabbe's adventure in Lyons had sent him packing to the airport.

The last member of this eclectic group of tourists was a compact, wire-haired kibbutznik known only as Sadeen. The word in Hebrew means "bedsheet," and the farmer from Galilee had acquired the nickname early in his army days, when he carried a white sheet in his combat ruck and always mummified himself before crawling into his sleeping bag. Sadeen was the youngest of the volunteers, having just turned thirty, but no small-unit mission could proceed without experienced hands such as his.

An immigrant from Uruguay, he had volunteered for service as a member of Chabalah Mootznachat, the airborne demolition section of the regular paratroops. He was quickly recognized as a natural genius with all manner of explosive materials, breezed through noncom and officers' school, and was sent to the Technion University in Haifa by the army. He was a captain in the reserves now, still frequently called up and attached to units being inserted deep into Lebanon. Demolition material was never foolproof; it could deteriorate or be lost in an airdrop; it could fail, but Sadeen never would. It was said that he could wander empty-handed into a sheep farm and come out with a burlap bag full of nitro cellulose.

He was not antisocial, yet he sat alone now near Eckstein at the far end of the tables, tinkering as always. He had emptied a glass salt shaker onto a napkin and was examining the inside of the metal screw cap.

All of these men, including Nimrodi, still easily scored *Aleph-Aleph*—double A—on the live-fire course at Mitkan Adam, the IDF's antiterror training facility. Among them, if they happened to shower together, one could have counted a total of nine bullet scars. For when they drew their weapons, whether on the slopes of Lebanon or in the back alleys of Europe, inevitably the opposition drew theirs as well.

Didi Lerner suddenly laughed. He threw his head back and barked, "*Royt*, mate," in his raspy Australian as he slapped the table. Amir Lapkin, who had obviously triggered this response, just twirled the end of his mustache and regarded Lerner curiously.

Eckstein turned his head from the balcony and glanced at his "recruits." These men were the real thing: not comic book heroes but the reluctant warriors who were Israel's most successful crop. They had proved themselves—not for glory or medals but for their cause, their comrades, their families, all entities that constituted that thing called country. They were half deaf from years of gunfire, but could still quick-march a hundred kilometers, and their combined hours of combat training were uncountable. Yet none of these factors was the decisive point that had made Eckstein reach out to them. You could train a man for years, but until he had actually been under fire, you knew nothing about him. Each of them had faced the devil, entered his darkened doorway at midnight, chased him through a cloud of flash and smoke, wrestled with his body close.

They were not violent men by nature, and Eckstein doubted if more than two of them had ever been in a fistfight. But in a *fire*fight, they would stand up and charge.

Benni caught Eckstein's attention and lifted his eyebrows in impatient concern. Eytan raised a finger to signal one more minute, then turned his attention back to the café's entrance. Then he smiled, reached out to his right, and snapped his fingers. Mike O'Donovan heard the fleshy click and walked over in response to Eckstein's wave.

"Are you feeling the odd man out, Michael?" Eckstein asked.

There was no point in denying the obvious. "First day at a new school," said the detective.

"You should get to know the men." Eckstein took O'Donovan's can of Imperial and swigged from it as if to demonstrate intimacy.

"I will," said the American as he glanced briefly at the seated contingent. "So who are we waiting for?"

"Roselli's courier. He will make it easier for you. I think you know him."

"Who is he?"

"That man." Eckstein jutted his chin toward the entrance.

O'Donovan placed his hands on the balcony rail and hunched to see better. His eyes widened as he stared at the entranceway.

Detective Jerry Binder was standing just inside the doorway. He was wearing a white German alpine parka splotched with intermittent leaf designs, shouldering a black Eastern Mountain Sports ruck, and looking around as if he had stumbled into the wrong dimension.

"Holy *shit*." O'Donovan whispered.

"Is he an asset?" Eckstein asked.

"Like *two* men," the American said, with barely concealed joy.

"Can you whistle?"

O'Donovan looked at Eckstein. Then he understood, stuck two fingers in his mouth, and issued a short, piercing blast.

Binder snapped his head up, brushed off an approaching waiter, and headed for the stairs.

O'Donovan's expression of stunned pleasure was still stuck to his face when he greeted the burly cop at the summit. He reached out his hand, and Binder crushed it briefly, but the big man was embarrassed by emotions and he pushed past as the younger detective followed.

"Jerry!" O'Donovan exclaimed in a sharp whisper. "How the fuck?"

"You think you're the only ex–SFer on Langley's roster?" Binder growled as Baum rose to greet him. "I was in Sphinx when you were still pissing in diapers."

"But how did Roselli know . . . ?"

"Fuckers never let you go," said Binder, although he was clearly proud to have been called upon once more. "Your Company buddy wanted a bag boy and somebody to watch your ass. Click click, clack clack." He mimed punching a computer keyboard. "Fed you in, came up with me."

"I don't believe you," O'Donovan scoffed. "You went down to Virginia and busted somebody's door."

"*Fuck* you, then," said Binder as he shook Baum's hand.

"A pleasure, once again," said Benni. "Though not a surprise."

"Same here," said Binder. "And we're calling you . . . ?"

"Schmidt."

"*Yawohl.*" Binder smiled and clicked his heels. "And I'm Alice in Wonderland."

"How did you get away?" O'Donovan pressed, meaning from Midtown North.

"Vacation time."

"The lieutenant must be duly pissed."

"Brace yourself. She'll probably ship us out to the Bronx."

O'Donovan laughed, something he had not done since Ruth's abduction. Binder's appearance had instantly reset his equilibrium, as if he had been stumbling lost in a dark forest and suddenly come upon his own twin, holding a flashlight and a map.

Binder opened his ruck and removed a large padded envelope, which he handed to Baum. Then he pulled out an empty chair and sat down between Shaul Nimrodi and Didi Lerner. Nimrodi turned to him and grinned around his onyx holder.

"Call me *Baba*," said Nimrodi.

"Call me Binder."

"A nickname would be better."

"Spider, then."

Nimrodi looked the American over, taking in his stiff black hair, large jaw, and the pectorals pushing at his parka. He was anything but delicate and arachnoid.

"Do you wear a tattoo?" Nimrodi asked.

Binder's eyes narrowed. "A tarantula. On my left hip."

"Yes." Nimrodi nodded. "It was just a guess," he assured the detective. "You are very large."

Binder grunted, then looked around the table at the other men, who were smiling, waiting for his response. "But I keep a low profile," he said.

Ari Schneller, who was taller than the American yet less physically imposing, laughed and reached across the table. The other men followed suit, offering their cool, rough grips and muttering first names only.

O'Donovan took a seat across from Binder, Eckstein pulled a chair up between Horse and Baum, and everyone shifted closer to the table's head. Without being assigned the task, Nimrodi turned his back to the group and straddled his chair as a lookout.

Benni opened the envelope and extracted one page of computer printout, three black-and-white photographs, a folded map, and a small rectangular leather case. The map was a restricted CIA terrain detail of the western sector of Algeria, bordering Morocco, but Benni could see that it was very large and he would not unfold it here. The photographs were aerial detail taken by a KH-11 satellite, or maybe an SR-71 Blackbird flyover. They appeared to be one-dimensional but were actually prints off two negatives exposed from cameras set at slightly different angles. In the leather pouch was a set of viewing lenses mounted on collapsible legs. When you set up the viewer above a photograph, the target area would appear in three-dimensional relief, as if you were hovering merely a thousand feet above the sharply defined structures, ground features, and human beings. For the time being, Benni left the viewer in its case.

"And so, gentlemen," said Benni in English as he flipped the photographs over and laced his fingers together upon them. "It begins."

The smiles had faded from the faces as the men leaned closer, straining to hear above the din from the soccer party below.

"First of all, we have very little time, so I am not going to bother with history for now. You should know that while my boss is aware of this project, it is a private affair, a deniable madness." Benni paused, unsure that his volunteers understood just how far removed they were from the cocoon of governmental sanction. "If we fail, there will be no rescue, no extraction. Each of us will have to 'escape and evade,' as the Americans call it."

No one reacted to this tacit offer to back out. The men regarded Baum with the blank impatience of smokers reading the surgeon general's warning on a cigarette box. To the Israelis, the concept of individual self-rescue was an anomaly. Binder and O'Donovan were ex-Green Berets, and their tradition was similar. They would all survive this as a unit or not at all.

"So there are two main objectives," Baum continued. "The first is the rescue of my daughter, Ruth, who is being held prisoner by Martina Ursula Klump and a group of her comrades."

Up until that moment, no one had discussed the true nature of the mission with any of the newcomers. These men were accustomed to being surprised at briefings, yet they had also been raised on the iron rule that if a family member was involved in a hostage predicament, they would automatically be scratched from a rescue mission manifest. Nimrodi, who had been listening as he faced away, slowly turned his head and stared at Baum.

"Yes," said Benni. "And the second part is no better. Klump is in possession of a small antiship weapon stolen from an American road convoy. In less than three days' time, we are scheduled to make an exchange off the coast of Morocco, Hizbollah's Sheik Sa'id for our own Captain Dan Sarel. She intends to stop that transaction."

A few mouths opened, someone lit up a cigarette. Sadeen put down his salt shaker and reached for a can of beer, and the popping tab sounded like a distant warhead impacting at the waterline.

"And so, my friends . . ." Benni lit up another Casa, coughed, and then looked at it as if he were holding a worm. "The problem is simple, no different from a graduation exercise at Bahd Echad." The reference was to the IDF officers' school. "Rescue the hostage and prevent her captors from taking further action."

Yes, it was a standard problem for elite Israeli units, but no one at the table accepted Baum's attempt to define the issue as "simple." The hostage was his own flesh and blood, and the images of possibly causing her death paralyzed the men into silence. Benni saw the hesitation in their eyes. He would have to convince them of his confidence, lead with strength, and they would follow.

"Chevrey," he said, using the Hebrew slang for "comrades." "Your pity will not save her. Nor your silence. Let's get to work."

Didi Lerner took up the cue. He dropped his fists on the table, shaking the various drinks.

"Awroyt," said the Australian. "First, let's eliminate problem two. Get the exchange postponed."

"Yeah," Amir Lapkin agreed. "Take the wind out of Klump's sails. Then we only have the hostage problem."

"Who is this Klahmp?" Sadeen asked in his Spanish accent. He was purely a demolition man and did not follow counterinsurgency current events.

"German terrorist," murmured Ari Schneller, seeming chagrined that she should hail from his mother country. "A real bad girl."

"Had a part in bombing our embassy in Buenos Aires," said Rick Nabbe. "It was Hizbollah vengeance for us killing Hussein Mussawi."

"And there's more," Eckstein interjected. "But it's irrelevant now. We'll give you her full CV later on."

"Good enough." Didi took a swig from a can of Pepsi. "So why don't we get the exchange put off?"

No one at the table replied. They knew the answer, but they chose to examine their fingernails. Benni had to prod them over the emotional hump.

"Well, why don't we?" he posed, and receiving no response, he raised his voice like a frustrated schoolmaster. "Class?"

" 'Cause Klump might get wind of it," Jerry Binder said.

Benni nodded. "And if she does . . . ?"

"She'll kill the hostage," Rick Nabbe blurted. His expression was pained, but it had to be said.

"Good." Benni slapped the table. "Just like any hostage problem. If Klump senses danger, she will kill Ruth. Let's get on with it! There isn't time for manners."

Shaul Nimrodi stood up and began to pace beside the tables, his cigarette smoke drifting behind his head. "He is right, my friends," he said. "Freeze your hearts. Think as you were taught to."

"Fine," said Ari Schneller as he summoned his hard side. "Where is the target area? What are the structures? How many men does she have? Vehicles, weapons, communications?"

Horse was holding Art Roselli's computer printout, comparing the information to a primitive map in his guidebook.

"They are located in the western Algerian Sahara, near a place called Taghit," he said. The men strained to understand his English, for his Russian accent was thick.

"Is it a built-up area?" Lapkin asked.

"Taghit, yes," Horse replied. "But the target area is dunes."

"Are they in tents?" Rick Nabbe shivered with the idea.

"Buried recreational vehicles," said Eckstein. "Like American Winnebagos."

"Jesus," Binder hissed.

"Numbers?" Schneller asked again.

"At least fifteen men," said Benni. "Maybe twice that."

Didi Lerner made a quick count of those present, eleven in all. "How many of us will go in?"

"Horse will not," said Benni. "And at least one more will stay behind for support."

No one noticed Horse's body go slack with relief. They were looking at Baum, who clearly meant that he himself *would* be going in.

"So that leaves nine of us," said Sadeen.

"Nine of us, and maybe *sirty* of *zem*," Rick Nabbe pondered in his Clouseau accent. "It hardly seems fair to zeh poor bastards."

A few smiles flashed around the table.

"We don't know the weaponry," said Eckstein. "But we should assume light arms and grenades. Maybe some hand-held antiarmor, and they could have night vision."

"What are *we* gonna use?" O'Donovan scoffed. "Penknives?"

"That will be my problem," said Shaul Nimrodi. "But for the moment, my friends, let us talk about climbing the Atlas Mountains."

The men looked at him curiously, then realized that he wanted the subject changed. A waiter was approaching from the top of the stairwell.

"Freeze-dried food for three days, men," said Rick Nabbe as he picked up Baba's hint.

"The Touring Club on Rue de Force Armées will know where to buy," Eckstein added.

"*Ça va, mes amis?*" the waiter asked as he approached the tables.

"*Oui, très bien,*" said Nimrodi. "*Une carafe du café, si'l vous plaît.*"

"*Noir?*"

"*Au lait.*"

"*D'accord.*" The waiter bowed and went away. A thundering cry rose up from the main floor. Morocco had scored.

When the din receded, Binder spoke up. "What's the range from here to the target area?" He pulled a face and waved some of Nimrodi's smoke away.

"Too far," said Eckstein. "But we'll relocate farther south tomorrow."

"Marrakesh," said Benni.

"And from there?" Schneller asked.

Horse raised his head from the computer printout. "It is approximately five hundred kilometers to the Algerian border." He handed the sheet to Baum.

Lapkin let out a low whistle as he calculated overland travel time. "What's the terrain like?"

"I believe the High Atlas range stands between Marrakesh and the border," said Nimrodi. He was facing the stairwell again, participating with his back to the group. "It is not a molehill, my friends."

"That's a day's travel time right there," said O'Donovan.

Benni was reading Art Roselli's page of printed information. It was a single sheet crammed with hard intelligence. There was no greeting.

REAL TIME DATA AS OF 0130 GMT. AIRCRAFT SET DOWN TARGET AREA LAT. 31°15–30N, LONG. 2°17–45W. SAT TRACK ON EMERGENCY TRANSPONDER INDICATES 12 HOURS NO CHANGE LOCATION. PASSIVE I.R. INDICATES TOTAL ENGINE SHUTDOWN, THREE HARD SHELTERS WARM AND ACTIVE, TWO VEHICLE ACTIVITIES, PERSONNEL FIFTEEN PLUS. SHORT RANGE COMMOS AT TARGET, NO LONG RANGE TRANSMISSION. PROJECTED WEATHER NEXT 72 HOURS MOD. WINDS 10 TO 13 KNOTS SOUTH SOUTHEAST, 18 TO 28 CELSIUS, CHANCE LIGHT PRECIPITATION. SURROUNDING AIR TRAFFIC SPARSE, INCLUSIVE ONE FLYOVER MILITARY AND . . .

"It appears," said Benni, "that Klump, some of her men, the hostage, and the missile landed by jet at the site. The aircraft was shut down, but its emergency beacon was activated, so we have a precise fix."

"Why would they activate a beacon?" Sadeen wondered.

"Yeah," Binder agreed. "They stupid?"

"A dangerous assumption," Eckstein cautioned.

Rick Nabbe looked at Baum. "Could your daugh—" He caught himself. "Could the hostage have done it?"

Benni shook his head. "She would not know how to do that."

"Coffee, gentlemen!" Nimrodi warned.

As the waiter appeared with a large steel carafe and a tray full of heavy glasses, Nabbe improvised more cover babble.

"I suggest we climb for two days, then get some photographs for the magazine."

"Super!" Didi agreed. "Then maybe we can pay for the beer." He pronounced it *bee-ah*.

The waiter left, and the smiles snapped back to tight creases.

"Then the crew must have hit the switch," said O'Donovan.

"Do we know how many crew?" Schneller asked.

"Two," said Benni. "Pilot and copilot."

"Shit," Lapkin whispered.

"Why shit?" Schneller asked him.

Lapkin turned on the tall blond man. "Don't you get it? The pilots aren't Klump's men. She hijacked them. They hit the transponder."

"Fuckin' A," Binder grunted. "Now you got *three* hostages."

This new reality enforced a somber silence. Rescuing one hostage alive was complex enough, but when you had three "friendlies," most probably physically separated, the exercise became a nightmare.

"The problems are tripled," Nabbe whispered.

"Or worse," Horse mumbled, for it was his distasteful lot in life to express the darkest scenario.

"Elaborate, *Soos*," Eckstein ordered.

Horse took off his spectacles and began to polish them with a napkin as he sighed. "Perhaps Ms. Klump set off the beacon herself. It could be a decoy to draw a party such as this one in, while she, the missile, and the prisoners have relocated."

Benni slumped back in his chair. He rubbed the knotted muscles at his neck and stared off into a void of fresh doubts.

"Christ, man," Binder snapped at Horse, and the little analyst cringed as if he might be devoured. "We can't assume that shit. We'll go fuckin' nuts."

"But it is a possibility." Nabbe defended Horse's theory.

"Full stop," Benni suddenly commanded as he raised a hand. "Spider here is correct. We have to assume the first case, the simplest one, or be paralyzed."

"Then you *still* have three hostages," O'Donovan reminded him, thinking now of the two helpless pilots.

"No." Benni tried to keep his voice even. "We have *one*. When she is secure, we go immediately to the secondary problem." It was clear that he was prepared to sacrifice the pilots. Had Ruth not been his daughter, he could have made that command decision and no one would have questioned his motives.

"So the men are expendable?" O'Donovan challenged. In his heart he was as willing as Baum to focus all efforts on Ruth, yet his selfish motive caused him to take the opposing tack.

Benni fixed him with a blazing stare. "If you wish, Michael, you can go after the pilots. The rest of us will follow the operational plan."

O'Donovan rubbed his jaw for a moment, then quickly surrendered. "Withdrawn," he said.

"Good," said Benni. "We will tend to them *if* we can."

"What's the additional range from the border to the target?" Nabbe asked.

"Approximately eighty kilometers," said Horse.

"Can we get our hands on some proper vehicles?" Schneller wondered.

"To the border, maybe," said Eckstein. "But we'd have to leave them there and penetrate on foot. And the Algerian frontier troops are not friendly, or bribable."

"Shit, people!" Jerry Binder exploded, then dropped his voice as Nimrodi touched his shoulder. "You got six hundred klicks of mountains, dunes, and fuck knows what else. You can have supercharged Land-Rovers and Suzuki dirt bikes, and you still ain't gonna make the timetable!"

The contingent erupted in an unruly babel of proposals and objections. They had arrived at the critical impasse. As with most special operations, it was not the point of engagement that was of major concern. The combat they were prepared for. It was the delivery that posed the problems.

"*Mes amis! Mes amis!*" Rick Nabbe waved his hands in the air until the men turned to him and slowly fell silent. "Why are we fooling ourselves, eh?" He smiled thinly and dropped his hands to the table. "We all know why we are here, do we not? There is no sea, so we are not frogmen. There is no snow, so we are not skiers." He looked across at Jerry Binder and offered the traditional inquiry posed at Forts Bragg and Benning. "What are we, Spider?"

A crease formed between Binder's brows for a moment. Then he smiled. "Airborne," he answered flatly.

"Correct. We are parachutists." Nabbe perused the rest of the group. "All of us." He focused on Eckstein. "That is why you summoned us. Correct, Monsieur *Tony?* This is why Didi is here." He jerked a thumb at Nimrodi's back. "And Baba. Is it not so?"

Eckstein grinned slyly at Nabbe and looked at his wristwatch. Then he frowned at the Breitling like a displeased platoon commander. "Not too bad, Rick," he said. "It only took you twenty-seven minutes to get it."

"Well, it would have been sooner." Nabbe shrugged and glanced around. "But I did not see an airplane."

Some of the men laughed. Of course they had the capabilities, the experience. They could certainly jump in, but drumming up a long-range aircraft and high-altitude equipment seemed utterly fantastic here.

"Perhaps God will provide," said Benni. He was also smiling now.

"Oh, really?" Nabbe exclaimed. "In that case . . ." He reached out for a napkin, placed it on his head, and began to mumble a prayer. "Airplane, pilots, parachutes, *mon Dieu.* Airplane, pilots, parachutes . . ."

More laughter burst from the faces around him, and someone snatched the napkin from his head.

"All right," said Benni as he returned the group to order. "So let us assume that we will make the target area." He realized as he said this how heavily indebted he was to Eckstein. Without Eytan's foresight during the recruitment phase, they would not be even dreaming now of success. He looked over at Eytan, who was speaking to Didi.

"But even if we exit over this side of the border," Eytan warned, "it's still a long way to target."

"We won't HALO," Didi instantly decided. "We'll HAHO." The distinction was between two types of free-fall insertion. With the first, High Altitude Low Opening, you dropped from the sky for a minute or two of whistling dive, then opened your parachute at only a marginally safe altitude, the entire exposure from exit to landing but a few minutes of air time.

With the second technique, High Altitude High Opening, you exited the aircraft, deployed the chute quickly, then navigated the ram-air canopy in formation with your teammates, extending the range for many kilometers.

"Oh, great," Binder mumbled. "We'll hop and pop, then freeze our dicks off for half an hour."

"That's why you told us to bring two pairs of *gatkes*," said Sadeen to Eckstein, using the Yiddish word for long johns. "Isn't it so, you *batardo*?"

Eckstein shrugged innocently. "And the Nomex gloves."

"Nobody told *me* to bring any of that shit," Binder complained.

"My apologies," said Eckstein. "You weren't on my manifest."

"You can have mine," Schneller offered to Binder. "I am cold-blooded." Binder snorted.

"The range is still too great," said Nabbe, the realities having temporarily squelched his enthusiasm.

"We will fly nap of the earth to the border." Nimrodi's deep voice wafted over his shoulders, for he was still facing away, sipping from a glass of café au lait. "Then we will run for altitude, make a wide arc into their territory, exit, and the plane will cross back before the Algerians can scramble." He actually had a modification of this plan forming in his mind, but he thought Baum was not mentally prepared for it yet.

"Baba," said Lapkin, "you're making me believe an airplane actually exists."

"There will be an airplane," said Nimrodi with a dismissive wave.

"And parachutes?" Didi asked doubtfully.

"Yes. It will be preferable to use parachutes," the small colonel said without irony. Someone emitted a shaky laugh.

"That's my project," said Eckstein. "And you'll use rip cords, Didi." He wagged a finger at Lerner. "No throw-outs."

Didi smiled back at him. The trend for experienced free-fallers was to dispense with rip cord deployment and open their main canopies by throwing a small pilot chute into the slipstream, which in turn dragged the rest of the assembly into a more graceful blossom. The pilot chutes were packed into long pockets on the lower right side of the backpack containers. Once, when he and

Lerner were jumping together, Eckstein had reached for his pilot and found it bunched and locked in the pocket. Didi, seeing Eytan's struggle, had tracked into him, latched onto his harness, and used all his might to haul the stubborn rag from its hole. The two men had deployed their chutes at less than five hundred meters altitude. Breathless, they had walked straight from the drop zone, finished off a six-pack of Maccabee, and never mentioned it again.

"So what about other gear?" Lapkin posed.

"Yeah," said Binder. "Like weapons."

"Working on it, my friend," said Nimrodi. His "work" apparently consisted of squinting past the tip of his cigarette into the cloud of an idea.

"Somebody make a list," Schneller suggested.

Horse produced a small writing pad, the orange-bound spiral notebook issued to IDF officers. Benni frowned at this breach of security, but then, Horse was not really a field man.

"Penlights," said Didi. "Electrical tape, black. Lots of it."

"Goggles," said Lapkin. "Blousing bands for sleeves and cuffs."

"Knives," said Schneller.

"Helmets?" Sadeen asked.

"No," said Eckstein. "Just the balaclavas you brought. Right?"

The men nodded. Binder rolled his eyes.

"Altimeters," Nabbe blurted. Then he clucked his tongue, realizing they would be impossible to find here.

"Me and Lapkin have ours," said Didi. "We won't need more, mate." With a HAHO jump, the men could simply agree on a count from exit to opening, then just pull and form up on the leader. If they could find him at night.

"Compasses," said O'Donovan. "We should all have one."

Horse scribbled furiously.

"Water." Lapkin began to count off on his fingers. "Some kind of energy rations, climbing rope, waterproofed matches, serious first aid." He avoided looking directly at Baum. "Hey, who's done medic's course besides me?"

Nabbe, Schneller, and Sadeen raised fingers.

"A surgeon's nightmare," Lapkin commented.

"A stretcher," said Benni. "In case we have to carry someone out." He tried to swipe the image of Ruth's body bouncing on rough canvas from his mind.

"Which brings us to the extraction problem," Didi offered.

"Let's forget it for now," Eckstein said. He did not want to stifle the momentum with harsher realities.

"Okay," Didi agreed. "But we should have a stretcher."

"Tent poles!" Horse suddenly blurted, then blushed at having spoken. But he finished the thought quietly. "You could buy a tent, then make a collapsible."

"Very good," said Benni as he touched the analyst's shoulder. "List it. And we will need packs too, to bring the gear down and carry it."

"Magazine pouches, or some sort of load-bearing gear," said Schneller, looking over at Nimrodi. "*Assuming* we'll have ammunition."

"You will carry them in jacket pockets, my friend," said Nimrodi curtly. "There will be no combat webbing. I am not a magician."

"We'll jump them in the packs, with the weapons," said Lapkin. "Then we'll break them out."

The safety-conscious Israelis were used to parachuting with their weapons swaddled in a canvas bag, so that no shroud lines could snag on the metallic protrusions. Unless, of course, intelligence predicted a "hot" drop zone, in which case the assault rifles would be slung and strapped down to the body. Americans always tended to jump "cowboy style."

"*My* weapon'll be locked and cocked and taped to my fuckin' hand," said Binder.

"What about commo gear?" Didi suggested.

"Better dig up a Radio Shack in this berg," said Binder. "Pick up some walkie-talkies. With earpieces."

"Note Spider's name next to that item," Benni said to Horse.

"Any chance of night vision?" Sadeen asked hopefully, though there was little hope of securing a pair of the expensive electronic goggles.

Benni pointed to one of his own eyes. "Only what you were born with, I am afraid."

"*You're* afraid," Nabbe said. "I am already pissing in my trousers."

"Speaking of which," said Eckstein. "Let's move on to the assault gear."

"Distractors would be nice," said O'Donovan. "Flash bangs." He was referring to a type of nonlethal hand grenade that would temporarily stun with its noise and blinding light.

"I'll do something," Sadeen promised.

"No frags, though," Schneller warned. "Not with hostages."

Sadeen nodded at him.

"How 'bout illumination?" Lapkin suggested. If the assault area was pitch black, it would be difficult to distinguish terrorists from captives. Under such circumstances, the assault group usually used tube-launched parachute flares.

"Flares?" Sadeen frowned. "I cannot promise."

"Emergency roadside stuff?" Didi suggested. "Better than bloody nothing."

"Good," said Benni.

"Let's work up a model," O'Donovan recommended. It was standard for special operations troops to construct detailed miniatures of the mission target.

"We will." Benni patted the small pile of photographs. "But tomorrow. We need to divide up responsibilities now, set transportation."

Horse reached out cautiously and slipped one of the photographs onto his lap. Then he opened the viewer case, extended the legs, and hunched over the lenses.

"You are forgetting something," Shaul Nimrodi suggested to no one in particular. He was watching two Moroccans exit the men's room, but they were hurrying to get back to the game, so he did not order the planning hushed.

"What is it?" Benni asked.

"The opposition," said the small colonel. "Who are they? Her men. What is their experience?"

Benni had wanted to postpone discussing this until some of the technical details were worked out. When you painted the enemy in flesh and blood, the mood of a planning session shifted. Young soldiers preferred to know nothing of the enemy's humanity, while experienced operators wanted every detail. But all of them grew somber when the heightened images reminded them that some, on both sides, would lose their lives at the moment of human collision.

Yet the subject had been raised, and all eyes were on him.

"Martina Klump leads a small group of freelancers," he said as he lit up another cigarette and blew out a cloud of acrid smoke. "They are not amateurs."

Eckstein continued Benni's brief. "They are an offshoot of Hizbollah," he said. "Trained and blooded in Lebanon. They have certainly seen action in the security zone." He meant the Israeli-controlled strip of southern Lebanon where IDF troops frequently clashed with the fundamentalists.

"They might have pulled off the consular bombing in Manhattan," O'Donovan added. "But we know for sure that they ambushed the missile convoy in Maryland, blew up the lead vehicle, and killed most of the Marines."

Lapkin and Sadeen raised their eyebrows, while Schneller murmured, "*Schweine*," in his native tongue.

"So they're not going to bloody break and run," Didi declared quietly.

"No," said Benni.

"Do they claim credit after ops?" Lapkin asked. "Call themselves something?"

"They didn't this time," said O'Donovan.

"They call themselves Yadd Allah," Benni said.

Nimrodi turned to him. He took the cigarette holder from between his teeth. "Yadd Allah?"

Baum closed his eyes and nodded once.

"Somebody translate," Binder demanded.

"It means Hand of God," said Eckstein. Then he looked down the table at Rick Nabbe, who was smiling rather foolishly. "Something funny about that, Rick?"

Nabbe did not answer immediately. His eyes were fixed on Didi Lerner, who seemed to know what the Belgian was going to say next. Nabbe scratched his nose thoughtfully.

"I once had a jump instructor who said that all parachutists are madmen. One life is not enough for them, so they are constantly trying to end it and begin again." Didi blushed, but Nabbe went on. "He said that parachuting is like committing suicide and being saved by the hand of God."

Didi took a swig from his Pepsi. "I believe I said the *nylon* hand of God," he corrected.

"Yes," Nabbe conceded. "I believe you did, *mon ami.*"

No one else spoke for a moment, as the men glanced inwardly at their own motivations, the psychoses that drove them through their lives, forcing them to commit acts that were reckless, or heroic, depending on one's viewpoint. The brief spell was broken by the mass scraping of chair legs from the floor below. The game was over.

Horse had finished examining the aerial photographs. Now he placed them facedown on the table and frowned deeply as he fiddled with the viewer. Benni was intimately attuned to the analyst's moods.

"Speak up, Horse," he ordered. "That is why you are here."

Chernikovsky was not called Benni Baum's Nightmare for nothing. It was his job to inform a team of how they might fail, not compliment them on their valor. There were no A's for effort in SpecOps.

"It will not work," he whispered.

"Say it out." Benni waved a hand toward the other men, even as a constriction gripped his chest.

"It will not work like this," Horse said in a fuller voice. "Klump's shelters are under the ground, set up in an open bowl of hard sand. Some air vents show, and a few sentries perhaps. But nothing else."

The men listened carefully; no one interrupted him. They seemed to be holding their breath.

"You cannot simply assault the position," Horse went on. "Even if you get close and silent-kill the sentries, you do not know in which shelter Klump has the girl." He could not bring himself to use Ruth's name. "Even if you can find the doors and blow them, there will not be enough time. These are not like exposed rooms, where you have windows and such options. They are buried trailers, most probably linked to form a tunnel." He looked around at the attentive faces, himself a lecturer doomed to a career of depressing speeches. "It will be like trench warfare, where you are funneled and the defenders have all the advantage." He paused for a moment and picked up someone else's coffee glass, the liquid trembling as he sipped it. "The hostage is probably guarded by an armed escort. And that man most certainly has his orders."

Silence settled over the contingent like mist in a graveyard, the recent adrenaline of plotting now pooling like a depressant in their bellies.

"Well, rain on my fucking parade," Jerry Binder whispered, but his tone held no malice for Horse. In fact, it was tinted with respect for a fellow professional.

"And so?" Benni rubbed both of his eyes with one hand. "Your conclusion, Horse?"

Horse sat up straighter in his chair. "The hostage must be aboveground when you assault," he said with conviction. "For some reason, Klump must bring her up." He turned to Baum. "I think, boss, that you must find a way to get her to do this. To make her *want* to do it."

Shaul Nimrodi slowly pulled out a chair and sat down next to Benni. He seemed no longer concerned that an intruder might eavesdrop. He was devoid of ideas and only praying that Baum's mind was still sharp, as sharp as it had once been in Beirut, in Suez, in the forbidden city of Petra, when they were young fools and their reflexes were as quick as viper strikes.

"Is there a way, my friend?" Nimrodi whispered.

Benni sat back and closed his eyes, folding his arms across his chest. He dismissed the throb at his temples, dissolved the image of Maya weeping over a fresh grave in Jerusalem. Martina had to bring Ruth aboveground. She had to *want* to do it, and the move could not be spontaneous. It had to be timed, planned. Such an act would occur only in response to an arrangement. An agreement. A deal.

"There might be a way," he murmured.

He could feel the shift in telepathies, hear the men's bodies angle toward him. He opened his eyes, to find his volunteers staring at him with the hunger of children who desperately want to please a parent. Benni placed his palms on the edge of the table.

"God knows I love my daughter," he said. "And God willing, Martina Ursula Klump loves her mother."

Chapter 18: New York City

By sundown, the interior of the black Jeep Cherokee had grown as cold as an Eskimo tribal tomb in the Alaskan tundra.

The vehicle's engine had been inactive for hours, the heating fans as still as the rusted props of a sunken scow, and it seemed probable that the battery's acid had been turned to the consistency of a snow cone. The comforting hiss of the jeep's AM/FM was strictly forbidden, so the plumes of exhaled breath rose to the roof and hung there in a silence broken only by the occasional muted crackle from a concealed transceiver. Although it was not yet 7:00 P.M., the winter darkness was as pitch as midnight, and the two members of the Joint Terrorism Task Force stared blankly from their alabaster faces, their bodies as stiff as the carp carcasses under glass at the corner fish market.

FBI Special Agent Jill Greene reclined against the tilted back of the passenger seat, a position she chose because otherwise her six-foot frame offered too much of a silhouette. Her blond hair was tucked beneath a down ski hat with ear flaps, which she referred to as her "Elmer Fudd," and the thick roll of a brown turtleneck was stretched over her sharp jaw. She would have opted for long johns, but if she had to run, it would be like sprinting in a diving suit. The rest of her was encased in a maroon ski coverall, and a nylon belly pouch held her ID and her Smith & Wesson automatic. She thought that she had never suffered a chill so deep, so numbingly painful, and she wanted to scream and slap her frozen body with her gloved hands. Yet her only movement was the curling of her toes inside her blue Nikes, for she was not about to reveal a single twitch of discomfort to her partner.

New York Police Department detective John de Vizio was not quite so proud. He sat hunched in the driver's seat, wearing a green down parka, over a heavy ragg sweater, over his Kevlar vest (which he used only in the winter months now), over a navy cotton turtleneck. He had also stuffed his middle-aged body into a black, bib-type ski overall and wrapped his lower half in a tartan wool blanket. He knew that Greene disapproved of the coverlet, because it would inhibit quick action, just as she would have sneered at his electric socks had she known about them. But he didn't really give a damn about what she thought. She was barely half his age; he had twenty years' experience on her and had waited out a thousand more sits than her few measly "surveillances"—as her snotty Feebie buddies called this kind of torture. He slapped his thighs, rolled to the left and right like a decked tuna, groaned, and looked over at her. She was sitting there like the goddamned Sphinx.

"Tell me you don't feel this, Greene," de Vizio snapped. "Tell me."

"I feel it, John."

"Yeah," the detective snorted. "You feel it."

"It's cold."

"This isn't cold. It's the dark fucking side of the moon."

Greene smiled. She did not express herself the way John did, keeping the foul language of her sorority days out of her lexicon now. She was going places in the Bureau, and a woman did not climb by emulating the crudities of male coworkers. But she enjoyed hearing his creative cursing, the way she imagined a reformed prostitute might nostalgically watch porno tapes.

De Vizio turned to her again.

"How do you do it, Greene?"

"Do what, John?"

"You haven't moved in a friggin' hour."

"Woman," she said simply, keeping her eyes focused down the street on the doorway to number 167 East Eighty-ninth. "Superior being. Extra layer of fat."

"Oh, *please*," de Vizio sneered. "Extra layer my ass."

"Yes," Greene agreed. "Yours does have an extra layer." That was about as far as she would descend into his world of bitter banter.

De Vizio broke off the contest and peered through the breath-fogged windshield. An elderly couple was approaching the entrance to the Edelweiss. He wiped a small circle of the glass with his glove, picked up the Olympus 35 mm, and propped the 300 mm lens on the steering wheel. He had 3200 ASA lab film in the camera.

"Don't bother," said Greene. "They can barely walk."

"If I don't, you'll probably turn me in," de Vizio mumbled. His hands were trembling, but he managed to get the shot. He dropped the camera on the seat. "Seven hours of friggin' nothing."

"It only has to happen once, John," Greene reminded him in the tone of an Academy instructor. "Then it's all worth it. Just *one* of her cell gets careless and crosses our path. The right man, at his wrong time."

"Lecture me. Seven hours with the Ice Queen, and now a lecture."

Greene smiled again. "You like me, John." She kept her eyes on the distant doorway. "I'm a pain in your butt, too young for you to have, too equal for you to control. But I'm good, and you like me."

De Vizio did not answer, although he made a sound as if he had just stepped in the horse droppings of a mounted patrol.

"I like you too," Greene continued. "You're just still mad because I pinned you in hand-to-hand."

"Oh, for Christ's sake! That's ancient history. You *pinned* me?"

"I did. Are you going to say now that you let me?"

"I had a fucking hangover the size of the Goodyear blimp."

"Nevertheless." Greene shrugged. "It's all an ego thing."

"*Hunh.*" De Vizio struggled with the cuff of his parka, trying to find his watch. "Goddamn FBI psychology horseshit," he mumbled as he peered down at the luminous dial. "How much longer on this damned bore?"

Greene glanced at him, then quickly refocused on the objective. Jack Buchanan had briefed the TTF teams on the importance of snatching just one human link in Martina Klump's network. Her hijacking of the navy's missile was no longer fresh, and it was confirmed that she had escaped the country with it. But it was also suspected that at least two members of her cell remained on U.S. soil, and her mother resided in the rest home just yards away. The terrorist ambush had been hushed up, no media were on it, and Jill knew that if she and John got lucky, the commendations would be issued quietly in the Director's office. Still, it would be quite a feather. . . . *How much longer?*

"Until we catch the motherfuckers," Greene suddenly growled.

De Vizio slowly turned to her. Greene *never* talked that way, and she returned his amazed look with a demure smile and a shrug.

"*Now* I'm starting to like you," he said.

A light rapping on de Vizio's window caused both officers to reach instinctively for their S & Ws. Yet they did not draw the weapons, their hands restrained by that nether zone of the brain where decisions teeter at the edge of fate. Friend or foe? Innocent bystander or cop-killer?

The man outside was not particularly threatening in appearance. He was clean shaven, wore a black watch cap, and was shifting from foot to foot in the cold. Even before he briefly opened his army field jacket to show the shield pinned to his sweater, de Vizio had decided: *One of us.*

The detective lowered his window halfway and offered a caustic greeting.

"If you're lookin' for a hot meal, you're out of luck, pal. . . . Ice coffee we can give you."

The man bent and smiled. "Have no fear, your relief is here."

Greene leaned toward the driver's side and looked up. "Do I know you?" she asked, preventing de Visio from uttering his common challenge of "Who the fuck are you?"

"Jim Sprengel." The man offered an ID wallet over the glass. "We're not with TTF. We're up from E Street." The FBI's administrative headquarters occupied a full block in Washington between E and Pennsylvania, but few agents actually worked out of the J. Edgar Hoover Building. "E Street" was just a cryptic mode of identification.

Sprengel glanced over his shoulder, and Jill Greene followed the gesture, spotting an old Chevy Malibu with District of Columbia plates double-parked a few car lengths back. Outside the tan car, a small figure in winter gear leaned back against the fender, arms folded. It appeared to be a woman, confirmed when she waved briefly and exposed a nylon belly pouch, the mode of pistol carry in vogue for female FBI undercovers.

De Vizio took Sprengel's ID, glanced at it, and handed it back.

"Buchanan wants all you people to come in," said Sprengel. "We're just picking up the slack tonight."

The mention of Jack Buchanan's name settled most of the doubts in de Vizio's and Greene's minds. Still, it was not SOP for them to be replaced by non-TTF agents.

"We didn't hear anything." De Vizio glanced down at the Motorola beneath the dash.

"So check it out," said Sprengel with some impatience. "We'd like to get off the street and hunker down. It's a bitch out here."

Greene gestured at the transceiver, and de Vizio reached under the dash, unhooked the mike, and rested it on the lower half of the steering wheel—this little gathering was blatant enough without him actually sticking a mike in his face. He pressed the transmit button and looked at Sprengel as he spoke.

"Teflon One to Base."

He waited, but the only reply was a burst of heavy static. He tried again.

"Teflon One to Base. Do you copy? Over."

Again there was a slight pause, then a longer burst of static in response. It sounded like the TTF dispatcher was trying to reply, but the voice was completely obscured.

"Fucking technology." De Vizio jammed the mike back into its slot. "Why don't they just issue kite string and paper cups."

Sprengel peered at the useless piece of equipment, then looked at the TTF members as if they were street cops with rust on their revolvers. He straightened up.

"Tell you what," he said. "No skin off my nose. You can sit here if you want to, but we're picking this up."

He turned and walked back toward the Malibu. De Vizio closed the window.

"Well, what do you think?" Jill Greene asked.

"All you Bureau types got poles up your asses."

"About *going in*, John."

"Oh." De Vizio drummed on the steering wheel. "We could find a pay phone."

"Let's."

The detective looked at his watch again. "Make you a deal," he said. "We were supposed to go another hour. Let's ride over to Mumbles, grab something hot, then call in. Everything's kosher, we hit the FDR Drive and pop the cherry on the roof." He grinned slyly at his partner, wondering if she would go for it. "We can be downtown in ten minutes flat."

Greene regarded him as if he were a fat little devil perched on her shoulder. She was always by the book, but his remark about anal agents had hit home. The small detour sounded all right. After all, there were people from Washington on site.

"Let's go," she said.

"You kidding?"

"Before I change my mind."

De Vizio started the Jeep. He looked back at the Malibu. Its headlights flashed once as it rolled toward his spot.

"French onion soup," he murmured as he pulled away. "Irish coffee." He could feel Greene smiling next to him as she flipped her seat lever and straightened up. "And you can tell me *all* about the Mistress Race, Eva Braun."

Greene punched him in the shoulder. . . .

Sprengel snuggled the Malibu up to the curb, but he did not kill the engine, and the Chevy's blowers held the interior at a comfortable fifty degrees. Those TTF people had good discipline, freezing their butts off like Russian snipers, refusing to show even a wisp of exhaust fumes. He almost felt guilty about the black box in his pocket, a close-range jammer that emitted hard noise on their UHF frequency, turning their reception to vegetable soup. But their efforts were irrelevant. He already knew the precise location of Klump's two remaining HOGs, and there was no chance of their showing up here tonight.

He looked over at the small woman beside him. She pulled off her wool ski hat, shook out her short brown hair, and unzipped her coverall. Lane's face was bony and masculine, but she had a voice that could have made big bucks for one of those phone sex outfits. She reached down between her feet and unzipped a long gym bag.

First, she pulled a full-size computer keyboard onto her lap, its cord unattached. Next, she came up with a Panasonic mobile cellular, placed it on the seat between herself and Sprengel, and plugged the power cable into the car's cigarette lighter. She removed a small headset with a boom mike from a vinyl case, pulled the unit onto her head, and inserted the jack into the base of the cellular. Finally, she took out a small clipboard with a flexible minilamp, and a hand-held Uniden transceiver. She looked over at Sprengel.

"Clear?" she asked.

He was scanning the far corner of Eighty-ninth and Third, where the red taillights of the Cherokee had swept around to the left. "They're gone."

Lane turned the power knob on the Uniden and brought it to her mouth. "Go, Ranger."

Half a minute passed, then headlights filled the Malibu with glare as a heavy square ambulance with Cabrini Medical Center printed on its flank cruised by and stopped at the foot of the Edelweiss's entrance. The vehicle's rear doors opened and a nurse in full whites and a long gray overcoat dropped to the pavement. She reached into the green cavern of the truck and pulled out a collapsed wheelchair.

From the passenger side of the ambulance cab, a tall man placed his polished shoes on the street and stood up. He was wearing a dark suit, a blue cashmere topcoat, and a fedora. A stethoscope glinted from the sides of his shirt collar, and he carried a black physician's bag. He closed the door, looked back up the street at the Malibu, and touched the brim of his hat.

The doctor joined the nurse at the sidewalk, helping her unfold the wheelchair. Then he mounted the stairway of the rest home, pressed the doorbell, and raised his black bag for the benefit of someone inside. The door buzzed open.

Inside the Malibu, Lane spoke into the walkie-talkie.

"Trigger Gamma, this is Alpha. Ranger is in."

She received two short clicks in reply. Then she hit the power button on the Panasonic, and the telephone's display glowed lime green. . . .

Closer to midtown Manhattan, Dr. Ernst Hoffmeyer's private practice was situated on the north side of Sixty-sixth Street between Park and Madison avenues. The doctor had gone home for the day, but his receptionist stayed on duty until eight o'clock. Because of Hoffmeyer's kindly demeanor and native, fluent German, many of his patients were elderly immigrants from the old country.

At the corner of Park and Sixty-sixth, a NYNEX telephone truck was parked next to an open manhole, the wide mouth protected from careless pedestrians by a half-circle of iron fence and a MEN WORKING sign. On the tailgate of the truck sat a young man wearing a white hard hat and bundled up like the Pillsbury Doughboy. He glanced down occasionally into the hole, but mostly he watched the street with the unblinking gaze of a stagecoach shotgun rider.

Down in the hole, a second man, wearing a miner's helmet with a beam lantern, replaced his own Uniden in its holster, then bent to a thick trunk of colored wires. It had taken him nearly two hours to find the Hoffmeyer leads, but he had them now, tagged and slightly stripped. He carefully clipped two alligators to them, checked the dial tone with his orange handset, then switched the connection to a cellular similar to Lane's but with a call-forwarding modification not yet commercially available. He hit the power button on the unit and looked at his watch. The cellular battery would drain off very quickly in this cold.

The physician who approached the reception desk of the Edelweiss was not Ernst Hoffmeyer, nor was he pretending to be. In fact, he had never met the man who was regarded by the Edelweiss residents as not only their doctor but their friend and confidant. This man presented his credentials as Dr. Peter Kradjel, a member of the cardiovascular staff at Cabrini.

"Good evening." He offered his hospital ID card to the rather cadaverous man behind the desk. "We are here for Mrs. Katharina Oberst."

"*Guten Abend*," the elderly watchman responded reflexively. He looked at the card and quickly handed it back. "Frau Oberst?" He rose halfway from his chair, peering over the counter at the wheelchair. The nurse smiled at him, and he sat back down. "She did not call down to me. Is she ill, Dr . . . ?"

"Kradjel."

"*Ja*, excuse me. Dr. Kradjel." The watchman dropped his eyes to his visitor's wide shoulders, his muscular physique. These middle-aged American professionals, spending so much time in gymnasiums. So undignified.

"It's not an emergency," said Kradjel. "She is scheduled for some tests, a cardio sonogram, *und so weiter*."

"Ahh." The watchman's eyes lit up. "*Sprechen Sie Deutsch?*"

"*Ein Bißen*." Kradjel smiled.

"*Sehr gut, Herr Doktor*," said the watchman. But he switched back to English, for it would not be proper to embarrass the physician if his linguistic talents were only minimal. "You will excuse my hesitation, but—"

"Of course." Kradjel fished inside his coat and produced a triplicate form on Cabrini letterhead, a test schedule with Katharina Oberst's name clearly delineated.

The watchman peered at the paperwork, even as he waved a hand as if such proof was unnecessary, "*Ja*, thank you." Still, he hesitated. He had worked for the civil service in Bonn for thirty years, and any deviation from procedure was hard for him to abide. He shifted uncomfortably. "I have no doubt about the tests, *Herr Doktor*. Absolutely no doubts. However . . ."

"You mean Dr. Hoffmeyer did not inform you?"

The watchman sagged with relief. "*Ja*, that is so! The doctor always notifies us of any such movements."

"Well, please," said Kradjel with grace and patience. "Why don't you call his office?"

"You would not mind?"

"Of course not." The physician gestured toward the old desk telephone.

"A moment, *ja*?" The watchman scraped a fingernail along a list taped to the countertop, and dialed.

In Hoffmeyer's office on Sixty-sixth street, the telephone did not ring. The receptionist was wondering why the damned switchboard had suddenly stopped lighting up like a Christmas tree, but she welcomed the respite and was flipping through a copy of *Vogue*.

In the freezing utility tunnel below the street, the telephone man's cellular also did not ring, but its LED blinked for the fifth time in as many minutes. He crossed his raw fingers, hoping this was the one.

Inside the Malibu, the cellular phone rang once again, its warble jarring because Sprengel had turned off the engine and the heater. Lane had already taken five calls from Hoffmeyer's patients and noted the messages on her pad. She threw her headset switch and began typing rapidly on the computer keyboard, affording the proper background ambience.

"Dr. Hoffmeyer's office."

"*Ja*, good evening. This is Mr. Franz at the Edelweiss Rest Home."

"How can I help you?" Lane sounded like a harried receptionist as she turned to Sprengel and nodded.

"Uh, we have a gentleman here," said the watchman. "A Dr. Kradjel from the Cabrini hospital."

"Dr. Hoffmeyer is in with a patient." Lane's tone suggested that it would not be wise to interrupt her boss. "Does he need to speak with him?"

"No, no, my dear!" the watchman sputtered. "Dr. Kradjel is here to take Frau Oberst to the hospital for some tests."

"Katharina Oberst?"

"Yes. Yes."

"Just one minute." Lane wrapped the small boom mike in the palm of her hand, looked over at Sprengel, and smiled. Sprengel held up a hand and, like a television-studio floor manager, waved it forward at her, each time showing one less finger as he mouthed, "Four, three, two, one."

Lane freed the mike.

"Dr. Hoffmeyer says to please release Mrs. Oberst into Kradjel's care immediately."

"Yes! Of course!" The watchman responded as only a Prussian can.

"And he says to thank you for your vigilance."

"Thank *you*, madam. Good evening."

" 'Bye now."

Lane stabbed the power button on the Panasonic, and the system went dead. Then she slumped back in the seat and exhaled one long breath. But she quickly recovered and picked up the Uniden.

"Trigger Gamma, this is Alpha. Contact is Go. Break it off."

She was answered by three mike clicks as the telephone man freed Hoffmeyer's line. Now she reactivated the Panasonic, unplugged her headset, and began to dial Hoffmeyer's receptionist. She and Sprengel would take turns until they had duplicated the intercepted calls. She squinted at her clipboard.

"Number one was a man calling for his wife." Lane grinned at her partner. "She has a vaginal infection."

"*That* I can handle," said Sprengel as he took the phone. . . .

Secure in the knowledge that he had followed procedure, the watchman had escorted Dr. Kradjel and his nurse to the elevator and returned to his station. He was not really surprised that Frau Oberst was experiencing heart trouble. No doubt the recent incident with that young woman, the shooting and the police, had shaken her up. It had certainly set the ancient tongues wagging throughout the rest home. As for Franz, he preferred the mundane, regular evenings when the residents were in bed by nine and he could work on his stamp collection.

The elevator opened and the nurse emerged, steering the wheelchair straight for the door. Frau Oberst's little form looked no larger than an oversized teddy bear, covered with a thick wool blanket, a large beret with a pearl stickpin pulled jauntily over her white curls. The doctor followed close behind, and he turned to the watchman as he passed.

"Thank you for your help," he said. "We'll have her back day after tomorrow."

"My pleasure." The watchman waved at his departing resident. "*Auf Wiedersehen, Frau Oberst! Viel Glück!*"

The doctor held the door as the nurse deftly spun the wheelchair and backed through. Frau Oberst was smiling, but she did not wave back at Franz, for she was busy unwrapping one of those small chocolate candy bottles, the kind that are filled with brandy. She seemed to have a whole box of them on her lap.

The ambulance driver bounded up the steps to help the nurse with the wheelchair.

"You two got it?" the doctor asked as the pair gently eased Frau Oberst down.

"No problem." The nurse and the driver said simultaneously, the clouds of breath puffing from their mouths.

The doctor walked around to the ambulance cab and got in. He took off his gloves and rubbed his hands together, then reached down to a trauma box, popped open the lid, and picked out a small Uniden identical to Lane's.

"Trigger units, this is Ranger. Wrap it up. We're on the road." He paused for a moment as he thought, then he keyed the mike again. "Alpha, you copy?"

Lane's voice crackled back. "Loud and clear."

"Call Bethesda. Tell the boys, 'The cookie's in the jar,' or some such hokey nonsense. Affirmative?"

"Roger that," Lane's voice replied. There was a smile in it.

"And Alpha," the doctor added. "One more thing. Deep-six the IDs. No souvenirs. You read?"

"Loud and sadly," said Lane.

"Out here."

The doctor dropped the Uniden back in the box. He sat back and sighed, then dug into his overcoat pocket and came up with a pack of Marlboros. He lit one and rolled the window down a crack, blowing smoke and steam into the frigid night.

This whole scenario was shaky enough, and he reminded himself to make sure that Sprengel and Lane followed through and destroyed the badges and identification cards. Relations between Langley and the Bureau were always borderline hostile, and it would not be good to have Company personnel caught with forged FBI documents. No, not good at all. As it was, when Jack Buchanan realized that someone had conned his TTF people off a surveillance, he would be running around like a monkey with its tailbone ablaze.

He reached into his shirt pocket, pulled out the Cabrini ID, and began bending the plastic rectangle like the credit card of a teenager who had abused the privilege. At his home in Virginia, he kept a secret collection in a floor safe, one small item from each of the covers he had used throughout his career.

But this mission was about as unsanctioned as a wiretap on the Pope, and Dr. Kradjel would have to expire without a trace.

He wondered if it would all be worth the risks, if it would pay off in the desert four thousand miles away. Baum's fax from Casablanca had been clear enough. It was a desperate request, almost a plea, but the logic seemed sound, and there was nothing to do but go for it. Clever, and still sharp, that Benni Baum. He hadn't lost it yet, and having no means to encrypt, he had typed out the fax in English characters, phonetically creating a long message in Hebrew.

"CHAVER SHELI. YESH LI BAKASHAH ELECHAH . . . My friend. I have a request . . ."

He reminded himself to give a copy to the cipher team, just to watch them sweat over it.

The rear doors of the ambulance slammed, and the driver hopped up into the cab and started the engine. The Malibu cruised by on the right. The doctor turned to the window at the back of the cab and slid it open as they began to roll. The nurse was seated on a side bench. She smiled and offered a thumbs-up.

He could see the old woman in the steel chair, its wheels clamped to the floor. She was playing with her treats, excited by the prospect of a small adventure, a respite from her days and nights, one upon the next, all of them the same.

"Keep her comfortable, Roxanne," Art Roselli said to the nurse. "Let's not get ourselves convicted for abuse of the elderly, in *addition* to kidnapping."

Fouad Ibn Khalid Fasjee had not slept in nearly twenty-four hours.

His eyes stung as he peered out through the blurred windshield of the Honda. The cold rain hammering the roof aggravated his headache tenfold, and the mealy taste in his mouth could not be salved by any food he forced into his jittery stomach.

It was not that his partner, Fahmi, who was snoring in a sleeping bag on the rear seat, had not offered to stand his share of the watches. It was just that each time Fouad had switched, he found himself tossing inside the damp cocoon like a bagged cat and wound up staring at the car's ceiling.

It was madness, to be parked here for days on the grounds of an American naval hospital. Yes, they moved the car from time to time, but they were forced to stay within sight of the main entrance. This, too, was foolishness, for it would have required a team of twenty to properly cover the building exits.

True, Martina had explained to them that their *presence* was the essential factor, proof to Colonel Baum that she still maintained a contingent on U.S. soil, a suggestion that he and Fahmi were only the tip of an iceberg of operatives. Yet as each hour passed, it appeared ever clearer that they had been abandoned as sacrifices.

By now the Americans had surely found the hidden hearse and limousine, taken fingerprints, logged evidence. Composites of himself and Fahmi were certainly in the hands of hundreds of policemen, detectives, intelligence agents. Federal prosecutors had amassed reams of charges, which, including the naval officer and police detective in New York, the Marines in Maryland, and Baum's daughter, added up to assault, murder, kidnapping, hijacking, theft, sabotage, and Allah knew what else.

He gripped the steering wheel and stared up at the stone hospital edifice, imagining that behind each darkened window, men with binoculars were laughing at him.

"*Koos ochtach arss,*" he cursed under his breath, then immediately admonished himself for his flagging faith. He summoned some logic, dredging up the calm that had saved him from bolting during three endless days and freezing nights.

He and Fahmi were still there, and unmanacled. There had to be a reason for that. No radio report or newspaper had mentioned any of the dramatic incidents, yet surely if Martina and the other men had been caught or killed, the American media would be celebrating in their typically orgasmic fashion, even if at first their government had suppressed news of the convoy ambush. And if Martina had wanted them to withdraw, she would have made contact through the relays. But the cellular phone in the Honda never rang.

The silence could mean only one thing. It was a stalemate. Martina still held the Minnow and the girl, Baum was still in his bed, and no one dared ignite a chain of explosive events.

He looked down at the telephone hidden in a small orange backpack, its wire snaking out toward the cigarette lighter, the plug nearly obscured by a pile of cold butts. Fouad had not smoked in nearly five years, but after the first maddening day on the hospital grounds, he had bought a carton of Kents and begun to ravage it, for there was nothing to do here *but* smoke. And wait. Yes, there was a way to make contact with Martina, an overseas number he could call to relay a message. But his instructions were clear: to use it only if Baum departed from Bethesda, which to the best of his understaffed knowledge had not happened. What other message could he relay? *We are here? Please tell us that you still love us?*

He almost laughed at his own pathetic weakness.

He relaxed a bit and stretched his sore legs. *Next time*, he decided, *if there is one, and Allah wills it, we shall rent a Lincoln.* In his mind he pronounced it *Linko-len*.

He reached into a paper bag and came up with a small bottle of orange juice. The citrus burned as it ran into his sleepless belly, and he reminded himself to tell Fahmi to switch to bottled water and buy some Alka-Seltzer.

He decided to turn the engine over and switch on the radio. Even though the American disc jockeys and the thump of their godless music were annoying, the sounds filled some of the void of his loneliness. He found it difficult to understand the English lyrics of Western pop, so he missed the irony of U2's soft lament.

> *Sleight of hand and twist of fate,*
> *On a bed of nails she makes me wait . . .*

A stalemate. Well, if they *were* intended as sacrificial lambs, while roped to this tree they seemed to be serving some purpose. God would surely reward such loyalty.

Fouad stared across the rain-washed roofs of the other parked cars toward the entrance of the hospital. It was early evening, and the lights blazed behind the high glass facade, the lobby draining of occupants as visiting hours ended. He had come to know the rhythm of the building: when the human traffic peaked and when it bled off; when the military staff changed shifts, the cleaners appeared and departed; how patients being dismissed were always taken to the front door in wheelchairs, no matter their condition.

In the past few days, perhaps twenty-five men fitting Colonel Baum's description had been escorted from the facility. For one reason or another, he and Fahmi had eliminated most of them, comparing the faces to the late Iyad's surveillance photographs; this one too fat, that one too slim. Some were met by large, happy families, while others had limbs encased in plaster casts. On three occasions, when he was really unsure, he had quickly called the hospital and asked if Mr. Benjamin Baum was still registered. Once, he was inadvertently patched through to Baum's room, and when the heavy voice answered with a fatigued "Yes?" he hung up.

Now his eyes suffered the curse of the exhausted watcher, his vision slipping into a watery blur. As he tried to summon the resolve for another painful hour, something behind the glass walls thirty meters away caused his nodding head to stiffen straight up. Without taking his eyes off the building, he gripped the steering wheel and leaned forward, then reached for the wiper switch and swept the blades once across the wavering windshield.

It was something about the way the three men walked, the composition of the trio. Two American Marine officers were striding across the lobby, approaching the door from the direction of the wards. Between them, they shepherded a third man. He was wearing a blue hospital robe, and the cuffs of his pajamas flapped above slippers. He was slightly shorter than his escorts, or at least appeared to be so, because they wore peaked caps, while he was hatless.

And rather stocky.

And bald.

"Fahmi," Fouad whispered as he watched the procession. Then, like a man who has lost his way in an unfamiliar suburb, he switched off the radio, as if the silence might help.

"Fahmi!" He nearly yelled, and he heard the alarmed gasp from behind as his partner jumped up.

"What? What is it?" Fahmi stuttered, wrestling to the surface of his dreams.

Slowly Fouad pointed out through the windshield. Fahmi slipped his head between the front seats and rubbed his eyes briskly, forcing them open, wider.

"Is that him?" Fahmi whispered.

The three men had reached the double exit of the lobby now. The first set of doors slid open.

"It is more than possible." Fouad looked to both sides of the exit, searching for a vehicle at the curb that might snatch Baum away from him. But no such car appeared to fill the role.

The outer doors opened, and the men stepped out into the driving rain. They did not look up at the sky, or pull their coats or robe closer about them. They did not hesitate.

They came straight on, heading for the Honda.

Fahmi spat an Arabic curse and arched back, fumbling on the floor for a knapsack, coming up with the Beretta that Mussa had left behind. He quickly checked the magazine, rammed it home, and chambered a round, the slide ringing like a hammer on a horseshoe.

"Put it down, Fahmi," Fouad ordered quietly. The marching men were much closer now, only ten meters away, but the reason for his urgent suggestion became clear to Fahmi as he looked up again.

From four other vehicles parked close to the Honda—cars that had appeared locked up and empty—other men had emerged, silently taking up positions at short range from Fouad's car.

They wore dark clothes and baseball caps, and beneath their open jackets they gripped the gleaming bodies of MP-5 submachine guns.

Fahmi slowly placed the Beretta on the back seat and raised his trembling palms.

The strange trio halted just off Fouad's front left fender. The wide bald man waited while one of the anonymous gunmen posted himself directly in front of the car, fully exposing the barrel of his weapon.

The bald man approached the driver's side, and Fouad's mouth opened even wider. He was stunned that Colonel Baum should have the audacity to confront him so directly, given the value of the human treasure that Martina held in her grasp. The audacity of Israeli officers was legendary, but this one was surely mad.

He rapped on the glass with a large knuckle.

Fouad rolled the window down, and his visitor bowed forward, nearly inserting his face into the car. The man was smiling. Not broadly, but the expression was one of great confidence, showing none of the fury that should have been present in the eyes of a nemesis. Rather, it was the arrogant pose of a magician who had just duped a nightclub audience.

The days of sleepless angst and poor nutrition suddenly fermented in the pit of Fouad's stomach. He stared up at the smiling face, then snapped his head down to the car seat, flicking his eyes over Iyad's photographs. Then he looked up again. He felt Fahmi's hot breath behind his ear.

The bald man spoke casually, in pure, unaccented American English.

"As you can see, young man," said the CIA officer, his voice raised a bit above the drumming of the rain, "I am not Colonel Benjamin Baum."

Fouad wanted to reply, to respond to this breach of Martina's demands with a powerful threat. But nothing emerged from the dry well of his throat.

"Colonel Baum is in North Africa," the man continued. "By tomorrow, Ms. Klump's mother will join him there." He paused to make sure the facts had been absorbed, then reached into the pocket of his robe and tossed a white card into Fouad's lap. "Tell your boss that Baum is willing to make an exchange."

Fouad forced himself to drag his eyes from the man's face. He looked down at the card. It held nothing more than a telephone number.

When he raised his head again, all but one of the men were gone. Vehicles were rolling out of the lot, and the driving rain spattered the hot skin of his cheek.

The lone gunman remained facing them from beyond the front bumper. He slowly returned his submachine gun beneath his jacket. But before he turned away, he raised his naked finger, pointed it, and shot Fouad between the eyes.

Chapter 19: The Mediterranean

General Itzik Ben-Zion was suffering a thundering sensory reminder that, compared to the gnatlike political machinations of the earth's human nations, the power of the sea was like the hoof of a bull elephant.

He had almost forgotten, for it had been so many years since that short summer between his high school graduation and his induction into the army. He had found work aboard a Zim cargo vessel sailing out of Haifa, and it was there, aboard that chunk of moaning steel, that he first realized how sailors were like airplane passengers, leaving logic at home while they trusted mechanical concoctions to see them through the cruelest whims of the heavens. He remembered how even the balm of August could suddenly betray. The sun would disappear, the blue sky would blacken, and the summer glass of the Mediterranean would boil into a million foam-topped knuckles. Now, in the midst of winter, the plain before him was a mass of gray-green welts, whipped into frenzy by some cosmic blender.

He stood just forward amidships of the *Aliyah*, a Saar 4.5 class missile boat of the Israeli Navy, gripping the starboard rail with his right hand, keeping his combat boots glued to the rolling deck. His left hand floated in the air for balance, a blue baseball cap hooded his eyes, the collar of his officer's jacket whipped around his neck, and he looked as if he were controlling the pitching vessel with his body.

Itzik had already spent so much time on deck that the *Aliyah's* crew had begun to refer to him as *HaGolesh Hametooraf*. The Mad Surfer.

By any maritime standard, the Saar 4.5 was not a large vessel. The shark-gray fast attack craft was merely sixty-two meters from the bow to the stern, where a contingent of naval commandos had lashed their rubber Zodiac and a *Snunit* assault craft. Yet crammed as she was with a complement of forty-five officers and men, plus four Gabriel Mark II surface-to-surface missile launchers, an OTO-Melara 76 mm gun turret, a Vulcan Air Defense System, a Barak surface-to-air missile system, various 20 mm, 0.5 inch, and 7.62 mm guns, and all the accompanying ammunition, stores, fire-control radar, electronic countermeasures, and antisubmarine warfare systems, her four diesels could still drive her light alloy hull at thirty-two knots. She also doubled as one of Israel's only "aircraft carriers," having a landing platform abaft the superstructure to service an Aerospatiale AS-365 Dolphin helicopter, which served a multipurpose role in ASW, target acquisition, and air-sea rescue.

She was a fast and formidable offensive craft, and her crew claimed she had all the sailing properties of an inflated condom powered by a skyrocket.

Itzik watched the bow as it rose lazily into the pale-purple sky, then dove forward into an arching wave, scooping hissing foam onto the deck. While the props struggled for a bite, the ship rolled hard to starboard, then to port, and the whole process began again, with each forward thrust the hull's impact sounding like an oil drum being pummeled by a rubber mallet. There was no rain from the high flat clouds, but the wind clipped off the wavetops, spewing up horizontal precipitation. Itzik almost smiled as he thought of the environmentalists fretting that man would soon destroy the earth. An hour at sea, and you quickly realized that man would destroy only himself and a few unfortunate fellow creatures, while the earth would hardly notice.

The ship proceeded on a northwestern course toward the Aegean, accompanied by two smaller Saar 4's, just dots on the puffy horizon far astern. Although the small patrol's destination was a point just off Cap Ras-Tarf, Morocco, it would follow a nauseating zigzag for the purposes of deception and arrive on station just an hour before the appointed rendezvous.

Over the next forty-eight hours, the *Aliyah* would steam due west past Crete, northwest toward Sicily, and west again between that island and Malta. Then they would turn northwest toward Sardinia, continue west for the Balearic Islands, and finally make a midnight run for the rendezvous point, code-named Gold Ring, just 1.5 kilometers off a deserted strip of Moroccan beach.

Unless the offer to exchange Dan Sarel for Sheik Sa'id was an Iranian idea of a geopolitical practical joke, a small "Liberian" trawler would be anchored there, and the deal would be consummated.

Itzik welcomed the cold, salty gusts that slapped his face and tried to take his hat. Unlike many landborne officers who were occasionally called upon to join special operations at sea, he was not on deck because he was ill. He needed to be alone, to ponder the operational pitfalls, and the crowded working quarters of the *Aliyah* offered no solitude. So he exposed himself to the elements, for he also suspected that he had lost some of his good sense and might benefit from a beating by Mother Nature.

Moonlight was galloping on toward the point of no return, with Itzik as its mad jockey. This was not some midnight rendezvous with a *shtinker* across the border, but a mission whose outcome would have international repercussions. With his final notification to the cabinet of a green light, events had begun to snowball. The navy's best crews had been assigned to the boats, the naval commandos had been ordered to supply security. The air force had laid on a squadron of F-16s to fly high cover above Gold Ring after a midair refueling, and finally, Itzik's own boss, the commander of AMAN, would be joining the chief of staff himself aboard a Boeing 707 monitoring station circling the site.

The churning in his guts was not the result of a volcanic sea. It was the idea that once again, his success, his career, his *life*, depended on the wherewithal of Baum and Eckstein, who had gotten him into this quicksand in the first place.

If only he had been able to act as he should, to think purely as a soldier, then the predicament of Baum's daughter could have been ignored, dismissed as a sacrificial casualty for "the good of the country." However, if Captain Dan Sarel was saved, while Ruth's life was lost, the newspapers would surely castrate Itzik for his pragmatic cruelty, even if the censors forbade mentioning him by name.

And yet—he was free to confess here before the thundering sea—it was much simpler than all that. Itzik knew the girl, she was a child too much like his own daughter, a fact that drew his heart toward the emotional dilemma he wished he could shun. He often despised Baum for his insubordinate brilliance and purity of motivation. But he simply could not imagine facing Ruth's grave, with her father's eyes upon him, if he did not give Baum and Eckstein every chance.

The worst of it was that all of this—Martina Klump, the wayward Minnow, Ruth's capture, Baum's desperate efforts—constituted secrets he had kept from his superiors. He stood there on the deck, and as it rolled to starboard he saw a ribbon for valor, and as it rolled to port the tribunal of a court-martial shimmered in the black swells.

"*Atah mishtazef, Itzik?* Getting a suntan, Itzik?"

Ben-Zion turned to see Ami Machnai approaching from the boat's Combat Information Center—*Merkaz Yidiaht Krav*—the MYK. Ami was the colonel in command of the *Aliyah*, a rank equivalent to captain in Western navies. It was common for missile boats to be piloted by former naval commando officers, and he fit the stereotypical bill with his full red hair, burned freckles, and clear green eyes of a kibbutznik from the seaside settlement of Sdot Yam. He was not as tall as Ben-Zion, but much wider, and Itzik wondered where the *Shayettet* had ever found a wet suit to fit his trapezoidal physique. True to his impervious commando blood, Ami was wearing light officers' trousers, canvas Palladium boots, and a sweatshirt cut off at the biceps. A baseball cap stenciled with the ship's name was pulled backward over his ginger curls.

"I came out for a smoke." Itzik had to shout above the roar of the sea, even though Ami stood at his shoulder.

"You should switch to a pipe," the boat commander suggested. "More naval." He was not holding on to anything, and he grinned as a sheet of spray whipped his face. "The men already think you're a closet squid."

Itzik shrugged. Guests aboard a Saar were usually regarded with disdain, but his apparent comfort caused the crewmen to treat him with unusual deference. "I can think out here."

Ami laughed. "What's the matter? You can't think where it stinks?"

Itzik smiled as well. He had spent the early hours inside the MYK as Ami and his deputies plotted the course on a map table. Far from the spacious, climate-controlled CICs aboard American vessels, the Israeli version was as cramped and foul as the brig of a Cuban rum boat. It held the captain's plotting table, the ship's navigational radar, three manned fire control stations, a Harpoon operator, a Vulcan operator, two *Lamed Alephs* (electronic warfare specialists), and a complement of standing officers. Watches in the MYK were long, demanding unflagging concentration, and the atmosphere during a sortie never cleared of stale sweat and the dense cigarette smoke of clashing brands. The deck was often strewn with candy wrappers, and the gas masks in their pouches swung and bumped against the bulkheads like the trophies of a maritime cannibal tribe. Although the crew wore headsets, the officers preferred to shout their orders, further thickening the cloud of tension.

The crewmen of the missile boats bitterly accepted their station in life. You did not volunteer for naval duty; you wound up there failing acceptance as a pilot, a paratrooper, or even a *tankist*. They were the orphans of the IDF, the Lost Boys, bent on proving it with their unfettered cursing, belching, and farting in the MYK. They sat at their stations in office-type chairs with unchocked casters, and often during rough weather they would roll over the toes of an officer and receive a painful head blow from the victim's hand microphone.

Itzik had visited just about every combat station in the IDF order of battle, but even he was put off by the Roman-galley atmosphere of the MYK.

"I don't know how you can work in there, Ami," he shouted as the bow split another high swell.

"Not too glamorous, is it."

"Far from."

"All naval vessels are like that."

"You mean *our* vessels."

"Tell me, Itzik." The boat commander suddenly gripped Ben-Zion's arm to steady himself, then released it. "Did you see the sentry in port?"

Ben-Zion thought back to the predawn boarding in Haifa. "So?"

"How was he armed?"

"An M-16."

"And an air rifle. Know why he has an air rifle, Itzik?"

"Tell me."

"For the rats." Ami smirked and shook his head. "What can you say about a service that inducts *rats?*"

"Time to transfer."

"Hey." Ami shrugged. "You get too old to dive with the teenagers." He meant his past glorious days in the *Shayettet.* "You have to do *something.*"

"I suppose."

"And I don't know about you up there in Jerusalem." The ship captain poked a finger into the general's wet shoulder. "But out here, we still see some action."

"Bull's-eye," Ben-Zion acknowledged, for while Itzik fought a silent war of nerves, Ami's battles were against oceans that gave no quarter and the constant attempts by seaborne terrorists to invade the Israeli coastline and slaughter civilians. Navy tradition held that if an FAC crew destroyed a terrorist craft, the men received a *chupar,* a gift, usually of the electronic-entertainment sort. The crews' quarters of the *Aliyah* had a brand-new color television and VCR, to match the ones already in the officers' quarters. They also shared a portable CD player.

Itzik heard a high-pitched oscillation from the stern, and he leaned back against the rail to see the rotor of the Dolphin spinning above the landing deck. Four air force crewmen in bright-orange helmets crouched below the chopper's fuselage, and as they quickly freed the tie-down straps, the vessel seemed to fling the Dolphin into the air. The red-and-white hornet turned, barely missing the main tower array, then scuttled forward past the bow. Itzik wondered how the pilots could hope to land it again in such conditions.

"What the hell is this?" he shouted.

"Vulcan test," Ami replied.

Itzik looked at the forward turret and its multibarreled 20 mm Vulcan gun. "In this weather?" He watched the Dolphin climb away in the distance.

"We don't choose the weather," said Ami. "We leave that to *Allah.*" He gave an Arabic twist to the consonants.

"Speaking of which," said Itzik, "how is our guest?"

Sheik Sa'id, the Hizbollah mullah who constituted the Israeli chip of the exchange bargain, was residing in the officers' quarters belowdecks. He had insisted on recostuming himself in the clothes he was wearing on the night of his capture in southern Lebanon. And so, despite the winter weather, he was now garbed in the gray cotton nightshirt and leather sandals he had hastily donned when the Sayeret Matkal commandos leapt over his balcony.

The man rarely spoke, except for his murmured prayers, and no one was sure if he considered the upcoming exchange a joyful day of liberation or a shameful surrender to which a chance at spontaneous suicide might be preferable. He was not allowed to wander free, for there were many small arms aboard, but the hatchway to the cabin was propped open as a sign of respect. Two recon captains from Sayeret HaDruzim, a battalion populated by Arabic-speaking sect members, were posted in the passageway. The men were not Moslems, but they could comfortably escort a Moslem cleric and feign appropriate deference to his position.

If Sheik Sa'id was pleased with his impending fate, he was not demonstrative. He lay on one of the thin bunk mattresses, holding a spar to avoid rolling onto the deck, while he stared up at the ceiling and stroked his black beard with his free hand.

"If the sea bothers him," said Ami, "he's swallowing his bile."

"He's been doing that for three years," said Itzik.

A loudspeaker on the flying bridge suddenly barked a warning.

"Stand by for a weapons test!"

The two men were very close to the forward turret. Ami turned to Itzik.

"Want to go in?" The cannon fire from the spinning barrels would be painfully percussive.

Itzik dismissed the offer with a heavy-browed look. Ami shrugged, hooked the toe of one boot around a vertical rail spar, and plugged his fingers into his ears. The general left his own ears unprotected. He had not yet been punished enough.

Up ahead in the bruised sky, the helicopter released the dot of an object, whose descent was instantly slowed by a white parachute as the Dolphin scampered away.

The forward turret came to life, whining on its gimbals while the black barrels of the Vulcan jinked up and down. The gun suddenly buzzed, and even though it was exposed to an infinite canopy of air, the sound was like being locked in the trunk of a car with a chain saw. Itzik flinched as the rounds spewed into the sky, the tracers forming a red beam like a laser at a rock concert, and the target disappeared in a powder of sparks and spinning debris. The gun had fired for only a second, but Itzik's head rang and his ears were deadened as if stuffed with dental cotton.

Four members of the naval commando contingent now appeared on deck, moving toward the stern and their black rubber Zodiac. They wore wet suits and BC vests, but aside from their flippers, masks, and snorkels, they carried no elaborate breathing gear. They would go into the sea if the returning Dolphin suffered a mishap.

Ami produced a Motorola mike from a base unit on his belt. He looked up at the sky as he spoke to the bridge.

"Chopper's coming in. Slow to ten knots."

"Ten knots, affirmative," the walkie-talkie crackled.

The boat slowed, but the swell action kept the flight deck flipping up and down like the tail of a beaver. The chopper appeared off the stern, hovering there as if the pilots were considering desertion to Crete. The air force ground-crew gripped their tie-down straps.

"Hold her straight and steady, Zvi," Ami ordered his driver.

Itzik shook his head. "It's like a hummingbird trying to ass-fuck a shark."

The pilots suddenly committed themselves, charging forward over the apron as they cut the power. The tail skid screeched across steel, the ground-crew men dodged and parried for their lives, and then the deck rose up and slammed the landing gear. The crewmen lunged in and captured the bird.

"*Metoorafim.* Maniacs." Itzik whistled as he touched the bill of his cap.

Ami was smiling and applauding. After a minute, the four naval commandos came walking back from the stern, looking disappointed at having been robbed of their adrenaline rush. . . .

Itzik's thoughts returned to the prisoner exchange. He wished the event were behind him, for the affair had already robbed him of enough sleep.

Sheik Tafilli, the negotiating partner for Hizbollah, had nearly scuttled the agreement just two days earlier. He had grown accustomed to dealing only with Benni Baum. At first the colonel's absence was explained away with a promise by the Israelis that he would reappear to dot the *i*'s and cross the *t*'s. Then Itzik was forced to admit that Baum had been hospitalized with a heart ailment, which was only a partial lie. When Tafilli balked, the general scrambled for a suitable replacement, dredging up a retired German-born former chief of AMAN's European desk. The man did not have Baum's style, yet he managed final closure on Cyprus. Tafilli was not happy, but he also had masters to please.

There should have been nothing more to attend to now than the operational details. But the specter of an unrestrained female terrorist—formerly, God help us, an AMAN asset—showing up at the party with a lethal gift broke a sweat under Itzik's arms.

Ami made a move to head for the galley, when Itzik put out a hand and stopped him.

"Tell me," the general said. "How are we going to work the exchange?"

Ami turned to Ben-Zion and squared his feet on the deck.

"Well, for security, all the commandos will have *Snuniyot* in the water." Each of the three missile boats carried a commando contingent, and their high-speed minicraft were mounted with MAGs and RPGs. "They'll stand off out of range, so we don't spook our cousins." He used the colloquial slang for Arabs. "We'll also have snipers, in case somebody gets careless."

"How the hell can a sniper work on one of these things?" Itzik wondered.

"They came up with some kind of gimbaled mount at Atlit," said Ami, meaning the *Shayettet's* not-so-secret headquarters. "You clamp it to a spar, then set in your M-21. It's kind of like that Steadicam rig they use in the movies."

"What about moving Sarel and Sa'id?"

"Well, you said Hizbollah wanted a flank-to-flank anchorage and a flexible bridge. But unless the water's still as the Dead Sea, that won't fly."

"So what then?"

"We'll use the Zodiac to take Sa'id over, and another to pick up Sarel."

Itzik considered this for a moment. "Let's send over Sarel's taxi first, so both men can board at the same time."

"Good idea," Ami agreed. "That's why you're the general."

Itzik ignored the compliment. "And what if it's like this?" He waved a hand at the wave crests.

"It won't be," said Ami. "*Shayettet* dropped a team in last week to check the depth and wave action at Gold Ring. Most we'll get is a one-meter chop." It was standard procedure to have recon teams precheck the site of any major mission. "But even if it does get rough," he assured, "we can use the chopper and the 996 people."

The Dolphin came equipped with a winch, and a team from the air force's pilot rescue Unit 996 was camped out belowdecks. If need be, Sheik Sa'id could be lowered to the deck of the Hizbollah trawler. Dan Sarel had been trained for extraction by collar.

"I'm not sure Sarel will be able to do it," Itzik said doubtfully. He had seen the condition of repatriated men before.

"Don't worry about Dan," said Ami. Until now, the boat commander had not mentioned the fact that he knew Sarel personally from years together in *Shayettet*, or that he himself had been captaining the vessel from which Sarel departed on the night of his capture. "When he sees my face, he'll probably jump in the water and swim for us."

Itzik did not reply. He doubted if Sarel would even be able to walk.

"Tell me something, Ami." Itzik tried to conceal his next query as a soldier's curiosity. "What kind of damage could a missile do here?" He looked up at the tower array of sonar disks and radar T's.

"A missile?"

"Ship-to-ship, let's say."

"Remember the *Eilat*." Ami recited the warning of vigilance to all overconfident boat drivers. In 1967, the Israeli destroyer *Eilat* had been sunk by a STYX missile fired from an Egyptian Komar FAC anchored in Port Said.

"Well, I wasn't really thinking of *that kind* of firepower."

"What kind of missile did you have in mind?"

"Something like a TOW."

"A TOW?" Ami took off his cap, scratched his head vigorously, and reset the hat again. "Haven't seen one deck-mounted yet, though they hang them from choppers all the time. A waterline hit could sink us."

"Quickly?"

"Quick enough. This fucking hull's like paper." As protective armor, the body of a Saar was worthless. She relied on her speed, maneuverability, and offensive weapons. "And a TOW usually kills everyone at the impact point," Ami added matter-of-factly.

"So if you had that kind of threat," Itzik posed, "what would be the safest station aboard?"

Ami squinted at the AMAN general. It seemed out of character for him to voice concern for his own skin. But then, maybe that was not the object of the question.

"The flying bridge." He jerked a thumb toward the open station above the MYK. "TOW operators usually go for the mass, in our case the hull, or the foot of the superstructure. The people up above would probably survive it, though they might get tossed into the water."

Itzik looked up at the row of plexiglass shields lining the forward bulkhead of the flying bridge. He doubted that he could coax Sheik Sa'id into climbing up the adjoining tower array to an even more secure roost.

"When we're five nautical miles from Gold Ring," Itzik decided, "let's put Sheik Sa'id up there. They'll want to see him anyway."

He looked down, to find Ami staring at him. The boat commander was not about to accept any further evasions.

"You know something," he stated flatly. "Don't you, Itzik."

The general pulled his eyes away, gazing past the pitching bow. At the horizon, the setting sun was filling the clouds with amber, while above, the blue night pushed it to the west.

By now, Mossad teams in Europe would be climbing into tractor trailers registered to cover corporations. On a relayed signal from Itzik to his Mossad counterpart in Tel Aviv, they would deliver the tons of agreed-upon spare parts to anonymous Farsi-speaking drivers. It was the first half of the deal, upon which the primary portion relied, but to Itzik it seemed too simple, too insignificant a demand. It troubled him in instinctive ways, like his occasional produce purchases in Machaneh Yehuda, when he would successfully bargain down a fruit seller, only to discover that the grapes were sour.

Sure, for months now his commander had ordered all AMAN field personnel to focus their intelligence gathering on Moonlight; report all rumors, search for the loopholes, find the catch. Yet there was no hint of an ambush, no smell of deception. The Mossad, with its much wider area of global operations, had likewise refocused many of its efforts, trying to uncover the dangers in what appeared to be a straight deal. Always reluctant to commit themselves fully to a position, the civilians had also given a green light.

And yet the nagging suspicion that the entire intelligence community was being led astray refused to free his mind. Moonlight would be a coup, but he worried that the gala event might be only a sideshow. He had been bred to think this way, for he had matured into the service on the heels of the Yom Kippur War, when a brilliant series of Arab deceptions had nearly resulted in cataclysm.

Martina Klump's role simply did not fit the play, her actions being an anomaly to the proceedings. Vengeance alone was not sufficient motive in which to frame her quest, for if she succeeded, the destruction would impact both enemy *and* ally. Perhaps it could all be attributed to simple synchronicity.

Itzik was not paid to entertain coincidence. And yet . . .

He looked at his watch. In one more hour, he would have to signal a "Go," and the flotilla would cross the point of no return.

He sighed, and as he watched the indigo ghosts scudding across the horizon, he answered the captain's question.

"I am the commander of AMAN's Special Operations, Ami," he said. "I know too much. And I never know enough."

Chapter 20: Skorpion

The impact of Martina Klump's palm against Ruth's cheek cracked like a lion tamer's bullwhip, echoing off the bulkheads of the small bedchamber and followed by a stunning ring in her left ear and a dull explosion in her brain. The power of the blow was further enhanced by its undeflected symmetry, for it had arrived completely unexpected, beginning with a hand resting casually on Martina's hip and ending as her arm suddenly arced through the air like a baseball bat.

In the instant following the slap, Ruth realized that there had been a warning. It was the way Martina opened the door and strode into the compartment, the sheen in her eyes and her labored breath. Her body seemed to contain a great pressure, and as Ruth rose slowly from the bed, Martina appeared to be gazing past her at something that colored her face and lifted her upper lip.

And suddenly Ruth was careening through space, her skull bouncing into the hard corner where the walls intersected. Her hair flew up into a spray of wild tangles, and she slid down onto the pillow, her legs splayed like those of a child playing jacks. Her cheek burned as if scalded by an iron, and she tasted a coppery froth of blood where her flesh had been slammed against her teeth. Yet her tears were not emotional, only smacked from their ducts, and she chose not to wipe them as she raised her trembling hand, cleared the hair from her face, and tucked it behind an ear.

"*Dein verdammter Vater!* Your accursed father!" Martina yelled as she paced at the foot of the narrow bed, pivoting in jerky twists of her body, her hands clutching at the air as if she were choking a ghost. She was wearing a black flight coverall stained with patches of oil and grit, and a pair of leather tanker's boots with ankle straps and cross-buckles clunked on the floor of the camper. The aluminum door to the sleeping compartment had remained open, and Martina must have sensed Youssef's concerned stare from up forward of the kitchenette, for she suddenly spun and kicked it closed. Normally the walls of the recreational vehicle would have reverberated with such a blow, but as it was buried belowground, only a heavy thud resulted, followed by the whisper of trickling sand.

Ruth flinched with this second venting of Martina's rage. Up until this moment, the woman had appeared to be unflappable, her cool demeanor under pressure almost admirable. In their brief encounters, she was civil if unsympathetic, her expression at times approaching a smile—a sign, Ruth assumed, of the woman's superior position in whatever gambit she was playing. The effect of Martina's confidence had been to drain Ruth's hope, dragging her through alternating hours of panic and despair.

But this was different. Something Ruth's father had done or said, or *failed* to do, had opened a fissure in the woman's armor, causing a regressive tantrum. For the first time since her abduction, Ruth felt empowered by Martina's unexpected violence.

She watched carefully as Martina suddenly stopped moving, facing a tall mirror on the door of the camper's closet. She reached up with both hands and briskly rubbed her short blond hair, ruffling it into a spiky plume. Then all at once she was tearing open the closet door, yanking out the black mourning dress of Ruth's recent travels. She looked at it, then flipped the hanger away and tried to tear the dress in half, but the cloth would not give. "*Scheisse!*" she screamed, and then she had a black, short-bladed knife in her hand, and she slashed the fabric into strips. She hurled the ragged heap into a corner, cursing like a sister who had decided that *this* Cinderella would *not be* going to the ball.

Ruth adjusted her position, moving her back against the rear wall of the trailer, setting her bare feet on the rough navy blanket. They had thrown her a pair of gray sweatpants and one of those dark-blue commando sweaters with elbow and shoulder patches, for there was no heat in the RV and the nights were very cold. They had taken her shoes.

She licked at the corner of her mouth, tasting the warm blood, then gently explored the gash inside her cheek with the tip of her tongue. She pressed her hands into the blanket, gathering a fold in her fingers. Martina was still holding the knife. Until this moment, Ruth had not thought herself capable of overpowering the woman. But if that blade came any closer, she would launch herself at Klump, crash her to the floor, and pummel her until they dragged her off the bloody body. The idea of it set her heart pounding at the cotton of her bra, and a cold rivulet of sweat snaked from her right armpit.

Yet Martina seemed to have forgotten that there was another presence in the compartment. She did not look at Ruth, who had become no more to her now than a flower vase smashed in a fit of frustration. She turned her back to the low bed and slowly sat on its corner, gripping the knife and pounding the hilt on her knee. Her back shuddered as she mumbled in German.

"*Mutti*, I am so sorry."

Ruth held her breath as she tried to overhear the whispered demons escaping Martina's mouth, tried to imagine why she should now invoke her mother.

"The devil take him and burn him in *hell* if he harms you." Her voice was like a child's whine, a thin plea choked with liquid. "I will save you, *Mutti*, I swear it. I will save you and still destroy their filthy bargain, and the only thing left for them to trade will be blood and bones."

The left side of Ruth's face throbbed, and a lump was rising under her hair where her head had struck the wall, but she pushed through the pain and tried to focus her concentration. The endless hours inside the cold metal cavern had exhausted her, dulled her, yet she realized that here was an opportunity. A small window had opened through which she might glimpse the truth of her circumstances, and she had to grasp the clues quickly.

What was the "filthy bargain" of which Martina muttered? What kind of "trade" would Martina's enemies hold dear, while she swore to turn the objects of barter into pulverized meat?

For most of Ruth's short imprisonment, she had been allowed to see nothing outside her chamber. Only once had she been taken out into the freezing desert night for an "exercise" walk around the compound, yet passing through Martina's sunken warren was enough to confirm that some sort of major operation was afoot, and her abduction only a side issue.

There were three long trailers buried in the sand, of the type used to pamper film stars on location shoots. As a former army intelligence officer, Ruth had visited hundreds of concealed observation posts, bunkers, and communications facilities, for the Israelis also had a penchant for digging. One such OP on the Egyptian border was so undetectable that she had walked unaware across its roof, while her escort from the engineering corps grinned proudly. The air exchange vents were concealed in tufts of prickly scrub, the head of a periscope inside a fiberglass cactus. It was easy for her to imagine how Martina's lair had been constructed.

A large semicircular trough had been dug into the sand, into which the RVs had been driven onto wooden planks. Duct tape and plastic sheeting had been used to seal the wheel wells, engine compartments, and roof-mounted air conditioners. You could not run the engines with their intakes obstructed, so electrical cables had been laid to the vehicles' external hookups, leading from a gas generator that hummed day and night. The pop-up emergency ceiling exits had been removed and vertical aluminum vent pipes inserted, capped with conical "hats" wrapped in earth-tone burlap. The trailers had been backed in catty corner, so that the open driver's door of each vehicle nearly met the tailgate exit of the next, the connections effected with sections of two-meter-wide flexible PVC water carriers, also sealed with plastic and tape.

When the sand was hoed back over the trailers, their roofs rested two meters below the desert surface.

The entrance ramp that led to the first vehicle was covered with a camouflage net and branches of scrub. This was the "action" trailer. The fold-down dining table just behind the driving station was being used as a plotting surface, but most of the other amenities, including the kitchen appliances, had been removed to make room for communications gear, equipment, and ammunition lockers. The walls were pegged with steel bolts supporting AK-47s, Hungarian AKMs, MP-5 machine pistols, and two RPGs. Martina's men sat on twist-up piano stools, monitoring radio traffic through headphones, cleaning grit from their weapons, or reading *Al Watan Al Arabi*. The cabin lights sometimes flickered as the gas generator choked on a bit of dust, the yellow glow reflecting off the high windshield and side windows, revealing the umber sand packed up against the glass. The pressed earth was lined with black crevasses and small rocks, a pattern suggesting a giant reptile hugging the camper to its belly.

The second vehicle was the living quarters for Martina's men. The ripe smell of chilled bacteria leaked from the humming refrigerator, and the scent of burned *zahtar* rose from the stovetop. The men had minimal access to water, and the dried sweat common to all soldiers' bunkers topped off the aromas. Every available horizontal space was covered with a well-used sleeping bag, including two fold-down ship bunks bolted to the wall where the kitchen table had stood.

The last trailer was clearly Martina's private quarters. She had not warmed the space with personal touches. There were no photographs, printed quilts, or tea cozies. However, the small dining table held a collection of maps, aircraft technical manuals, a copy of the German weapons magazine *Visier*, a pistol-cleaning kit, and a box of Tampax. She had given up her bedroom in the rear for use as Ruth's cell, after first stripping it of every item that might be used innovatively by a prisoner. A heavy dead bolt had been added to the bedroom door.

Nowhere in the complex had an emergency escape tunnel been constructed. Martina expected her men to fight and die with her where they stood.

During Ruth's brief passages through this submerged trailer park, she did not glimpse assault diagrams, catch the men preparing dastardly disguises, or overhear the proper names of Israeli or European cities popping through their Arabic. Rather, it was the atmosphere that convinced her of a countdown, the silences of men anticipating action, settling private accounts. It was the same pre-mission intensity she had witnessed often, always as an observer, guilty in her safety. That emotion was certainly not present now, but she could still smell an operation on the brink of its launching.

Whatever Martina was planning, she clearly thought that holding Ruth would assure noninterference. This in turn meant that somehow Ruth's father, and therefore AMAN, could foil her operation. The conclusion had to be that Martina's target was an Israeli one, perhaps the "trade" of her incoherent mumblings. Yet here Ruth's reasoning ground to a halt. There were not enough pieces. As always, her father's lust for secrecy had left her in the dark.

"Oh, Papa." Martina was whispering now, rocking slightly as if trying to control an abdominal pain. "*Please* forgive me, Papa. I should never have let her leave home. I exposed her, I know it—it was *so* stupid." She called herself *Trottel*, a retarded idiot. She roughly smeared the end of her nose with the back of her fist. "But I *will* get her back, I *swear* to you."

Ruth stayed still as an ice statuette, which was how she had come to feel, given the winter desert days, hardly discernible from the nights. The gloom of her metal cavern did not change with the course of the sun. Her watch had been taken, and her only point of time reference was the top of the air vent. A section of chain-link fence covered the ceiling hatch, but through it she could see the undercap of the conical hat, and as the sun moved, the light inside the tube faded to a shadowless black. She shivered constantly and her nose ran, and now the bruising of her face triggered a further flood. Without warning, she sneezed.

Martina leapt up from the bed as if reacting to a gunshot. She spun on Ruth, regarding her as though the young woman had just crawled in through a window.

"You think he is going to save you, don't you?" she said, her voice still heavy with her moments of remorse. "You think he is going to come in here and whisk you away." She snorted once through her nose. "Or maybe that stupid policeman, yes?"

Ruth just watched her, focusing on her eyes even as the blade flashed with Martina's gesticulations. Early on she had found the opportunity to ask about Michael's fate, when Youssef allowed her to use the small toilet between her chamber and the kitchenette. He refused to respond, and she failed to read the truth in his eyes, yet now Martina's slip revealed the wonderful reality. Michael had survived. He was out there somewhere, maybe together with her father. Forces were gathering on her behalf, oh, *yes*.

"Perhaps he will," Martina speculated, her body easing into a more casual posture as she regained some composure. "Your father is a very resourceful man." She looked up at the ceiling as she tapped the knife blade on a fingernail. "Isn't he?"

It was time for Ruth to answer. She had to speak, or lose the power she had gained by refusing to cry out with Martina's blow. "Yes, he is," she warned.

Martina nodded as she inspected the dirty crevices of the trailer, frowning like an interior decorator in a shelter for the homeless. "Ah, that's nice to hear," she said. "A daughter's pride."

Ruth knew enough about the woman's early loss of her own father to be wary of every step in this emotional minefield. However, she had no idea that once, when Martina was barely out of her teens, she had looked to Benjamin Baum as a substitute for that lost paternal care.

"A father's love is also very powerful," she suggested carefully.

Martina dropped her pale eyes to Ruth's face. "Really?" she asked as if, having lost that gift, she could not imagine it.

"I think parental love is the most powerful of all," Ruth said, realizing with a twinge that she might not live to adore a child of her own.

"And you think your father loves you?"

"Yes." It was a selfish love, but was there really any other kind?

Martina's expression did not change, though she lowered her gaze to Ruth's mouth. The two women were separated only by the length of the bed.

"Your lip is swelling," she said.

Ruth raised her hand to touch the bruise, then stopped halfway and returned her palm to the blanket.

"You could use some ice," Martina suggested.

"That would be good. Thank you."

"We have no ice here," Martina said flatly. She waved a hand through the air. "I do not allow it. The freezers function, but I forbid such luxuries. Men are like children. Give them a treat and they immediately go slack and lazy, expecting toys and presents and affection."

Ruth said nothing. She had a fleeting image of Martina as a mother, a shiver of pity for any child of hers.

"He loves no one," Martina said. She looked down at her hands and, discovering oily grit beneath her fingernails, began to clean them with the point of the blade. "Your father. He is not capable of it."

Ruth stepped blithely into the trap, a scoff of arrogance. "Oh? You know him so well?"

"I know him much better than *you* do, my dear!" Martina yelled without warning as she thrust the blade forward, causing Ruth to bang her head back against the wall. "*Much* better!"

"You must be very perceptive, then," Ruth responded quickly, trying to assuage Klump before she erupted again. Her calf muscles bulged as she prepared to parry a lunge.

"Perceptive?" Martina sneered. "*Perceptive?* You think I am some kind of deluded clairvoyant? I know him from experience, *years* of it. He is not a man. Or yes, he *is*, with everything that implies. A lizard, hiding beneath a rock. A liar, a betrayer, a deceiver by trade!" She stopped yelling and slowly straightened up. Then she shook her head and laughed once as she turned and gently closed the closet door. "You don't know, do you?" she whispered in genuine empathy.

"It is true that my father is some of those things," Ruth offered, although Martina's vehemence confused her, warning of some strange connection that she could not imagine. "He is an intelligence officer. Spies are not princes."

Martina's fingers were set to the glass of the mirror where she had pushed it home. She stood there looking at her own face, and then she began to laugh, throwing her head back and giving full vent to it.

"No!" she exclaimed, as her shoulders shook. "They aren't, are they?" Her mirth subsided, and she touched one eye with a finger, inspecting a wrinkle in the looking glass. "Nor princesses," she said. "I suppose it was better for you to be ignorant. I was that way too as a child." She examined the other eye. "Then I discovered the truth much later, and I tried to make up for it, to compensate for his crimes. You can never do that, you know."

Ruth realized that attempting to defuse Klump's bottled rage only fanned the embers, so she held her silence. Yet more than that, she sensed a desire on the woman's part to regain control, to sway power, if not physically, then with unsettling revelations. But what could this woman know about her father that she herself had not imagined at one time or another? That he had killed? That he had sent others to be lost, or captured, or tortured for their secrets? These were all notions she had suppressed, even while admitting their existence. She watched as Martina opened the zipper of a chest pocket, removed a box of cigarettes, and lit one up with a lighter. She assured herself that there was nothing the woman could really say to surprise her, until Martina blew a ring of smoke into the mirror and stunned her breathless.

"Your *father*," she said. "I was fucking him while you were still in kindergarten."

The words entered Ruth's brain, bursting into a blaze that she immediately tried to extinguish by twisting their meaning. It is a rare child who can accept her parents' sexuality, and even when her own adolescence reveals the nature of desire, somehow mother and father are forbidden carnality. Of course, her father was just a man, but he was not a sexual one aside from *Eema's* bed, and even there she assumed their lovemaking to be clumsy and brief, an occasional renewal of their vows. So Martina had to mean something else, she reasoned, as her body held itself impossibly still. The woman meant that she had been outwitting him, defeating him, eluding him since the beginning of her career.

"Yes." Martina turned from the mirror and nodded to her prisoner. "He was trying to turn me." She looked around for a place to perch, then remembered that she had ordered the stool and every other loose item removed. She backed up to the entrance door and slid down to the floor, draping her wrists across her raised knees, the knife dangling from her right hand, the cigarette from her left. "It was in Paris. I was very young. Younger than you are now." She took a drag and blew a stream of smoke at the ceiling. She was in no hurry. Her audience was not going anywhere. "I was very confused, inexperienced. I did not yet have any convictions. And you know how men are. They sense these things, like sharks when there is blood in the water."

She is making it up, Ruth decided, even as a knot began to twist her stomach. *It's very good, sounds very real, but it is only a cruel game. You're expected to protest, to deny it. Don't jump in.*

"I thought he was a wonderful lover." Martina laughed at her own childish foolishness. "Until later, of course." She smirked. "But it worked for him then, I admit it. That is why old men want the young girls. There is power in it, and of course a child such as I was has little with which to compare." She looked at Ruth, savoring the young woman's mesmerized stillness. "When I had doubts, he fucked them right out of me."

Although Ruth's chest was folding in on itself now, her sternum like an iron bar obstructing her heart, she refused to give Martina the gift of a reaction. With the strength remaining in her pained cheek muscles, she smiled, even as her lips trembled.

Martina waved smoke away from her face. "Oh," she said as she lifted her chin. "You don't believe me?" She shrugged. "Of course not." She raised the knife and looked at the black blade. "Should I describe his cock for you? I still remember it well, and I assume you have seen it." She lowered the weapon. "Or maybe not. Come to think of it, I never saw *my* father's, though of course I was very small when he killed himself." She placed the cigarette in her mouth and raised a finger as if an idea had struck her. "How about other things? Old wounds and such you *would* have seen." She touched the finger to her right breast. "He had a small bullet scar here. I have heard he has another one in the belly, though he is fat now and it is probably difficult to find." She put her hands to the floor and steadied herself, raising her ankles into the air and crossing them as she looked at Ruth through the open diamond of her legs. "I used to put them around his neck when he fucked me. He liked that." She closed her eyes, smiling as she began to thump her head rhythmically against the door. "I can still see that hairy chest pounding at me like a train. Sometimes I thought he was going to *kill* me." She stopped moving and opened her eyes. "He used to sweat so when he fucked."

Ruth's chin quivered and her eyes were squeezed shut, but she would not cover her assaulted ears. She had gathered the blanket in her balled fists, and she summoned images to drown the pain: the purple perfume of bougainvillea in Jerusalem, the pastels of her summer dresses. Her brothers chased a soccer ball through Independence Park, and she kept up with them, even though she fell and scraped her shins, and they were proud of her. She smelled the smoke of a scout campfire mingling with the pines of the Jerusalem Forest, and she and Gabi were alone on a soft blanket, the stars peeking through the branches, and though it was the first time and they were only sixteen, it was not ugly, it was not coarse. It was so sweet, so beautiful, the softness and warmth and the wonderful cry of melding souls.

She heard the awful woman coming to her feet, the heavy boots clunking as she began to pace. And still Ruth fought to keep the images, to fight off the attack as a tai chi master might, absorbing and dissolving it with the better sides of life.

"Of course, the penis has no real power," Martina announced as she ground some form of desert insect with her boot. "It is a retarded thing that answers to the basest stimuli. Don't you agree?"

Ruth heard the gentle hush of the Mediterranean waves in summer, the comforting *pok-pok* of beach paddleballs. She felt the cold of a lemon Popsicle on her lips.

"It is uncontrollable," Martina continued with sarcastic pity. "Anything can send it flying—coarse underwear, a child's body, even the hanging of its own master." She stopped moving and lifted her arms, as if preaching to a congregation of militant feminists. "All of the *true* strength is in that which *grips* the penis, because a vagina is a part of a woman's brain. Men know this, my dear, and they fuck with fear and anger, because they realize that in those moments they are puny servants, clutched by fingers that wield the power of the universe." Her blade and the burning ember of her cigarette nearly touched the ceiling. "They are in creation's cauldron. They are lost."

She remained in this pose for a moment, then placed her hands to her waist. She cocked her head and looked at Ruth, surprised to find her soliloquy unappreciated, the young woman's eyes open and full of fire.

"*Du verdammte Fotze*," Ruth snarled.

Martina took a step backward, opening her mouth in feigned shock. "*Cunt?*" She clucked her tongue in disapproval. "Shame on you. Apparently you missed the point of my sisterly lecture."

"You stupid bitch." Ruth touched her wounded mouth now, as if to show that her only pain was physical. "You expect me to believe that drivel?" So what if her father did have such a scar on his chest? That fact was probably recorded in the dossiers of ten intelligence services.

"Believe what you wish." Martina shrugged.

"Go to hell." Ruth shifted, moving her back to the side wall and turning her face away. "You know nothing. Ten minutes of research, and I could make up a fantasy about *your* father."

Martina sighed. "I suppose." She flipped the knife in the air and caught it by the handle. "Yes, of course. You are correct." The blade spun again. "Research." Now she tried for two spins. "*Research* told me about that dog you had when you were little. A dachshund, I think. *Schatzi* was his name? He was killed by a milk wagon." She looked for a new trick, trying to balance the blade on the tip of her index finger. "And research told me about your mother, Maya, and about Yosh and Amos. I also found out quite a bit about your house in Abu Tor—in the *files*, of course. Two floors, very Turkish and medieval. It once belonged to a pasha, I remember. Very pretty." She caught the toppling knife and suddenly smacked her forehead with the other hand. "Oh, no," she exclaimed. "That was not in the files! Your father drove me by it. *Twice.* Very unprofessional of him, a terrible breach of security. But then, he was still in the recruitment phase with me. Flowers and fucking and trust-building and all that. *You* know."

"I'll kill you!" Ruth screamed as she leapt to her feet on the bed, her fists clenching and her eyes wild.

In one quick stride Martina had her right boot on the mattress and the knife point pressing into Ruth's chest, just a millimeter short of breaking skin and piercing flesh.

"Sit down," she ordered. Yet Ruth's grief and rage kept her frozen at the point, unsure if she wanted to break Martina's wrist or pull the weapon into her already wounded heart.

"Sit!" Martina yelled, and the force of her voice trembled the light fixture. A frantic pounding at the door added to the din, as Youssef had become alarmed for his mistress. "*Hör auf!*" she yelled, and the knocking stopped. She looked up into Ruth's eyes. "Unfortunately, I have to keep you alive for now. But there is nothing in the rules about carving my name on that pretty face." She angled the blade, pressing forward and down until Ruth was forced to lower herself or bleed. Ruth's bottom met the bed, and their heads returned to more proper positions of warden and charge.

"Take off your pants," Martina commanded.

Ruth could not meet the woman's eyes. She stared at the midriff of her flight suit, slowly shaking her head. Her tears overflowed and rolled off her cheeks.

"No," she whispered. "No."

"Take them off."

"*No.*"

"I am not going to rape you, you silly shit!" Martina shouted. "You are simply far too arrogant for me. Now take them *off.*"

Ruth's fingers trembled as she untied the drawstring of the sweatpants, then slipped them down to her knees. Martina dragged them over her feet, tossing the bundle onto the tattered dress in the corner, as Ruth covered her face with her hands.

Martina straightened up, keeping the blade extended in warning.

"Now, tell me which of us is the stupid bitch," she said quietly. "Me, a simple woman who did not even finish her schooling. You, the great student of psychology. And still, a plain fact of nature turns you into an unthinking, quivering worm."

Ruth dropped her hands and placed them on the bed. But the tears still dripped off the end of her nose, and her chest shuddered.

"Those are the simple facts, my dear." Something like pity colored Martina's voice. "*That* is the truth of your father's legacy. I should have learned it long ago, but I trusted him, allowed him to betray me, to send me into a den of thieves and murderers, to live like them, to *become* one of them." She shook her head. "And then I trusted him *again*, just once more, and he proved his character and tried to finish me."

Ruth sobbed once. She turned her hands upward, her fingers contracting in small twitches.

"You should have learned it too, my dear." Martina sighed. "A girl like you, raised in a society like yours. They bring you up to be so strong, so independent, while blinding and paralyzing you with foolish, idealistic poetry."

Martina held the knife in position, while she looked around to find her cigarette. It was burning on the floor, and she crushed it with her boot. Then, with her free hand, she took the box from her pocket, extracted a fresh cigarette with her lips, and lit it. She plucked it from her mouth and held it out.

"Go ahead," she offered. "You smoke. I saw you in the restaurant, with your detective."

After a moment, Ruth accepted the smoke with fluttering fingers. She inhaled and coughed.

"He is not for you," Martina said. "Handsome, yes. Perhaps gallant. Maybe you would even have married such a man, but it would not have worked. That kind of passion is fleeting, my dear. Believe me, I know. We should stick to our own kind."

Ruth's breathing had slowed to a shallow rhythm. She no longer sensed the physical pain in her face, for the injuries of her mental violation were far more serious. The woman's words ran through her now like a slowly drawn coping saw. She took the cigarette from her mouth and tried to focus on the ember.

"And please don't try anything with that," Martina warned. "I've been burned before." Even so, she backed up a step, for her tactical instincts were always tuned. After all, she was a smart Catholic girl trained by Jewish warriors. She placed her left hand on her hip.

"So," she said. "You are enlightened now. But you must still be wondering what this is all about."

Ruth's head was so heavy, as if it had been pumped full of liquid mercury. She looked down at her bare legs. The sweater was not long enough to cover her, and she saw the white triangle of her underwear and pressed her forearms over it, holding one hand steady with the other as the smoke from the cigarette rose into her face.

Yes, she had been wondering, through every sleepless minute since being tossed in here like a rabid pet. What else was she to do? They offered her nothing to pass the time. No radio, for a local broadcast would tell her where she was. Lebanon? Syria? Libya? And nothing to read, for perhaps they thought her resourceful enough to effect a lethal paper cut. Like most fresh prisoners, she had spent the first few hours pacing, resisting, trying to reason it out. And then the temperature had forced her into bed, although sleep was not even a remote hope. Without a clue to the woman's plans, there was no way to guess how long she would be here. A week? A year? Five? Her fear of execution had settled into a bearable ache, for she knew the histories of many war prisoners and hostages. If you were kept alive for a day, then the chances were good that you would be spared, used as leverage. *I'm young*, she told herself. *I can survive this. I will recover when I am free again. They won't give up until they find me.*

In the emotional agony of the last few minutes, she had nearly crossed the breaking point, wanted to die. But that was gone now. She wanted to live to smell the flowers of home, feel the sun on her cheeks, be touched by a cherished kiss. If for no other reason, she had to survive and discover the truth.

"Yes," she whispered. "I was wondering."

"Well," said Martina, pleased to have a receptive audience again. "It is not very complicated, and there really is no reason why you should not know."

Ruth was not heartened by Martina's willingness to confide. When terrorists took off their masks, it did not bode well for their hostages.

"Your people are very anxious to conclude a prisoner exchange with Hizbollah." Martina had taken to flipping the knife again. "I, of course, do not work for either side. I am my own woman." She failed to mention a third party, for her own inability to identify her employer weighed heavily on her today. "My mission is to destroy that exchange. Which I will do, believe me."

Ruth nodded as she kept her focus on her cigarette. A prisoner exchange. She struck the curiosity from her mind. She needed to be responsible only for her own life now.

"I took you merely as an insurance policy," said Martina.

Something drove Ruth to speak now. Maybe it was her army training, the tradition of challenging the status quo, the Israeli habit of questioning all statements that failed to satisfy. When terrorists took a hostage, the prisoner's compatriots were temporarily immobilized. You could secretly kill a hostage and still buy yourself weeks of time.

"Why am I alive?" she asked.

Martina stopped toying with the knife. "I told you," she said, as her eyes darkened. "A bargaining chip." Yet she also realized the balances and rhythms of these kinds of gambits. Her timetable was very short, the final action nearly in play. She could have killed the girl upon arrival at Skorpion, while her unknown status still maintained its effect. Yet she had spared her, and did not know why. The girl sensed the weakness, and that brought the bile into Martina's throat. Now the relayed message from Fouad had paralyzed her ability to act. She began to pace again, barely taking a full step to the right before she turned to the left.

"I would have let you go," she snarled. "But your fucking father thinks he is so smart! The bastard has no respect. He will stop at nothing. My mother is an old woman. She is frail. She is ill. She knows *nothing*."

Ruth slowly raised her head. Now she understood. Now the pieces dropped quickly into place as her hope began to simmer. *Your mother's life for mine!* she wanted to scream, even as she held her peace. *Oh, Abba. You will stop at nothing for me!* She watched the woman losing control again and carefully turned up the fire.

"As I said," Ruth whispered. "A father's love . . ."

"Don't flatter yourself!" Martina shouted as she spun on her, the blade leaping out close to her nose. "With him it is merely a tactic!"

This time Ruth did not flinch. The fear jackhammered in her heart, but she knew that for every scratch inflicted on her face, her father would find this woman and rend a triple vengeance upon her. *He loved you?* she challenged silently. *Used you, yes, and threw you away when you proved to be the trash that you are.* She was unarmed, half naked, yet all the arrows were in her quiver.

"If you harm me," she warned, "he will kill her."

Martina screamed, cocking her left hand back. Yet Ruth did not duck, only closed her eyes to take the blow. They were forced open when, instead, the woman's fingers gripped her jaw, crushing her cheeks against her teeth. The still-fresh wound shot lightning into her skull as Klump's face came in very close.

"I shall deal with him," she promised, in a hiss like a steam valve. "But don't expect to get out of it alive."

She held Ruth for a long moment, then slowly drew her hand away. She barely made a sound as she turned, picked up the dress and the sweats, stepped quickly through the door, then slammed it so hard that the mirrored closet bucked open, swinging on its hinges.

Ruth lifted her hands and looked at them. They were quivering like autumn leaves in a swift wind. She took a last puff from the cigarette, then ground it into the wall.

Her eyes slowly scanned her cell, just once more. She would start at one corner and pull and scrape at every scrap of steel molding, any part that might give, snap, open a hole, offer a weapon, something to dig with, or to kill with.

She finally knew one thing for certain. She had a stay of execution. She had to search in earnest now for a breach, a weakness in her prison, a means of escape. A way out.

Freedom, onto a continent she could not even identify.

Chapter 21: Marrakesh

Benni Baum's fingers were wrapped around the throat of an oily green cobra, the lipless jaw nearly touching his mouth, the flat nose hissing electrically close to his ear. He stared at the head, wishing he had the power to crush the stubborn vertebrae, seeing how the horrible tail coiled around his forearm and shivered in concert with his own tremble. Of course, he was fully aware that the object of his loathing was only a telephone, yet he saw in it that same devil's serpent he had held so many times before, whispering lies into its willing mouth.

A telephone had so often served as a conduit for his inventions that counting the sins would be hopeless, but *this* one had certainly been the worst of all. A cozy chat with his wife, relayed through Avraham's office in Washington—for that was the method from "friendly" Arab states. His unsuspecting Maya, off to a picnic with their boys, home on leave, had hardly sighed at the news that her husband would be delayed in the States, so pleased that at least he and Ruth had managed a reconciliation. And how *is* our wayward New York scholar? Oh, she's fine. He had smiled into the phone while his mind screamed: Our *baby* may be dead already, most certainly *will* be if I don't *do* something, and heaven forgive me, it is all my fault.

Oh, she's fine. . . .

He suddenly rose from the bed and hurled the instrument across the room. But its plastic tail was resilient, uncoiling and then snapping back, so that the satanic head flopped on the brown coverlet and lay still, hissing satellite static.

Benni stood there breathing heavily as the muted chatter in the room fell to stone silence. He swore to God that if the Holy One would get him out of this, just this once, he would never, ever lie to Maya again.

Then he realized that he was lying to God.

Eytan walked to his partner and touched him on the shoulder, the kind of exploratory contact you use with a wounded animal. Benni did not turn. He stood there looking down at the bed, where his girth had pulled the coverlet into a delta of wrinkles. He looked at his hands, his watch, the seconds ticking onward, the minutes flipping over.

Close by, Sadeen, Rick Nabbe, and Ari Schneller sat on the hotel room carpet, around a low glass coffee table. The CIA map covered the tabletop. The men held felt pens, but they did not mark the map itself, which would have been a breach of operational security. Instead, they had taped thick plastic wrap over the detail, on which they drew their arrows and circles and X's, which was also how they would trace their individual assault and escape maps. You could hold such a device up to the moon and read it quite clearly, or destroy it quickly in one long pull.

A wastebasket overflowed with wads of plastic wrap, for the men had been plotting and discarding vehicle approaches to Klump's camp from the north. Now, in the wake of Baum's sudden violence, they sat in silence, fiddling with their pens, like children who have witnessed a parent's weeping.

Eytan's fingers finally penetrated, and Benni straightened up. This would not do, not at all. He had to reject the sympathy, throw off guilt, cover his despair and panic, for they would poison his men. He had to command, not collapse. He turned, brushed past Eckstein, and strode to the table, looking down at the work as he pulled a pack of Rothmans from his pocket. He lit up. These you could smoke without coughing to death, at least not immediately. He put his knuckles to his hips, and when Sadeen began to speak, he said, "Shhh." The commander was working.

Before forcing his recalcitrant hands to contact Maya, he had taken the long-awaited call from Art Roselli. It should have bolstered his hope, which had taken a beating during the early-morning ride aboard the Marrakesh express from Casablanca.

"The fruit is on ice," Arthur had said modestly. "But it will not keep for long."

So Roselli had actually managed to take Klump's mother, a terrible risk for the American, the mark of a true friend. Yet he could go no further than that. At any rate, Benni had never intended to take possession of the old woman in turn. But now the bluff had to be played out. Martina had "purchased" the product, and if it did not appear to be deliverable, her rage would have no bounds.

"Your friend agrees to the nuptials," Arthur had said. "At 0100 hours her time zone, her place. That's thirty-six hours from now."

Roselli's Bethesda ploy had also worked, although exactly how Martina's HOGs in America then contacted her, were recontacted, and in turn advised Arthur was of no real interest to Benni. But he admired the CIA officer's professionalism, had a flash fantasy of the two of them going into the private sector together. Perhaps Miami. That would be a nice, balmy, neutral place to work, though if you lost your daughter, no sun could warm you anywhere on earth.

In agreeing to the swap, Martina had also relayed her coordinates. The information was superfluous given Langley's overflights, but it was comforting as confirmation. Still, her choice of a time for the exchange of loved ones, just five hours before Moonlight, signaled that she would not allow this glitch to sway her purpose. Arthur had strongly suggested that she turn over the Minnow along with Ruth. Martina's final relay had been the clipped advice that he perform an impossible act of self-fornication.

For an hour the men in the room had batted about the options, finally deciding that a vehicle would have to be driven south along the Ben Zireg-Taghit road, arriving after the bulk of the team was already in position at the target. Yet this task would require a minimum of two men—one to drive and one costumed as an old woman, a ploy that had to serve until the range was very close. It was not a terribly original tactic, having been used at Entebbe with a repainted Mercedes and an Israeli double for Idi Amin. And like most brainstorms, it seemed flashy and brilliant at first, until a careful review revealed its foibles.

Benni looked over at O'Donovan, who was leaning against a low bureau, arms folded, rubbing his unshaven jaw. The bandage was gone and makeup covered his bruises, but there was still a lump at the bridge of his nose that made him look like a Dublin Jew. O'Donovan's silences told Benni that the man did not trust himself to contribute objectively. His feelings for Ruth were much more than a crush.

Benni squinted at the high glass doors that formed the far wall of the room. The ground floor of the Hotel N'Fis opened onto flowered walkways. Beyond them, an expansive swimming pool failed to seduce most winter bathers, yet a slim Frenchwoman in a black bikini rose from her chaise longue and gracefully arced into the emerald water. Horse stood before the sliding doors, his rounded posture tensing as he watched her, as if he were participating in a funeral while a ballerina pirouetted among the gravestones.

"Horse!" Benni suddenly shouted, as he clapped his hands together. "Why the hell don't you say it?"

The little man did not move. He sighed. "You know what I am going to say, Benni."

In fact, everyone else had already reached Horse's conclusions, but all were delaying the self-disappointment.

"So why are you letting us concoct this foolishness?" Benni challenged his analyst. "What do I pay you for?"

Horse slowly turned from the window, but before he could speak, Nabbe tried to lighten the blow.

"I have an idea," the Belgian offered. "Why don't we just shoot Horse and get on with it?"

No one laughed. Horse shrugged, accepting his life's sad lot. "Okay," he said. "It stinks."

"Of course it stinks!" Benni boomed, as if he had known it all along. "It cannot work. We would have to get a truck across at Figuig, and given the range, it would have to leave here *now*."

"Correct," said Horse.

"So why don't we go in, split up, and hijack one on the ground?" Schneller suggested.

Nabbe hummed as he considered this.

"And if there is no vehicle traffic at that hour?" Horse posed. "If the Algerians are all snuggled around their televisions for a soccer match?"

"He's right," said Eytan, who had taken Benni's place on the flank of the bed, leaning over his knees and pulling at the end of his short ponytail. "Klump has to *think* we are making the delivery, *without* our actually air-dropping a Land-Rover."

"Yes," said Benni. He placed his hands behind his back and walked to the glass doors, gazing out at the pool and the gardens. There were still so many preparations to be made, but this was the crux of the matter. Martina might not bring Ruth up until she actually saw the approaching vehicle. "Let's scrap it and start again."

Sadeen raised his head from the map. "Did someone say *scrap*?"

"*Oo-ah*," Nabbe warned. "The engineer is thinking."

Sadeen got up quickly from the floor. "Is there an ironworks in the Casbah?"

Eckstein raised his head. "It's north of the Djemaa el Fna. Why?"

"Never you mind." The sapper shouldered his small green ruck. "I think I've got it."

"You'll get lost," Eckstein warned. "Pick up Mustaffa at the café." Inside the walls of Marrakesh's old city, a foreigner could not move without being assaulted by "guides." You had to hire one or be badgered into immobility. "But tell us what's up first."

"Yes." Benni turned hopefully from the window. "What do you have in mind?"

"You can forget this part." Sadeen smiled as he made for the door. "I have solved it. Leave it to me and go on."

Before anyone could question him further, he had trotted out of the room.

"Leebit do me angoahn." Nabbe mimicked Sadeen's Spanish slur.

"Hey," Schneller growled. "Let him be. I've never heard him promise anything and not deliver."

"Mr. Hearthstone?" Benni begged his partner's opinion. There was still time to stop Sadeen.

Eckstein lifted his hands. "We're all living in a bloody fool's paradise." His speech was still colored with the Briticisms of his Ethiopian cover. "Let the joker tinker."

"All right," said Benni, relieved to be unburdened of at least one problem. He turned to Nabbe, Schneller, and O'Donovan. "You three should get moving. Find your partners and work quickly. We meet at 1800 for review." He looked the three men over. They had shed their mountain parkas, for the sun was strong in this desert oasis, but even in their colorful T-shirts, denims, and sneakers, they still looked to him like commandos on holiday. "I wish we had some women," he muttered.

"Benni!" Schneller bucked his head back. "*Du altes Schwein.*"

"For *cover*, you idiot," said Eytan.

"Well, perhaps we can pick up some Swedish blondes," Nabbe offered enthusiastically.

"Don't try it." Benni wagged a finger. "You will think you are picking *them*, but they might be baiting *you*." The Moroccan Sûreté was skilled in honey-trapping Westerners.

"*Oui, mon colonel.*" Nabbe saluted, then switched to Clouseau as he beckoned Schneller. "Follow me, Kato."

Benni stopped them.

"Schneller, let Michael go first. You and Nabbe clear him for tails." They tried to leave again. "And Michael," Benni called, as O'Donovan stopped halfway out the door. "Only bottled water for you. And no fruit. Your stomach may not tolerate the microbes here."

O'Donovan almost smiled. "Yes, *Abba*," he said. His eyes and Benni's met, their thoughts converging on the last time they had both heard Ruth utter that endearment. Baum broke the spell, waving the three men out with both hands.

Eckstein looked at his black Breitling and snapped up from the bed. "So where the hell is Didi?" he muttered. It was warm enough in Marrakesh that he had shed his leather flight jacket, and now he wore only his sleeveless NYU sweatshirt, black jeans, and the canvas boots. He walked over to a corner writing table and picked up Horse's pad, reviewing the equipment list for the tenth time.

"Do not worry," said Horse. "It is probably just traffic." He welcomed the opportunity to buck someone up rather than shatter illusions.

"Are you sure he was able to close the deal?" Benni asked Eckstein. He poured himself his fourth cup of coffee from a room-service tray.

"Of course," said Eytan. "Even if they decided to haggle, he would have just kept peeling off bills."

Between Itzik Ben-Zion's departure from Casablanca and the midnight rendezvous at the Café de France, Eckstein had not been idle. He had already recruited a proper team, but they could not be dropped onto the target with bedsheets and kite string. He could have had Lerner and Lapkin bring in the gear, but the risk of confiscation at the airport was too great. He had to acquire it on the ground.

Every country that has a military airborne unit finds itself hosting at least one civilian parachute club, for some veterans cannot kick the habit. At the Syndicat d'Initiative on Boulevard Mohammed V, a kindly woman informed the "Englishman" that such a club existed at the civilian strip at Tit Melil, though she had no idea if they were still active. Tit Melil was only ten kilometers southeast of Casablanca.

He did not bother to rent a car, because with time so short, he might have to ask directions en route, leaving a calling card each time he opened his mouth. So he hired one witness only, the Grand Taxi driver Abderrahim.

Abder was a fountain of information on many subjects, suggesting all sorts of alternatives should "Anthony" fail in his quest at Tit Melil. Although Eckstein was a detached and quiet man, one of his assets as an intelligence officer was the ability to metamorphose his somber appearance. He could mobilize a disarming smile and carefree tone, and by the time Abder had urged his coughing green Mercedes onto the palm-lined thoroughfare of Moulay Ismael, Eckstein had already been invited to his sister's wedding.

They joked about women in French, while Abder pounded on the strip of Persian carpet that covered his dashboard and honked at sputtering mopeds and horse-drawn carts. They soon turned off onto a long private road and parked before a two-story white stucco building. Abder got out of the car, reached back in for a red pillow, and went to take a nap under the trees.

Eytan trotted up the concrete steps to the second floor, passing beneath a black propeller mounted over a doorway. Inside the Aeroclub, there was a bar immediately to the left, and his hopes rose when he saw a framed poster of a military parachutist.

"*Bonjour, mon ami.*" He greeted the barman, who was wiping a coffee glass.

"*Bonjour.*"

"*Où est le club des parachutistes?*"

The barman smiled, but it was more an expression of pity. "*Là-bas.*" He pointed.

Eytan strode along a catwalk outside the building, past a modest control tower atop silver girders. The tarmac strip, about a thousand meters long, rested between flat plains of farm furrows. You could bring in a C-47 here, but there were only two Cessna 150s parked on the apron. The orange wind sock stood stiff and horizontal. He walked down a flight of stairs to a large open hangar with a beautifully painted sign that bore a winged crest and the words *Aero-Club Royal De Casa Blanca*.

Three men sat playing cards just inside the hangar.

"Hello, mates." Eytan flashed his smile as he decided on English. People generally assume that if you are linguistically limited, you are also probably harmless.

"*Allo*," replied the youngest of the three. Like most Moroccan men, he sported a slim black mustache. He was wearing a shiny olive flight jacket.

"Could you tell me where the parachute club is?"

The young man rose from his chair, and Eytan followed him back out into the sunlight.

"It is there." The man pointed to a shuttered hangar next door with a small black plaque mounted beside the closure. Eytan squinted. The parachute club was "Royal" as well. "But we are closed."

That bit of news was a blow, but the use of the pronoun was a plus.

"Oh?" said Eytan. "Too windy?"

"*Non, mon ami*." The man laughed. "Too poor. Our aeroplane is broken."

"Bloody pity," Eytan commiserated, although he did not need a plane. That would be Nimrodi's problem.

"Are you a *parachutiste?*" the man asked, as he donned a pair of Ray•Bans.

"Sometimes." Eytan stuck out a hand. "Anthony Hearthstone."

"Hakim Azziz." He had a strong, cool grip.

Eytan opened one pocket of his flight jacket and handed Hakim a business card. It was printed with generic gold parachute wings, the words *Airborne Operations Group*, and a London address and telephone. The phone was physically located in an import-export office in the West End, but it automatically forwarded calls to an answering machine and fax in Jerusalem.

"My mates are having a meet down in Beni Mellal next week," Eytan said. "We were hoping to rent some gear. Some of us are coming a long way."

"Rent?" Hakim's eyebrows lifted above his sunglasses. He understood the word, but the concept was an anomaly to skydivers.

"Well, you know." Eytan shrugged, somewhat embarrassed. "The boys are getting a bit old and lazy."

Hakim laughed. He began to walk toward the hangar, fishing in his trouser pocket for keys. "We do have some parachutes," he said as Eytan eagerly followed along. "But no plane, so no *parachutism*. I could not lend the equipment. The members are not here."

"Well, we would pay them, of course," said Eytan as Hakim opened a large padlock. He leapt up to a steel chain and raised the corrugated door.

The hangar was dark. The smell of cold oil and cylinder solvent hung in the still air. A white Norman Islander jump plane occupied most of the space, but its cowling was off and its engine sat on the stained cement floor like a defective artificial heart.

Hakim led Eytan around the wingtip to a pile of dark bundles lying on a wooden pallet. He kicked one of the zippered kit bags, as Eytan winced.

"You see?" said the Moroccan. "We have maybe twelve here. Some student Telesis, some PD Sabres, a Glide Path Nova. But I believe it is not legal to rent them."

"I think we could pay five hundred per rig for the week." Eytan wondered how long the chutes had been huddled like that in the dank space. But then, what was a little canopy rot between friends? "We'll need ten." That would give Didi Lerner at least one extra to cannibalize.

"Five hundred?" Hakim turned to his newfound, wealthy friend.

"American dollars," said Eytan. "Five thousand altogether."

Hakim stroked his mustache. "I would have to ask the members."

"And of course I would leave you with a deposit," Eytan pressed. "Full replacement price, in case they are damaged."

"Or stolen?"

"You never know." Eytan shrugged innocently. "But if that happens, you can hand your mates two thousand apiece and tell them to buy new rigs. Right?" He looked at Hakim, who had removed his sunglasses but could still not read the Englishman's eyes in the gloom. *Or*, Eytan thought, *you can chop your padlock, plead robbery to your friends, and buy yourself a sports car.*

Hakim suddenly decided he needed a smoke. Eytan gently took his elbow and led him away from the gear.

"Tell you what." Eckstein opened his other jacket pocket, flipped through a large wad of bills, and peeled off five American hundreds. "You take this as a down payment. Tomorrow morning at seven, one of my mates will be here with the rest of the money." He was not concerned that Hakim and company might try to roll Didi for the cash. He pitied them if they tried. "You give him the chutes, and he'll sign any rental paper you want." For twenty thousand, he reckoned Hakim would drum up a typewriter and hire a secretary. He gripped the Moroccan's hand, the cash forming a bond between their flesh. "Is it a deal?" Eytan smiled. "Jumper to jumper?"

Hakim was at a total disadvantage. He had nothing to lose. The Englishman was obviously *toqué*, perhaps even a criminal. Hakim could call in the Sûreté, but then he would lose a small fortune.

"We do business," he said, lifting his chest to show his honor.

"Bloody good," said Eytan. He clasped both of Hakim's shoulders. "Tomorrow at seven, then." He released him and walked briskly away, turning back only to call out, "Don't be late. And no dirty laundry!"

Hakim smiled and waved. He looked down at the money, then held one bill up to the sun. *No dirty laundry*. What in Allah's name did that mean . . .?

Horse began to gesture excitedly, and Eytan turned from the writing table. Didi Lerner was hustling quickly from the direction of the hotel's reception lobby, across the wide pool patio, his bald head twisting as he scanned for room numbers. Spotting Horse, he took a hard left through the gardens and leapt over a goldfish pond. Horse just managed to haul on the glass door in time for him to bound into the room.

"Bloody fucking piece of shit Mitsubishi," Lerner spat, as he landed on the carpet and shook a spray of water from one sneaker, which had trailed into the pond. He was wearing khaki shorts and a black T-shirt that said *Blue Sky Ranch* and showed three nude skydivers clasping each other's limbs. The shirt was glued to his body with sweat.

"Good of you to join us." Benni smiled at him.

Lerner unshouldered a canvas gym bag, tossed his sunglasses onto a soft armchair, and went straight for the refrigerated bar. He pulled out a bottle of orange juice, finished half of it, and wiped his lips with his wrist. "Where did you get that fucking truck?" he growled at Eckstein.

"Abderrahim, the cabdriver." Eytan grinned. If Didi was only bitching about the transport, then everything else was all right.

"What is he?" Lerner demanded. "Your bloody cousin?"

"I don't *think* I have any Berber ancestors." Eytan tapped a finger on his lips. "I'll have to check."

"But you *did* acquire the gear," Benni fished anxiously.

"Ah course I got the bloody gear. Would I drive five fucking hours from Casa with an empty truck?" Lerner backed up with his orange juice bottle and slumped into the soft chair, then quickly arched as he felt the glasses under his rump. He pulled them out and looked at the twisted frames. "Bloody hell," he snapped. "And don't expect any change back from your dollars, Herr Schmidt." He turned to Eckstein. "Your Hakim is one slick, happy bugger."

"No matter." Benni crossed his wrists and flagged his hands. "Horse, you can put the balance in the safe."

Horse picked up the soft attaché and went to the sliding closet in the entrance foyer. The main reason Benni had selected the N'Fis as his base was that only the first-class hotels had private safes in the rooms. The funds were crucial to this operation, and he did not want the men wandering around with large sums, or raising the curiosity of desk clerks with deposits and withdrawals from the boxes at Reception.

"And you should see this stuff," Didi carried on. "The bloody colors. We'll look like a flying circus."

"But you think the gear's okay?" Eytan's amused expression further annoyed Lerner.

"Buggered if I know," he complained. "I'll have to repack everything and hope to hell I don't need rigging tools."

Eytan thought for a moment, his smile fading. They would need a large open area and some sort of clean mat for repacking the chutes. "We'll have to do it tonight," he said. "Find someplace outside of town."

"It'll take three hours minimum," said Lerner. "Me and Lapkin together." He looked up at Eckstein with a frown. "You don't remember how, do you?"

Eckstein had not made a free-fall jump in three years. Military jumping was easy. You just threw yourself out and let the static line do the rest, a dope on a rope. However, skydiving was a complex skill, and his abilities were purely functional. He could remain stable, turn right and left, track on a vector, and pull. But he could no longer trust himself to pack properly. He shrugged sheepishly.

"Wanker," Didi mumbled. "Well, I'm not touching the reserves. We'll just have to play Russian roulette."

"Why can you not do the same with the main parachutes?" Horse asked foolishly as he walked back from the safe.

"Have you seen the cars on these roads?!" Didi shouted, making Horse wince in confusion. "This gear belongs to *Moroccan* skydivers." A country's vehicles were evidence of the general cultural regard for things mechanical. The choked cities and dusty highways were filled with sputtering, sloppily repaired hulks.

"Repack the mains, Didi," Eytan agreed.

"Bloody royt," said the Australian as he finished his juice.

"Where is the truck?" Benni asked.

Didi threw a thumb over his shoulder. "In the front lot. I gave the doorman a hundred green and told him I'd double it tomorrow if nobody touches that rattling piece of shit."

"Should we not post someone?" Horse asked Benni. He was afraid to look at Lerner.

"It will have to do," said Benni.

"Yeah," Lerner snapped. "We're not the Queen's Own Guard."

"All right, people." Eytan was looking at his watch and snapping his fingers. "On to the next." He picked up his Ethiopian ruck and slung it as he walked toward the door. Benni joined him. The colonel was wearing a white safari shirt, and Eytan opened one of his breast pockets and stuffed the equipment list inside. Benni turned to Lerner, who was still slumped in the chair.

"Well?" he said. "You two have a project."

"Just five minutes," Didi promised, "and we're off." He frowned at Horse. Being paired with the mousy analyst was not his idea of the perfect marriage.

Horse called out to Benni. "What about my groceries?"

"Oh, yes," said Baum as he stopped again and turned. "Give us the list."

"Brown sugar, salt, flour, parsley, and food coloring." Horse looked at his fingers. "Oh, and a large piece of hard cheese, also some cheesecloth. And white glue."

"Got it," said Eytan, and he and Benni went out.

Lerner looked at Horse. "What's all that for, then?" he asked as he turned the skydiving T-shirt inside out.

The analyst was folding up the terrain map. He would also sweep the room and carry all incriminating scraps with him when they left. As a rule, he felt intimidated by the field expertise of the men he worked with, but when they encroached on *his* territory, he could be surprisingly brusque.

"I am going to bake a *bloody* cake," he snapped.

The city of Marrakesh lies in southern Morocco, at the foot of the Atlas Mountains, whose ridges are brushed with snow even in summer and firmly encapped by a dangerous mantle in December. The low plaster buildings jut up from a wide, flat plain of huge rectangular plots which alternate between lush grove patches and barren sand, as if the sultan Youssef Ibn Tachfin could not decide if he preferred to settle in desert or garden. The walls of the old medina, within which wind an impossible labyrinth of souks, are high, thick, and perfectly symmetrical, their pastel orange-pink so breathtaking under the Maghreb sun that most of the buildings encircled by them have been similarly washed in emulation. And the other prevalent color of Marrakesh is a glistening emerald green, as the underground irrigation *khettara* still feed the parks and gardens with cold mountain water. So from any small distance, Marrakesh resembles carved cubes of salmon flesh on a bed of kale.

There were other cities in Morocco, such as Ouarzazate and Er-Rachidia, which were in closer proximity to Algeria and might have offered a more convenient departure base. But they lay at the edge of disputed territory, where roving bands of Polisario still raided, and their streets were filled with wary garrisoned soldiers. Marrakesh, on the other hand, was still a tourist mecca, her citizens striving to import and sell every matter of Western convenience. Benni had decided that its cultural stew would provide the best natural cover for his men, and the ingredients needed to improvise the basic tools of warfare would likely be found somewhere in the winding alleyways of mysterious stalls.

Jerry Binder was happy to be in Marrakesh, at least relative to the claustrophobic mode of arrival he had just endured. The alleged "express" from Casablanca had stopped at every puny hamlet, pisspot, and goat crossing, and by the time he finally hopped down from the old red-and-yellow electric car, he had sworn to attend a Crosby, Stills and Nash revival and machine-gun the whole damned bunch, for he could not expunge the old hippie tune from his brain.

Binder quick-marched along the concrete platform of the Marrakesh station, a large stuffed duffel bag over his shoulder, his mountain ruck and German parka packed away. Whenever he was off duty from Midtown North, his fashion tastes leaned toward shades of black: cowboy boots, jeans, tight-fitting T-shirts that displayed his torso. But Baum had pointed out that his appearance was too Ramboesque, so he had switched to blue jeans, high-topped Reeboks, and a white golf shirt. Now he looked more like a personal trainer en route to a job at one of the big hotels.

The driver of a tan Petit Taxi stuffed Binder's duffel into the back seat and was pleased to hear the American say, "The Mamounia, my man," as he squeezed his muscled bulk into the front. The Hotel Mamounia was a very luxurious place, and latching onto one of its guests for a few days could cover a month's rent in the *ville nouvelle*.

They drove quickly along the wide thoroughfares of the Avenues de France and de la Ménéra. Binder did not respond much to the driver's chatter, but when he saw the wide-open gate of the medina walls at the intersection of el Yarmouk and el Fetouaki, exactly as Eckstein had described it, he smiled. Jerry did not often reflect on his Judaism, but he was an ardent admirer of Israel's military machine, and so far these *Landsmen* were proving to be pros.

The driver dropped him off inside the circular drive of the hotel. Binder watched him pull away, then shouldered his bag, went back out onto Houmane el Fetouaki, and began to walk. The duffel was not light, but he had often humped a lot more and much farther.

He had been waiting outside the Camping Oasis in Casablanca when it opened in the morning, and was not surprised to discover its supplies barely fit for a Cub Scout troop. Still, he had managed to find the GI duffel, ten garrison belts, and a pair of plastic canteens and pouches for each. He also bought seven cheap lensatic compasses, which was all they had. Alice packs would have been a wonderful find, but Eckstein had assured him that the Marrakesh bazaar would have plenty of large camel-leather backpacks. Then he was quickly on his way back to an electronics store on Allal ben Abdallah, where he spotted a Realistic three-watt walkie-talkie with a telescopic antenna, which would be good for the dunes, and promptly cleaned the shop out of its inventory of four. They did not have external jacks, but he bought earplugs for them anyway, figuring that Sadeen could bypass the noisy speakers. He left the clerk desperately trying to sell him a Discman and hustled for the train station at Casa-Port.

Binder kicked out a nice pace now along el Fetouaki, following Eckstein's brief, keeping the Koutoubia mosque to his left and bearing straight on at the traffic circle. His hard expression beneath wraparound sun visors brushed off a couple of eager boy guides, and there, as described, was the gas station across the open square, and the flophouse Hotel al Charaf, soaking up the fumes. "Ahh. Home," Binder said to himself with satisfaction. "Fucking Israelis must have a color shot of every Arab street corner on earth."

He gave the desk clerk sixty-five dirhams for a room overlooking the street, bounded up the stairs, and barely inspected the showerless cubicle as he stuffed the duffel under the bed, went out with his ruck, and locked the door. He made the clerk's day as he handed him "forty American."

"Listen up, Mohammed old buddy," Binder said as the clerk smiled at him and squinted. "I'm climbing in the Atlas tomorrow. Anybody touches my stuff…" He drew a finger across his own throat and made a gurgling sound. The clerk laughed, but Binder raised his sunglasses to show his eyes, and the young man nodded somberly.

Outside in the sun, Binder found O'Donovan leaning against a lamppost. As he passed him, he said, "Speaking of blades . . ." and the two men paired up, heading for the souks.

The Djemaa el Fna cannot really be compared to the municipal squares of any other cities on earth. Bordered on the south end by the respectable structures of banks, apothecaries, and the post office, the remaining three sides feather off into establishments of questionable legality. The expanse of its sun-bleached asphalt could rival the parking lot of a sports stadium, but no vehicle can easily maneuver there, for the el Fna is constant host to an undulating circus of snake charmers, magicians, potion hawkers, jugglers, freelancing tour guides, and stiletto-wielding hash dealers. While in the center of the square crowds surge from one entertainer to another, the circumference is lined with canvas-shaded tables offering orange slices, chicken hearts, lizard tails, and turtle broth, all to the accompaniment of *tareejah* drums, cobra flutes, and the distant calls of muezzins from the minarets.

Amir Lapkin and Ari Schneller hardly had to wander beyond the borders of the el Fna to acquire everything on their list. They had linked up at Lapkin's hotel room, emptied their gym duffels, and headed for the fray, quickly latching onto a Moroccan teenager and giving him one hundred dirhams to serve as "bodyguard."

Lapkin filled his carryall with cans of lentil soup, burlap bags, plastic cigarette lighters, five boxes of large Ziploc sandwich bags, and a rectangular drum of cooking oil. Schneller bought penlights, dark twine, batteries, black electrical tape, shoe polish, two dozen lollipops wrapped in red cellophane, shaving brushes, a large roll of insulated alarm wire, a dozen mini-screwdrivers, five small cans of electric motor oil, and three pairs of striped flannel pajamas.

Their guide was very disappointed, for he had trotted around behind the foreigners dreaming of his commissions when they would finally wade into the jewelers' souk, which they never did. But Lapkin gave him another hundred dirhams just for waving off the flies, and he and Schneller trotted back to the Hotel de Foucald, just south of the el Fna, their duffels clinking and clanking.

They encamped on the pink plaster balcony of their second-floor room and began to work.

Lapkin's first task was to create *guznikim*, the primitive but reliable beacons that IDF troops use for everything from marking targets to landing choppers. He opened ten soup cans with his Swiss Army knife, flushed the contents down the toilet, and affixed a disposable lighter to each one with electrical tape. Then he cut ten squares of burlap and stuffed them in the cans, sealing them in sandwich bags. Tonight he would fill the cans with sand, leaving a wick of exposed burlap, and soak the contents with cooking oil. A man could light his *guznik*, later smother it with his boot, let it cool, repack it, and drop it in his ruck.

Schneller went to work on weapons-cleaning kits, even though Shaul Nimrodi had not yet come up with so much as a cap pistol. He laid out ten

Ziploc bags, filling each with a screwdriver and a meter length of alarm wire with a small eye fashioned at one end. Using the scissors of Lapkin's knife, he cut squares of cleaning patches from the pajamas and trimmed the shaving brushes until only hard bristle remained; in every other bag, he enclosed a small can of oil. Team partners would have to share.

The men worked together to modify a pair of penlights for each member. One would be taped to the back of the jumper's left wrist, the bulb toward his fingers, so that as he gripped the parachute-steering toggles above his head, the next man in formation could track him. The spare would be closed in a pocket and secured to the buttonhole with a length of twine, as would the compasses and any other tool in danger of being dropped. The penlight bulbs were white, so Lapkin and Schneller happily sucked on lollipops after stripping the red cellophane and taping new covers over the lights. The illumination kits were finished off with a roll of electrical tape, an extra battery, and three meters of twine.

Schneller looked up from his work when something caught his eye through the slats of the balcony. It was Benni Baum's bald head bobbing through the park as the colonel and Eckstein crossed onto Avenue el Mouahidine.

"*Eekon l'mizdar hamefaked,*" Schneller murmured in Hebrew. "Prepare for the commander's inspection."

"Watch your language," Lapkin warned in English.

There was a soft rap on the room door, and Lapkin went in off the balcony.

"Password?" He smiled behind the closed door.

"Canada is just a suburb of Detroit," came Eckstein's voice.

"Fuck you." Lapkin chuckled as he turned the lock.

Eckstein came on through. He saw that the men were working out on the balcony, yet the sensation that events were too quickly swallowing them all caused him to stop for a moment and examine the room. The salmon-colored wall plaster was peeling, showing white patches like the sunburned skin of a Scandinavian. A single bare lightbulb hung from a wire, and the two small beds were steel military types, their white sheets scarred by ironing burns, gray woolen blankets rolled at the feet. There were no pictures or posters of any kind.

He knew that every man on this team had encamped in such places before: flophouses, barracks, bunkers, bombed-out buildings in foreign lands. Like himself, they had lain on lumps and stared at ceilings not their own, seeking elusive sleep as they wondered if this would be the final bedroom of their lives. He had brought these men to this, and that stone of responsibility caused him to swear, once again, that he would quit this game and never ask another man to volunteer.

Lapkin seemed to read Eckstein's mind, for he patted the major's shoulder and said, "Hey. At least it isn't mud."

They went out onto the balcony.

"Should I stand at attention?" Ari Schneller looked up from his growing pile of packages.

"Thirty push-ups," said Eckstein as he bent to examine one of the cleaning kits. "Looks good, gentlemen."

"A season at Sanur," said Lapkin, referring to the paratroopers' training base, where recruits were taught anal-retentive attention to their gear.

Eckstein stood. "We were just at the Gallia." This was another small hotel in the "budget" area of the medina. "Didi's almost finished with the stretcher. Made it out of a two-man tent."

"Born to sew," Lapkin commented. Lerner's rigging skills were such that he could have made a wedding gown from a cargo chute.

"And Horse is making mud pies," Eckstein added.

"*Entschuldigung?* Pardon?" Schneller often lapsed into the mother tongue with Eckstein.

"The assault model," said Eckstein. "You should see him. I'm sure he has toy trains at home."

Lapkin smiled at the image of Horse laying tracks in his Jerusalem flat.

There was not very much for Eckstein to do here. As team leaders, he and Benni had to flit between the assigned safe locations, checking progress and coordinating activities. Yet these men did not really need baby-sitting. He made to leave. "You two need anything?"

"Weapons," Schneller and Lapkin said simultaneously, then looked up at each other and laughed.

"Slingshots all right?" Eckstein deadpanned.

"Just the ingredients will do," said Lapkin. "Wishbones, condoms, and marbles."

"Maybe by tomorrow night." Eckstein smiled at them. "See you at eighteen hundred."

Benni and Eytan walked along Avenue el Mouahidine, occasionally sidestepping as one of a cloud of moped riders would peel off, run right up on the sidewalk, and plug his rattling machine into a rack of scooters. Although the two men were clearly Europeans, none of the young locals tried to attach himself to them, for they moved too purposefully, eyes unattracted by the exotic surroundings. So often in the past they had diffused the dangers of operations with blustery jokes or false bickering, yet today they moved in silent sobriety, minds focused on a problem the likes of which no sadistic IDF scenario planner could ever concoct. They summoned every tactic developed through experience, yet in the end, both knew, the outcome would be in the hands of luck and fate.

"She'll be all right," Eytan said quietly as they reached the large traffic circle at the corner of Bab Agnou.

Benni did not respond.

"And if not," Eytan continued, "we will go with her."

Benni stopped walking, forcing his young partner to do the same, and he looked up into Eckstein's face. Could it be that Eytan was saying what Baum himself had not yet confessed? That if Ruth died, her father would not go home alive, and Eckstein understood that and would join him in a ritual self-sacrifice? No, that could not be. Eckstein had his own wife and son. He could not possibly hold Ruth's life so dear, no matter his brotherly love for her. Yet he had seen Eytan commit acts of suicidal heroics, wondering if a therapist might someday discover Eckstein lived in a world of hidden emotional pain and only survived this life because the opportunity to leave it properly had not yet presented itself. No. He simply meant they would save Ruth, or die trying. That was normal. That was acceptable.

Eckstein pointed to the green awnings of the Café Glacier la Victoire. "I'll be in there, overcaffeinating," he said as he walked away.

Benni crossed the circle to the Grand Hotel Tazi. Compared to the rest of the team's pensions, the Tazi was deserving of its title. The rooms were relatively large, the necessity for a good work space having been Sadeen's only request.

Sadeen cracked open the door to his second-floor room. Whenever possible, operators on foreign soil never occupied higher floors. If your operation was blown, you had to be able to drop to the street.

"*Hola, Padre.*" The sapper smiled as Benni slipped through. The room faced northwest, and the afternoon sunlight was diced by a wrought-iron window guard. Sadeen's yellow T-shirt was stuck to his back, he wore tan gym shorts above his bare feet, and his curly brown hair was matted by soiled finger combing. He dropped to his knees on the tile floor and continued working.

The place looked like an anarchist's laboratory. The twin beds had been pushed aside, exposing a strip of open floor, along which Sadeen had laid out the components for his "flash-bangs." There were long rows of various-width containers—soda cans, sink cleansers, vegetable tins, deodorant dispensers—some of them already bisected or drilled, their discarded contents forming an unimaginable brew in a plastic garbage can. Three soup bowls held different types of wood screws next to boxes of cornstarch, a tub of roofing tar, spools of electrical tape, three bags of children's marbles, rolls of toilet paper, a dozen rubber balls, pliers, scissors, and a carpet knife. Benni looked over to one of the beds, upon which lay two black *jallabiyas* and a large plastic bag full of fireworks. The pyrotechnics were sold openly in the Djemaa el Fna, but the two boxes of Winchester twelve-gauge Express surprised him.

"Where did you get the shotgun shells?" Benni asked.

"Mustaffa," Sadeen answered as he sliced a rubber ball in half. "The Berbers are bird hunters, you know."

"Yes."

"How did Eckstein find that kid so fast?" Sadeen was clearly pleased with his "guide."

"Eytan has been here before," said Benni. In fact, Eckstein maintained a link with the mountain tribesman by sending him the odd gift, as he did with all his local assets in foreign lands. The Berber guides were constantly being shaken down by plainclothes Marrakesh police, and Eytan had once sprung Mustaffa from jail with a hefty bribe.

"Guess so," said Sadeen. "You mention Mr. Anthony, and the kid's eyes light up."

"How are you going to use them?" Benni turned one of the red shells in his fingers.

"Well, first I was going to go electric, with a battery, impact switch, and some sort of filament or flashbulb as igniter." Sadeen chattered rapidly, enthused about his improvisations. "But that is too risky, so I decided to keep it simple." He held up half an empty cleanser container. He had worked a hole in the aluminum bottom cap and forced just the brass primer case of a shotgun shell through. "Impact detonator, mix of powder from the shotgun shells and the fireworks, then a head of cornstarch for a nice air burst."

Benni frowned. "They will detonate when they hit? Just like that?" He was versed enough to know that the primer would need a robust striker.

"Of course not," Sadeen scoffed. He slipped half a soup can over the cleanser tube, a snug fit. A screw had been twisted into the can bottom, and he picked up half a rubber ball and held it over the end. "Striker pin, just like on a parachute flare, but with an aerodynamic nose." The standard infantry flare was a long aluminum tube with a primer on one end. You simply reversed the end cap with its hidden striker, slipped it over the primer, and slammed the tube down onto your knee to fire it. "I will glue marbles around the primer for weight and put kite tails on the back ends for stability." He gestured at the black *jallabiyas*.

"Of course," Benni murmured. He had a vision of them all hurling canisters that would then just lie there like bouquets at a leper colony wedding.

"He is going to kill us all, *mon colonel!*" Rick Nabbe's voice echoed from the bathroom. Benni stepped carefully across the floor and stuck his head into the cubicle. Nabbe was sitting on the toilet, making waterproof match containers from plastic film canisters, gluing matchbook flints to the insides of the caps. He looked up at Benni and grinned. "I prefer to die with dignity."

Benni backed out of the bathroom and shut the door. Nabbe's matches and Sadeen's powder were better kept segregated.

"So? What about the truck?" Benni asked Sadeen reluctantly.

"That piece of brilliance is being worked on as we speak." The engineer smiled as he sliced open a shotgun shell. "Don't you trust me?"

"Do I have a choice?"

"No."

Benni sighed. He started for the door, and then his insecurity got the best of him. "Sadeen? Are these things going to work?"

The engineer looked up at him and batted his eyelids like an offended debutante. "*Amigo*," he said, "if I had but two more days I would give you LAW rockets and claymores."

Benni nodded and went out. . . .

At the Hotel al Charaf, Eckstein was admitted into the lair of Binder and O'Donovan. He waved a hand through air thick with paint fumes, but the stench would pique no one's curiosity, as the al Charaf lay just beside the busy petrol station.

Ten camel-hide backpacks hung like smoked hams from a white clothesline stretched between the window grates, their skins spray-painted black. The floor was covered with the pages of a daily Arabic newspaper, upon which nine *kochmers*, the ritual Berber knives, were also laid out for painting. Binder sat on the edge of one of the beds, staring at the knives with regret. He was a blade aficionado, and the *kochmers* were quite beautiful, with curved, silver-plated scabbards, camel-bone hilts, and silver belt rings.

Binder stood up. He was wearing a garrison belt with canteens and had linked one of the knives to the eyelets over his left hip. The big detective turned like a clumsy fashion model.

"Check it out, baby," he said. "Spider of Arabia."

"Very nice," said Eckstein, squinting at the polished silver. "They'll see you coming from three kilometers."

"I'm *gonna* paint them," Binder whined defensively. "It's a fucking shame is all." He drew the blade cross-handed and showed it to Eckstein. The point was good, but the steel edge was so flat you could barely have sliced watermelon with it. "You'd have to go right to the heart or throat with this thing. Won't cut for shit."

"Then why didn't you buy kitchen knives?"

Binder looked embarrassed. " 'Cause these are *scary*," he said as he slid the blade home again.

"Ahh, the psychological edge."

"Fuckin' A." Binder picked up a can of spray paint, then bent over the newspaper and stroked across the knives with a long black plume. "Sacrilege," he sighed.

Mike O'Donovan came out of the bathroom. He was wearing his white dress shirt, which had been laundered in Casablanca, a pair of khaki chinos, and brown laced shoes, just purchased. His hair was washed and combed, and he had touched up his bruises.

"Better move, huh?" he said to Eckstein.

The Israeli looked at his watch. "Yes. Your flight is at 1530."

"Terrific," Binder complained. "He goes flying while yours truly does all the homework." He gestured at two large shopping bags printed with the green crosses and crescents of a pharmacy.

"Benni will help you," said Eckstein as he moved with O'Donovan to the door.

"Send him up," said Binder.

A few minutes later, Baum came into the room and locked the door.

"Skipper." Binder greeted him as he continued to dull the scabbards.

"Spider," Baum replied. He picked up the shopping bags and dumped their contents on the empty bed. Then he sat down and sorted through the piles of gauze rolls, white tape, square bandages, surgical scissors, anti-infection cream, and Vaseline tubes. He laid out ten Ziploc bags and taped a Band-Aid to each for easy identification as a first-aid kit.

"Do you mind if I smoke?" he asked.

Binder shrugged. "Go ahead." The spray can rattled as he shook it again. "I'm already sucking gas."

Then Benni thought better of lighting up in the aerosol haze, so he plugged an unlit Rothman into his mouth. He cut a coil of rubber tubing into equal lengths for tourniquets, then fashioned quick-tying field dressings from pads and strips of gauze. The whine of mopeds and the friendly shouts in Arabic drifted up from the street, and he tried very hard not to envision the kinds of wounds upon which his no longer sterile concoctions might soon lie. He had once seen a woman shot, and he closed his eyes as he remembered the ragged puncture blaspheming her smooth flesh.

Picking up a rubber rain poncho, he began cutting out squares for sucking chest wounds. . . .

The ride to the Marrakesh airport at Menara was only a few kilometers over the fine wide road to Asni, yet as Eckstein and O'Donovan sat in the back of the Mercedes cab, they both wished they could further shorten the trip with distracting chatter. But all the hollow bits of small talk had been swept away by their cerebral storms.

Eckstein had made a reservation for O'Donovan with a French pilot who flew sightseeing tours over the area. If Nimrodi succeeded in bringing in a transport plane, it would first land at Menara. But the Marrakesh facility was controlled by the Royal Moroccan Air Force, and you could not have nine combat-clad parachutists traipsing across the tarmac to board a strange jump plane. The craft would have to land, refuel, lift off again, and almost immediately declare an emergency. Then it would briefly set down again somewhere close by, load the men at that rendezvous point, radio the tower that only a warning light had malfunctioned, and be on its way over the Atlas range.

It was O'Donovan's idea to enlist the aid of a local pilot, for they could not just trot over to the tower and ask for the coordinates of potential emergency landing sites. When he heard that the pilot was French, he insisted that he be the one to go up for the survey. Eckstein pondered the American's strange demand as the two men rode in silence, their windows open and their heads turned outboard to the passing palms. O'Donovan smoked, while Eckstein wished that he could.

"What makes you think you'll have rapport with this pilot?" Eckstein asked. Then he glanced at the back of the cabdriver's head, a signal to keep the conversation cryptic.

"I don't," said O'Donovan. "The French hate us. We saved their asses too many times."

"And that's a plus?"

"He'll react to a challenge from me. It's a knee-jerk ego thing. I'll just have to mention Normandy, and he'll probably buzz the tower."

"I hope that's not what you have in mind."

O'Donovan did not answer. He was watching a fat tourist trying to mount a camel in an olive grove. The animal spit at its driver, who was thrashing its forehead with a switch.

Eckstein breathed in the mixed scents of desert dust and prickly pear cactus, spices that brought sense memories of home. His thoughts turned to the many hostage-taking incidents that had ended with Israeli commando raids. More often than not, one or more of the hostages died in these attempts, but the decision to raid rather than negotiate was still lauded by politicians and public. In this case, there would be no political capital. Ruth's life was the only reward.

"I've known her since she was a child," he murmured as he stared at nothing and the breeze chilled his neck.

"She's not a child anymore," O'Donovan said after a moment. Then he realized his response was defensive, an inappropriate suitor encroaching on a close-knit family. His voice dropped to a near whisper. "What was she like?"

"Much the same." Over the years, Eckstein had met some of Ruth's few boyfriends and lovers. She was selective, and he realized that he would probably never meet the Michael O'Donovan to whom she had been attracted, for those aspects of the American's character were certainly suppressed now and might be burned away forever in the coming firefight. "Smart, headstrong, direct," he added. "Warm, when you're worthy of it. Her beauty has only grown."

"Then she hasn't changed," O'Donovan said. He turned to the Israeli, and for a moment he had the urge to grip the man's hand, to give and gather strength from it. Instead, he tossed his cigarette from the window and laced his fingers together over his knee. "I just hope this will all be worth the effort," he sighed, meaning that Ruth would still be alive when they got there.

"There are some men who would risk their lives to snatch the *Mona Lisa* from the Louvre," said Eckstein.

O'Donovan nodded. "Now, *that* would be stupid," he whispered. . . .

The pilot of the single-engine Cessna 207 was a tall ex-Parisian named Philippe Ducrocque. He wore a tan cloth flying jacket over khaki trousers and leather boots. His hair was salt and pepper, gold-rimmed Ray-Bans were set upon an angular face, and indeed the corners of his long mouth curved up at the ends, giving him the look of a lizard with a secret.

"No photographs, please," said Ducrocque as he taxied the airplane. He glanced at O'Donovan's camera and gestured at the military side of the field, where four Fouga Magistere trainers were parked on the apron. O'Donovan covered the camera in his lap, as if the device had been known to jump up and take its own pictures.

The failing sun was thickening the haze as the Cessna took off into the west, and O'Donovan noticed a red plastic sign in French, screwed to the left dash plate of the cockpit: *Do Not Exceed 147 Knots with Doors Off.*

"Is this a jump plane?" he asked, as Ducrocque leveled off at five hundred meters.

"It was." The Frenchman adjusted the engine mixture. "But I am not a jump pilot. I purchased it for charters and surveys." The American had paid him fifty dollars for a twenty-minute tour, and that was not much air time for wandering about. "What would you like to see?" he asked above the engine drone.

"Well, coincidentally, I'm looking for a DZ."

"A *Dee Zee?*"

"Drop zone. I'm a skydiver."

"The military has a club at the glider strip at Beni Mellal."

"Where's that?"

"Approximately two hundred kilometers from here."

O'Donovan looked down at the small pink cubes of Marrakesh. "Too far," he said. "I'd like to jump close to the city, so I can hop back to my hotel or get right back to Menara for another lift."

The pilot shrugged. "Well, there is no 'DZ' here."

"How about Amanouz?" The CIA map indicated a long flat plain bisected by a dirt road just ten kilometers southeast of Menara, but only a pilot could tell you if it would eat up an airplane or not.

"Amanouz?" Ducrocque looked over at his passenger. "There is only a dirt road out that way."

"Could you land there?"

"In an emergency. Not for sport."

"Let's have a look."

Ducrocque was already raising his watch as O'Donovan waved a hundred-dollar bill in the air. The Frenchman glanced at the money, shrugged again, checked his compass, and banked gently to the right.

O'Donovan reached into his trousers and pulled out another bill.

"Tell you what, Monsieur Ducrocque. Set it down at Amanouz, and we'll make it an even two hundred."

The Frenchman's half-smile now bent to an angry gash. "I cannot do that," he said. "It is illegal, unless I have a true emergency. Your money cannot buy everything, you know." He increased the angle of his bank, clearly offended, and heading back for the airport now.

"Okay, okay." O'Donovan threw up his hands and sighed. He did not need Ducrocque to actually dirty his tires at Amanouz, but he *did* have to see that it could be done, get the Frenchman to commit to it. The Cessna was large and could handle up to eight sport jumpers. If it could make it into

Amanouz, then most other STOL aircraft could as well. He switched his tone to one of nostalgic regret. "You know," he said, "I used to read Saint-Exupéry. High school French. I guess he made me think French pilots would try almost anything."

Ducrocque bridled. "Saint-Exupéry was more of a writer than a pilot," he scoffed.

O'Donovan smiled, leaning over one knee as he turned to the Frenchman. "And what are you, Philippe?" he challenged. "More pilot or taxi driver?"

Ducrocque's face curdled. He stared at the arrogant American for a moment. "*Suce-moi*," he said quite clearly. "Blow me." Then he yanked the throttle back, jammed the yoke in, and twisted hard to the left, as O'Donovan's camera crashed to the floor and they dived toward Amanouz. . . .

It took Shaul "Baba" Nimrodi less than two hours to purchase landing rights at Menara, as well as the air corridor between Marrakesh and Ouarzazate, and then again from Ouarzazate to Zagora. It was a narrow passage, and it would be open for only a limited time on the following night, but he was confident that the Royal Moroccan Air Force would be ignoring the odd blip on their radars.

The Menara terminal was a long, spacious rectangle of polished tile floors and rarely frequented shops, for the facility hosted only two commercial flights per day. Not far from the main entrance was a small coffee and brandy bar, across from which neat tables and chairs of bent black wood were arranged over the floor. Wearing a gray cotton suit, white shirt, and red wool tie, Nimrodi spent the first hour chatting in Arabic with the old barman, a Berber who had to come down from the mountains each day to support a large family.

Nimrodi could have trotted up to the flight plan office and tried simply to file for his incoming aircraft, but if the Moroccans were anything like Israelis and refused him on a whim, the plane would be impounded as soon as it landed. So he chose to wait and appeal to the fiscal requirements of the man in charge.

Air force officers drifted in and out of the café area, and at last a lieutenant colonel appeared, taking a corner table and opening a copy of *Le Monde*. He was a slim, pleasant-looking fellow in his mid-thirties, who aside from his shoulder insignia wore no wings or decorations on a freshly pressed khaki uniform. Nimrodi recognized the burden of command, for with it comes isolation.

The barman raised his eyebrows toward the officer.

"*Le commandant?*" Nimrodi asked.

"*C'est lui*," whispered the old man.

Nimrodi slid off the stool, carrying a small leather hand satchel of the type popular with European men. With the exception of a couple of Scandinavian trekkers, the café had emptied, and he approached the officer and offered the standard Arabic greetings, chest palming and flowery politesse. He pulled out a chair and ran up his false flag in mellifluous French.

"I am a member of the King's own security detachment, *mon cher colonel*," Nimrodi began, and as the officer closed his newspaper and regarded his guest with astonishment, the Israeli embellished. He explained that on the next evening, a transport plane would arrive from Atar in Mauritania. The aircraft would be empty, and the colonel should feel free to inspect it. Nimrodi, who had not yet offered a name, would then board that aircraft and fly to Algeria. Could he expect the colonel's cooperation in this confidential matter?

"Of course," the officer replied, although he was wedged between his penchant for orders and the risk of offending a member of King Hassan's entourage. "But I will have to inform my superior officer."

Nimrodi clucked his tongue. "The King, Allah be with him, would regret that." He edged a bit closer. "You see, we are determined to prevent an assassination attempt by Algerian fundamentalists conspiring with the Iraqi Mukhabbarat." Nimrodi produced his Iraqi passport in the name of Ahmed Tabri and flipped it open to show his photograph. "As you can see, we intend to penetrate and destroy these monsters. My mission is, of course, a state secret. Allah willing, I will return." He shrugged and put the passport away. "If the forgers of our Sûreté are what they claim to be."

By this point the colonel's eyes had widened substantially. "But this is very dangerous for you," he whispered.

"As is *your* role," Nimrodi warned. "But for your courage and cooperation, His Majesty has approved a 'field' bonus." He placed his hand satchel on the table, opened the zipper, and spread the metal lips with his fingers, revealing a thick stack of green bills. "It is only ten thousand dollars," he apologized. "But this is also a matter of patriotism, *mon cher ami*."

The officer reached for his demitasse. It trembled slightly as he sipped, the neglected *café noir* as cold as river mud. He could refuse and possibly face a hanging. He could agree, and if it turned out that he had aided and abetted an impostor, the same noose would fit the crime. Yet there was a third option: He could write up a report, seal it, hand it to his second in command in the presence of a witness, and if everything turned out all right, he would take it back and destroy it. His wife would not be displeased, and he might even receive something shiny from Rabat to decorate his uniform.

The officer wet his lips. "I shall do my duty."

Nimrodi told him the ETA of the incoming aircraft, skipped the emergency landing, and described the way points of its subsequent navigation.

The Moroccan nodded, but he hesitated for a moment. Then he touched the leather satchel, slid it to his side of the table, and lowered it to his knee.

Nimrodi smiled, not too brightly, and he swiveled his head toward the bar. Eytan Eckstein had taken a stool there, viewing the entire transaction in the wall mirror. Eckstein briefly raised a thumb over his shoulder.

The Moroccan colonel saw it all, and he began to breathe very hard. Nimrodi reached out and patted his hand.

"Do not worry." The Israeli smiled. "*C'est kascher, comme disent les Juifs.* It's kosher, as the Jews say."

The wadi of Oued Issil is not completely dry in the winter months. A small trickle of mountain water gurgles through its winding cracked vein, and in a rainstorm that stream can flash into a rushing swell. But tonight the stars flickered high above the wide trough, and although a chilled breeze blew from the north, the carved walls offered enough protection so that a rigger could unfurl his nylon without it being dragged away.

The wadi was a comfortable hike from the road to Had Abdullah Rhiate, where Didi had parked the white Mitsubishi on the shoulder and Ari Schneller had jacked it up, removed a tire, and leaned it against a fender in the unlikely event that a wandering police car might find its location an oddity.

Only Didi, Lapkin, and Schneller had traveled with the truck, for it would not do for a local shepherd to witness a contingent of healthy men streaming from the vehicle like a circus act. Nabbe, O'Donovan, and Binder had hiked along the wadi at spaced intervals from the outskirts of Marrakesh. Eckstein, Nimrodi, and Mustaffa the Berber guide had been dropped by cab in the middle of the Issil oasis, then walked due south through the palm groves until they reached the wadi and doubled back north. No one knew from which direction Baum was coming, until he appeared from the southwest over a hard dune.

Mustaffa set up shop on a plateau overlooking the road. He made a small wood fire, then covered it with a large inverted steel bowl, upon which he spread thin pancakes of dough to make the bread of the Bedouin called *fatir*. The fire might draw attention, but it was a natural evening pastime for a Berber. With a whistle, he could summon Mr. Anthony and his friends, who would quickly gather round, playing the crazy foreign campers.

One by one the men approached the truck and carried a parachute bag up over the long crest of sandstone and down into the wadi. Didi and Amir unfurled a long blue roll of produce trucker's plastic on the hardpan beside the running stream. They worked on the chutes with penlights in their mouths, and Didi grunted and cursed each time he found a frayed suspension line, a worn canopy cell, or a butterfly snap that looked like a relic from the early Christian era.

The ram air free-fall canopies bear little resemblance to their round military progenitors. The standard paratrooper's chute is a marginally steerable mushroom of material and suspension lines, while the ram air is a highly maneuverable portable glider. The ram air assembly is complex, its web of seams, lines, slider and air brakes as daunting as the wiring harness of a Jaguar. Due to the covert nature of his travels, Didi had not been able to import his full rigger's kit, the steel punches, awls, grommet dies, and vise grips that would have set off airport alarms. But he had risked carrying his bags of rubber retainer bands, an assortment of high-grade sewing needles, "E" thread, and ripstop tape. Still, he prayed that he would not find major structural failures. He had a camel bag filled with Moroccan carpenter's hardware, but it would be like repairing a racing car with bicycle parts.

Despite Eckstein's trepidations, Didi was pleased that most of the rigs were equipped with throw-out pilot chutes. The two rip-cord-activated rigs were missing their cables, and the containers had been closed with rusty twists of steel wire. Tomorrow he would have to fashion rip cords from moped brake cables, and handles from short lengths of PVC pipe.

The men who had never used a throw-out would learn to do so right here on the ground. Those who had never flown a high-performance PD Sabre would solo tomorrow night. There would be no practice jumps.

Shaul Nimrodi, who had rigged a few thousand military chutes in his day, was a great asset to Lerner and Lapkin. He marched around the area with an unlit cigarette plugged into his holder, inspecting the containers and affixing small squares of masking tape to spots that needed Didi's attention. He quietly ordered the other men into support positions, maneuvering them to stand inside the harnesses, lift the piggyback rigs, and lean back gently to provide tension on the lines as Didi and Amir untangled.

The men were no longer fresh. They had begun the day at dawn, traveling by bus, train, and truck from Casablanca to Marrakesh. The afternoon had been filled with intense preparations, and they had just spent two hours in a dark corner of a restaurant called L'Étoile de Marrakesh, whispering "what if"s to each other as a belly dancer undulated on a small stage at the far end of the room.

"What if there are sentries outside the perimeter?"

"We'll try to take them with knives."

"What if the perimeter is mined?"

"We'll disarm a path if there is time. Otherwise, we'll regroup and come straight down the road."

"Suppose they're wearing Kevlar?"

"Go for the legs and finish them close. You'll never make a head shot."

"Suppose they won't bring Ruth up?"

"Benni will have to show himself and try to negotiate."

"Suppose *none* of them are aboveground?"

"We're fucked."

Horse had not been present for this planning session, and for once his somber inquiries were sorely missed. But he had taken his "groceries" back to the N'Fis and was presumably working with Roselli's aerial recon photos.

Jerry Binder was seated on a large rock just across the narrow stream. He was watching Lerner and Lapkin work, and while he admired their skill, he was superstitious about certain practices.

"When you find one for me, Didi," he said, "just leave it. I pack my own gear."

Didi grunted without looking up from his labors. "With pleasure."

"But you will let him check the canopy first, Spider," Nimrodi cautioned.

"Yes, Baba," Binder replied with mock obedience. "And speaking of equipment checks . . . Weapons, baby. How about some *tools* for this cluster fuck?"

"They will be aboard the airplane," Nimrodi patiently reiterated as he inspected the container of a Para Flite XL Cloud. The Cloud was a large canopy popular with military HALO teams. "And there will be one for every man, my friend."

"Great," Binder complained. "Could you be less specific?"

"I am sorry, Spider," Nimrodi said without a hint of genuine apology. "But my telephone conversations with Atar could not be *more* specific, given their *en clair* nature. My associates understood the requirements, and they will provide."

"Jesus," Binder whispered.

Ari Schneller's German accent drifted down from the wadi wall behind Binder, which he had mounted to look out for intruders from the south. "I thought you Special Forces people are supposed to be experts on all foreign weapons."

"We are," said O'Donovan, who was helping Lapkin by kneeling on a deployment bag. "Spider's just a baby."

Binder muttered an obscenity.

"So where is our friend *le cheval?*" Nabbe gripped a fistful of suspension lines so that Didi could apply a rubber retaining band. No one had seen Horse for hours.

"He will be along," Benni murmured. He was pacing over the winter-hard sand bed just upstream of the packing mat, his silhouette outlined by the glow of a cigarette in his cupped hand. He glanced occasionally at the labors of his men, but he did not offer to assist, which Eckstein found distinctly out of character. Though the major kept his peace, he suspected the reason for Baum's distance.

"And what about Dr. Einstein?" O'Donovan wondered. Sadeen had left L'Étoile halfway through the planning session, having been beckoned to the street by Mustaffa.

"He's making a bloody truck from egg cartons," Didi mumbled as he worked.

"Balloons," Binder offered. "It's an inflatable, like in the Macy's parade."

"No," Nabbe corrected. "I think he is out hunting nachos. He is tired of lamb stew."

"Speaking of which." Eckstein squinted in the dark, trying to thread "E" cord through a curved needle for Didi. "Don't let me forget rations tomorrow." He had drawn up a list of hard chocolate bars, raw potatoes, sucking candies, and other items high in sucrose and starch, low on salt.

"If you do forget," Nabbe warned, "we will have to cook you, *Cordon Algérie*, although you are a brooder and will probably be sour."

The thin sound of a tooth-and-finger whistle broke from the direction of Mustaffa's lookout. For a moment, the men froze. "Keep working," Benni said. He motioned to Eckstein, and the pair climbed over the wadi lip and hurried up the grade.

Mustaffa was squatting near his fire and looking off toward Marrakesh. A pile of fresh *fatir* loaves sat on a straw mat, and the burry-headed boy was smiling as if party to a secret. Eckstein and Baum joined him as he pointed up the dirt road, which twisted between rows of prickly pear.

"*Ein Lastwagen,*" he said, for German was the foreign language he had studied in school and his mode of communication with Eckstein.

As Eckstein and Baum peered into the distance, a pair of very bright headlights emerged from a curve, and they were forced to squint. The sound of badly timed cylinders and the hollow rattle of a cheap truck body reached them on the wind.

"It's just a van," Eckstein whispered.

"Or a jeep," Benni cautioned.

The vehicle came on more quickly now, then all at once its lights extinguished, the engine gunned as if struggling over an obstacle, and a strange jumble of piping was racing up the shallow grade. It stopped halfway up the slope as Eytan and Benni rose to their feet, mouths agape.

Sadeen was beaming as the pair approached him. They walked around the Autobecane moped and stared. Across the handlebars, a length of steel pipe had been slipped through plumber's T's, which were welded to the bike. In turn, a pair of large headlights had been clamped to the pipe ends, their wires leading to a chain-saw battery strapped to the fuel tank. At the right rear of the moped, the exhaust pipe was covered by an empty olive oil can, drilled with a pattern of small holes and girdled by a heavy link chain.

Horse came walking up the grade. He had dismounted on the road and was carrying a large camel-hide suitcase. And he was smiling.

"I think it will work," he said as he approached. "Perhaps as close as two hundred meters range. At that point he will stop. Klump will have to show herself."

Benni rubbed his jaw, and even though he shook his head, he said, "It might."

"And how are you going to jump this sculpture?" Eckstein asked warily.

Sadeen raised his palms proudly. "The whole thing comes apart. We will seal it up in a camel rug, and I will go out with it. Like a stripped-down fifty-caliber." He dismounted the contraption and lifted it easily. "It weighs about the same."

Eckstein had himself jumped with MAGs and 52 mm mortars, but never a fifty, and certainly not HAHO. "Let's see what Didi says."

They helped Sadeen roll the moped down into the wadi, whereupon a raucous discussion ensued as to its viability. However, Baum and Eckstein attested to the effectiveness of the ruse, at least as a time buyer, and Sadeen ended the argument by calling for a better suggestion.

"Hijack," Schneller insisted.

"That will also be my preference," Sadeen agreed. "But if no *real* vehicle appears, we will have this option."

Nimrodi, the master of loadmasters, had the final word.

"Didi will give you the largest canopy," he said to Sadeen. "We will drop you first, but the rest will not form up on you. And if that thing gives you any trouble, you will cut it away, my friend."

The engineer grinned and bowed to the colonel.

O'Donovan let out a low whistle. He was watching Horse, who had gently laid his suitcase on the packing mat and opened it. The men gathered around and murmured their approval.

His model of Martina's camp could have been constructed by an architect. It was nothing like the quickly assembled sand tables usually presented by field intelligence officers. The slopes, contours, and dunes of the target were rendered in hard brown plaster, the mounds of the submerged trailers topped with cardboard conical vents. Where every bush and cactus appeared in the aerial shots, they were mimicked by parsley sprigs, and every significant rock was a glued-down pebble. A jet aircraft had been carved from cheese, then covered by a net of dyed cheesecloth. Another such net obscured a hole past the northeast boundary of the camp. The access road was a strip of pasted salt.

"Bloody fucking excellent," Didi whispered as he went back to work. Most of his rigging had been accomplished, but there were two chutes left for repacking.

"Well, we're all here," said Eckstein. "Let's work on it now." He helped Horse move the model off the packing mat and onto the flat sand. Though the men were tired, they did not complain, for aided by the appearance of familiar tools, they had begun the self-deception necessary to undertake the venture. They gathered around the model and sat in a semicircle.

Eytan looked for Benni, then spotted his partner sitting by himself on a large slab of granite. The moon had breached the peaks of the Atlases, and it bathed Baum in a gray shroud as he looked up at it, his fingers playing a slow minuet on his knees.

"It is time for confessions, gentlemen," Benni said.

The men fell silent, turning their heads to the colonel, wondering what he had in mind.

"Okay." O'Donovan tried to break the spell. "I took a buck from the church basket when I was seven."

No one laughed.

"I have never made a free-fall jump in my life," said Benni.

The men stared at their commander in shocked silence.

"*Encore?*" Nabbe whispered.

Benni turned on his rock. He was looking down at his feet like a schoolboy. Had the light been more generous, his blush would have shown.

"Tel Nof, yes," said Benni, meaning the standard military jump course at the airborne school. "And the occasional refresher, of course. I did the father and son thing two years ago." If your son was a paratrooper and your legs were still good, it was a family tradition. "But free fall?" He looked up and tried to work a smile. "No, my friends. Never."

The men watched, realizing from Benni's expression that he was not revealing fear. On this operation he would probably agree to jump with an umbrella. His confession was that of a slow runner, the worry that he would hold the team back, be unable to keep up. He might fail to deploy and thereby diminish their numbers, or wander off into the sky while they went on to try to rescue his daughter. Without him.

Didi and Amir rose from their labors and walked quietly to the edge of the circle. The men looked up at them, while the pair glanced at each other and then focused on Baum. He had purposefully concealed a truth they should have known. They were not angry, for they understood, and the plea in Baum's eyes was too much to bear.

"No worries," said Didi. "Me and Lapkin will take you out, AFF style." Accelerated free fall was a technique used to quickly advance novice skydivers, but it usually entailed hours of instruction. "We'll pull the rip cord for you, and you'll just follow the group."

That was it. Decision made. Problem solved. The two riggers returned to their work, although, excluding Horse, every man there was remembering his first free falls. They had not been made at night, nor with combat gear, and certainly not at the head of a deep-penetration raid.

Jerry Binder had come down off his rock and was squatting at the edge of the circle. In his heavy New Yorkese, he began to sing his macabre version of a Bob Seger tune.

Like a rock, fallin' from the sky,
Like a rock, I ain't gonna cry,
Like a rock, no better way to die,
       Like a rock . . .

Chapter 22: The North Atlantic

Dr. Ali-Hamza Asawi should have been the happiest man in Tehran.

For five long years he had dedicated all of his intelligence efforts to the success of Project Mahdi, whose commission by a small inner circle of the Revolutionary Council had laid him naked under their scrutiny and whose outcome would determine his future in all aspects. Five mind-straining years, not to mention the germinal phase, for before verbalizing his concept to a single soul, he had spent six months thinking, planning, studying the tactical intelligence histories of Western powers, devising and discarding plots, distilling fantasy from probability.

And then, when his confidence outweighed his doubts, he had presented the essence of Mahdi to Larijani, the Presidential Adviser on Intelligence Affairs. And finally he had been honored to lay the plan before Rafsanjani himself, holding his breath until the presidential nod tipped the scales. Apparently, Asawi's fussing over a proper code name for the project had been wise, for "The Rightly Guided One" appealed to the president's belief that nuclear power was somehow divine.

Then the work had begun, each step in the process carefully masked by open diplomatic and trade efforts. While thinly covered consular officials were inquiring about technical components on the open market, SAVAMA agents were photographing Soviet Strategic Rocket Forces in the crumbling republics. While the foreign minister signed nonproliferation pacts in Paris, Asawi's men were bribing hungry Kazakh officers in Alma-Ata. While the arms of Hizbollah were being twisted into unnatural postures, and a German terrorist was being primed for a deceptive drama, the bunkers of Isfahan were being readied to receive a smuggled prize from the forests of Semipalatinsk.

So at last, here he was, less than a day away from the glory of Mahdi's birth.

He should have been having his Dior double-breasted pressed and his Bally loafers polished, alerting his staff that he would soon be taking a well-deserved holiday. He should have been preparing his home to receive government well-wishers and gifts of accolade, as he joyously anticipated his status as the honored guest at a presidential reception. He should have been the most envied intelligence officer in the Persian capital.

Except that he was nowhere *near* Iran.

The iron rail of the three-hundred-foot trawler seemed as cold as a block of dry ice, yet Asawi welcomed the chill against his sweating palms, a surviving shred of dignity the only thing keeping him from pressing his forehead against the metal as well. He could no longer stay in the ship's small infirmary, and there was no point to it, at any rate. How could you find relief when, lying on a tattered bunk, you had to brace every limb against the bulkheads to keep from being pitched to the floor? So he had staggered out onto the work deck to inhale deep drafts of brittle Atlantic air. The crumbs of salt crackers that failed to settle his stomach were glued to his gums, and he watched the empty fishnets swinging over holds still reeking of tuna oil. The tattered red and white stripes and single star of the Liberian flag whipped from a guy wire, as if that African slum still hoped to become a state of the Great Satan, and the masthead drew crazy figure eights in the purple sky.

Asawi was stunned again to see the green wave crests arch impossibly high, and he understood how novice sailors sometimes hurled themselves into the sea, for anything seemed better than remaining on this pitching platform. The strings of drool began to gather at the back of his throat, and he was able to suppress the inevitable only because a Hizbollah guard, wearing a black slicker and a Kalashnikov, turned from his position at the bow and smiled arrogantly at him.

Asawi pressed his shivering lips together and managed to turn them up. The guard faced forward again, and Asawi tried to focus on the man's figure being drenched in spray. Yet this was unlike a road vehicle, where you could mitigate motion sickness by focusing into a middle distance. Here the foaming panorama flung itself across the bow every which way. He closed his eyes, yet that only made it worse, like lying in a darkened bedroom with a raging hangover.

A drink. What he would have given for a Dewar's on the rocks. But that was hardly a possibility aboard this rattling can stuffed with unwashed religious fanatics. Perhaps he should have been grateful, for at least he had not suffered a full two weeks aboard as the trawler waddled from the Gulf of Oman, through the Arabian Sea, the Indian Ocean, around the Horn of Africa, back up through the South Atlantic and finally to the winter waters off the West African coast, where it steamed in circles now, waiting for a single-burst transmission relayed through Beirut. The men of Hizbollah were hard, primitive, their company a wretched bore, as their conversation rarely varied from Koranic platitudes. But they were not foolish.

As Mahdi progressed, the Israeli prisoner had been moved from the Bekaa Valley to a secret location in Iran near Bandar' Abbas. He had been loaded aboard ship, then secretly deposited in Somalia, hidden inside a modified tractor crate, and flown to Gambia, while the boat continued to make its way. If the

Israelis intended to renege on their agreement, they would most likely attempt a raid on the high seas, where their commandos would find themselves assaulting a prizeless vessel. Yet the proof of their sincerity was in the ship's undisturbed cruise, and Dan Sarel was picked up again in Banjul.

Asawi had neither expected nor wanted to witness these transactions. He had always thought to receive progress reports via encoded transmission, while he sipped champagne and snatched a flimsy from a motorcycle messenger. Yet apparently Sheik Tafilli, the Hizbollah negotiator, had grown tired of walking a lonely point out there in the face of his hated Israelis. Tafilli had convinced his own commander, Sa'id Abbas Mussawi, that their Iranian paymasters could be trusted only if one of them, preferably of considerable rank, came along for the ride.

And so Asawi had received the ghastly news from Larijani himself. He was to leave Tehran immediately and be flown to Cape Verde, a small pile of typhoid-riddled islands off Senegal. He had packed only his dress clothes, assuming that at the very least his accommodations aboard ship would be fitting. But when the Liberian trawler *Wologisi*, rust dripping from its scuppers and its stench preceding its arrival, butted up against the docks in Praia, he realized that he was overdressed for the occasion.

"*Kíf hâlak yâ sídi?*"

Asawi barely heard the voice inquiring after his welfare, for the roar of the sea seemed to be coming from inside his head. Yet he managed to turn, heard the bang of knuckles on hollow steel, and looked up.

Sheik Tafilli was bending over the rail of the *Wologisi's* bridge. In port he had discreetly worn a British pea coat, watch cap, and fisherman's boots. Now he had switched to an Egyptian commando tunic, a black-and-white kaffiyeh wrapped tightly around his face. His black beard dripped sea spray, his teeth flashed as a web of lightning stabbed the horizon, and Asawi had the distinct sensation of watching one of those jingoistic American Chuck Norris films on cable television.

"*Ilham' dilla,*" Asawi managed, though he felt no gratitude to God for anything at the moment.

"You have a radio message," Tafilli called. Unbelievably, he lifted a green apple to his lips and took a large bite.

"What did it say?"

"Red Tide."

Asawi nodded, then turned away and gripped the railing again, watching the near sea as it formed another wave that would have unnerved an Australian surfer. *Red Tide.* That was it, then. The Israelis had transferred the equipment.

Now the Jews would steam full ahead toward the rendezvous point, no doubt beneath an air umbrella and accompanied by a small armada, for that was their foolish wont, to focus exorbitant power on the recovery of a single soldier. Despite their reputation, they had limited resources, and thanks to the Syrians they were constantly on guard along their northeastern borders. So any major foreign operation drew off remaining intelligence and reconnaissance power.

The final stage of Mahdi had arrived, and he had always dreamed of issuing the order from the subterranean control rooms of the Defense Ministry, surrounded by envious generals of the Revolutionary Guard. Yet here he was, the joy sucked out of him by the twisting voyage aboard this stinking scow, and instead of being filled with pride, he was brimming with nausea. He turned back and looked up at Tafilli.

"Send them *Sunlight*," he called.

The sheik cocked his head, then pulled the apple away from his mouth. "You do not wish to come up and send it yourself, Doctor?"

Asawi thought for a moment. Yes, that would be proper, and the SAVAMA recipients might ask for his call sign as confirmation. But he was very afraid that if he stepped into the stuffy wheelhouse he might lose control of his stomach, and he could imagine nothing worse than having that image passed down through the ranks of Hizbollah like some tribal legend.

"It is all right." He waved weakly to Tafilli. "Just send it, please."

"*Mitl mâ bitrîd.*" Tafilli shrugged and disappeared.

Sunlight. Asawi hoped that there was none of that now in the mountains near Alma-Ata, that the peaks of Kazakhstan would be smothered in cloud and the roads hidden from prying satellites. A chicken truck containing the detached forty-kiloton nuclear warhead of a Soviet Scud-B would begin to race astride the Kazakh border, toward the point where Russia and Iran linked at the shores of the Caspian Sea. Sometime between midnight and dawn, it would encounter the well-paid renegades of the Kazakh engineering corps, who would guide it from a darkened beachhead onto a pontoon bridge and into the hold of a former American LST. The landing ship would pass quickly into Iranian waters, where it would be boarded by naval troops and hoist the green-white-and-red colors long before reaching Rasht.

He looked down at his soaked blue suit, the fine wool stained with disgusting yellow gobs of his breakfast. Despite the cold, he left his rain slicker open, for there was not enough air in the entire Atlantic to cool his fever. But at least the boat would stop its spiraling now, steam for the Mediterranean, and perhaps find a calmer sea there. Yet if he was suffering here on the open deck, he wondered how the Israeli commando was surviving the final hours of his imprisonment below. . . .

Captain Dan Sarel had not been given the slightest hint that his freedom was imminent. The naval commando had been moved so often during the uncountable years that he had ceased to wonder or ask. Asawi still marveled at the man's reported intransigence, and like a research biologist in possession of a fascinating mutant, he was reluctant to let SAVAMA give him up, except that the reward was far greater than Hizbollah's worthless Sheik Sa'id.

The Israeli was only a husk of his former self, half dead and devoid of all emotions except defiance, SAVAMA had not been able to elicit a decent sentence from the man, so they had destroyed him instead. The physical tortures, which brought him to the brink of death, were followed by hospitalizations. His recovery periods were then followed by experimental assaults, weeks of exposure to sound effects, during which he was straitjacketed so he could not protect his ears. And then he was bathed in stretches of utter silence, until the process was resumed with the truncheons.

"We will exchange you when you talk," Sarel's interrogators had promised him over and over. The commando remained unimpressed. Five years from the date of his capture, he was shown a glossy color folder. It was an appeal to the international community, printed by his wife and showing the six-year-old daughter he had known only as an infant. He spilled whatever tears he had left, and his captors waited optimistically as he murmured his first long soliloquy.

"She will live with the memory of a dead hero, but not with the shame of a living coward."

He was worthless, except for his reduced weight in exchangeable flesh.

And now, if only there were a way to be sure that Mahdi would take place unopposed, Asawi would somehow postpone the prisoner exchange, for he was convinced that he was sailing to his own death. As a removed tactician, his plot for a double deception had seemed brilliant, although now he was sure he had indulged in unnecessary machinations. Yes, the insertion of Martina Klump into the picture had been brilliant, the Americans and Israelis chasing after her like hornets from a trampled nest. And of course he could not be certain, until it was all over, if their misguided focus had indeed kept Mahdi safe. Yet he cringed at his own stupidity, for there was no way to recall the woman, to order her to stand down. She was out there somewhere, still determined to destroy this symbolic bridge of peace between old foes. And he, an intelligence guru whose focus was the acquisition of a nuclear warhead, had neglected to install a fail-safe mechanism to save his own life!

He almost laughed at the irony of his predicament, then immediately felt his knees buckle as he remembered the morning's grim revelation. As they set sail from Praia, Tafilli had escorted him on a tour of the *Wologisi*, as if the disgusting vessel were the flagship of a Greek cruise line. Aside from the Portuguese crew, who were highly paid to ignore their armed passengers, thirty battle-hardened Hizbollah roamed the decks and passageways. They swaggered about with assault rifles and miniature Korans, bathed in the blessing of *a fatwa* issued by Fadlallah himself, enjoying the temporary delusion that the Party of God now had a navy.

In the engine room, Asawi had first noticed the stack of green ammunition crates, which did not seem particularly unusual for this party, except for the strange snake of white cable that wandered off from them to another part of the ship. In a narrow passageway just outside the locked brig in which Sarel was trussed, he had seen another pile of such crates, and again the white cable. And finally, in the wheelhouse, he had been introduced to Tafilli's second in command, who perched upon a third pyramid. Between the man's legs the cable came to an end, crimped into a trigger housing secured only by a brass safety ring.

Asawi's breath quickened as he recognized the "electrical cable" as primacord, but he asked about the crates' contents anyway.

"Oh!" Tafilli smiled at the Iranian's sickened expression. "Many, many kilograms of TNT. Should the Jews fail to deliver Sheik Sa'id, or attempt to board us beforehand, or afterward, we will of course martyr ourselves and as many of them as possible. Allah would so will it. Don't you agree?"

But Asawi did not respond, for his inner ear chose that moment to react to the motion of the boat, and he fled to his quarters.

He had lain there gasping on the bunk, stunned by the fact that this woman Klump did not *need* a sophisticated missile to destroy the exchange. A properly placed rifle bullet would do the trick or, God forbid, the carelessly discarded cigarette from one of these fools! He hoped that if Klump survived to set her sights on the exchange, she would be able to tell the difference between an Israeli missile boat and a tuna trawler. But he was quite unsure that she would care; she might indeed make her selection with the toss of a coin.

The engine noise changed as the *Wologisi* set a new course and drove with the wind toward Gibraltar. Asawi gripped the railing harder as he looked up at the roiling sky, a gathering rain adding insult to injury. He had served the revolution with dedication, but his sacrifice was not limitless, like the blind passion for Paradise of these violent primitives. Yes, he had traveled the world in style, tasted foreign wines and infidel women, but that was all essential to his success. He prayed when he could, but of course he did not self-flagellate on *Ashura*, for when in Rome one did not face the senators with a bloody forehead. He treated his wife with the respect due a Moslem woman, spoiled his six children when he saw them, made sure to lavish gifts upon both his mistresses. He was almost of a royal caste. He owned a horse farm and rode English style. And now his greatest passion, that for secrets shared by few or none at all, could wipe it all away in a horrible flash.

For no one but Omar the Palestinian was aware of Asawi's double deception. He had not even informed Larijani of this brilliant end run, letting him believe that the exchange alone would be enough to mask Mahdi. He had planned to reveal it only if Klump managed to destroy the exchange, which would have set the Revolutionary Council to dancing in the president's reception hall. And they might yet dance after all, while his carcass was nibbled by the fishes.

He found himself praying that the Israelis and Americans would succeed where he had failed to anticipate. . . .

Near the stern of the vessel, where the galley hatch opened onto a deck covered by coiled hawsers, Omar Bin Al-Wafa sat near the port rail in a metal folding chair. His diminutive elderly form was swathed in a blue woolen blanket, and rivulets of rain ran from his beret, over his spectacles, and into his mustache, but all in all he appeared to be enjoying the ride. The heels of his shoes were locked against a cross-spar, and as the ship rolled he occasionally thrust out his arms for balance, smiling as he remembered accompanying his grandchildren on a roller coaster.

Omar had also not volunteered for this trip. Ali-Hamza Asawi, raging in near incoherence from somewhere in Tehran, had ordered Omar to accompany him. Apparently, the doctor was projecting his own frustration, blaming Omar for an impossible predicament, though the old man had merely followed his orders to the letter. It was Omar who had voiced reservations regarding the command and control of Martina Klump, while Asawi had waved his concerns away. Perhaps the Iranian was finally understanding that manipulations bred their own monsters, and deception had a price tag.

Yet Omar had his own secret, a private one that could easily have been read in his expression, had any other fool been on deck to witness it. He was happy, perhaps more so than he had been in years. For once again he was a young foot soldier on the front lines, though he faced the risks with the relaxed enjoyment that accompanies the old age of courageous men.

The fact that Iran would finally join the nuclear club did not please him, but it was an inevitable event with or without his participation. What *did* please him was the fruition of this exchange, for regardless of its motivation, he believed that every such act would create converts to the possibilities of peace. Yes, he served his masters in their fundamentalist zeal because he had no choice, but his deepest secret hope was that inevitably his Palestinian brothers would find their way home, and he knew that that would not really be accomplished by obliterating the Jews. Peace, although still far away, was twinkling on the horizon. And each time enemies took each other's hands across a table, for whatever reason, it became much harder to snuff it out.

Unlike Ali-Hamza Asawi, Omar was not convinced that Martina Klump would succeed here. He had watched her eyes, and they were not the windows to a fanatical soul but the confused and blurred lenses of a lost child. She would err, because her will was impure, and no doubt her opponents would take advantage of her weaknesses, poor girl.

Omar bent forward in his chair, grasped the rail, and peered forward along the deck. He wiped his spectacles with the soaked end of his scarf and clucked his tongue at the distant figure of Asawi hunched over the rail. He pitied the young man, for there was no strength in a hollow heart. Omar was a modest man of God and could accept any fate that might befall him. Asawi was a shell of political platitudes that quickly fled, leaving nothing with which to face Allah's judgment. The Iranian adored only power, and here in the stormy cauldron of a might much greater than man's, his love appeared to have failed him.

The *Wologisi* had an ancient ship's bell that hung from an iron arm somewhere above the galley. The Portuguese cook rang it to signal meals, and it bonged heavily now, its steady voice a comfort above the sea roar and the thrum of the engines.

Omar snapped open his pocket watch. Yes, it was lunchtime, and he was hungry. As he struggled up from his chair and turned toward the galley, he stopped and slowly shook his head in empathy.

Asawi's back was bucking uncontrollably as he vomited into the sea.

Chapter 23: Amanouz

A slim pink strip of the failing sun lingered like a smile in the wake of a pretty woman, then slowly faded behind the distant crest of Sidi Moktar, and as with all deserts everywhere, the night came on quickly and the earth surrendered its warmth. From the darkened plain of Amanouz the lights of Marrakesh were a soft yellow halo on an umber blanket, yet they were enough to silhouette the black bird that rumbled onward through the sky, and as Benni Baum's men bent beside the dusty road to ignite their oil beacons, they stared in wonder at its familiar form.

In an age when none of humankind's mechanical fabrications was built to last, by rights no Douglas C-47 should have been airworthy. Yet the awkward transport planes called Skytrains by the Americans, Dakotas by the British and Israelis, and Gooney Birds by one and all still flew, hauling medical supplies across African mountain ranges just as they once had over the Chinese Hump, dropping skydivers over Florida just as they had delivered paratroops over Sicily, Normandy, and the Mitla Pass.

It was a craft that had not been manufactured for over forty years, and whenever it settled onto a tarmac, it brought with it the shapes and sounds of another time, long gone, a time when the corners of flying machines, the wingtips and canopies and engine nacelles, were smooth and fat and round. In the year of this Dakota's birth, it would still have been acceptable to refer to an airplane as a female, and she would have been a Rubens model, full bodied and lazy looking, with big twin props that angled up when her rump settled, and fat, bouncy cartoon tires that squealed as the rubber sprayed up waves of sandy pebbles.

Baum's men had come to expect that Shaul Nimrodi would deliver the goods. They had anticipated a Twin Otter, hoped for an Israeli Arava. But this was not merely an airplane. It was a time machine, an amulet of airborne success.

The Dakota pilots were grateful for the landing zone markings of the primitive illumination cans and set down just before the first *guznik*. And as the camouflage-mottled hulk roared past the flickering flames, Jerry Binder placed a boot over his soup can, smiled widely, and said, "Nimrodi, you wonderful sonuvabitch."

The Dakota's tail wheel dragged up a stream of dust and its brakes reined it in fifty meters past the last beacon, and as it sat there with its big Pratt

& Whitneys rumbling, the men snatched up the cans with gloved hands and sprinted for it.

They had slung their parachute bags like knapsacks and then the camel rucks above, so that the blackened hides bounced against their necks as they thundered down the shoulders of the road, converging toward the cargo door on the port side near the tail. Sadeen and Schneller hustled with the carpet-swaddled moped between them, looking like contestants in an absurd game show relay race.

As the men neared the airplane, Shaul Nimrodi's face poked from the door. He had dropped a small hook ladder from the opening, but it did not nearly reach the ground, and O'Donovan, who was first to arrive began to shuck his gear.

"No!" Baba shouted as he stretched out his hands through the dark hatch. "Come! Up!" The small colonel set his feet astride the doorframe. O'Donovan, who was squinting in the dust of the prop wash, got a boot tip onto the bottom rung and was stunned to find himself yanked up and into the fuselage. Everyone and everything was inside the ship within ninety seconds, with the exception of Baum, who stood below the ladder and wriggled out of his gear, hurling it up to Nimrodi like a shot put. Horse stood beside him on the road, his hands jammed into the pockets of Binder's huge white alpine jacket, which had been temporarily entrusted to his care.

Baum made a fluttering hand motion to Nimrodi as the engines revved higher. Nimrodi ducked back inside, quickly counted heads, and popped out like a jack-in-the-box. "*Yallah!* Let's go!" he yelled.

Benni leaned close to Horse's ear. "Okay," he shouted. "Get in."

Horse snapped his head back, his eyes bulging. He had fully expected to stay behind, sweep the hotel rooms again, drive the Mitsubishi back to Casablanca, and then find his way home. Maybe by *ship.*

"What about the truck?" he yelled back feebly.

Benni put a hand around the little man's neck and pulled him close. "You think I'm going to leave you here to a friendly interrogation?"

"But Benni."

"Get in! That's an order! You've been suspended, not *discharged.*"

A flicker of headlights appeared on the road from the direction of Had Abdullah Rhiate.

"*Nu?!*" Nimrodi shouted as Baum slammed Horse on the back and knocked him against the ladder. The analyst scrambled aboard, and then Eckstein's hands appeared, thumb-locking with Benni's as he pulled him in. Nimrodi reached out for the ladder, hauled it up, and slammed the hatch.

The men had expected a respite while the Dakota turned and taxied back to set itself up for takeoff. They were slumped on the green steel benches, slowly doffing their gear and catching their breaths. But the pilots were already facing into the wind, and even though the track to Amanouz made a forbidding left turn only a thousand meters ahead, they stood on their brakes and committed their throttles.

The men had no chance to properly position themselves or use the crash belts dangling from the troop benches. As the Dakota gathered speed and its tires bucked over ruts, they reached out for something metallic, and hung on. The thunder of the engines and the battering of the undercarriage set up a din like a motorcycle trapped in a barn, and the forward momentum tumbled O'Donovan sideways onto Binder's lap.

"You know what I hate about this life, Jerry?" he yelled up to his partner as the big man gripped him by his jacket front.

"Tell me." Binder grinned.

"No adventure."

Then the tail of the airplane lifted from the road, leveling the fuselage. And seconds later, she roared into the night sky with the cliché sound of a cinematic airplane, the run-up thunder easing to a fading drone as if the classic craft were actually flying *away* from the men, rather than *with* them in her belly.

"I'm gone," she purred. "I'm gone. . . ."

Nimrodi pushed himself away from the aft bulkhead, where he had been held against the lavatory door by the takeoff G's. The airplane was climbing steadily now, for the lower slopes of the Atlases rose quickly after Amanouz, and he struggled forward inside an oversized green parka like a man wading through a rushing river. The Dakota bucked against the updraft from the ridges below, and he reached out for a cross-spar to steady himself. As in most military cargo planes, the interior offered hundreds of handholds, for it was built as a skeleton of vertical ribs and horizontal spars covered by a metal skin. Bundled winch ropes hung down from pulleys, and the short ends of cargo straps swung from pins like the grips on an old subway train.

This Dakota had first served the British Royal Air Force in operations over Arnhem, then the Israel Air Force, and it was now leased back to Akorda, the company that ferried for various African nations while serving the interests of AMAN. On the outside it displayed no insignia but an international call sign, and all the interior Hebrew instructions had been painted over. Yet the original warnings in English remained, stamped in white between the ribs: EMERGENCY, DON'T STEP, and NO REST, as if a picayune graffiti artist had been at it with a stencil set.

Nimrodi placed a hand on the shoulder of Didi Lerner, who was seated in the closest port position to the cargo door. He bent to a narrow window, peering through the scratched Perspex.

To the north, the flat plains of the Bahira lay like a massive brown carpet dotted with the star clusters of Tamelelt, Dar Ould Zidouh, and even the distant El-Borouj. But the lights of the towns were beginning to blur as Atlas mist swept past the Dakota's thick wings, and below, the black copses of trees began to show feathers of snow. Nimrodi pushed away from Didi and stepped carefully along the floor.

Along the left-hand bench, Lapkin, Nabbe, Eckstein, and Baum had spaced themselves out at comfortable intervals. On the right, Horse, Sadeen, Schneller, Binder, and O'Donovan had done the same. The men had quickly recovered from the takeoff melee, and although they knew that their flying time would approach three hours, they sought refuge from the tension by fussing over equipment. The parachute bags were arranged, the large camel rucks set between their feet and opened for reinspection. Sadeen and Schneller sat with their boots on the Motobecane, considering whether to lash it to the deck.

Nimrodi pulled himself past the empty radio-operator and navigator stations and on into the cockpit. The two men who sat in the left and right seats were past middle age, but they handled the oversized wheel yokes with the relaxed confidence of youthful fighter jocks. The pilot had been born in South Africa, the copilot in Zimbabwe, yet each had served a full career in the Israel Air Force and then found himself unable to stay earthbound. No longer restricted by military convention, they wore white roll-neck sweaters, heavy leather flying jackets, and peaked caps, from which their gray hair bristled.

The copilot turned his head as Nimrodi braced himself in the doorway. In Mauritania they communicated only in English, and he did so now out of habit.

"We just radioed Menara. Claimed a miraculous recovery and thanked them for their understanding."

"Good," said Nimrodi. "Now they will leave us alone for the rest of the night."

The pilot pulled his headphones down around his neck and grinned. "Who did you get to now, Baba?"

"The base commander." Nimrodi bent to look through the narrow cockpit windshields at a pair of jagged white peaks that seemed anxious to serve as the Dakota's grave. "He thinks it is his national duty."

"And what about return clearance?" asked the copilot.

"We will not be coming back," said Nimrodi. "At least not this way. And I will need you to execute some more fancy landings."

"*Some?*" The copilot checked the altimeter and looked at a chart board strapped to his left thigh.

"Yes. Is that all right?"

"Well, I'd rather be in bed," the pilot complained. He pronounced it "bid," as South Africans do.

"Liar," Nimrodi accused. The Dakota bucked hard as it entered a white wall of cloud, and then the peaks appeared again, closer.

"Those first ones are the Atlases," said the pilot as he pointed. "The big one beyond is Jbel Sarhro. It'll feel rough, but it's an easy go." He leaned toward his left-hand window and pointed down. "We just follow the road to Ouarzazate and then again to Zagora. After that it's a straight run over dunes to the border."

"And you will stay low till then?"

"We'll give the Bedouins a fright," said the copilot.

Nimrodi rubbed his hands together. "So where are my provisions?"

"In the left heating vent and behind the right panel in the loo," said the pilot. "Your suppliers looked like Barbary pirates."

"They *are*."

"There's a drill in the navigator's box. And hurry up so we can get some heat going again."

Nimrodi turned to go, then stopped. "By the way," he said. "Can either of you fly a corporate jet?"

The pilot and his partner looked at each other, then back at the colonel. "We can fly anything with wings and an engine," said the South African.

"Good." Nimrodi slapped the doorframe.

"Baba?" the copilot called.

"Yes?"

"*B'atslacha*," he offered in Hebrew. "Good luck."

Nimrodi bugged his eyes in mock surprise. "*Ma? Atah yehudi?* What? You're Jewish?" The pilots laughed as he went out.

Below the folding navigator's table there was a large metal toolbox, and Nimrodi extracted a battery-powered screwdriver from it. He walked back into the cargo compartment, grinned at Benni Baum and pointed up at the ceiling. A pair of boxy aluminum air ducts ran the length of the cabin, and Baum, Eckstein, and Nabbe rose from the bench and pressed their palms against the left carrier. Nimrodi hopped up on the bench, quickly extracting screws and dropping them into his jacket pocket. Then he gently peeled away one side of the duct, reached inside, and removed a long package of burlap closed with twine. He tossed it across the cabin to O'Donovan, who immediately began to tear at it like an orphan who had never experienced Christmas.

By the time the duct was empty and Nimrodi had begun to reset the screws, the cabin floor was strewn with strips of burlap and twine. The men were huddled around four CAR-15 Colt Commandos—the collapsible versions of the M-16 assault rifle—and one mini Uzi with a wire stock, and Schneller, grinning at Nimrodi and shaking his head, held a British Parker-Hale M85 sniper rifle and was obviously unconcerned that jumping with the long-barreled weapon might prove a dangerous undertaking.

The Dakota's engines were still running flat out, and the Atlas winds slapped the undercarriage, so O'Donovan had to yell.

"That's only six, Baba."

"And mags, baby," Binder added as he stuck a thumb up the empty magazine well of one of the CARs.

"Ammunition would also be *très désirable*," said Nabbe.

Nimrodi ignored them, making his way back to the lavatory. He squeezed inside and quickly removed the right fuselage panel with the power tool. Between the ribs, cardboard boxes of 5.56 mm, 9 mm, and 7.62 NATO rounds, both standard and tracer, were stacked up to his waist. Above them, piles of black magazines were laid in like brickwork. And finally, three FN Browning High-Power pistols in Cordura holsters were duct-taped to the wall. Nimrodi motioned to Horse, whose facial color was resembling the olive hue of the cabin, and the little man staggered to him, forming the head of a chain as Nimrodi passed the ammunition.

Had the men been idle passengers, the turbulent motion of the Dakota would have begun to take its toll by now. Had they been sport skydivers, or even regular paratroops on a long jump run, that strange phenomenon called jumper's slumber might have come into play, where the brain realizes that the body is about to perform an extremely unnatural act and suddenly anesthetizes its host, slumping him into a sleep of denial. But they were overburdened with equipment problems, and they welcomed them in an adrenal frenzy.

All of them were wearing military-style jump boots, for you could not quick-march over dunes in a skydiving sneaker. Even Binder had instinctively packed his Vietnam jungle boots. They also wore various types of fatigue trousers: some standard IDF with the markings blotted out, some old-style American jungle cargoes. They removed their footwear, pulled thick rubber bands over their ankles, and bloused the cuffs to deny the cold winds at altitude. They opened their trousers, pushed them down to expose their thermal underwear, and passed around one of Didi's rigger blades, cutting short slices in the waistbands and cuffs of the thermals. The extra layer would be essential during the drop, but once they began to march, the heat would quickly build and choke them. Upon landing, they would now be able to quickly drop their fatigues and shred off the thermals without removing their boots.

Each man was wearing a heavy sweater, some of which had been dyed darker during the last day in Marrakesh, and over those were the dark mountain anoraks in which they had convened in Casablanca. Binder, having loaned his white alpine to Horse, had bought an old U.S. M-52 field jacket from a rack in the *souk*.

They bound their cuffs down to their forearms with electrical tape, then used another length to affix the penlights to the backs of their left wrists and checked the bulbs. They pulled black balaclavas onto their heads, then slipped their goggles over to hang around their necks. Didi and Amir had the lightweight Kroops they always traveled with, while Mustaffa had come up with rubber-coated industrial models for everyone else. Sadeen had drilled small holes in all the lens tops to prevent fogging.

Baum and Eckstein oversaw a weapons preparation session, working their way along the cabin. The CAR-15s were not new, but they were very clean and their actions seemed fine. The men field-stripped them and inspected the firing pins. Out of habit, precaution, or superstition, they took out their cleaning kits and worked on the barrels. Nabbe, who was a world-class pistolero, gladly accepted one of the High-Powers, as did Lapkin. Baum, who was a very mediocre shot with any weapon, took the third. The mini Uzi happened to be Didi's favorite, and he had snatched it up like a possessive toddler.

"Standard night loads," Baum said to Sadeen, who passed it on throughout the cabin.

"What's 'standard' for you guys?" O'Donovan asked Eckstein. It was not a challenge. Both he and Binder appreciated the need for continuity.

"In the thirty-round mags," said Eckstein, "load only twenty-nine." The Israelis were wary of overloading magazine springs. "First two in should be tracer, so you'll know when you're out. Then three regular and one tracer all the way through."

"Makes sense to me," said Binder. The CARs had come with only seven magazines apiece. He would have preferred ten, but he was happy not to have been handed a crossbow.

"How am I going to accurize this thing?" Schneller was looking over the Parker-Hale. It was fitted with a 4>10x Pecar scope, but there was no way to know if it was correctly mounted.

"It has just been used at three hundred meters," Nimrodi called to him. "At that range or closer, you will be all right, my friend."

Schneller raised an eyebrow. What had Baba been doing in Mauritania? Hunting wild boar? No matter. His word was clearly gold.

With their magazines fully loaded, the men stood up and held on to the pitching fuselage as they worked out how they would carry them in their pockets without rattling. Horse, whose fear was undiminished, as he could not participate in these distractions, suddenly decided that the litter of burlap and ammo boxes was unseemly, and he took a steel vomit bucket from beneath a bench, got down on all fours, and began to collect the mess.

Didi came off his bench by the cargo door and straddled the cabin floor. "All right," he called. "You can put one mag in your trouser side pocket. The rest go back in the rucks."

The men sat down and reluctantly parted with their ammunition. Lerner crossed to O'Donovan and stood him up to use as a mannequin. The CAR-15 was equipped with a web sling, which he pulled to its full length and draped over O'Donovan's right shoulder and diagonally across his back, so that the weapon rested horizontally just below his crotch, barrel to the left and away from where the throw-out pilot chute would deploy. He knelt and flipped the American's camel ruck around so that the flap was away from him, helped him step through the shoulder straps, slid the ruck up his legs, opened the flap, rebuckled it around the CAR, then tightened up the rifle sling until the pack was covering his groin and the weapon lay across his pelvis.

Now he opened O'Donovan's parachute bag, lifted out a purple Telesis container, and freed the harness straps. He helped him into the rig, then spun him around, threaded the leg webs through the camel-ruck straps, clipped them, and cinched them up until the detective groaned. As he closed the chest band, he could feel O'Donovan's heart pounding, which was just fine, as only a robot or a psychopath would have reacted indifferently to the procedure.

He held O'Donovan by the shoulders and looked him over.

"I think it's good, Mike," said Didi, for the first time addressing O'Donovan by his Christian name. "Don't you?"

"Feels okay." The American hopped up and down to check the slack in the rig. It was solid, and as all the rucks had been very carefully packed, nothing banged or rattled. "But a quick release would be better." When a military jumper went out with equipment, it was usually in a special bag snapped onto D rings on the harness. After his chute opened, he released the bag, and it would fall to dangle below him on a five-meter rope. This method had added benefits at night because you could hear the bag hit first and know that your landing was imminent.

"Don't like 'em with ram airs," said Didi as he turned O'Donovan and inspected him from the back. "The pendulum screws up maneuverability, especially near the ground when you need it. Spread your legs." O'Donovan obeyed and Didi reached through, pulling on the ruck to see if it might obstruct the main deployment. "Don't try a stand-up landing, but avoid a PLF if you can. Just come in and sit down, like you're sliding into home plate. Better to take off a piece of your arse than bust up your legs or ribs."

Binder reached up from his seat and tugged at Didi's elbow. "Hey, boss. Why don't we just sling the weapons barrel down and under our harnesses?"

Although Didi smiled, it was clear that he considered the jumpmaster's decisions inviolate. "Because I don't know you, mate, so I don't trust you. You get a malfunction at night, you'll be scrambling for the cutaway and wind up hauling on the bloody trigger grip, wondering why the fuck your reserve won't deploy."

Binder raised his hands. "*No más, no más.*"

Didi turned to look at Lapkin and Nimrodi, who were seated back near the cargo door. Both men shot him a thumbs-up. He stepped to the front of the cabin and turned aft, raising his palms. The Dakota had ceased its constant pattern of banks and turns, and having passed over Jbel Sarhro, it was descending more gently toward the lower plateaus of Kem Kem. The men stood and began slinging their weapons as Didi had done to O'Donovan.

Nimrodi and Lapkin worked from the back of the plane, while Didi rigged from the front. Baum and Nabbe were easy, as their High-Powers fit inside their closed rucks. Binder was given the stretcher, which Didi had designed to be no larger than a quartet of poster tubes, and it was added to his ruck flap below his CAR. Schneller was a real challenge, until Nimrodi and Lapkin decided to tape the long Parker-Hale to his left thigh with ripstop, beneath the leg strap and barrel up, with the sling wound around his trunk. They cut a swath from a parachute bag and enshrouded the scope using electrical tape, then urged him to try for a dead man's PLF onto his right leg when he hit.

At last the three riggers stood scratching their chins over Sadeen. They all wished now that they had vetoed his crazy moped idea, for there were too many ways in which the bulky package could kill him. Didi had initially thought to tie the moped frame to two harness points, with a third umbilical of climbing rope from it to the leg straps. Sadeen would cut the joiners and let the bike dangle below him. But now the Australian hesitated. He knew that as Sadeen jumped, the moped's carpet would immediately catch the wind, and he would somersault. It might flip up and smash his chest or his jaw. He could not picture a proper attitude with which Sadeen could exit the aircraft.

"Let's can the whole fucking thing," Didi said bitterly.

"You can't," Lapkin argued in his ear. "It'll throw off the plan, kill everyone's morale."

"It'll kill *him* if we do it," Didi snapped.

"He is correct," said Nimrodi. "We must find another way."

Sadeen looked up at them, having lost a measure of cockiness, awaiting their verdict. "And there is this too," he said, holding up his ruck and the CAR-15.

"Excuse me, gentlemen."

Didi and Amir parted to admit Horse's pale face. The analyst had been listening to the discussion, and since no options seemed to present themselves, he shyly offered a suggestion.

"Sadeen is wearing the big parachute, with the rip cord. No?"

"Yeah," said Didi. "I gave him the Cloud. So?"

"And he will be the first one out. Correct?"

"Yeah? Yeah?" Didi was exasperated by Horse's diffidence.

"Say it out, *Soos*." Baum had waddled over to the group.

Horse pushed his glasses up onto his nose. "Well, why don't you have him jump like the Americans do from helicopters? Rig the backpack and the weapon as you wanted, then the moped over that, then seat him in the doorway with his hand on the rip cord. He can just roll forward, fall straight down, and pull. No?"

No one said anything at all for a moment, then Nimrodi grabbed Horse and kissed him on both cheeks like de Gaulle presenting the Croix de Guerre. Didi slapped Horse on the back and cried, "You brilliant little wanker! I'm gonna buy you a *crate* of Foster's!"

Horse grinned sheepishly, privately recoiling at the nauseating notion of so much beer.

"That's why he gets the big salary," Baum said proudly as he struggled away under the weight of his gear.

The heavy drone of the Dakota's engines changed to a lower thrum, and Nimrodi crouched at a window. For a moment, he saw nothing but the swirl of close cloud, and then the curtain shifted instantly to black as they broke through the ceiling. They had cleared the High Atlas, passed over Zagora and Jbel Tadrart, and were still dropping lower. The vast wastes of Kem Kem and beyond that the Hamada du Guir stretched to the horizon, undisturbed by a single beacon of light. This tract of desert was a coarse quilt of hard plateaus and wadis. The night sky was moonless but full of stars, and their light washed the floor in hues of brown and purple, a sun- and wind-battered flesh lined with jagged black veins. The landscape moved quickly past the wingtip as the pilots flew a modest nap of the earth at two hundred meters.

Nimrodi moved back past the cargo door and donned the jumpmaster's headset. He spoke to the pilots and then caught the attention of the men in the cabin, tapped his watch, raised an index finger, and made a single circling motion with the digit.

One hour to go.

The overhead cabin lights went out and were replaced by the ghostly red glow of mission bulbs, which had the effect of subduing everyone. Benni scanned the cabin. An hour was an eon for men en route to such a venture, too much time to think.

They had spent most of the day paired off, reviewing procedures with their partners, getting to know each other's habits. *I shoot from the shoulder as I move. I will yell "Magazine!" when I'm empty and reloading. If you're shooting prone and I want to pass you close, I'll tap you on the head on the way, so hold your fire.* They were seated in those pairs now, Baum with Eckstein, O'Donovan and Binder across the cabin. Schneller could no longer sit properly with the Parker-Hale strapped to his leg like a splint, so he half reclined on the starboard bench, while Nabbe sat across the way.

Didi and Lapkin worked over Sadeen, who was seated on the floor with his back against the starboard aft fuselage. His legs were spread and his ruck and rifle lay between them. The riggers had inverted two vomit buckets and set them on either side of his legs, then laid the cocooned moped across so it applied no pressure. They cut holes through the rug and tied the frame to his harness, then taped a hook knife into the palm of his left glove. The drop line was a length of 11 mm climbing rope, which Didi now coiled with a packing band.

In a field operation, it would have been the time for Benni, as mission commander, to stand up and speak, issue words of encouragement, God and country and all that. But this brief respite had the effect of allowing his exhaustion to bloom, and the weight of his equipment was doubled by the measure of his doubts. Unlike the other men, he was not visited by the natural apprehension over the trustworthiness of his parachute. If he did not survive the jump, then at least he would not have to face the horror of losing Ruth. But he somehow knew that he *would* survive it, and he mustered some strength with the oath that if he was to die, it would be at his daughter's feet and no less than that.

"Eytan," he said.

"Yes?"

"Tell them to review again with their partners and blacken their faces."

"Right."

"And remind them that anyone who gets lost is to go for the nearest road and dump everything but his passport. No weapons. Bury it all."

"Got it."

"And one more thing."

"What?"

Benni squinted off into an undefined distance. "Thank them for me."

Eckstein looked at him, then turned to Nabbe, and Benni's orders were passed along like a game of "telephone."

The men came up with tins of shoe polish and began to work on each other's facial features. The Israelis were not terribly artistic, while Binder and O'Donovan would have made a chameleon proud. Nabbe crossed the cabin and knelt in front of Schneller. He worked on the big German's forehead for a minute, then motioned for everyone to have a look. He had spelled out the Hebrew word *friar*, slang for "sucker."

Didi showed up in front of Baum. He was wearing his rig, including the ruck with the mini Uzi tucked away, but he moved as easily as if he sported only a track suit.

"Change of plans," he said. "I want Amir to be last out, so he can shepherd anyone who strays." He turned to Eckstein. "You and me'll take Benni out. Think you can do that?"

Eckstein was far from being qualified to AFF a novice, but he had been the man in the middle a number of times and knew how it went. This was not the time to demur. "Talk to me," he said.

"You just take his left side, right hand on his leg strap and left on his upper sleeve. Good grip, don't let go for shit. We'll probably flip over, so just give us a good arch until I get us right. When I pull for him, just track away and open. So far?"

Eckstein nodded. He was wearing his gloves, and he took one off and wiped his palm on his fatigues.

"Now, we won't be in the door for long," Didi added. "But you'll have to float."

Eckstein would have to brace himself *outside* the aircraft until Didi was ready.

"And don't pull him, Eytan. I'll push from the inside." Didi smiled, pinched Eckstein's cheek, and walked away.

Nabbe nudged Eckstein and handed him a tin of brown shoe polish. Eckstein took the flat can and stared at it for a moment, thinking of how easily some men could discard their good sense, defy their own survival instinct. Perhaps it was a mutant gene, the same cerebral fissure that drove lemmings over a cliff. That might be true, but a catalyst was also required, and he had no doubt that here that fuel was love, his and Benni's and O'Donovan's for Ruth, the rest of the men's for Baum, and even the feelings that Binder would deny he felt for his NYPD partner. Only that kind of power could allow them to ignore the probabilities of failure, for in truth this mission was like an impossible billiard shot attempted by a talented amateur. If the ball went in the pocket, it would not be due to skill.

He looked up to find Benni's face turned toward him. They held each other's gaze as Eytan began to smear the polish across his friend's wide features, and then Benni closed his eyes.

Didi went to Nimrodi at the cargo door, took the headset from him, and sat down. He slipped the folded CIA map and a small calculator from his pocket and laid them across his knee. He was wearing an illuminated MA3-30 metric altimeter on his left wrist, and he used the light to aid him as he began to rework the ranges.

"Hullo, mate," he said into the mike. "This is the jumpmaster."

"Hey, you sound like an Aussie," the pilot said brightly.

"Was."

"Late of Johannesburg myself."

"What's the range?" Didi asked.

" 'Bout twenty-two minutes to the border."

"Winds?"

"At sixteen thousand feet we'll have eighteen knots from one sixty-three degrees south-southeast. Beni-Abbès is broadcasting twelve knots below ten thousand feet."

"Meters, if you don't mind."

"Divide by three, multiply by point six, mate."

Didi smiled as he did so. He began to calculate the average forward speed of all the ram-airs, which was about 25 feet or 5.4 meters per second, versus a 10 FPS rate of descent, and taking the split wind speeds and altitudes into account. If they ran with the wind, they would be in the air for twenty-six minutes and cover twenty-three kilometers over ground. Didi had hoped for a north-south wind so they could drop well north of Klump's lair and pass high over it for a quick survey before landing, but the elements were against them.

"Sorry, mate," he said to the pilot. "You're gonna have to go in deep, twenty-three klicks southeast of the target on the wind line."

"No worries," the South African assured in mock-Aussie vernacular.

"I'm gonna drop one man early." Didi peered at the map. "About three kilometers north of Jbel el Akhal. Then the rest of us in one stick."

"All at sixteen thousand?"

"Right."

"You're going to be dizzy," the pilot warned. That altitude was a borderline oxygen jump.

"We'll wake up on the way down," said Didi. "What's the temperature up there?"

"Are you going to scratch this thing if it's freezing?"

"No."

"Then don't ask, *mate*."

Didi grinned and reworked his calculations once more from the beginning.

Rick Nabbe had to pee. He wanted very badly to hold it until he landed, but he knew that he would never make it, and the idea of gliding with a stream of urine frozen to his leg was not appealing. Nimrodi saw him struggling with his ruck and sprang to help him, but the Belgian was still wearing his chute when he squeezed into the lavatory, searched desperately for his penis between the choking leg straps, and finally gasped, "*Mon Dieu!*"

The Dakota was beginning to climb rapidly again as Nabbe struggled back to his seat and rerigged his ruck. Didi listened in his headset and looked up at the men. He drew an imaginary line with one hand across the floor from right to left, then flew over it and up with the other. They were crossing the border. He beckoned Baum and Eckstein, and they struggled up and came to him. They sat near the door as Lapkin got up and shifted toward the cockpit.

Nimrodi was standing in the aft section, holding on to a cargo strap. He patted the top of his head and pointed to his eyes. The men rolled their balaclavas down over their faces, which suddenly gave them all the appearance of masked bank robbers. They pulled their goggles up and adjusted the straps, then pushed them onto their foreheads.

A heavy bell rang twice inside the cabin, and as is always the case in paratroop transports, it was like a Pavlovian signal that set the men's hearts to thumping wildly in their chests. Even as the inevitable approached, the body always prayed to be somehow saved from this madness, but the ringing of the warning klaxon extinguished all hope of reason.

Didi stood up, pointed at his watch, and raised ten fingers. The men nodded and checked their gloves, their fatigue cuffs, the jacket closures near their throats. Their movements were jerky, frenetic; they needed to get on with it. Didi pointed to the penlight on his left wrist and switched it on. The men mimicked him. He was wearing a second one on his right wrist, next to his compass, and he turned it on as well, showing both his lights to the men over outstretched fists. *I'll be the one with two lights.* They nodded again like a squad of deaf-mutes.

He listened in the headphones for a moment, then made a fluttering motion with one hand. He held up ten fingers, then eight more.

Binder turned to O'Donovan and rolled his eyes. "Christ!" he shouted above the straining engines. "Eighteen-knot wind."

O'Donovan quickly estimated their forward glide speed. "Don't forget to turn back into it for the landing," he shouted back.

"Fuckin' A."

Didi lifted his palms twice, and the men struggled to their feet. Lapkin came down the line and herded them to the port side of the cabin, where they huddled close up to each other like frightened cattle. They automatically performed an equipment check, searching each other's packs for loose closure pins, pilot chutes half out of pockets, a wayward buckle that could snag a suspension line.

Lapkin checked each man over again, running his fingers across their rigs as he reminded them to deploy their chutes five seconds after the exit, no matter their body position. As he approved each man, he slapped him on the head. Goggles came down and were pulled tight once more. They were breathing heavily now. The sudden rise to altitude had bathed the cabin in a steel chill. Sweat ran down their rib cages.

Didi slipped off the headset and handed it to Nimrodi, who would be staying with the airplane. He pulled his black hood over his face, set his goggles, and checked his altimeter. He cocked his head at Nimrodi, and together they removed the cargo door.

Horse nearly screamed when the thunder roared into the plane. He backed up on the starboard bench and wrapped his fingers around the seat in a death grip, but he could have yelled his head off and no one would have heard him. The blast of black wind howled through the door, carrying the unfettered engine roar with it. The vomit bucket toppled over, and the cardboard litter went whipping around the cabin like the pranks of a poltergeist. "No! Don't do it!" he wanted to yell as he saw Didi drop to his knees and stick his head right out the open hatch like some mad gremlin. The jumpmaster stayed there for a moment, looking down into the void, and as the wind tried to suck him out, he stuck one hand back in the cabin and held it like a blade, signaling to Nimrodi.

"Come left," Nimrodi shouted into the headset.

The Dakota banked gently, though the noise level seemed to rise. Didi signaled again.

"Straight and level," Nimrodi yelled.

The pilots complied.

The warning beacon by the doorframe glowed red. Didi came back in and duck-walked to Sadeen, who crabbed forward on his hands and heels beneath his ridiculous burden as Nimrodi and Lerner lifted the tires of the encased moped. The contraption was not going to fit straight on through, so Didi kept Sadeen at an angle. The sapper's boots cleared the forward corner of the hatch, where the slipstream immediately snatched at them, bending his legs and flapping them like a rag doll. Nimrodi, who had donned the team's spare chute, for there was every chance that he could be dragged out now, was holding Sadeen's harness and leaning back with everything he had. Didi took Sadeen's right hand and placed it tightly around the rip cord handle as he bent his mouth to the engineer's ear and yelled something. The sapper nodded vigorously. The red lamp went out, the green jump light blazed, and then he was gone.

Didi dived to his knees again and looked down. The rest of the men held their breaths, waiting for the verdict. Lerner snapped back inside and shot them a thumbs-up.

They had three minutes now. All the time in the world. He looked at his watch, then motioned Eckstein to come to him.

Eckstein skirted the howling doorway in a wide berth, edging up carefully to the rear frame as Nimrodi gripped his harness. He did not look down but focused back into the cabin as the wind hammered his chest, threatening alternately to knock him back inside or drag him out.

Didi went for Baum, nudging the colonel's bulk so his rump faced Eckstein and his feet were positioned near the doorstep, one before the other like a surfer. He placed both of Baum's hands around the forward frame, one atop the other, while he gripped him by the leg strap and checked to see that Eckstein was doing the same. He looked up at Eckstein and lifted his jaw twice.

Very, very carefully now, Eckstein removed his left hand from the doorframe and quickly switched it to the overhead sill, gripping hard with his fingers inside. He edged past Benni's rump, catching a glimpse of the Dakota's huge horizontal stabilizer, which would surely impale them all. He set his boot heels to the doorstep and backed out a bit, where the wind immediately tried to take him away. But nothing could make him let go of Baum, and his other fingers clamped the sill with the power of a maniac on angel dust. He could feel his ponytail wagging madly from the back of his woolen hood, and he looked down to see Benni's black head and goggles pointed forward like those of a crazed motorcyclist. As he stole one glance at the fuselage gleaming under the starlight and the big prop spinning like a demonic blade, he felt his legs begin to quake uncontrollably in the cold. And then something very strange happened. He had the unspeakable urge to laugh. No sound emerged, and the only result was a death's-head grin as his cheeks were smeared back over his face, but he felt it rise in his chest and wondered what it meant.

He heard someone calling to him and looked down. Didi's face hovered inside the door above Baum's head, mouthing, *"Moochan?"*—"Ready?"—in Hebrew. For much as in lovemaking, in which you usually orgasm in your native tongue, you parachute in the language of instruction.

Eckstein nodded vigorously.

"Echad!" Didi began the count, and the trio leaned out.

"Shtayim!" he shouted, and they leaned back inside.

Whatever he yelled next was lost as he launched them from the door.

Ari Schneller did not hesitate. Even with the restraining bulk of the Parker-Hale, he immediately dove headfirst after the clump of flailing arms and legs. Then Nabbe, Binder, O'Donovan, and Lapkin raced after him like summer swimmers arcing into a warm pond, and Nimrodi dropped into the jumpmaster's posture, sticking his head out and watching for the chutes until the Dakota banked away.

Baba stood back up, brushed off his hands, and smiled at Horse, who was still collapsed in shock on the bench. Nimrodi pointed down at the discarded cargo door in the aft section.

"Come, my friend!" he yelled. "Give me a hand."

Horse looked at the door, then at the strangely empty cabin, then up at the black mouth of the hatch, still raging with the wind. He raised a quaking finger to request just a short break, then crawled toward the lavatory, while Nimrodi laughed. . . .

There are parachutists who claim that the act is addictive not because of its thrilling flirtation with death but in fact for quite the opposite reason, that it fulfills a visceral desire for birth in reverse, a return to the womb. A newborn is forced from a weightless world of gentle sensations and muted sounds into a cacophony of sensory assaults that will surround him for the rest of his natural life. Every jump plane is a mirror of that confusing world in microcosm, a crowded, horrendously noisy tube of jostling bodies and multiplied fear, until the jumper dives through a narrow portal and into sudden silence, an unfettered weightlessness in endless space, no need to speak or to be heard, a few minutes of rushing wind and the whispering flutter of fabric.

Eckstein was utterly disoriented by the night, for he could discern no up or down. And he did not care. The relief was upon him, for he had passed into another dimension, and there was only the rush of air and the flapping of cloth, both muted by his woolen falcon's hood. He suspected that he was on his back, for he had seen the black underbelly of the Dakota pass over his head and disappear between his feet, but he focused only on his hands and the leg strap and sleeve bunched in his gloved fingers. The rest was up to Didi.

The octopus of arms and legs suddenly flipped over, and Eckstein arched harder, knowing he was face to earth now as his head was lifted back on the air column. He released Benni's sleeve and extended his left hand, still keeping a grip with his right, and he marveled to see Baum stretch his arms in a Superman pose exactly as he had been instructed. He looked for Didi, then saw the jumpmaster's right-hand penlight across Baum's shoulders as it lifted briefly. The red light streamed as Lerner brought it in to pull Baum's rip cord, there was a tearing sound, and Baum was yanked from his hands. Eckstein instantly placed his palms flat along his sides and tracked away as he felt for his pilot chute knob and hoped it would emerge from its pocket.

Schneller's sniper rifle acted as a stubborn impediment to his grace. He could not arch properly and slowly rolled onto his left side, which was just fine with him as he drew out his pilot chute and watched it race up into the stars, which blurred into sharp stripes of light as his main blossomed hard and beautifully.

Nabbe was on his back. The air had caught the ruck between his legs and rolled him over his head. He made one attempt to flip, but the count was up and he deployed. He saw the pilot chute launch between his legs and he knew what was coming, gritting his teeth as he was spun head over heels and lynched by the opening shock. He shook his addled head and looked up, expecting to see shredded nylon. But it was all there, and he muttered, "*Elohim*, it's cold," as he reached for the web toggles.

Binder arched perfectly, held it as he counted, drew his left hand in to his forehead for balance, reached down with his right, and pulled. The explosion of fabric sounded right, felt good, and he immediately reached up for the toggles and yanked on them until the slider came down the lines and he whispered, "Yessss."

O'Donovan was spinning like a top. His position had felt all right, but without a horizon, he had not realized that he was in a rapid flat turn to the right. His shroud lines were twisted together like a dishrag. He could not raise his head, assumed a full malfunction, and was just putting both hands to the cutaway when his body suddenly stopped and bounced. He looked up. It was all there.

Lapkin clucked his tongue impatiently. He was hanging beneath his chute at half brakes, trying to count his flock. It was very difficult to pick them out, but as a bank of thin cloud drove across the landscape far below, the square flat mushrooms were thrown briefly into silhouette. They were all over the sky. Someone to the right was making a slow full turn, clearly unable to find his comrades. Another man was heading off due west.

Three hundred meters forward and below, Didi must have realized the confusion, for beneath the small black shape of his canopy, a flashing red X blinked as he crossed his wrists vigorously behind his head. He continued this for a full minute, and gradually, very gradually, the men spotted him and formed up in a ragged staircase of canopies.

"Maybe," Lapkin whispered in his native Canadian. "Just maybe." And he released his brakes and flew.

Benni could not believe the cold. With his thick Germanic bulk, it was something that rarely bothered him, but after a few minutes of descent his entire body was quaking. The harness was terribly uncomfortable. His legs were numb, and the wind at his back made his thermal underwear completely ineffectual. For all the layers, his sweater, and his jacket, he might just as well have been wearing cotton pajamas, and he imagined that a slim man such as Eckstein might shatter like an ice statuette when he landed. But Benni's hands and arms were working, and he followed Didi's every move like a faithful dog after its master.

The wind died at a thousand meters. Completely. One minute it was driving all of them like an express train, the dunes below moving quickly between their boots, and the next minute they decelerated to only the speed of their chutes, their sliders flapping languidly above their heads.

There was nothing to be done about it. Didi knew that at least a stingy breeze survived, and he picked out a flat trough of ground between two high dunes, passed it at two hundred meters, and then gently turned back for it, twisting his head to see that his flock followed.

He knew that the men were stunned by the cold of the endless descent, sapped of the energy to control their landings properly. He gathered all his own strength, sped in hot, and flared half a meter above the ground, uncrossed his ankles, and stood up. The chute tried to billow, but he was already dropping his harness as he turned.

They came in with all the grace of crash dummies, someone racing past him to smash into a dune, others falling short and dropping out of sight. Baum flared too high and dropped straight down like a rock, but his instincts returned and he managed a parachute-landing fall in the sand. Eckstein made a good show of it on the left, plowing up a plume of sand with one foot as his canopy flapped like the wings of a dodo and he slid into a cloud of dust. Schneller's rifle pitched him forward onto his face, as Didi winced. The others touched down in the darkness beyond his vision, except for Lapkin, who made a wild hook turn just above and then raced in to flare and stand up just meters to Didi's right.

Astounded by their survival and ecstatic to be grounded again, the men struggled up and hobbled around on their frozen legs, pulling their chutes down, doffing their harnesses, bundling them up and kicking sand over them, until they were buried and briefly mourned.

Didi waved his penlights, and the men began to gather with their rucks and weapons. Baum limped forward first, rubbing his thigh but moving quickly.

"Do we have a count?" he whispered as he neared.

"Not yet," Didi replied in kind. "Give it a minute."

Schneller came out of the shadows, his ruck already slung, tearing the canvas from his rifle scope. Baum peered up at him. The German's face had encountered a rock. His goggles were gone, and two streams of blood ran from the bridge of his nose down over his cheeks like a witch doctor's tattoo.

"It's all right." He grinned at Benni. "It's warm."

Eckstein appeared carrying his ruck, his CAR-15 already slung from his neck and a magazine in the well.

Nabbe, who had overshot the DZ, came walking back, covered in sand from head to foot and picking cactus thorns from his backside. Binder and O'Donovan showed up together on the run.

The ground temperature was as balmy as an autumn eve in Vermont, but they were all still shivering from the torturous ride. Benni took over now.

"Get the thermals off," he whispered. He saw the hesitation in Nabbe's face. "Do it," he ordered. "Then put your web belts on and finish one canteen per pair. We don't want any sloshing." No one balked. They were dehydrated from the adrenaline and the extreme cold. Benni switched his penlight off, and everyone followed suit. "Roll your caps up. Lose the goggles. Men with the walkie-talkies, stick the earpieces in and fix them with a Band-Aid. Set your weapons and magazines up."

Benni bent to his own ruck, a signal that he was through for the moment. After six long minutes, O'Donovan and Eckstein were standing up, then moving to help the others.

"Mike and Eytan," Baum whispered from the ground, where he was taping a walkie-talkie to his left ruck strap. "Go up to that high dune and get a fix."

The two men jogged away with their weapons and compasses. They struggled up the promontory on the northern rim of the DZ, nearly crawling in the loose sand near the twenty-meter summit. Falling to their knees, they looked over the top.

Below them the dune sea sloped down and away into a wide gray bowl of undefined shadow. Beyond that to the northwest, the light of the stars picked out the lower ridges of a long range of mountains. A slim black line followed the curves of the foot—the Ben Zireg–Taghit road. Somewhere between their position and that road, Martina's camp lay in the folds of the Sahara.

Eckstein flipped open his compass. O'Donovan pulled a small pair of rubber-coated binoculars from his pocket.

The American scanned to the northwest. He picked out a small cluster of buildings and some meager lights just beyond a huge mound of sand. The Grande Dune. And the village was the only evidence of humankind on the horizon.

He lowered his glasses and pointed. "That *has* to be Taghit," he whispered. "But if we're on our mark, it should be over *there*," and he swung his arm due west.

"I know it," Eckstein said.

O'Donovan looked at him. They scrambled backward and hurtled down the slope. . . .

The men were nearly ready. They were crouched around Baum like Boy Scouts at a campfire, listening to his admonitions as they tightened ruck straps and adjusted weapon slings.

"Okay," said Baum. "Lock and load."

The pings of bolts and charging handles sounded like a car crash in the night, but it had to be done.

Eckstein and O'Donovan appeared on the run. Benni looked up at them.

"We're short by three kilometers," Eckstein panted.

"Five from the target," said O'Donovan.

Benni rose to his feet. He raised his wrist and peered at the luminous face of his watch.

Midnight.

Five kilometers.

Over dunes.

Without a word, he burst through the huddle and began to run north. The men raced after him across the sand.

Chapter 24: Skorpion

Ruth was awakened by the sudden burst of silence.

For five days and nights, the engine of the gasoline generator had idled incessantly in the distance, at first the constant coughing of the cylinders grating on her terribly, compounding her inability to find comfort or rest. Then she had begun to accept the machine, grateful for the energy it supplied to the only light in her prison. And finally its hum pervaded her being, a pulse in the background assuring her that she was still alive, like the sound of her own breath.

She had not been able to sleep at all until after her "discussion" with Martina. Prior to that she had retreated to the bed for warmth only, the blanket over her head to shield her from the harsh electric light, and she accomplished nothing but a constant squirm, as her life did not flash before her eyes. It crawled.

Yet after the wounding of her face, the adrenaline surge of their encounter, and three hours of frantic searching, during which she failed to devise a single practical weapon or escape tool, she finally collapsed. She slept throughout that afternoon, her nostrils briefly alerting her to an open can of cold soup and three loaves of pita that were set inside the door. She crawled to the meal and finished it with the groggy indifference of necessity, then returned to her slumber.

She sat up with a gasp in the utter stillness, rubbing her eyes roughly as she feared for a terrible moment that they had poisoned her into blindness. The generator had died and with it the light. The chamber was almost completely black, except for a gray cone of starlight that reflected off the sand above, into her air vent, around the aluminum shaft, and down to the floor, where the shadows of the grating drew the soft lines of a cage.

She slid her back up against the wall and hugged the blanket over her chest. For a moment, the tomblike silence gave her hope, an ironic wish that she had been abandoned, that for some reason Martina and her HOGs had fled. But slowly other sounds began to come to her, echoing softly from beyond the door, from somewhere in the warren of trailers. Boot steps thudded dully back and forth. The voices of men called urgently to each other. Her ears were open and receptive as a hound's now, and she discerned the ring of metallic slings, the dull clicks of catches and springs, palms slapping against pressed steel, and the heavy ramming of bolt carriers and breeches.

She had heard those things before. They were the sounds of death.

She threw off the covers and jumped up from the bed, the freezing floor stinging her bare feet as she thrust her hands into the darkness and found the door. She pressed her ear against it, but quickly turned and stared up at the air vent.

The engine was starting again. She waited, but the bulb did not come on. She stepped slowly into the cone of watery light and squinted up into the vent.

It was not the same sound as the generator. It was different, a heavy whine beginning slowly, then rising in pitch as if someone were squeezing it. She searched her memory for a match. It might have been the engines of the jet, but the thumping oscillation that accompanied it now denied that option.

Then she remembered. Martina had said *Hubschrauber.* Helicopter.

She waited for a moment, expecting to hear the whopping of the distant rotor blades blur into a roar, then recede as the machine lifted away. Yet nothing changed. The turbine continued to spin at a constant rhythm as if just warming up. Waiting.

Ruth began to pace in a tight semicircle inside the weak conus of light. Martina's men preparing their weapons? A helicopter standing by? They were the signs of a coming battle, perhaps an assault on the prisoner exchange, or her removal to some other location.

Yet Martina still had to deal with Ruth's father if she did not want him to harm her mother. Did she plan to go to him, dragging Ruth along to a rendezvous? Was *he* on the way *here*?

Ruth stopped suddenly and stared down at the skin of her legs, a shivering pale blue in the gloom of her cell, and her fingers spread wide like the claws of an alarmed cat as it hit her. Martina led a team of sacrificial fanatics. There was no fear in fundamentalists and no honor among terrorists. As soon as she had her mother safely at her side, she would turn them loose to kill Ruth, her father, and anyone else who was with him.

Michael.

"No!" she yelled involuntarily, and then quickly covered her mouth. She stuck her fingers into her matted hair and squeezed her eyes shut. As long as she stayed in this miserable hole, she was serving Martina's interests. She was a pawn. She was bait. Her imprisonment shackled her father's hands, making it impossible for him to secure the prisoner exchange. Her existence threatened that of some poor Israeli prisoner of war. And worse than that, every moment that she stayed here brought her own father closer to his end, and hers would surely follow.

Rubbing her arms, she suppressed the urge to scream like an ensnared wolverine. She had to try again. Ruth had no illusions about surviving in the desert night for very long, but if she could just get away, even for a short while, she could hurl Martina's plans into turmoil.

She squinted at the door. She had spent an hour in the morning trying to pry off its frame, work its hinge pins out, which only resulted in curses and broken, bloody fingernails. But she had not tried to *ram* it.

She stepped up on the bed and bounded quickly to the rear wall, bending into a sprinter's stance, ready to charge. Then she dropped her head, her hair hanging as she swallowed a wretched sigh. The door was heavy aluminum. It was not going to splinter like hollow wood. She might dent it superficially, but only after nearly breaking her shoulder.

She snapped her chin up, swept the hair from her face, and stared at the air vent again. A metal grate, like a section of chain-link fence, was sandwiched between the roof and the bottom of the wide tube. She had wanted to saw at the links, yet her quest for a tool, anything with a rough edge, had proved fruitless. But she had not *pulled* on it.

She jumped down off the bed, reached beneath the frame, and dragged it to the edge of the ray of light. Then she hopped up onto the foot of the mattress, turned, pushed the sleeves of the woolen sweater up over her elbows, crouched like a competition swimmer, and jumped.

The links rang as she hooked her fingers through them. A metal joint caught her flesh, and she bit down on her lip, but she held on. Her bare legs swinging above the floor, she looked up into the vent. The grate flexed as she swung, and she quickly switched her grip, bringing her hands closer together at its center. A trickle of blood ran down her right palm; she ignored it.

She began to swing now in earnest, feet apart, back and forth until she had a good arc going. Then she arched hard on the backswing, held her breath, sped forward, and grunted hard as she rolled her hip sockets and jammed her feet to the ceiling on both sides of the grate.

She froze there for a moment, stunned that she had managed it, stuck to the ceiling like a bat in a cave. Her legs were pressing outside her elbows, and she shifted her feet wider for better leverage. Then she pulled.

Nothing significant happened. The grate bent a bit, and she heard the whisper of loosened sand, but that was all. She let her head flop back while she breathed, her back muscles straining. She had pulled only with her arms.

"Your *legs*, you idiot," she whispered, and she bent her head into her chest, focused every ounce of strength into her thighs, and willed herself to stand erect.

She came to her senses on the floor. She had plunged straight down onto her back, the air knocked from her lungs. She gasped in the first breath as she felt the pain at the back of her skull, then realized with a shock of joy that the grate was lying on her chest, her fingers still locked around the links.

The grate was, in fact, a piece of chain-link fence, a section cut just wider than the mouth of the vent. It had been placed over the ceiling hole, the aluminum vent tube on top of that, and strips of burlap laid around the joint before the earth was shoveled in. Ruth had completely bent the grate, pulling it through the ceiling. But its edges had levered the vent upward, leaving a gap the height of a head.

She pulled herself painfully to her elbows and looked up. At first only a light drizzle of sand hissed from the edges of the hole, bouncing onto her sweater like sprinkled sugar. And then it happened.

The roof of the trailer was buried beneath two meters of the Sahara, half a metric ton of sand, and it plunged for the opening, a sudden avalanche of liberated grit. It sprayed from the hole like a black torrent from a fire hose, and Ruth took a faceful of it before she slapped at it with her hands and rolled away.

She scrambled into a corner near the door, spitting ground rock from her mouth and shaking her head violently to dislodge it from her eyes and ears. It was in her throat, and she bent over and retched, the reflex bringing tears that she smeared away with her palms.

Even in the pitch dark of her cell she knew what was happening. The light was completely gone, but she could hear it well enough, a roar like a ton of grain gushing from a kibbutznik's silo. It was not like an hourglass. It was like a river rushing through the open window of a submerged car.

She waited for two full minutes, crouched and utterly still, hoping that the current would run itself out. Then, for a split second, it slowed, and a brief stab of gray light revealed an enormous pile already nearing the ceiling. Then it all went black as it began anew.

Ruth was no longer cold; sweat ran freely down her ribs. Her pulse was bursting in her throat, and her breath was labored. She tried to tell herself that there was plenty of air, that soon it would stop. Just like with a submerged car, the fluid would reach a certain level and then pressurize itself, leaving a breathable bubble.

But no! this was not water, and the chamber was not sealed. It was open at the top, and the sand would keep coming until it entombed her. Or she stopped it. Or fought *through* it.

She closed her eyes and dived at the mound, scrambling up as the torrent pounded her face and hair, gasping as she tore at the peak with her cupped hands and the spray pummeled her, mocking her feeble efforts.

She should have allowed the pile to find its own form, to peak until it pierced the ceiling hole, for it would eventually have corked itself. But the panic was on her now and she slapped at the sand and pulled as she wept freely, the tears masking her face in streams of silt.

She backed out of the mound, gasping for air, her legs crumpling under her as she knelt in the cool pile that had already smothered the entire floor. She rose and waded through it to the door, pounding on it with both fists as she cried, then slumping against the aluminum, her trembling cheek pressed up to the metal.

"*Abba*," she groaned. "Oh, *Abba*."

She turned her back to the door and leaned there for a moment, catching her breath, her very last breath. She was going to die. Oh, yes. That was clear. That was what God had in mind for her. By either Martina's hand or his own.

She preferred Martina's hand.

She charged the mountain again. It was so huge now that she sank into it up to her hips. She fought her way up the slope and punched the cone away, cursing and screaming at it as she swept it to the side and it instantly grew again. She crawled up farther and bent her head as it assaulted her, snatching open the neck of her sweater and molesting the flesh of her chest with pummeling fists of broken rock, flooding over her hair and mashing it to her neck, while the exposed tips of her ears were bent down and the skin where they joined her skull started to tear. It pounded her with the power of a waterfall in hell, hammering at her burning biceps, vacuuming the last air from her lungs. And then her shoulders froze in spasmodic exhaustion, her flailing arms slowed, she could not pull her legs from the monster's grip. And finally she collapsed, her forehead in the crook of her elbow.

The sand enshrouded her, like blizzard snow over a fallen deer.

It stopped. As quickly as it had begun. One final torrent, a following trickle, and then nothing. Not one grain. Silence.

Ruth tried to raise one arm. It came free and her fingers scratched the air. Her nose was completely closed off, but her mouth was open to a small hollow, her upper teeth embedded in the jagged powder. Her lungs burned with the pain of oxygen starvation. She tried to raise herself on one hand, but it just plunged in up to the elbow. Then she pulled it out once more, laid the whole arm flat, and rolled with everything she had.

She lay on her back, her nose just inches from the ceiling hole, and she opened her mouth and took in great gasps of the cool air swirling in through the vent. She coughed in agony, and a mist of grit sprayed out over her swollen tongue.

She slowly lifted her hands to the lip of the hatch, aware as she gripped it that her fingers were caked with blood and earth. She pulled with her trembling arms and sat up into the opening, her hair streaming sand, like some mythical she-monster rising from a lava pool, and she was inside the vent.

She squinted up dizzily at the conical cap. If she could just get her feet out and up onto the edge of the hatch, she could probably straighten herself and push the cover off. She sat for a moment, quieting her heart, gathering strength.

Then she realized that the vent tube was sitting flush to the roof. She reached and pushed the aluminum. The entire thing toppled away from her and clanged, leaving her to stare dumbly into its fallen mouth.

She came to her senses. She was out. She had to move. *Right now.* She put her palms to the roof and pushed to free her legs. But the effort was unnecessary, as she suddenly felt her hair clamped in a hand, and she screamed as she was lifted free in one mighty pull.

She staggered backward, but a large palm held her spine erect. She squinted into a darkness absolute, yet gradually she discerned the shapes of human forms.

She was surrounded by Martina's HOGs. Their silhouettes showed the bulky shapes of combat webbing strapped to their bodies, black kaffiyehs on their heads, and weapons in their hands. Their smiles offered the only available light.

Martina stepped in front of her face.

"Welcome to the party," she said. "I was just coming to get you."

Sadeen had broken three of his ribs.

It was foolish and unnecessary and he could have avoided it, but almost immediately after his big XL Cloud deployed successfully, he had fallen prey to superstitions such as rarely distracted his engineer's brain. The dark-blue canopy fluttered above him, and the Dakota's engines faded quickly into the limitless ink, and he was alone. It was so dark and so cold that he felt like an astronaut expelled from a space shuttle, and he reached down from the toggles and pulled the woolen chin of his balaclava over his mouth.

Didi had scavenged a triangular altimeter pillow from one of the other rigs and mounted it on Sadeen's chest strap, taping a lensatic compass to it with ripstop. The sapper looked down at the luminous face and made a slow right turn until he was heading at 343 degrees north-northwest.

Amazingly, the moped was still there, laid across his legs like a giant half loaf of pita. Its weight and the force exerted by his forward glide pressed it against his ruck, forcing the pack between his legs so that they were splayed like a wishbone, the CAR-15 chafing his pelvis. Now was the time to reach down and quickly cut through the taut loops that held the bike to his harness, letting it fall to the end of the climbing rope so he could glide comfortably. But he had the vivid premonition that if he did so, he would lose the contraption. Or, if it remained with him, he would not be able to control his landing and it might smash against a rock. All for nothing. Why screw up a good thing? he asked himself.

A rushing layer of gray cloud moved below him, and he could not yet discern ground features, yet he was unconcerned. Didi had told him to just maintain his heading. By the time he crossed the area of Klump's camp, he would be able to clearly see Taghit and the road to Ben Zireg. Given his early exit, he would merely have to land in the flats on the east side of the road, set up the bike, and drive south.

Lapkin had given him his altimeter. At three thousand meters, his lungs ached and his body felt like a lump of frozen fish carcass. The shadowed ripples of dunes began to show themselves below, and as he descended, his speed became apparent as they moved more quickly past his splayed boots. Then the temperature rose perceptibly, almost like the thermocline as a diver rises into warmer waters, and he wriggled to free his frozen blood.

At one thousand meters, he was quite sure that he passed over Klump's camp and grateful that Didi had split his slider, for the small square sail above his head would otherwise have been flapping up a racket in this wind. The black line of the road was very clear now, and he turned due north to avoid crossing it.

The dunes no longer looked so soft and creamy as he neared them. They all leaned with the prevailing Sahara winds, but their crests were blown into jagged tufts like the eyebrows of old Russian men, and the black steel wool of prickly brush poked up from denuded troughs. As he began to speed toward the ground, he wished that he had released the moped, and while regretting that lack of decision, he forgot to turn back into the wind for his landing.

He flared instinctively at his usual altitude, which was also a mistake, for the added weight of his gear muddled the response of the chute and he came in impossibly fast. The moped smacked into a rill of sand and his body flipped over it, his face braking the forward roll as his forehead impacted with the ground. He actually heard the crack of bone from inside his body as it rippled up from his left side into his head.

He could not move, for he was still roped tightly to the bike, his legs splayed in the air and his chest arched into the sand. He felt the chute billowing out in front, jerking at his harness, and the pain came in a nauseating wave.

He was afraid to raise his left arm and puncture a lung, so he slowly drew it into his body, burrowed his right hand under his neck and across, felt for the hook knife, and tore it from his left palm. Then he began to cut at every line and web strap he could find.

It took a full five minutes until he was finally standing, bathed in a chill, slimy sweat, the pain in his left side clawing at him with every breath. The chute had snagged on a large clump of black sage, and he just watched it undulate like a beached jellyfish, knowing that he should bury it. The Autobecane lay on its side upon the open slab of shredded carpet. He tore off his hood and his goggles, which had left a deepening bruise around his eyes, like a raccoon's mask, and staggered out of the ruck.

He looked at his watch. It was 0026, nearly half-past midnight. From somewhere deep inside he found anger and summoned it, for it was the only drug he had to fight the agony. He freed his weapon, shortened the sling, draped it over his neck, and got a magazine into it. Then he tried very hard not to yell as he bent down and righted the moped.

He straightened out the handlebars, cursing them for doing this damage to him, and he did not bother to try to rig the dual headlights, not yet, as he slung his ruck over the brake handle and began to push.

He was in a slight depression, whose edges rose enough that he could see nothing beyond. He stopped and leaned the Autobecane against his thigh as he panicked momentarily, dug into his pocket, found the compass, discovered that he was headed almost due west, and continued. The tires sank into the sand, and he had to lift the handlebars to make progress, a strain that caused him to breathe even harder, which pressed the soft tissue of his left lung against a very sharp splinter of rib.

He was panting, nearly swooning, when he crested the bowl, but the panorama gave him a thrill of renewal. The mountain range was very close, its starlit ridges running north and south, rising away from him into blackness. The empty road lay there, not even a hundred meters down a shallow slope of hard-packed sand.

With a grunt, he pushed the moped forward, and much to his relief it rolled well now, the tires hardly sinking in this stretch of slope that had recently seen a brief winter shower. Halfway down the grade, it picked up so much speed that he decided to mount it, trying hard to keep his chest erect as he did so, biting his lip as he flipped the ignition switch and engaged the clutch.

Nothing happened. The thing did not even turn over. Not a single cough.

He stuck out his heels and skidded to a stop, reaching down to pump the primer as he exhaled as much air as possible. Then he pushed off again, gathered speed, bounced over the shoulder, and managed to hold it as he turned south on the macadam, released the clutch again, twisted the throttle.

Nothing.

It was finished. There was no way he could pedal it into ignition.

He cursed in a stream of Spanish hisses as he braked and stopped in the middle of the road. He looked at his watch. In twenty minutes, the entire mission would depend on the appearance of two headlights he would fail to deliver. Schneller was right. It was a ridiculous idea. His own Technion University egotistical idiocy had doomed them all.

Then he noticed something in the road. It was his own shadow, the silhouette of his CAR, the curls of his hair, growing sharper, stretching out before him.

He jumped off the moped and threw it to the road, kicking the tire so it spun as he moved into the dead center of the macadam, knelt there, laid his weapon down, and smothered it with his body, spread-eagled and in genuine, undramatized pain. He heard the vehicle approach, felt the glare of its lights, then the steady throb through the road as it stopped. A door creaked. A pair of soft-soled shoes whispered up to him. He did not budge until the hand touched his shoulder, and then he rolled and sat up like a corpse in a horror film, grabbing the sleeve of a stunned Algerian driver as he set the barrel of the CAR into the base of the man's throat.

Sadeen knew that the *lingua franca* here was French. But he did not have French. All he had was a smile.

"*Buenas noches, amigo*," he said.

To an infantryman, sand and snow are much the same, a nightmare of impediment to any reasonable progress. You may be in quite a hurry, even commence your march with a self-deceptive sprint, yet before too long the fingers that grip your boots will set your legs on fire and turn your muscles into quivering blubber. On a snow-cursed landscape, there is a slight advantage, because exertion raises your body temperature so that, as long as you move, freezing to death is a delayed danger. But in the desert, your only solace becomes the hope that you will soon either faint or be killed in action.

Benni and his men no longer ran. They slogged. Their numbing glide of not an hour before had become a pleasant memory, their reluctance to shed their thermal underwear a joke. Their fatigues were stained with black amoebas of sweat, their gloveless fingers slippery on trigger grips; their polish-smeared faces shone like oil slicks in a third world seaport, and their breaths streamed behind their heads like the contrails of meandering jets. Each of them had done this before, many times. Yet that did not stop them from wishing they were naked now, barefoot, wearing their gear above loincloths like Amazonian spearmen.

The desert sky was crowded with stars, and the purple-gray dunes and troughs were well defined, though maddeningly featureless in their repetitiveness. But the men were not in danger of wandering off course, for with their compasses they were on the mark. In addition to that, and of no comfort in the least, the heavy whine of an aircraft turbine reached out to them like a siren's summons from the target's vector.

But they were still well short, and Benni knew it. Eckstein was keeping count. Every soldier knows the measure of his stride, and Eckstein's was sixty full paces to every hundred meters. Yet in this sucking Sahara they were stumbling in baby steps, and it seemed ages between his raising of fingers to mark each kilometer.

They had split off into pairs now, maintaining contact via panted whispers into their walkie-talkies. That was as planned, but their original concept to encircle Klump's camp from the western, southern, and eastern flanks had to be abandoned. They were approaching from the southeast, and there wasn't time.

Benni had ordered Schneller and Nabbe into a classic Israeli infantry "banana." They would swing out to the right, climb the eastern flank of Martina's "bowl," and set up like a light machine gun team, their marksmanship with the sniper rifle and the High-Power hopefully compensating for the lack of a MAG. Didi and Amir would use the shadows of the camouflaged jet to infiltrate close into the southeastern quadrant, while O'Donovan and Binder mounted the berm fifty meters farther west along the southern boundary. Baum and Eckstein would approach directly opposite the semicircle of sunken trailers.

If there were antipersonnel mines, the first detonation would prove it. If Klump had enough manpower to lay out ambushes, a gunshot would be evidence enough. Either way, they no longer had the luxury of probing, and the agreed-upon response was simply to charge.

Benni fell to his hands and knees near the top of a dune. He was exhausted beyond imagination, yes, but a heavy smoker who could still play a full intramural soccer match was not about to be taken out of the World Cup of his life. He had dropped as a result of instinct, and his right elbow poked into the sand as he kept his High-Power out of it. Eckstein came up and knelt to his left, the sweat from beneath his rolled balaclava running off the end of his ponytail, onto his ruck.

They both squinted forward, over perhaps another quarter-kilometer of dunes, beyond which lay a straight ridge that appeared to have been formed by some sort of plow. Between that and the next row of dune crests lay a horizontal oval of black, like the surface of a large pond of oil into which they could not see. The distant horizon was feathered with the dark ridges of receding mountains and the peak of Jbel Es-Seba.

Eckstein, panting like a dehydrated retriever, nudged Benni and pointed to the right. At the southeastern curve of the dark bowl, just beyond a dune shaped like a rump, the tip of a steel tail gleamed in spite of its camouflage net. The two men looked at each other. Their heart rates rose even higher.

Baum was reaching to key the mike button of his walkie-talkie, when he and Eckstein both snapped their heads to the left. The southern berm of the camp stretched away into the western darkness, but its narrow tail there was suddenly aglow with the bouncing reflections of an approaching vehicle.

"*Sadeen*," Eytan whispered, and to Benni it sounded like a Talmudic blessing. Then he looked at the remaining tract of desert, and it became a cabalic curse. He jabbed the mike button.

"*Kahn Nylon*," he began in Hebrew, then quickly remembered O'Donovan. "This is Nylon. Five is here. Move!"

"Two here." O'Donovan's voice crackled in Benni's wet earpiece. "We're hauling."

"Three," Didi whispered.

"Four," said Nabbe. "Do not try it without us!"

Eckstein jumped up and grabbed Baum's antenna, but he was barely able to jam the whipping shaft down into Benni's walkie-talkie as his burly mentor disappeared from his hands like a fleeing ghost.

Sadeen's new acquisition was a white Renault half-van, its cab like the front of a small sedan, with a bulky box in the back that had the Algerian postal *PTT* stamped on its sides. He wished now that the driver had been a woman, preferably an elderly one, for he could have sat her beside him and possibly bought Benni another minute or so. But he was grateful enough for what Providence had provided and only hoped that he had made the proper left turn. He was not worried that the driver whom he had frightened off into the dunes would summon the police. The fellow would be hiking until dawn before he saw another soul.

The wide, flat wadi looked right, its surface spaded over for vehicles, the rising side berms resembling those of Horse's model. He drove with his right hand and worked the strange dashboard shift with it also, for he could not raise his left arm at all now. He tasted the metallic film of blood in his mouth, and he coughed as little as possible. The driver's strange white *tagelmoust* covered everything but his eyes and reminded him of Afghan mujahideen. His CAR lay across his lap, the barrel pointed at the left door.

He had assumed that Klump would have posted men along the passageway to meet him and was surprised that no one appeared. But then, she was waiting for Baum and her mother, and she knew that the colonel would give her nothing until he saw his daughter.

Every rut in the road was a blade in his left chest. He did not believe that he would die from this injury, though God knew he might shortly sustain more serious wounds. He could not have cared less. He was on time, and in just a few more meters he would have done his bit.

The passageway suddenly opened into a wide mouth, the right-hand berm stretching on while the left curved away. He took his foot off the accelerator and braked, then put the clutch in and set the gear in reverse, just holding. In the distance, the yellow beams of his headlights picked out the hulk of the netted jet. To his left, figures retreated from his offending light like shy vampires.

He did not move, except to very slowly slip his right hand around the trigger grip of the CAR, thumbing the safety to full auto. It suddenly struck him that Baum and company might be still out there, wandering around the Sahara, and the idea that he had crashed this party alone nearly made him laugh.

Then he saw the girl, and nothing was funny anymore.

She was standing at the edge of the pool of his beams. Her legs were bare, she wore some kind of a sweater, and she looked as if they had keelhauled her through a pool of quicksand. Her head hung down and her long hair was encrusted with strips of plastery grit, but still he could see the shine of her eyes. He began to breathe heavily. It was the Latin fury rising in him, and he no longer felt his ribs at all.

Where are you, Benni? he growled inside his head.

A voice called out from the darkness. A woman's voice, but it was not Benni's daughter, and it was not in a language he understood.

"*Wo bist du, Baum?*" the voice demanded.

Now, Benni, Sadeen breathed. *Now!*

Another figure entered the light just behind Benni's daughter. Short blond hair and a hand that crawled over the girl's shoulder and gripped it.

For God's sake, Benni!

Martina was blinded by the headlights, but her handicap did not frighten her. She was protected by a human shield as unassailable as titanium. Mussa stood to her left, Youssef to her right, and the rest of her men crouched in blackness to all points of the compass.

What she did feel was an oncoming eruption of rage, for the truck just sat there like an abandoned ship, no sign of life, only the rumble of its old engine. The arrogance! Did Baum think she would wait there forever like some stood-up schoolgirl?

"Let me see her!" she called louder, in English now.

Nothing.

"All right," she whispered through clenched teeth. She stepped closer to Ruth and stuck her hand through the mat of her hair, gripping the warm throat where the girl's pulse pounded. "What were you saying about a father's love?" she growled as she pushed down with a violent wrench of her fingers.

Ruth fell to her hands and knees. She began to sob as Martina cocked the P-38 and placed the barrel against her skull.

Schneller's first shot missed Martina completely. But considering that he had just crested the eastern dune, flopped onto his belly, and aimed for less than two seconds, the impact to Youssef's left jaw was really quite amazing. The huge man jerked and slumped to the ground just before the report of the 7.62 mm cartridge echoed through the bowl, and then everything else came down like an avalanche of fire and thunder.

Close-quarter combat is nothing like its cinematic depiction, in which an editor carefully assembles points of view so that an audience can follow along. A gunfight, especially at night, is much more like a road accident on the autobahn, a ten-car pileup whose drivers snatch up bits of images and sounds through their terror, items burned into the memory like random cuttings from a jerky old news-reel. Some of it you recall forever, especially those stark tableaux frozen by explosions and muzzle flashes. But mostly it is a private, claustrophobic experience, in which your hearing is quickly deadened by your own gunfire, your nostrils and lungs fill with burning gases, the screams are unrecognizable as your own, and you are locked inside your own private little box of violence.

Benni charged. He had sprinted even harder toward the berm as the bowl beyond filled with the lights of the truck, and as he scrambled up the embankment, his eyes breached the top and he was faced with the horrific vision of his daughter going to her knees. He never slowed. He instinctively yelled, "*Kadima!*" as both a rally to his men and the blatant offering of himself as the better target. His boots slammed down onto the flat bowl and a terrible cry emerged from him, for he heard Schneller's shot and thought it was Martina's pistol. But then Ruth was scrambling toward him, and he thundered toward *her*, arms and legs flying like a stampeding bison, and he saw nothing else at all.

Eckstein was very close to his left flank, O'Donovan and Binder just twenty meters to the right, and despite Benni's motivation, O'Donovan's was equal, and his young legs longer.

Martina had her choice of targets, though merely a millisecond in which to make it. Rounds from the left were kicking up near her feet, but the weapons of the charging shadows before her had not yet flashed, because the girl was between them, crawling in the sand. Yet they would begin firing over her form in the next second. The calm of the changing game came upon her as she realized that she had been duped. All right. A point for you, my ex-beloved.

One figure emerged first into the light. A woolen cap flew from his head, and she recognized the blond policeman from New York. How *romantic*. How pathetically *galant*. Shoot the girl? Or leave her with an endless nightmare?

She squatted quickly and held the P-38 out between her knees. *This is not a snowy rooftop game of hide-and-seek. And you only get* one *warning*.

She shot O'Donovan twice in the chest, and his momentum carried him flat onto his face, his legs in the air, a wave of sand pluming over his shoulders.

Benni dove, his arms in front and his back arched hard as the white blisters of Kalashnikov muzzles opened up directly before him. He landed on top of Ruth, his chest slammed her backside down, and she grunted out a great moan. He grabbed for her bare feet, banging one ankle with his pistol as he folded them roughly under his arms, jammed his thighs together over her head, and tried to bury her like a tortoise protecting its soft-shelled newborn.

Martina leapt behind Mussa, who was standing to her left, erect as a figurehead on the bowsprit of a sailing ship. He was absolutely expressionless, wondering only who would inherit his role as Martina's protector, for there were no more Hawatmeh brothers, and he raised his MP-5 to his shoulder. From their two opposing angles, Binder and Eckstein swung to him and fired in bucking double taps until he arched beyond their muzzle flashes, then they both went prone and continued firing as Martina bear-hugged the body that slammed backward into her chest, fell with it, and spooned up against Mussa in death as she had refused to do when he lived.

With Schneller's first shot, Sadeen had stamped the accelerator of the Renault, swung the wheel to the right, skidded in reverse, and hit the brakes. His headlights swept across the ragged line of Martina's men. Peripherally, he saw Baum dash across the bowl, with Eckstein a close second, but his attention was fused to the closer group of HOGs, who, apparently offended by his breach of night etiquette, opened up on him with everything they had. He vaulted for the right-hand door and scrambled out onto the ground as the windows exploded above him and the Renault bucked like a police van being pummeled by a crowd of rioters.

Although Didi and Amir had reached the encampment before anyone else, they had the farthest to go now in order to close the range. They had crouched in the black shadow beneath the wings of the Falcon. Yet when Sadeen's truck appeared, they were momentarily confused and went instantly to their bellies. The growing whine of the distant chopper turbine made it possible for Lapkin to put his mustache to Lerner's ear.

"Looks like Sadeen went for the Schneller option."

Didi nodded, then glanced up at the jet's fuselage, wagged a warning finger at Amir, and pointed out toward the eastern rim of the bowl. Lapkin understood: no firing till we are clear of the airplane. It was the only available taxi in sight, and they did not want to use it as cover.

Schneller's first shot launched them from their cover, and now the gunfire was a squall as they sprinted from their corner of the bowl, trying to get clear of Binder, who lay between them and the scurrying shadows against the northern dune wall. The lights of the truck exploded, and they kept on, then zigzagged wildly as a pistol spat at them out of the sudden blackness. . . .

Salim and Yaccub had backed up behind the two standing vents of the trailers. Eckstein, functionally deafened now, was holding them there with his CAR, shifting quickly from left to right and getting off quick doubles. Every fourth round trailed a neon pipe of red light, some of them sparking off rocks and careening up into the night, and from somewhere behind the riddled truck Sadeen's CAR joined in, echoing Eckstein's weapon like an admiring younger brother. The two HOGs dueled back with their AKs, firing less disciplined bursts through the heavier Kalashnikov throats, until Schneller killed each of them with a single shot from the Parker–Hale. His Pecar was not a night scope, but the men illuminated themselves nicely with the bursts from their own weapons.

Nabil, Martina's explosives technician, had chosen to hunker down behind the fallen vent of Ruth's trailer, next to a quivering radio operator called Idri. They each had Makarov pistols but had not fired a shot, choosing instead to scrape troughs for themselves with their wriggling bodies. Yet they were lying on the roof of the trailer, whose shallow surface of remaining sand offered no further cover, and the aluminum vent pipe banged and rolled with every impacting round. When a red stream of tracer passed through the tube and struck the sand in front of Nabil's face, he jumped up and ran.

The dunes at the northern flank were ten meters high, but he was already halfway up the slope when, for some reason, he stopped and turned. The truck was beginning to burn, reminding him of the Marine Hum-Vee that had been destroyed by his briefcase bomb. In the flicker of its flaring gasoline he could see a man, who he did not know was Eckstein, lying on his stomach and reloading a short assault rifle as he yelled something. It was an easy shot, one final blow for Martina before he escaped, and he raised the Makarov.

Nabbe, who had been sniping with his High-Power alongside Schneller, was up on his knees, reloading, when he saw the distant silhouette on the dune slope. His palm was still slapping the magazine home when he arched the weapon around and up, released the slide, and got off three quick shots one-handed at an impossible night range of one hundred meters. The shadow rolled down the dune.

At the northeastern corner of the bowl, a trough had been plowed through the dunes, leaving a high-walled, forbidding black tunnel. As the Renault's headlights burst under impact, Martina rolled away from Mussa's bloody corpse, sprang up, and ran for the tunnel's mouth, firing spaced single shots at the two shadows charging her from the direction of the covered jet.

She disappeared into the passageway, but Muhammed and Riyad were not quite so quick. They trailed her by only five meters, sprinting in long hurdlers' strides. Didi dropped to one knee, Amir stamped to a stop in strange baby steps just to his left, and they led the figures with the mini Uzi and the High-Power for two full seconds before releasing a flurry of single shots. Muhammed and Riyad sprawled.

The firing stopped, all forty-six seconds of it, the echoes of the last shots fading away like heavy, stuttering nostril sighs. The immolated Renault bathed the bowl in eerie campfire flickers, and the stench of burning rubber and powder gases drifted along with the pale haze of gun smoke.

Binder rose cautiously to his feet. He removed a magazine from his CAR and looked at its lips. Two tracers lay in the metal folds. He grunted, pocketed the magazine, and jammed another into the weapon, thumbing the bolt latch. He looked to the right, where Didi and Amir had flattened themselves up against the right frame of the tunnel mouth after checking two strewn bodies for signs of threat. He looked to the left, where O'Donovan lay still on his chest, his right hand stretched out to the side, palm turned up. The wind ruffled his hair. His weapon was plowed into the sand, the stock sticking partially upright. There was a ragged tear in the back of his ruck.

Eckstein jogged across in front of Binder, waving up at Schneller and Nabbe, urging them off their dune to intercept the woman. A small man, Martina's surviving radio operator, got up shakily from behind the fallen aluminum air vent. He was not wearing his kaffiyeh. He raised his hands and placed them behind his neck.

Binder walked to him, drawing the *kochmer* from its sheath as he did so. Idri, who had never seen a Berber so large and ferocious looking, lost control of his bladder and sank to his knees, babbling prayers of mercy. Binder stopped just before the lowered head. He sheathed the blade, walked around the kneeling man, stopped again, and fired a round into his right calf muscle.

"That oughta hold you, motherfucker," he said as he walked away from the scream.

Benni rolled off Ruth. She gasped as if she had been drowning again, but when she tried to rise, he pushed her flat as he scanned his surroundings. "Not yet, *Ruti*," he panted.

Sadeen limped up to him, silhouetted in the flames of the burning vehicle.

"Your moped grew," said Benni.

"It got excited." Sadeen smiled weakly.

"Watch her," Baum ordered, and he trotted away.

Didi and Amir were hugging the right frame of the tunnel mouth, Eckstein on the left. Binder was squatting next to Eckstein, opening his ruck.

"Amir," Benni called quietly as he ran up. "Go see to Michael." He said it flatly, fearing that Amir's ministrations would be unrewarded gestures. Lapkin sprinted away.

"Anyone go in besides her?" Eckstein asked across to Didi. He thought he was whispering, but he was nearly shouting.

"Not that I saw, mate."

"But who knows what scumbag lurks?" Binder posed the question as he rose with two of Sadeen's flash-bangs in his hands. He frowned at them, reversed the primitive caps, unfurled the tails, and sighed. "Give my balls for an M-26," he said as he hurled the grenades, putting football spins on them, one right after the other, up and over into the roofless trough.

The devices had the effect of stunning Binder, for he did not believe they would actually detonate. But they did, with high-pitched hollow bangs and a blast of yellow light that bounced off the trough walls like camera strobes. Eytan and Didi charged in, firing.

No one was in the passageway. Martina was gone, sprinting in the direction of the whining turbine and a pickup truck parked halfway between her camp and another wide hole, which, until only an hour before, had been covered by a pegged-down net.

Schneller had scrambled down the far slope of his dune, which was very steep, and he lost track of Nabbe when the Belgian tripped and went head over heels like a clumsy skier. The tall German hit flat sand, ran around a plowed-up embankment, and nearly toppled into the woman.

He skidded to a stop and quickly brought the long rifle to bear, yet he hesitated for a moment. She was loping along through the dark and hardly broke stride as she turned toward him, first shot him a look of empathy for his inferior reflexes, then shot him with the P-38. The 9 mm round punched through the wooden stock of the Parker-Hale and into his right side, knocking him flat back like a snow angel.

She picked up her pace and ran past the truck. Jaweed and Ali, the blond and the redhead who had butt-stroked Del Ray and shot Humason on the road through Ironsides, were crouched in the back of the pickup behind the wooden sign that said FOLLOW ME. As Martina flew by and the distant figures emerged cautiously from the tunnel, they opened up on full auto with their AKs.

The heavy Russian rounds split off chunks of plowed-up rock and geysers of sand as Eckstein and Didi dove to their bellies and rolled up against the sides of the trough. Some of the projectiles were green tracer, and they whip-cracked in the dark air overhead. Binder was trying to crawl forward to them on his elbows, and Eytan waved him off violently. Ruth was safe. This was no time to die. He held his CAR away from his body and got off a meaningless, blind burst.

"Where's the fucking air cover?" Binder yelled amid the cacophony of ricochets and Eckstein's short-barreled explosions. Eckstein thought he heard Didi laugh.

Rick Nabbe was not amused. He poked his head around a low sand nipple and saw Schneller lying on his back, then winced as a pair of white barrel bursts leapt out from the dark hulk of a truck just a stone's throw away.

He wriggled out of his rucksack, quickly checked his magazine, jammed it back into the High-Power, slithered backwards, and began to run. He swung out to the right, his head bent low, dodging clumps of sagebrush, the incongruous black ring of a discarded tire. The whine of the turbine was shifting even higher now, and it seemed that weak bolts of lightning were bouncing up from a wide hole up ahead, but he cared only for the AK barrels that hammered away to his left.

He went to his stomach, crawled over a low dune, and found himself nose-to-grille with the pickup. Then he rolled to his feet, duck-walked along the driver's side, and stopped with his back against the cab, taking a deep breath as the brass casings from one of the guns streamed out over his head.

He stood up, gripping the pistol two-handed. *Terribly unsporting*, he thought, then shot both men twice between their shoulder blades.

He spun his head when he heard the rotors biting hard into the air, then opened his mouth as the tail of a snow-white Bell 212 helicopter rose from the ground not fifty meters away. The main rotor appeared, and the aircraft floated straight up, then tilted, filling his eyes and mouth with grit as he threw up an arm to protect his face.

He staggered forward, squinting into the roiling haze as the Bell turned on its axis, mocking him with the bold black letters of the UN stenciled arrogantly on its flank.

He raised the pistol and squeezed the trigger. The hammer clicked on an empty chamber as the chopper roared off into the night.

At 0212, Nimrodi brought the Dakota in on the Ben Zireg-Taghit road. He had told Baum that he was going to do it, circling over the Moroccan side of the border and then coming back in for them, no matter what happened. Benni had vigorously objected, insisting that if they survived the action, they would improvise a way out: find a vehicle, march overland to the border, dig up one of Klump's trailers, and drive it.

"Oh, yes, my friend," Nimrodi had scoffed. "You and your wounded will be fresh as daisies and ready for automotive *excavations*, while the entire Front Islamique du Salut closes in on you!"

For once Benni was grateful for equality of ranks, for he could not overlord a fellow lieutenant colonel.

The men did not really need their *guznik* landing beacons, for Nabbe had parked the pickup truck on the shoulder beside the cutoff to Martina's smoldering camp, and he flashed the headlights and then left the high beams on. But they had laid out the flaming soup cans anyway, as a signal to Nimrodi that it was they who awaited him and no others, for they had no radio contact with the plane.

The black silhouette of the Dakota was a comforting sight, but no one jumped up to run to it this time. Its tires screeched on the cracked road well to the north, sending up sprays of pebbles that hammered a racket on the wing bottoms, and then it crept slowly toward them like a wary raven.

They lay off the eastern shoulder in a shallow depression, spread out in a full circle, weapons outboard. Some of them chewed bits of chocolate bars. O'Donovan lay on his back on the assembled stretcher, his ragged chest wounds patched to the best of Lapkin's abilities. He was covered now by Binder's field jacket, his breaths shallow and bubbling, his pale forehead beaded with sweat. Ruth sat close to him, her ruined fingers trembling gently through his hair. Her shoulders shook despite the warm shroud of both Benni's and Eytan's anoraks.

Sadeen's chest had gone completely stiff now, and he had to lie on his back, where he tried to will his body into using only his right lung. He rested his head on Schneller's thigh. The big German's wound was not life-threatening, Martina's round having passed through a "love handle." He held one of Benni's field dressings over the entrance hole, while a gauze pad soaked up blood from his back, and he and Sadeen kept each other going by arguing over whose injuries were worse.

Binder fidgeted as he scanned every dune on the eastern horizon. He regretted having wounded Martina's survivor, wishing he had killed him outright. He did not like loose ends, though he had trussed the man, gagged him, and dumped him in the passage to Klump's underground lair. He and Eckstein had wanted to go down into the trailers to load up on "intelligence materials," but Baum would not allow it. He himself had taught Martina to booby-trap such attractive prizes.

Benni took his arm from Ruth's shoulders and jogged to the Dakota, with Eckstein close behind. Nimrodi jumped down from the cargo door, and he did not need to ask if Ruth was all right. Anything else would have shown instantly on Baum's face. They began to shout at each other over the rumbling engines.

"*Nu?*" Nimrodi looked up at Baum. "Are you waiting for an invitation from the Prime Minister?" His black onyx holder was jammed between his teeth, but he could not light his cigarette in the prop blast.

"She got away," Baum shouted.

"Who?"

"The woman," Eckstein yelled. "In a chopper. Probably with the missile."

Nimrodi looked at his watch. "We can try a radio relay to Ben-Zion, maybe through one of the Moroccan airports. Though I've been declaring emergencies all over the sky and have certainly used up all my favors."

"And even if we could," Benni said.

"He would have to postpone the exchange," Eytan finished.

Nimrodi looked at them, then up at the airplane. "Do you think you could catch up?"

"Maybe," Eckstein said. "She was in a Bell 212." The cruising speed of a loaded Bell was 161 mph. The empty Dakota could do 204.

Nimrodi sighed, although no one heard it. "What about the jet?"

"It looks all right," said Benni. "But what do I know? It will have to be towed out to the road, and there isn't time."

Nimrodi suddenly turned, leapt up to the cargo door, and wriggled inside. After a moment he came back and jumped down again, followed by the copilot, and then Horse, who glanced around wildly as if he had just been dropped into a panther cage. Baba placed his hands up on Benni's and Eytan's shoulders, pulling them close.

"Like this, then," he yelled. "You two take the Dakota. I will get everyone else into the jet. Like civilians; no weapons, no equipment. Just passports." He paused. "You did not find the charter pilots?"

Benni and Eytan shook their heads.

"We will fire up the emergency frequency and declare ourselves the stranded victims of a hijacking," Nimrodi continued. "Will your friend be monitoring?"

"I'm sure Arthur has been sleeping at Warrenton." Benni meant the CIA's communications facility in Virginia.

"Good. If we can get it off the ground, we will just hop to Bechar, sit on the runway, and scream for the American consul. And if not, we'll drag it out onto the road here, lock ourselves in it, and broadcast to every airport in the Mediterranean."

Benni and Eytan looked at each other. Nimrodi shook them hard. "Do not worry," he shouted. "No one will dare touch us!"

Benni looked down at the road. The High-Power, still unfired in anger, gleamed from the holster strapped to his belt. He hiked up his trousers.

"Okay," he shouted. "I'll go get Ruth."

Eckstein caught his elbow. "No, Benni." He held Baum's eyes with his own. "She'll be safer here, with Nimrodi."

Benni opened his mouth to object, but Nimrodi placed a hand on his chest.

"Yes." Baba smiled. "*Everyone* is safer with me."

It was true. An entire parachute brigade would swear to it.

The small colonel released Baum, grabbed Horse by the sleeve, and ran off with him as the copilot trotted behind them.

Benni hesitated. He could not leave without speaking to her, and he stared longingly past the wingtip of the airplane. Then he saw her in the halo of the pickup's headlights, standing anxiously with Nimrodi as he spoke to her, touching her sleeve, and she sprang away, running toward her father.

The Dakota pilot clanged the jump warning bell like an impatient trolley driver. Eytan pulled at Benni, who turned to find his partner bending, with his fingers intertwined. Benni reached up for the doorframe, stepped into Eytan's stirrup, and struggled inside. He pulled Eytan up after him, then pushed him aside as he lay in the doorway, his arms reaching down as Ruth ran up in her bare feet.

"*Abba!*" she shouted.

He reached out and took her face in his hands. "Ruti, go with Nimrodi."

"*Abba!*" she cried again. The streams were flowing freely over her cheeks, and she reached up to press his hands against her, as if she might seal them there with her tears. She began to walk as the Dakota revved and started its roll.

"I will see you in Jerusalem," he yelled as he clasped her harder. "I swear it!"

"But *Abba,*" she choked, "you always lie."

"Not this time." He tried to smile at her as his heart pounded against the steel floor. "Not *this* time," he shouted.

She could not keep up, and she backed away, arms still outstretched as the roaring engines lifted her matted hair.

And then she vanished into the darkness.

Chapter 25: Cap Ras Tarf

Benni Baum's stamina tried to desert him over the wide Plateau du Rekkam, and although his shoulders were jammed between the narrow doorframes of the Dakota's cockpit, his head began to nod, his fingers went limp, and he would have pitched backward but for Eckstein, who reached back from the copilot's seat and grabbed him by the belt buckle. He snapped awake, not altogether surprised that his body finally sought refuge, for his child was out of mortal danger and it begged him to shut down. He would have liked to comply, but as Itzik Ben-Zion had pointed out, he was much like Mary Shelley's eternal experimenter, and the deadly creature of his own concoctions was still very much at large.

He squinted through his stinging eyes at the dark tables of rock and patches of trees, that seemed to rush the cockpit and then dissolve below in a blur, and he wondered how the pilot could possibly maintain the reflexes to fly so low after such a grueling night. Yet he certainly appreciated the man's efforts, which were not the showy aerobatics of an old airman. Benni had told the pilot that they were engaged in a mortal air race for the finish line at Cap Ras Tarf. As the Dakota's speed efficiency was greatest where the props could bite the thickest air, that was why they now seemed on the verge of shredding treetops.

In the absence of caffeine, Benni lit up a cigarette, which trembled in his fingers, for every muscle in his body was twitching on overdrive. Eckstein looked up at him longingly, sighed, and succumbed at last, sticking out a hand. Benni could have refused, helped Eytan maintain his nicotine celibacy, but he handed him the butt. It was wholly a personal choice. Like suicide.

The approaching strip of northeastern Morocco began to glow now with a dull pink burnish beneath a quickly paling sky, and Benni tried very hard not to glance at his watch. But the clock face just above the pilot's knee intercepted him. He had often looked up into the bright-blue sky of midday to find the strange appearance of the lunar crescent. Just like that unsettling phenomenon, the morning sun was about to shine on Moonlight.

We could just make it, he thought, though the idea that they might also arrive to find a smoldering catastrophe at sea made him want to scream, "Come on!" like a teenager stuck behind an old man driving a jalopy. Still, they were very lucky that their flight had so far been unopposed. They had monitored only one alert, at the Algerian air base at Beni-Abbès just as they crossed safely back into Morocco. Thereafter, the towers at Boudnib, Taza, and just now

El Aleb had called out challenges to them. Eckstein had answered casually in French, using Nimrodi's call sign as Ahmed Tabri and referring them back to the base commander at Menara. No one had ordered them to set down, though that was small comfort as Benni fretted over Nimrodi's ability to safely shepherd his people from the mouths of the wolves. The images of O'Donovan's wounds and his daughter witnessing his pain caused him to grind his teeth, his previous jealousy over their affair bathed in the glare of his conscience, like a pervert caught by a policeman's flashlight.

He looked down at Eckstein, who seemed to be trying to will the Mediterranean to appear on the horizon. His partner was filthy, his fingers black with paraffin burns, his face still streaked with brown shoe polish, and his blond hair caked with dust like that of a reserve tank commander. Hunched forward in the old leather seat of the Dakota and wearing the bulky headphones, he looked like a mercenary running drugs for a cartel. Baum was grateful that there was no mirror in which to face his own visage.

"Do you think they made it out, Eytan?" Benni asked above the engine roar.

"No," Eytan replied without turning his head. "Not yet. I'd be amazed if the Algerians just let them fly away."

"Thank you for your honesty," Baum groaned.

"But, Benni, even if they *are* all taken in, do you think Algiers will fuck with them while Roselli is raising an international ruckus?"

"No."

"Then let's shut up and concentrate on Martina."

Benni grunted as he reached up and rubbed his face. The hand, already stained with Schneller's blood, came away smeared in brown grease. He wiped it on his oatmeal sweater, which had been sloppily dyed black.

Concentrate on Martina, yes, that was the exercise now. To focus on her madness, her sociopathic cruelty, her near execution of Ruth. To suppress the nagging suspicion that she had certainly been able to kill his daughter, yet had made the conscious choice to abstain. Ignore the fantasy that Martina's taking of Ruth was the vengeance of a spurned lover, and place it in one of those other categories he used to justify the ruthless acts of his profession. This was not the time to pan for Martina's qualities of mercy. She had shot Michael O'Donovan point-blank. But then, she had not shot Benni, although that should have been her first choice. And it was not her lack of reflexes that had kept her from pulling the trigger on Ruth.

No matter. For in truth, Benni did not really expect ever to see Martina again. Yes, she had taken off in a helicopter whose United Nations camouflage was clearly designed to stay the trigger finger of anyone who might shoot it down. And he had little doubt that the Minnow was aboard the Bell. But unless Martina had crossed that threshold where a desire for self-destruction devoured reason, she would assume that her intended target had gone to full alert. She would grudgingly choose escape. She would choose life.

They would arrive in a cold sweat to Cap Ras Tarf, while she would never appear. He found himself wishing that for her. And he was secretly ashamed.

There had been no sign of the helicopter since their flight from Algeria, though that was evidence of nothing, really. She would not have crossed back into Moroccan territory, for her refuge was in the skies of a country rife with Islamic fanaticism. If she *did* intend to carry out her mission, she would fly due north through Algeria and cross back into Morocco only at the final stage, along the coast at Saida. Her necessity to detour was the only hope they had of intercepting her, given her substantial head start.

Eckstein suddenly raised his left arm and pointed forward. Benni squinted through the windshield, yet he saw nothing to warrant his attention. They had just passed over the last large forest of cedars and pines at the foot of the Rif Mountains, then the highway that links Melilla to Tangier had flashed underneath, its predawn truckers probably rubbing their eyes after witnessing this aeronautical ghost roar overhead. Before them lay a valley of wheat and corn, then the last dry ridges of the eastern tail of the Rif.

"Do you see it?" Eytan excitedly called out to Benni.

"What?" He craned his head. "What?"

"There's Dar-Kebdani," the pilot said, pointing to a casbah nestled in the ridge folds. "It's nine hundred meters there, so we have to get over it anyway." And he gently pulled the yoke toward his chest.

The Dakota began to climb, and Benni finally realized why his partner's enthusiasm had revived.

The tops of the ridges dropped away. Beyond them an endless blanket of wispy fog curled to the horizon, and as he watched, the morning sun melted it, and there was the hard blue face of the Mediterranean Sea.

Martina saw the sea as well, yet from her vantage point on the right-hand assault bench of the Bell 212, it was much closer, only meters away, the soft curls of its dawn swells rushing past the windows. To her left, the long strip of winter beach was empty, for it was too early for even the hearty old Moroccans who raced each morning to the cold surf in the belief that the exercise prolonged their lives. In the cockpit, her mercenary Sudanese pilot delicately twisted the collective, and past the white globe of his helmet the coastal bluffs curved away to the north. She could see a small phallic structure poking up from a cliffside at the end of the peninsula, and she came off the end of the bench and stuck her head into the cockpit for a better look. Beyond the bluffs, perhaps one kilometer out to sea, the flat gray silhouettes of small vessels were slowly clustering. She reached out and knocked on the pilot's helmet.

"Set down in the surf just beyond the lighthouse," she ordered.

The helmet dipped twice.

She climbed back into the assault compartment and hauled on the right door latch, pulling the heavy sliding panel halfway back as the cold wind rushed into the cabin. Then she put her right foot on the bench, which was a double affair so that troops could sit back-to-back facing both doors, and swung her left leg over the spine as if mounting a small pony.

She straddled the piping for a moment, leaning forward, gripping it with her hands. Closing her eyes, she breathed in the scents of brine and fishes that washed over her face as the wind fluttered her coverall and lifted her tousled hair. Almost dreamily, she reached down to her left to touch the nose cone of *Der Fliegende Fisch*, where it rested on the floor in its flotation skirt. The optical sight had been stripped of its protective plastic, the trigger and tracking toggle banded to the launch casing for her convenience. Nabil had run checks on all the circuitry and inspected the warhead. The device was armed. A flip of the safety, and it would be ready to leap into its maiden flight.

Martina had not even entertained the notion of retreat. She did not see that option as the better part of valor. She had had plenty of time during the night flight to plan a means of escape, to forswear this final act, yet she had not done so. Instead, she reflected silently on the loss of her men, mourning for their devotion snatched from her. Her mother had been used as a pawn, while surely remaining unharmed. But Martina's family had gone to its grave.

Alone within her private silence, unbreached by the vibrating flight, she had realized that her enthusiasm to use the missile had not really waned, for the lust had never really been there. It was an apolitical act, pushed along by the very personal motives only occasionally glimpsed by her for their hard truths. Her will, her furies, her brief loves and rages, all were festering wounds unsoothed by her cries for something she could never have. As the helicopter flew and she knew that each kilometer brought her closer to her own end, her life had not raced before her eyes. She had carefully summoned it, dredged up every year, each rare joy, and the larger balances of sorrow.

And although there were a thousand images of cruelty, hardships, and violence from which to choose, only one picture refused to fade. It was the vision of Benni Baum throwing his body over his daughter's, hiding her, protecting her, smothering her with his love. It was the stark realization that not since her fifth birthday had there been, nor would there ever be, someone who would do that for *her*.

She opened her eyes and looked down at her right leg. The thigh pocket of the coverall was half open, the butt of the P-38 protruding from the zipper. She lifted her father's pistol out and looked at it, touching the barrel lightly with one finger. Then, as the lighthouse flashed by the windows and the Bell began to slow and settle, she lofted the pistol through the open door, where it twisted like a boomerang and did not return.

The Dakota banked hard to the left at Pointe Afraou, and Benni scrabbled for the cockpit doorframe as his spine jammed into the steel. They had come down off the ridges like a hotdog skier, twisting through the wadis as the pilot dove to pick up speed. Then a flat strip of brush-strewn plateau appeared and almost instantly dropped away into a blink of beach, and they were out over the water. The pilot skidded around the turn like a drunk and came back on line, where the low waves foamed against the shoreline. The thatched roofs of a small seaside resort poked up briefly from the dunes and rushed past the left wing, and within seconds Eckstein was clutching at the cockpit dash and shouting.

"There!" He stabbed his finger madly. "There!"

The sun was high enough now to dazzle the sea with sparklers of white light, and just beyond the point of Cap Ras Tarf a small flotilla of vessels—two larger ones almost prow-to-prow and smaller shapes buzzing about like water flies—was haloed in the glow.

"Get on the emergency frequency," Baum snapped at the pilot.

"And call bloody who?" the Dakota driver asked as he tried to squeeze more power from the throttles.

"The air force'll have a 707 in the air," said Eckstein. "They'll be monitoring the international tethers."

"Eytan!" Benni gripped Eckstein's shoulder so hard that the major winced and looked up at him. Then he quickly snapped his head forward again when he saw the shock in Baum's eyes.

The finger of a lighthouse was quickly growing into a stone forearm, and just beyond that, the spinning rotors of a white helicopter flashed up streamers of sunlight as the craft settled into the surf.

"For God's sake, man!" Benni yelled, and the pilot fumbled with the radio transmitter and tossed a hand microphone into Eckstein's lap.

"Moonlight, Moonlight, this is Bavaria calling. Over." Eytan nearly shouted into the mike, hoping that one of the AMAN officers aboard the communications jet would recognize his old departmental code name. He had barely released the button when Benni snatched the mike from his hand.

"Moonlight, this is Baum," Benni spat, abandoning all covert caution. "You have an emergency. There are unfriendlies in your area—I repeat, unfriendlies in your area. Acknowledge."

There was no danger now that the ships would back away from each other. It was far too late for that, and Martina certainly knew it too.

"Moonlight," Benni began again. Then he shouted, "*Ach, Scheisse!*" and threw the microphone to the floor as the shadow of the Dakota enveloped the helicopter not twenty meters below, and then the white wasp was gone. *Behind* them.

"Set it down!" Baum shouted to the pilot.

"*Where?*" the South African twisted his head from left to right. "In the water? We don't even have a hundred meters of straight beach."

"Damn you!" Benni pounded a fist on the doorframe in exasperation.

"Over there!" Eckstein pointed to the left, where just past the line of low bluffs the plain of sand and brush looked reasonably flat.

The pilot looked left, made his decision, then banked hard to the right. Baum began to curse him again as he was slammed against the doorframe. But the pilot was merely setting himself up for an approach, swinging out briefly over the water.

"I'm coming around," he warned as he stamped the rudder pedals and hauled on the yoke. The engines howled as they dragged the big airplane into a skidding left turn, and Benni struggled to hang on.

"Go strap in," Eckstein shouted to Baum.

"Strap in your bloody *self*," the pilot yelled, for Eytan was now being smeared into the right corner of the cockpit by the force of the wild turn.

Benni hesitated as the line of rocky bluffs grew large across the windshield, but there would be only seconds of straight and level flying, so he staggered quickly back into the cabin, fell onto the port bench, and fumbled for the crash belt. As soon as the catches clicked, he twisted around toward the window, catching a glimpse of the chopper as its rotor kicked out an expanding circle of sea foam and its skids dipped into the shallow waves licking at the beach.

He was thrown back as the Dakota banked hard to the left once again, then straightened out, and he heard the engine roar drop suddenly to a rumble of low power rasps.

"Crank that hard!" he heard the pilot yell to Eckstein. And then they were floating, settling gracefully, the nose lifting and the floor tilting as scrubs of sand thorns reached up to the windows and the sky was snatched up and away like a magician's cape.

There really was nowhere to land the airplane properly. The sandy plateau was scarred with deep drifts and nubby seaside vegetation. The wind was still hard from the southeast, and the pilot was using every muscle he had to keep the right wing down.

With his bowels in his throat, Benni welcomed the crash, for otherwise they would roll to a stop far away and too late. The big tires dumped into a trough, the right wing came up and was immediately butted by the wind, so it kept on rising while the tail lifted, the propellers bit into the sand, and huge waves of yellow grit pinwheeled over the wings as the nose tilted over and punched into the ground.

Benni pulled himself up onto his left elbow. He unstrapped his crash belt, fell to his knees, and immediately began sliding along the floor toward the cockpit. He threw his hands out for the doorframe.

Servos were whining crazily. The windshields had spidered from impact compression and there was the reek of spilling aero gas. Eckstein was slumped against the control panel, his arms hanging down and his head turned to the left. A gash on his forehead was already expressing a thin stream of blood that ran past his nose and over his upper lip.

The pilot was bracing himself against the panel with one hand as he fumbled to unstrap himself. He twisted around and saw Baum in the doorway.

"I'll get him out," he mumbled as he returned to his efforts. Baum seemed to be frozen there. "He'll be all right!" the pilot yelled, clearly furious at having destroyed his beloved aircraft. "Just go!"

Benni turned and propelled himself away from the cockpit. He stumbled against the port cabin wall, for the plane was pitched up at a crazy angle, and he used the vertical ribs to pull himself along until he found the emergency window exit. He reached up, grabbed a cross-spar, lifted his legs, and kicked into the Plexiglas with all his weight and muscle. The window and the exit panel exploded out of the fuselage, and his momentum thrust him through the narrow rectangle, where the flesh of his upper arms was rent right through his sweater by the sharp metal.

He felt no pain as his feet collapsed under him, his knees banged onto the wing, and he squinted hard in the sudden burst of daylight. Then he began to slide forward and managed to flop onto his back and twist in toward the fuselage, narrowly avoiding impaling himself on one jagged blade of the curled-back propeller.

He fell into a pile of sand just forward of the wing. The cockpit door popped open, and he saw the heels of the pilot's boots. He did not wait. He struggled to his feet and began to run.

A strange and terrible silence enveloped him as he found his bearings and sprinted toward the sea. No roaring engines, no gunfire, no unnatural disturbance of the morning calm but the pounding of his boots in the sand, the ragged wheeze of his own breath, and the soft hammer of metal against bone as his holstered pistol flopped against his pelvis. The wind was at his back, and it curled the tips of salt grass in the dunes, stole the sounds of the sea from him. His panic mounted, for he could not hear the helicopter's rotor, nor would he hear the launch of the missile, or its impact, until it struck its mark and whispered back to him with a dull boom.

His fists were striking at the air and his thighs were on fire as he neared the edge of the bluff, and for the first time ever he thought that his heart might finally explode, for he could feel it swelling inside his aching chest, the sweat dribbling over his face and into the neck of the sweater that strangled him.

He reached the edge of the cliff, and the helicopter came into view, the size of a horizontal thumb, vibrating there at the edge of the water. And beyond it, in a perfect flat trajectory, the two vessels were touching prows in an Eskimo kiss on the dazzling blue horizon. He never took his eyes from the white machine, not even as he leapt into the air and smacked his spine onto the steep face of the bluff, jamming his heels into the sand as he slid and watched Martina's small figure wrestling the Minnow from the open door of the Bell into the surf. Something jagged tore across his back as he struck bottom and was up again, nearly sobbing through his gaping mouth, dragging the pistol from the holster as he pounded across the flat sand.

She was up to her hips in the water, gently turning the missile on its floating skirt, her distant figure still so small, too small, and Benni breathed like a man in the throes of a nightmare where he could run forever and remain in place, unable to flee from or catch the monster that was himself. The helicopter lifted away, ruffling Martina's hair and drenching her in spray, and she ignored it as she bent to the Minnow and extended a cable, as if she were starting a lawn mower. Yet Benni knew it was the launch trigger. He could not remember if a round was chambered in his High-Power, and he pulled it out, cocked the slide, and raised it as he ran. And he tried to yell, yet nothing emerged but a feeble grunt of air.

She sensed him then. She straightened up and slowly turned her head. Her right hand was on her hip, and she briefly regarded his clumsy athletics with the disdain of a gazelle for a rhinoceros. Then she turned back to the Minnow and leaned to its sight.

He began to fire, and his yell came to him, though it contained no human word. The pistol bucked at the end of his arm, the explosions sledgehammering his head as he ran through the smoke, and still her narrow back would not flinch. He fired again, and she stood up stiffly, her head arching to search the sky. He fired again, and she twisted and lay down in the water.

He walked now, but his finger could not be ordered to desist, and it kept on pulling until Martina's hand floated away from her trigger and Benni's slide locked itself back, refusing to continue its complicity.

The echo of his last shot breathed away over the sea. Benni dropped the pistol, took one more step, and crumpled to his knees.

Then he collapsed onto the cold sand as the fringe of a wave crept up to him and tiptoed around his body.

Epilogue: Jerusalem

The Athenian edifice of King Solomon's Temple has long since vanished from the high plateau of ancient rock, a summit upon which Abraham once raised his blade to sacrifice his son, his hand stayed by an angel stunned to witness the power of human fundamentalist fervor. Now the Moslem shrine of the Mosque of Omar squats on toppled slabs of the dead king's pride, its golden dome the city's centerpiece, its circular floor a moat of murmurs where pious men touch their foreheads into the dust of Maccabean bones.

There is little left of Solomon's glory, just one small section of the temple's western retaining wall, albeit spectacular in itself, a high and wide brickwork of huge slabs of granite. And it is to this shuttered gateway to the biblical past that Jews are drawn from every continent, bowing their heads in prayer, caressing the rocks with trembling fingers, whispering their wishes into seemingly indifferent geology.

Yet perhaps there is a clue here to the legendary prowess of the Israeli intelligence services, a hint of traditions inherited by Jewish agents. For, spurred by tribal custom, men and women silently approach the Western Wall, clutching scraps of folded paper scrawled with prayers in countless tongues. The cracks in the towering stones bristle with these messages, for this is the Lord's mailbox, his chosen people's dead drop. It is a portal to heaven through which slip prayers For His Eyes Only, in private codes he alone can decipher.

The early winter morning was a cold one, though not bitterly so, for patches of the sun chased shadows of cloud across the flat pink slabs of the wall's great forecourt. The wide-open floor, bordered by the structures of the Old City, was fairly empty now, for the celebratory crowds had not held the field for long. Captain Dan Sarel was finally home, but he was in no condition to be lofted on gleeful shoulders, and without his presence the parties dispersed in reluctant solemnity. It was a quiet morning, leaving only the fervently religious and the recently bereaved.

At the farthest corner of the courtyard, beside the wide stone staircase that leads up to the Jewish Quarter of the Old City, a quartet of tired travelers had gathered. This inner corps, their heads bent toward each other like physicians at a loss, was watched discreetly by an outer ring, a few nonmembers standing well back, hunched politely in the chill.

Didi Lerner, Amir Lapkin, and Rick Nabbe were not present. They had already reentered their lives: Didi to salvage his law boards, Amir to trim neglected hedges, and Nabbe to the pistol ranges in Frankfurt. Jerry Binder's flight was just touching down at JFK, while Sadeen and Schneller lay in adjoining beds in the military wing of Tel Hashomer Hospital, arguing over a game of rummy. Shaul Nimrodi was going to spend the day spoiling his three daughters before heading back to Mauritania. And Horse, of course, was where he should have been, at SpecOps headquarters in the Russian Compound, cleaning out Benni Baum's office.

Perhaps of all those in the small group, Art Roselli should have appeared the most relaxed and triumphant. After all, he had returned his elderly kidnap victim safely to her rest home in New York, no worse for wear. The two surviving members of Martina Klump's cell were being arraigned in a District of Columbia federal court. And the Minnow was presently being loaded aboard a U.S. Navy cargo plane at Ben-Gurion Airport. But Roselli's tired eyes displayed no pleasure, for although he, too, was going home, he would also be accompanying a friend.

He bent to Ruth and kissed her softly on the cheek, then took her hand and held it as she looked up at him. The wind lifted her hair and dappled her face with a deceptive glow. He cleared his throat.

"I'm going to get him a commendation," Arthur said. "The one he should have had for Desert One." Then he lowered his gaze from Ruth's glistening eyes and murmured, "I know that means nothing to you now."

She opened her arms and came to him, hugging his waist, her head against the parka over his wide chest as she tried to smother his guilt.

The Falcon had actually lifted off the road near Taghit, despite some bullet punctures in the fuselage, and they had enough fuel to make it as far as Tlemcen. But seeing O'Donovan's condition, Nimrodi decided to set down at Bechar and had begun radioing for an ambulance and a trauma team almost immediately they were airborne.

O'Donovan had regained consciousness for a moment. He lay on the floor of the jet, his head cradled in Ruth's arms. It was as if he had been reviewing his life through each labored breath and found the balance of it meaningless, for he opened his eyes, looked up at her, and whispered, "But *you* were something. . . ."

They almost lost him at Béchar, but a skilled French surgeon saved his life, though not his spine. The AP wires were carrying a story of an American tourist wounded and paralyzed by Algerian fundamentalists, which was more or less the truth.

Ruth spoke into Arthur's chest. "But it will mean something to *him*," she said. Then she backed away, polishing her cheeks with the backs of her fists.

She swept a lock of hair behind one ear as she tried to smile. Arthur stuffed his hands into his jacket pockets and summoned a casual expression that failed to touch his eyes.

"So you're going back to the Rotten Apple?"

"Have to finish my degree," said Ruth. "And Michael will need me, at least for a while."

Roselli turned to Benni Baum.

"It's a good thing you didn't push her to stay, Baum." Then he saw Benni's frown and warned, "You know what happens when you push kids."

Benni shrugged. "They go in the opposite direction."

Roselli nodded. "Parental Law of Physics." He stuck out a hand, which Benni took and gripped for a long time, saying everything with his fingers, until he finally released it.

"Arthur?" Baum searched for an exit from his emotions. "Did you hear anything about the Falcon pilots?"

"The Red Crescent picked them up in the dunes near Igli. They almost didn't make it. The pilot had the copilot over his shoulders, the older one carrying the younger one."

Benni grinned. "Isn't that how it always is?"

"*Chantareesh.* Bullshit," said Eckstein as he punched Baum lightly in the shoulder.

"You're wounded," Benni warned, pointing at the fresh sutures in Eytan's forehead. "But I'll still take you to the mat."

"Children," Ruth scoffed, and she and Eckstein exchanged full glances.

A large blue Mercury with diplomatic plates had rolled through the security gates at the southern end of the forecourt. Arthur saw it and sighed as he shook Eckstein's hand.

"Until whenever," he said.

"Not too soon," said Benni, for their reunions were becoming heart-straining events.

"*L'hitraot, chevrey.* See you again, comrades," said Arthur, and Ruth took his elbow and walked him to his car.

Eckstein reached up and plucked absently at his ponytail.

"When are you going to cut that wretched thing off?" Benni chastised.

"When Anthony Hearthstone comes out of the bush."

"At the rate you work, it'll be down to your waist."

But Eckstein did not hear him. He was squinting off past Roselli's car, where a young raven-haired woman was crossing the stones quickly, a small child grasping her hand. The little boy suddenly hopped in the air, tore his hand from his mother, and began to run, his blond bangs flying as his wispy cries reached them.

"*Abba! Abba!*"

And Eckstein was flying toward him, his leather jacket flapping as they collided, and Eytan swung the laughing child around and around in a blur of small sneakers and quick kisses to his laughing face.

A cloud of smoke drifted around Benni's head, and he turned to find the towering figure of Itzik Ben-Zion. The general was back in uniform, snuggled in a rakish fur-collared officer's jacket, his boots and insignia polished. He had come from a congratulatory breakfast at the Prime Minister's residence, and the warmth of accolades seemed to have returned his youthful posture. Yet he had not just arrived. He had waited in the shadows until the group dispersed, uncomfortable with their apparent intimacy.

"Why did you call me, Baum?"

Benni had signaled Itzik's digital display beeper with "Meet me at the Wall. *B. B.*" Just as with Vietnam veterans in Washington, such a summons could mean only one location in Jerusalem.

"I wanted to introduce you to Arthur Roselli," said Benni. "Without him, you might just be shark bait now."

Itzik followed Baum's eyes to the receding car. He was a man of curious double standards, happy to bathe in glory, while pretending outwardly to disdain it. And never thanking others for performing their duties.

"I'll ask the Washington embassy to throw him a party."

Benni opened his mouth to retort, then shut it partially and murmured, "Nice idea."

"It's confirmed, by the way," said Itzik as he continued to stare through his cigarette smoke. "The exchange was an Iranian setup. A diversion, while they took possession of a warhead." He dropped the cigarette and ground it under a boot.

Benni looked down. They had discussed this fresh intelligence while sailing back to Haifa aboard the missile boat. The Moroccans had, of course, quietly blessed the exchange taking place in their waters off Cap Ras Tarf. And they had also allowed the naval commandos to come in and pick up Baum, Eckstein, and their pilot, in exchange for the rumpled yet recoverable Dakota. The signals from Jerusalem had begun to reach Ben-Zion while they were still at sea, but Benni had pushed the disheartening news away. Until now. He closed his eyes.

"I am praying it was one of the Blackstones," he whispered.

Itzik paused for effect. "Yes. Luckily," he said at last, and Benni's shoulders slumped in relief.

Blackstone was a highly secret project of the Mossad, though as chief of AMAN's SpecOps, Itzik was privy to it and had once sent Baum to a coordinating session between the services. As the Soviet republics began to crumble, the Israelis feared that nuclear warheads might be "lost" in the shuffle. A Kazhak Jew and former artillery officer, who had emigrated to Israel, had been reinserted back into his homeland, tasked with seeking out the inadequately guarded missiles. Wherever and whenever he dared, he had managed to insert a small microchip into the guidance circuitries of the warheads. The chips were dormant and would remain so until activated by lasers from American satellites. They would then reflect a weak homing signal.

"They were going to get their hands on one eventually," said Itzik. "But at least this lot's detectable, if we ever decide to repeat Osirak." He meant the Israeli raid on Baghdad's nuclear reactor, condemned by the world at the time and blessed ex post facto by the Allied Coalition when the winds of Desert Storm began to blow.

Benni said nothing. That would be someone else's problem now.

"I have to get back to the office," Itzik said, but as he turned he gestured at Eytan, Simona, and their son. "His flight back to Africa is first thing tomorrow. And he had better be on it."

"I am not his baby-sitter, Itzik," Benni protested.

"No." The general looked down at him darkly. "You're his Svengali."

He began to walk toward the northwestern corner of the forecourt, where another wide flight of stone stairs led up into the Arab Quarter, through a maze of winding stalls, and out Damascus Gate, a short stroll to headquarters. Benni signaled to his own family, a plea for a moment more of patience. Yosh and Amos, resplendent in their pilot and paratrooper uniforms, were crushing Ruth between them, as Maya laughed and tried to pull them apart. The Baums had made no move to approach Benni and Itzik. They did not care much for Benni's boss.

Benni caught up with the general, whose long strides made that a challenge.

"You're sure you want to join Eckstein," Itzik said disapprovingly as his boots clicked on the stones.

"Yes."

"Africa is not the Côte d'Azur."

"He needs me there."

"I shouldn't let you." Itzik sighed. "You two are dangerous together."

"And apart." Benni smiled.

As they reached the foot of the stairway, a pair of passing recruits saluted the general in mock formality. He ignored them as he began to climb.

"You'll have to sign the long form," he warned. "Put off the pension."

"I'll sign."

"And you'll have to wrap up the Moonlight and Tango files."

"Done."

Itzik ascended in earnest now, taking two steps at a time. Benni slowed and stopped, watching the tall man's back.

"And what about your retirement party?" the general called, though he did not turn or wait for a reply. He strode through the security gate, past the elderly pocketbook and parcel inspectors in their rumpled fatigues, and he disappeared into the Old City.

Benni put his hands into the pockets of his leather coat and slowly turned away. He stood for a moment, regarding the black-clad Hasids davening at the foot of the high wall. He looked up at the rooftops of the northern quarter, where Israeli flags whipped in the wind and rifle-toting troops strolled along the parapets. He turned his gaze to the southern stone ramp that led up to the Temple Mount, where a line of kaffiyeh-swathed men rose toward the Al Aksa Mosque.

He might be growing older, but the Middle East was not. It plodded on, perhaps making some progress, two steps forward, one step back. Here and there a lonely flag of truce, a brief cool handshake, a reluctant kiss. Yet, like a stubborn marriage, essentially unchanged.

He began to descend the stairs, breathed in the perfume of Jerusalem pines, smiled slightly, and whispered:

"It will have to wait."